Action Hero!

Written
& drawn
by

~~Jim Smith~~

Barry
Loser!

First published in Great Britain
in 2023 by Farshore
An imprint of HarperCollins*Publishers*
1 London Bridge Street, London SE1 9GF

www.farshore.co.uk

HarperCollins*Publishers*
Macken House, 39/40 Mayor Street
Upper, Dublin 1, D01 C9W8, Ireland

www.waldopancake.com

The moral rights of the author and
illustrator have been asserted.

ISBN 978 0 0084 9724 8

Printed in Bosnia and Herzegovina
1

A CIP catalogue record for this title is
available from the British Library.

Stay safe online. Any website addresses listed in this book are correct at the time of going to print. However, Farshore is not responsible for content hosted by third parties. Please be aware that online content can be subject to change and websites can contain content that is unsuitable for children. We advise that all children are supervised when using the internet.

MIX
Paper from
responsible sources
FSC™ C007454

This book is produced from independently certified FSC™ paper
to ensure responsible forest management.
For more information visit: www.harpercollins.co.uk/green

HUGELY ENJOYABLE, SURREAL CHAOS
-Guardian

Will make you laugh out loud, cringe and snigger, all at the same time
-LoveReading4Kids

Waterstones Children's Book Prize Shortlistee!

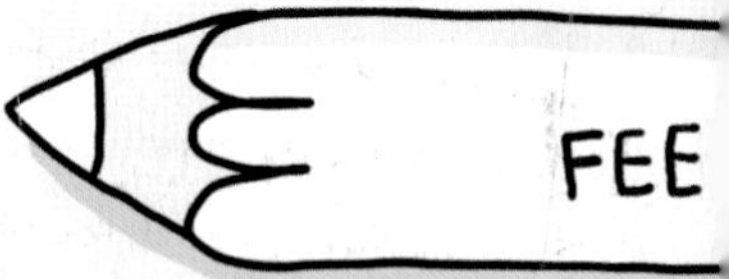
FEE

SCHOLASTIC
Lollies
LAUGH OUT LOUD BOOK AWARDS
WINNER!

The review of the 8 year old boy in our house... 'Can I keep it to give to a friend?' Best recommendation you can get
-Observer

The Roald Dahl Funny Prize Winner!

WHAT'S NOT TO LOVE?
-Sun

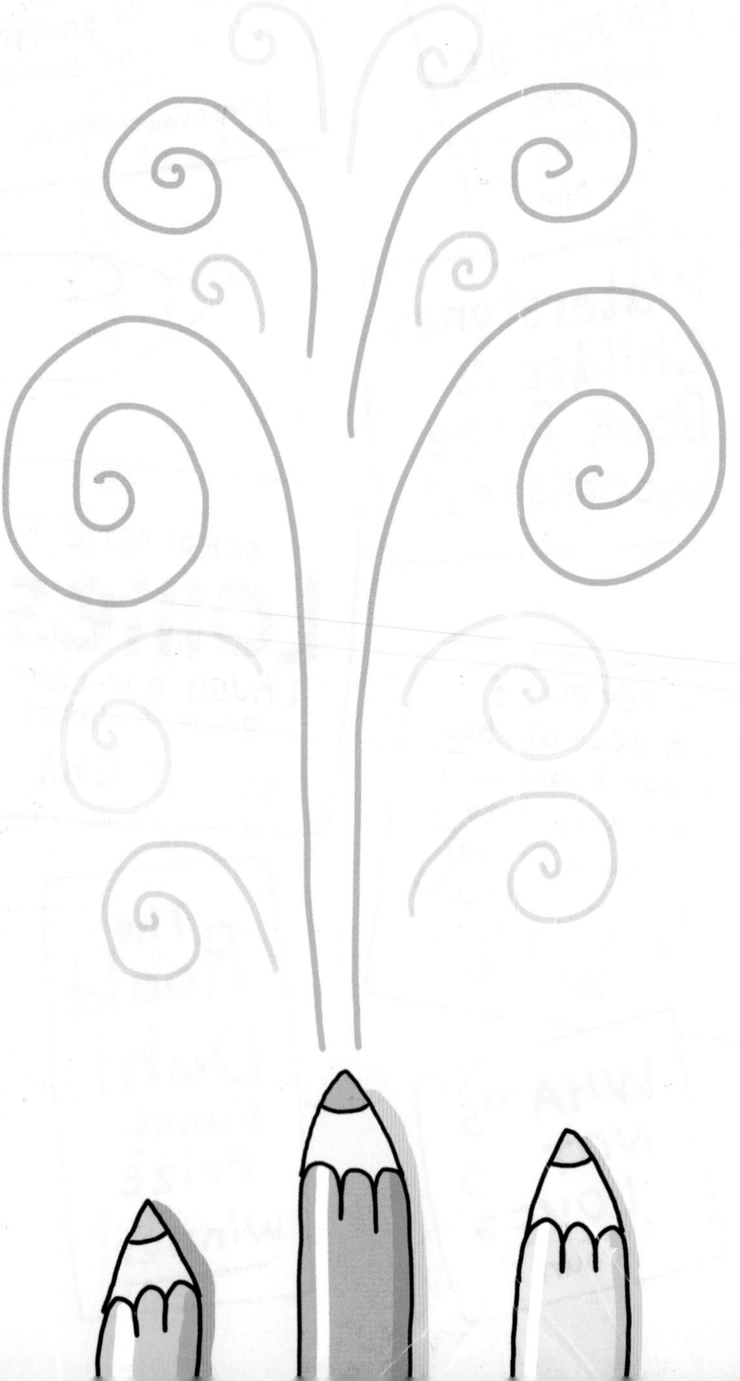

Contents

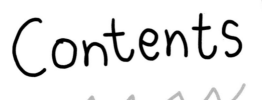

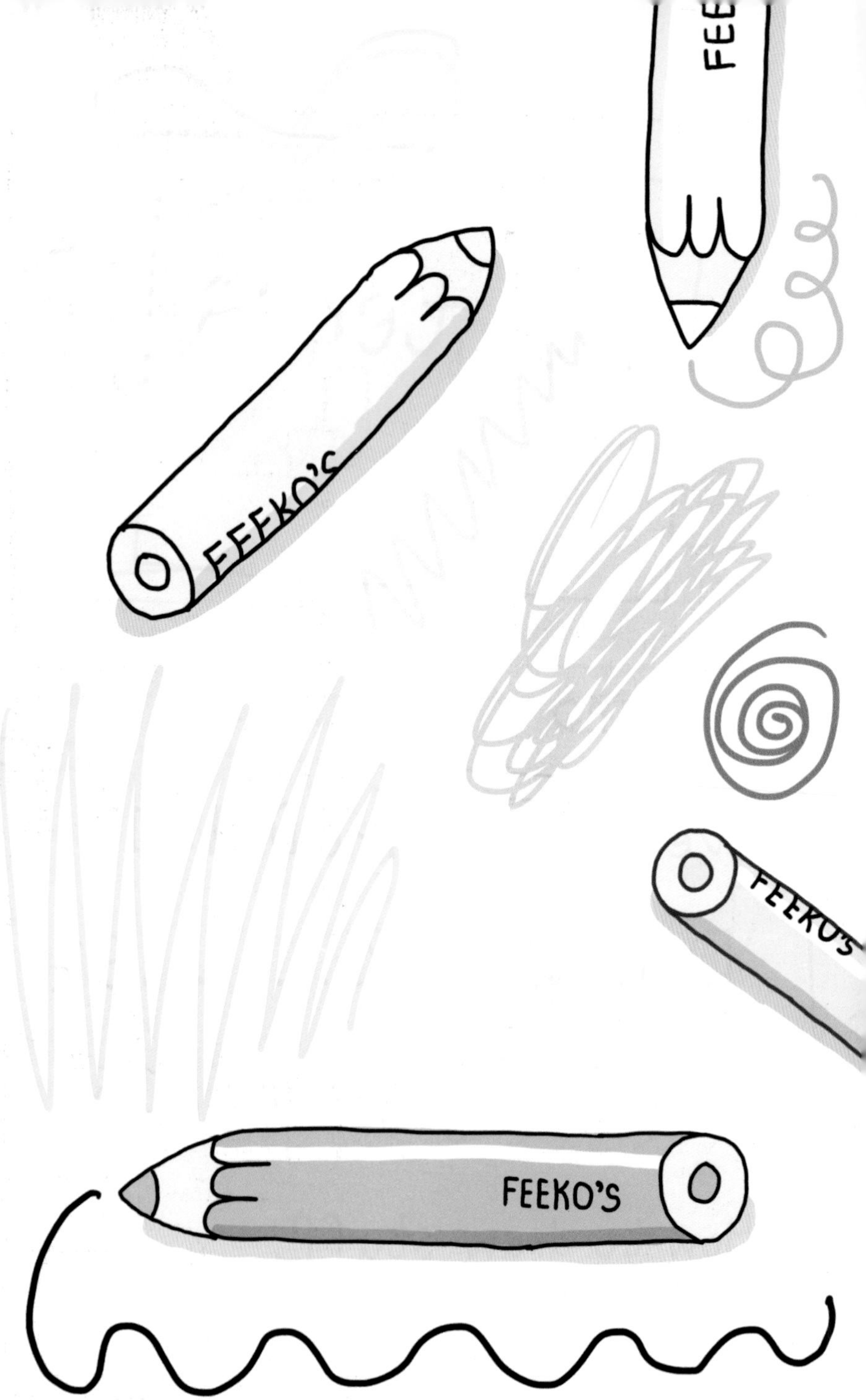
FEEKO'S
FEEKO'S
FEEKO'S
FEEKO'S

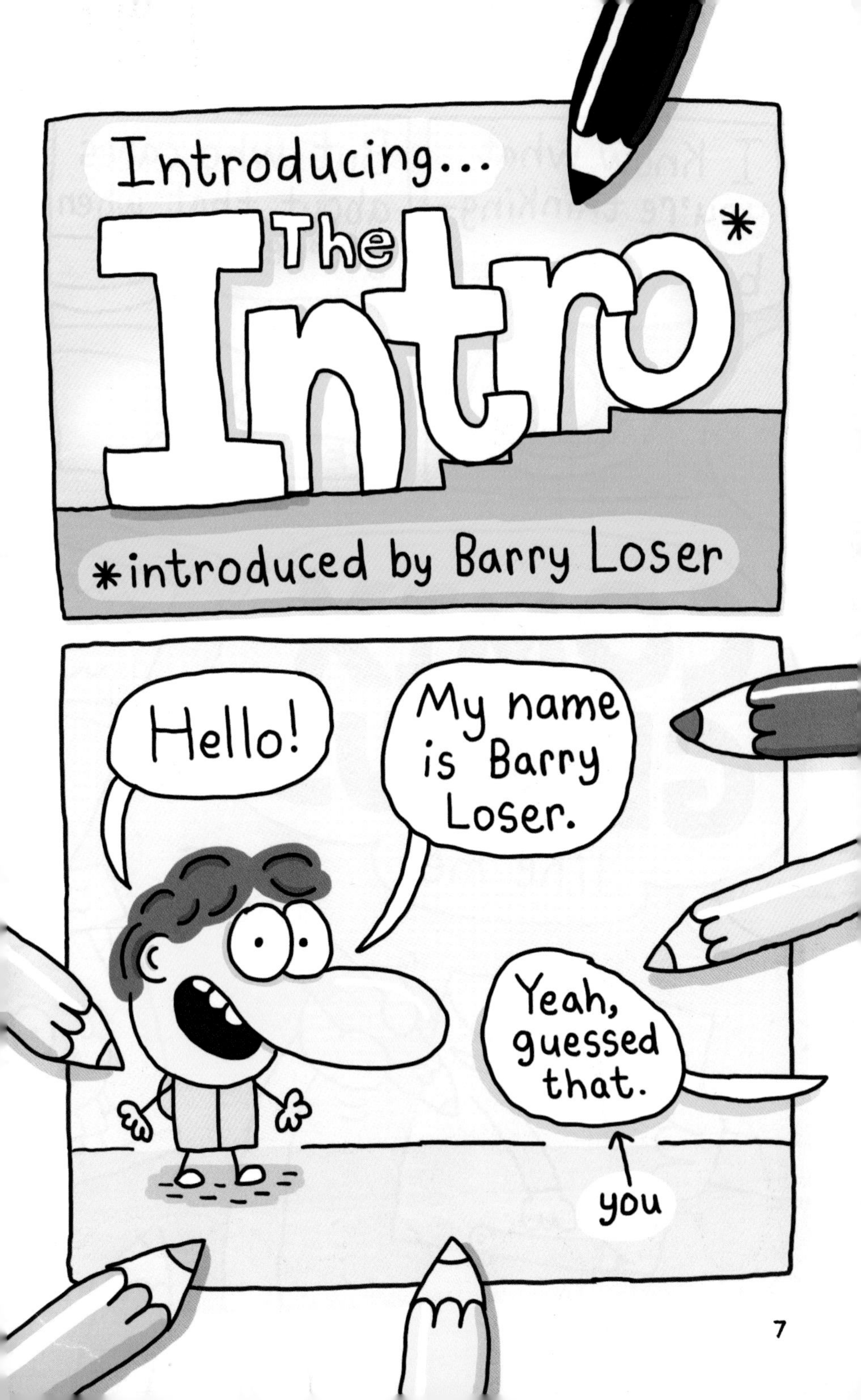
Introducing...
The Intro*
*introduced by Barry Loser
Hello!
My name is Barry Loser.
Yeah, guessed that.
you

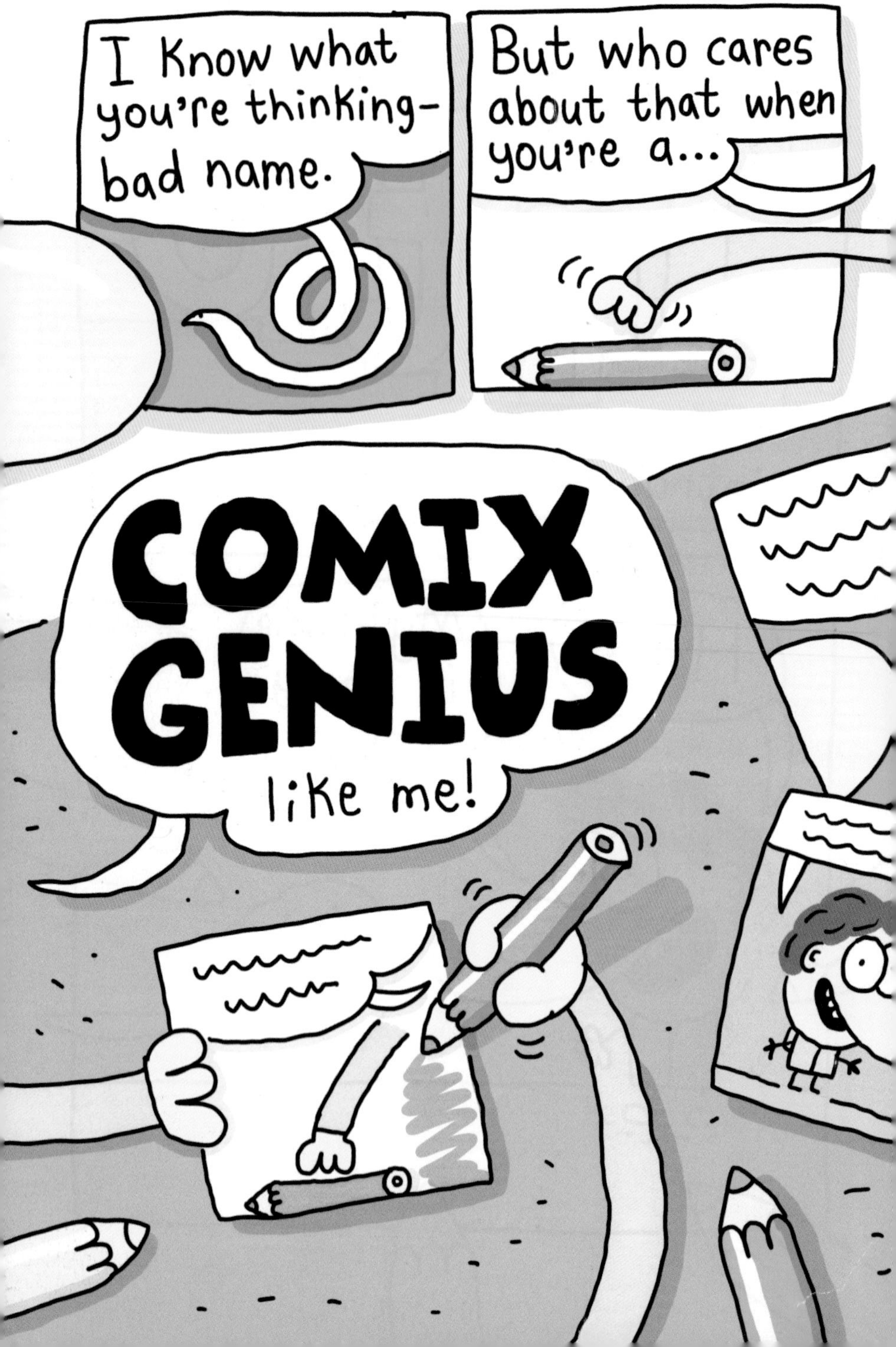
I Know what you're thinking- bad name.
But who cares about that when you're a...
COMIX GENIUS like me!

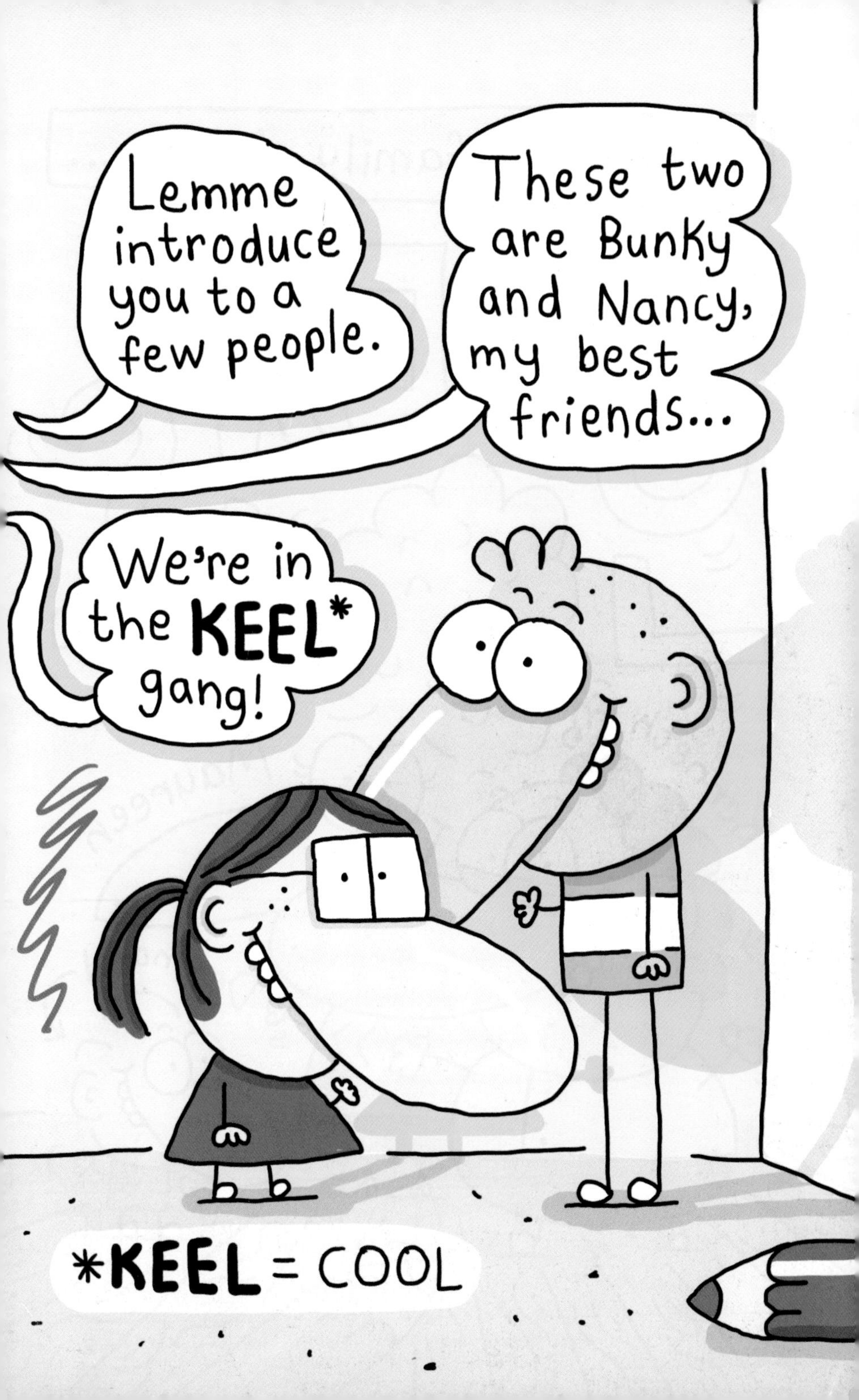
Lemme introduce you to a few people.
These two are Bunky and Nancy, my best friends...
We're in the KEEL* gang!
*KEEL = COOL

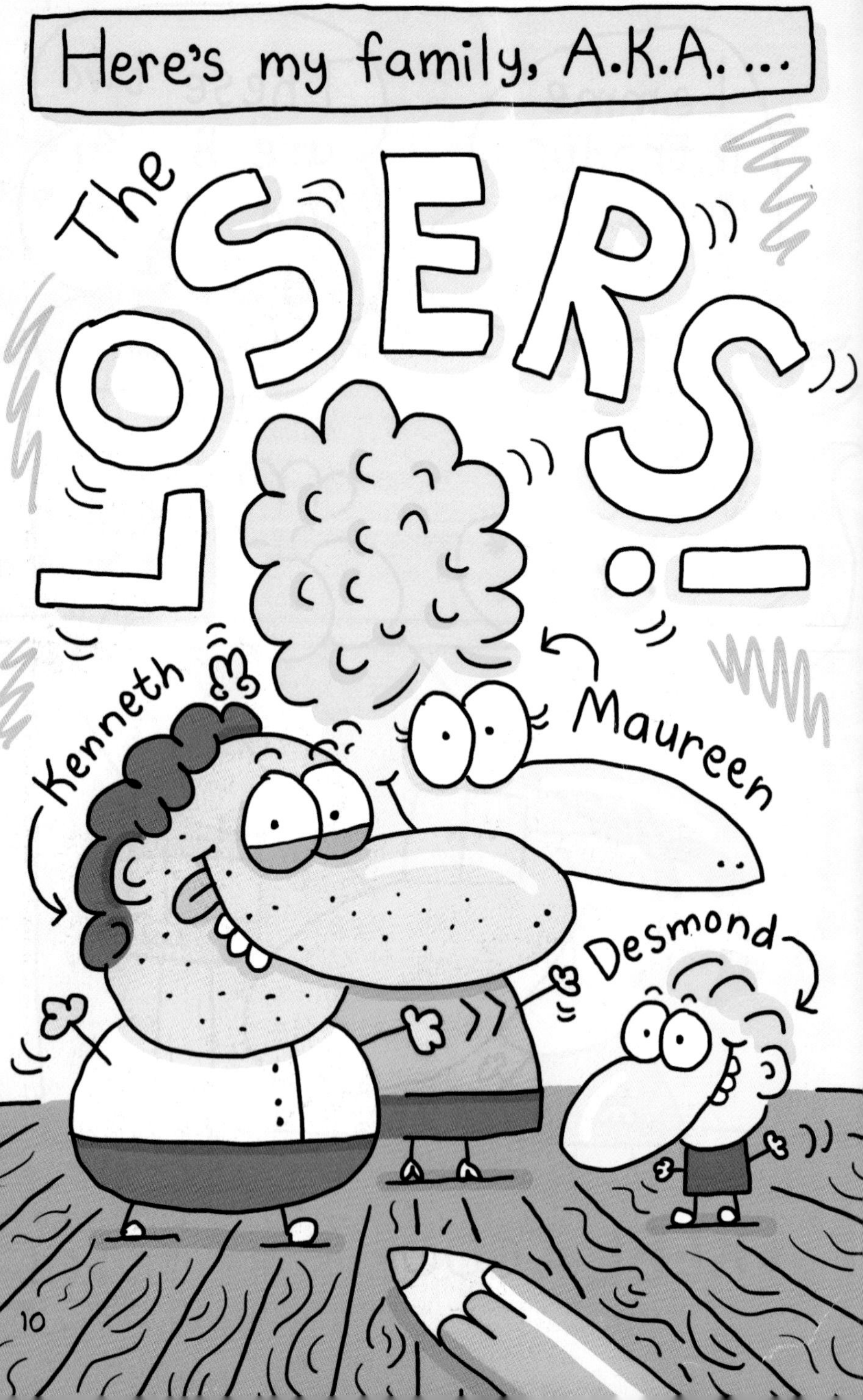
Here's my family, A.K.A. ...
The LOSERS!
Kenneth
Maureen
Desmond

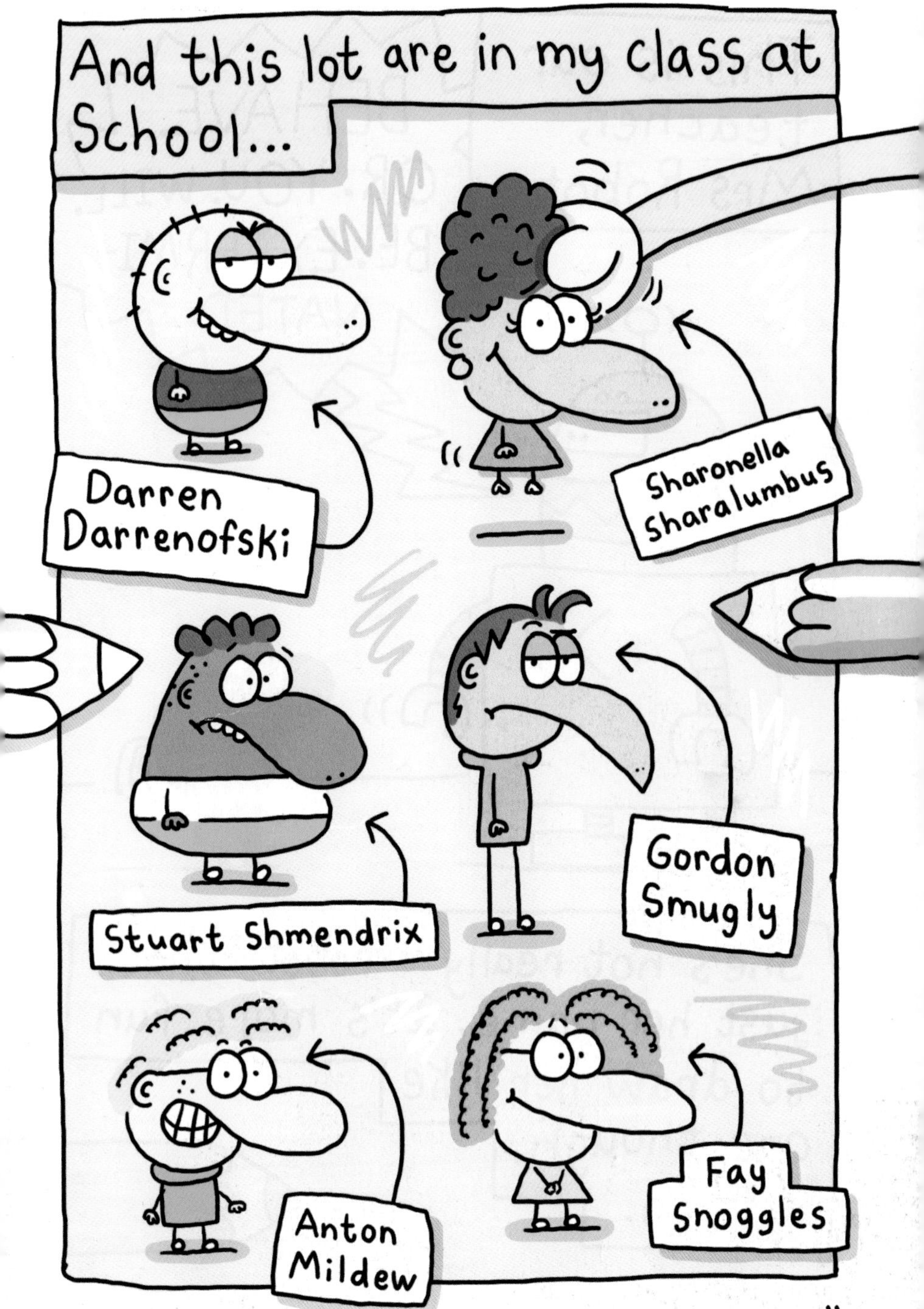
And this lot are in my class at School...
Darren Darrenofski
Sharonella Sharalumbus
Stuart Shmendrix
Gordon Smugly
Anton Mildew
Fay Snoggles

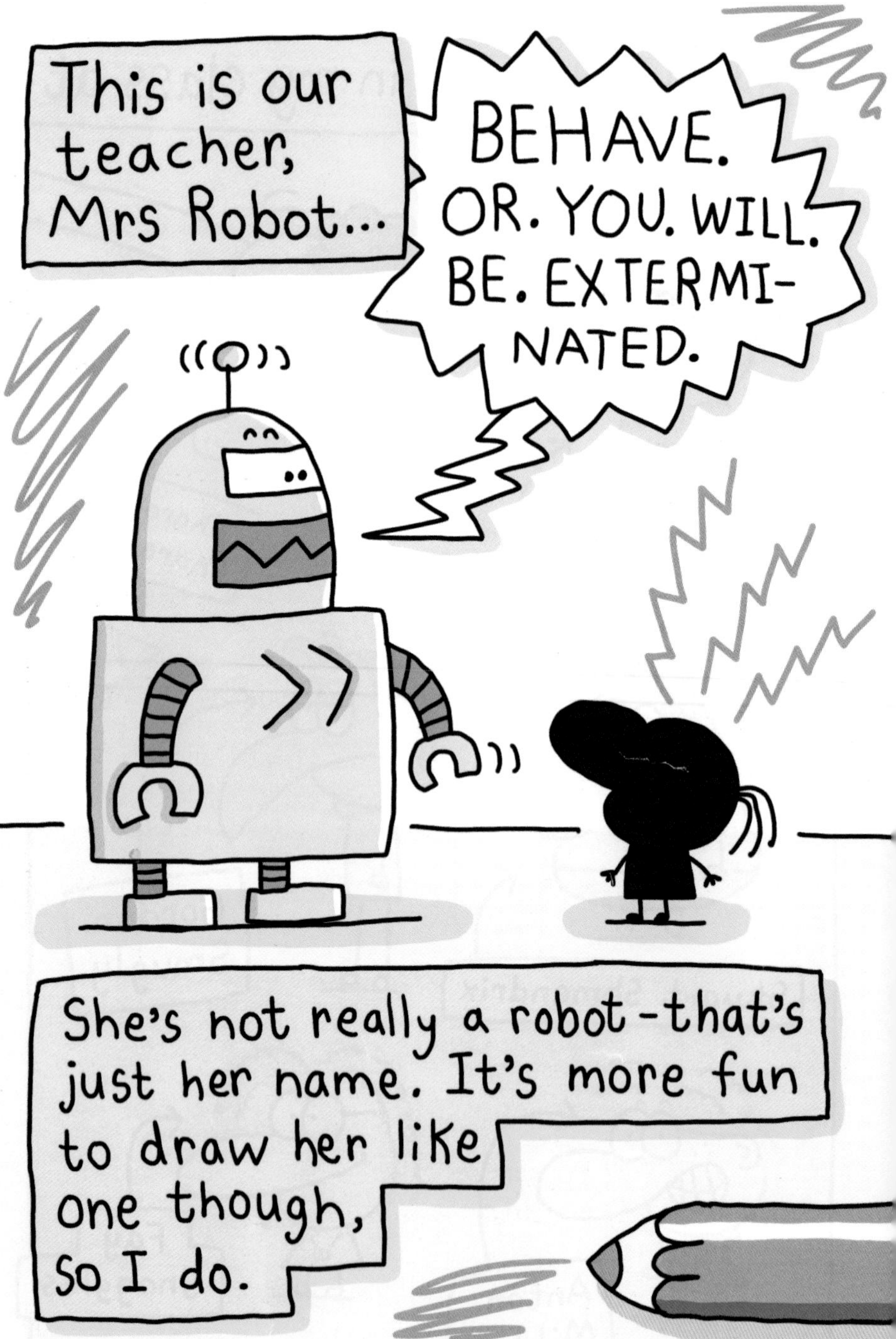
This is our teacher, Mrs Robot...
BEHAVE. OR. YOU. WILL. BE. EXTERMI-NATED.
She's not really a robot - that's just her name. It's more fun to draw her like one though, so I do.

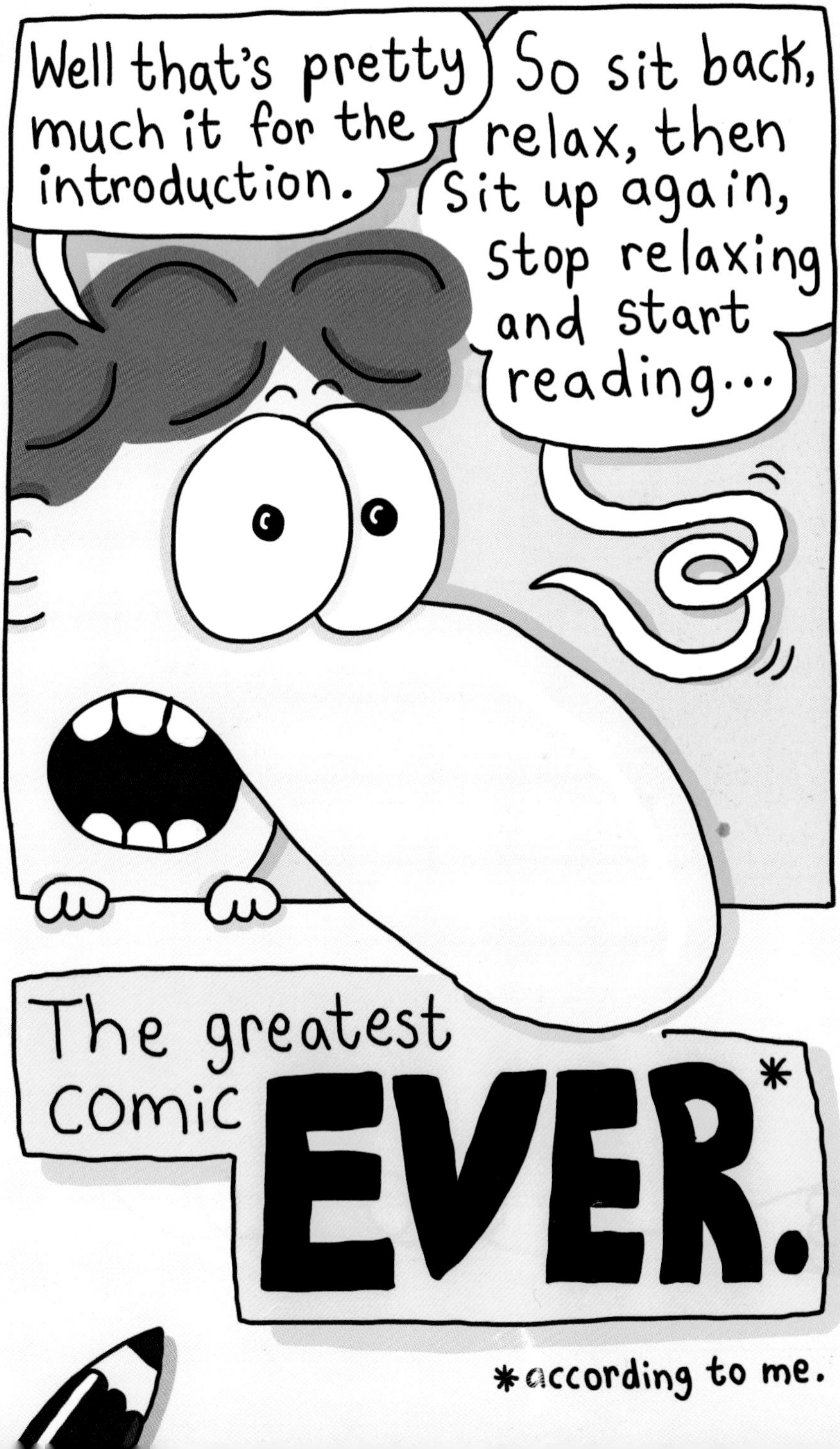
Well that's pretty much it for the introduction.
So sit back, relax, then Sit up again, Stop relaxing and Start reading...
The greatest comic EVER.*
*according to me.

Write
something
on this
page.

Episode 1

Vending Machine Dad

Very early one morning...

Pssst! Barry!

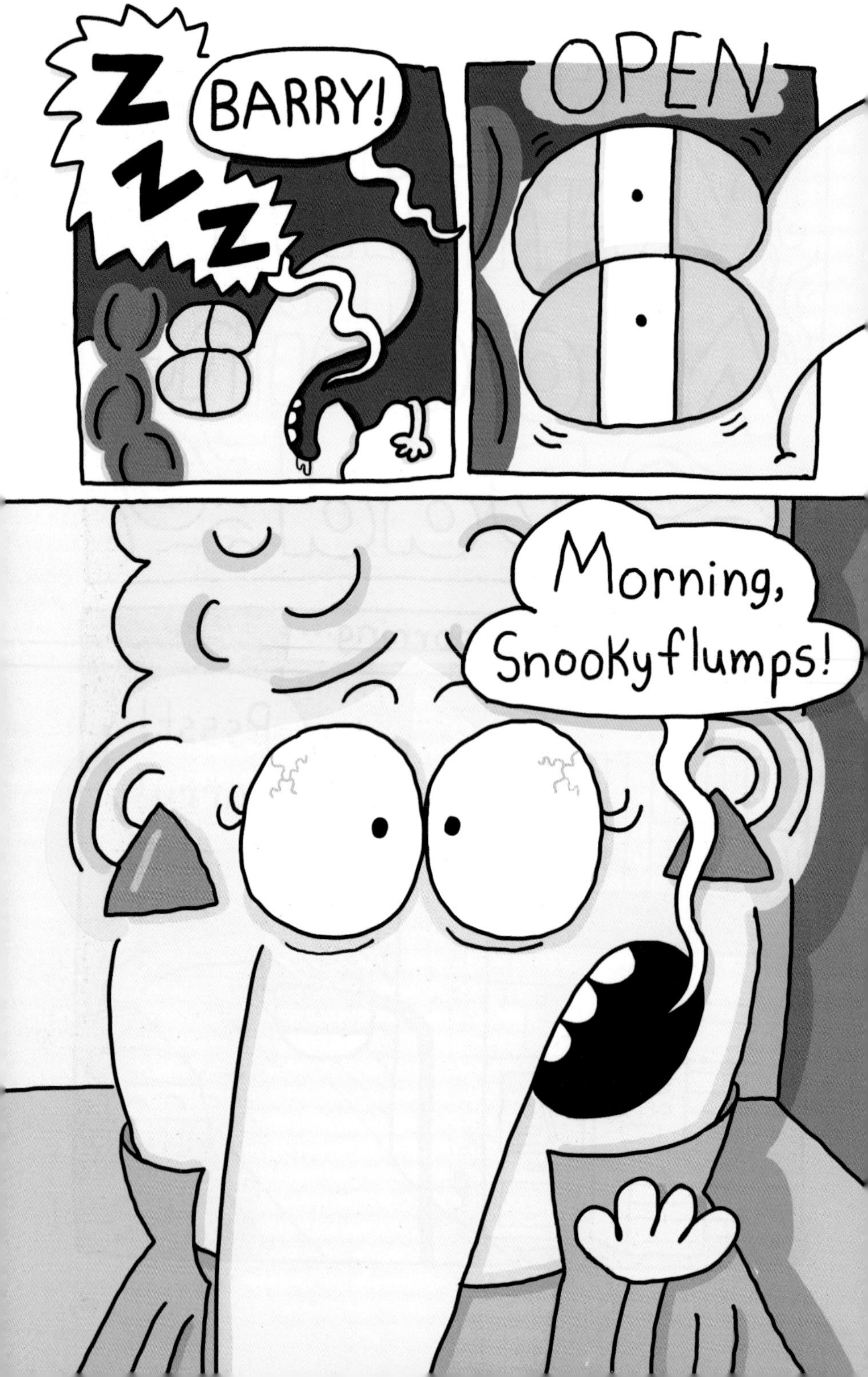
ZZZ
BARRY!
OPEN
Morning, Snookyflumps!

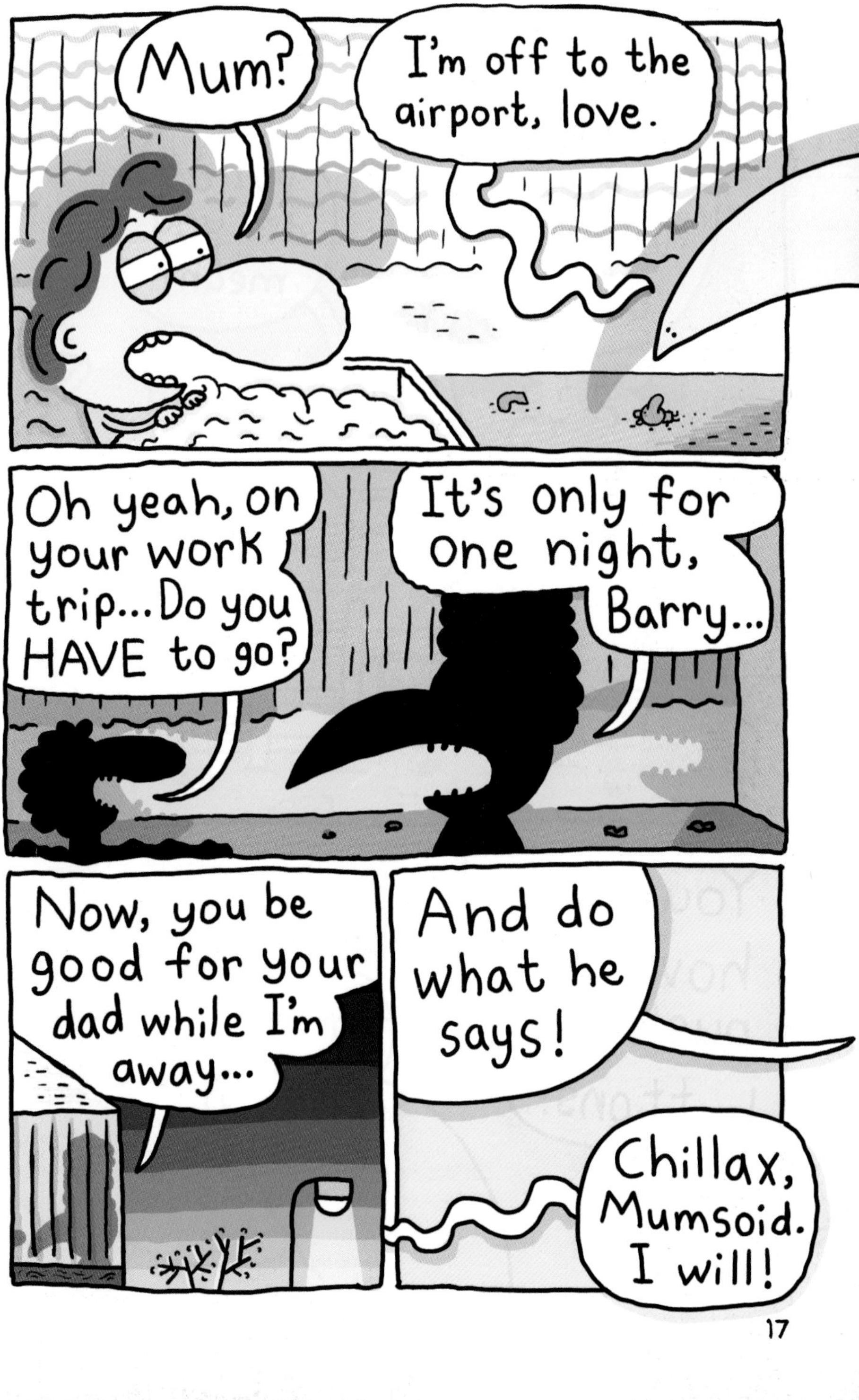
Mum?
I'm off to the airport, love.
Oh yeah, on your work trip... Do you HAVE to go?
It's only for one night, Barry...
Now, you be good for your dad while I'm away...
And do what he says!
Chillax, Mumsoid. I will!

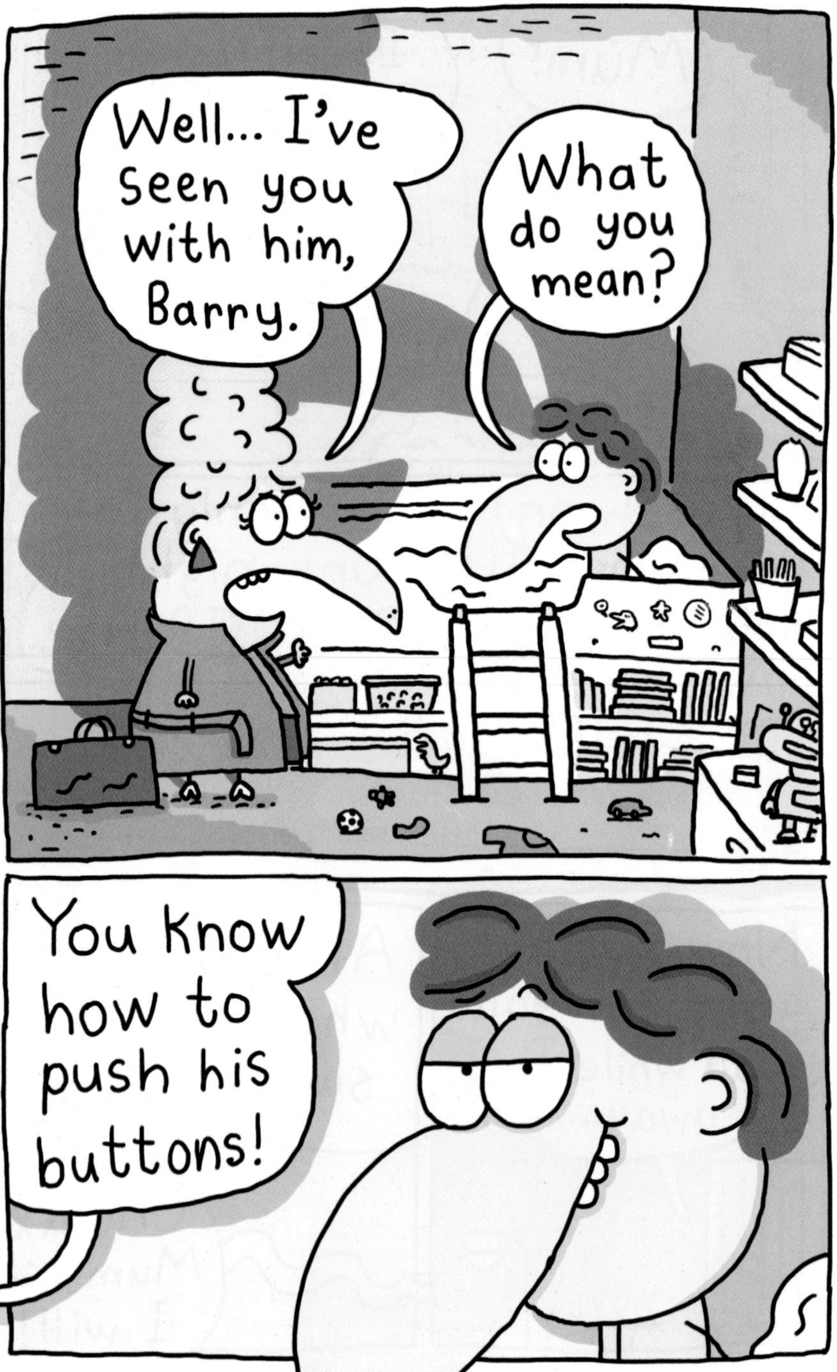
Well... I've seen you with him, Barry.
What do you mean?
You know how to push his buttons!

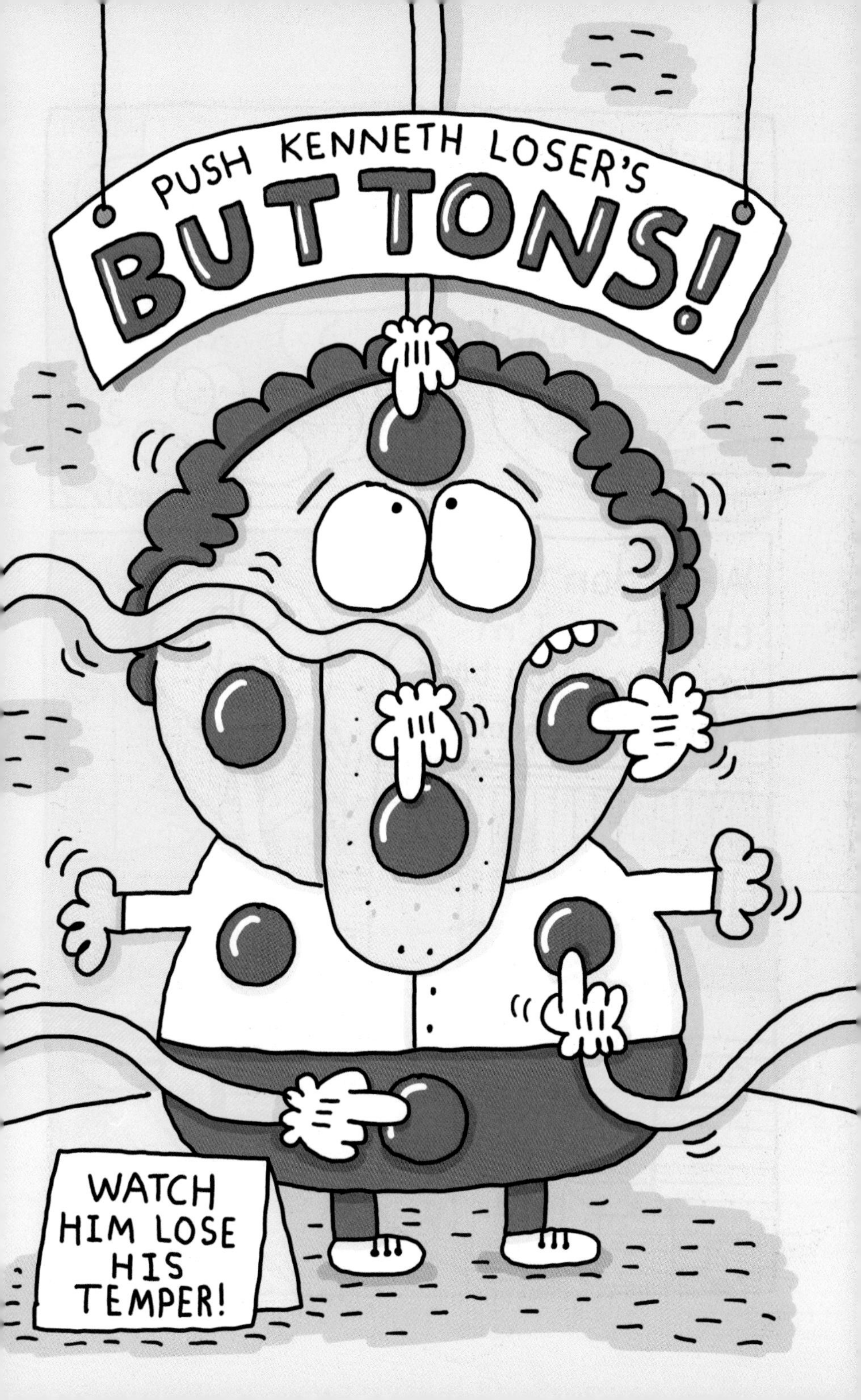
PUSH KENNETH LOSER'S
BUTTONS!
WATCH
HIM LOSE
HIS
TEMPER!

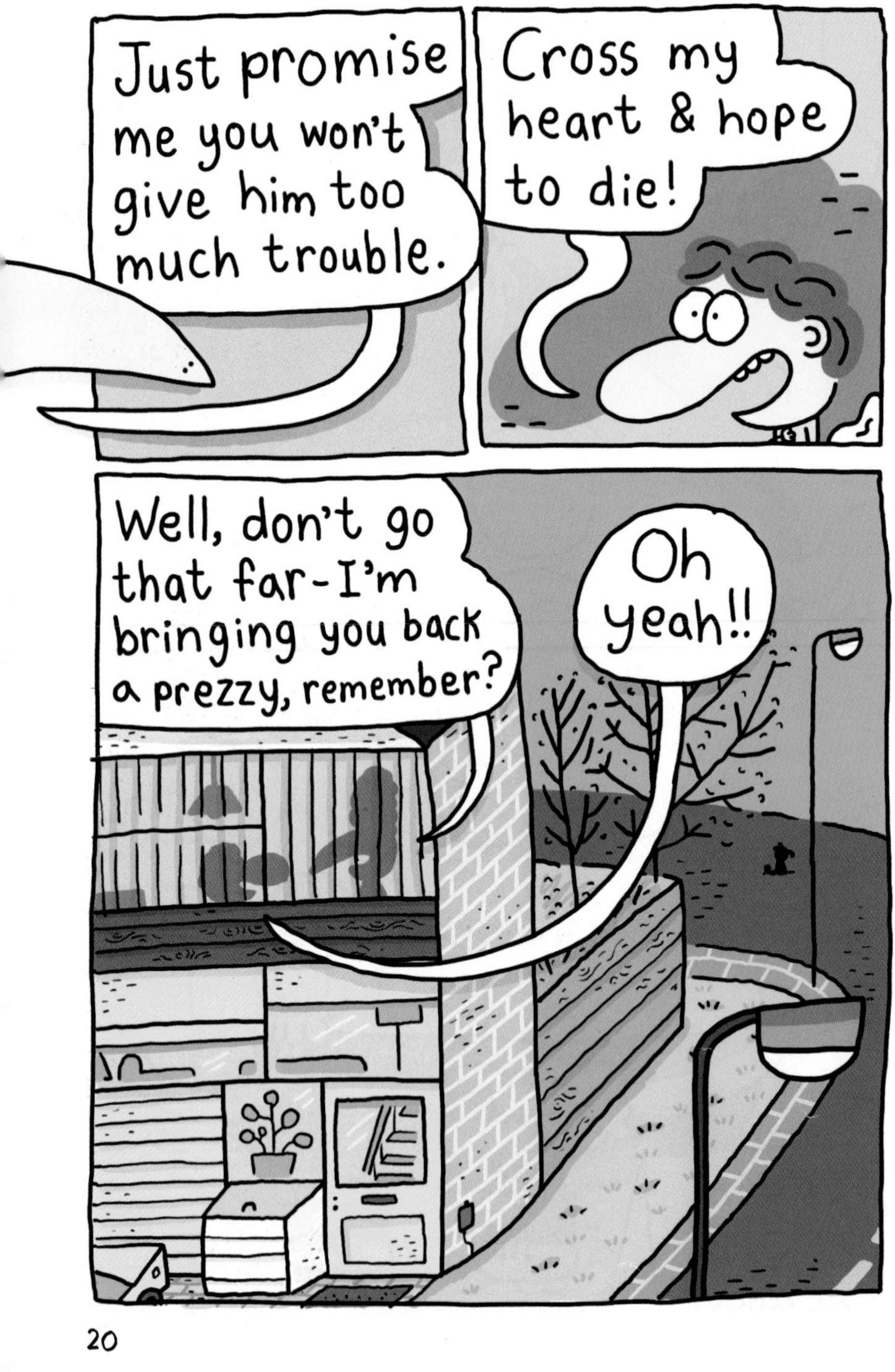
Just promise me you won't give him too much trouble.
Cross my heart & hope to die!
Well, don't go that far-I'm bringing you back a prezzy, remember?
Oh yeah!!

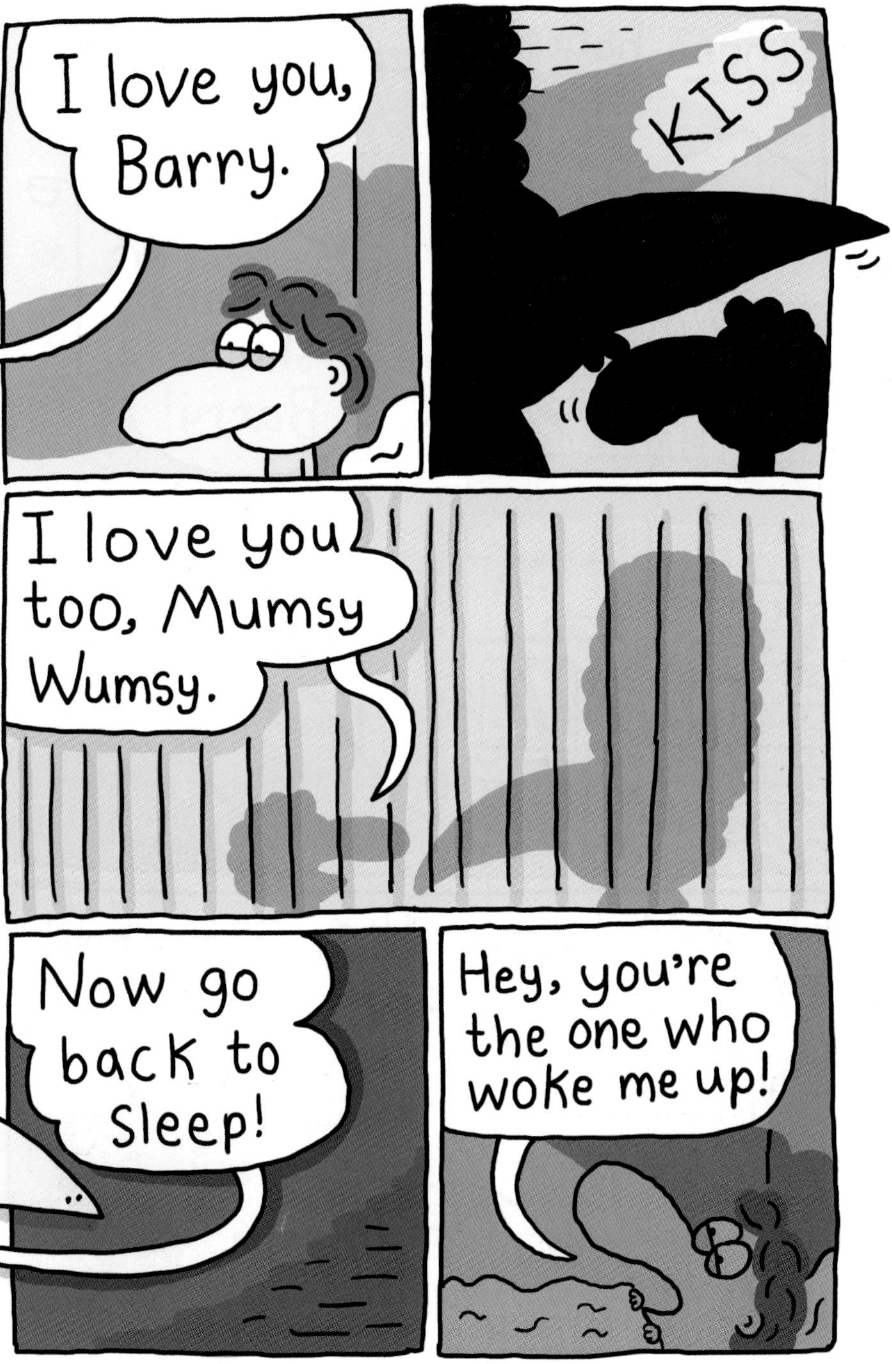
I love you, Barry.
KISS
I love you too, Mumsy Wumsy.
Now go back to sleep!
Hey, you're the one who woke me up!

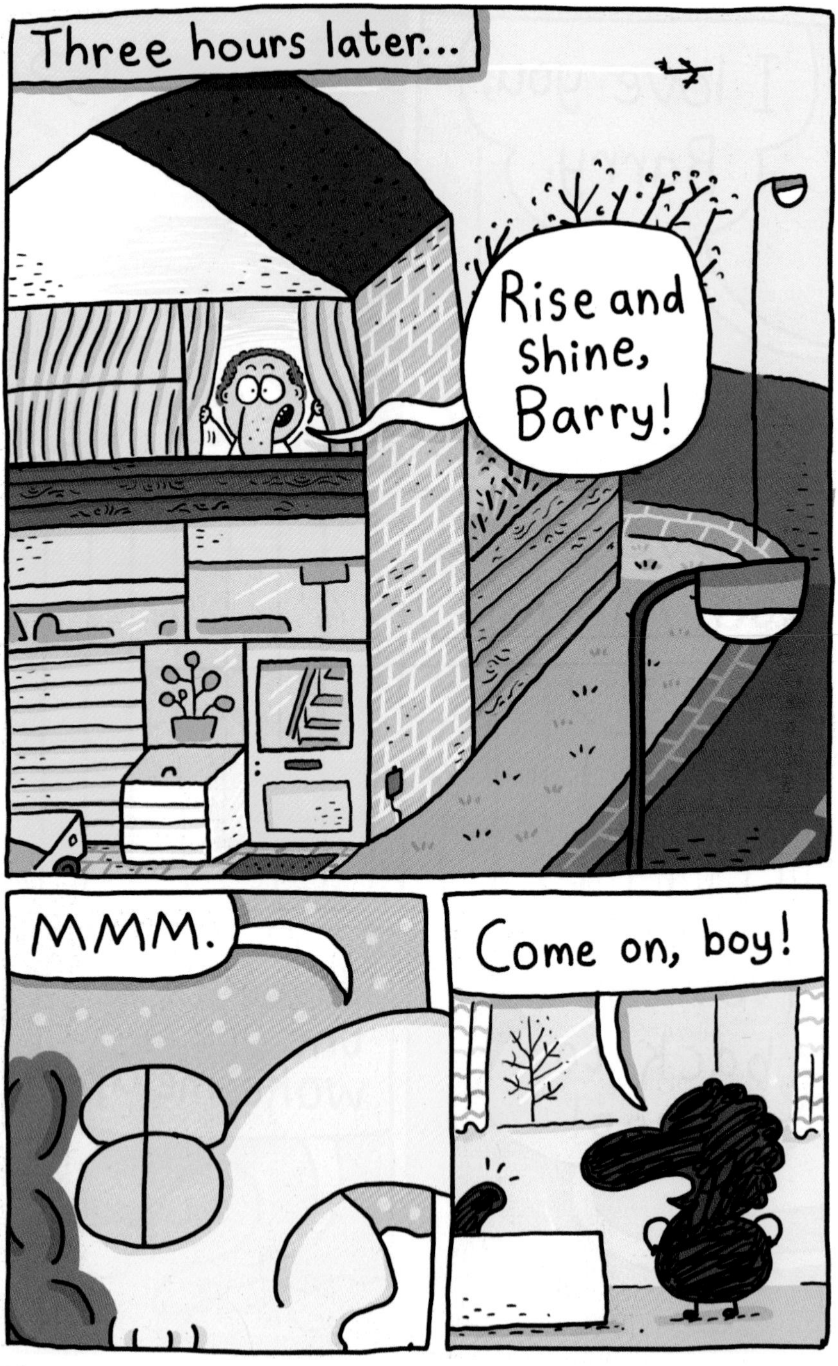
Three hours later...
Rise and shine, Barry!
MMM.
Come on, boy!

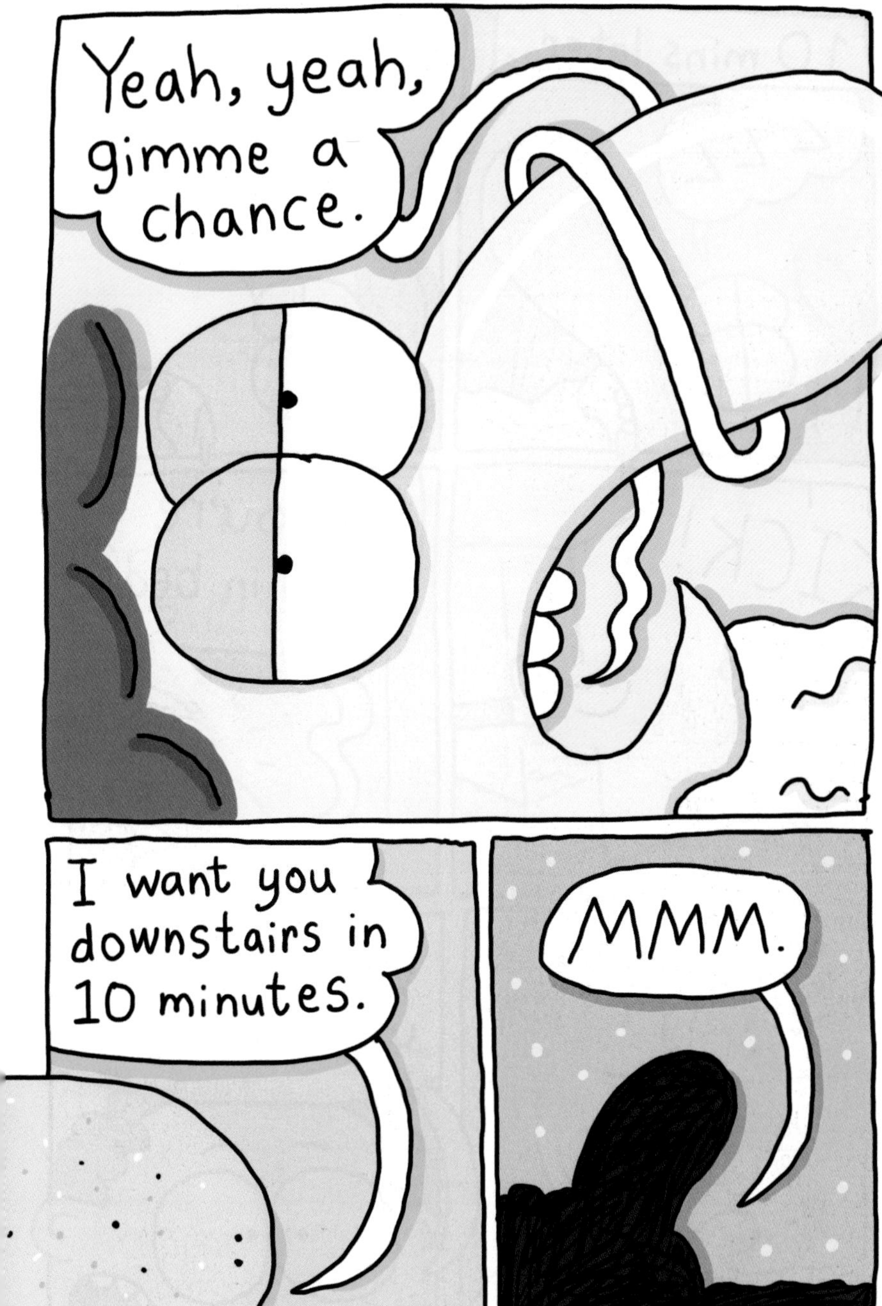
Yeah, yeah, gimme a chance.
I want you downstairs in 10 minutes.
MMM.

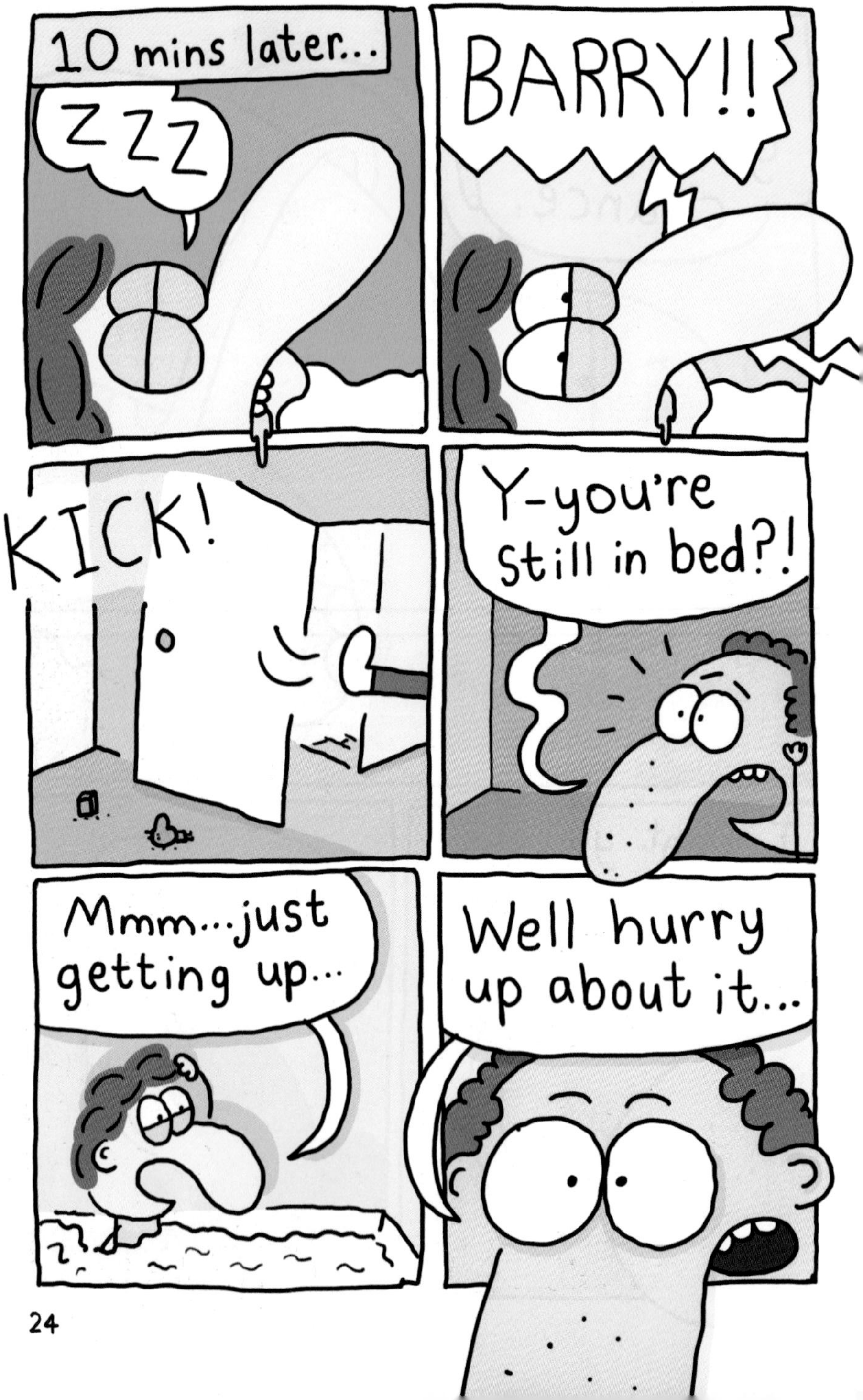
10 mins later...
ZZZ
BARRY!!
KICK!
Y-you're still in bed?!
Mmm...just getting up...
Well hurry up about it...

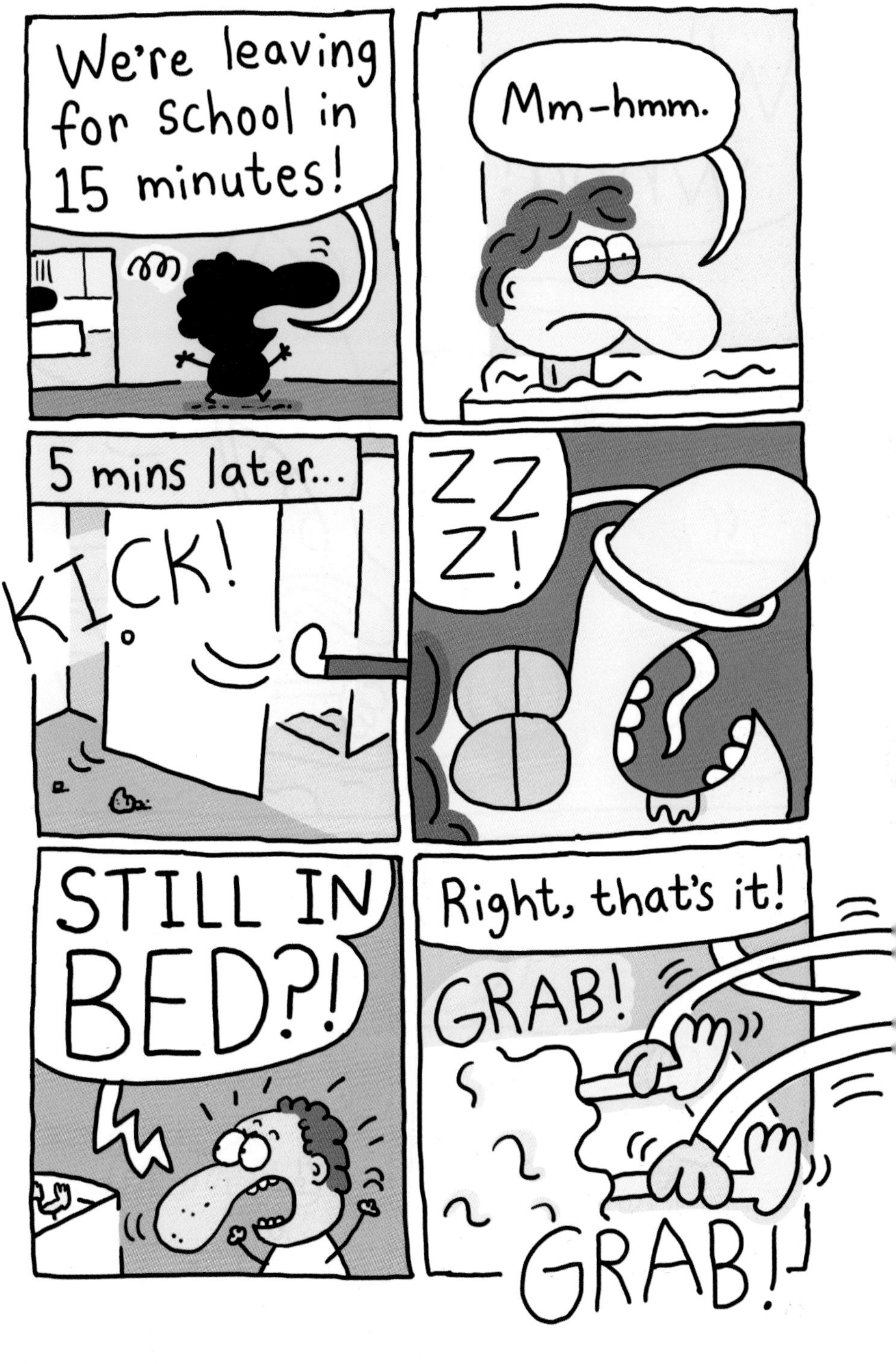
We're leaving for School in 15 minutes!
Mm-hmm.
5 mins later...
KICK!
ZZZ!
STILL IN BED?!
Right, that's it!
GRAB!
GRAB!

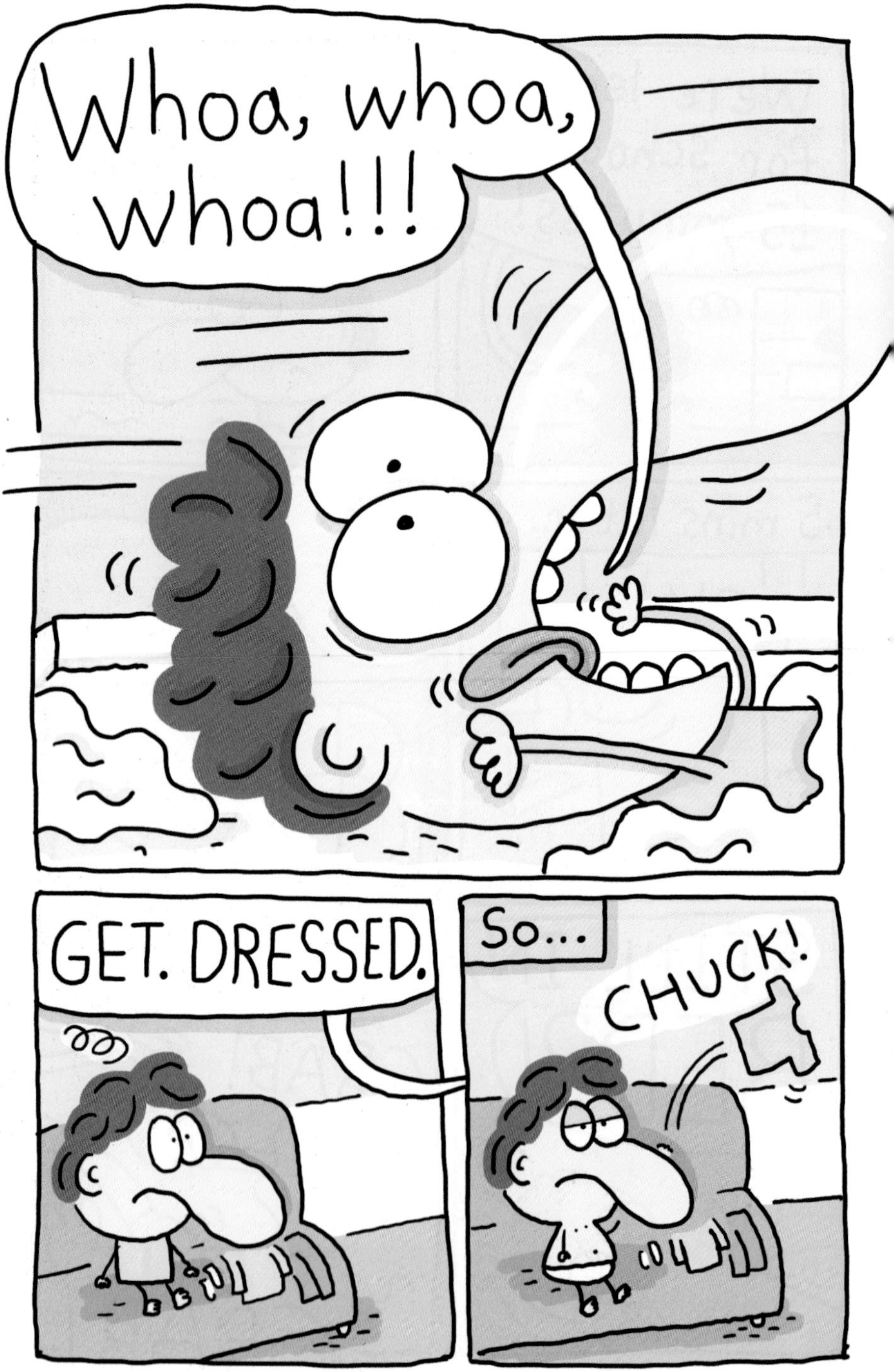
Whoa, whoa, whoa!!!
GET. DRESSED.
So...
CHUCK!

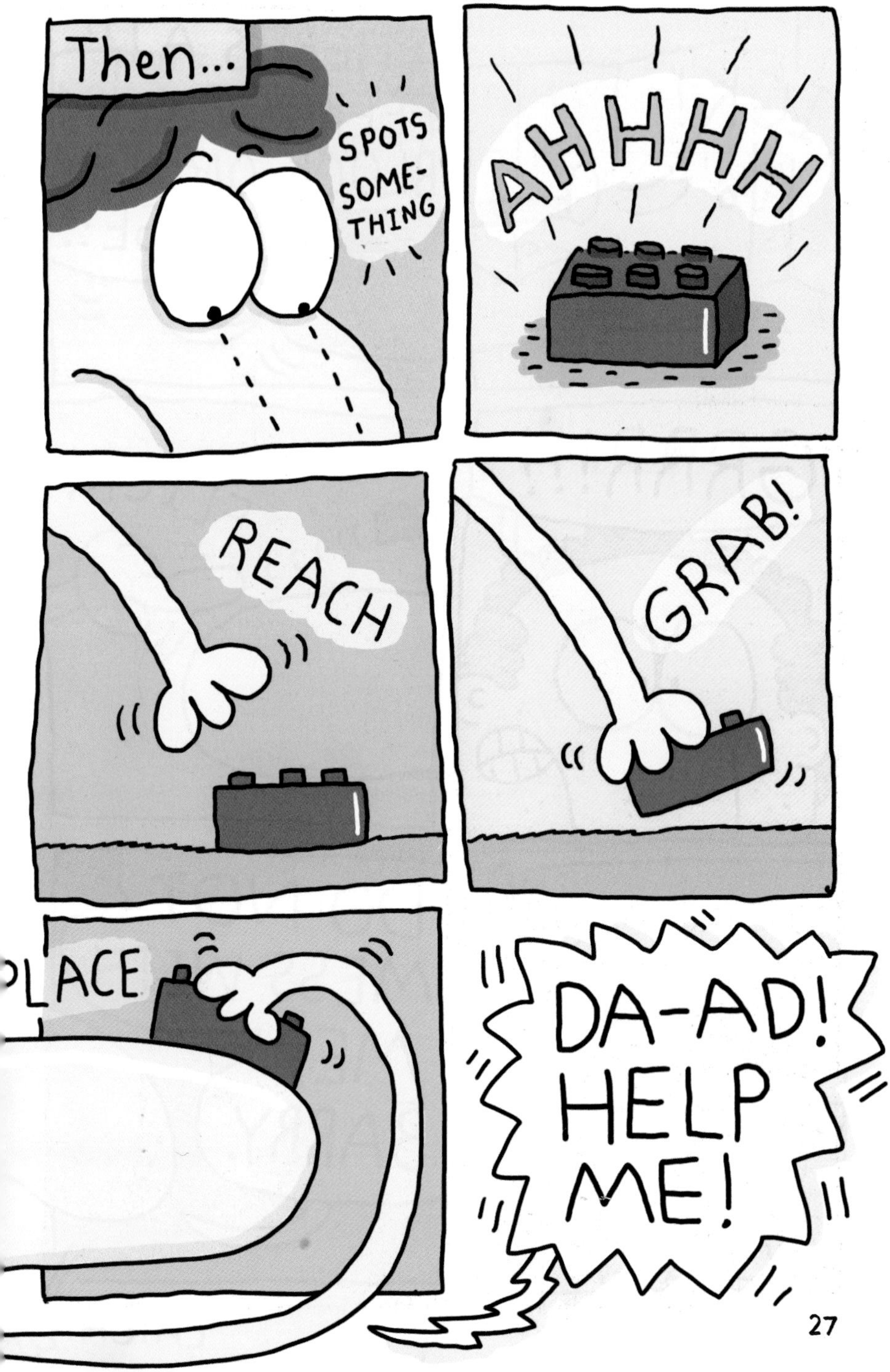
Then...
SPOTS SOME-THING
AHHHH
REACH
GRAB!
PLACE
DA-AD! HELP ME!

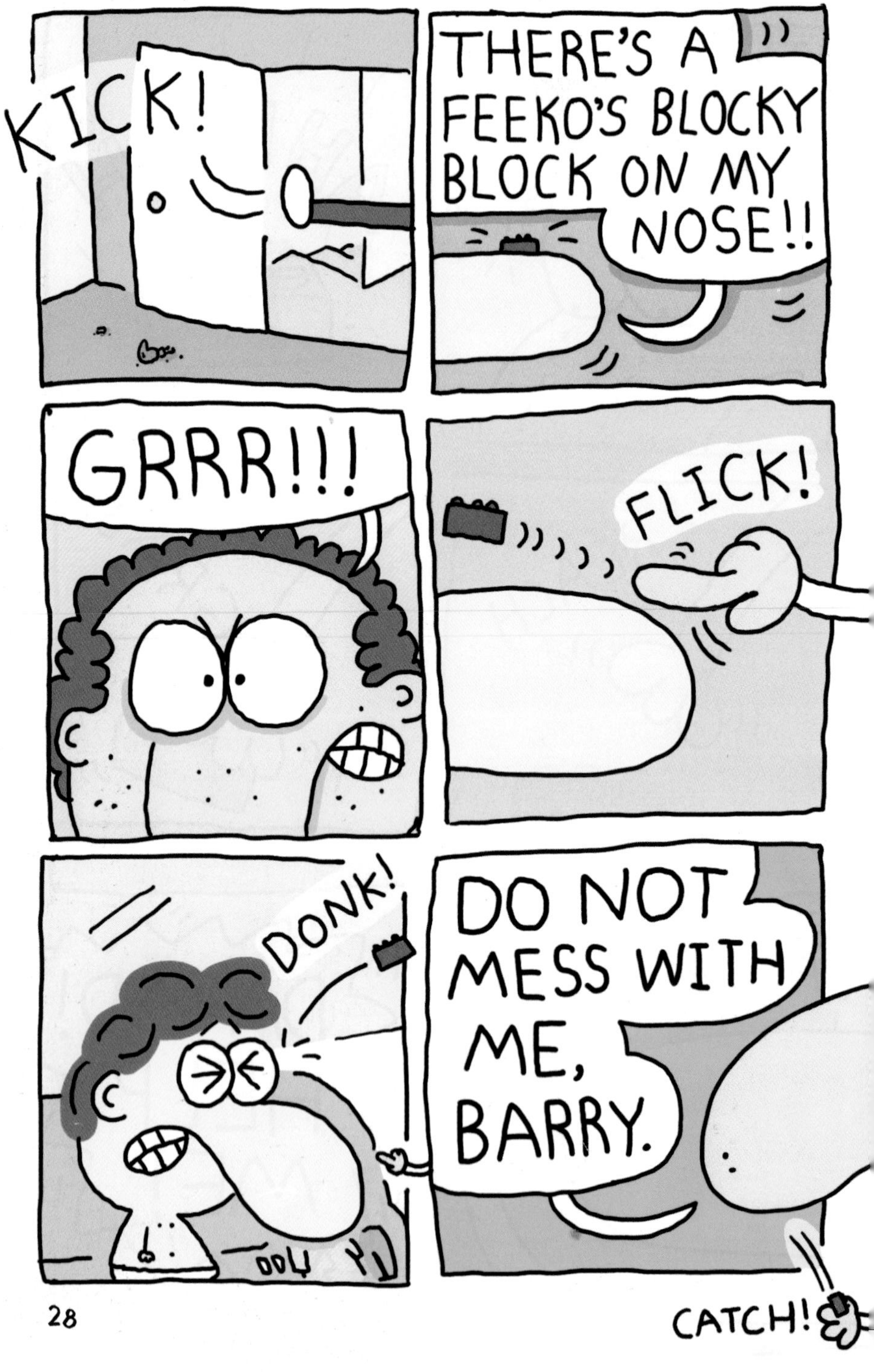

KICK!
THERE'S A FEEKO'S BLOCKY BLOCK ON MY NOSE!!
GRRRR!!!
FLICK!
DONK!
DO NOT MESS WITH ME, BARRY.
CATCH!

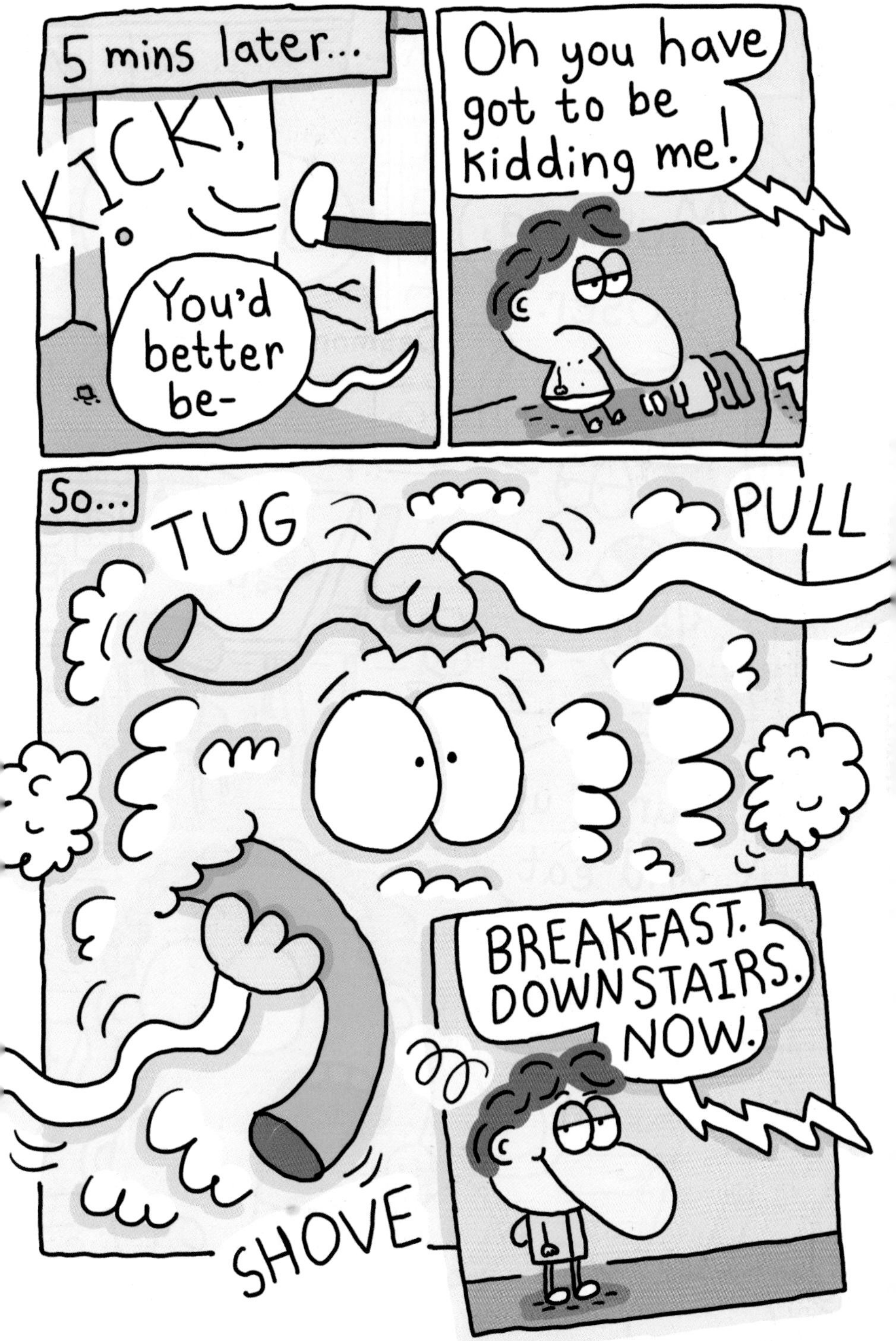
5 mins later...
KICK!
You'd better be-
Oh you have got to be kidding me!
So...
TUG
PULL
SHOVE
BREAKFAST. DOWNSTAIRS. NOW.

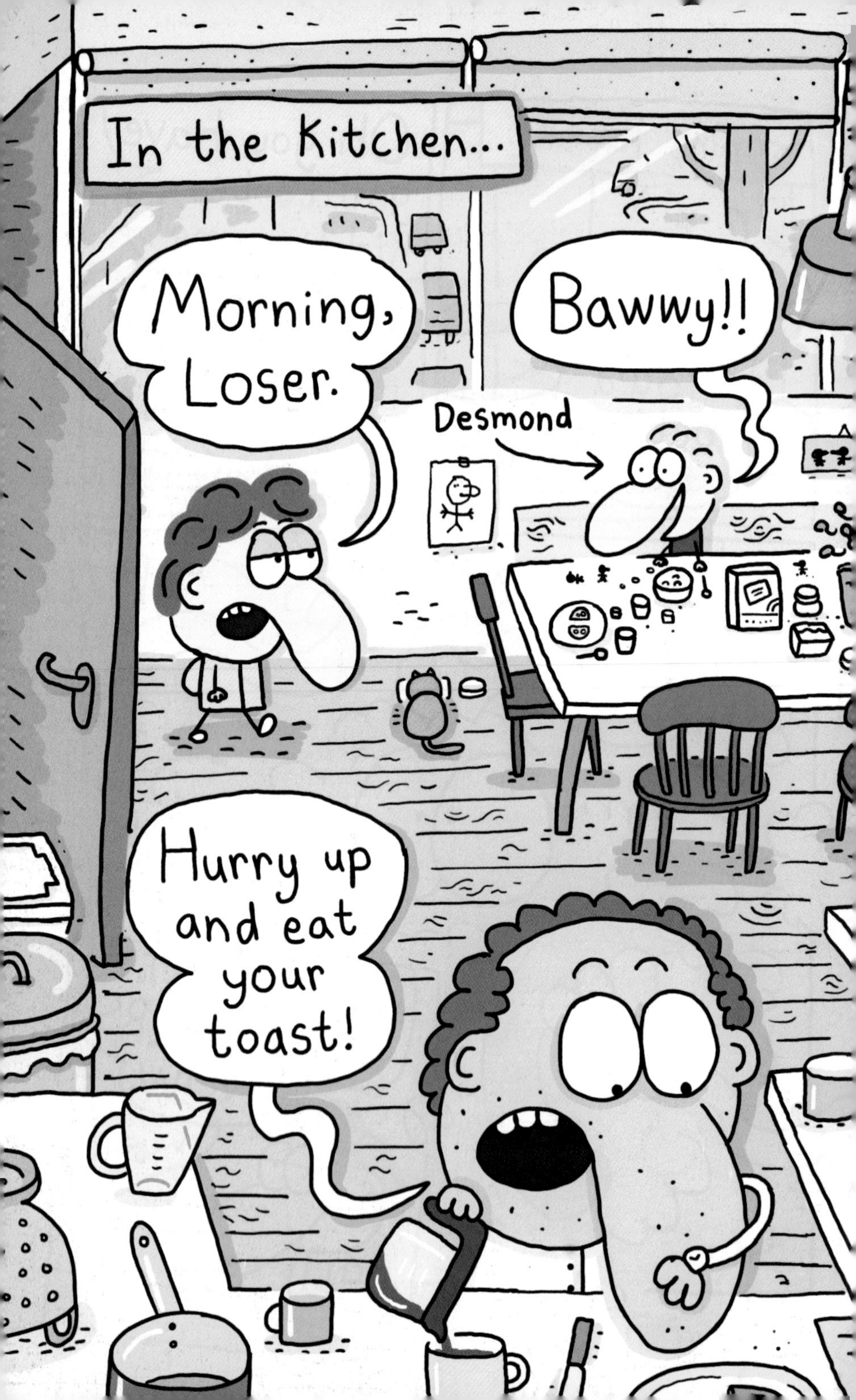
In the Kitchen...
Morning, Loser.
Bawwy!!
Desmond
Hurry up and eat your toast!

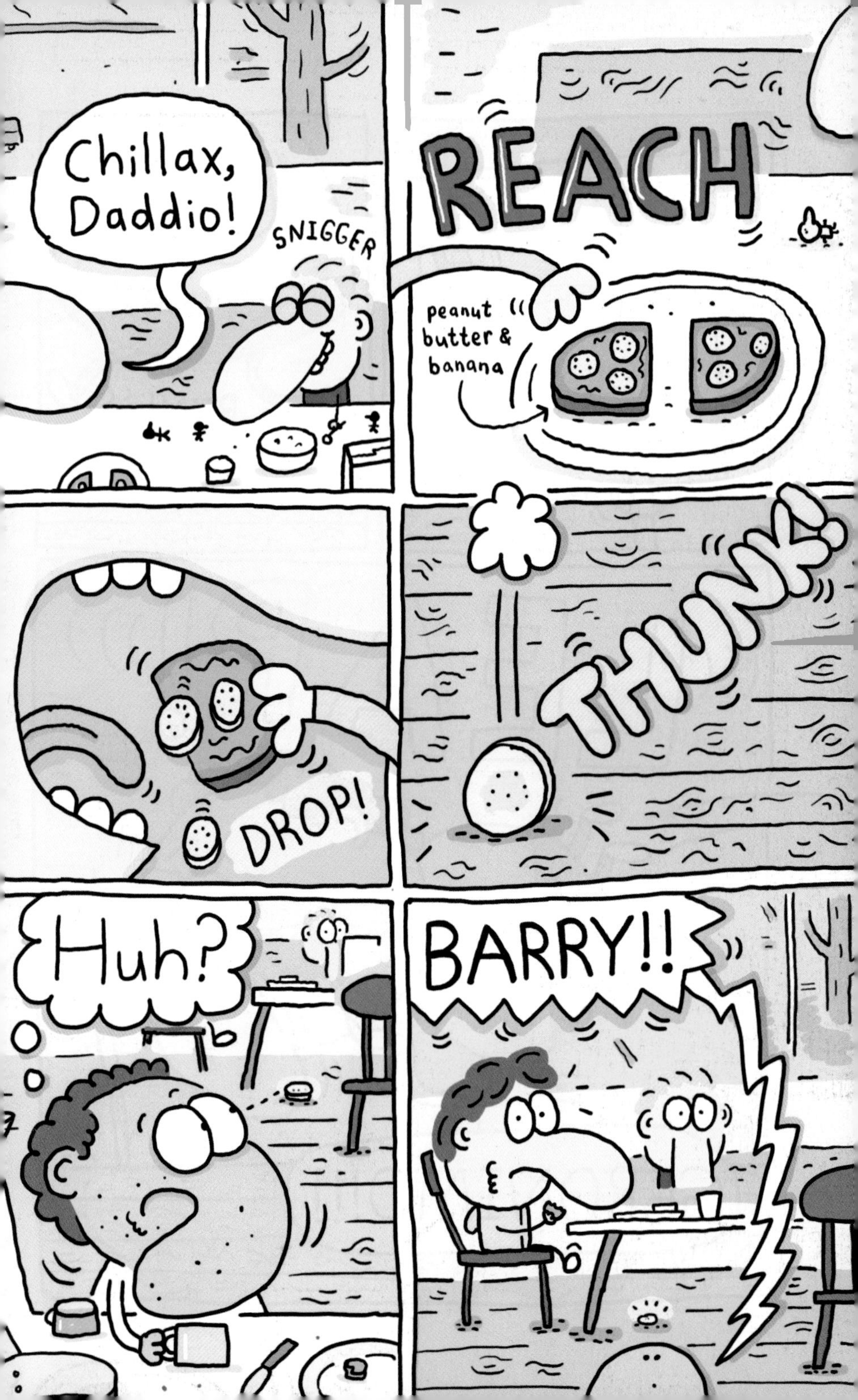
Chillax, Daddio!
SNIGGER
REACH
peanut butter & banana
DROP!
THUNK!
Huh?
BARRY!!

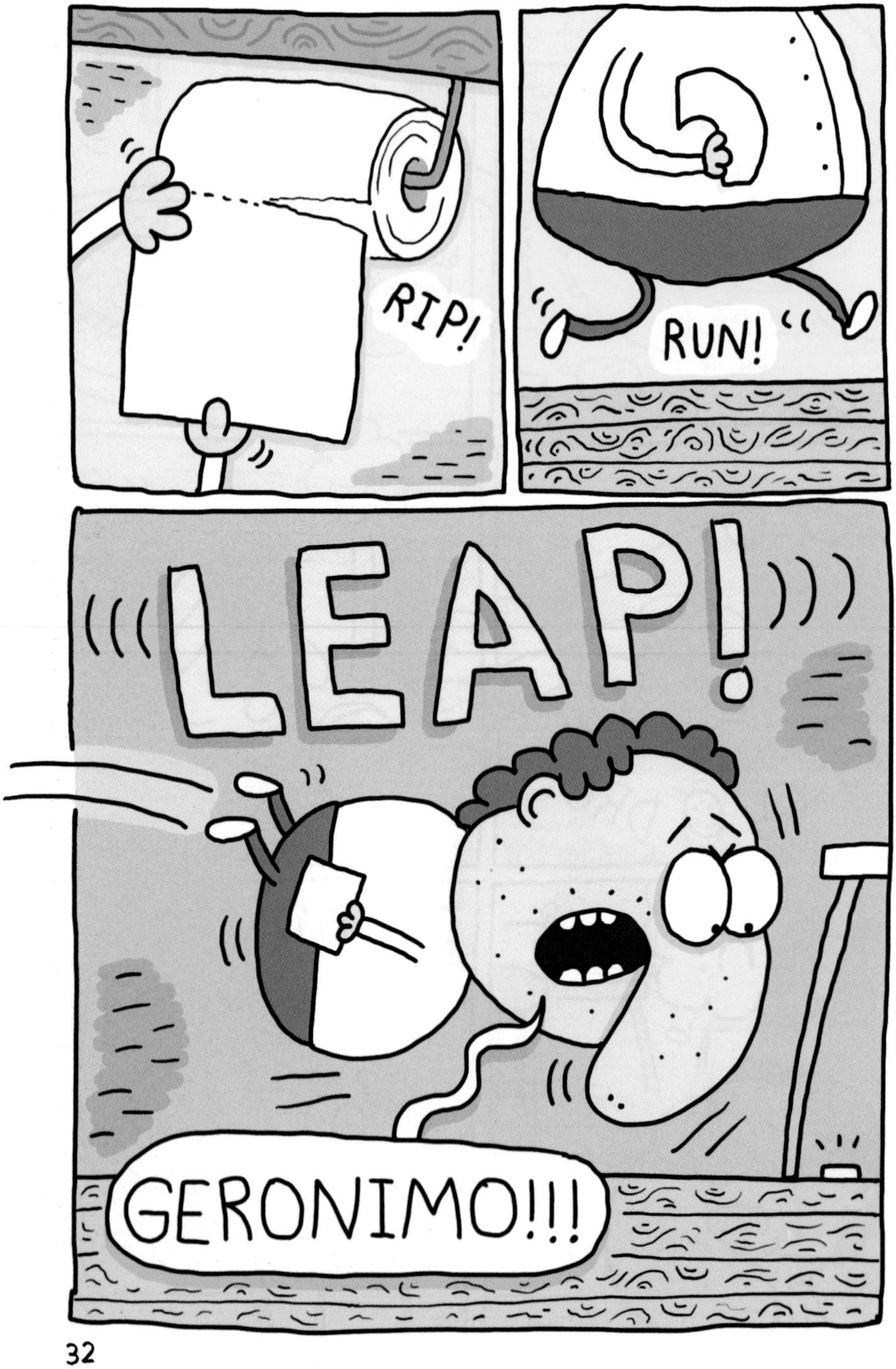
RIP!
RUN!
LEAP!
GERONIMO!!!

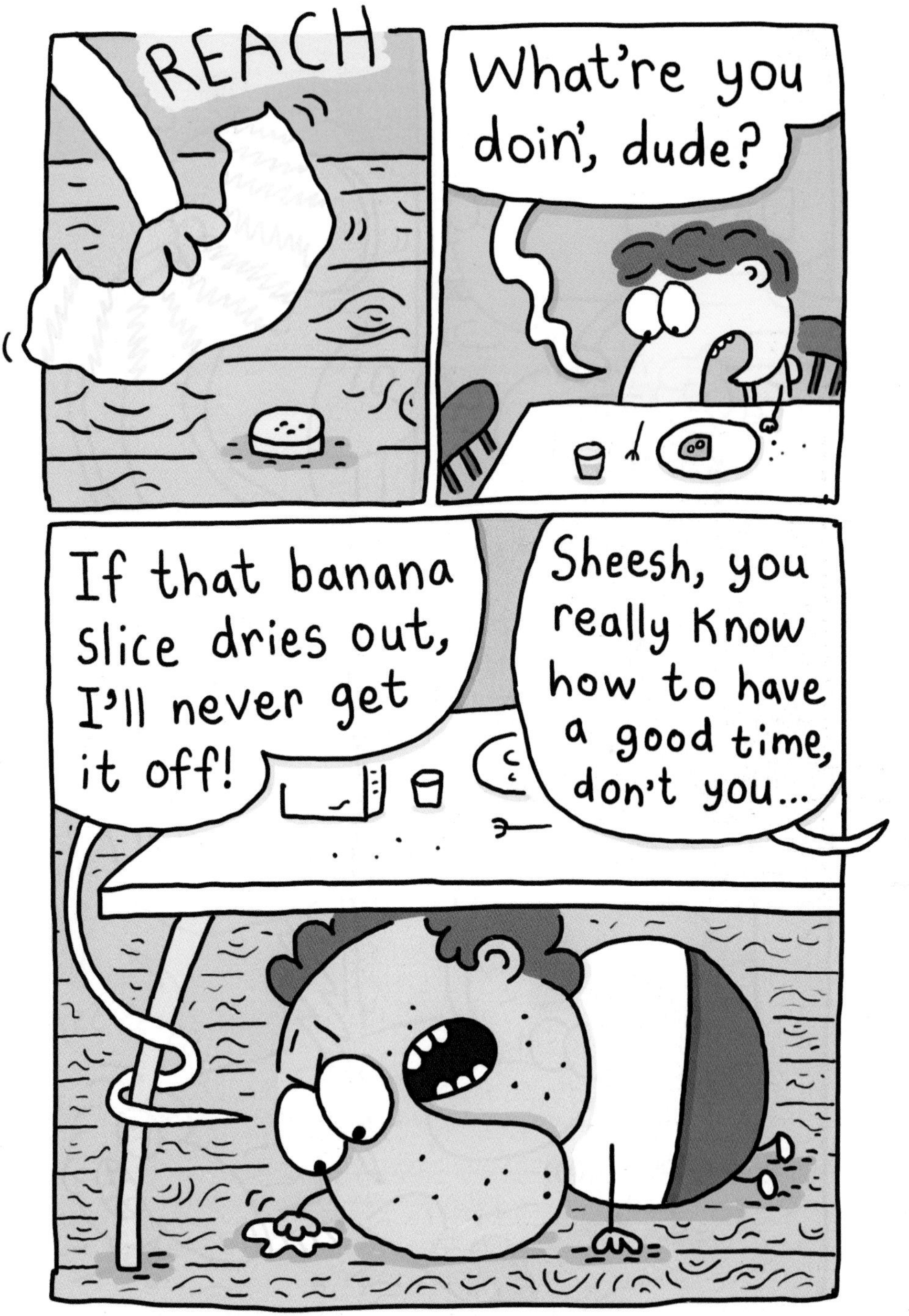
REACH
What're you doin', dude?
If that banana slice dries out, I'll never get it off!
Sheesh, you really know how to have a good time, don't you...

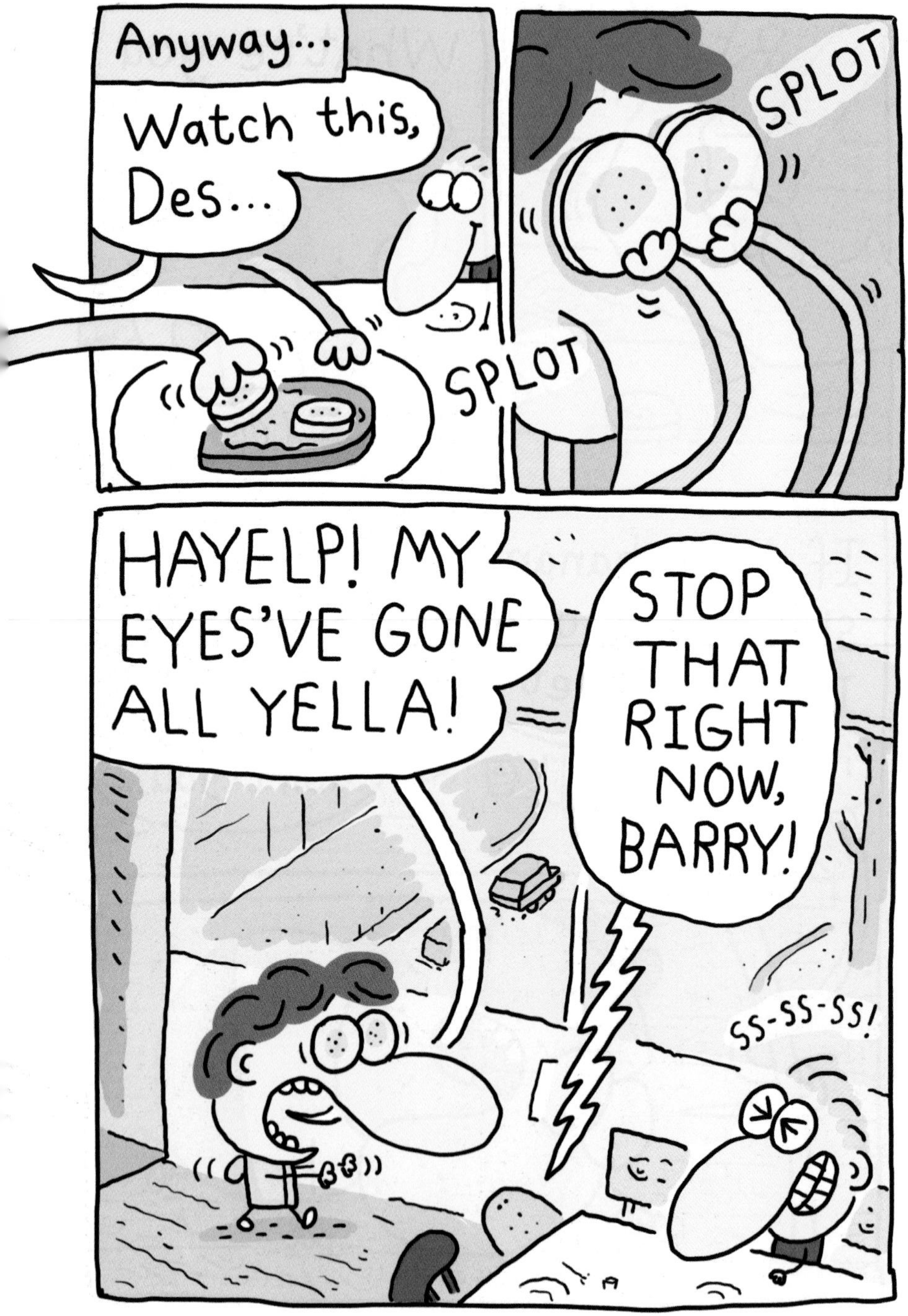
Anyway...
Watch this, Des...
SPLOT
SPLOT
HAYELP! MY EYES'VE GONE ALL YELLA!
STOP THAT RIGHT NOW, BARRY!
SS-SS-SS!

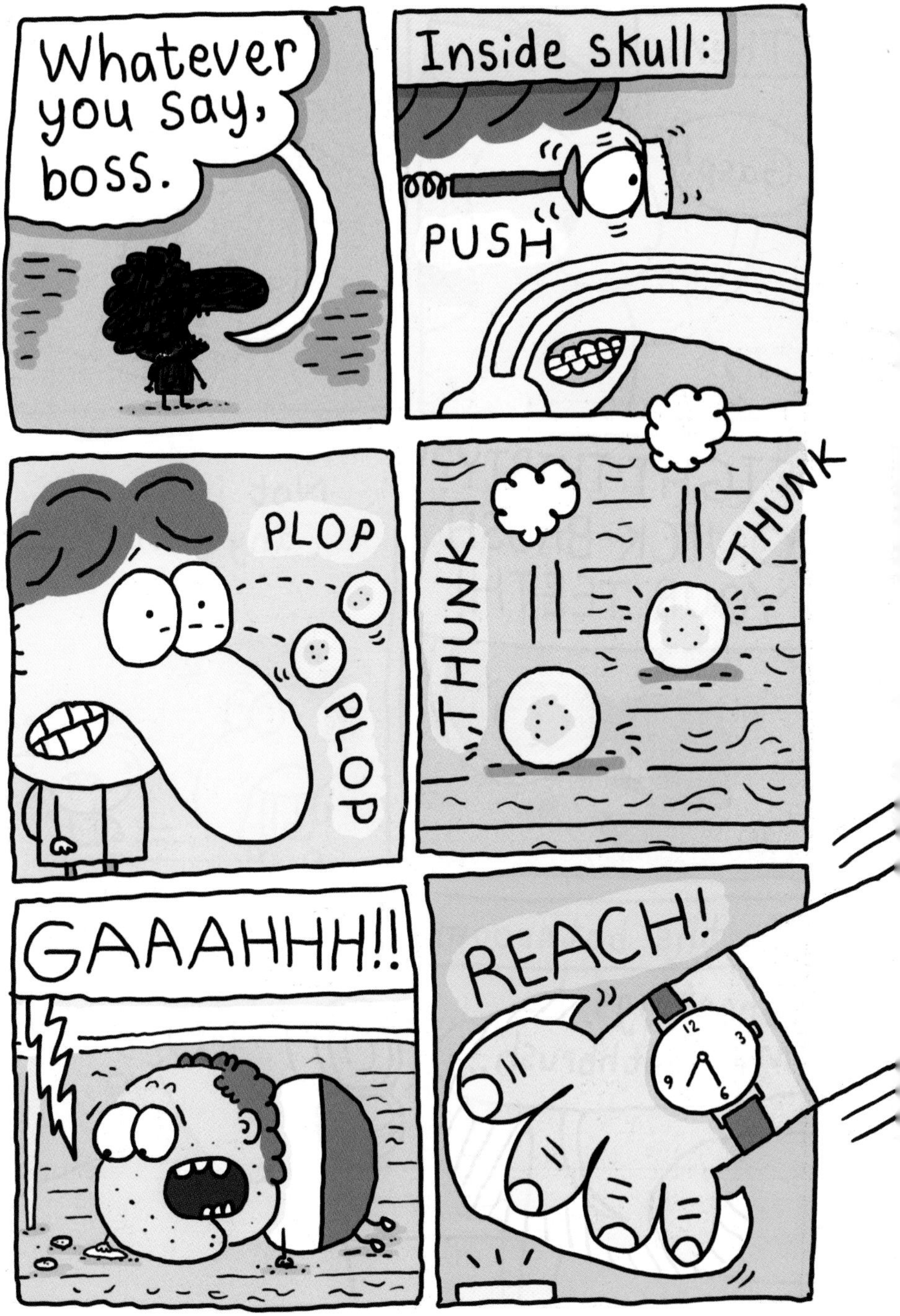
Whatever you say, boss.
Inside skull:
PUSH
PLOP
PLOP
THUNK
THUNK
GAAAHHH!!
REACH!

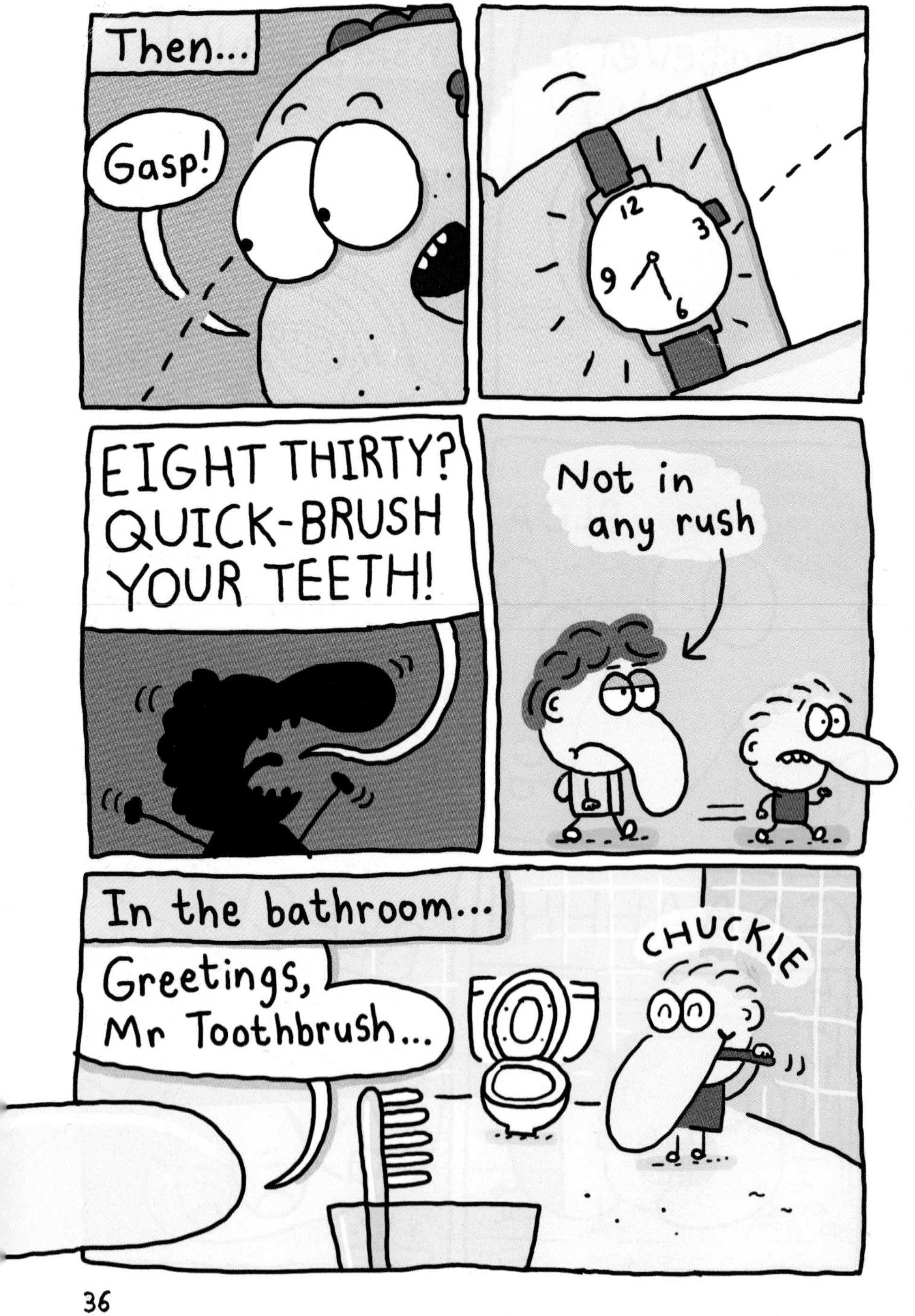
Then...
Gasp!
12
3
9
6
EIGHT THIRTY? QUICK-BRUSH YOUR TEETH!
Not in any rush
In the bathroom...
Greetings, Mr Toothbrush...
CHUCKLE

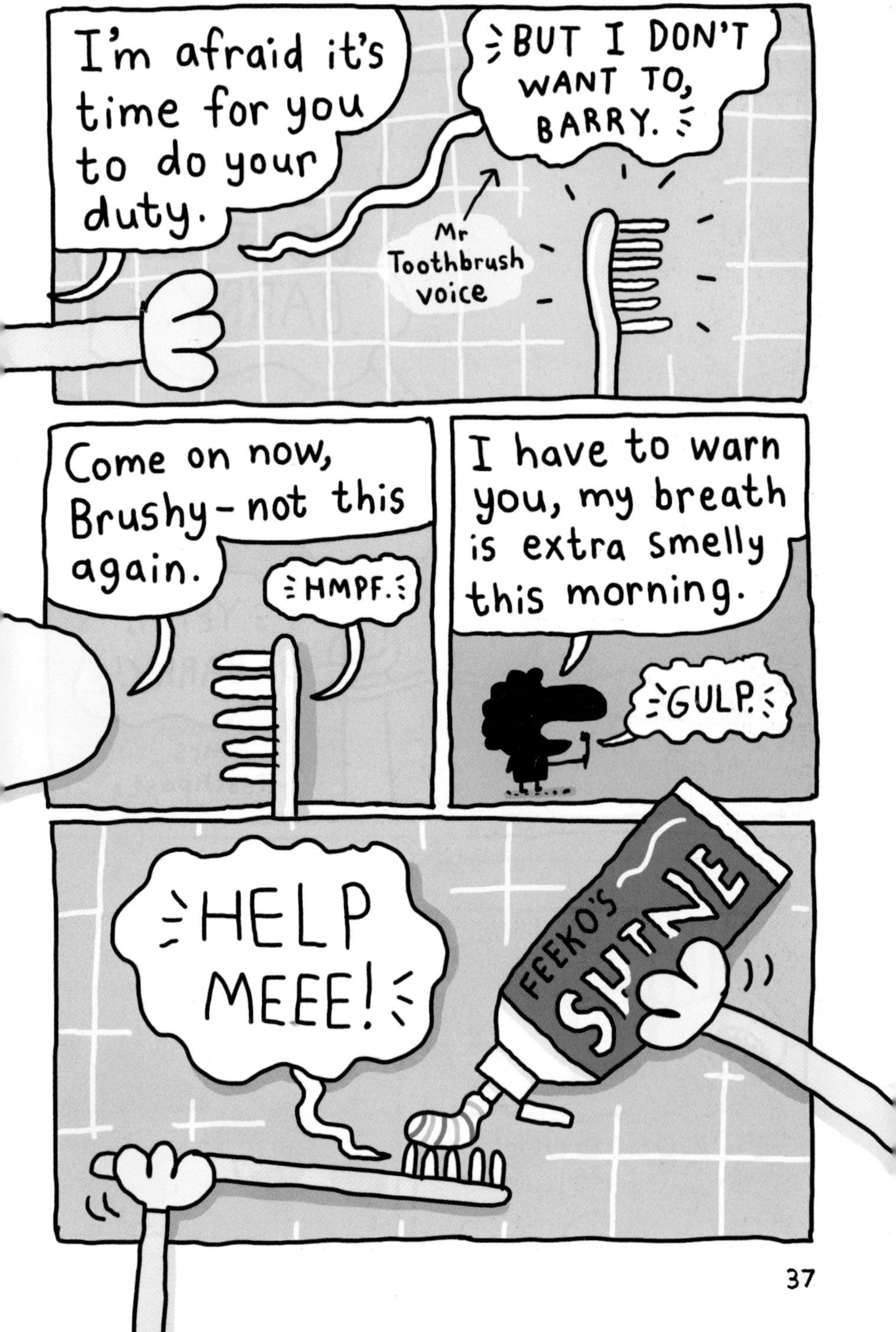
I'm afraid it's time for you to do your duty.
BUT I DON'T WANT TO, BARRY.
Mr Toothbrush voice
Come on now, Brushy - not this again.
HMPF.
I have to warn you, my breath is extra smelly this morning.
GULP.
HELP MEEE!
FEEKO'S
SHTNE

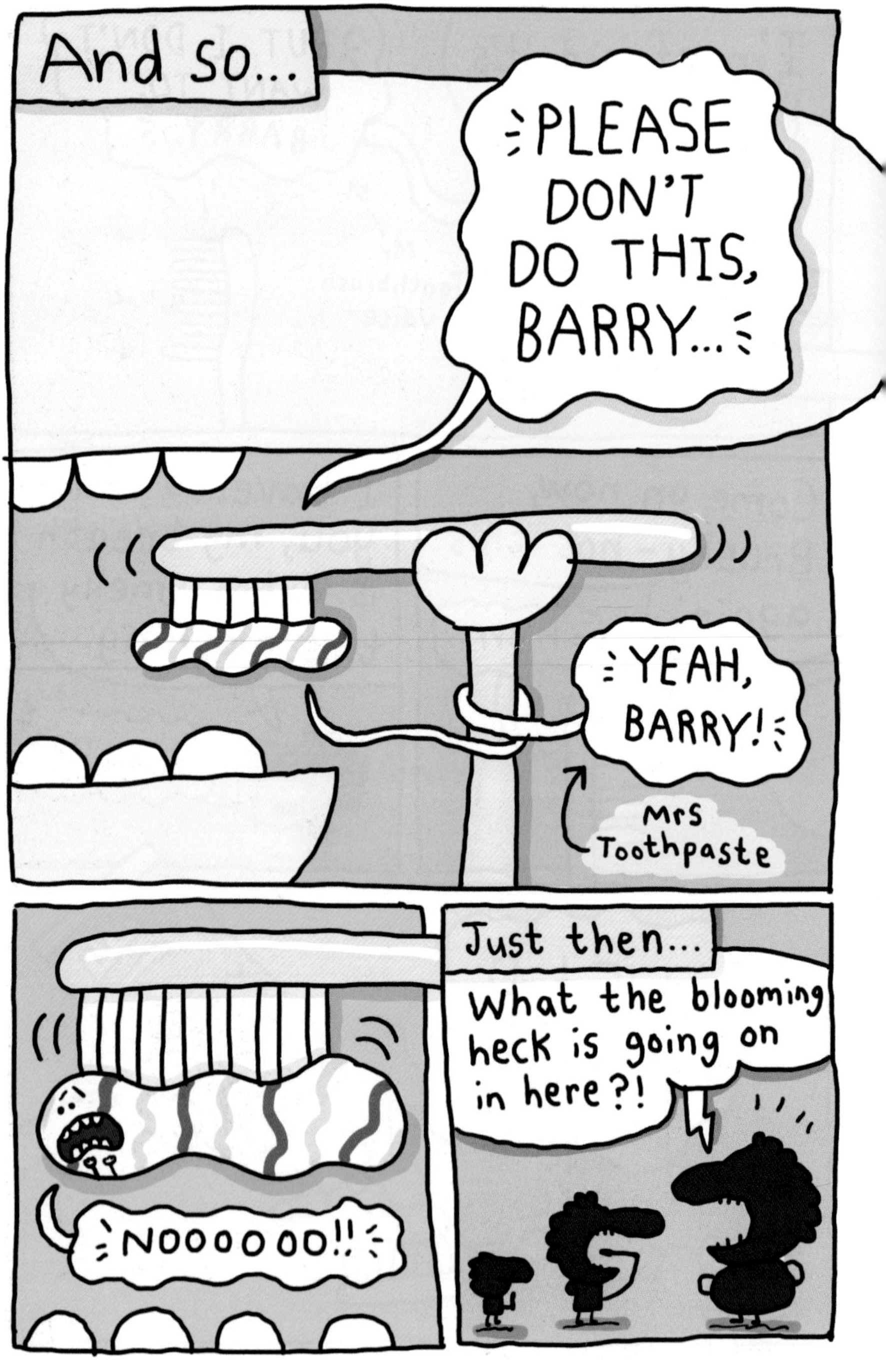
And so...
PLEASE DON'T DO THIS, BARRY...
YEAH, BARRY!
Mrs Toothpaste
NOOOOOO!!
Just then...
What the blooming heck is going on in here?!

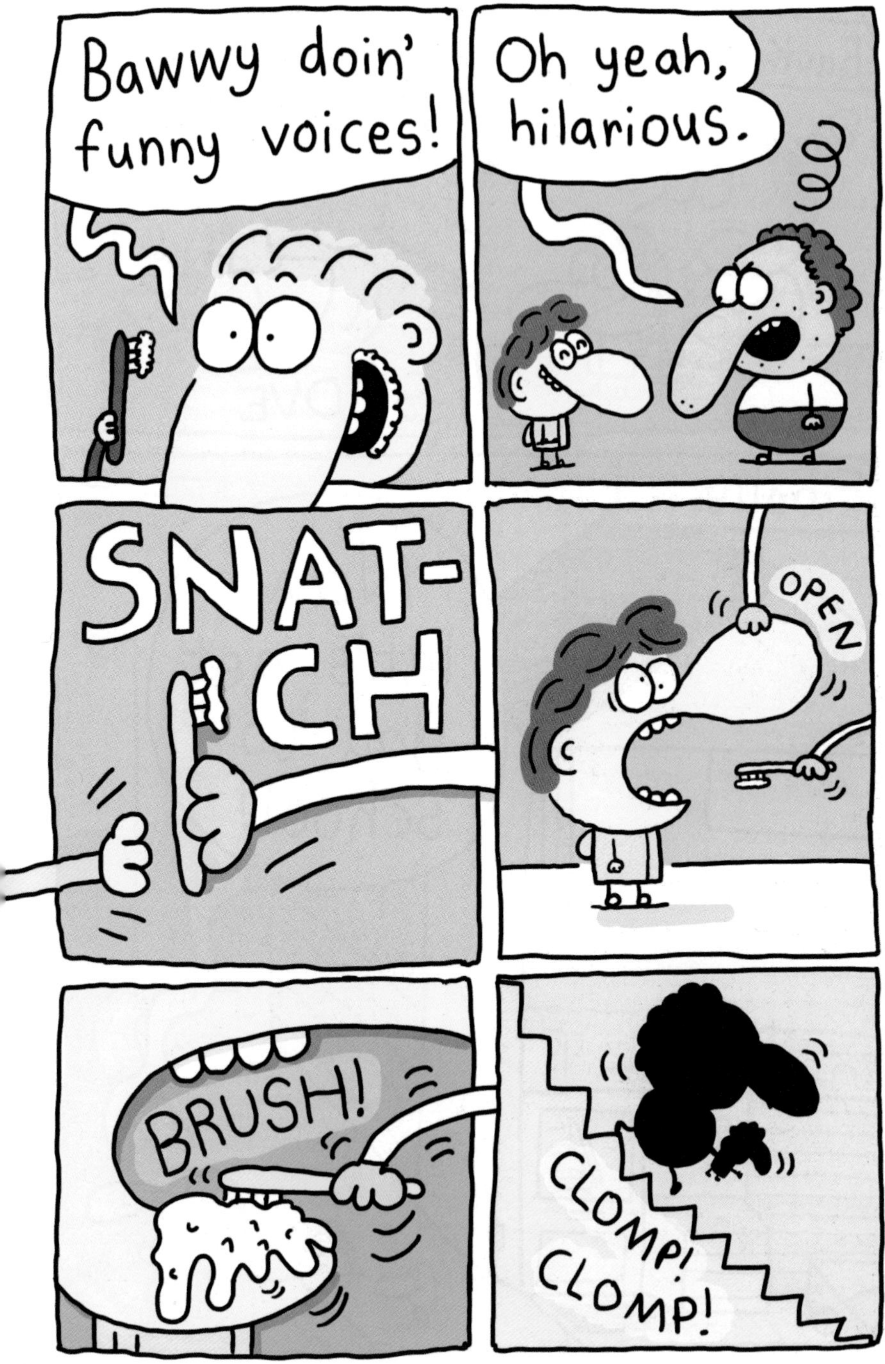
Bawwy doin' funny voices!
Oh yeah, hilarious.
SNAT-CH
OPEN
BRUSH!
CLOMP! CLOMP!

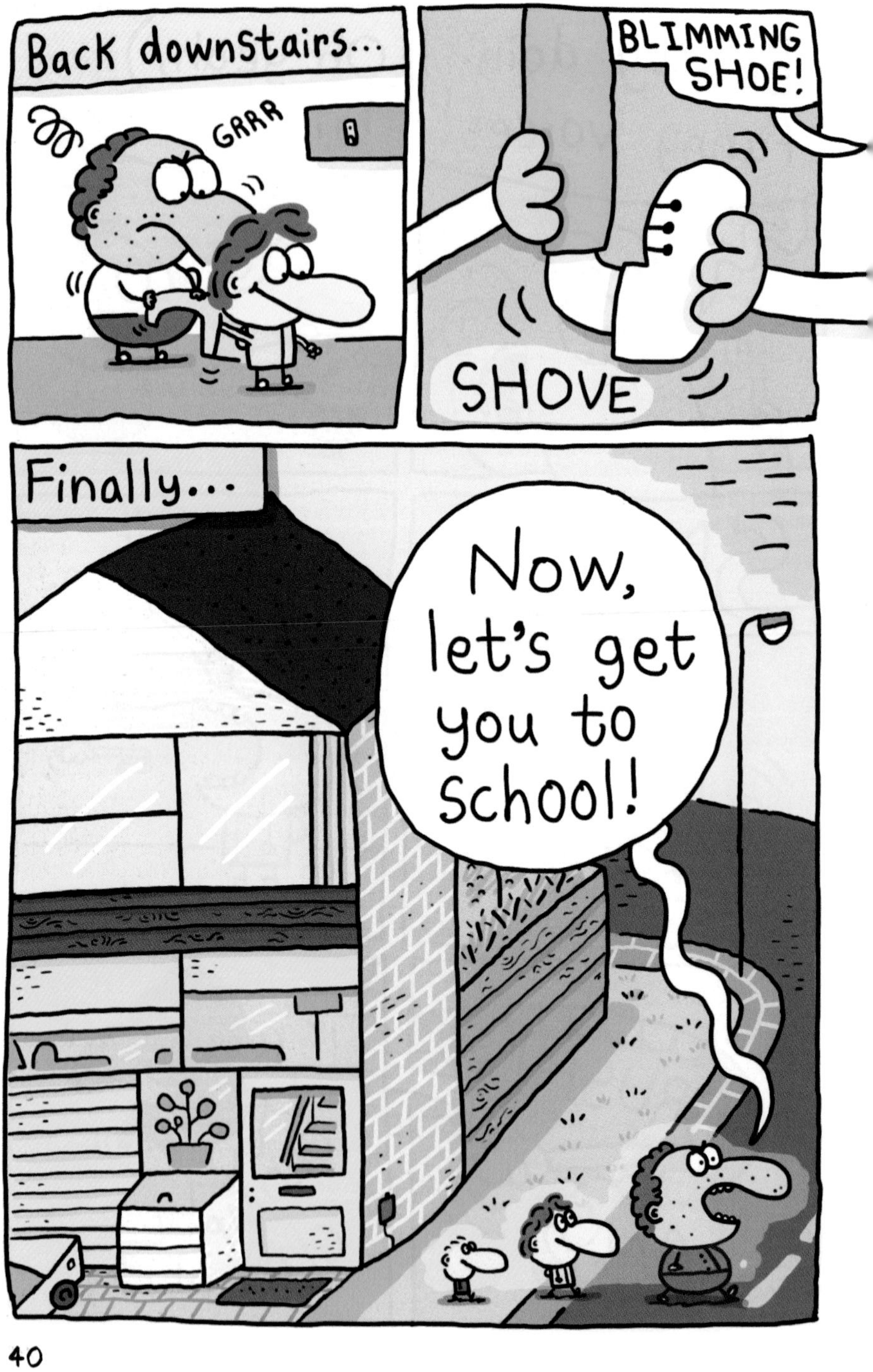
Back downstairs...
GRRR
BLIMMING SHOE!
SHOVE
Finally...
Now, let's get you to school!

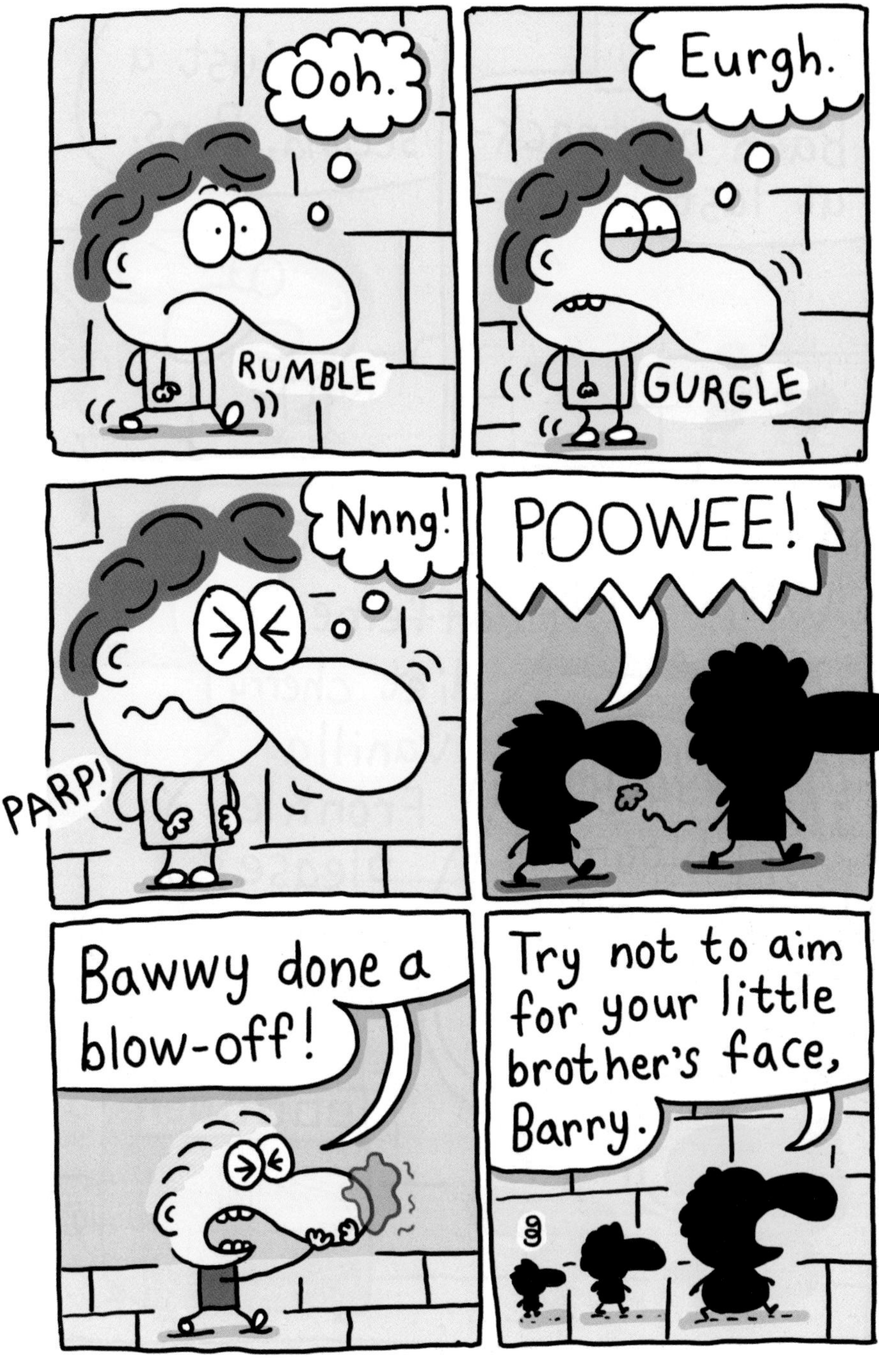
Ooh.
RUMBLE
Eurgh.
GURGLE
Nnng!
PARP!
POOWEE!
Bawwy done a blow-off!
Try not to aim for your little brother's face, Barry.

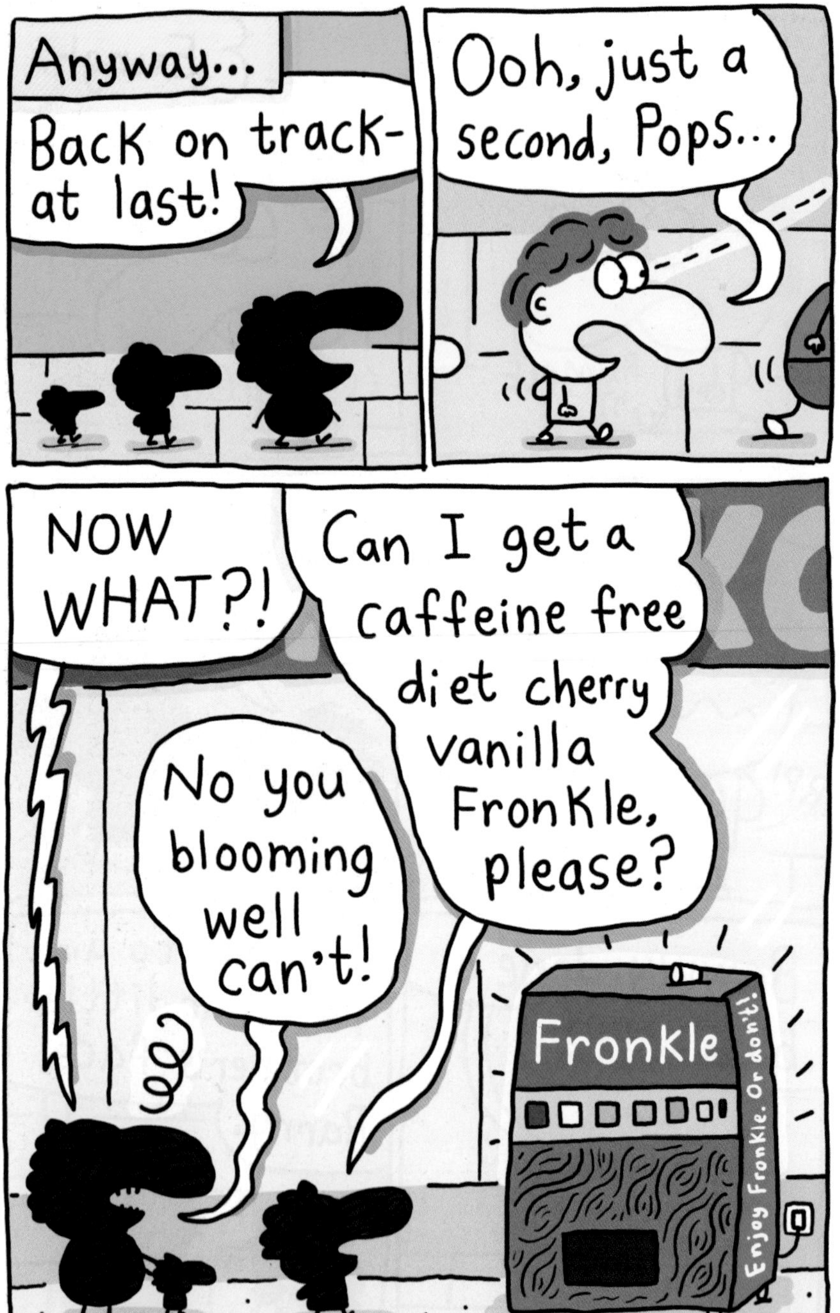
Anyway...
Back on track- at last!
Ooh, just a second, Pops...
NOW WHAT?!
Can I get a caffeine free diet cherry vanilla Fronkle, please?
No you blooming well can't!
Fronkle
Enjoy Fronkle. Or don't!

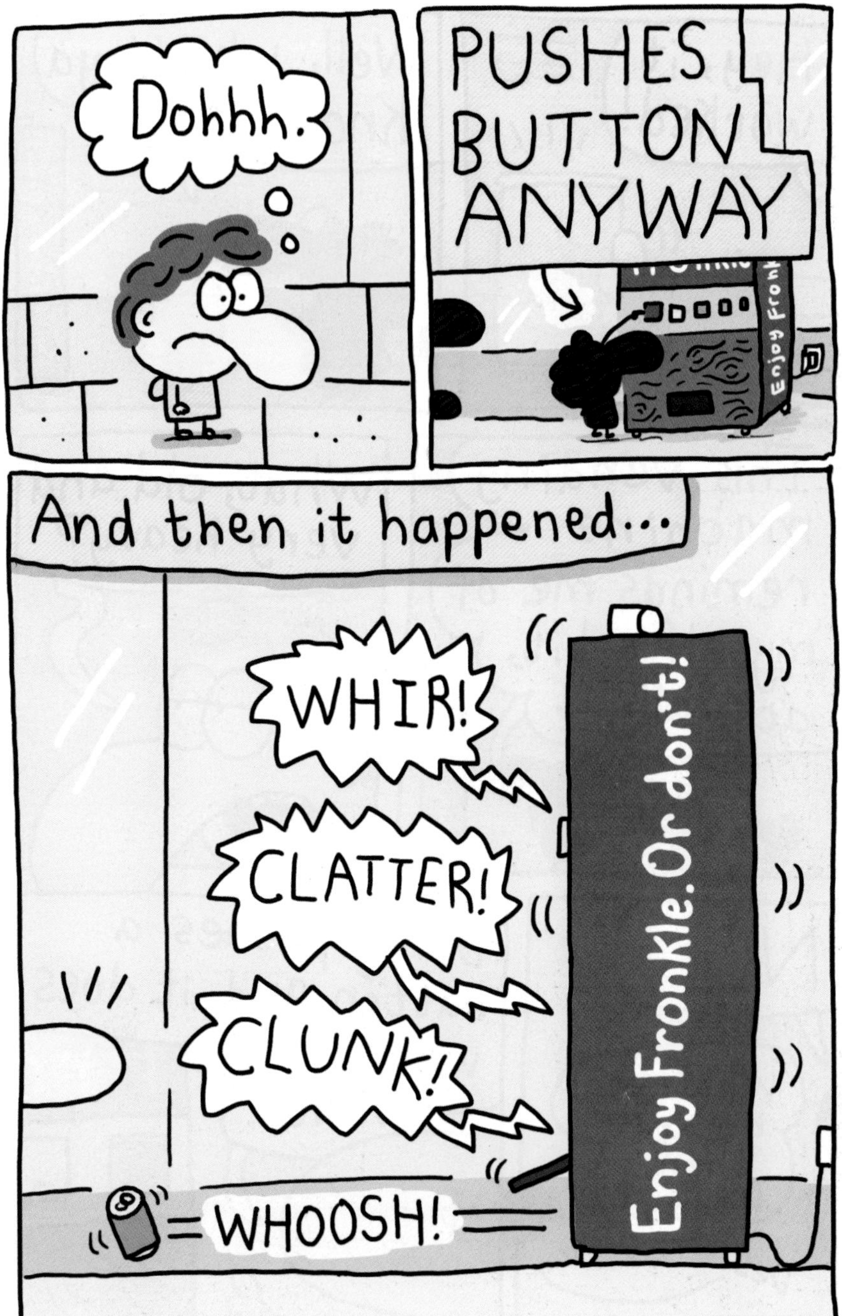
Dohhh.
PUSHES BUTTON ANYWAY
Enjoy Fronk
And then it happened...
WHIR!
CLATTER!
CLUNK!
WHOOSH!
Enjoy Fronkle. Or don't!

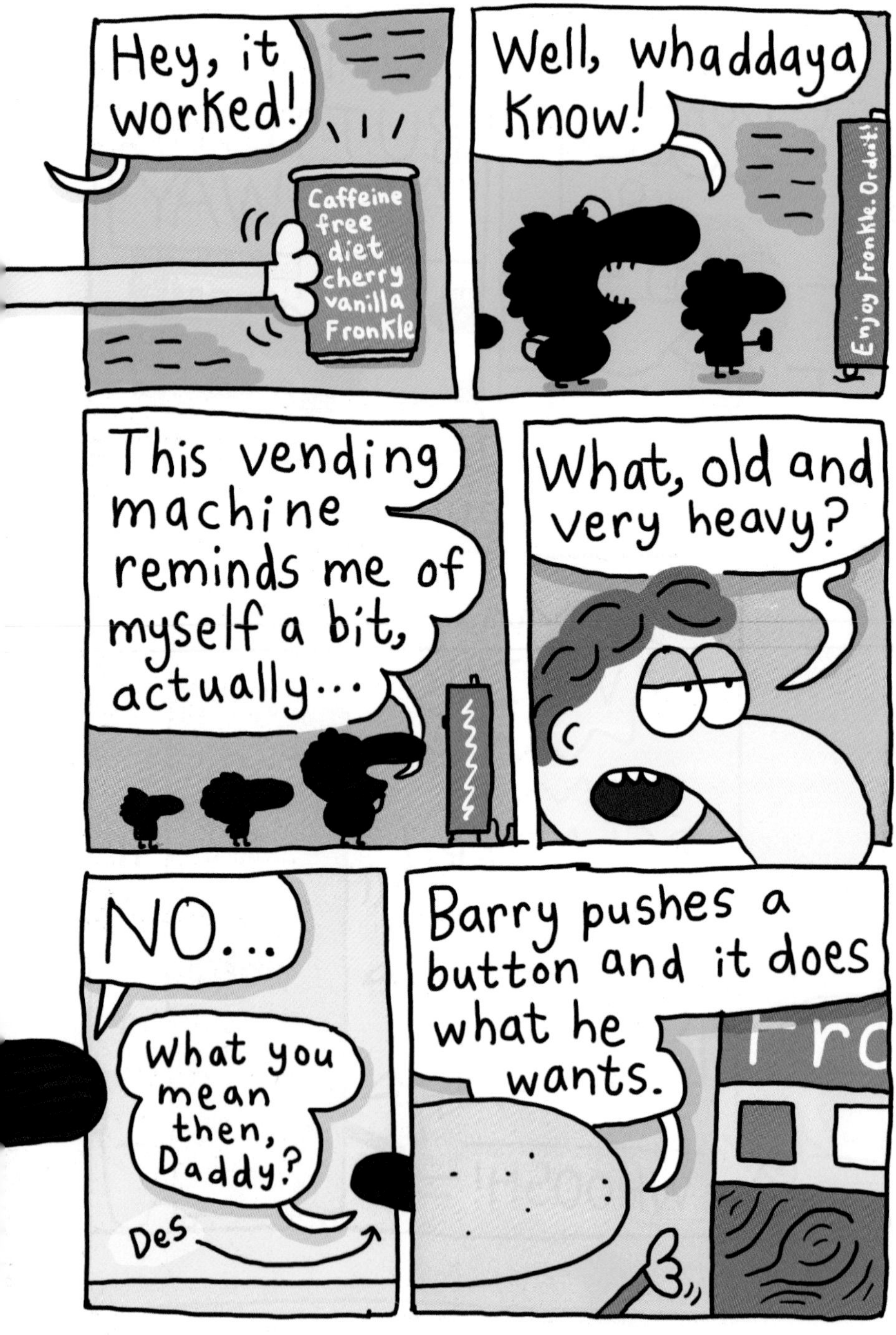
Hey, it worked!
Caffeine free diet cherry vanilla Fronkle
Well, whaddaya know!
Enjoy Fronkle. Or don't!
This vending machine reminds me of myself a bit, actually...
What, old and very heavy?
NO...
What you mean then, Daddy?
Des
Barry pushes a button and it does what he wants.
Fro

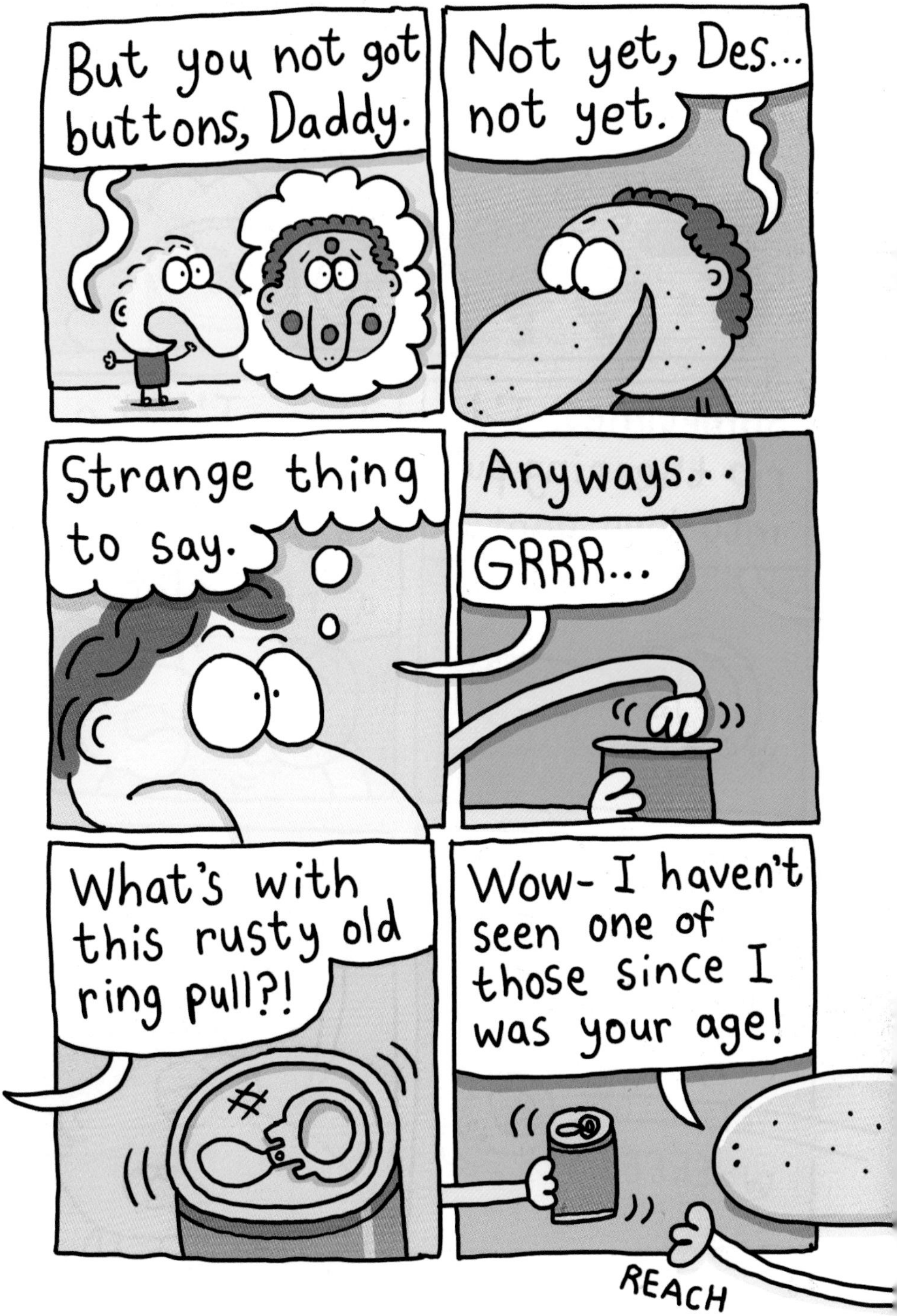
But you not got buttons, Daddy.
Not yet, Des... not yet.
Strange thing to say.
Anyways...
GRRR...
What's with this rusty old ring pull?!
Wow- I haven't seen one of those since I was your age!
REACH

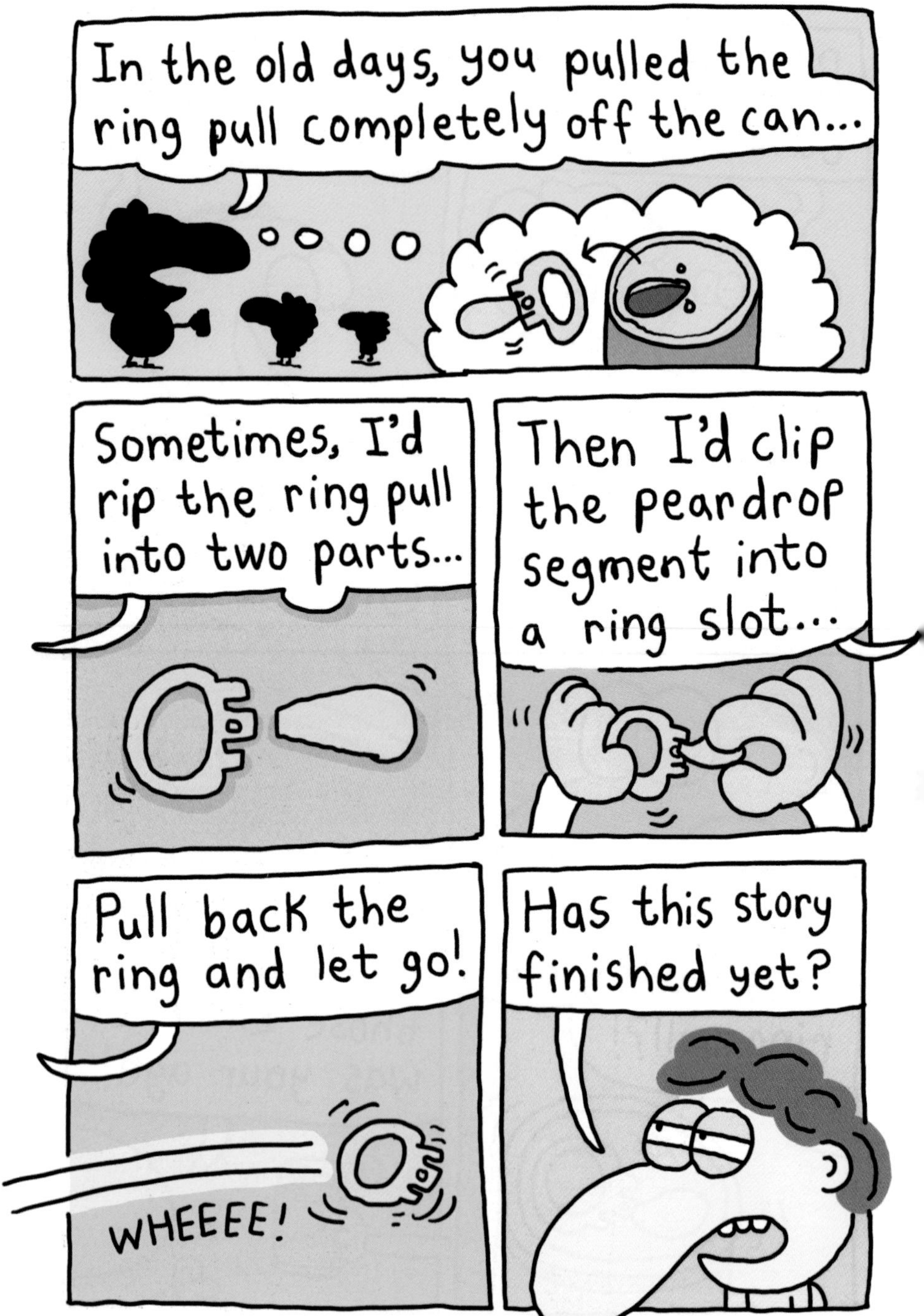
In the old days, you pulled the ring pull completely off the can...
Sometimes, I'd rip the ring pull into two parts...
Then I'd clip the peardrop segment into a ring slot...
Pull back the ring and let go!
WHEEEE!
Has this story finished yet?

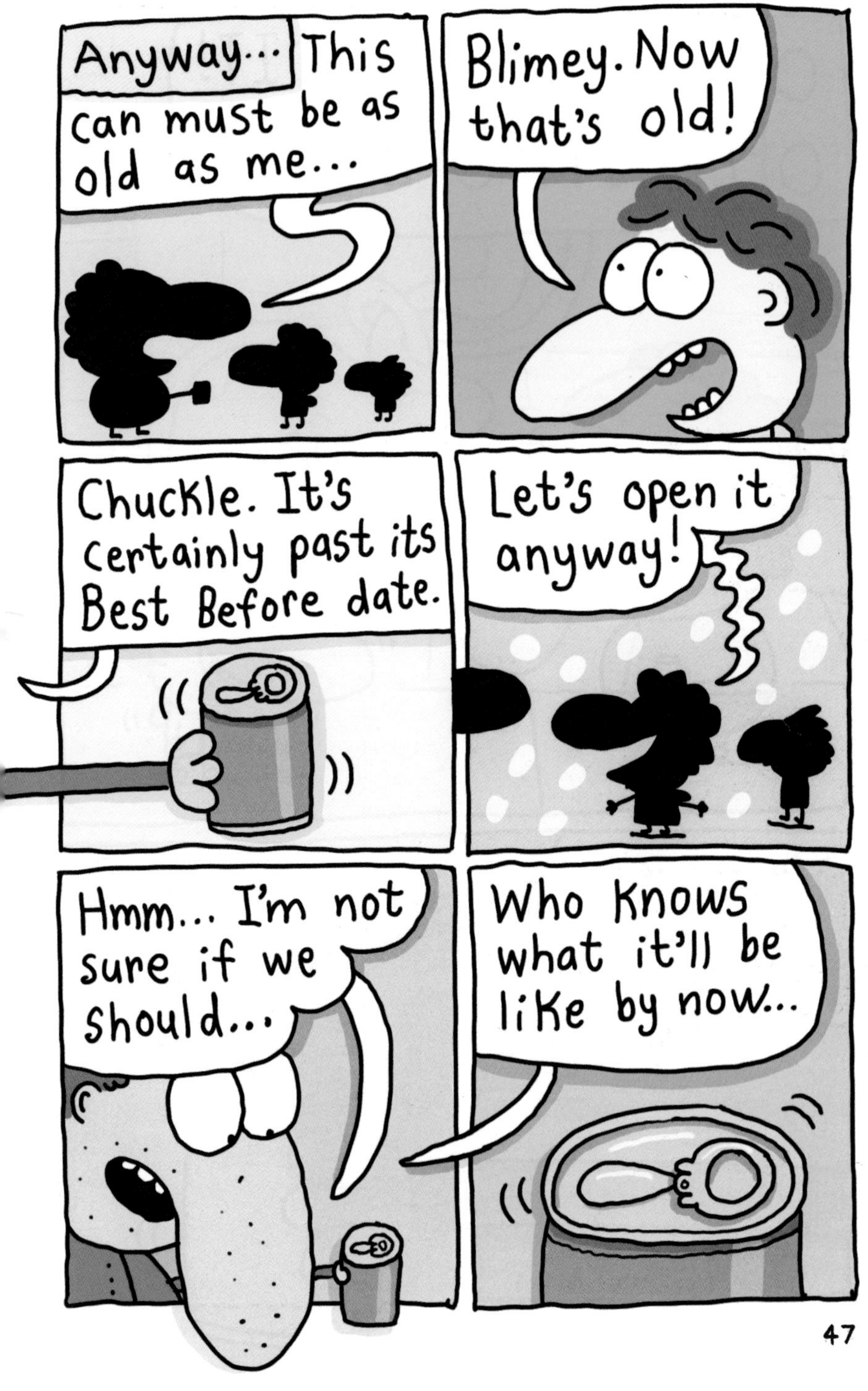
Anyway... This can must be as old as me...
Blimey. Now that's old!
Chuckle. It's certainly past its Best Before date.
Let's open it anyway!
Hmm... I'm not sure if we should...
Who knows what it'll be like by now...

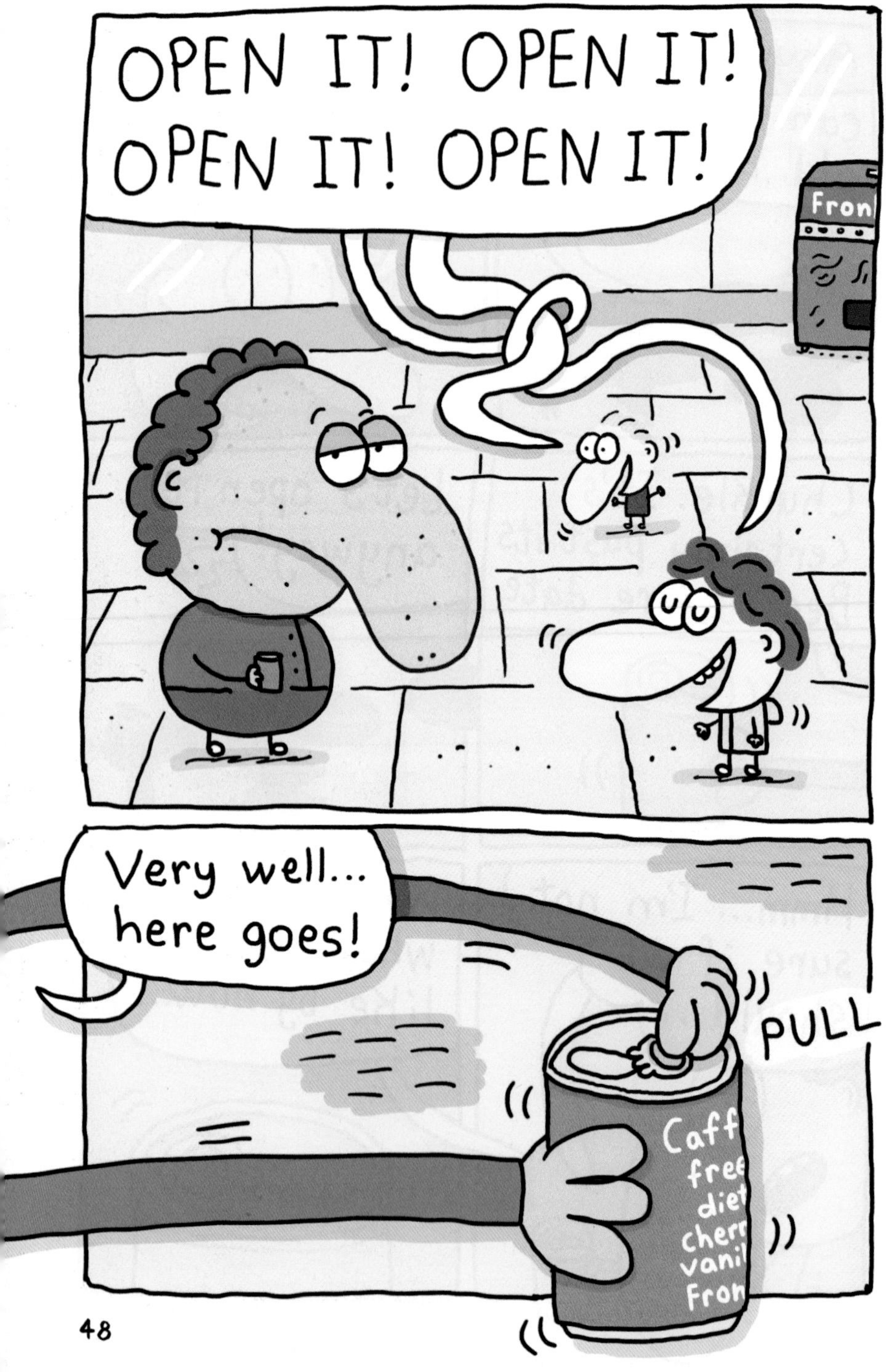
OPEN IT! OPEN IT! OPEN IT! OPEN IT!
Very well... here goes!
PULL

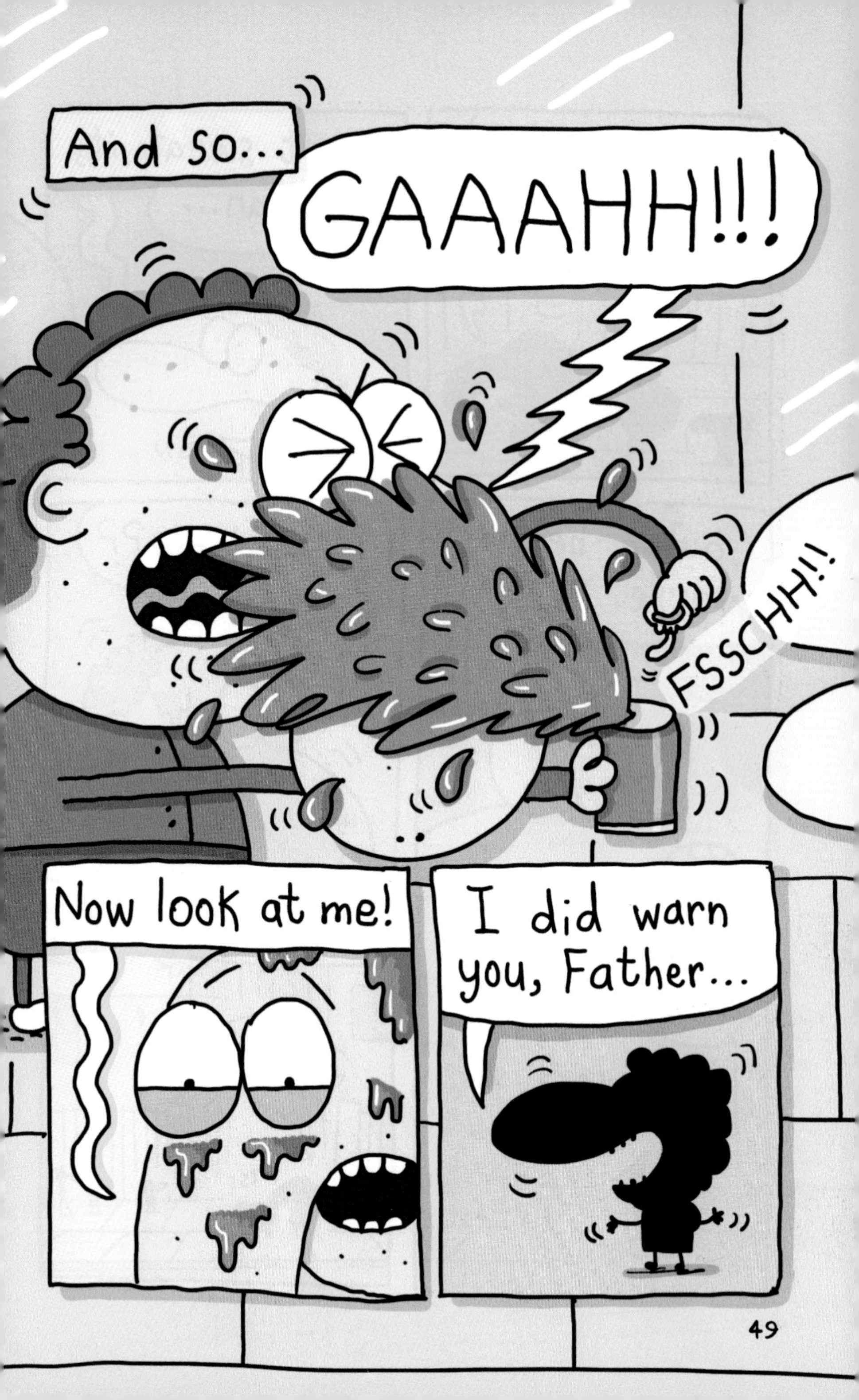
And so...
GAAAHH!!!
FSSCHH!!
Now look at me!
I did warn you, Father...

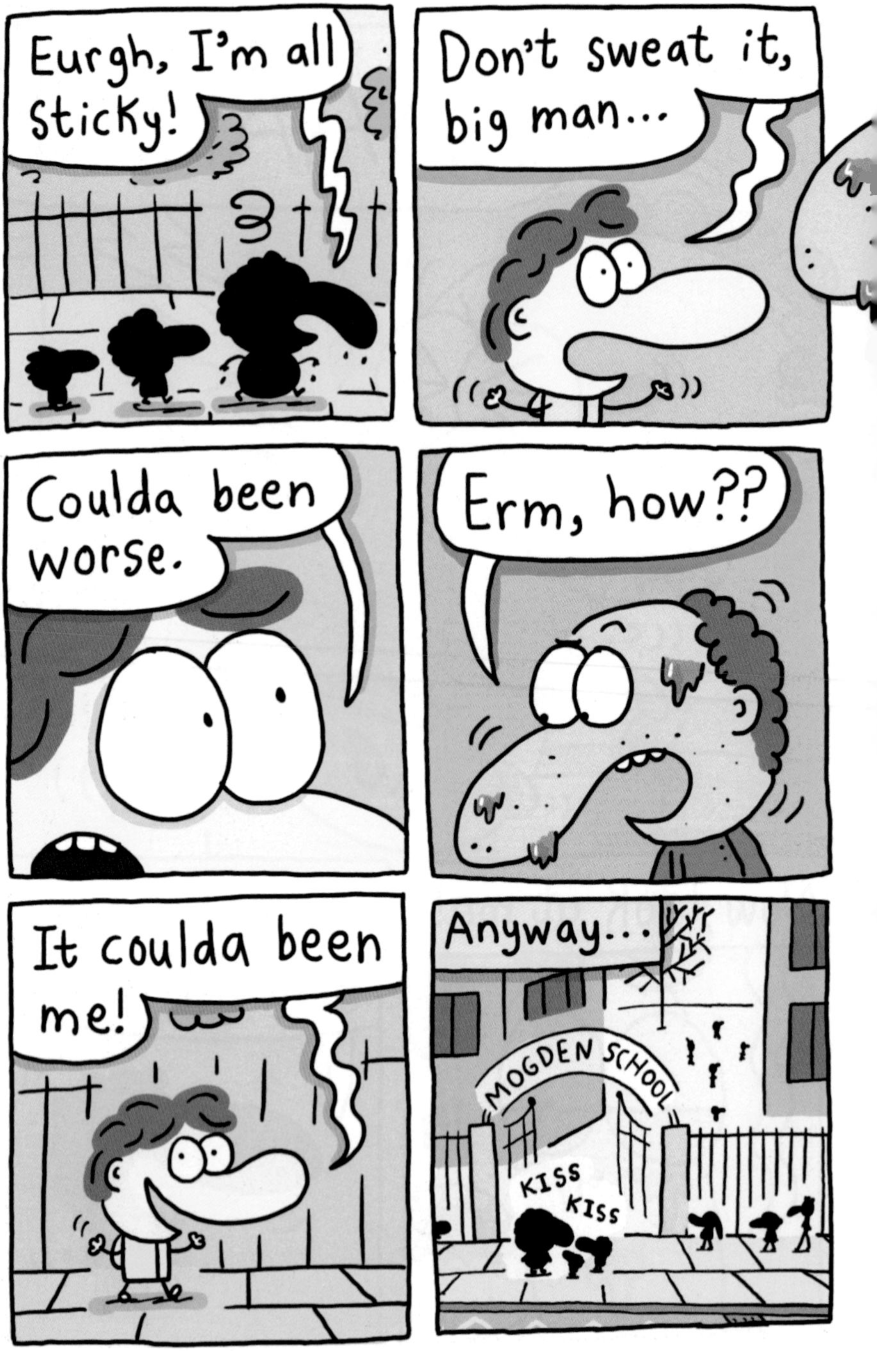
Eurgh, I'm all sticky!
Don't sweat it, big man...
Coulda been worse.
Erm, how??
It coulda been me!
Anyway...
MOGDEN SCHOOL
KISS
KISS

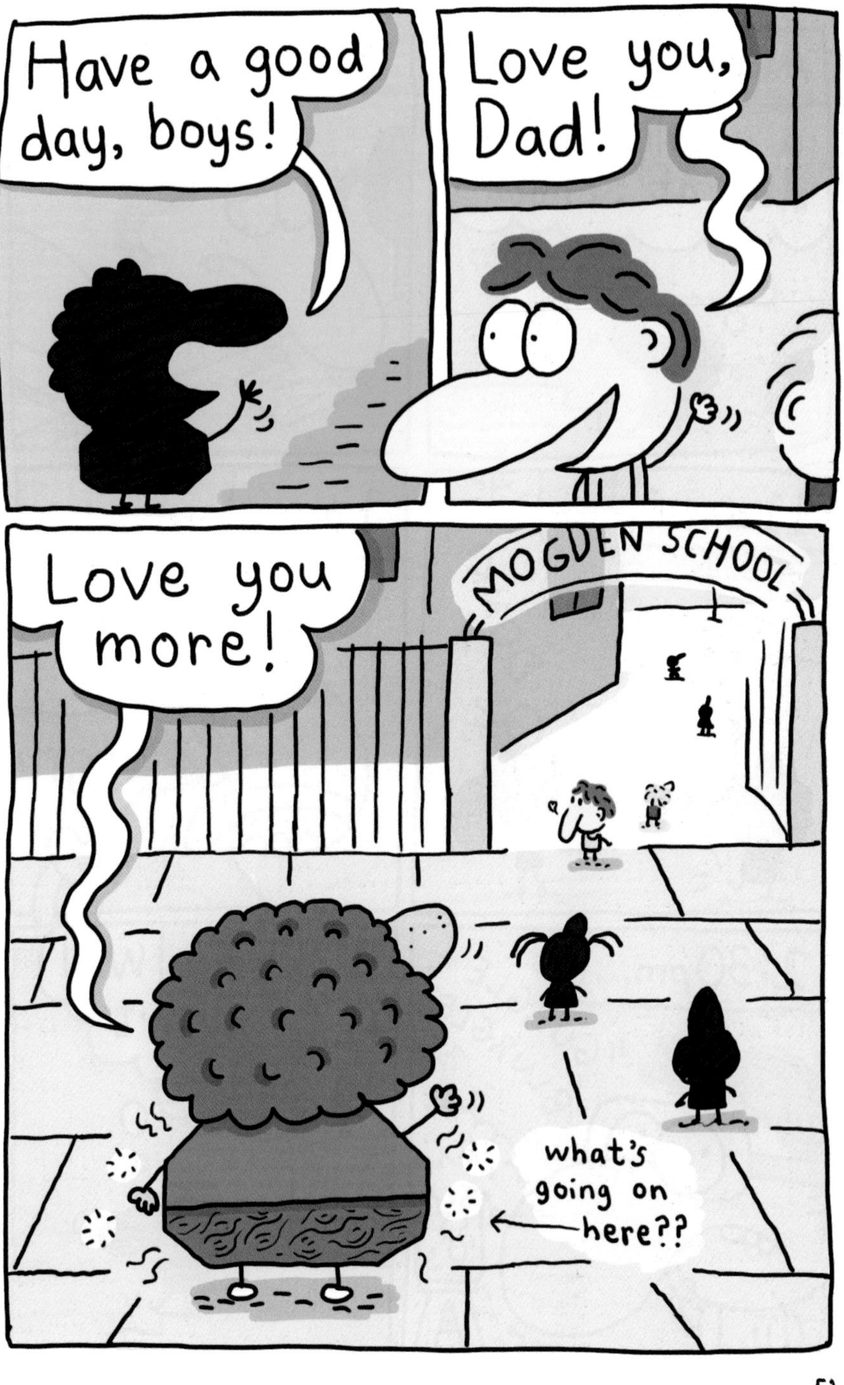
Have a good day, boys!
Love you, Dad!
MOGDEN SCHOOL
Love you more!
what's going on here??

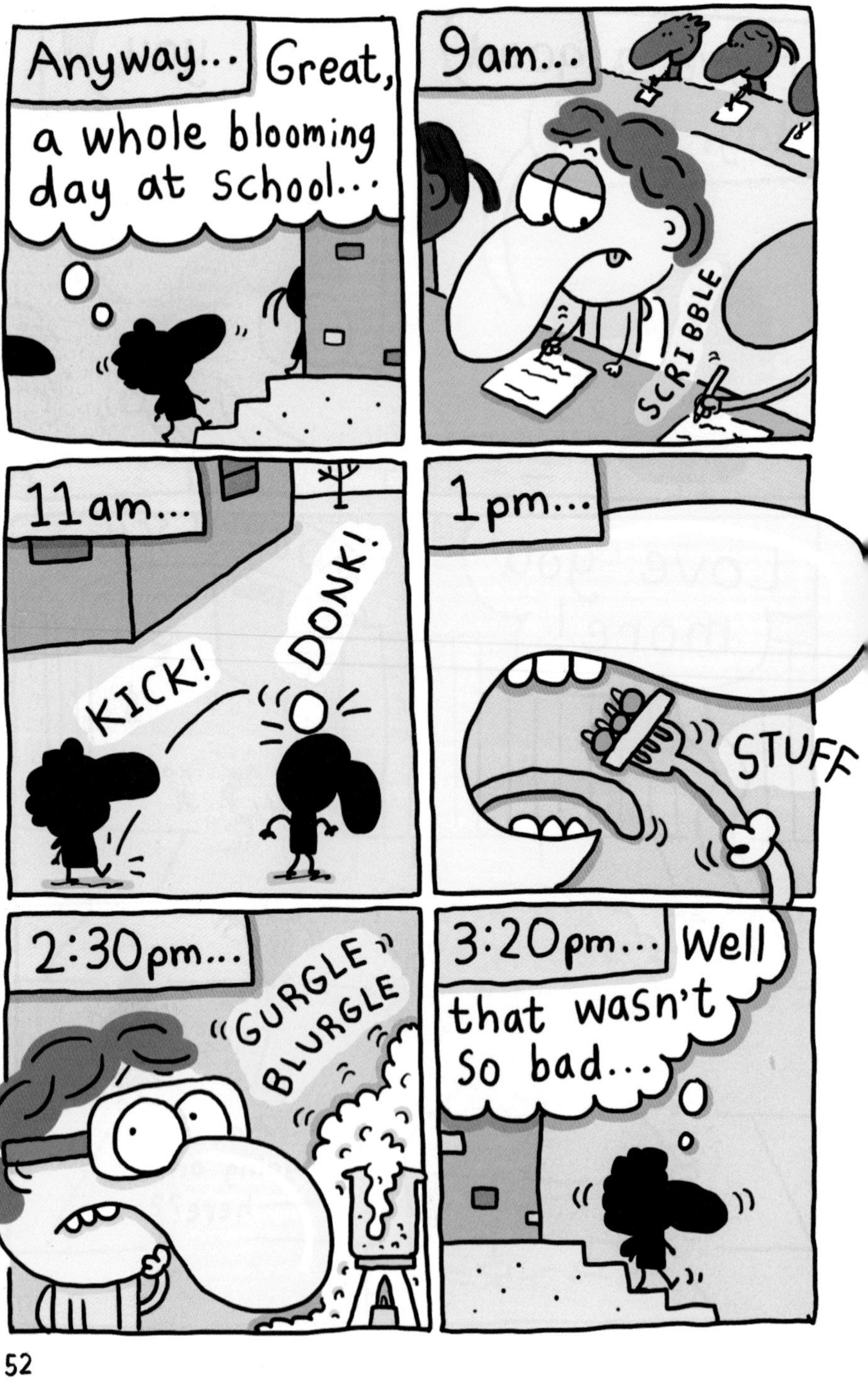
Anyway...
Great, a whole blooming day at school...
9am...
SCRIBBLE
11am...
KICK!
DONK!
1pm...
STUFF
2:30pm...
GURGLE
BLURGLE
3:20pm...
Well that wasn't so bad...

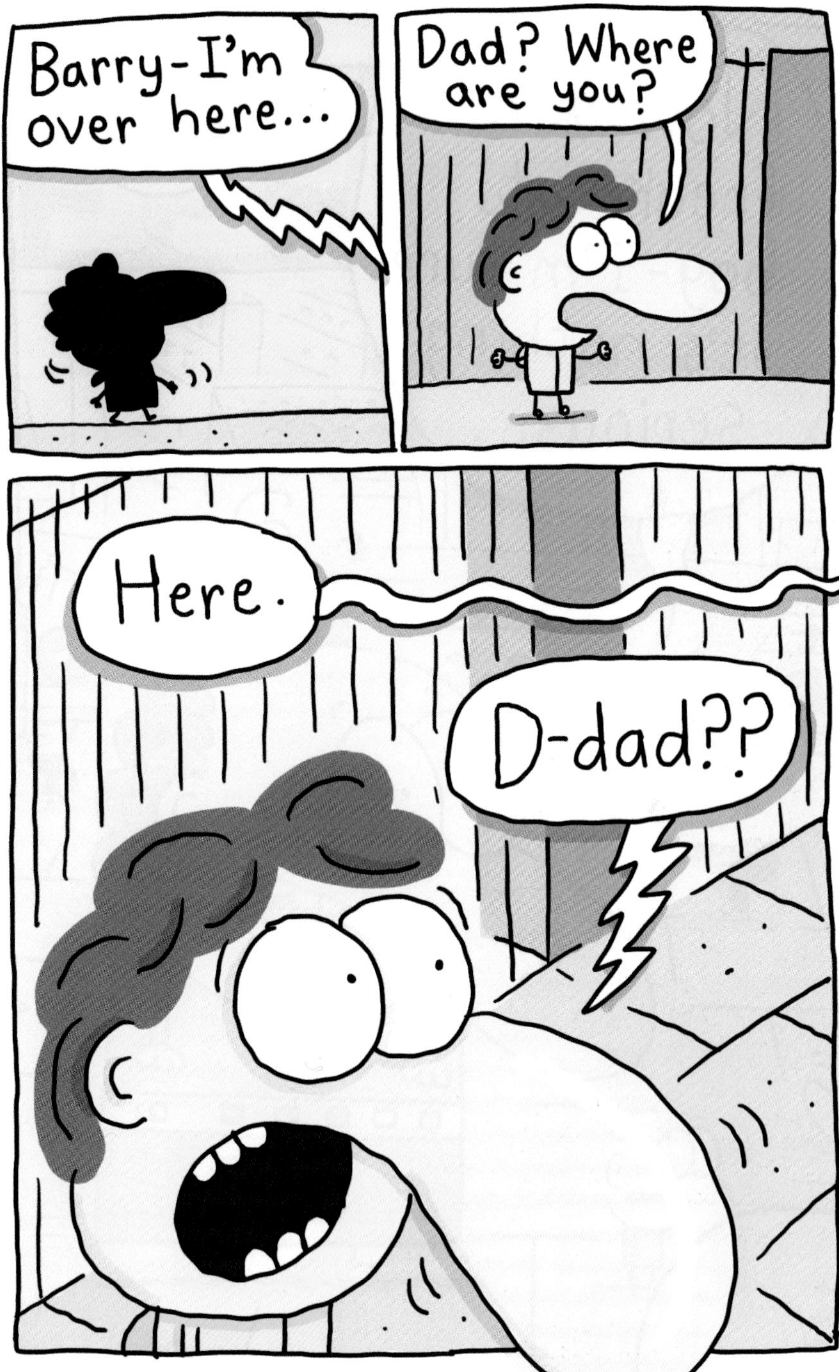
Barry- I'm over here...
Dad? Where are you?
Here.
D-dad??

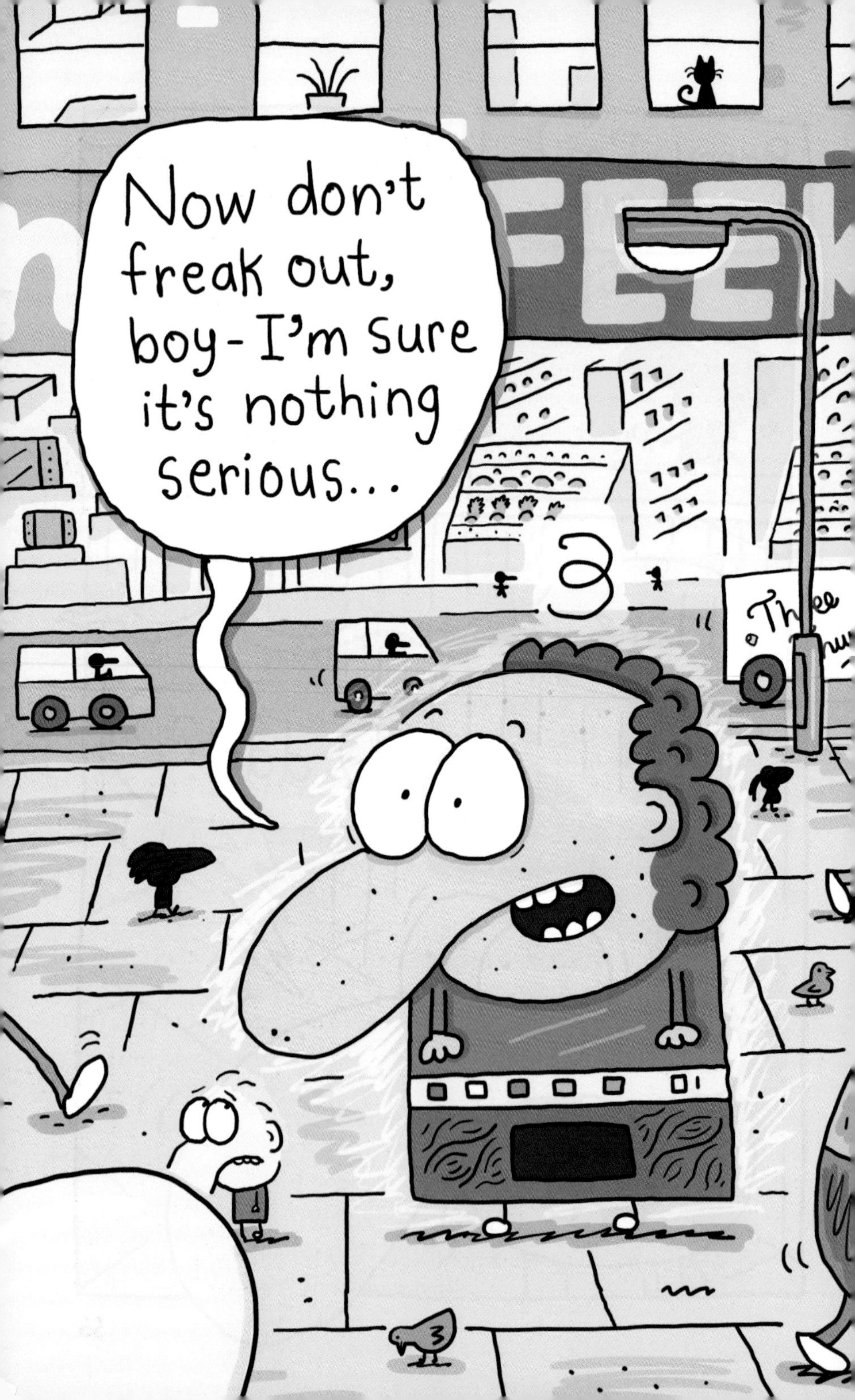
Now don't freak out, boy - I'm sure it's nothing serious...

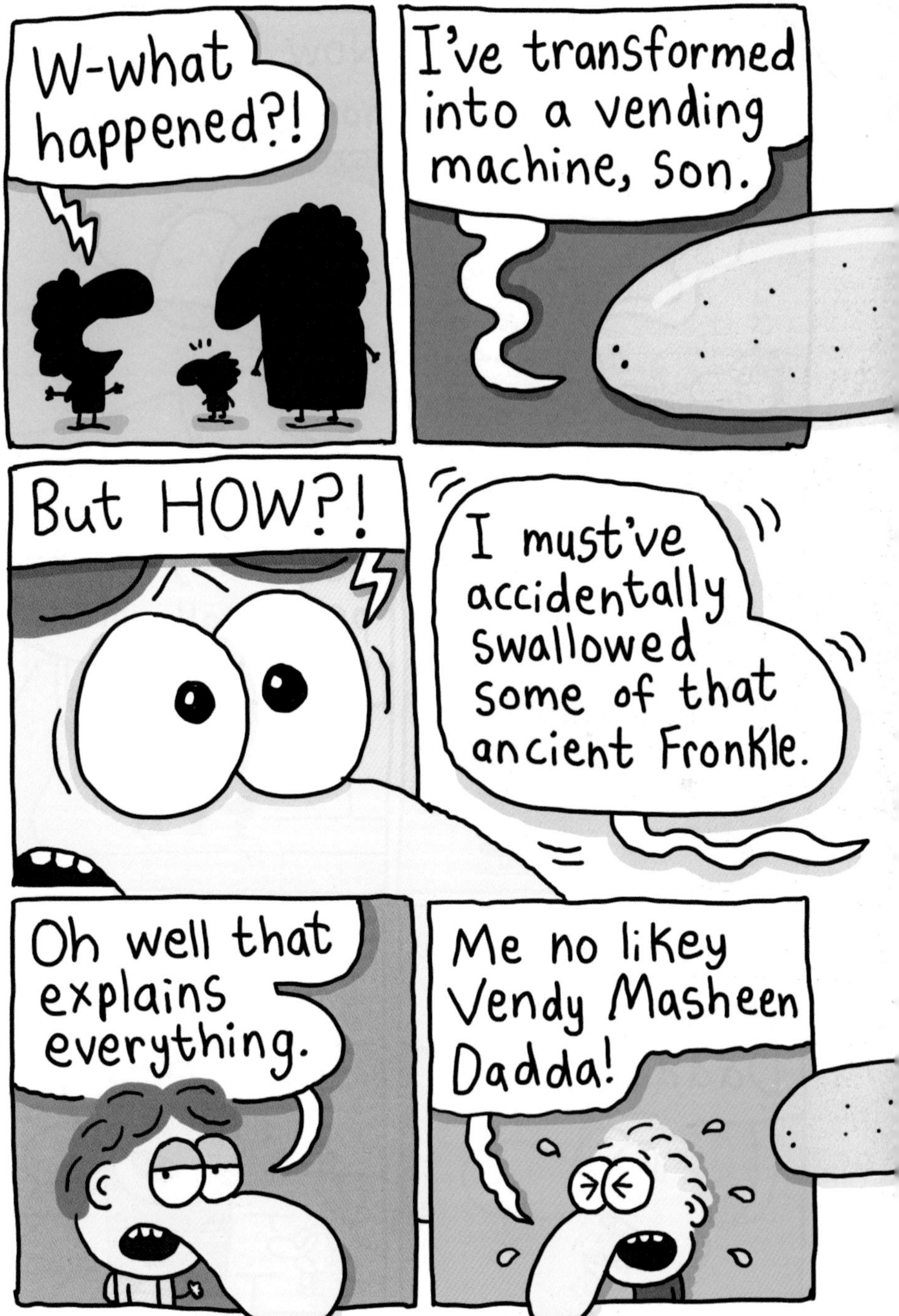
W-what happened?!
I've transformed into a vending machine, son.
But HOW?!
I must've accidentally swallowed some of that ancient Fronkle.
Oh well that explains everything.
Me no likey Vendy Masheen Dadda!

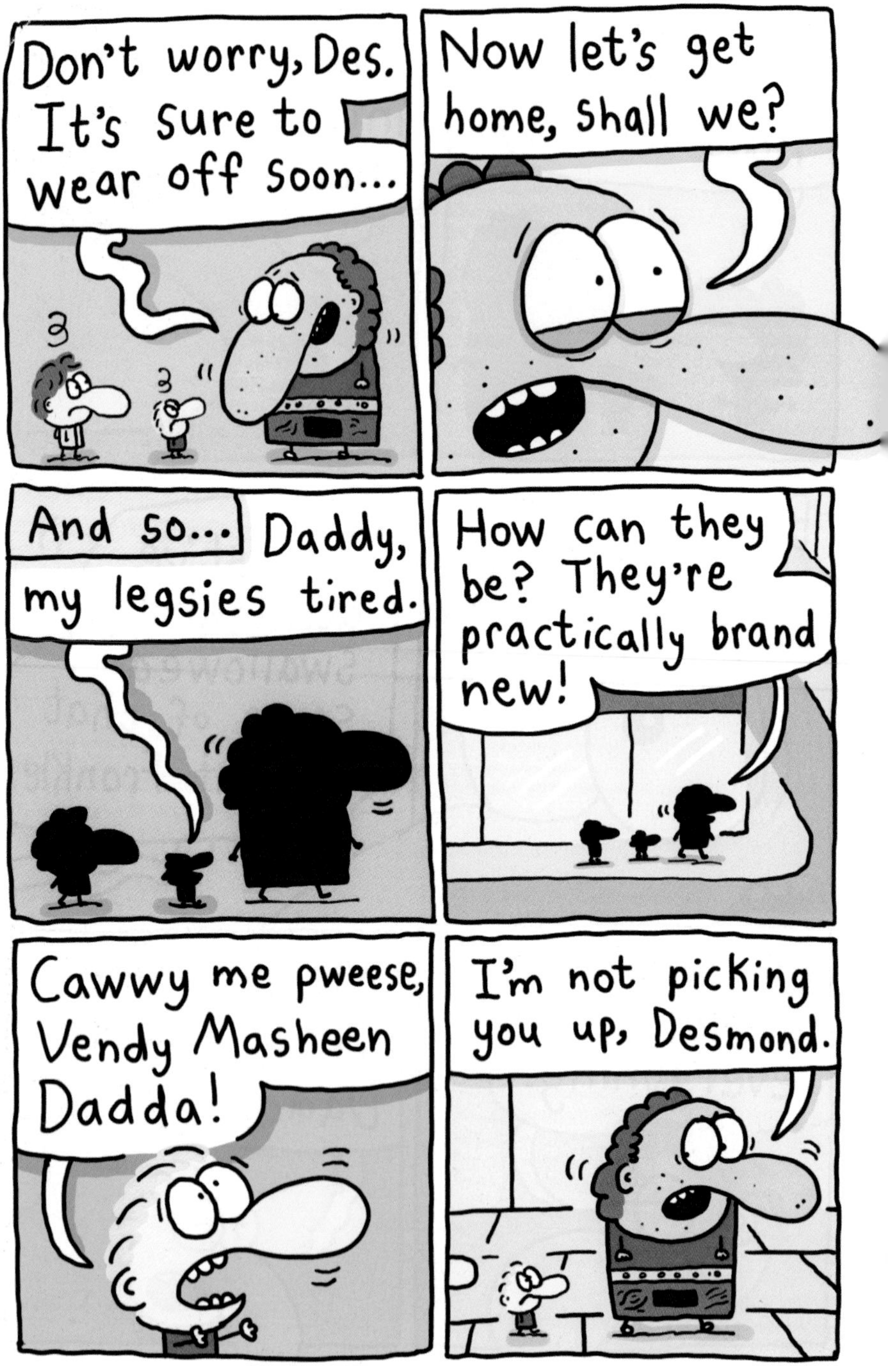
Don't worry, Des. It's sure to wear off soon...
Now let's get home, shall we?
And so...
Daddy, my legsies tired.
How can they be? They're practically brand new!
Cawwy me pweese, Vendy Masheen Dadda!
I'm not picking you up, Desmond.

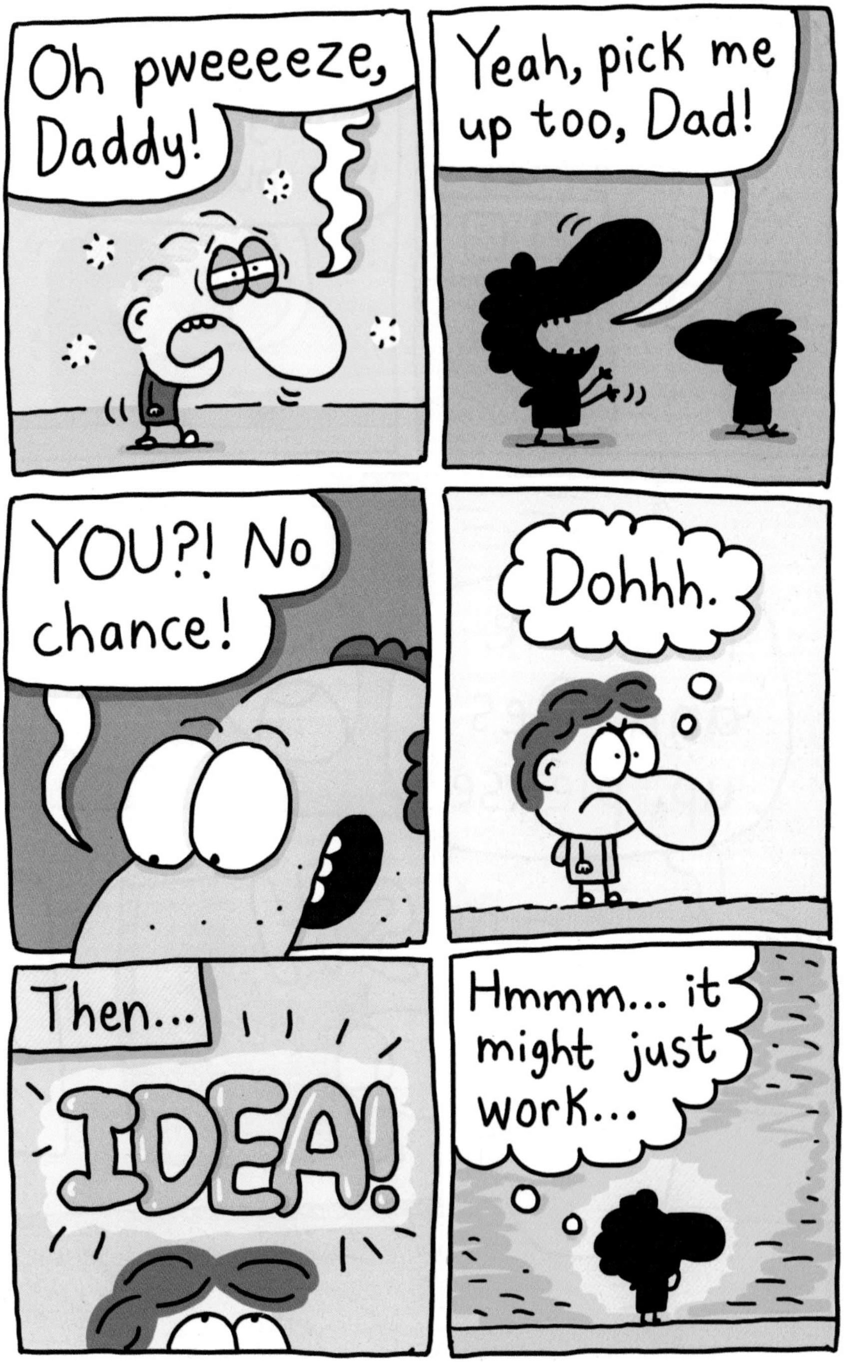
Oh pweeeeze, Daddy!
Yeah, pick me up too, Dad!
YOU?! No chance!
Dohhh.
Then...
IDEA!
Hmmm... it might just work...

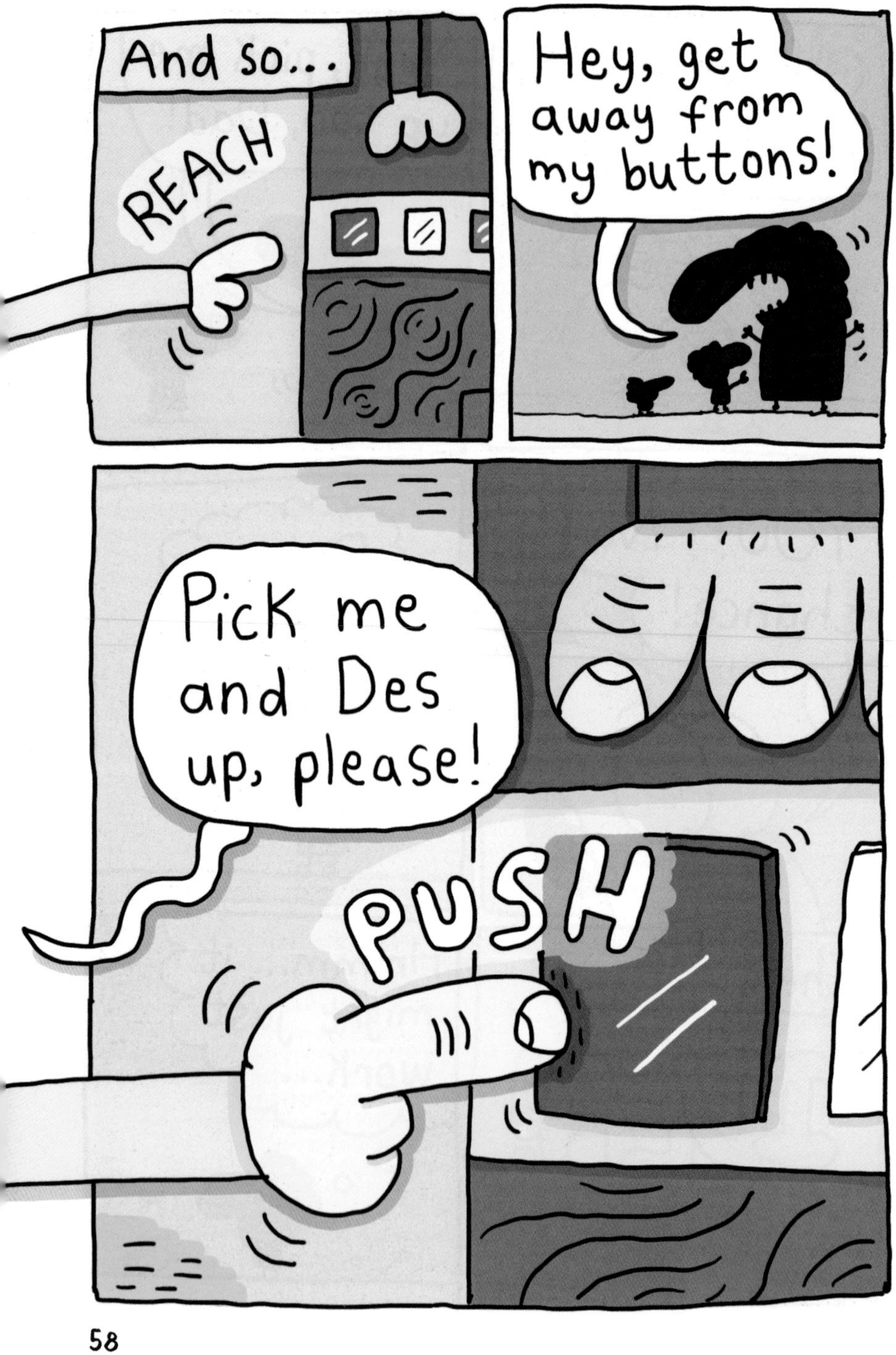
And so...
REACH
Hey, get away from my buttons!
Pick me and Des up, please!
PUSH

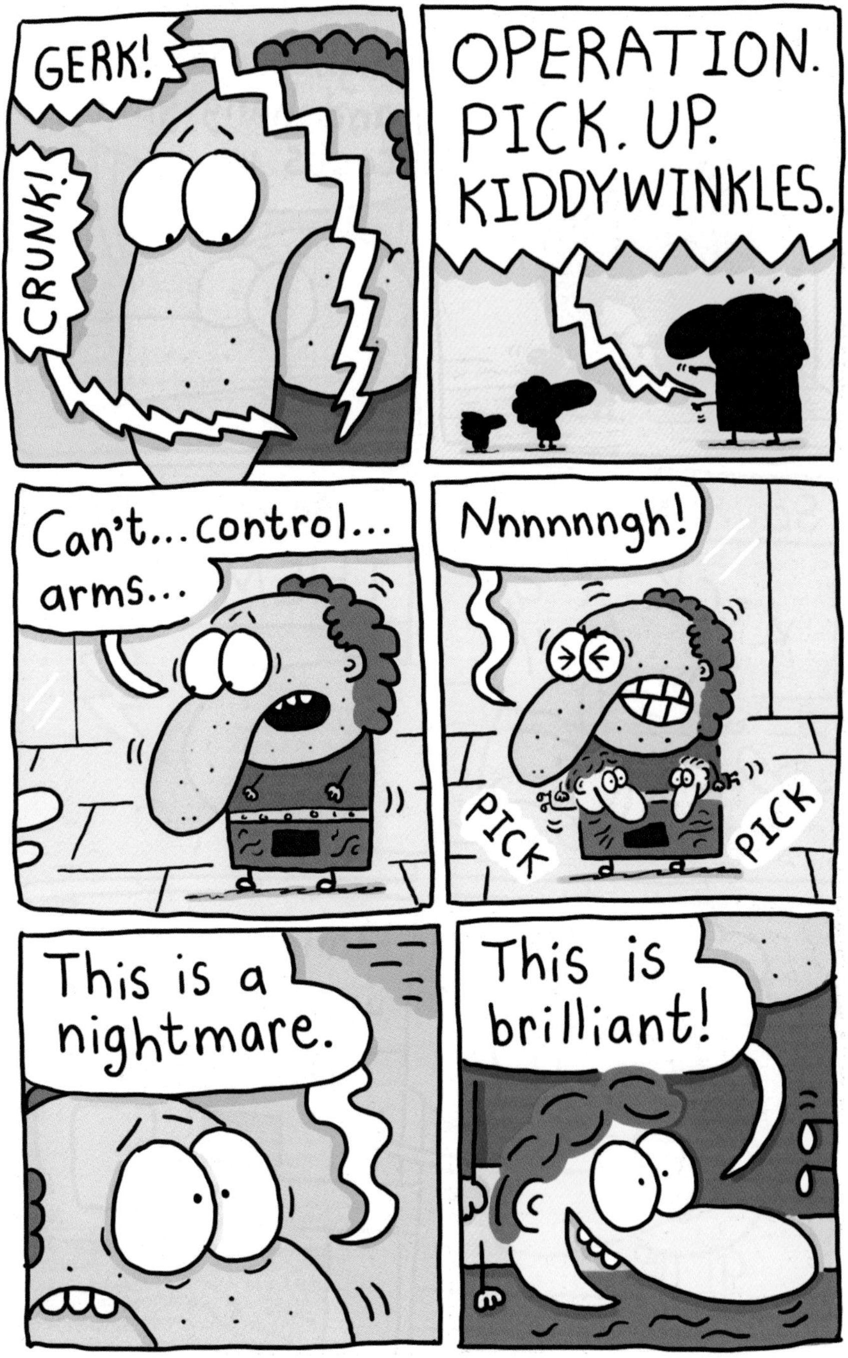
GERK!
CRUNK!
OPERATION. PICK. UP. KIDDYWINKLES.
Can't... control... arms...
Nnnnngh!
PICK
PICK
This is a nightmare.
This is brilliant!

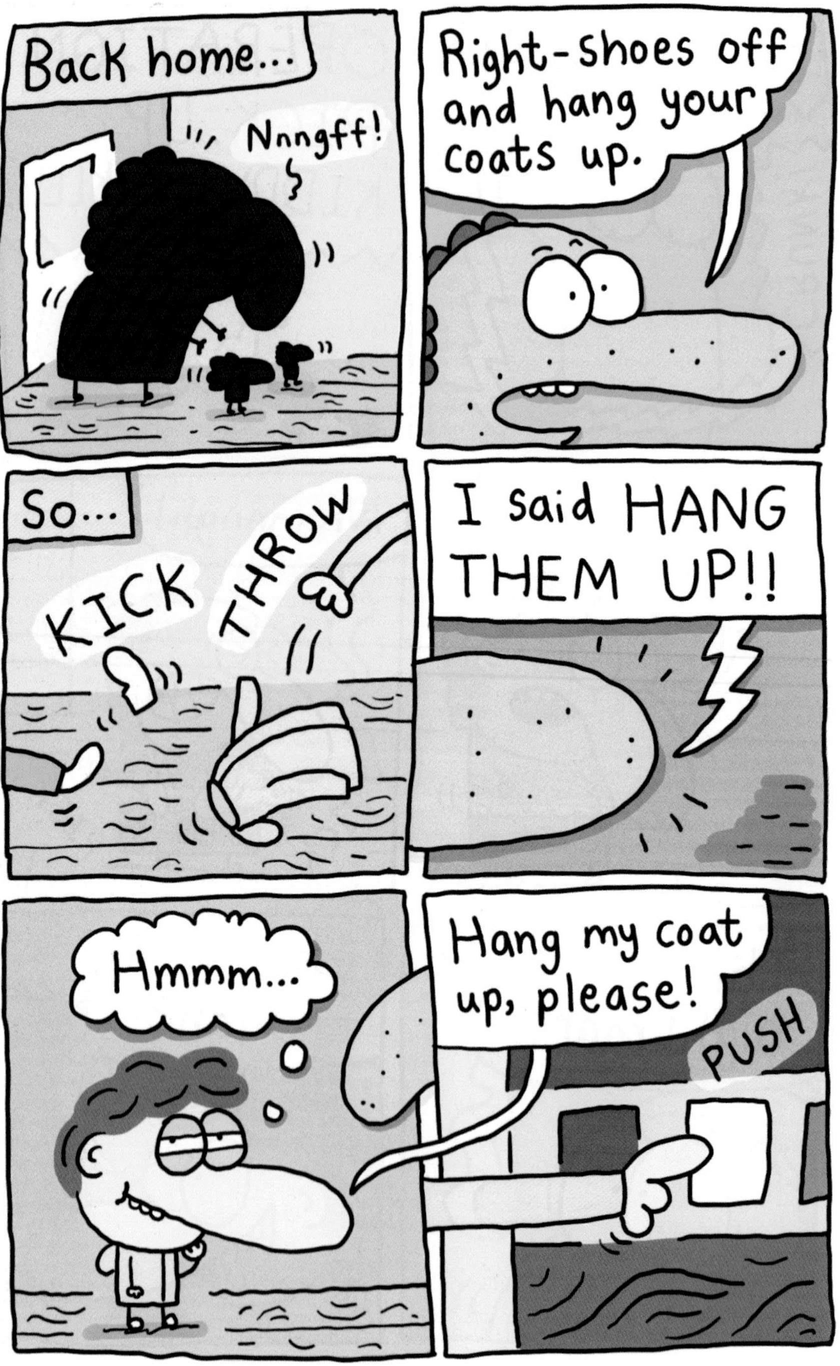
Back home...
Nnngff!
Right-shoes off and hang your coats up.
So...
KICK
THROW
I said HANG THEM UP!!
Hmmm...
Hang my coat up, please!
PUSH

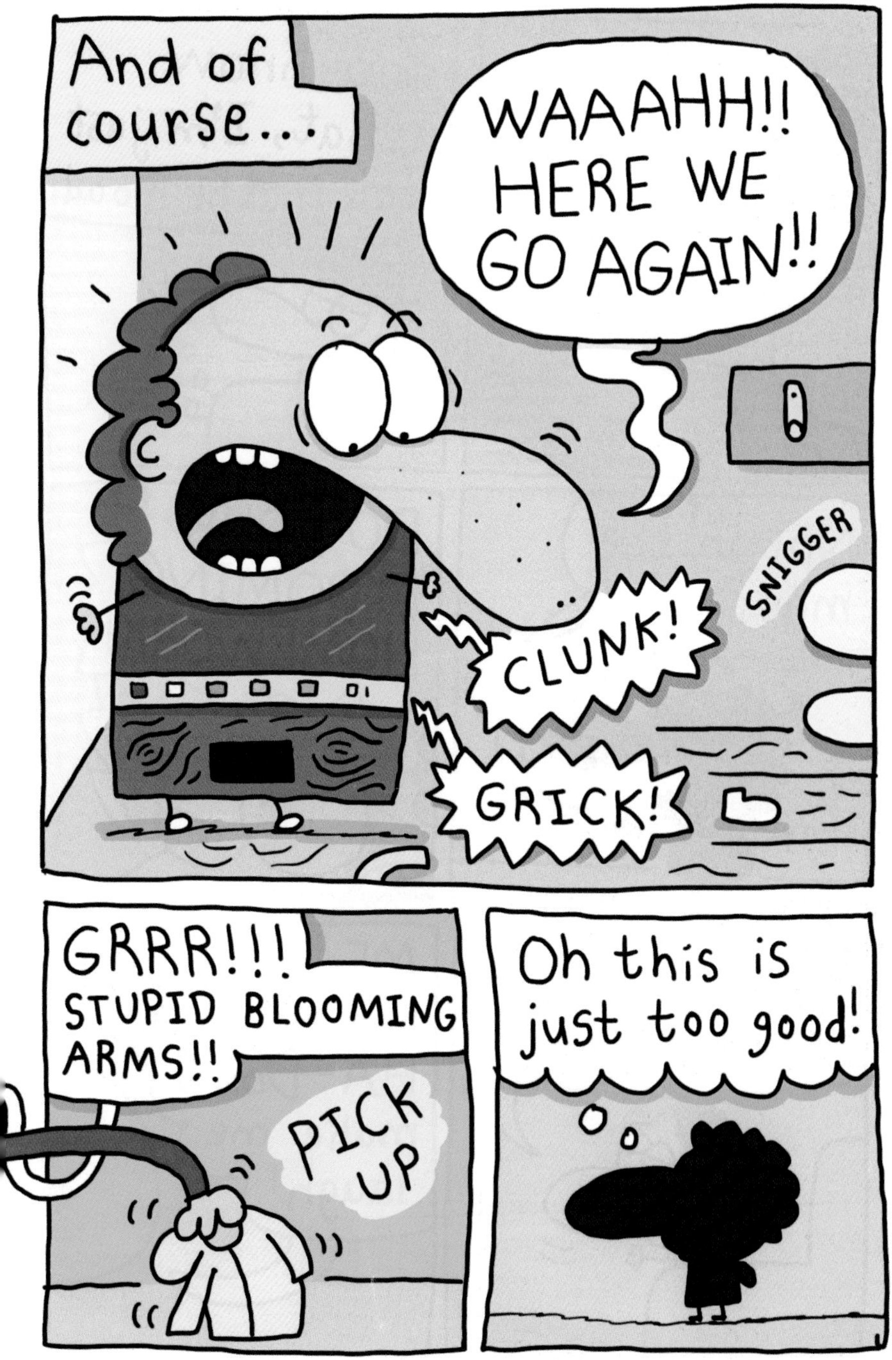
And of course...
WAAAHH!! HERE WE GO AGAIN!!
SNIGGER
CLUNK!
GRICK!
GRRR!!! STUPID BLOOMING ARMS!!
PICK UP
Oh this is just too good!

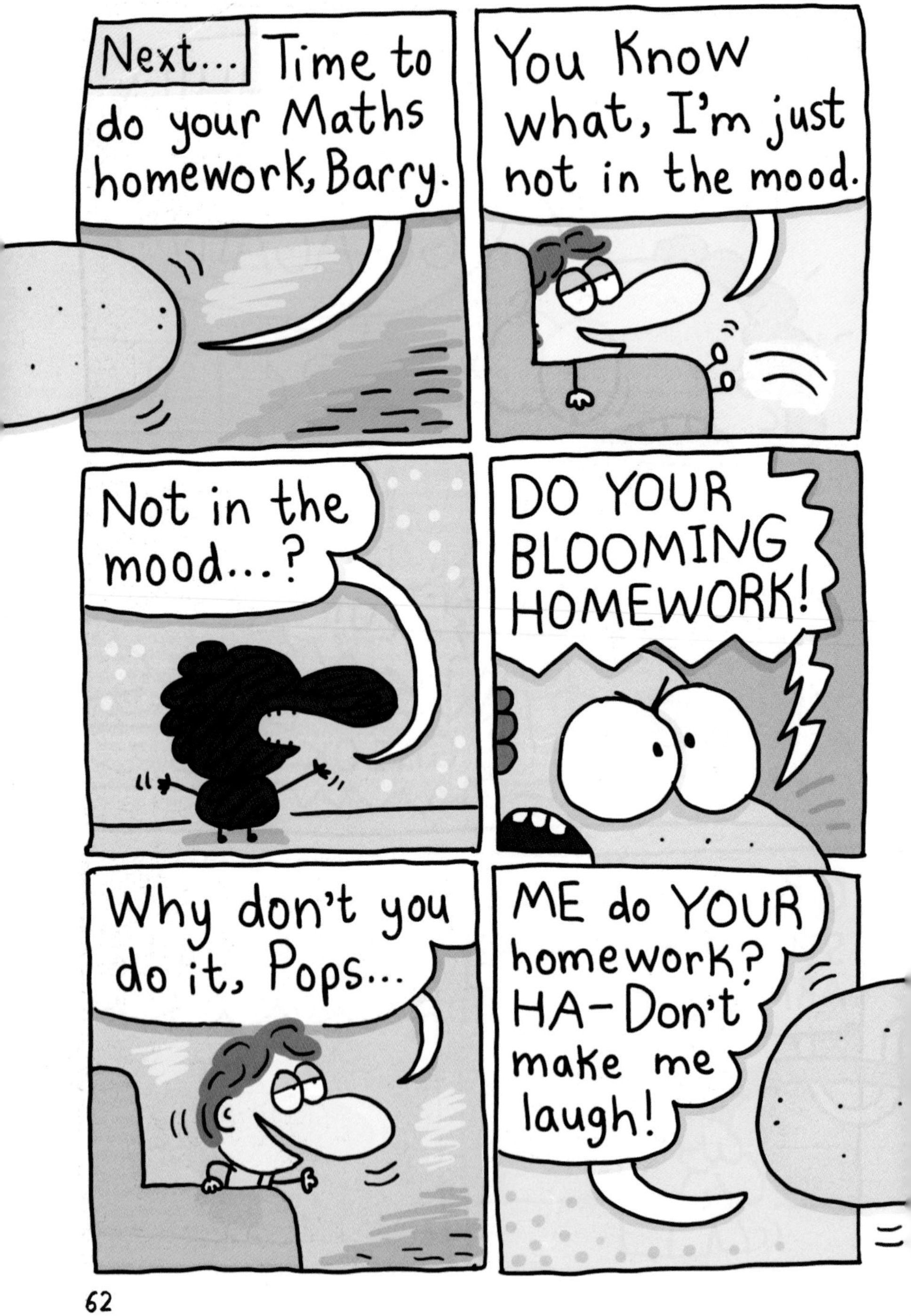
Next...
Time to do your Maths homework, Barry.
You Know what, I'm just not in the mood.
Not in the mood...?
DO YOUR BLOOMING HOMEWORK!
Why don't you do it, Pops...
ME do YOUR homework? HA-Don't make me laugh!

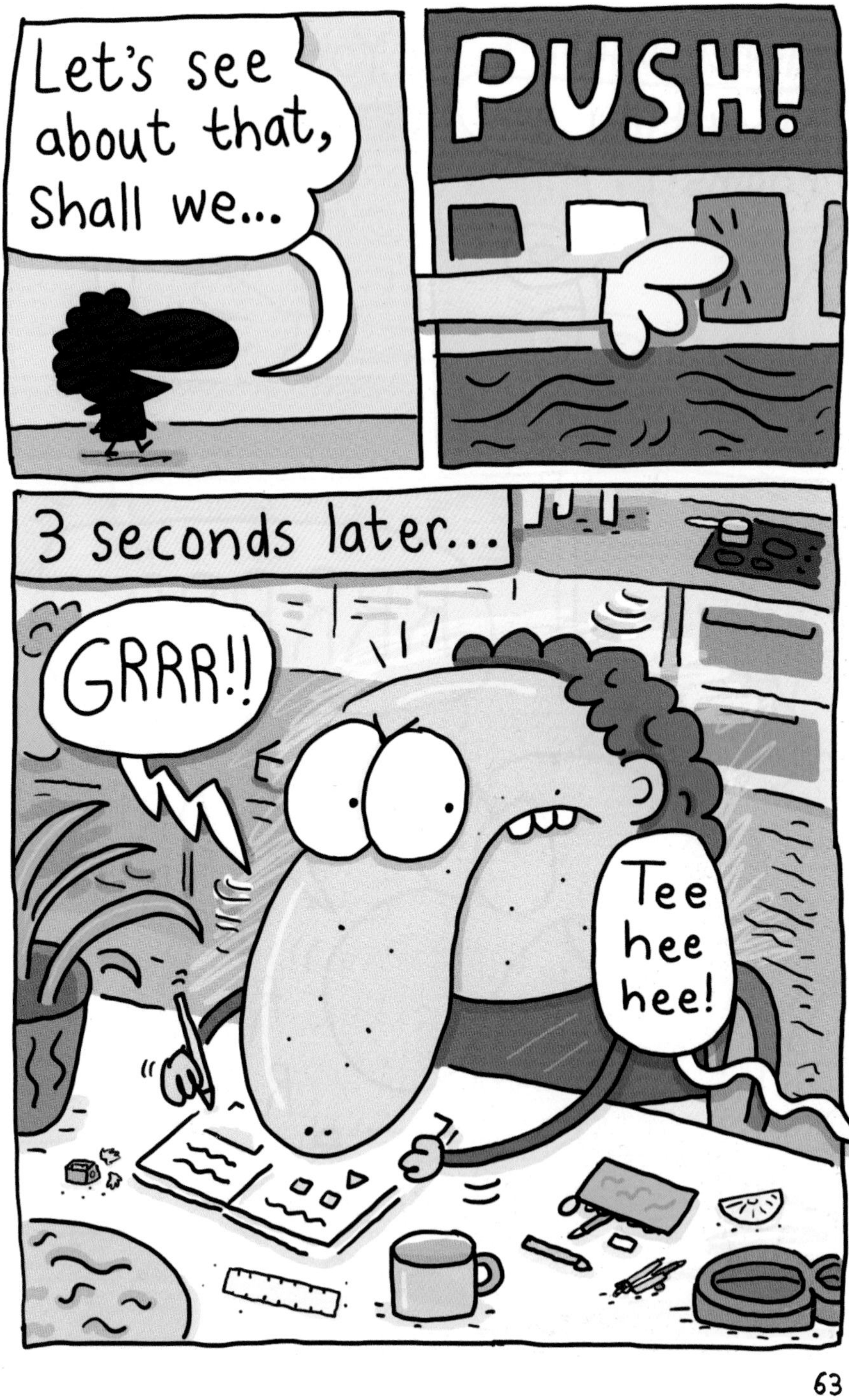
Let's see about that, shall we...
PUSH!
3 seconds later...
GRRR!!
Tee hee hee!

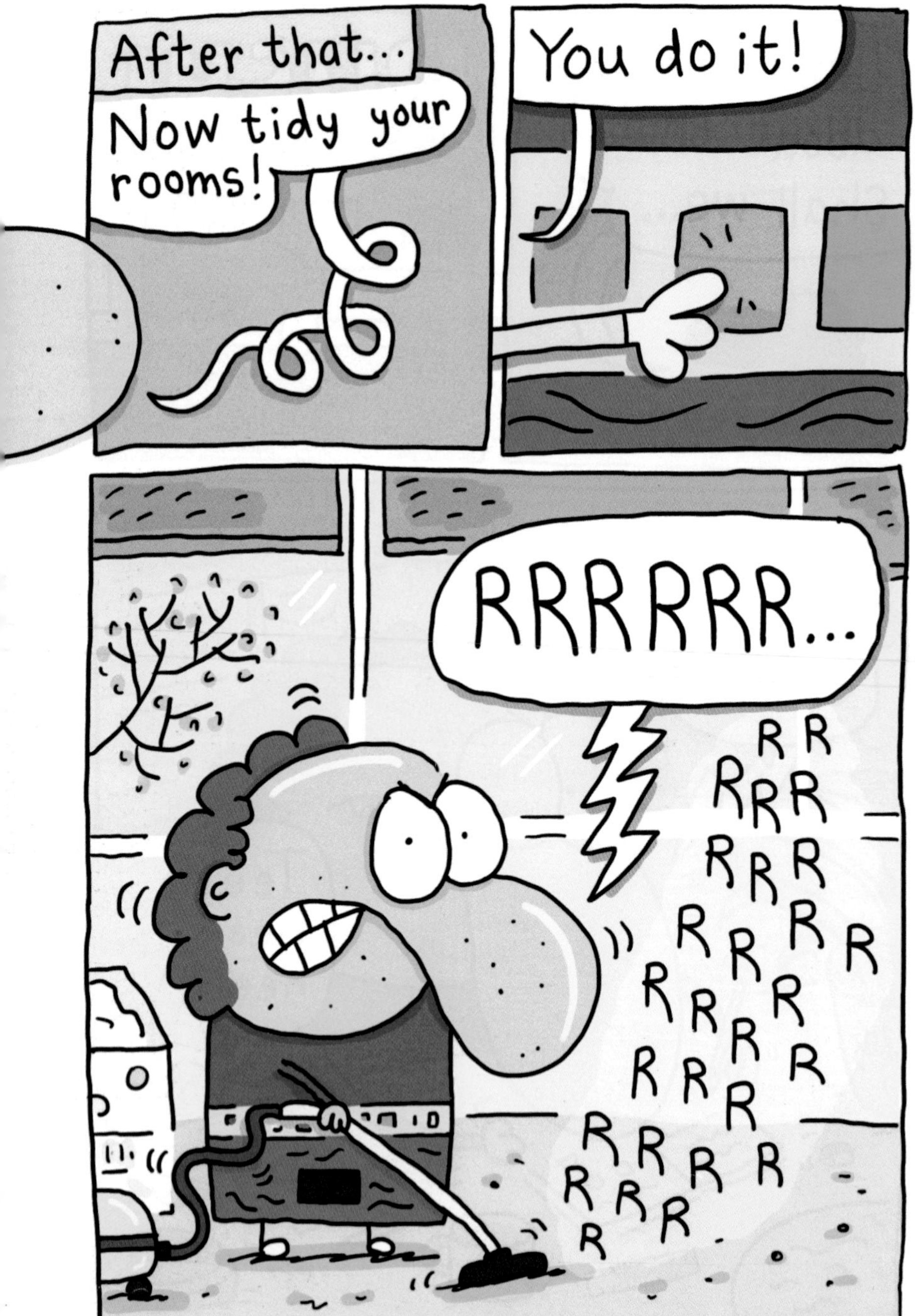
After that...
Now tidy your rooms!
You do it!
RRRRRR...
R R RRR RRR RRRR RRR R RRR R RRRR RRR R

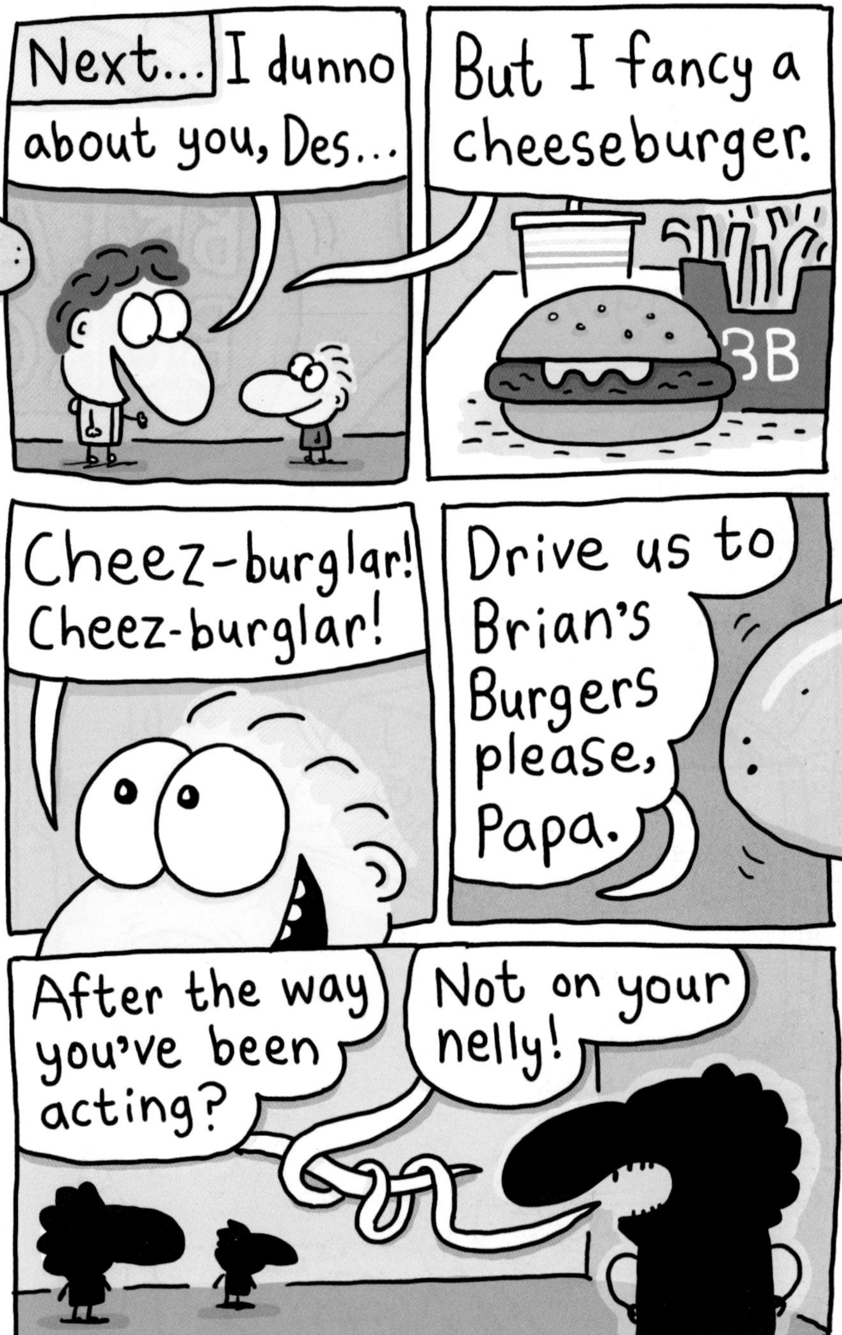
Next...
I dunno about you, Des...
But I fancy a cheeseburger.
Cheez-burglar! Cheez-burglar!
Drive us to Brian's Burgers please, Papa.
After the way you've been acting?
Not on your nelly!

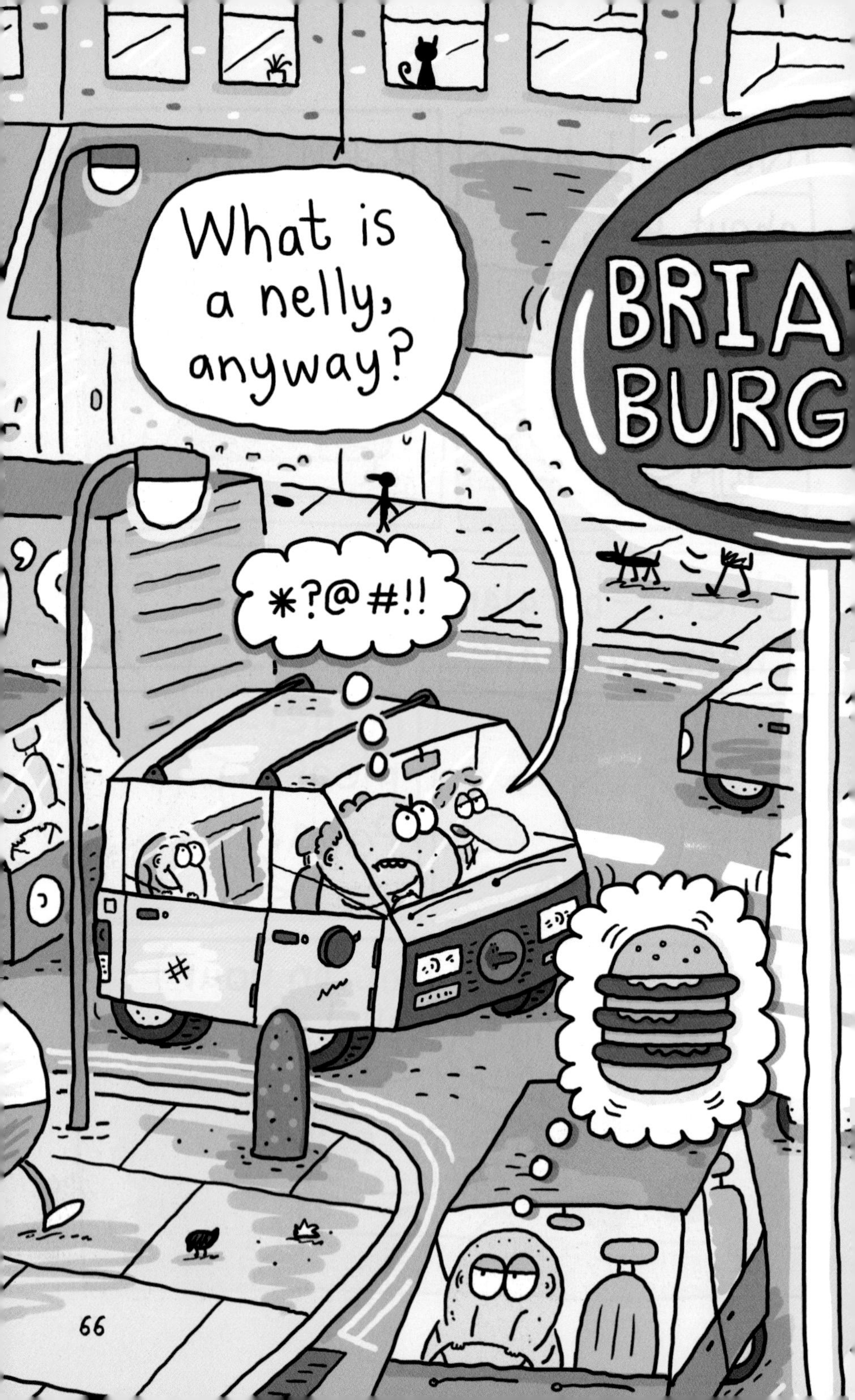
What is a nelly, anyway?
*?@#!!
BRIA
BURG

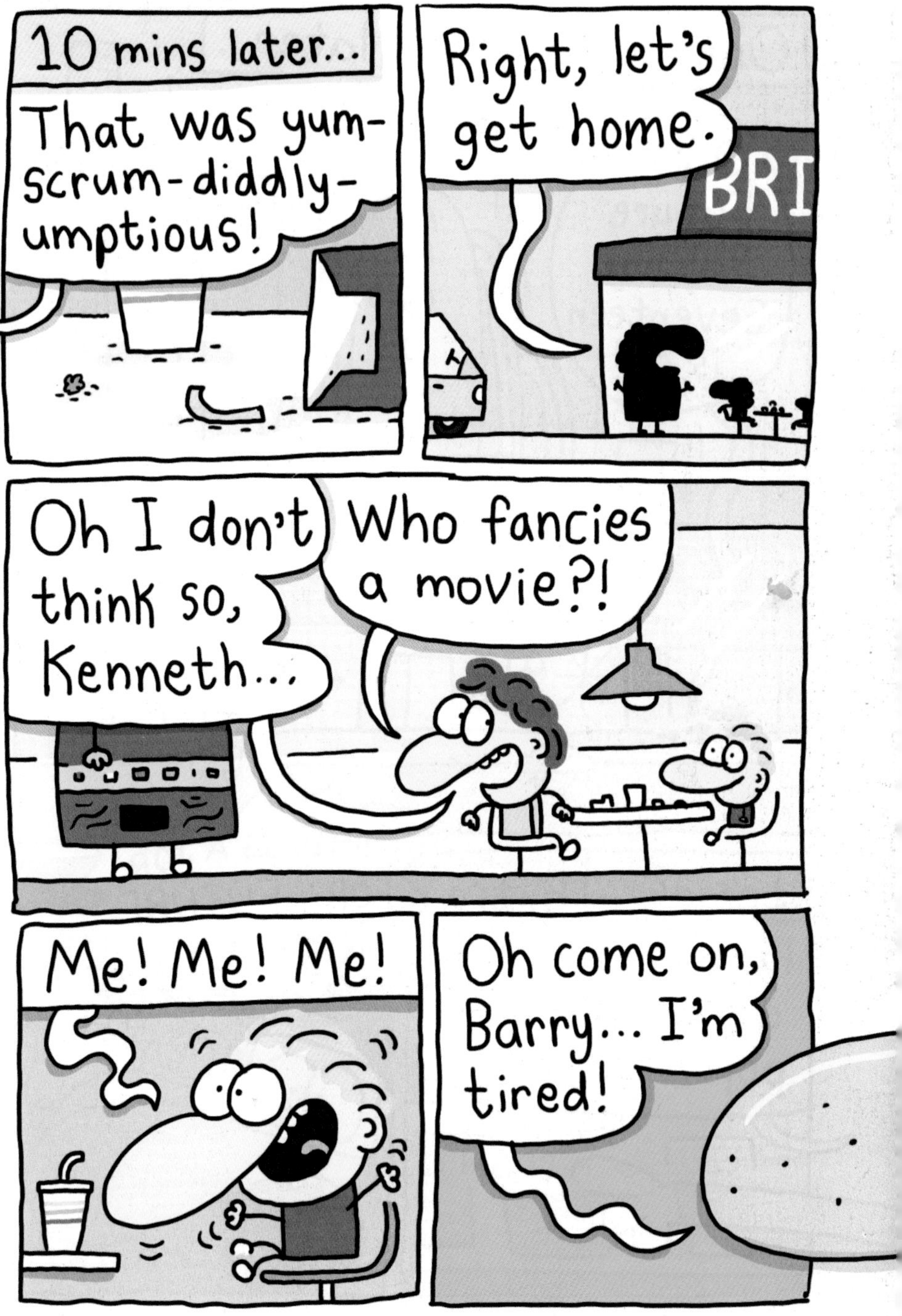

10 mins later...
That was yum-scrum-diddly-umptious!
Right, let's get home.
BRI
Oh I don't think so, Kenneth...
Who fancies a movie?!
Me! Me! Me!
Oh come on, Barry... I'm tired!

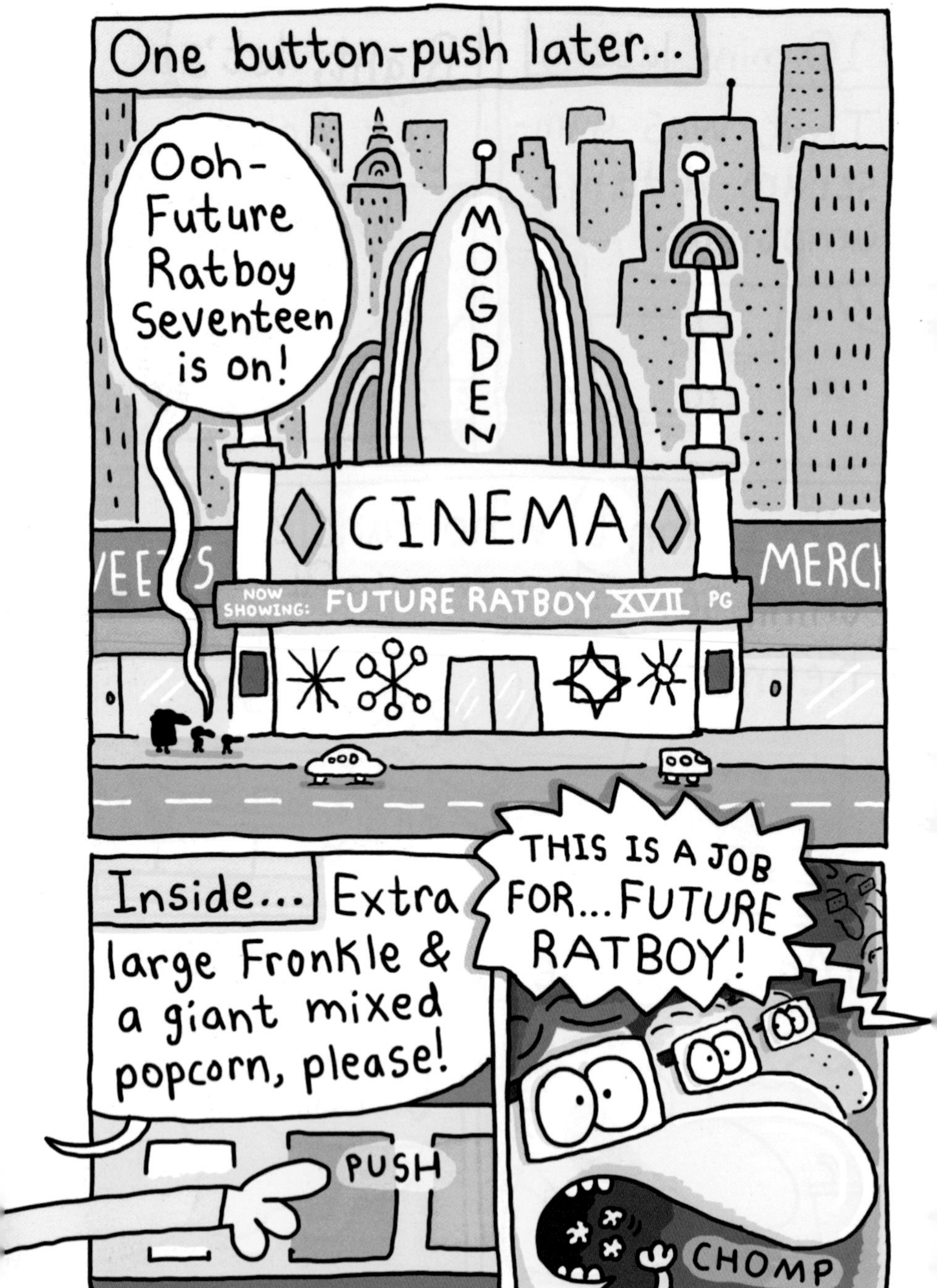
One button-push later...
Ooh- Future Ratboy Seventeen is on!
MOGDEN
CINEMA
NOW SHOWING: FUTURE RATBOY XVII PG
MERCH
Inside... Extra large Fronkle & a giant mixed popcorn, please!
PUSH
THIS IS A JOB FOR... FUTURE RATBOY!
CHOMP

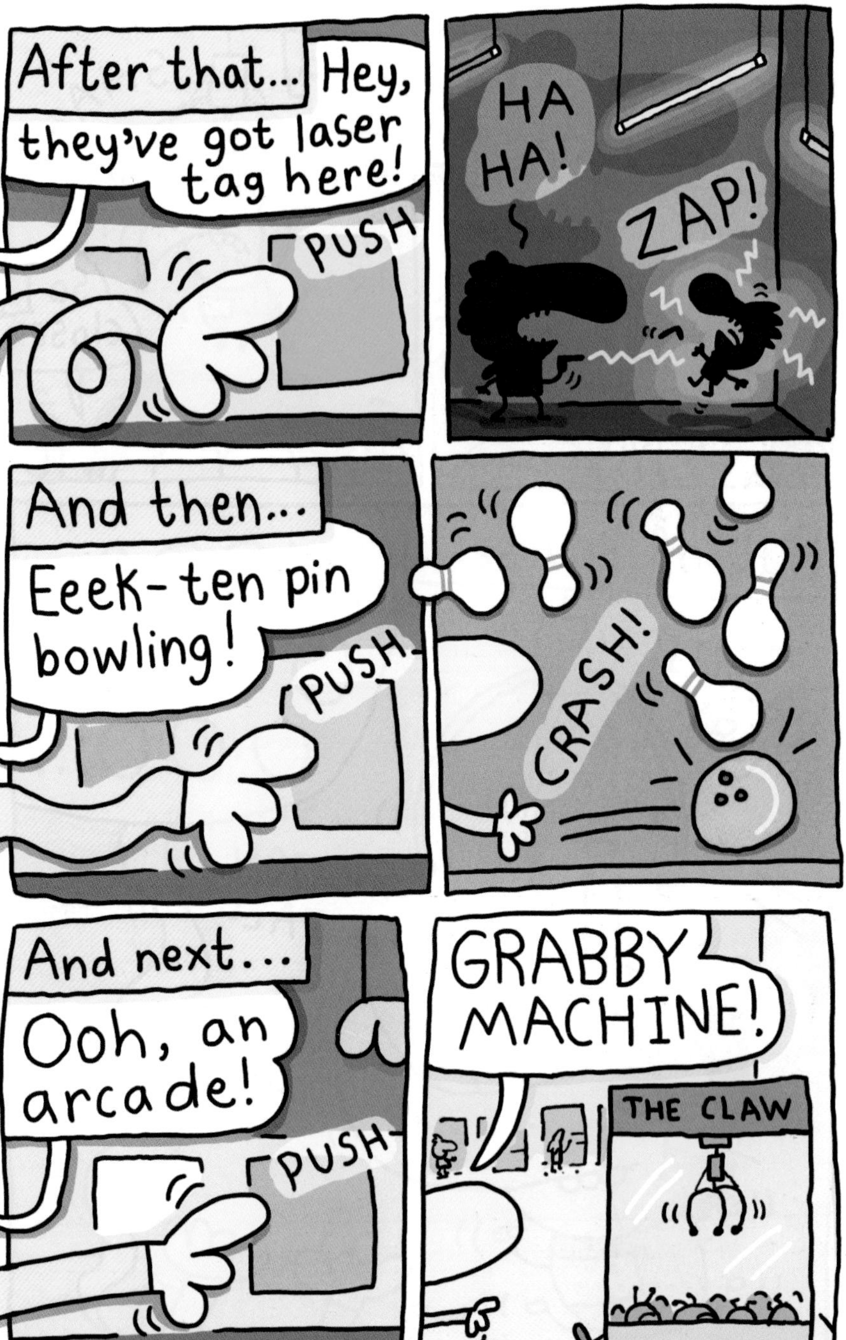
After that...
Hey, they've got laser tag here!
PUSH
HA HA!
ZAP!
And then...
Eeek- ten pin bowling!
PUSH
CRASH!
And next...
Ooh, an arcade!
PUSH
GRABBY MACHINE!
THE CLAW

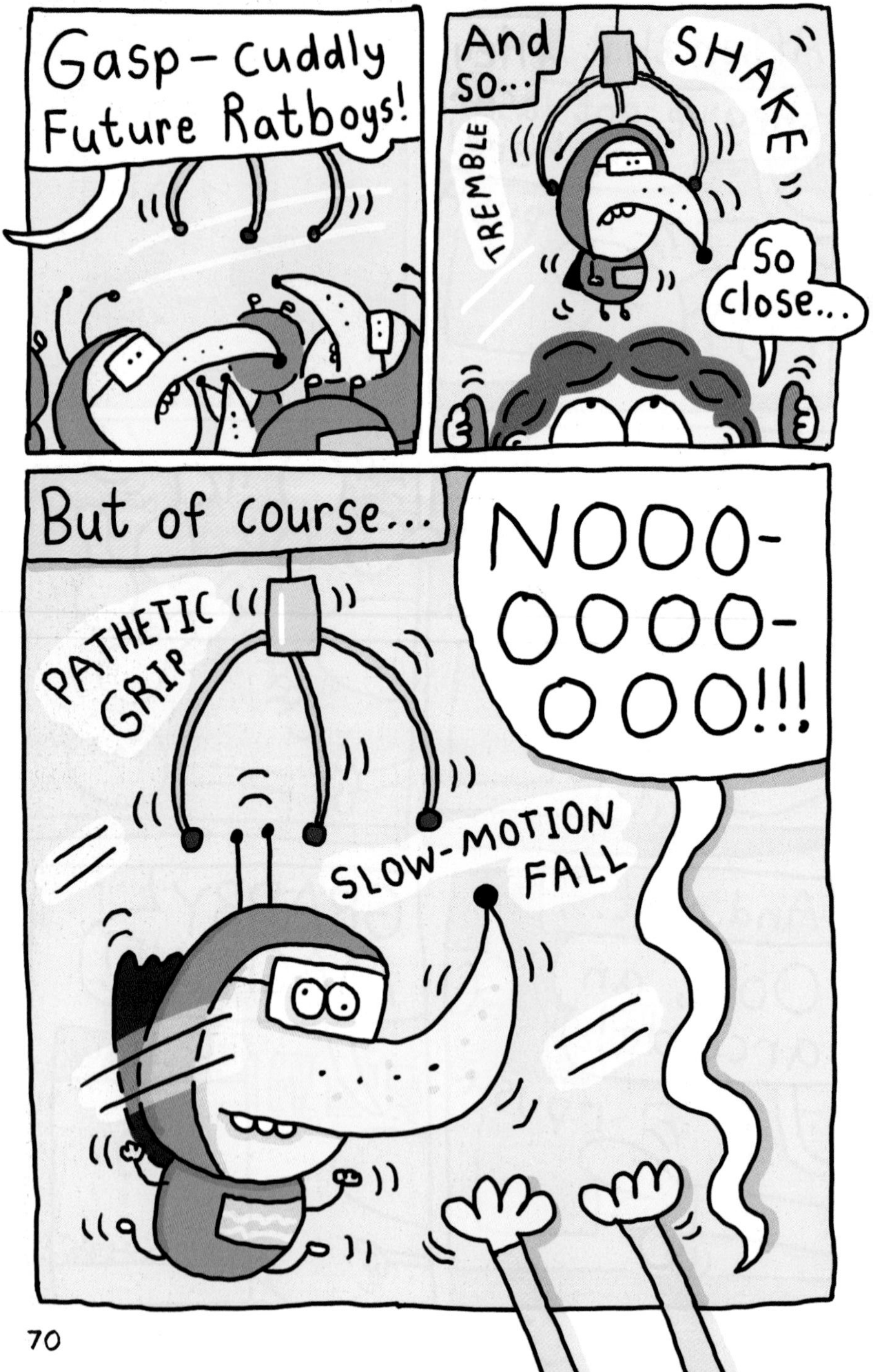
Gasp – cuddly Future Ratboys!
And so...
SHAKE
TREMBLE
So close...
But of course...
NOOO-OOOO-OOO!!!
PATHETIC GRIP
SLOW-MOTION FALL

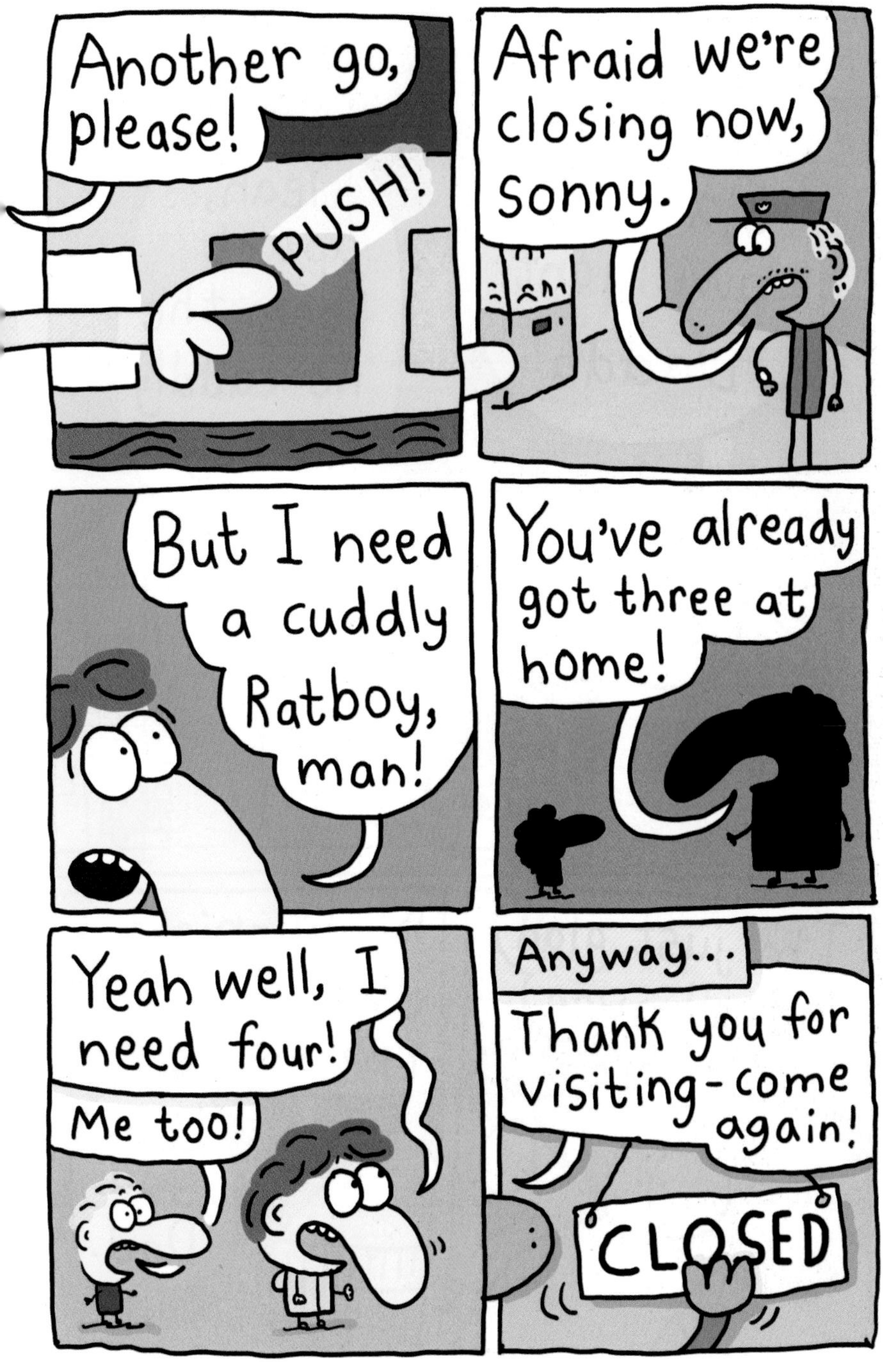
Another go, please!
PUSH!
Afraid we're closing now, Sonny.
But I need a cuddly Ratboy, man!
You've already got three at home!
Yeah well, I need four!
Me too!
Anyway...
Thank you for visiting - come again!
CLOSED

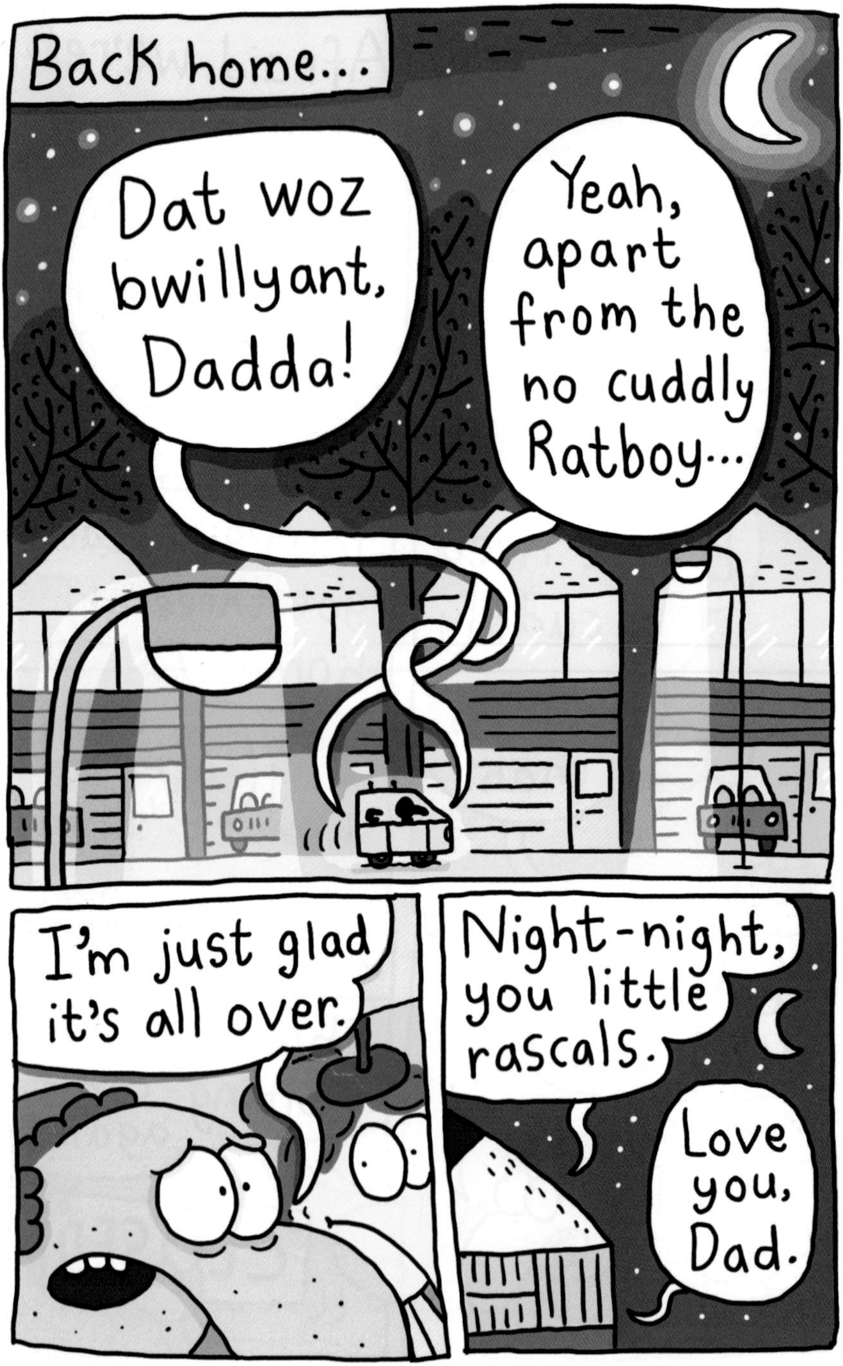
Back home...
Dat woz bwillyant, Dadda!
Yeah, apart from the no cuddly Ratboy...
I'm just glad it's all over.
Night-night, you little rascals.
Love you, Dad.

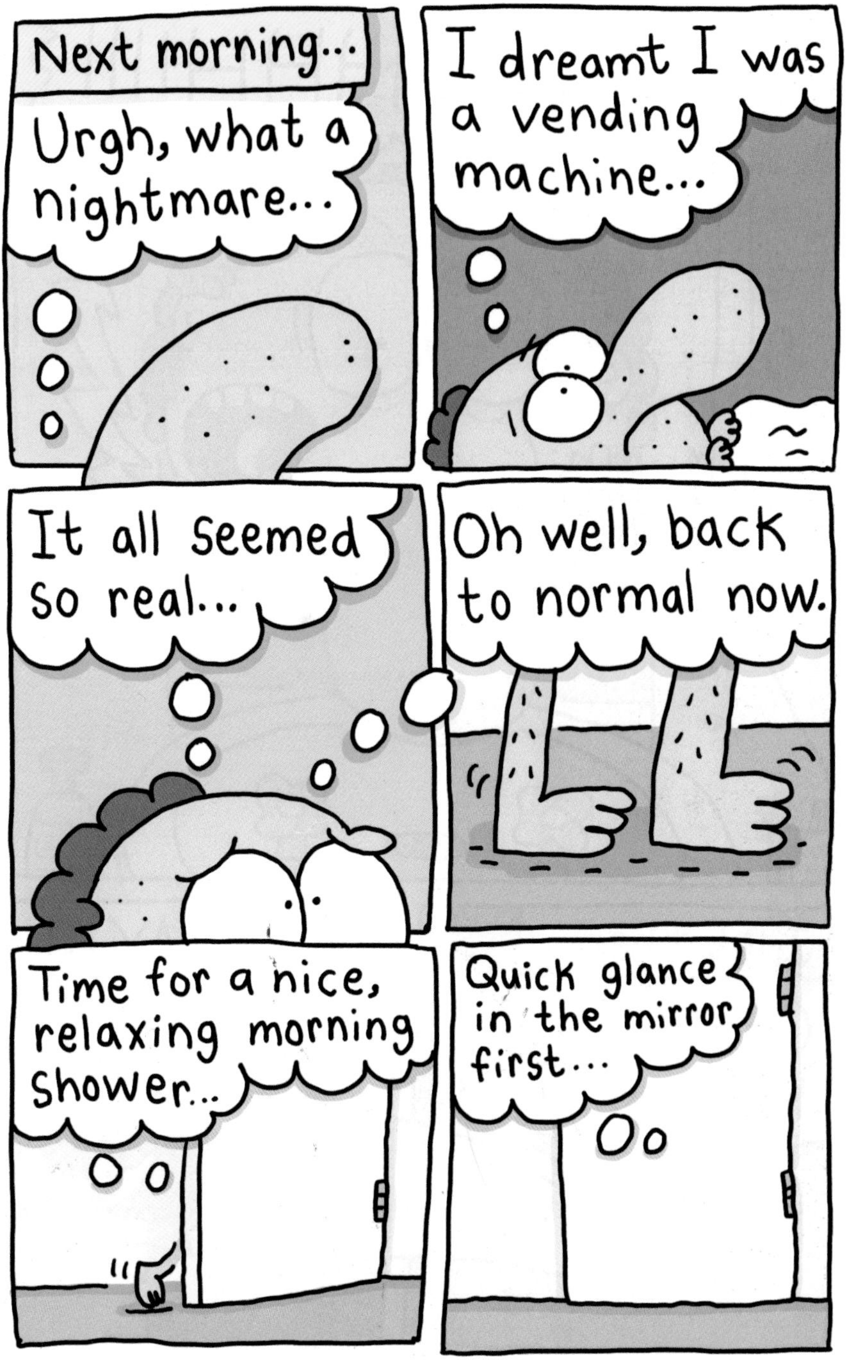
Next morning...
Urgh, what a nightmare...
I dreamt I was a vending machine...
It all seemed so real...
Oh well, back to normal now.
Time for a nice, relaxing morning shower...
Quick glance in the mirror first...

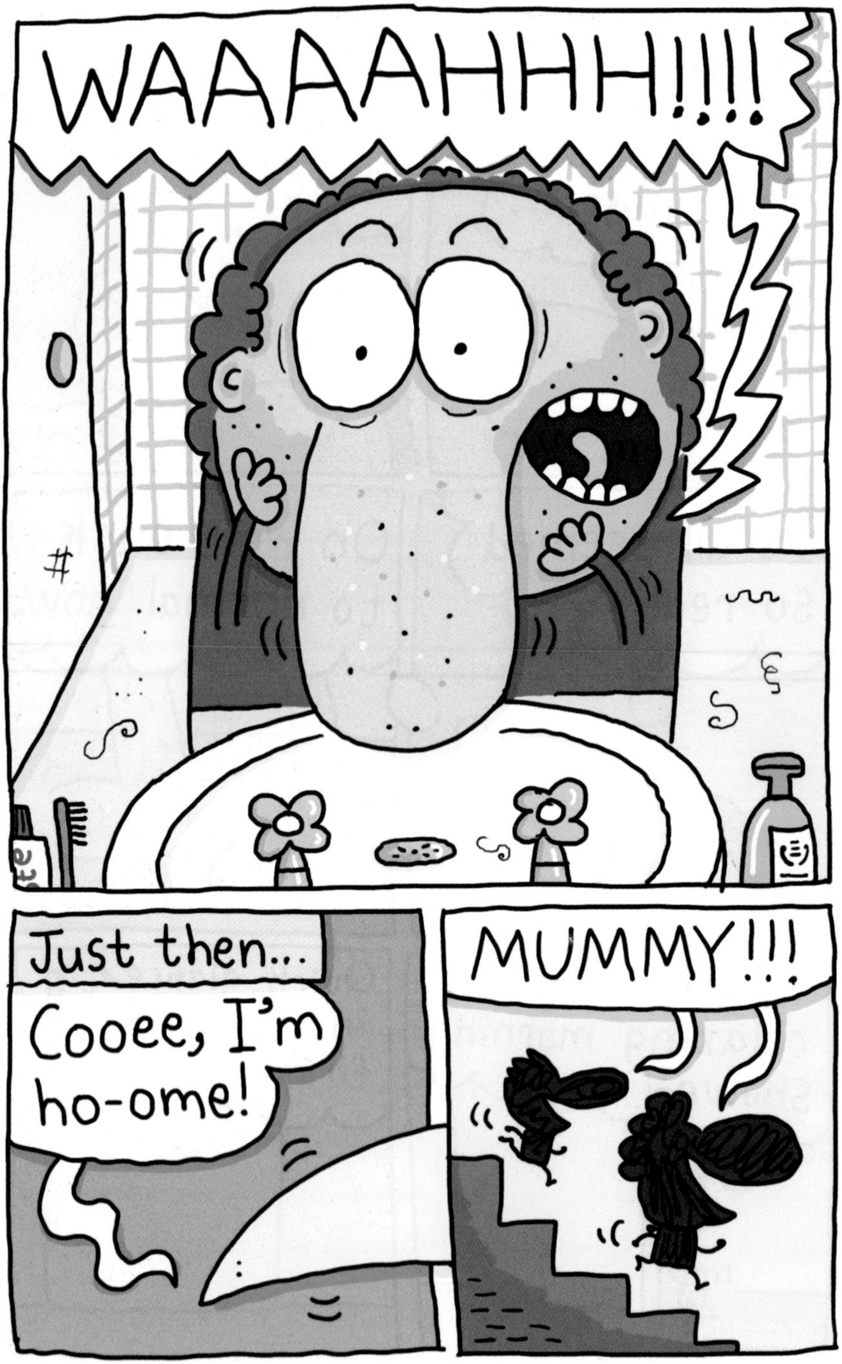
WAAAAHHH!!!!
Just then...
Cooee, I'm ho-ome!
MUMMY!!!

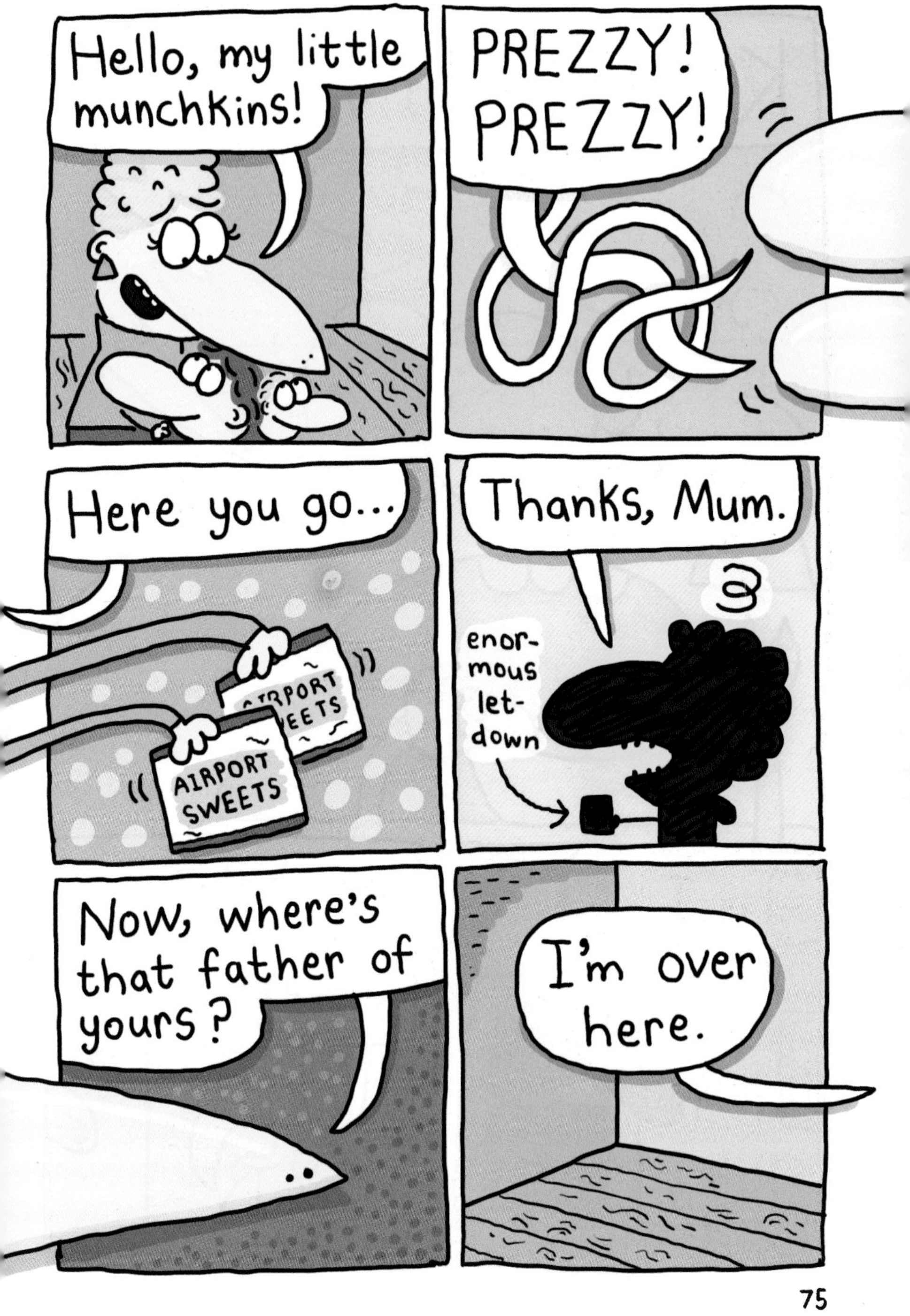
Hello, my little munchkins!
PREZZY! PREZZY!
Here you go...
AIRPORT SWEETS
AIRPORT SWEETS
Thanks, Mum.
enormous let-down
Now, where's that father of yours?
I'm over here.

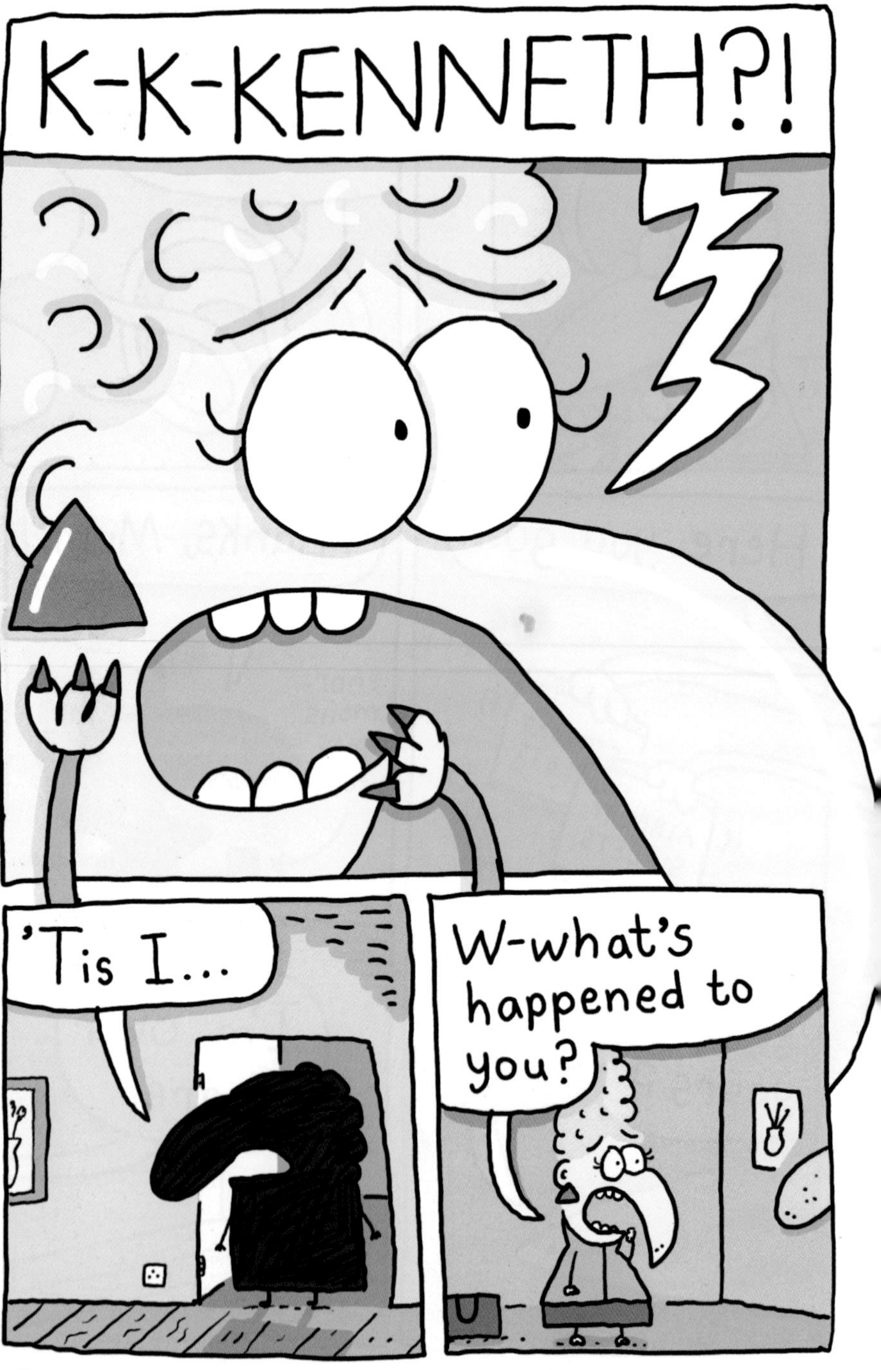
K-K-KENNETH?!
'Tis I...
W-what's happened to you?

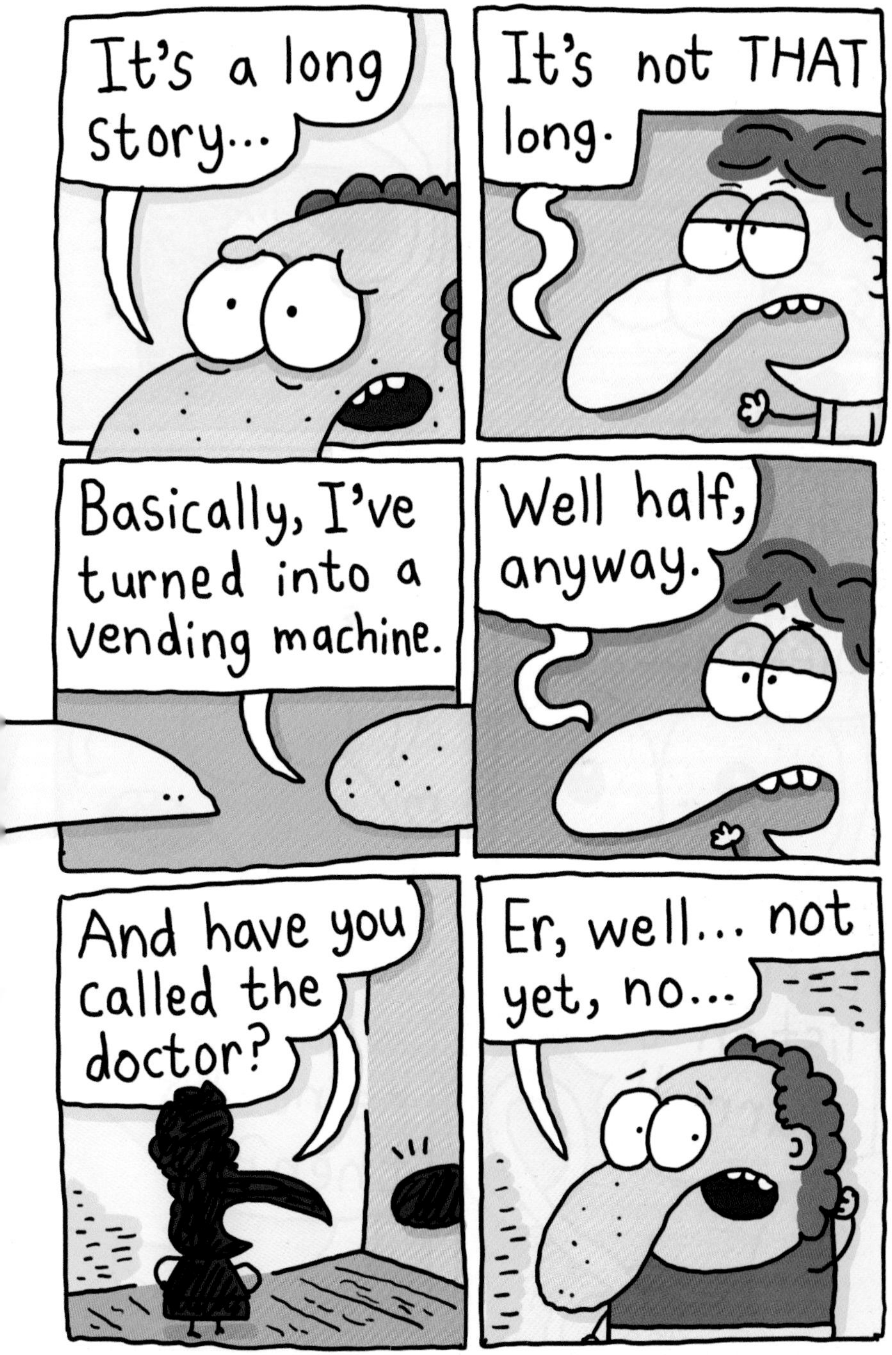
It's a long story...
It's not THAT long.
Basically, I've turned into a vending machine.
Well half, anyway.
And have you called the doctor?
Er, well... not yet, no...

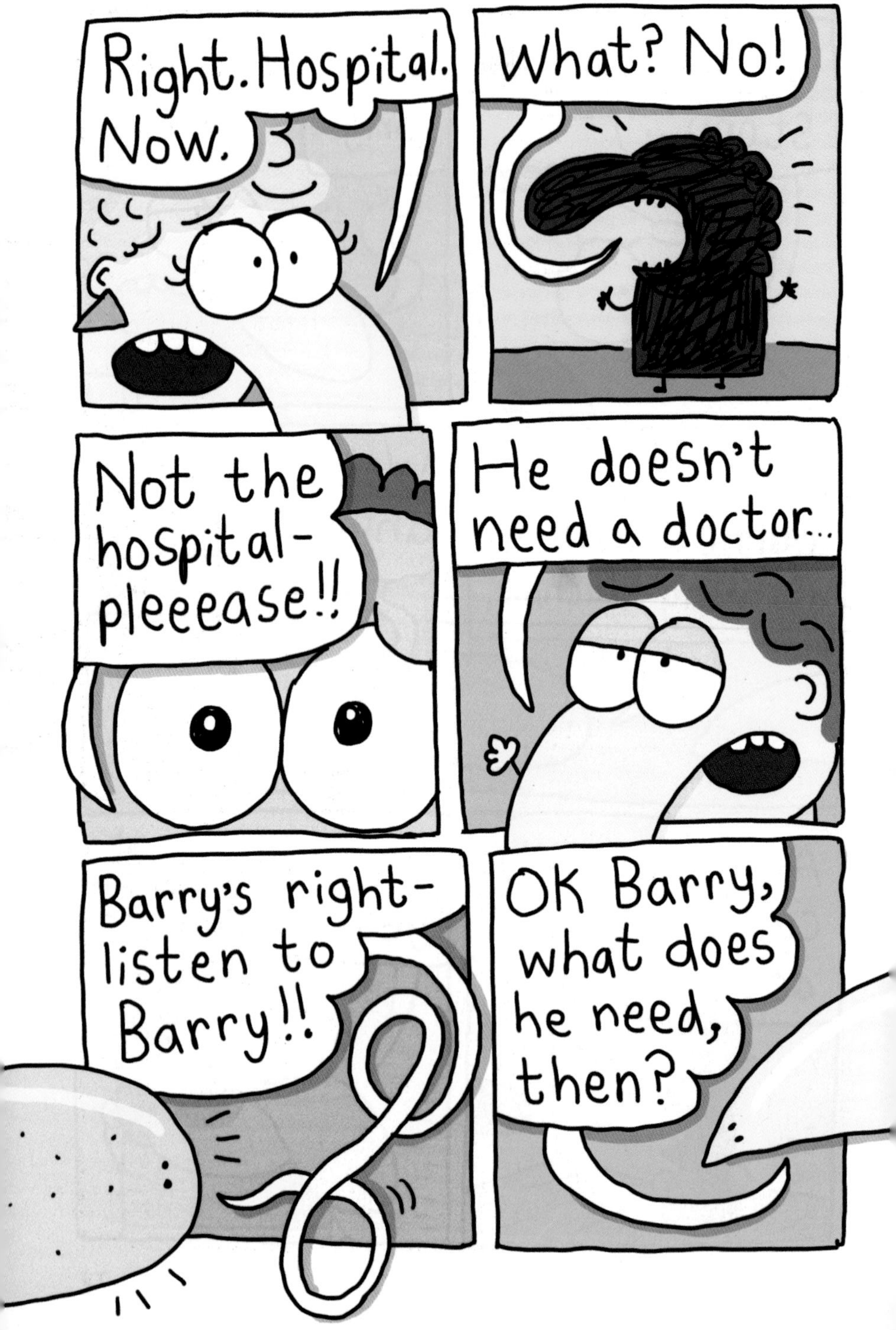
Right. Hospital. Now.
What? No!
Not the hospital- pleeeease!!
He doesn't need a doctor...
Barry's right- listen to Barry!!
OK Barry, what does he need, then?

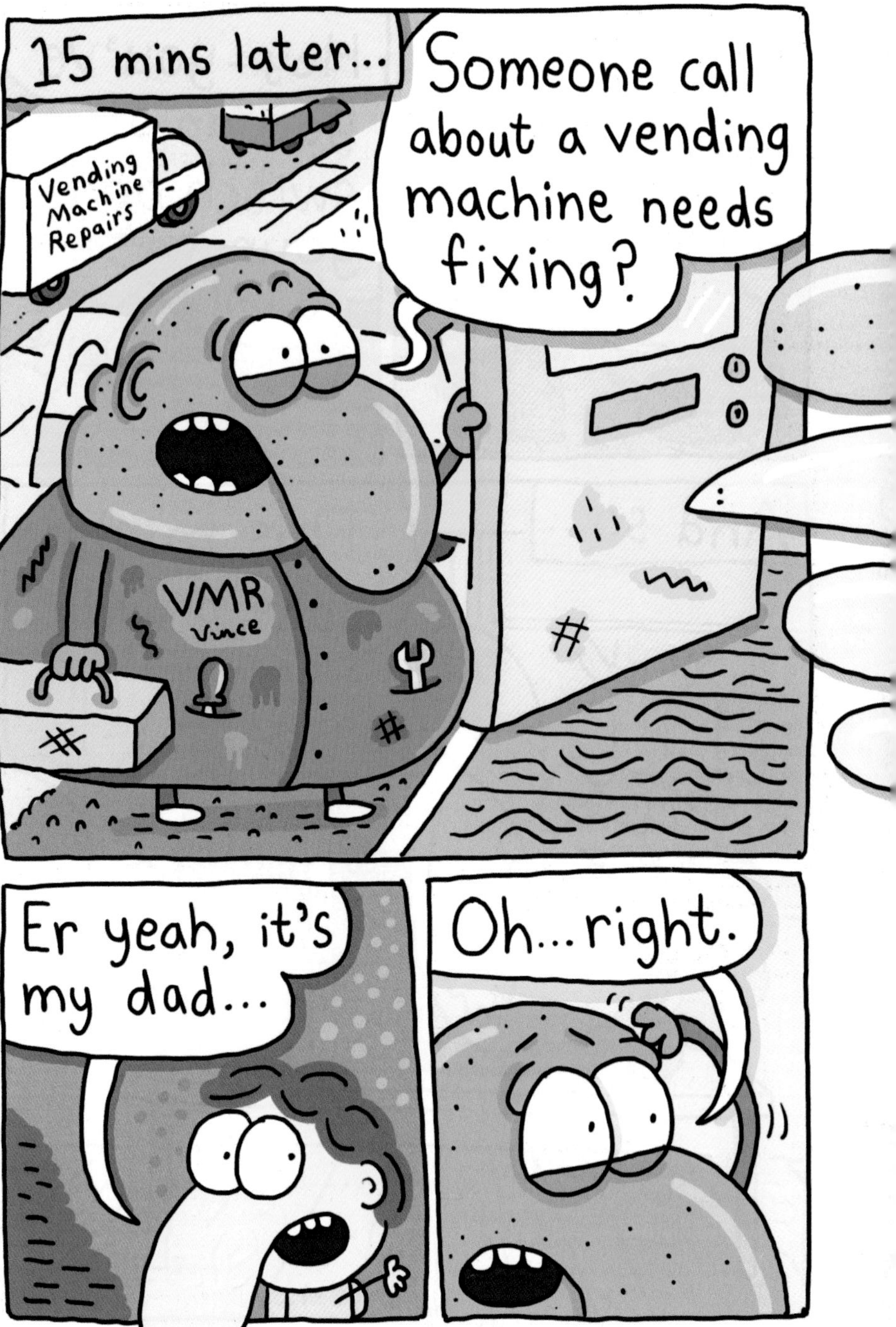
15 mins later...
Vending Machine Repairs
Someone call about a vending machine needs fixing?
VMR
Vince
Er yeah, it's my dad...
Oh... right.

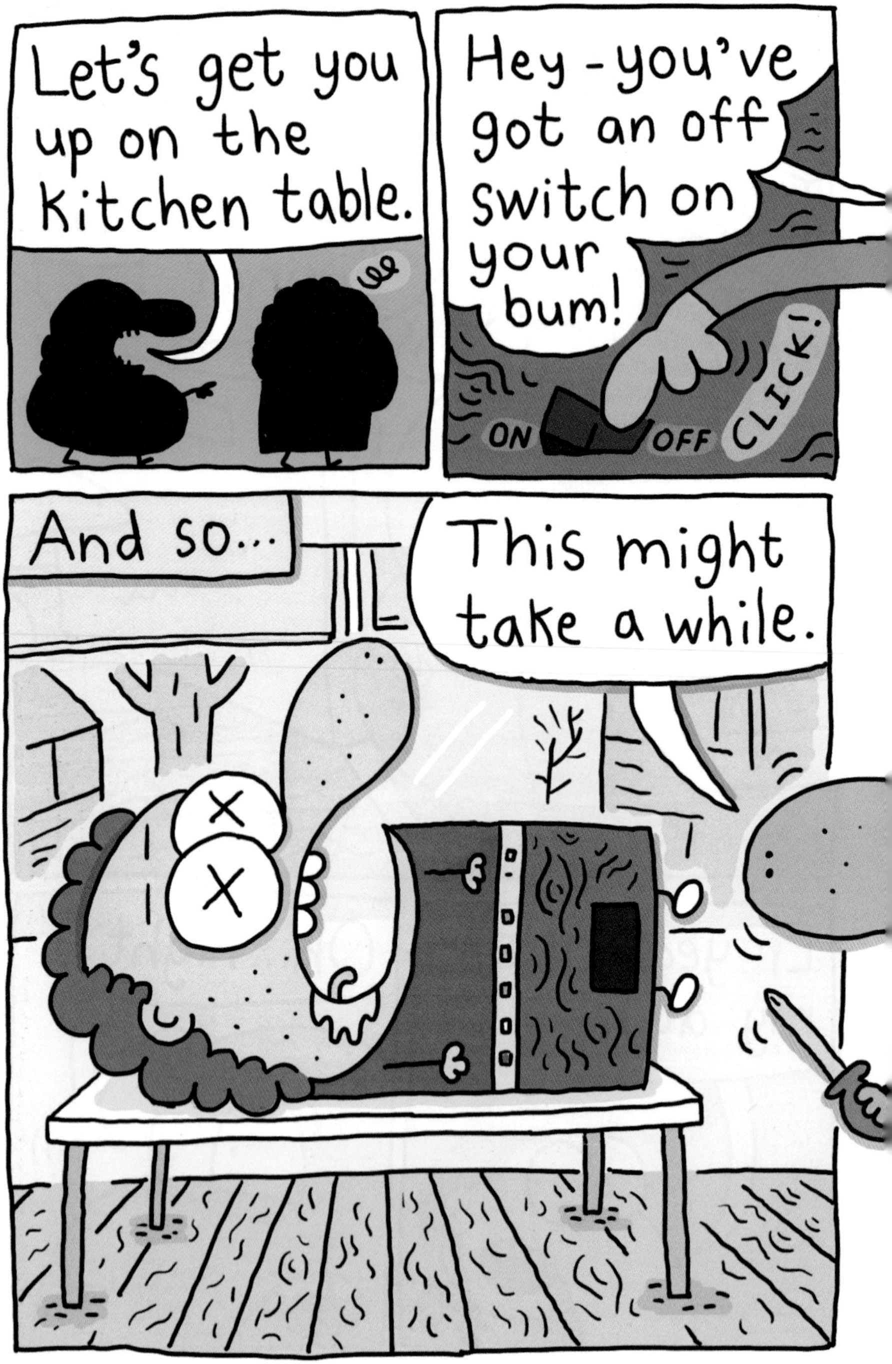
Let's get you up on the kitchen table.
Hey - you've got an off switch on your bum!
ON
OFF
CLICK!
And so...
This might take a while.

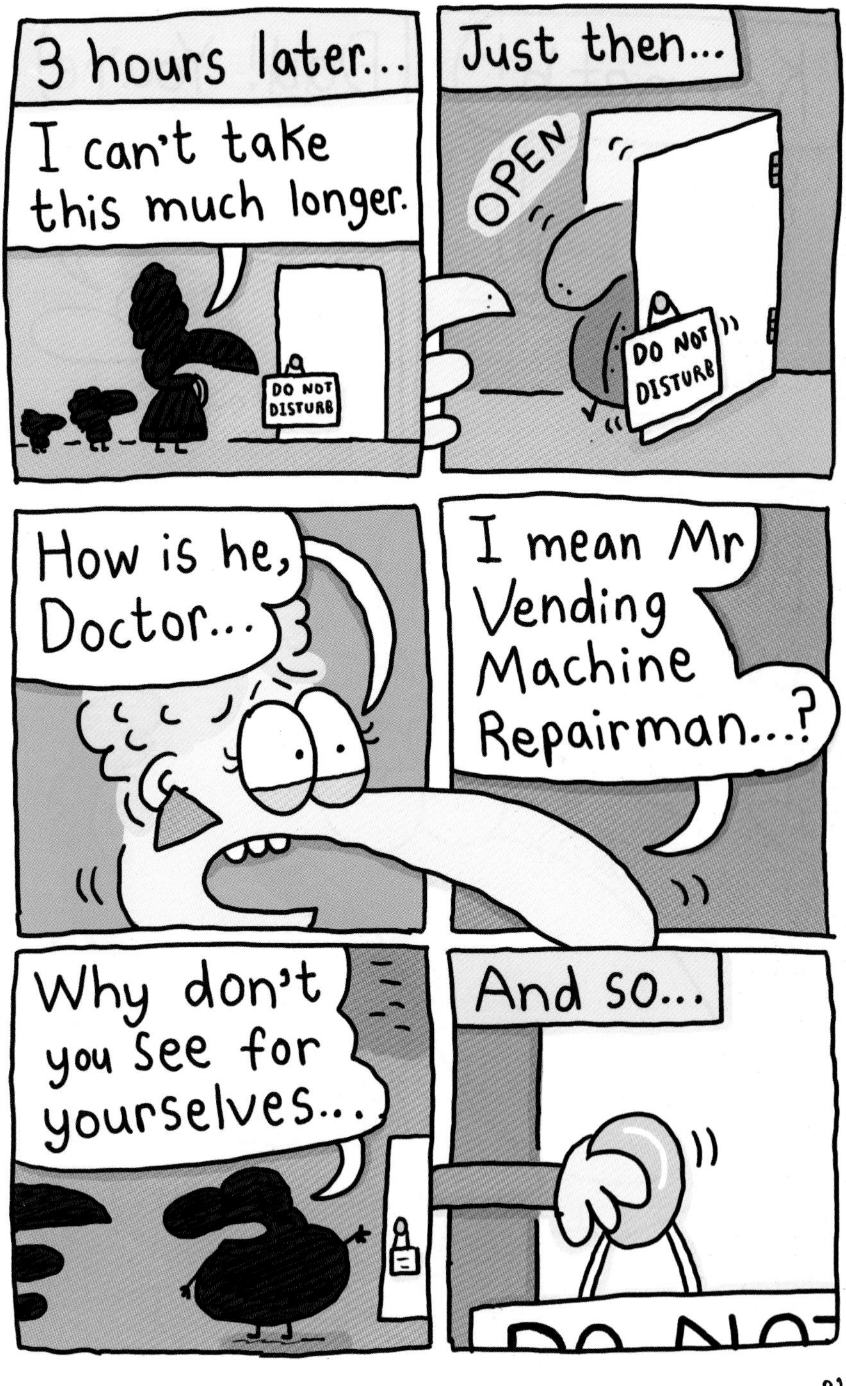

3 hours later...
I can't take this much longer.
DO NOT DISTURB
Just then...
OPEN
DO NOT DISTURB
How is he, Doctor...
I mean Mr Vending Machine Repairman...?
Why don't you see for yourselves...
And so...
DO NOT

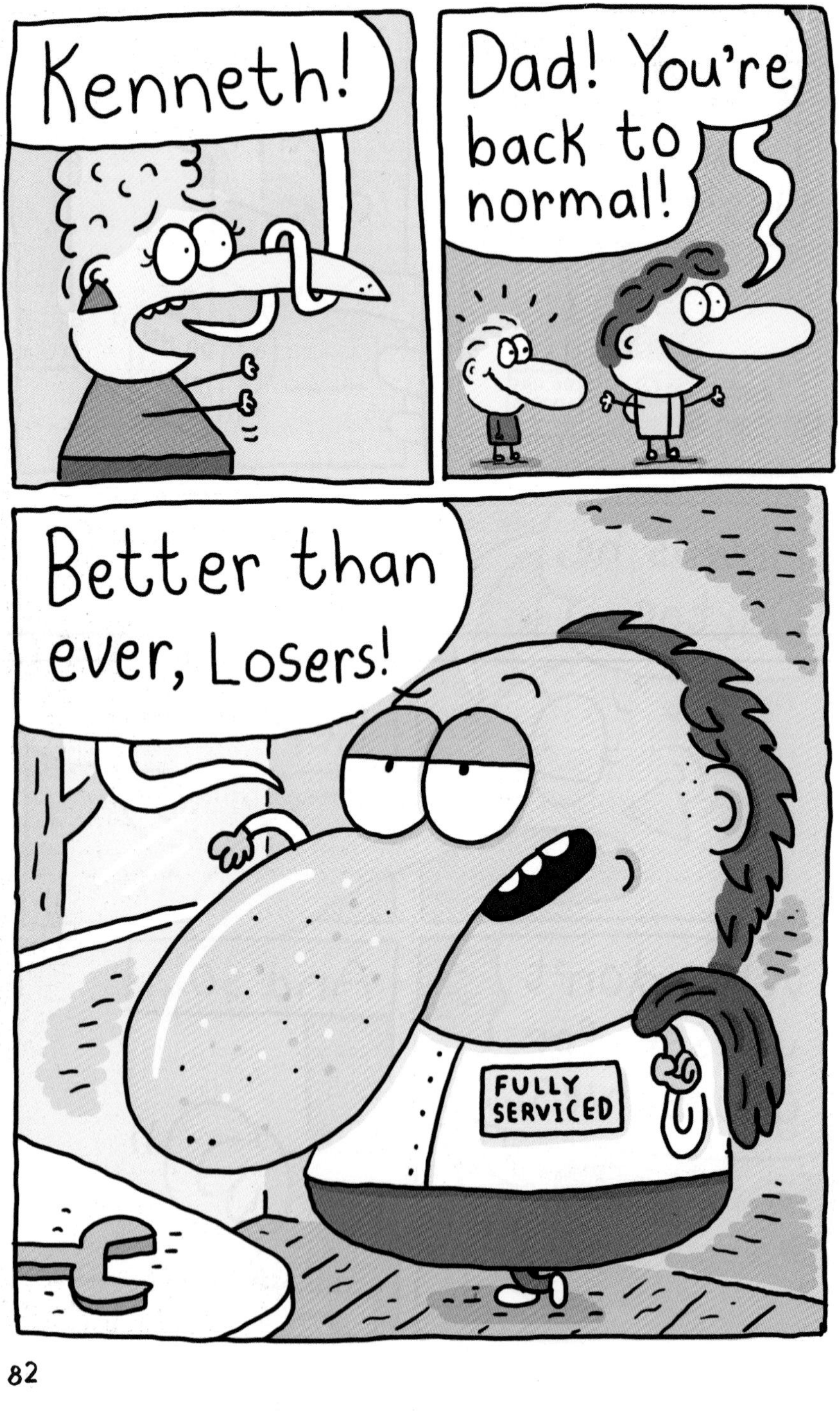
Kenneth!
Dad! You're back to normal!
Better than ever, Losers!
FULLY SERVICED

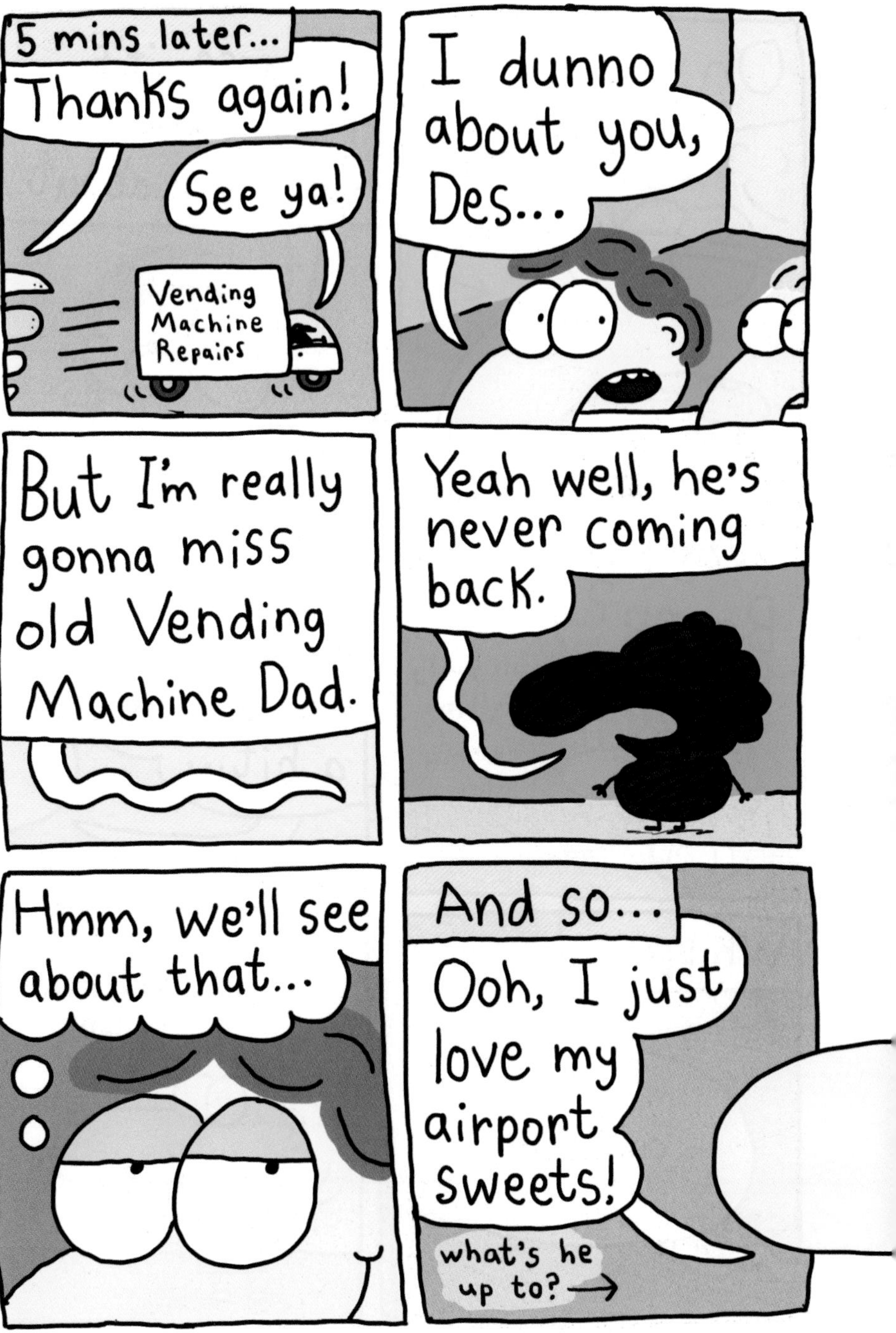
5 mins later...
Thanks again!
See ya!
Vending Machine Repairs
I dunno about you, Des...
But I'm really gonna miss old Vending Machine Dad.
Yeah well, he's never coming back.
Hmm, we'll see about that...
And so...
Ooh, I just love my airport sweets!
what's he up to?

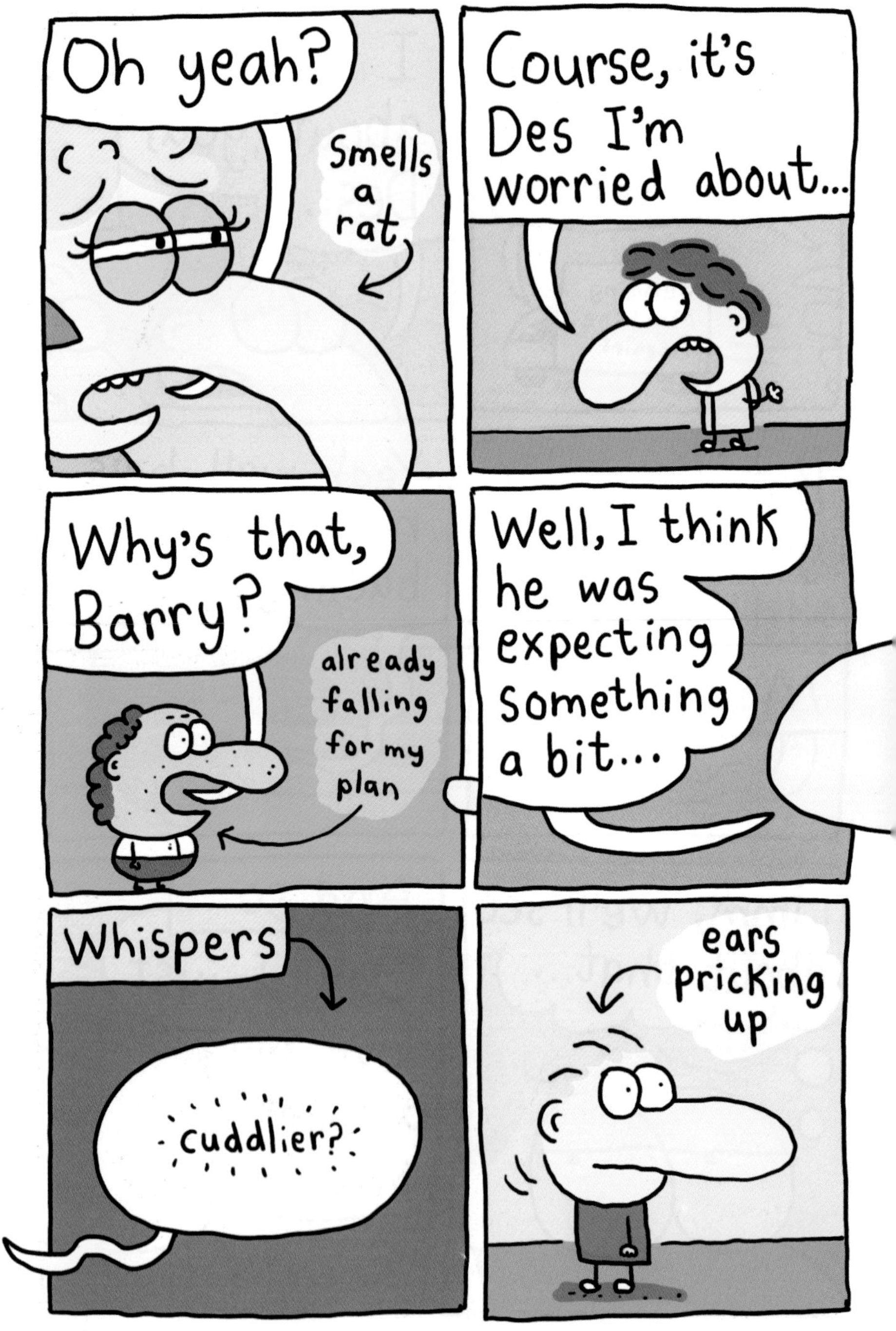
Oh yeah?
Smells a rat
Course, it's Des I'm worried about...
Why's that, Barry?
already falling for my plan
Well, I think he was expecting something a bit...
Whispers
cuddlier?
ears pricking up

And so... Did me heer sumboddy say 'cuggly'?

No, no, Des. Nobody said 'CUDDLY'.

whispers again:

He really wanted a cuddly Future Ratboy...

Ratboy...
Ratboy...
Ratboy...

doing echo

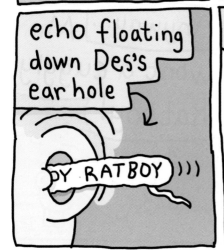
echo floating down Des's ear hole

DY RATBOY)))

And so...
Hey, me wontid a cuggly Future Ratboy!

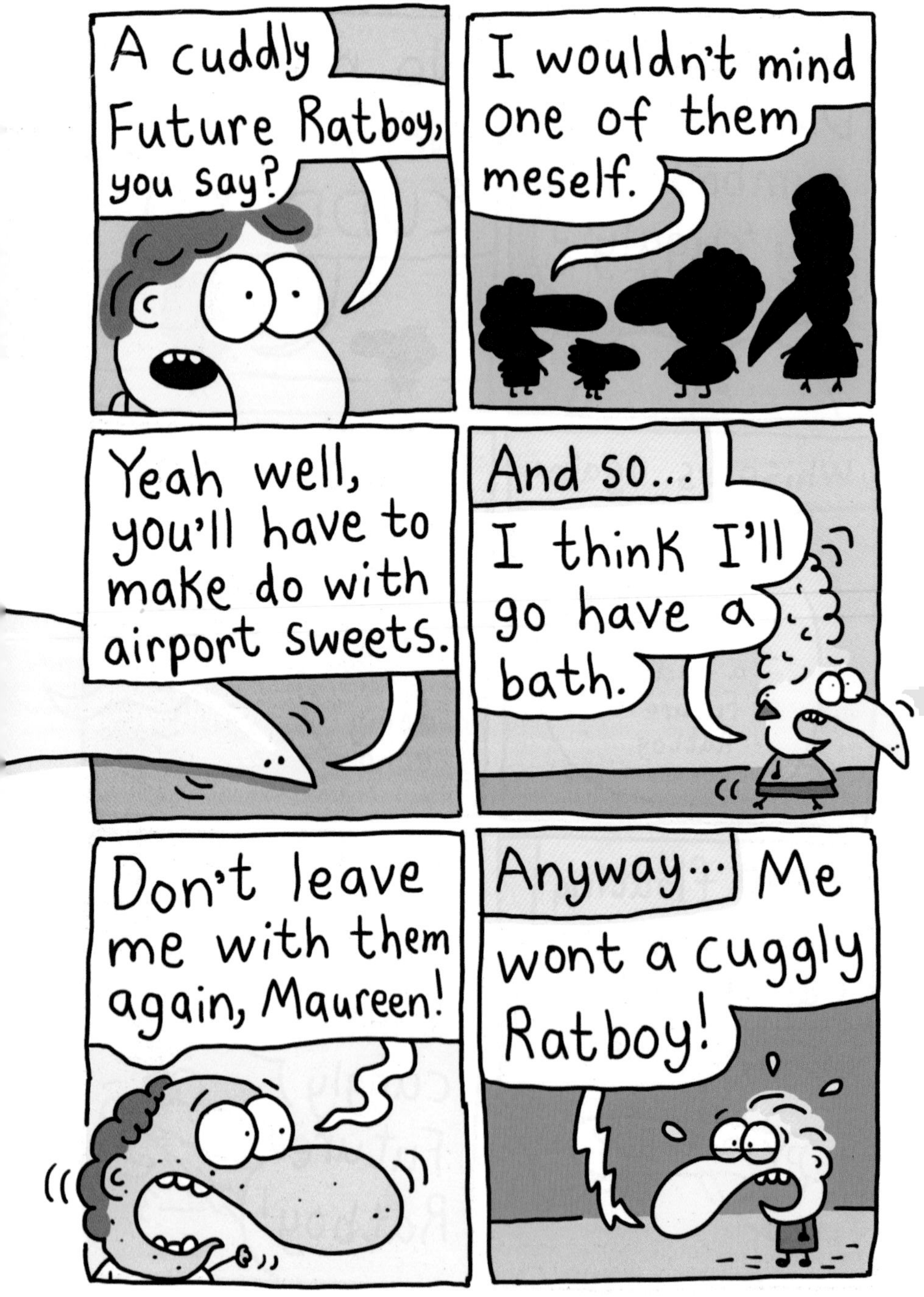
A cuddly Future Ratboy, you say?
I wouldn't mind one of them meself.
Yeah well, you'll have to make do with airport sweets.
And so...
I think I'll go have a bath.
Don't leave me with them again, Maureen!
Anyway...
Me wont a cuggly Ratboy!

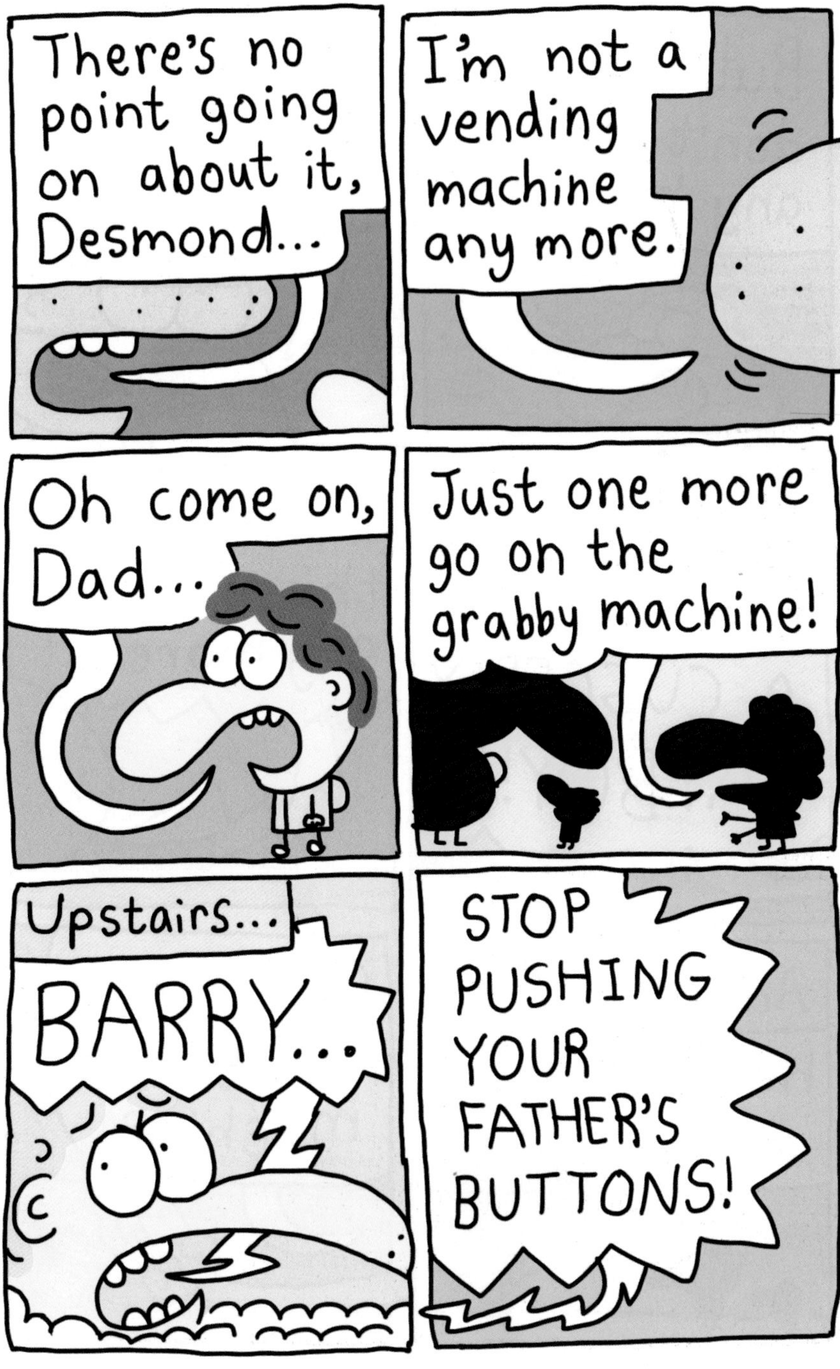
There's no point going on about it, Desmond...
I'm not a vending machine any more.
Oh come on, Dad...
Just one more go on the grabby machine!
Upstairs...
BARRY...
STOP PUSHING YOUR FATHER'S BUTTONS!

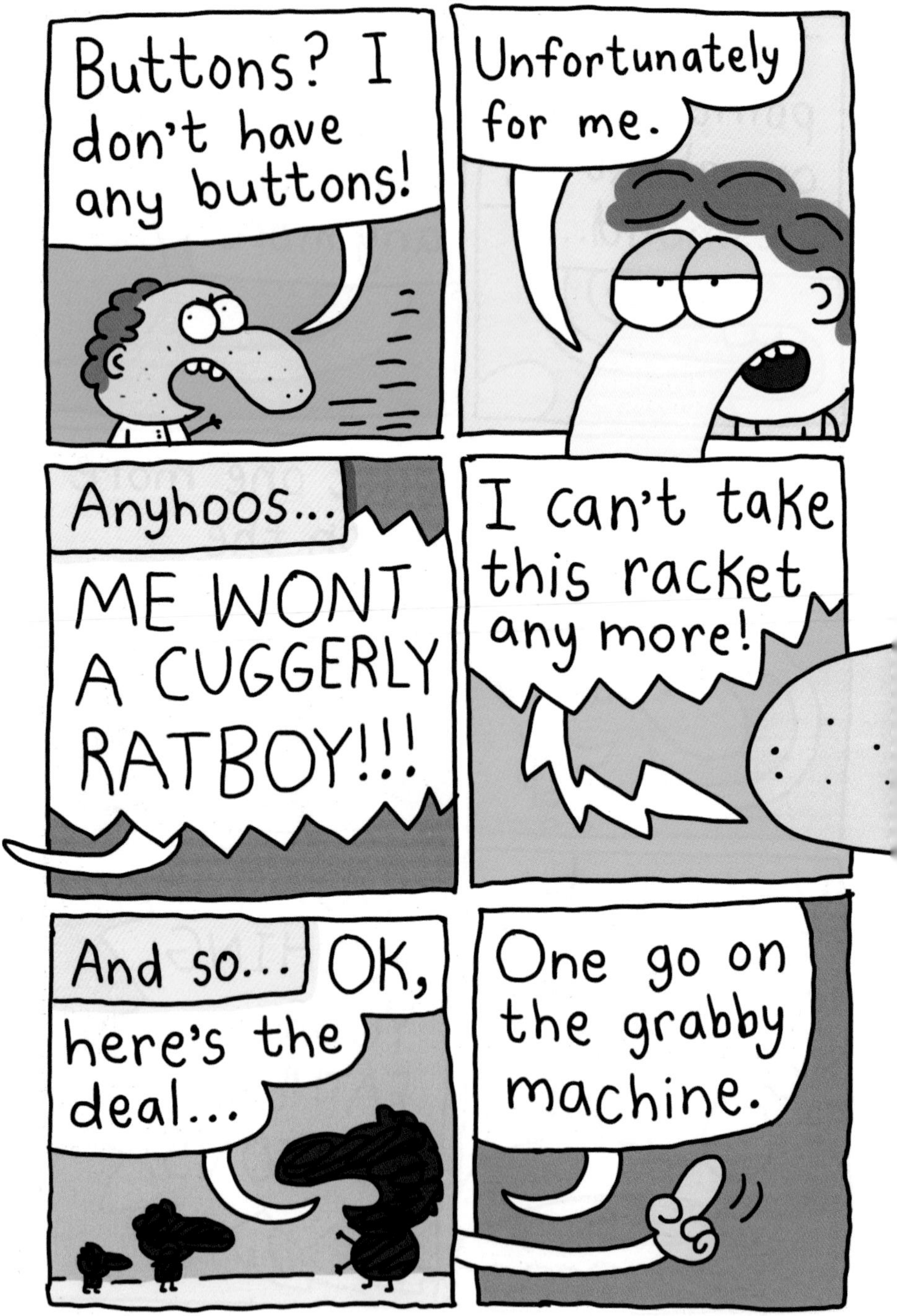
Buttons? I don't have any buttons!
Unfortunately for me.
Anyhoos...
ME WONT A CUGGERLY RATBOY!!!
I can't take this racket any more!
And so...
OK, here's the deal...
One go on the grabby machine.

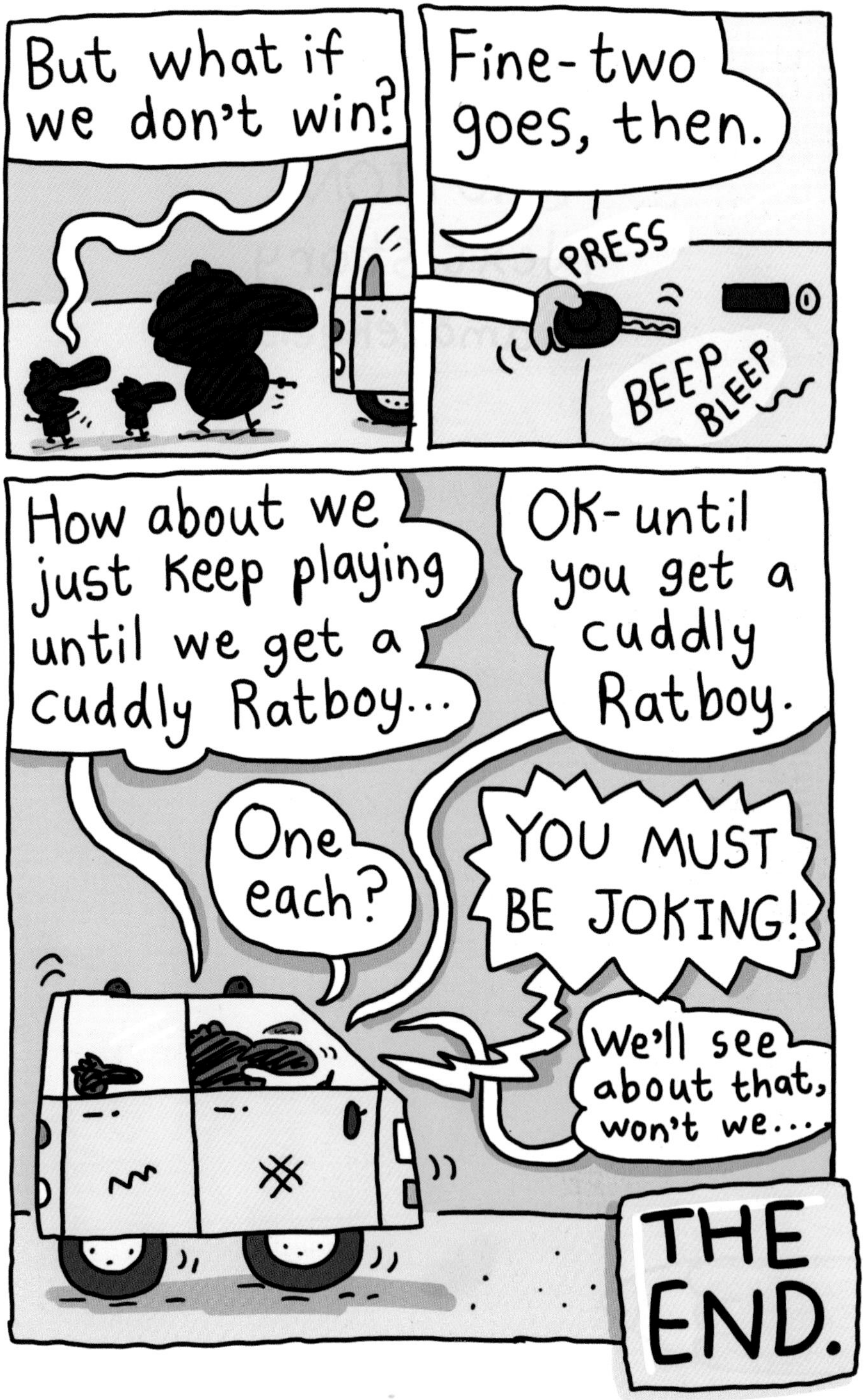
But what if we don't win?
Fine-two goes, then.
PRESS
BEEP
BLEEP
How about we just keep playing until we get a cuddly Ratboy...
OK-until you get a cuddly Ratboy.
One each?
YOU MUST BE JOKING!
We'll see about that, won't we...
THE END.

CAUTION:
Next Story
is amazekeels.

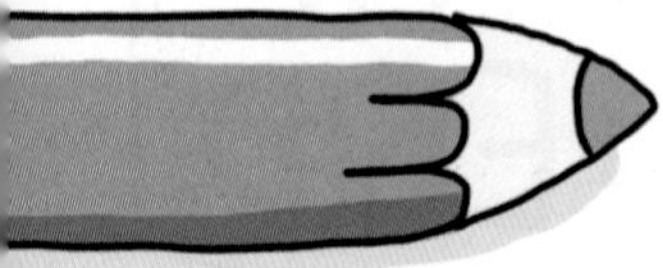

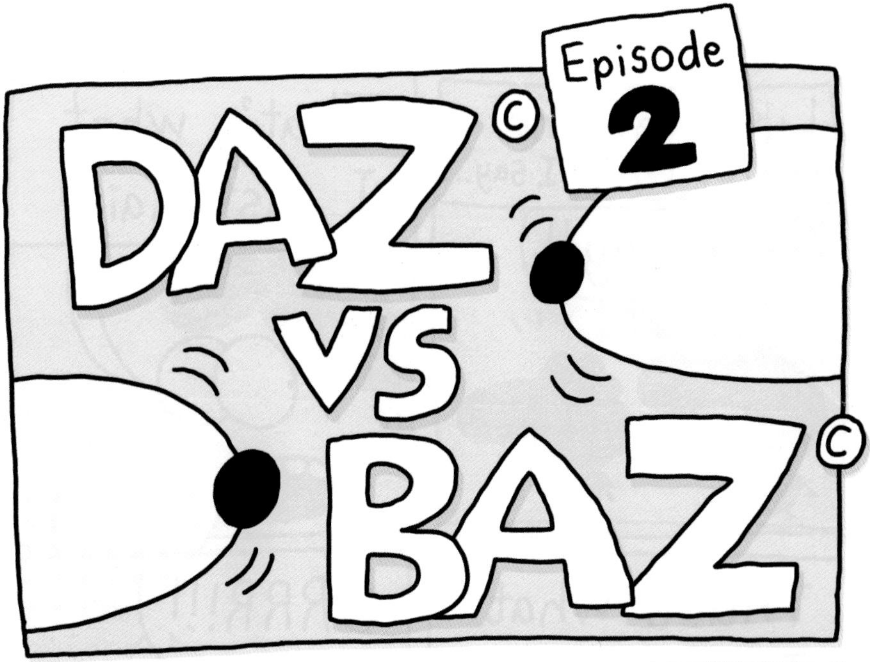
DAZ©
Episode 2
VS
BAZ©

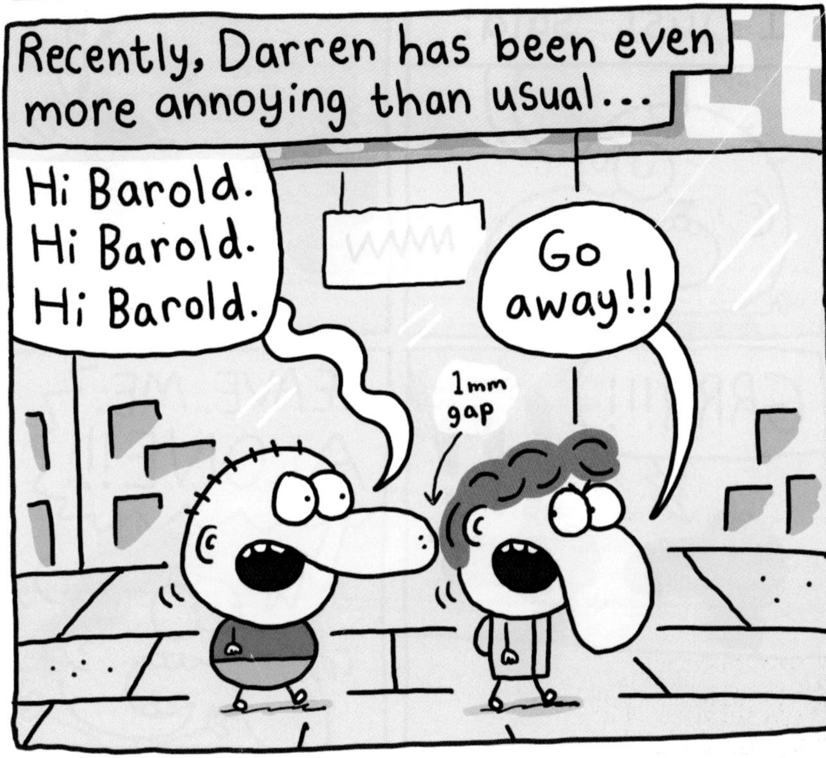
Recently, Darren has been even more annoying than usual...
Hi Barold.
Hi Barold.
Hi Barold.
Go away!!
1mm gap

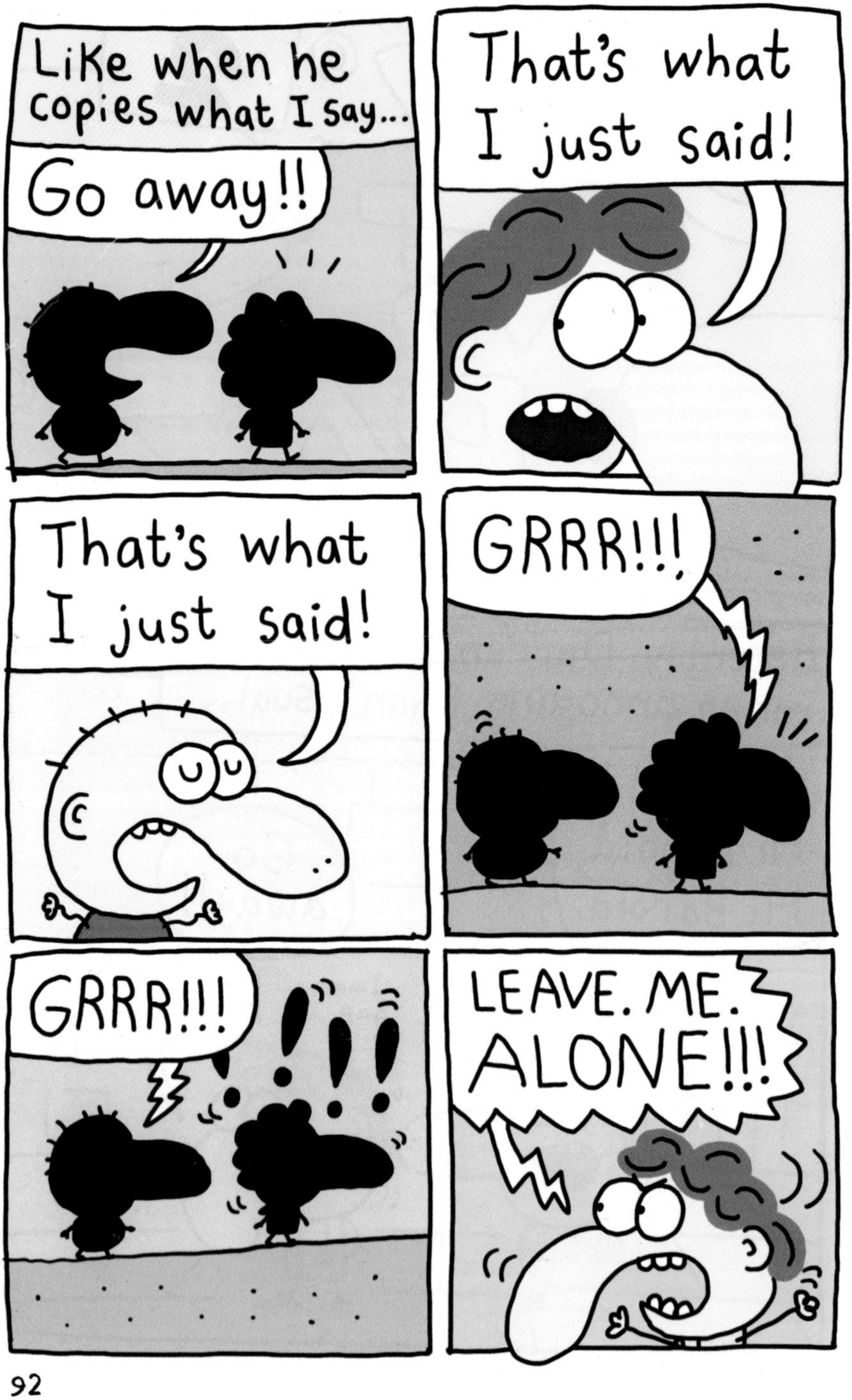
Like when he copies what I say...
Go away!!
That's what I just said!
That's what I just said!
GRRR!!!
GRRR!!!
LEAVE. ME. ALONE!!!

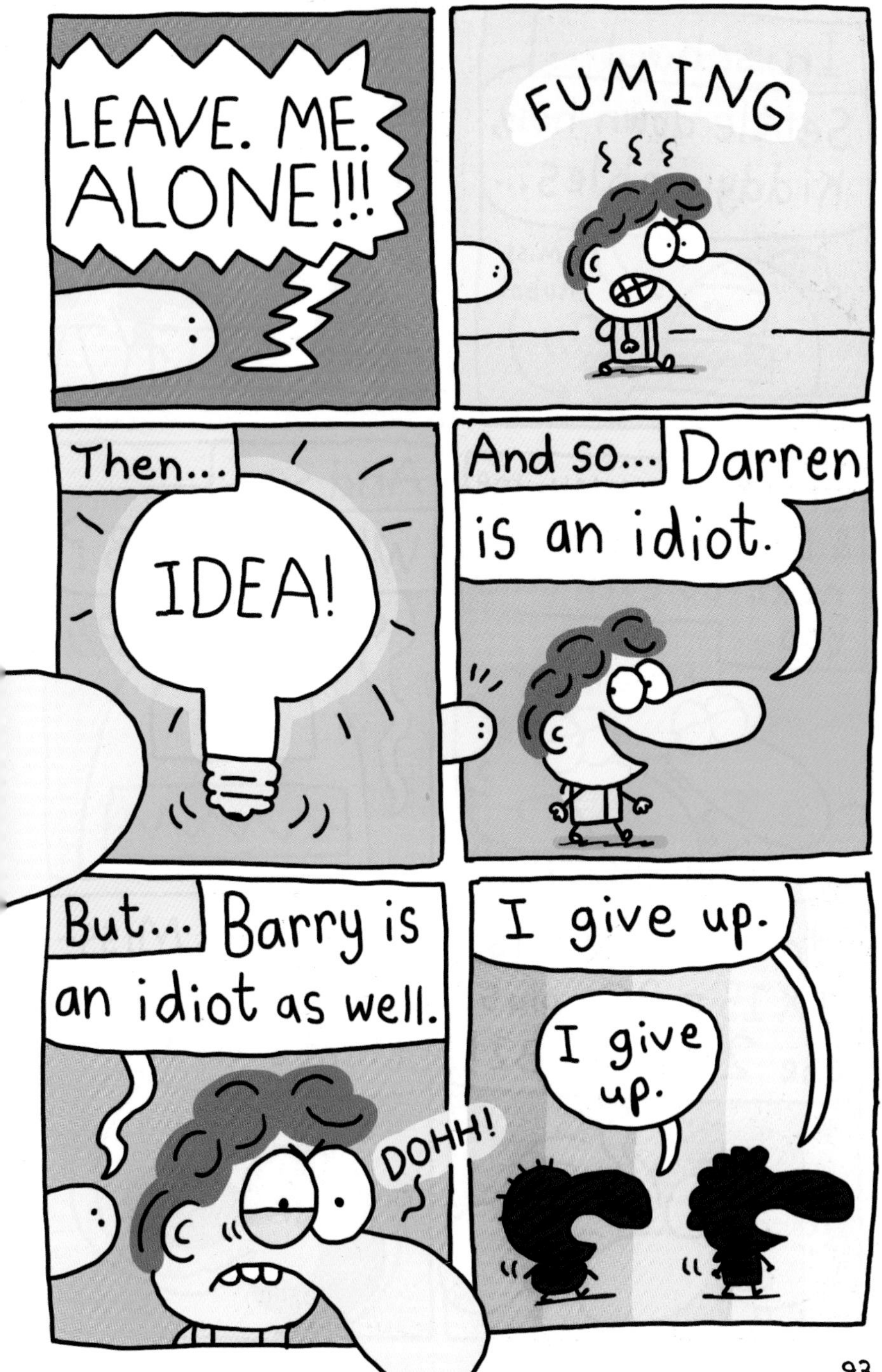
LEAVE. ME. ALONE!!!
FUMING
Then...
IDEA!
And so... Darren is an idiot.
But... Barry is an idiot as well.
DOHH!
I give up.
I give up.

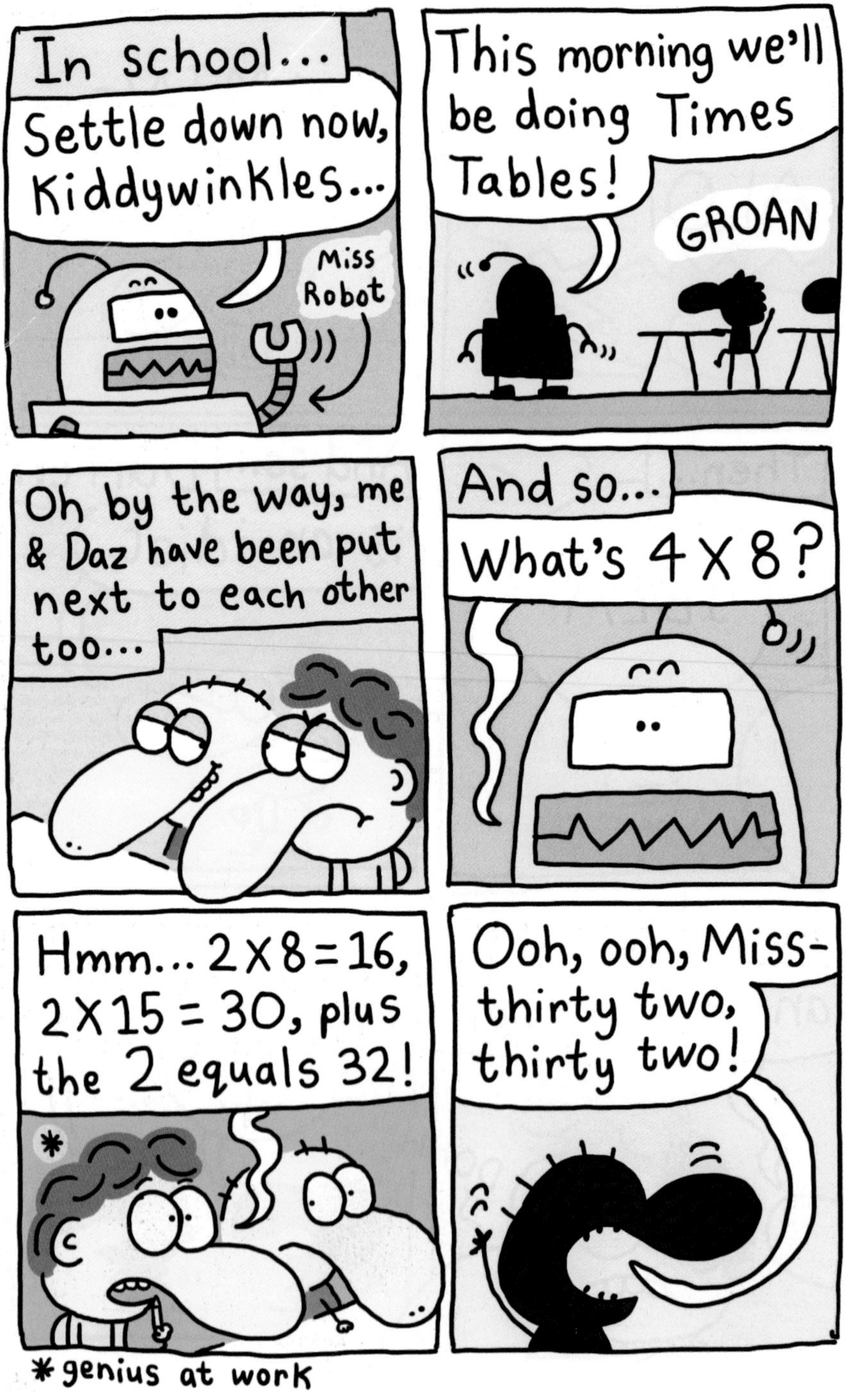
In school...
Settle down now, Kiddywinkles...
Miss Robot
This morning we'll be doing Times Tables!
GROAN
Oh by the way, me & Daz have been put next to each other too...
And so...
What's 4 X 8?
Hmm... 2 X 8 = 16, 2 X 15 = 30, plus the 2 equals 32!
*
Ooh, ooh, Miss- thirty two, thirty two!

*genius at work

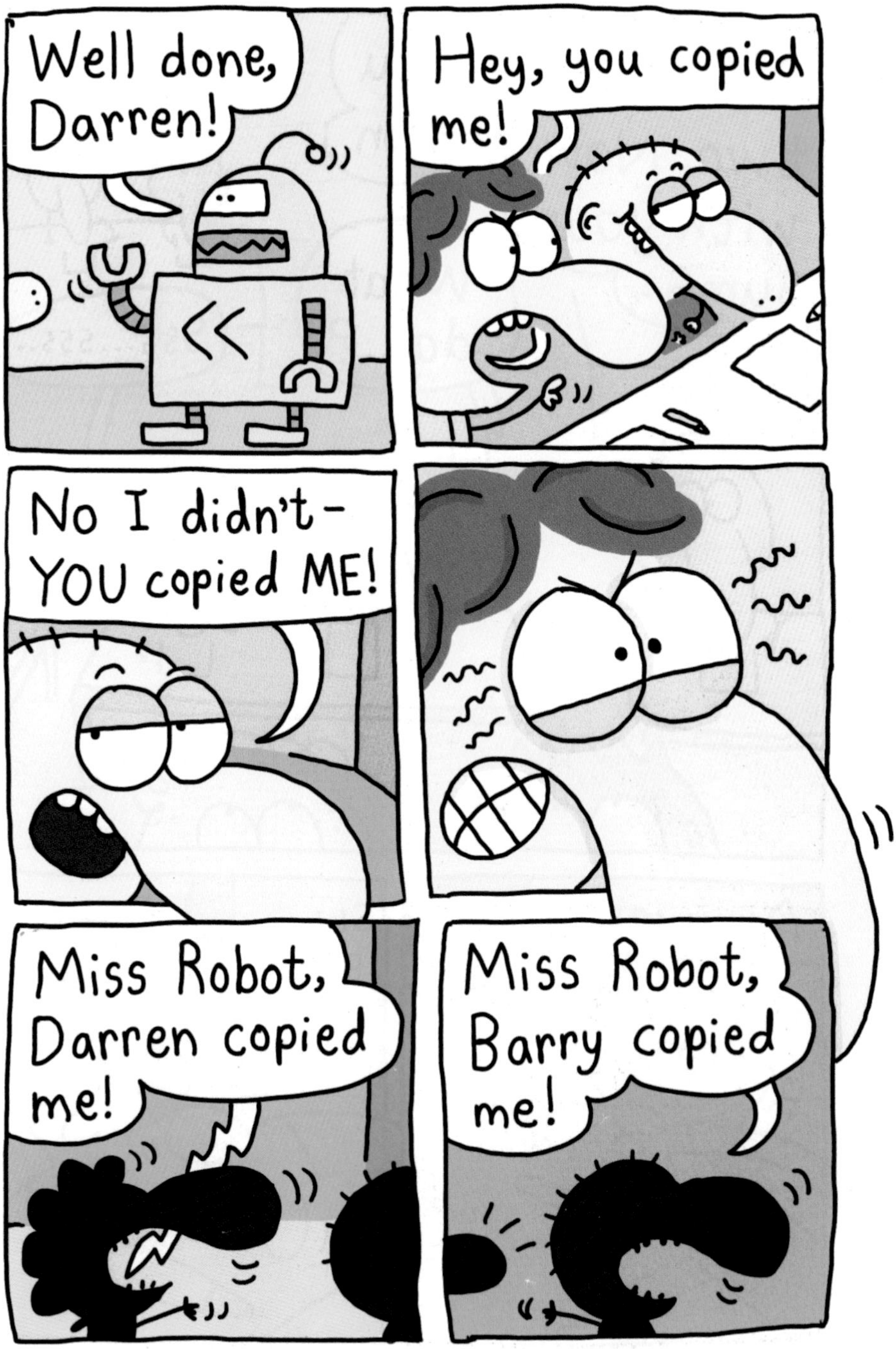
Well done, Darren!
Hey, you copied me!
No I didn't- YOU copied ME!
Miss Robot, Darren copied me!
Miss Robot, Barry copied me!

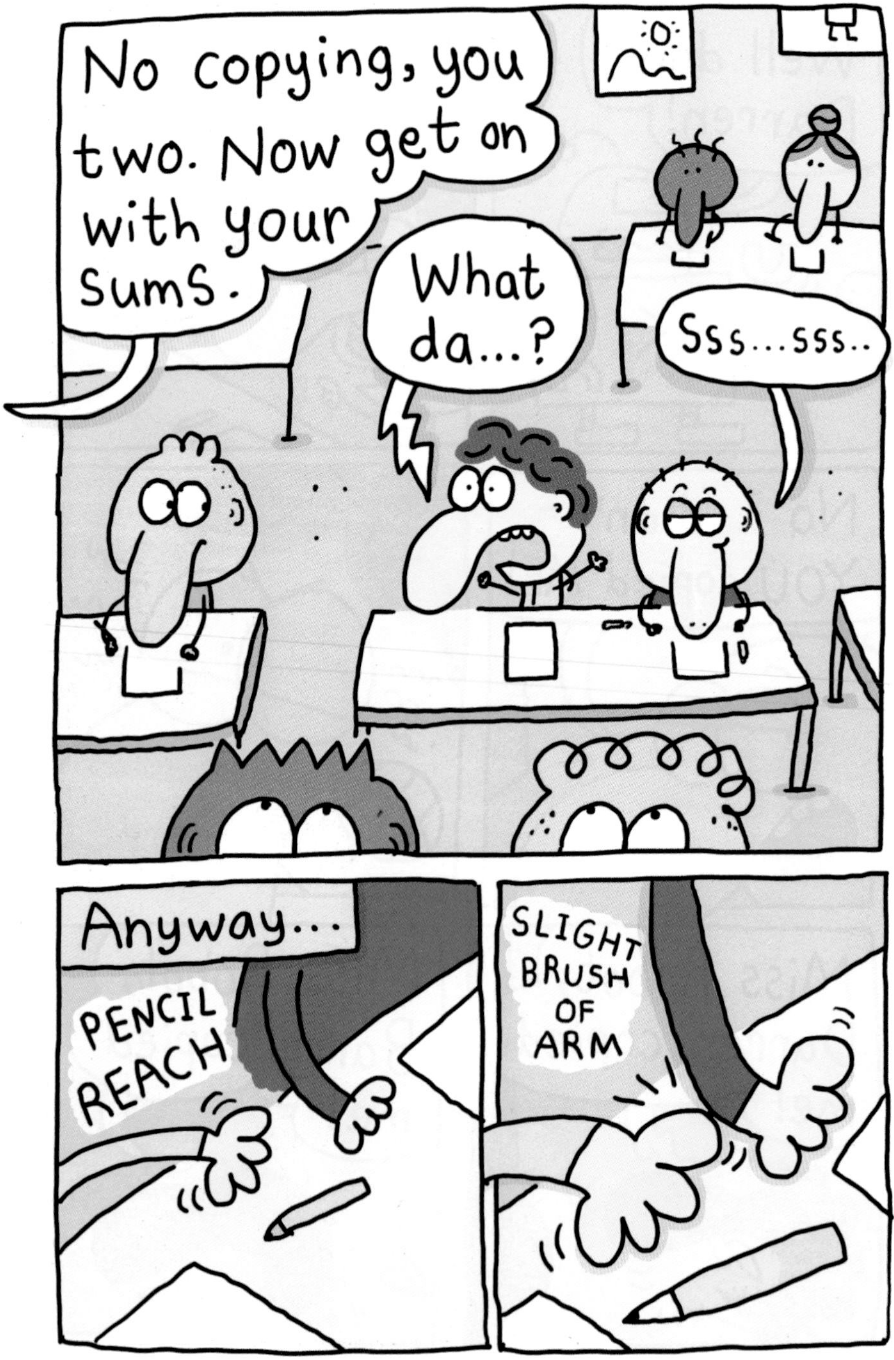
No copying, you two. Now get on with your sums.
What da...?
Sss...sss..
Anyway...
PENCIL REACH
SLIGHT BRUSH OF ARM

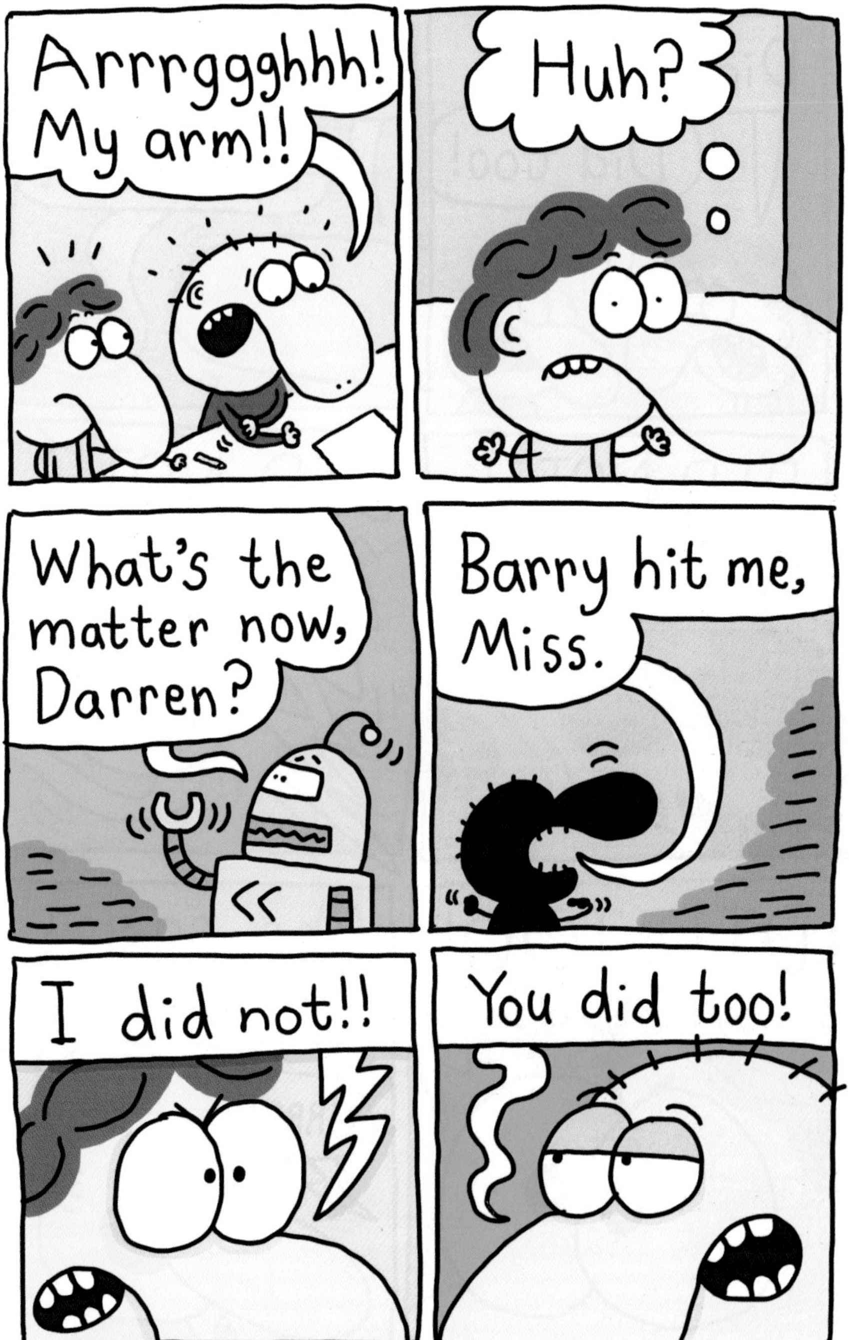
Arrrggghhh! My arm!!
Huh?
What's the matter now, Darren?
Barry hit me, Miss.
I did not!!
You did too!

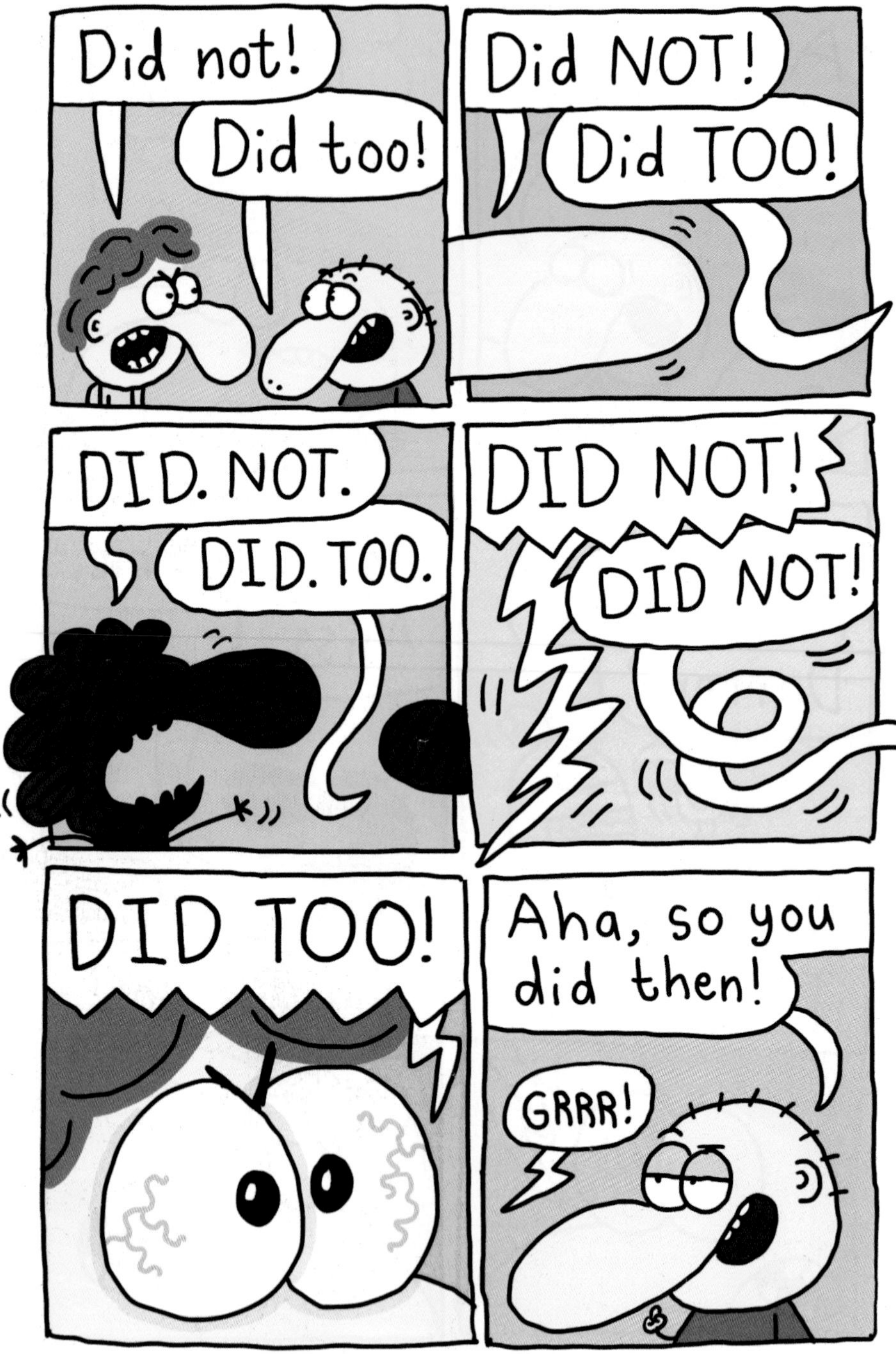
Did not!
Did too!
Did NOT!
Did TOO!
DID. NOT.
DID. TOO.
DID NOT!
DID NOT!
DID TOO!
Aha, so you did then!
GRRR!

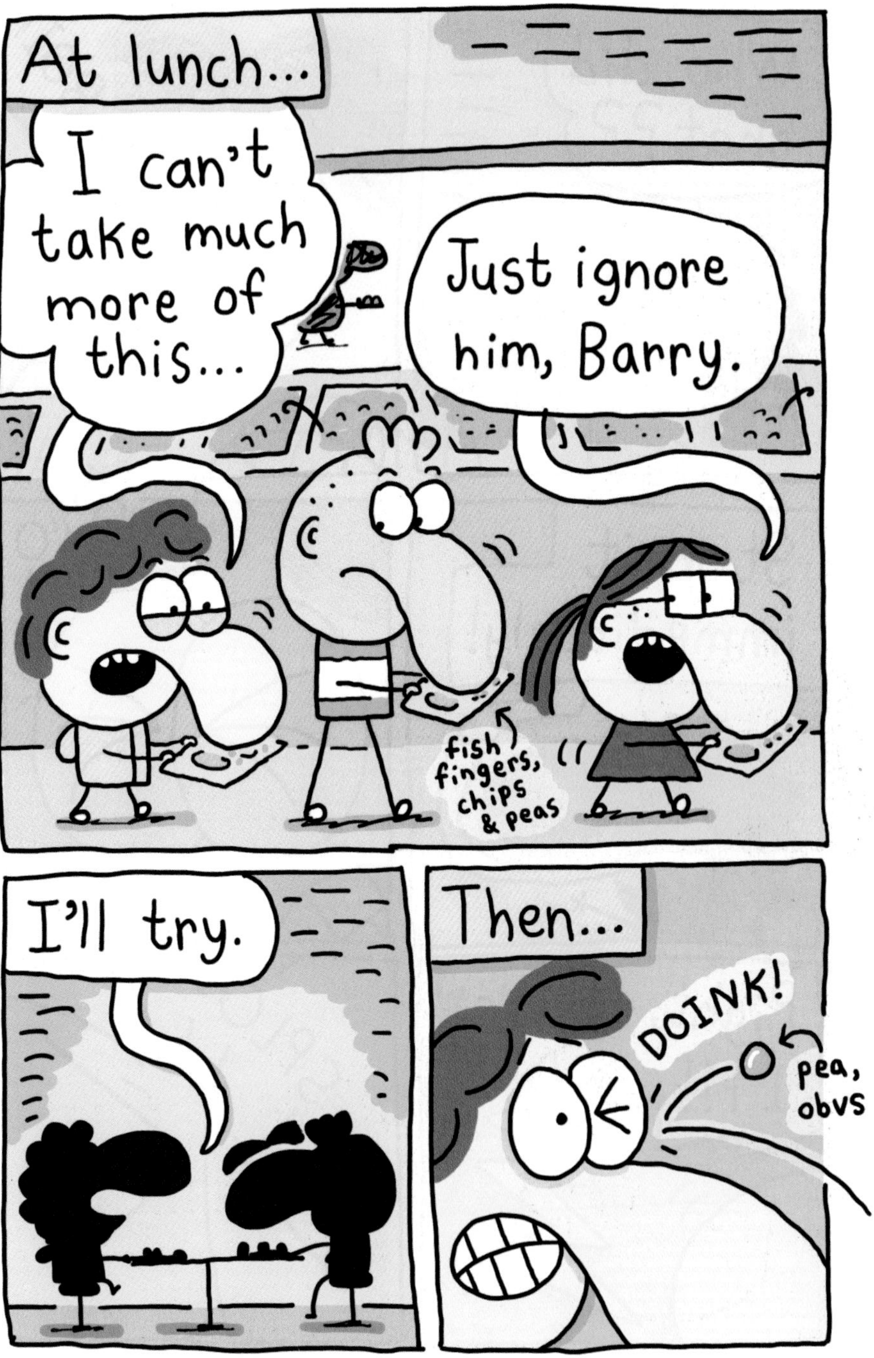
At lunch...
I can't take much more of this...
Just ignore him, Barry.
fish fingers, chips & peas
I'll try.
Then...
DOINK!
pea, obvs

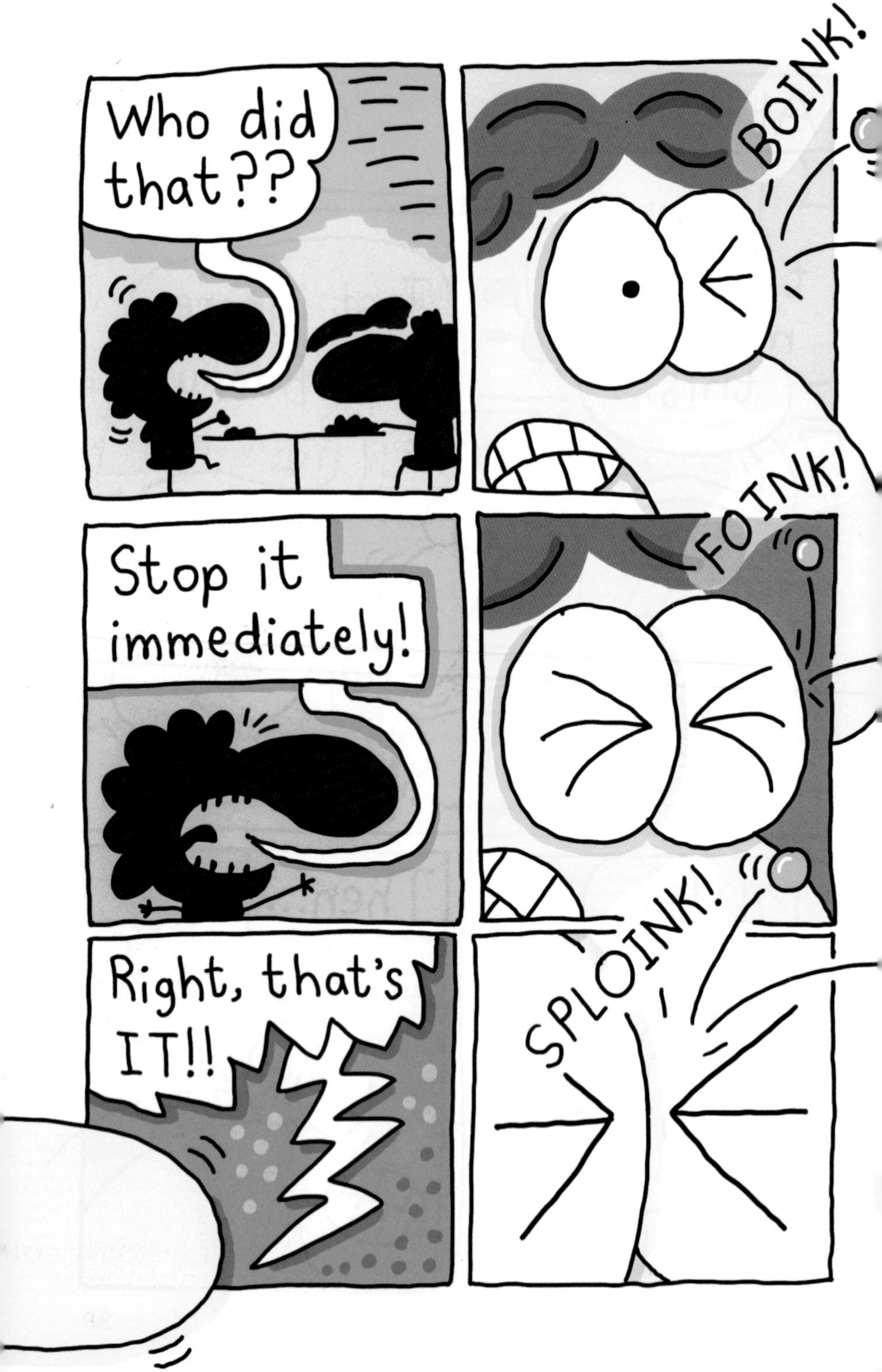
Who did that??
BOINK!
Stop it immediately!
FOINK!
Right, that's IT!!
SPLOINK!

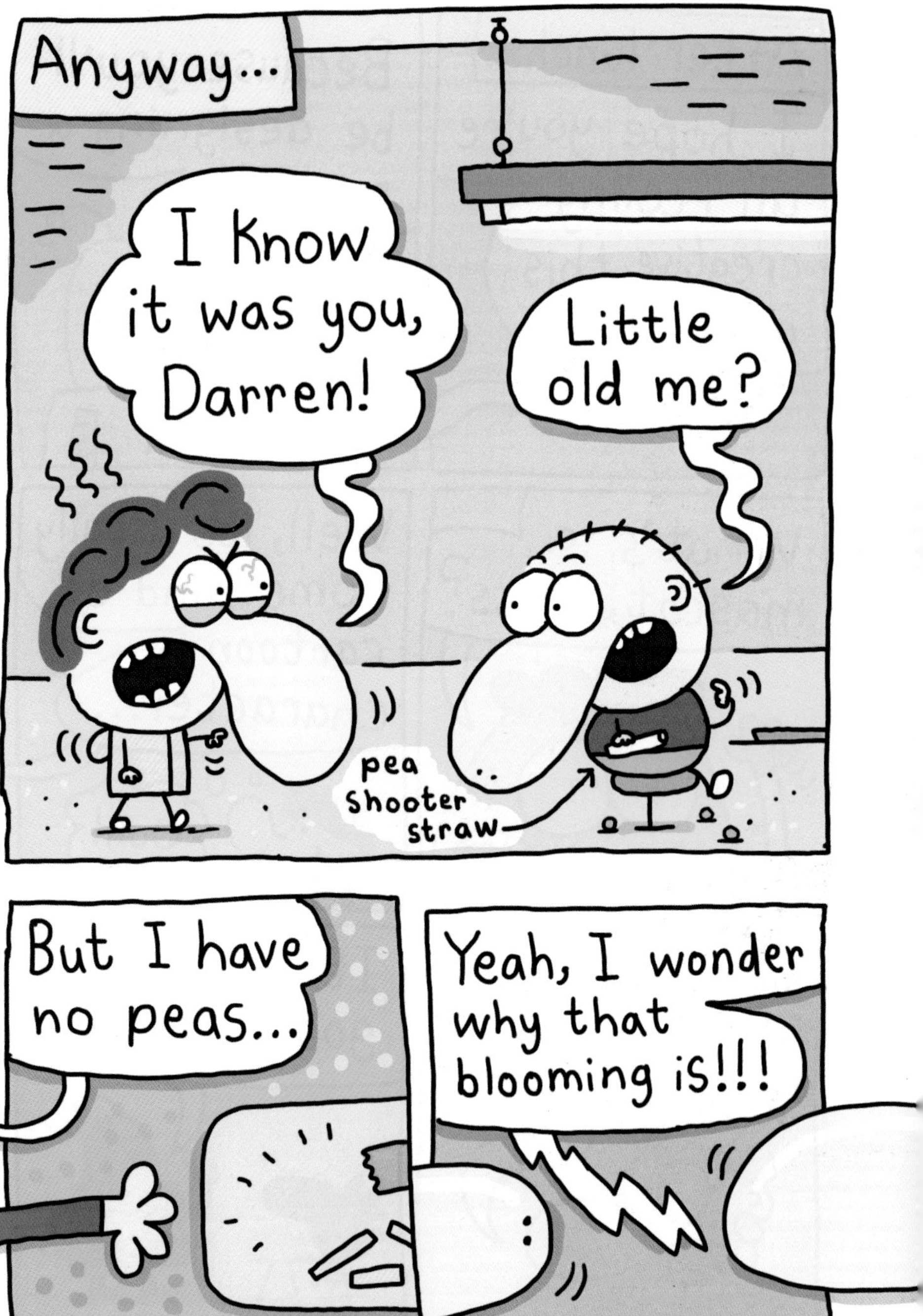
Anyway...
I know it was you, Darren!
Little old me?
pea shooter straw
But I have no peas...
Yeah, I wonder why that blooming is!!!

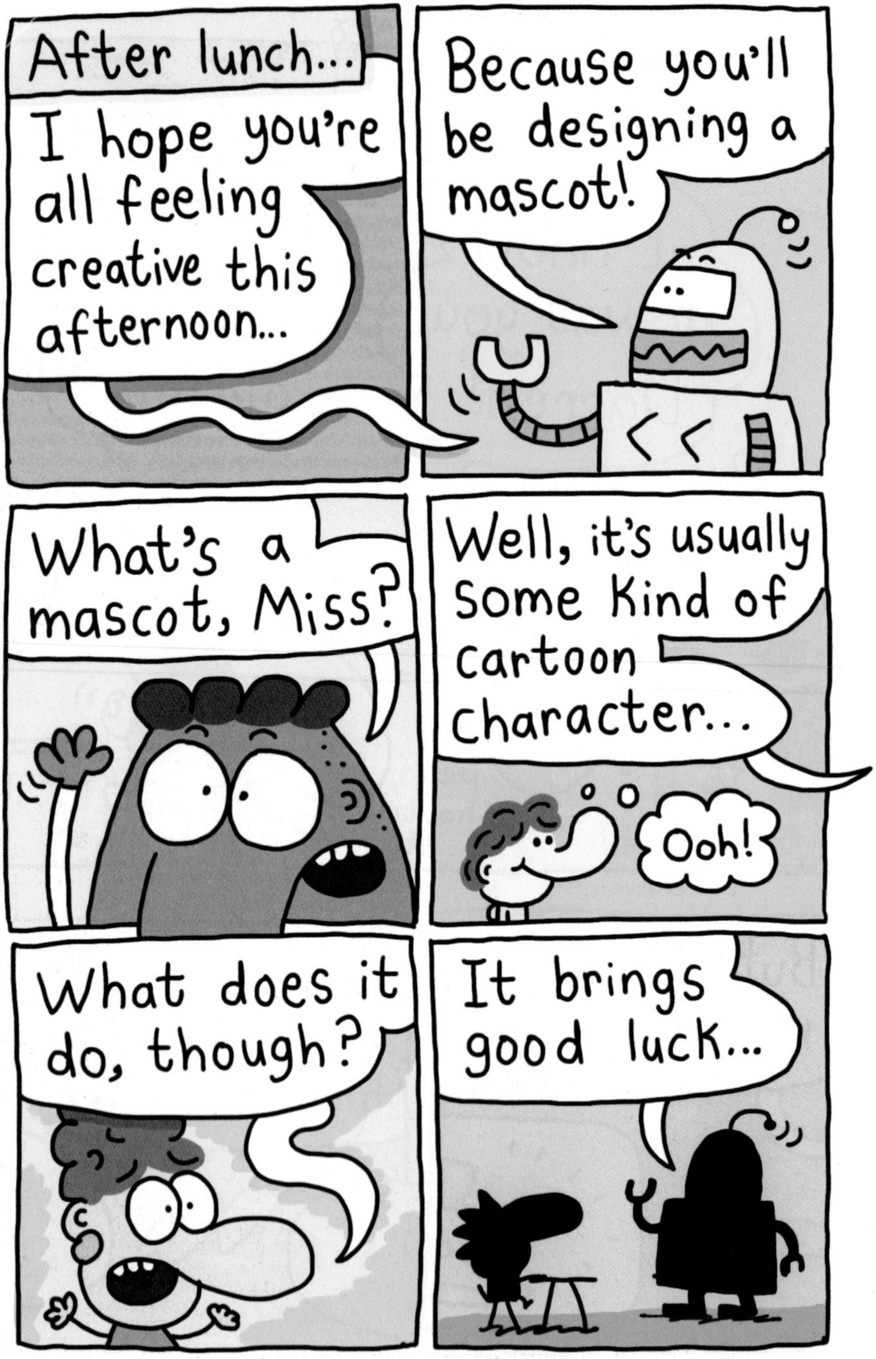
After lunch...
I hope you're all feeling creative this afternoon...
Because you'll be designing a mascot!
What's a mascot, Miss?
Well, it's usually some kind of cartoon character...
Ooh!
What does it do, though?
It brings good luck...

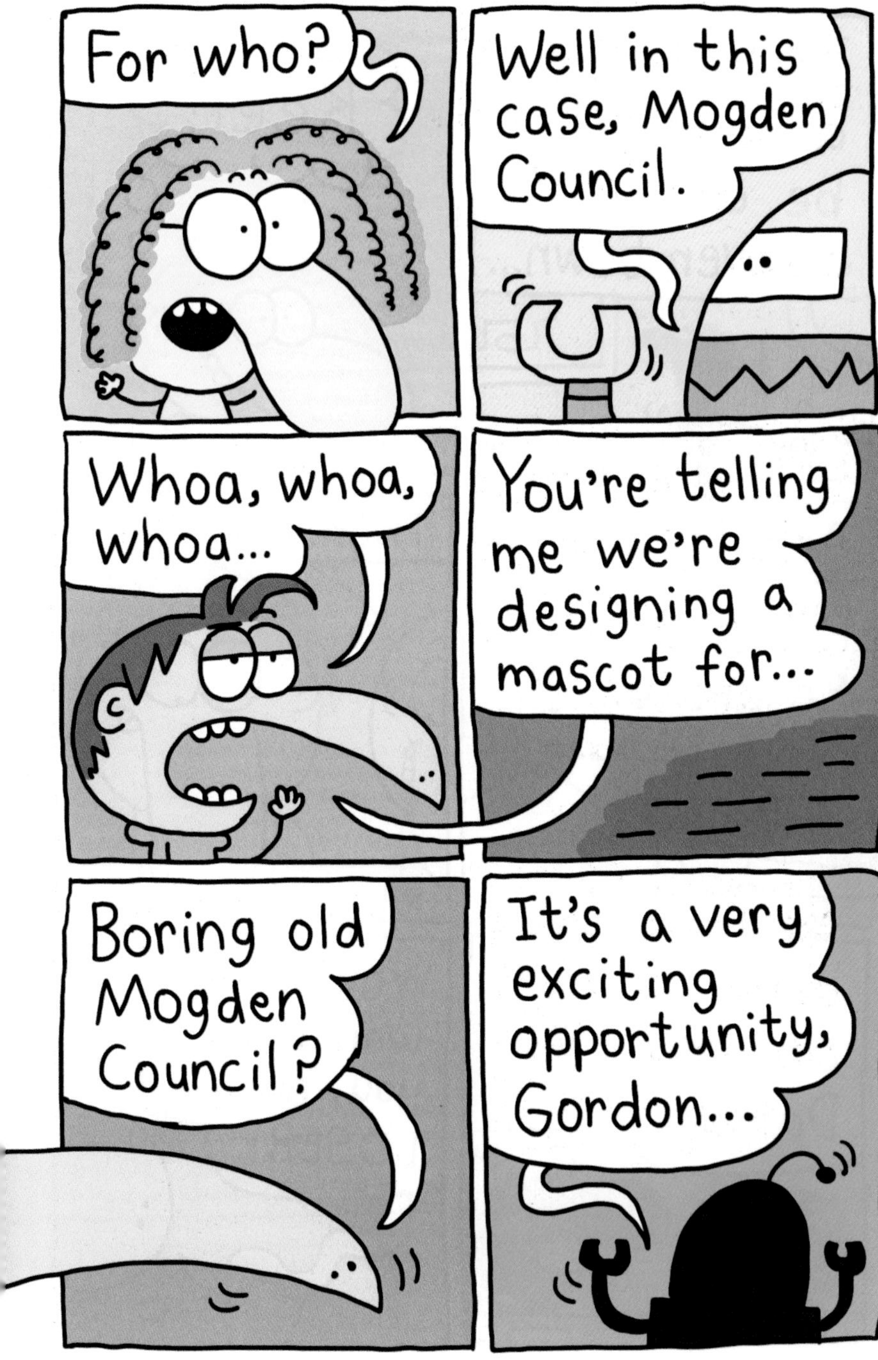
For who?
Well in this case, Mogden Council.
Whoa, whoa, whoa...
You're telling me we're designing a mascot for...
Boring old Mogden Council?
It's a very exciting opportunity, Gordon...

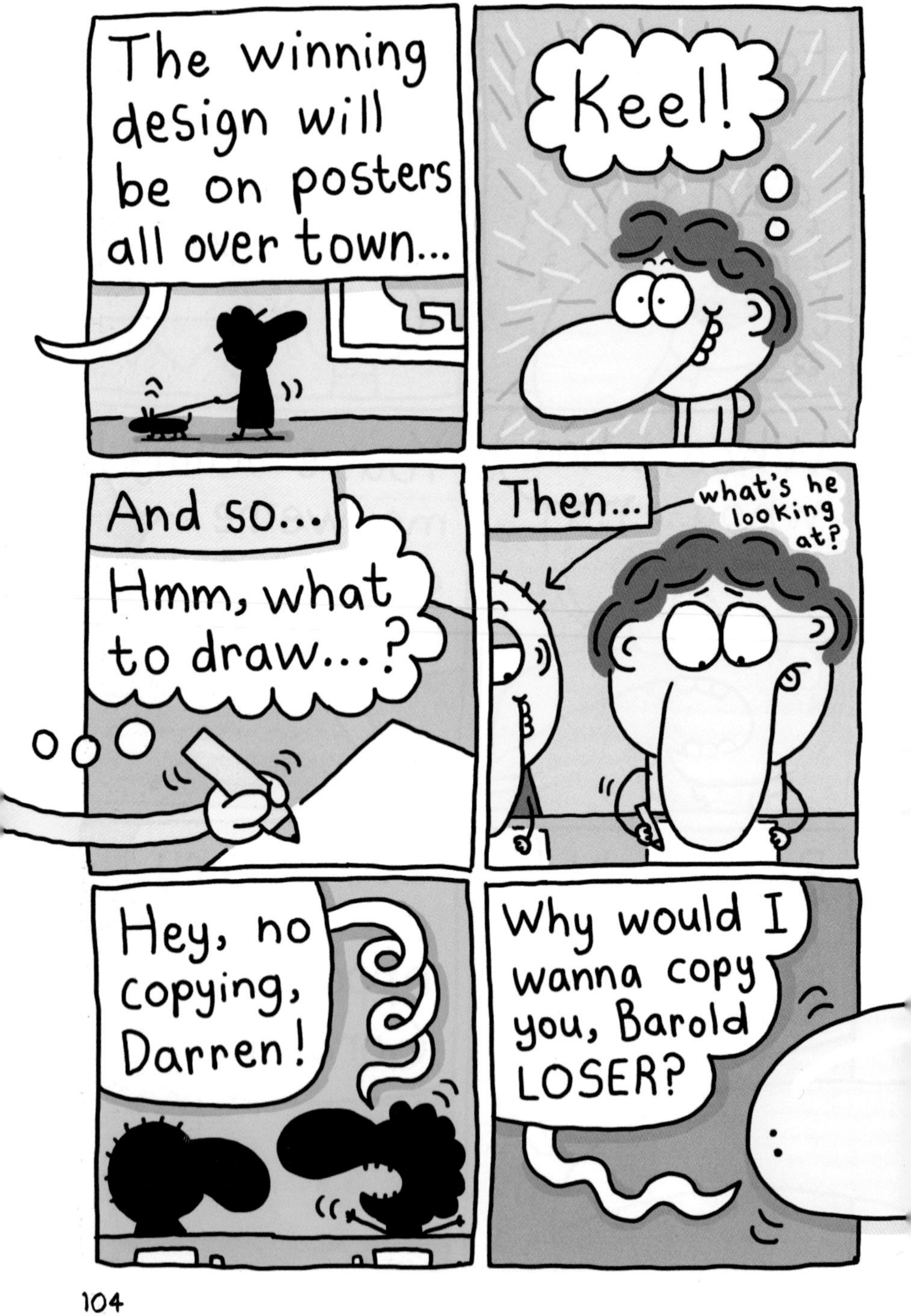
The winning design will be on posters all over town...
Keel!
And so...
Hmm, what to draw...?
Then...
what's he looking at?
Hey, no copying, Darren!
Why would I wanna copy you, Barold LOSER?

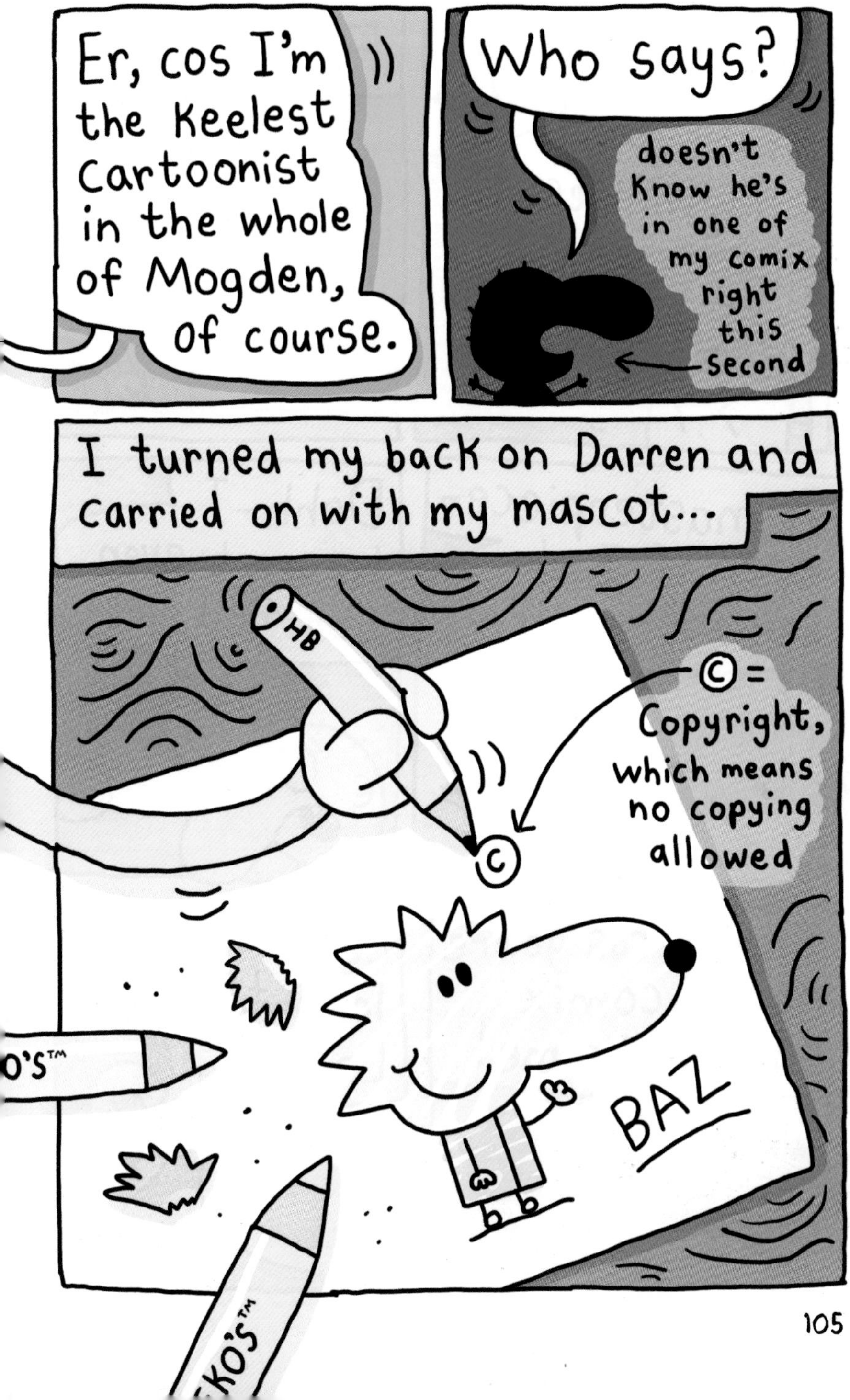
Er, cos I'm the Keelest cartoonist in the whole of Mogden, of course.
Who says?
doesn't know he's in one of my comix right this second
I turned my back on Darren and carried on with my mascot...
HB
© = Copyright, which means no copying allowed
BAZ
O'S™
EKO'S™

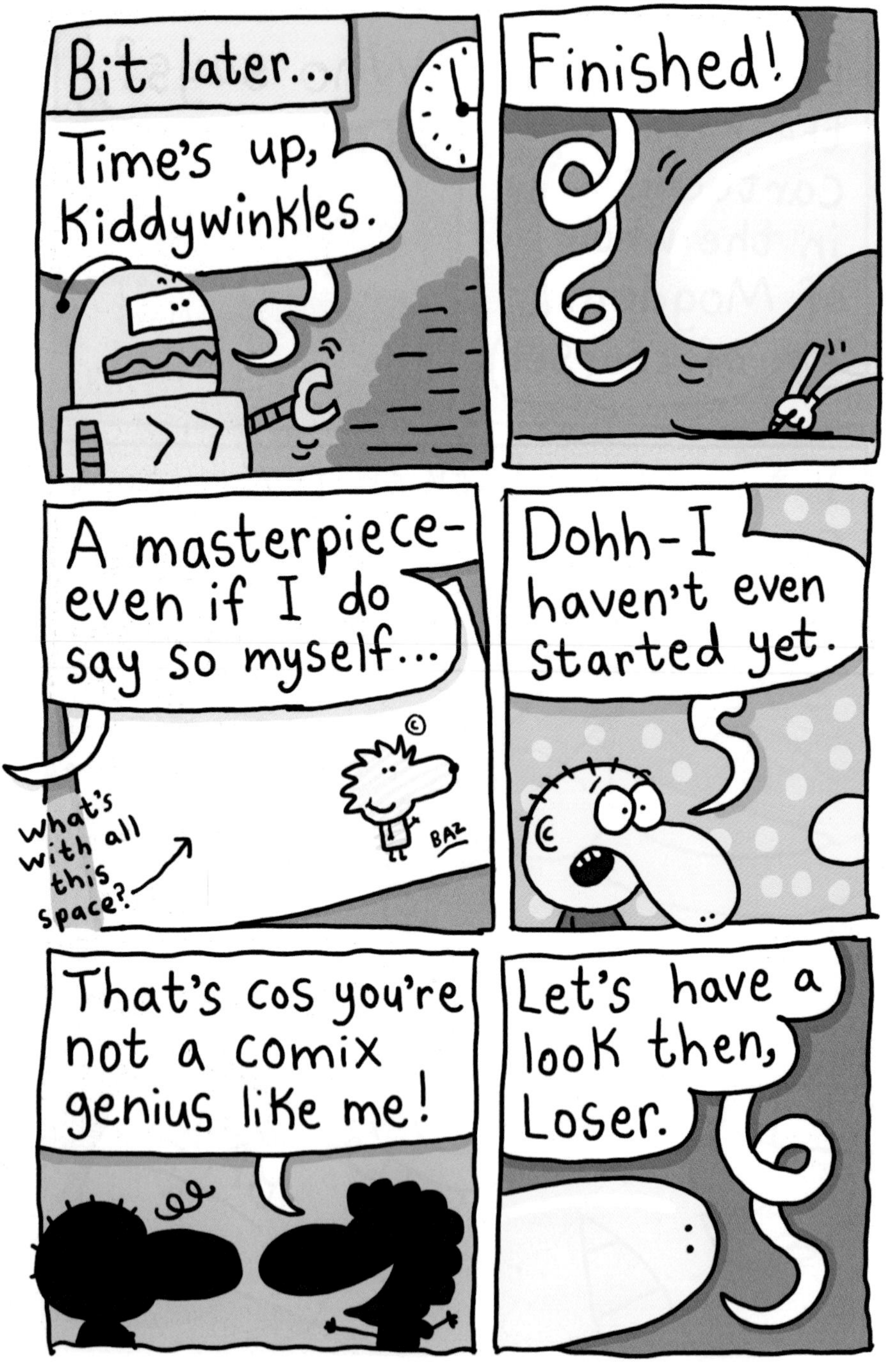
Bit later...
Time's up, Kiddywinkles.
Finished!
A masterpiece- even if I do say so myself...
what's with all this space?
BAZ
Dohh-I haven't even started yet.
That's cos you're not a comix genius like me!
Let's have a look then, Loser.

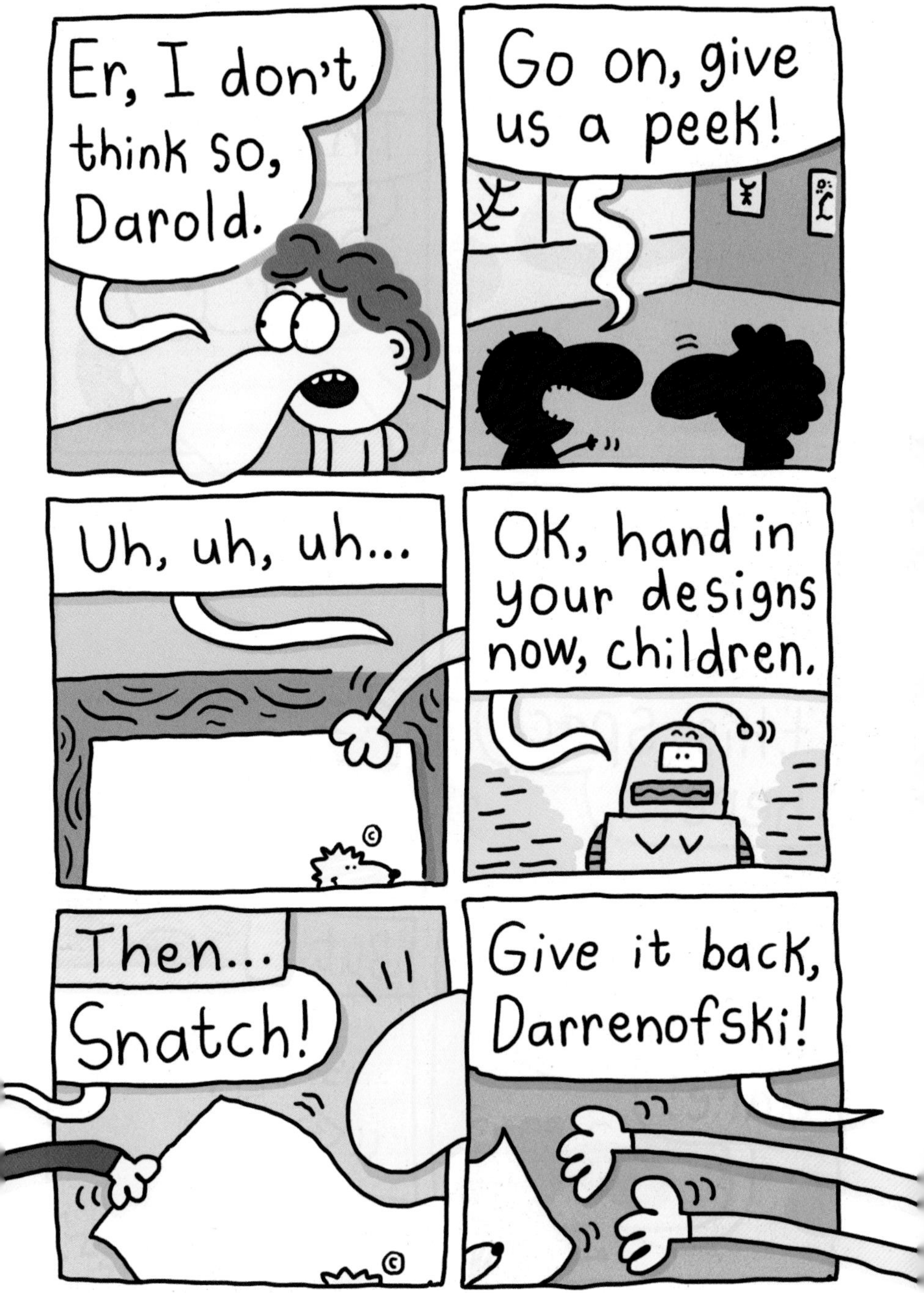

Er, I don't think so, Darold.
Go on, give us a peek!
Uh, uh, uh...
OK, hand in your designs now, children.
Then...
Snatch!
Give it back, Darrenofski!

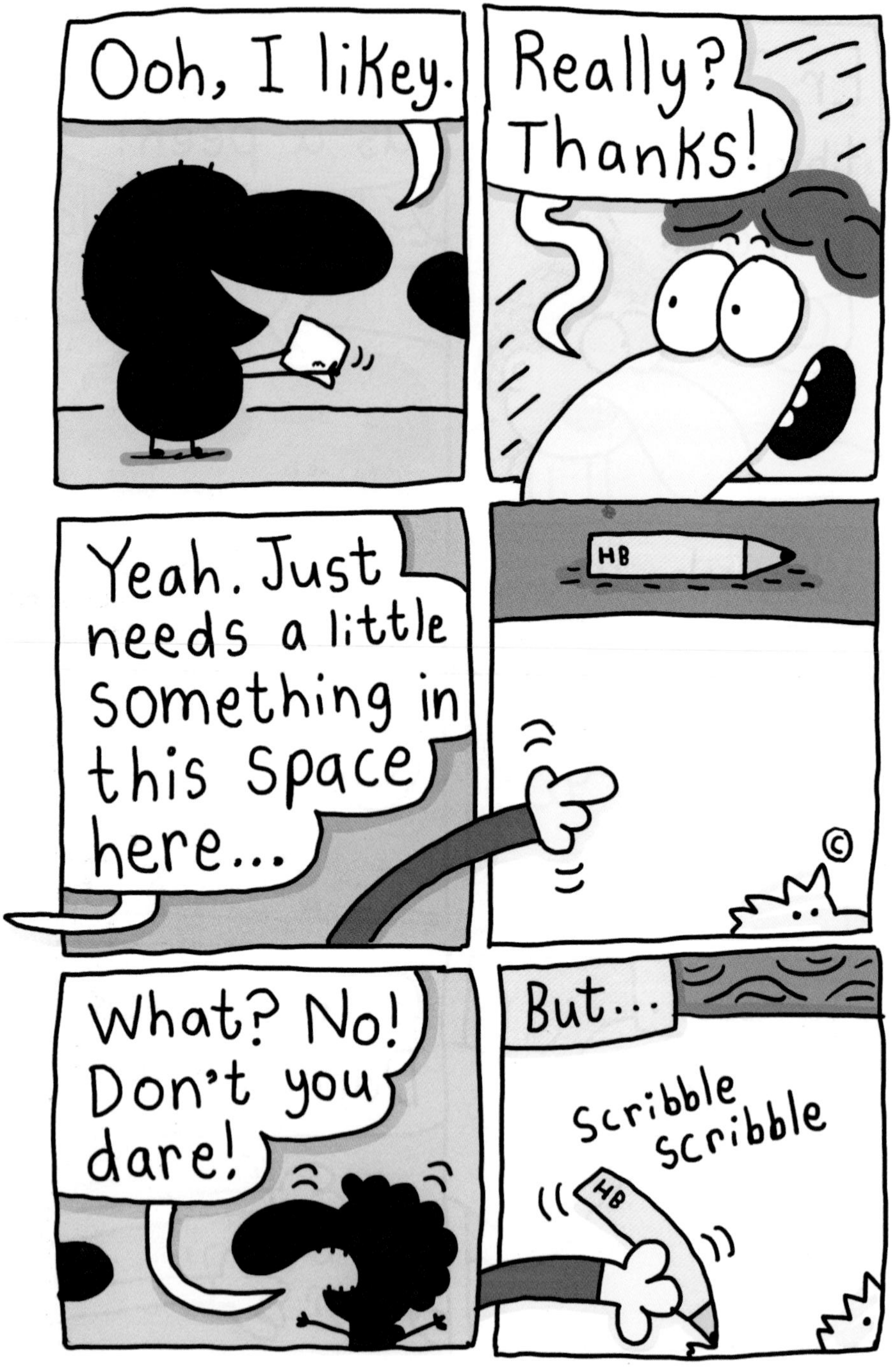
Ooh, I likey.
Really? Thanks!
Yeah. Just needs a little something in this space here...
HB
©
What? No! Don't you dare!
But...
Scribble scribble
HB

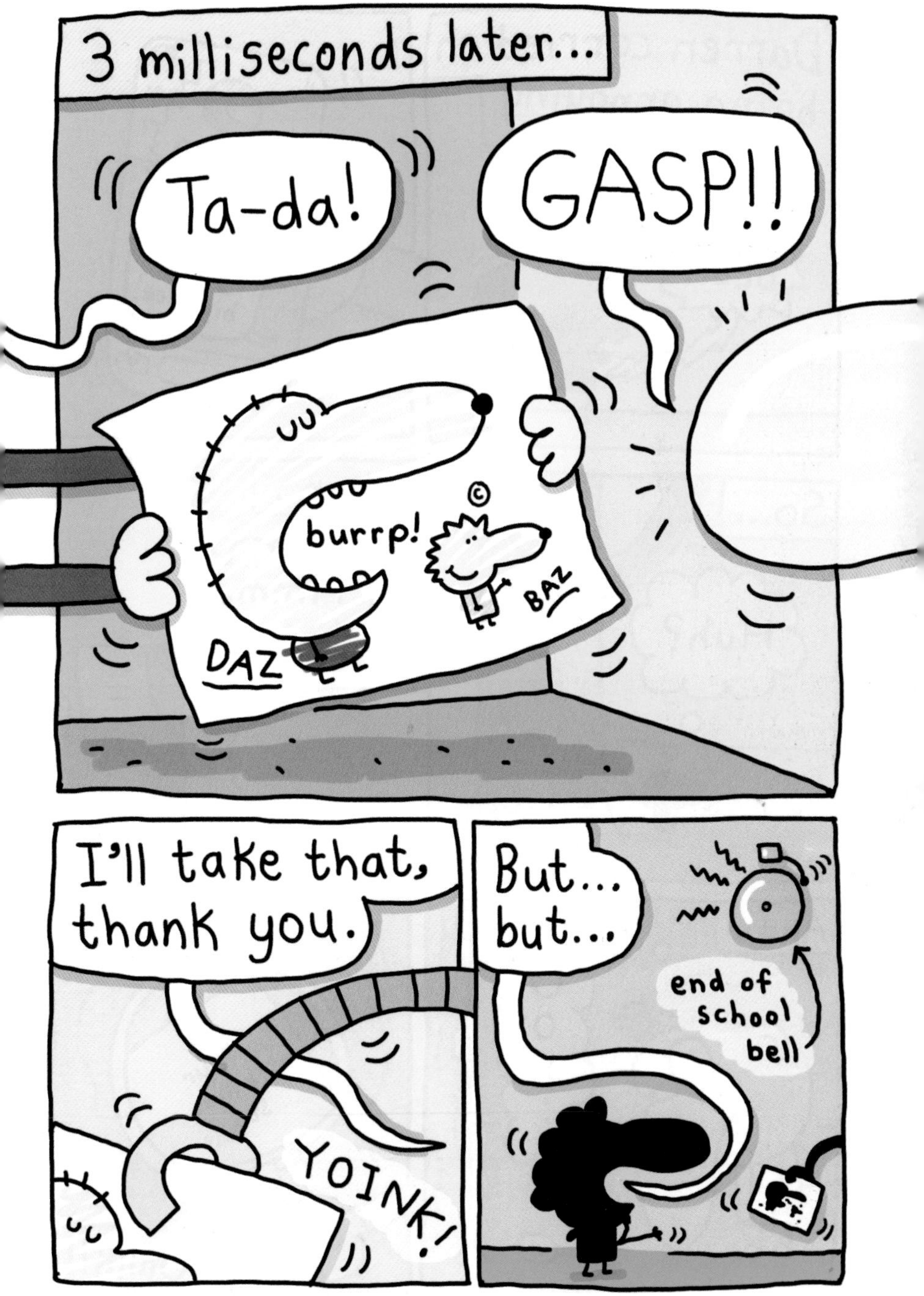
3 milliseconds later...
Ta-da!
GASP!!
burrp!
©
DAZ
BAZ
I'll take that, thank you.
YOINK!
But... but...
end of school bell

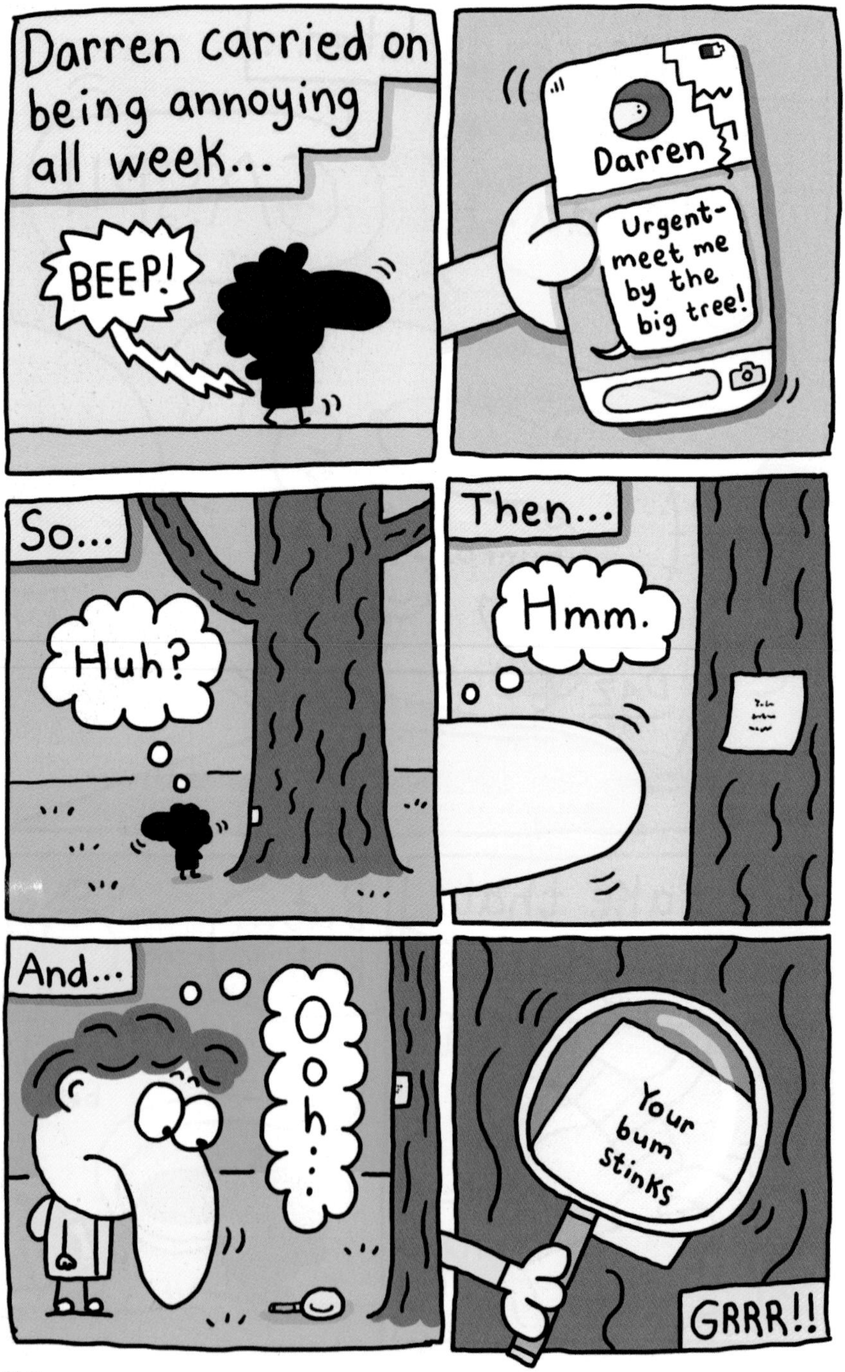
Darren carried on being annoying all week...
BEEP!
Darren
Urgent- meet me by the big tree!
So...
Huh?
Then...
Hmm.
And...
Ooh...
Your bum stinks
GRRR!!

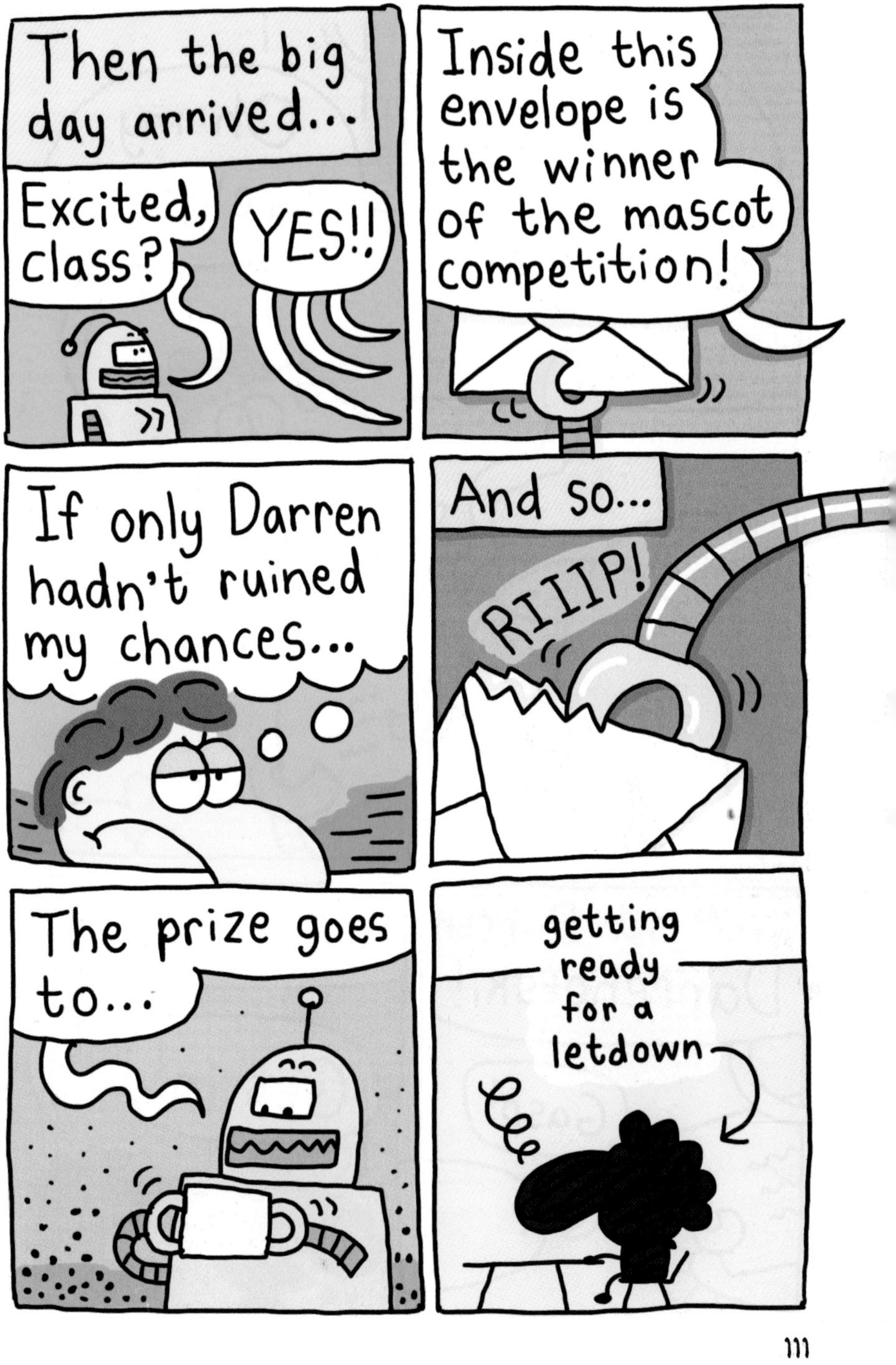
Then the big day arrived...
Excited, class?
YES!!
Inside this envelope is the winner of the mascot competition!
If only Darren hadn't ruined my chances...
And so...
RIIIP!
The prize goes to...
getting ready for a letdown

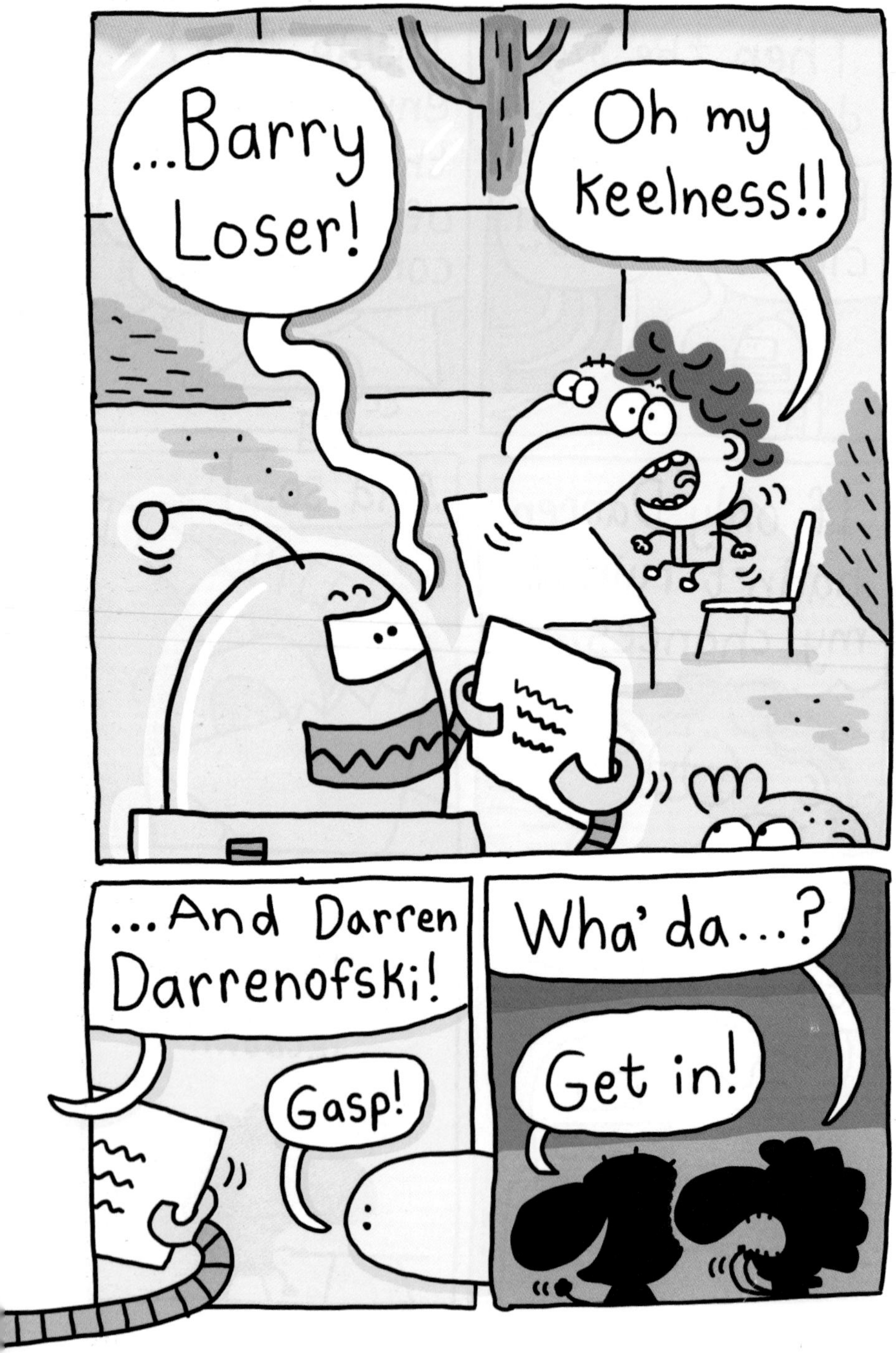
...Barry Loser!
Oh my keelness!!
...And Darren Darrenofski!
Wha' da...?
Gasp!
Get in!

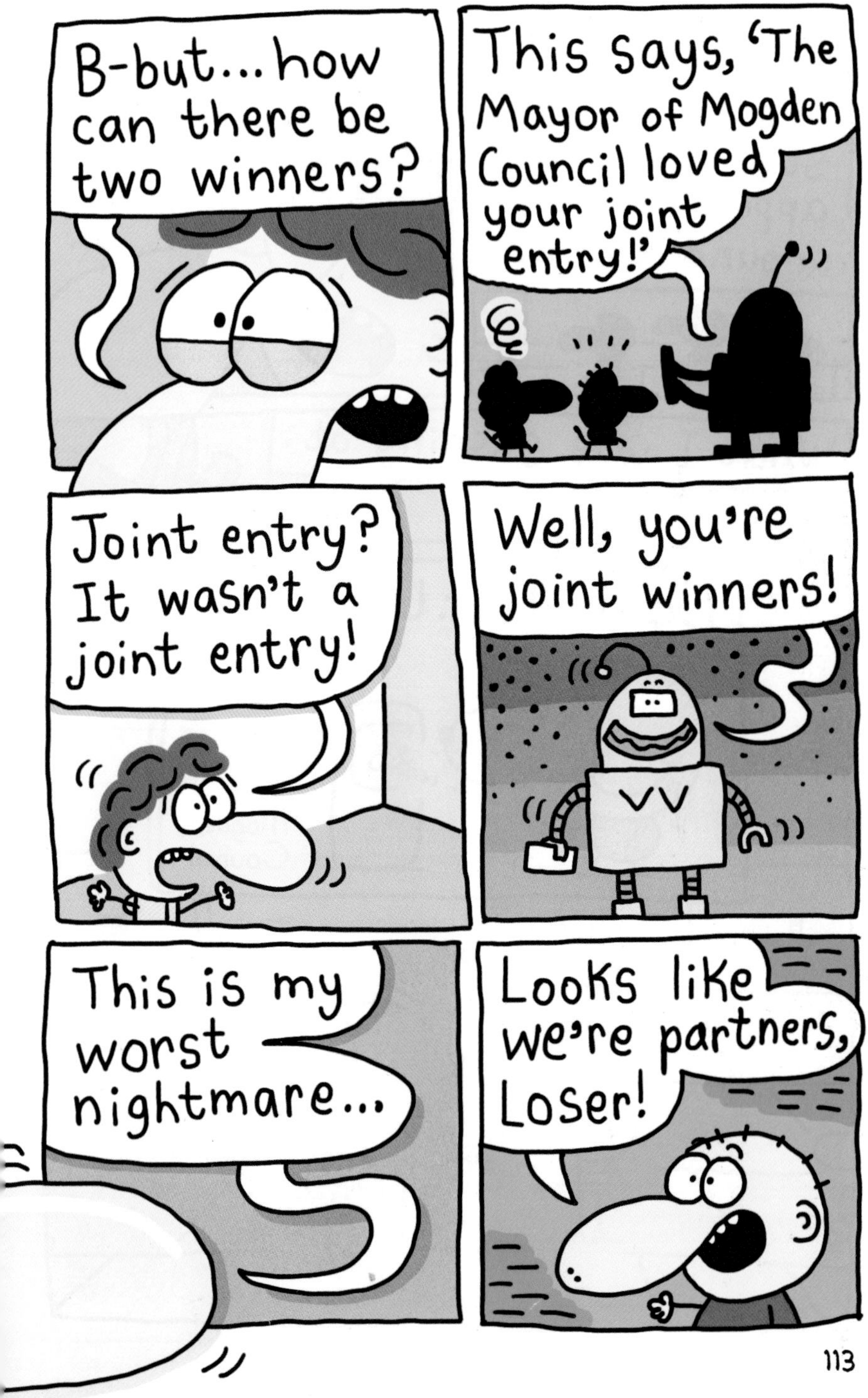
B-but... how can there be two winners?
This says, 'The Mayor of Mogden Council loved your joint entry!'
Joint entry? It wasn't a joint entry!
Well, you're joint winners!
This is my worst nightmare...
Looks like we're partners, Loser!

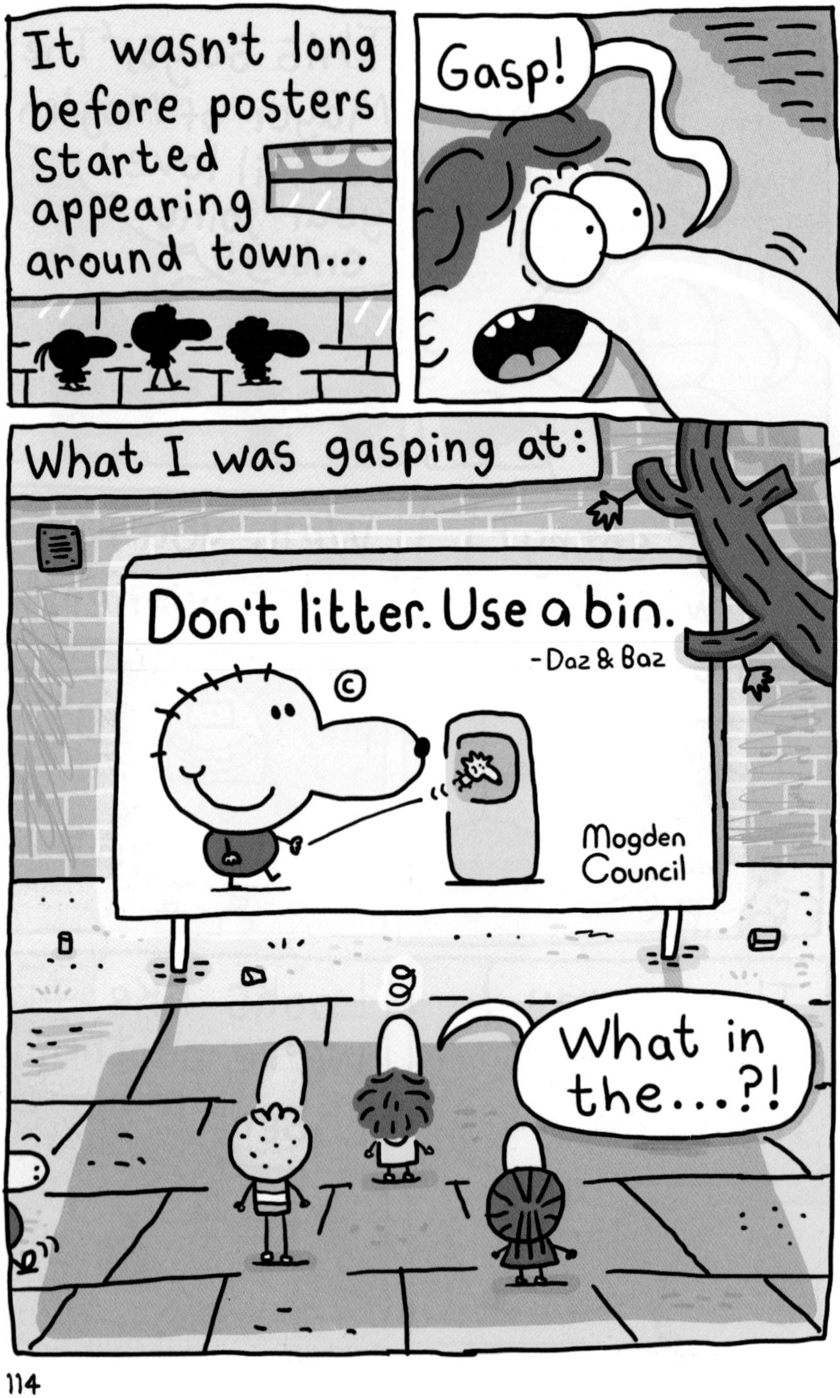
It wasn't long before posters started appearing around town...
Gasp!
What I was gasping at:
Don't litter. Use a bin.
-Daz & Baz
©
Mogden Council
What in the...?!

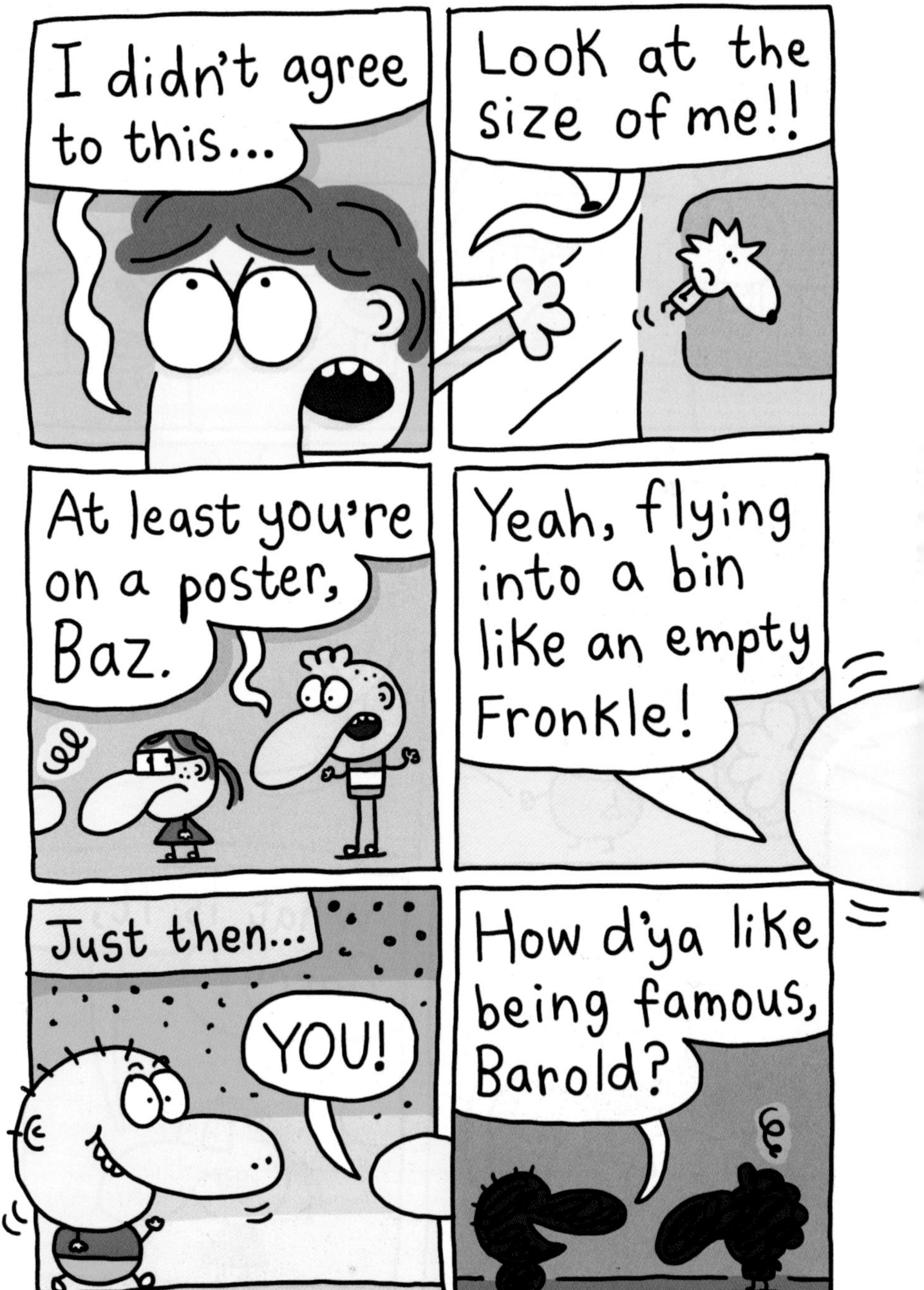
I didn't agree to this...
Look at the size of me!!
At least you're on a poster, Baz.
Yeah, flying into a bin like an empty Fronkle!
Just then...
YOU!
How d'ya like being famous, Barold?

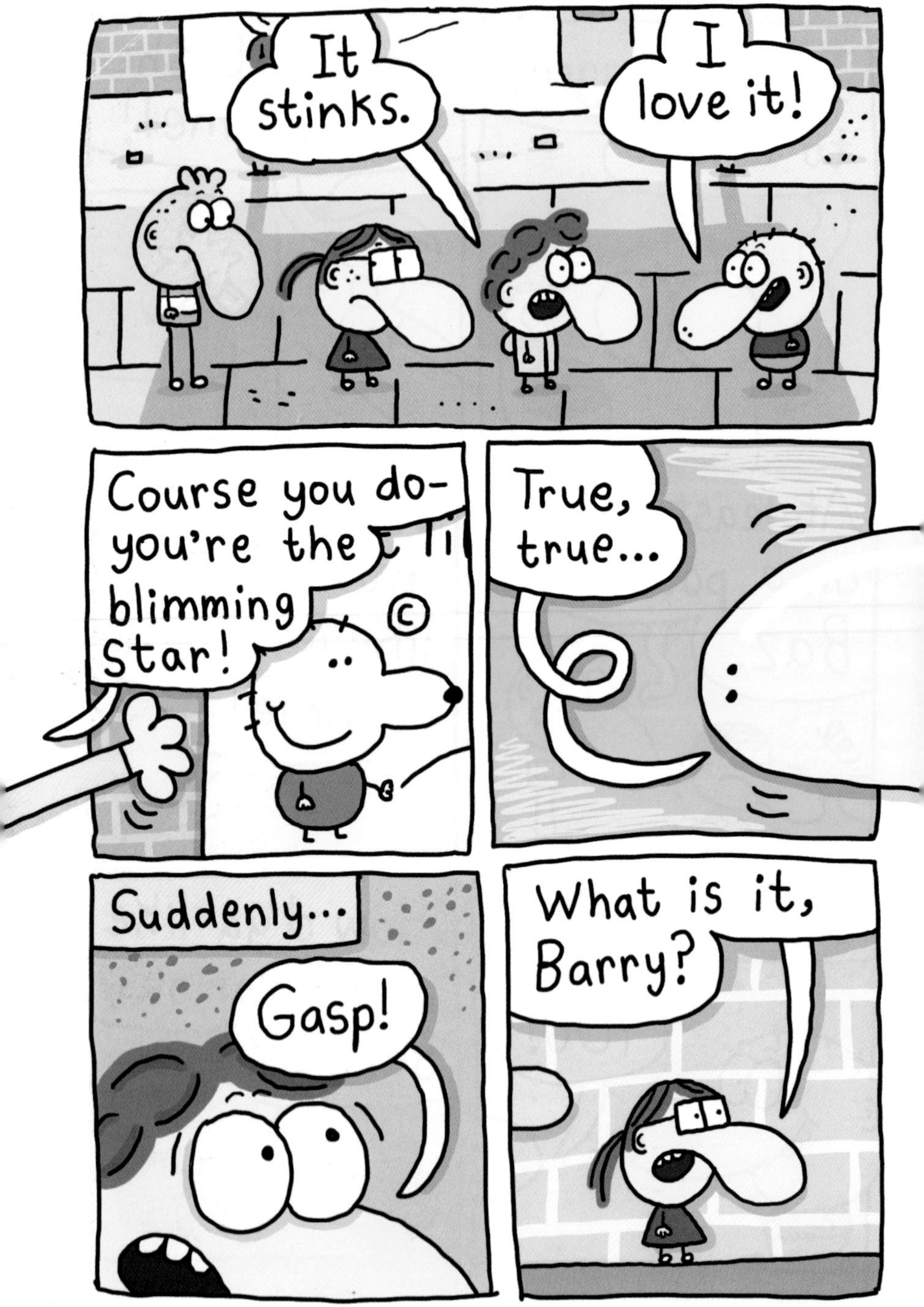
It stinks.
I love it!
Course you do- you're the blimming star!
True, true...
Suddenly...
Gasp!
What is it, Barry?

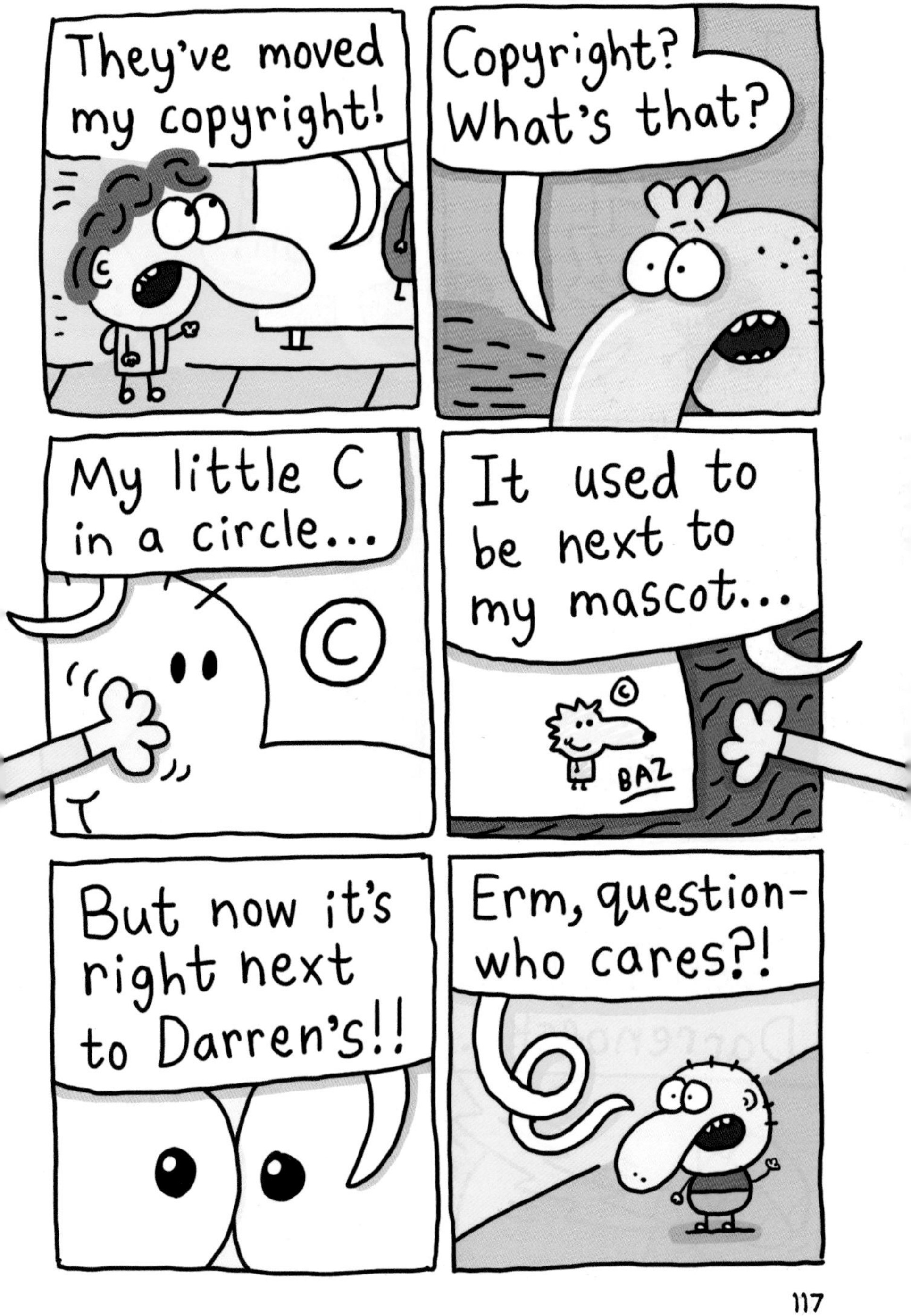

They've moved my copyright!
Copyright? What's that?
My little C in a circle...
©
It used to be next to my mascot...
©
BAZ
But now it's right next to Darren's!!
Erm, question- who cares?!

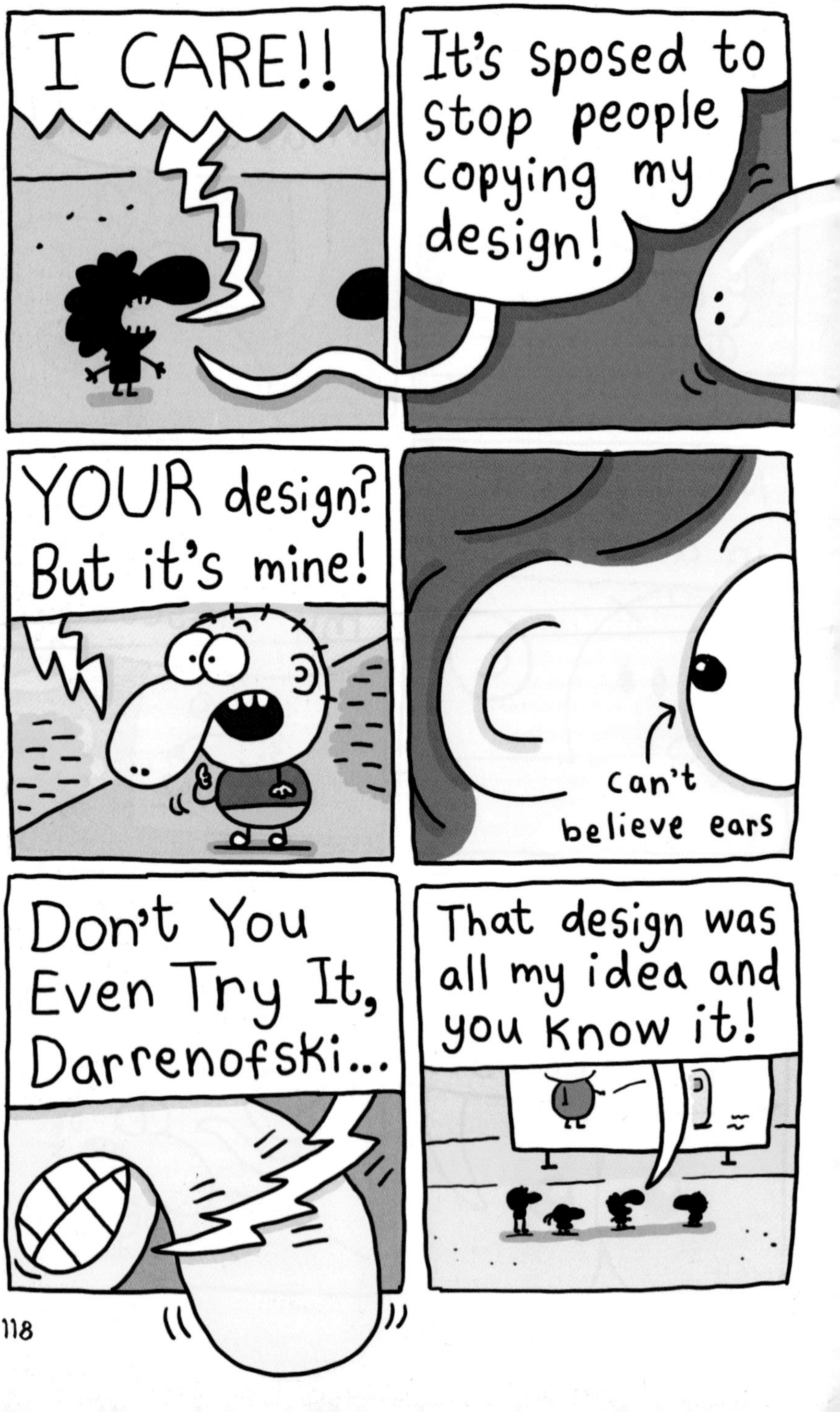
I CARE!!
It's sposed to stop people copying my design!
YOUR design? But it's mine!
can't believe ears
Don't You Even Try It, Darrenofski...
That design was all my idea and you know it!

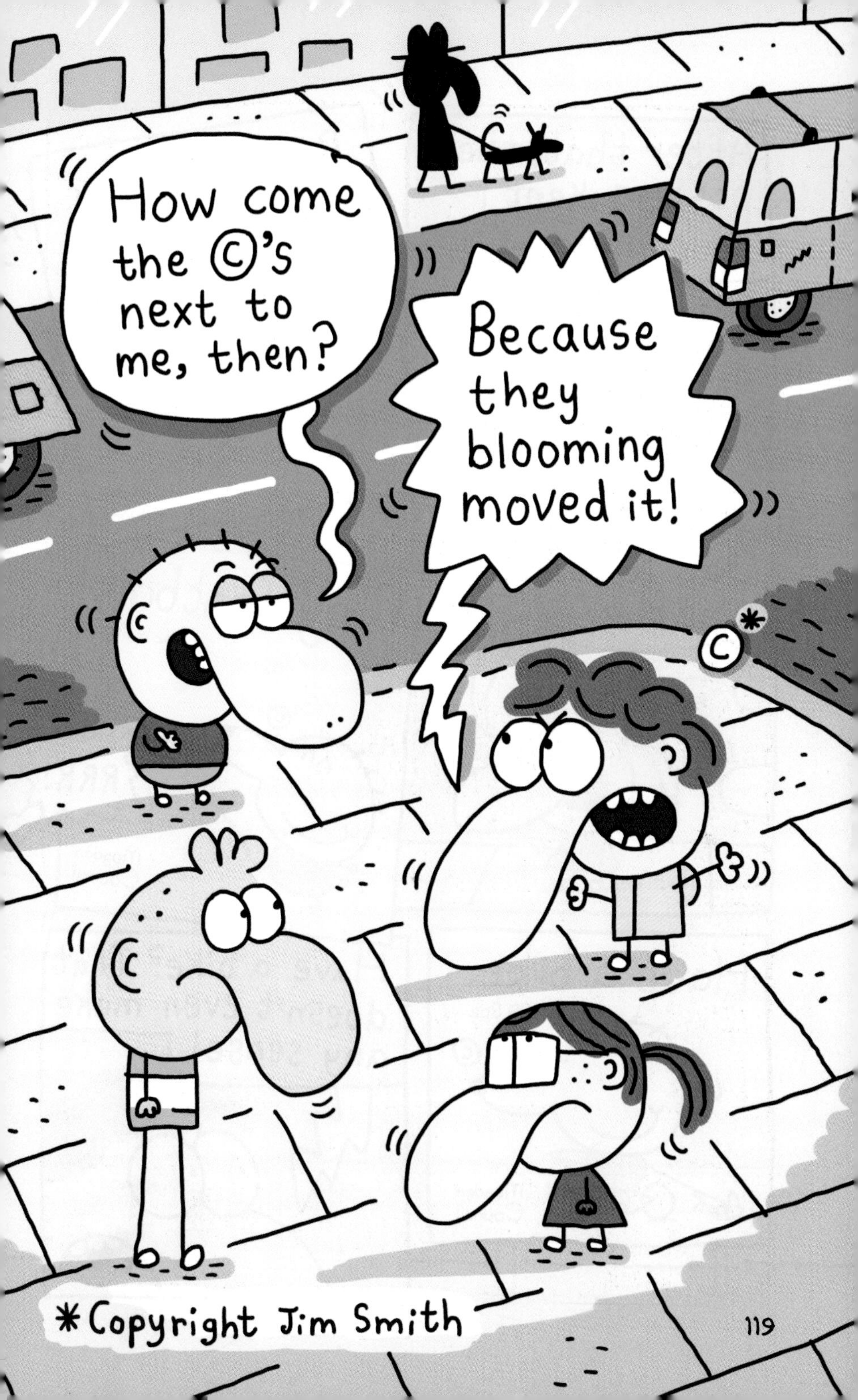
How come the ©'s next to me, then?
Because they blooming moved it!
©*

*Copyright Jim Smith

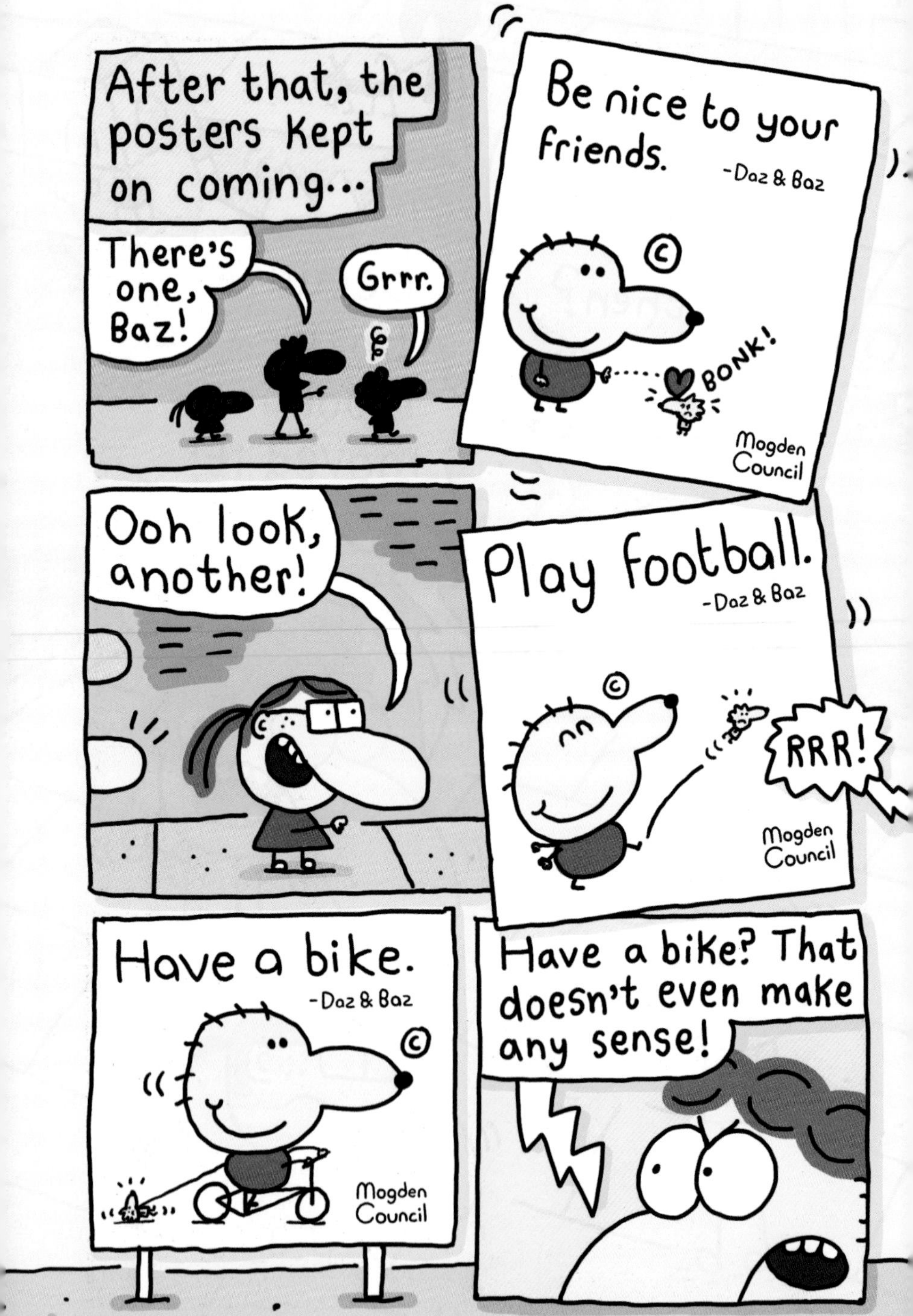
After that, the posters kept on coming...
There's one, Baz!
Grrr.
Be nice to your friends. -Daz & Baz
©
BONK!
Mogden Council
Ooh look, another!
Play football. -Daz & Baz
©
RRR!
Mogden Council
Have a bike. -Daz & Baz
©
Mogden Council
Have a bike? That doesn't even make any sense!

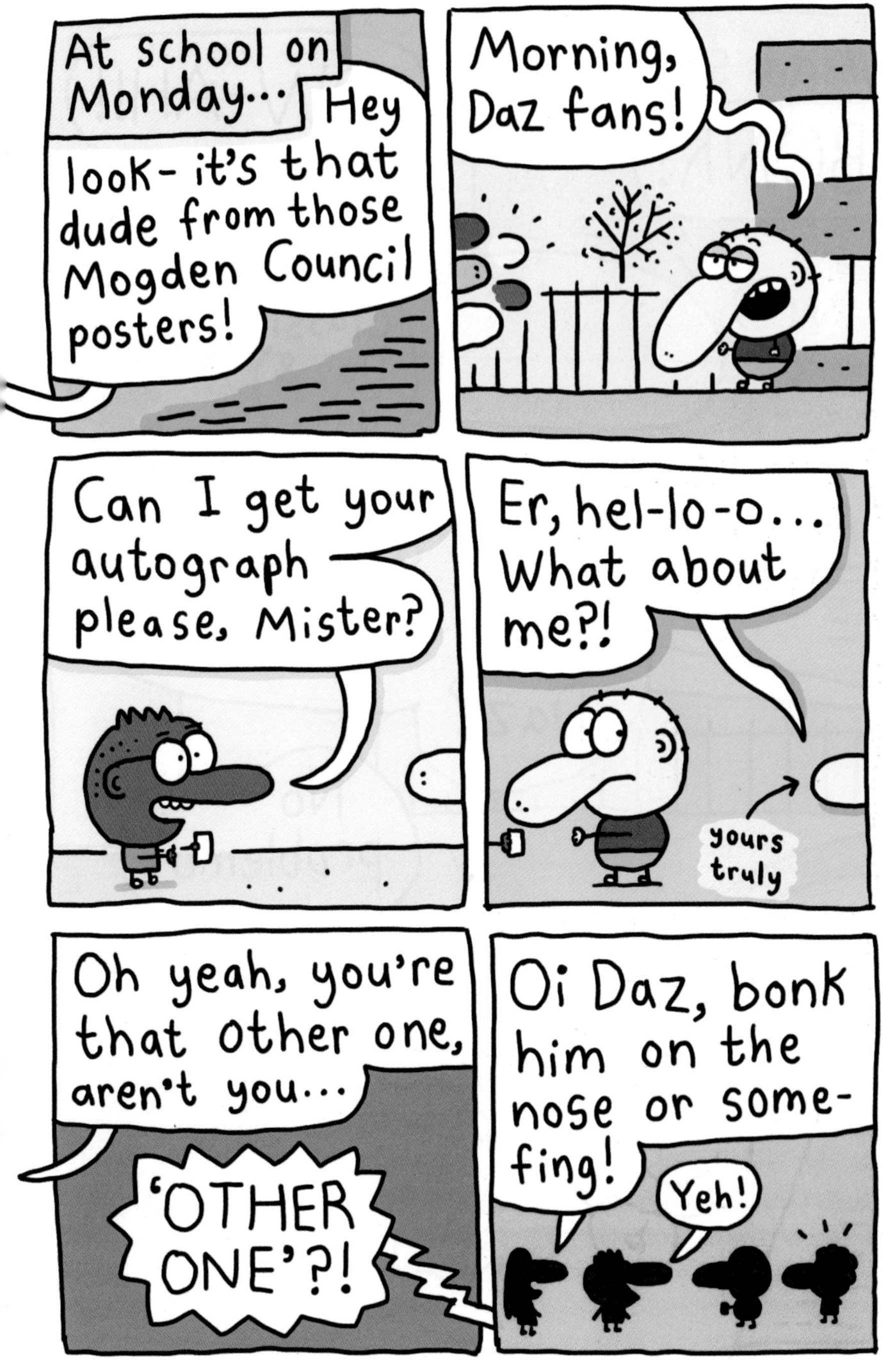
At school on Monday...
Hey look- it's that dude from those Mogden Council posters!
Morning, Daz fans!
Can I get your autograph please, Mister?
Er, hel-lo-o... What about me?!
yours truly
Oh yeah, you're that other one, aren't you...
'OTHER ONE'?!
Oi Daz, bonk him on the nose or some-fing!
Yeh!

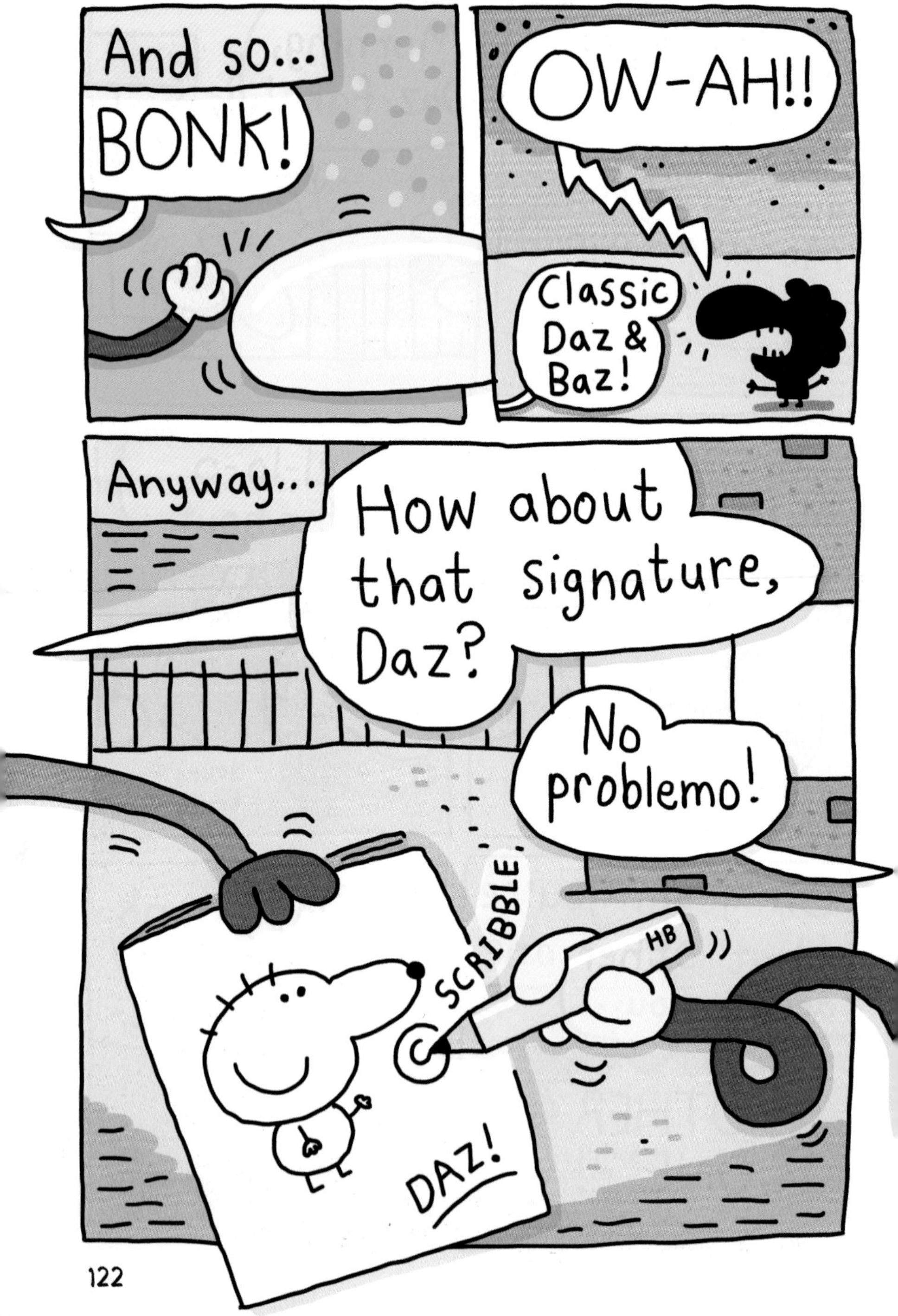
And so...
BONK!
OW-AH!!
Classic Daz & Baz!
Anyway...
How about that signature, Daz?
No problemo!
SCRIBBLE
HB
DAZ!

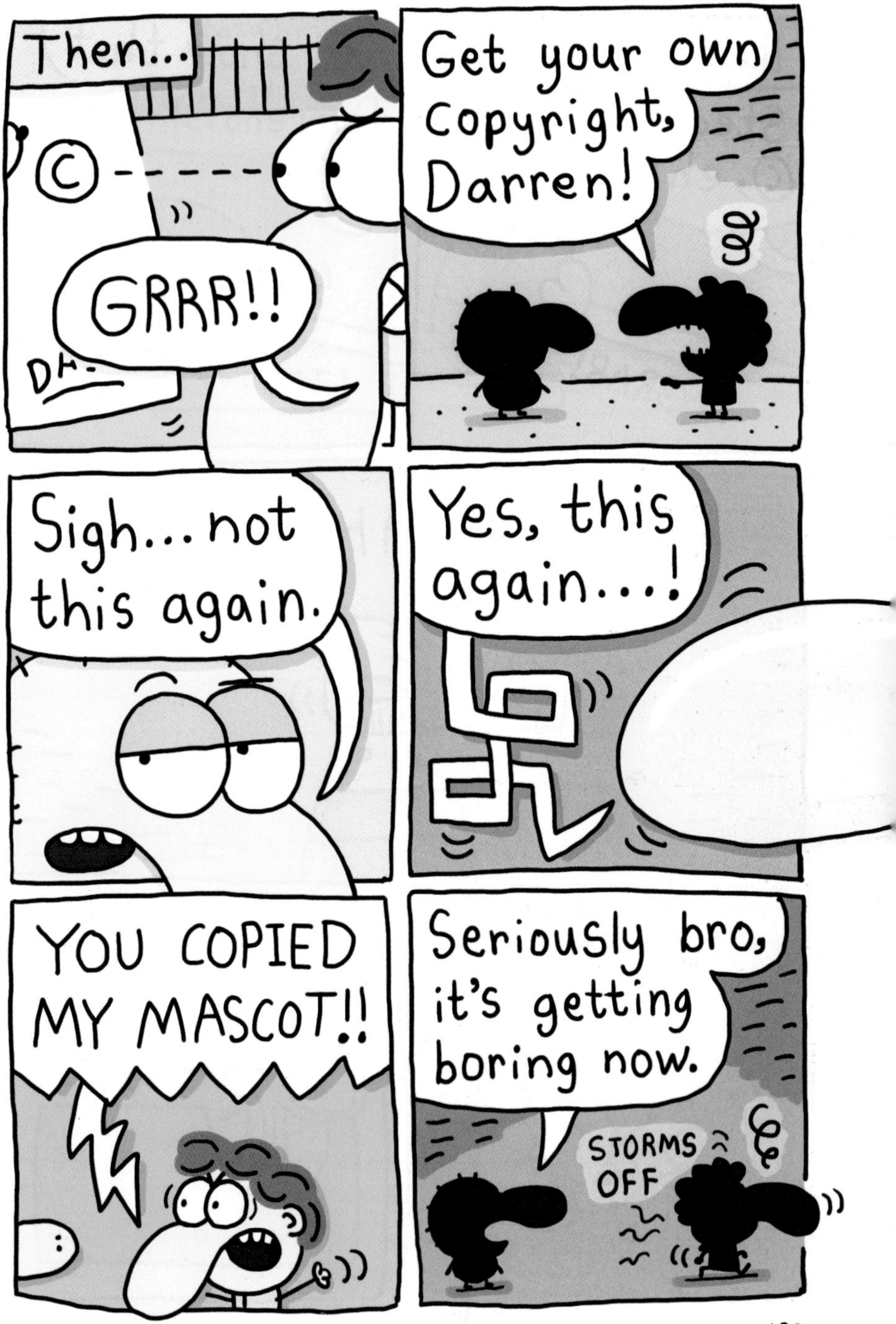
Then...
GRRR!!
Get your own copyright, Darren!
Sigh... not this again.
Yes, this again...!
YOU COPIED MY MASCOT!!
Seriously bro, it's getting boring now.
STORMS OFF

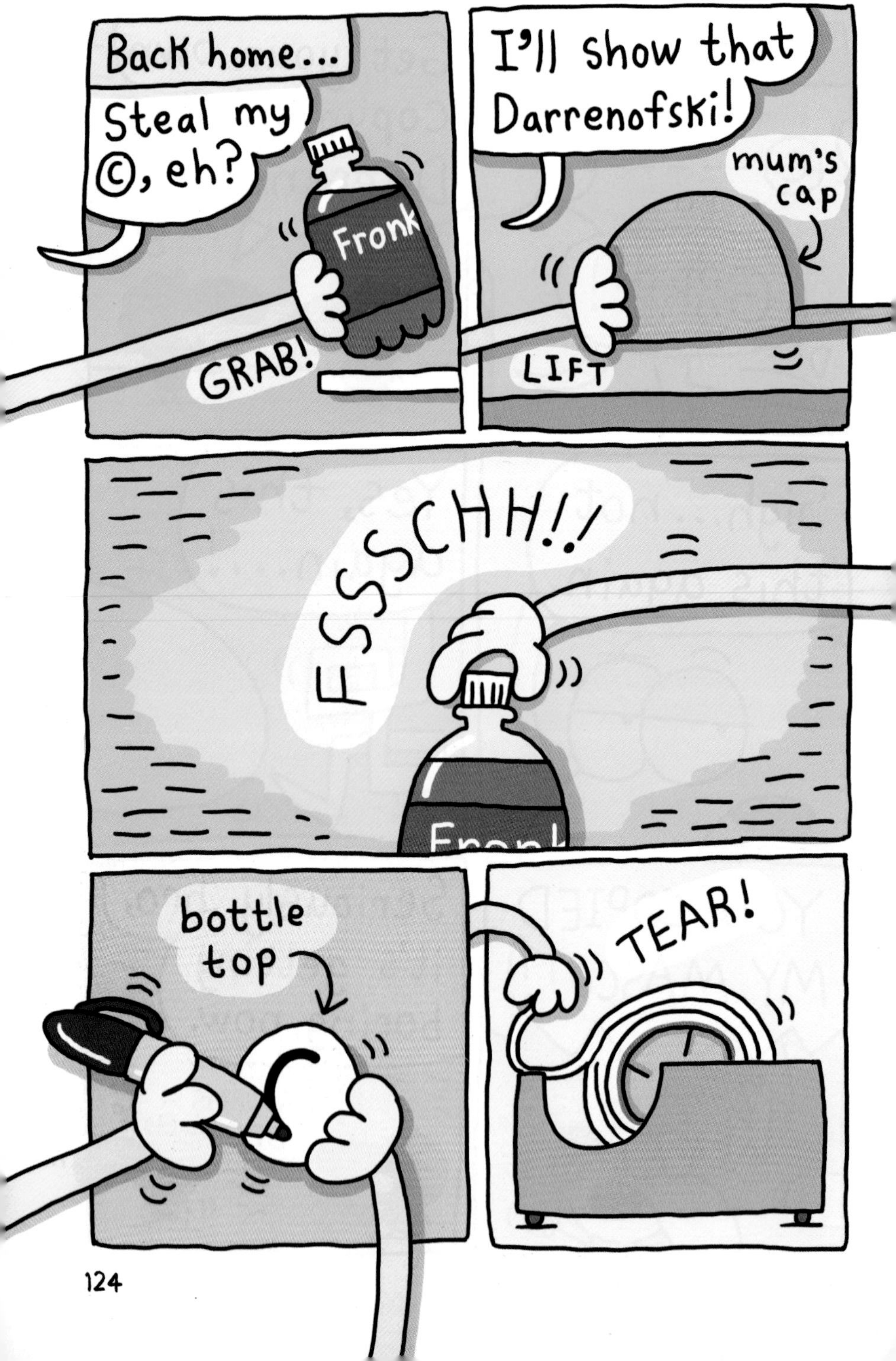
Back home...
Steal my ©, eh?
GRAB!
Fronk
I'll show that Darrenofski!
mum's cap
LIFT
FSSSCHH!!
bottle top
TEAR!

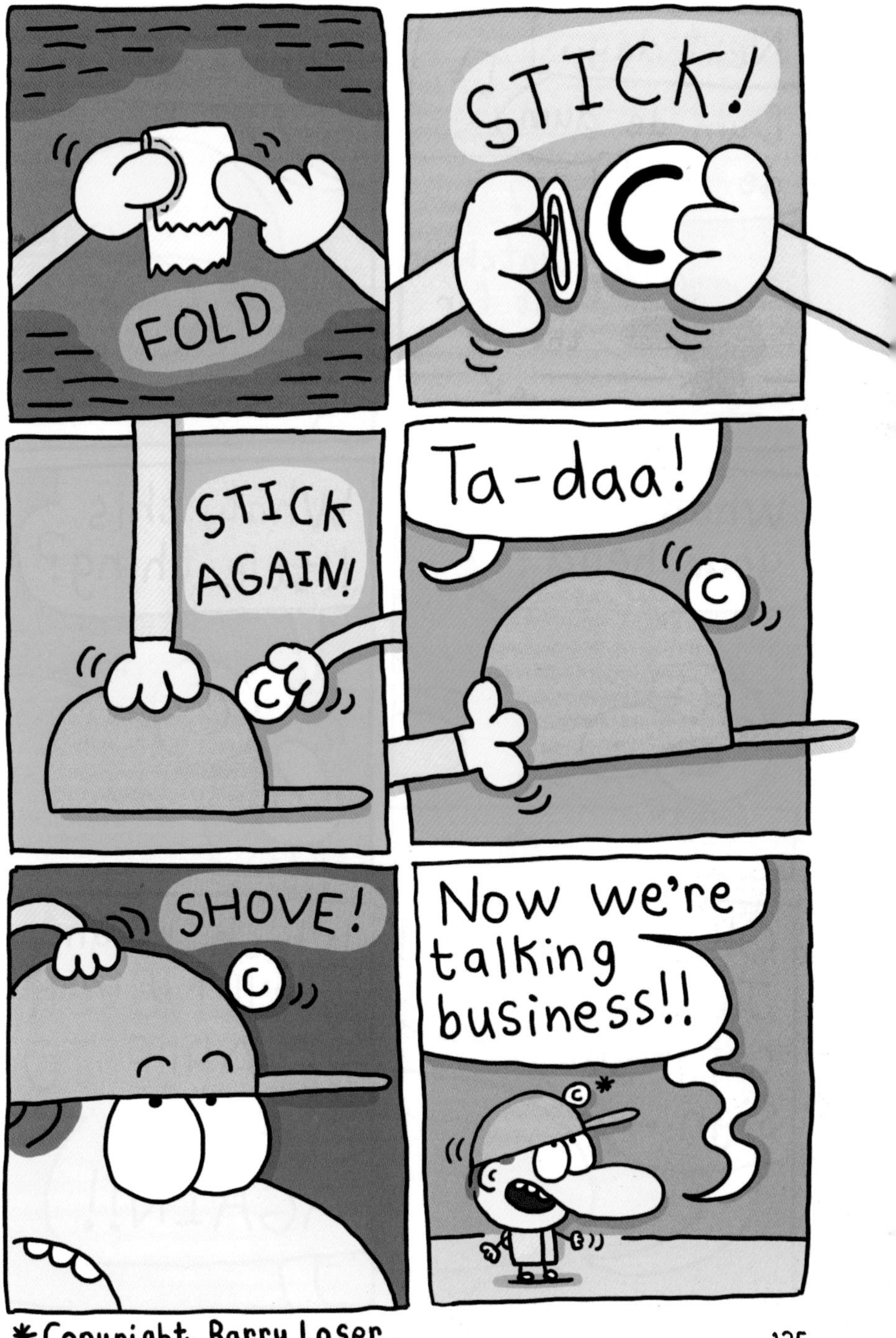
FOLD
STICK!
C
STICK AGAIN!
C
Ta-daa!
C
SHOVE!
C
Now we're talking business!!
C*

*Copyright Barry Loser

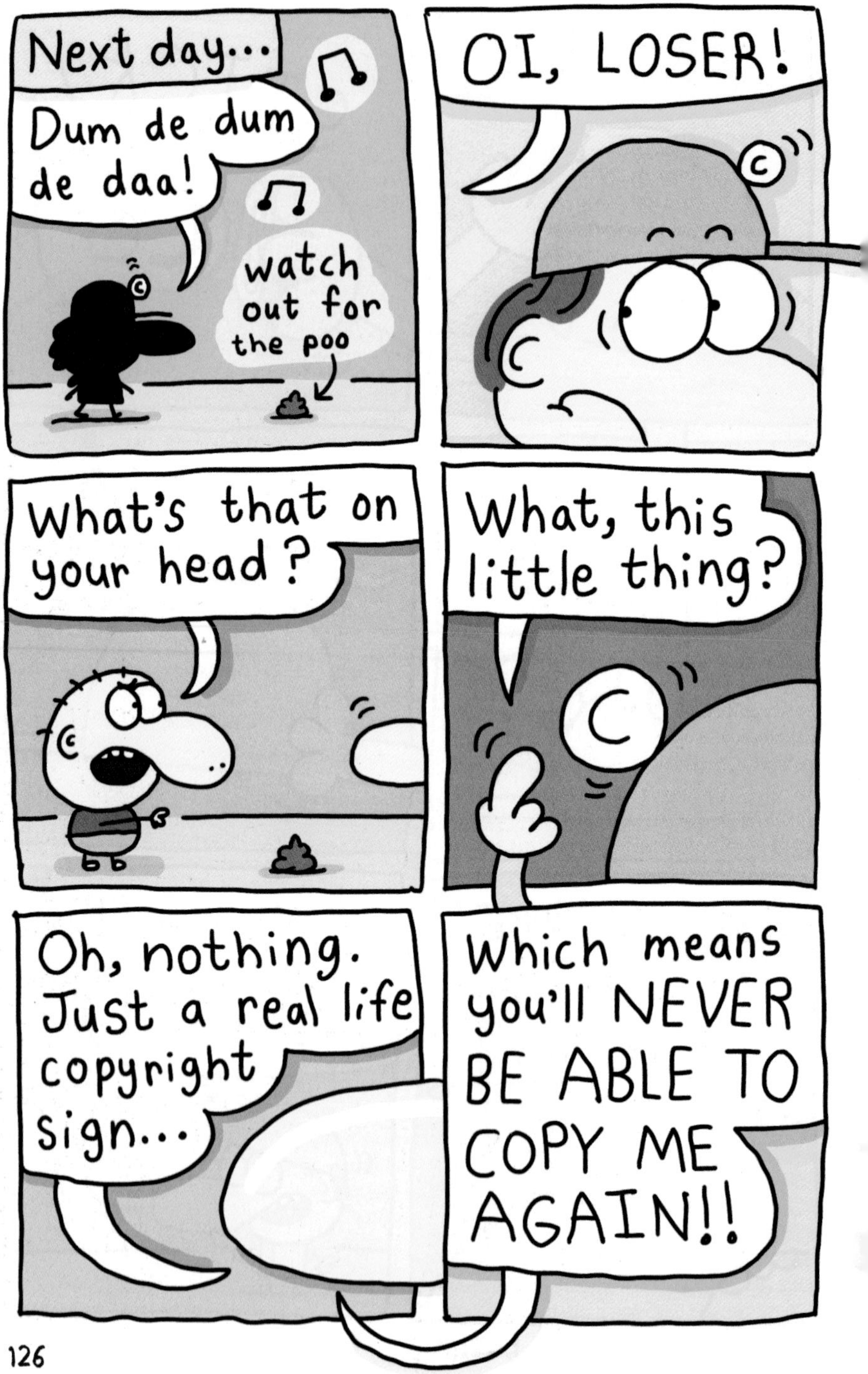
Next day...
Dum de dum de daa!
watch out for the poo
OI, LOSER!
What's that on your head?
What, this little thing?
Oh, nothing. Just a real life copyright sign...
Which means you'll NEVER BE ABLE TO COPY ME AGAIN!!

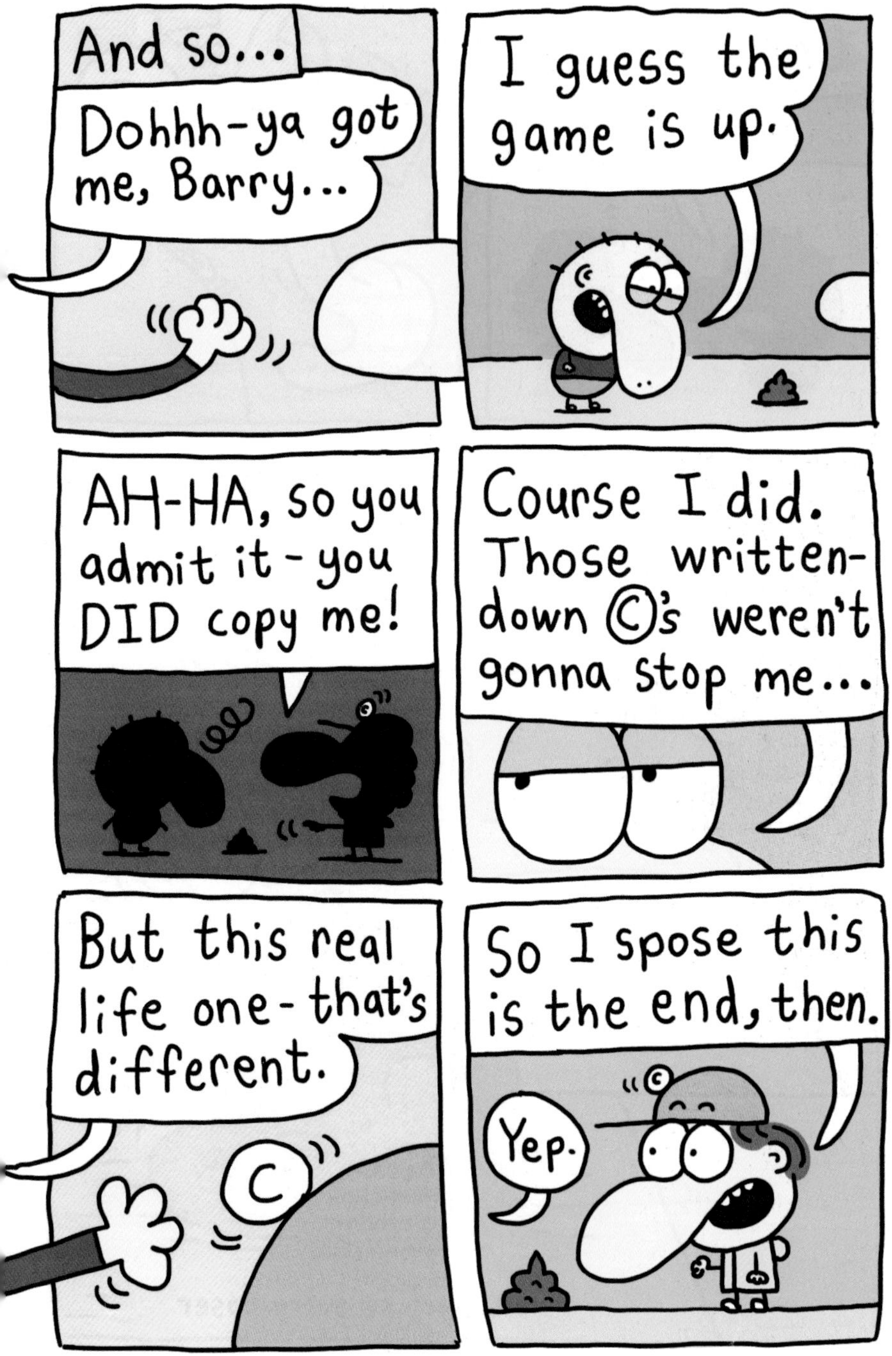
And so...
Dohhh-ya got me, Barry...
I guess the game is up.
AH-HA, so you admit it - you DID copy me!
Course I did. Those written-down ©'s weren't gonna stop me...
But this real life one - that's different.
C
So I spose this is the end, then.
Yep.

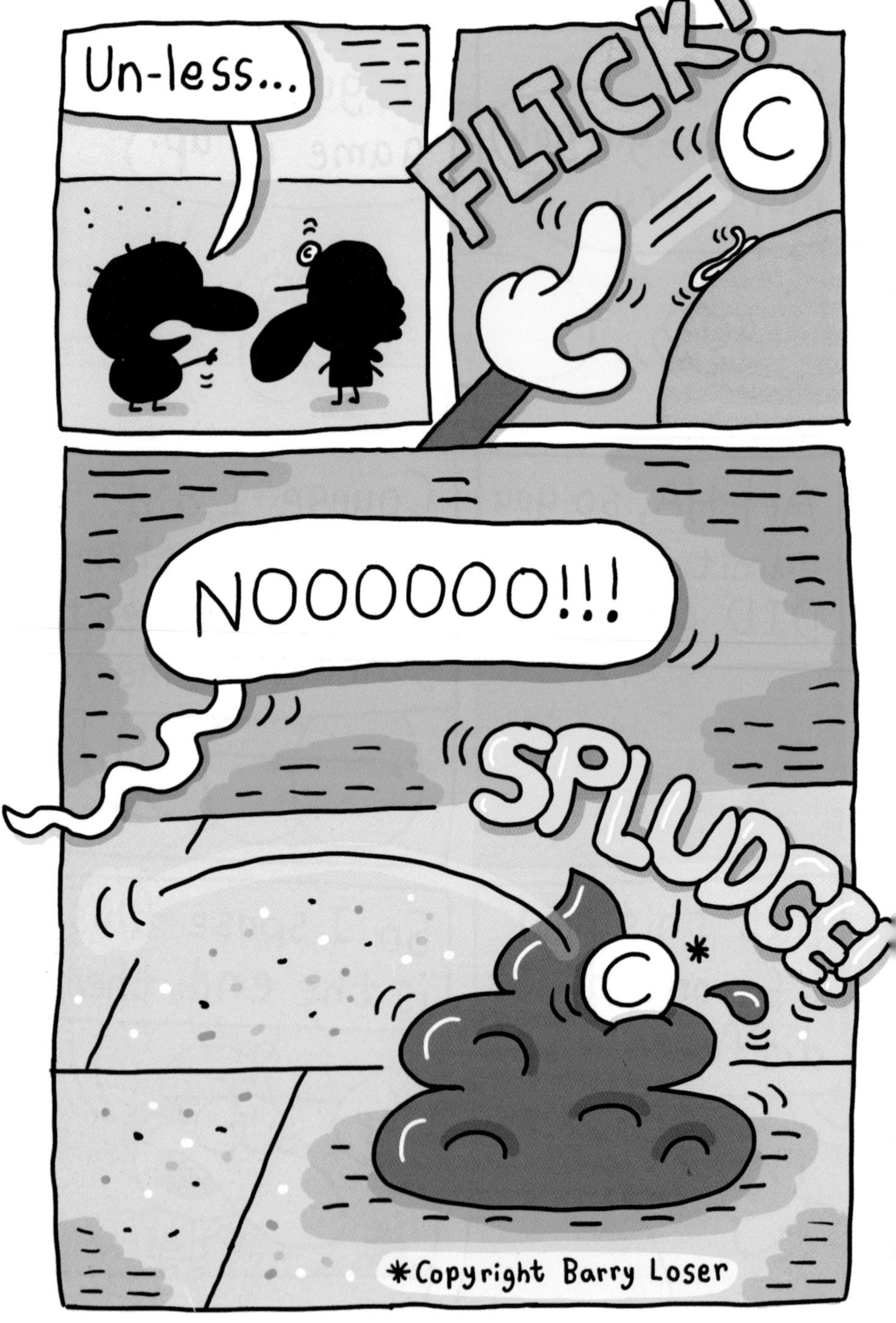
Un-less...
FLICK!
NOOOOOO!!!
SPLUDGE!
*
*Copyright Barry Loser

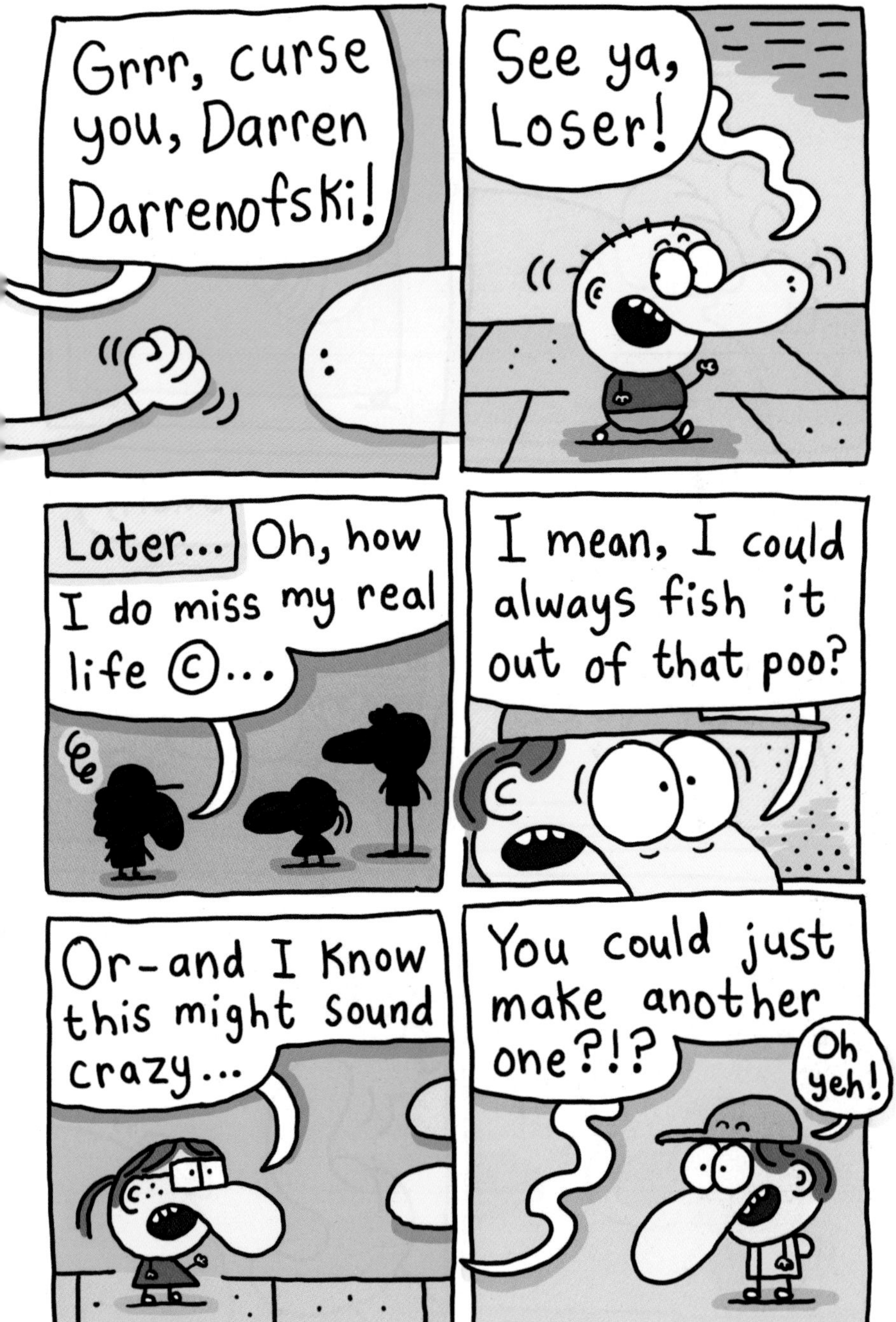
Grrr, curse you, Darren Darrenofski!
See ya, Loser!
Later...
Oh, how I do miss my real life ©...
I mean, I could always fish it out of that poo?
Or-and I know this might sound crazy...
You could just make another one?!?
Oh yeh!

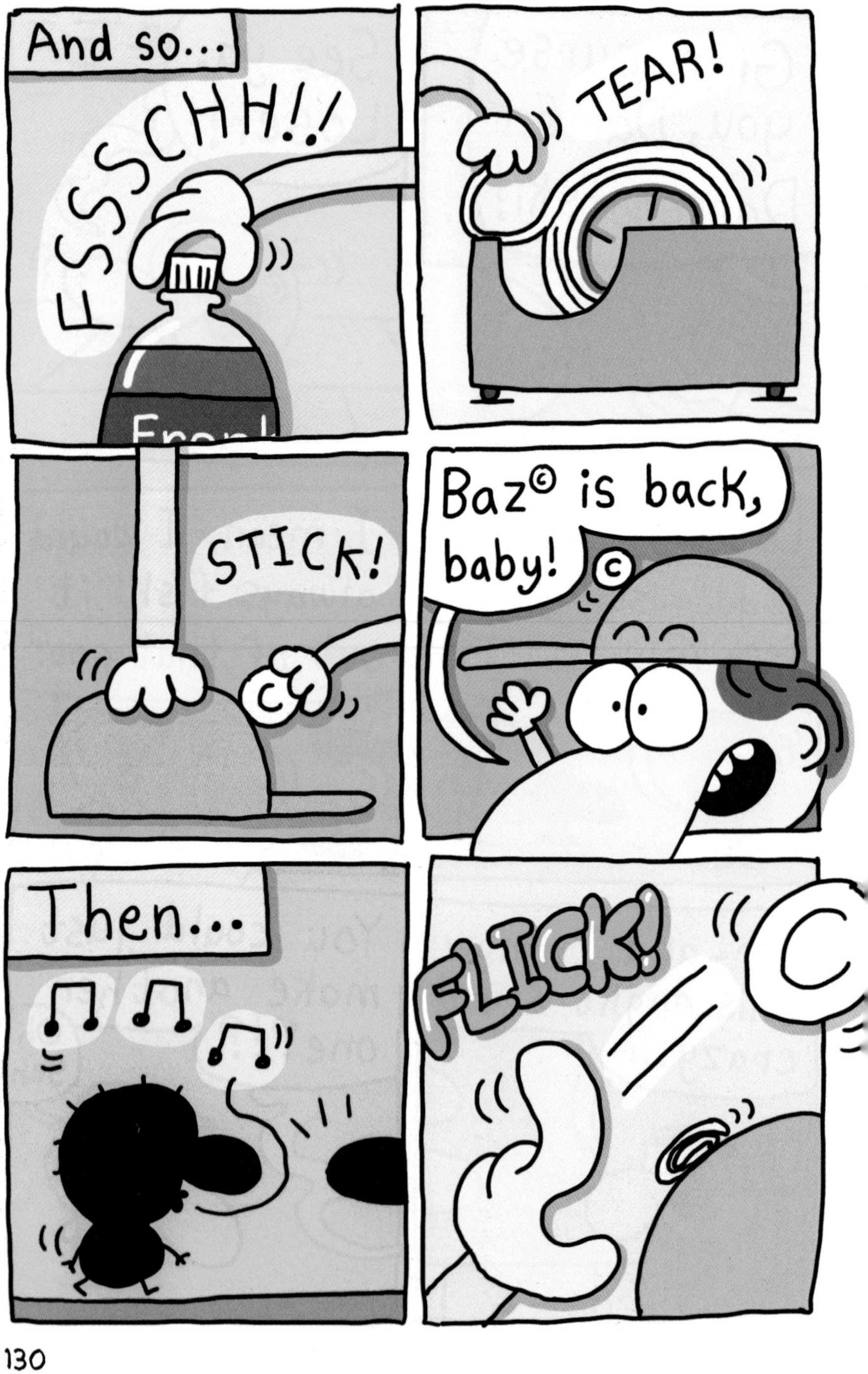
And so...
FSSSCHH!!
TEAR!
STICK!
Baz© is back, baby!
Then...
FLICK!

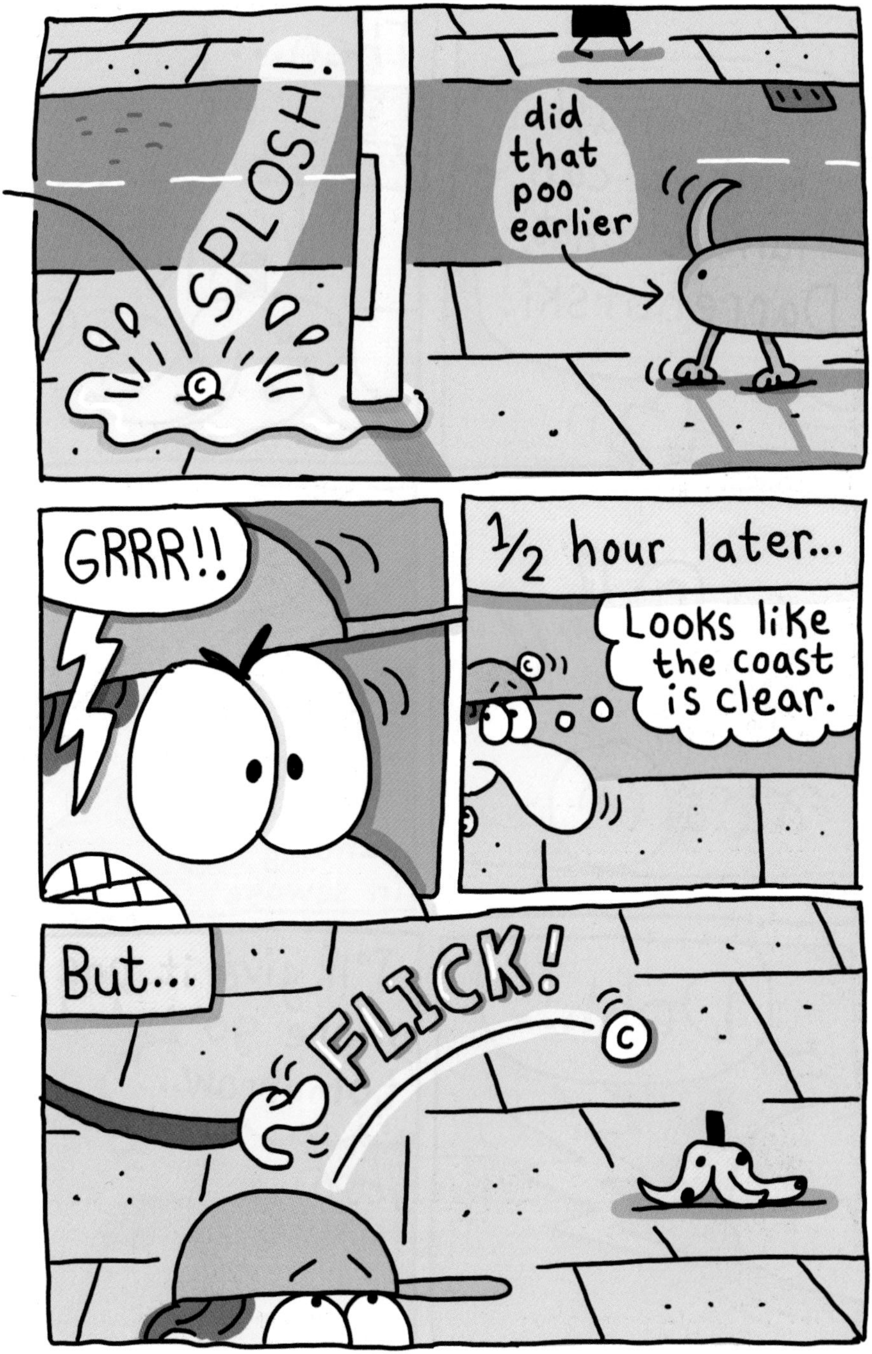
SPLOSH!
did that poo earlier
GRRR!!
1/2 hour later...
Looks like the coast is clear.
But...
FLICK!

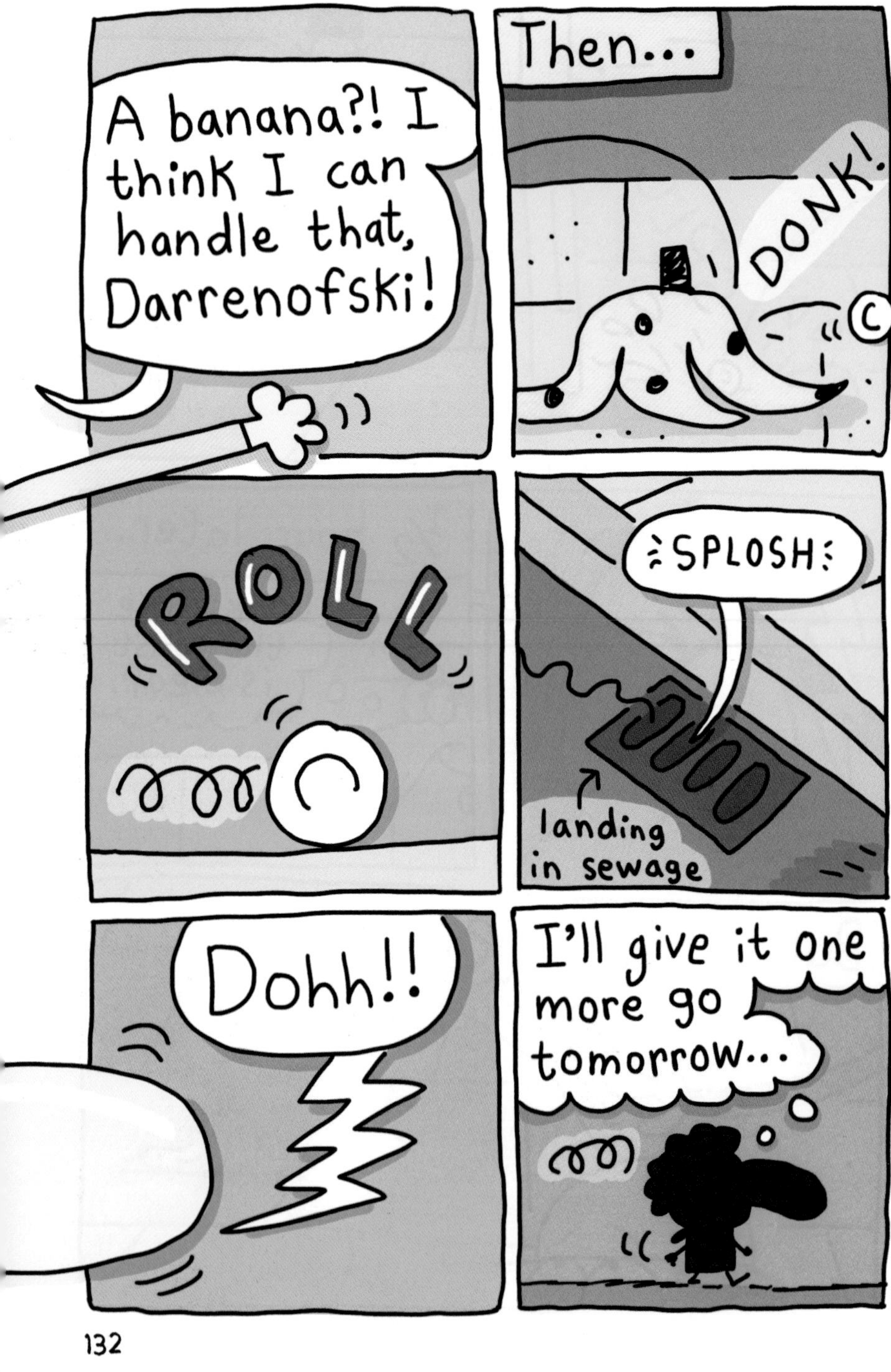
A banana?! I think I can handle that, Darrenofski!
Then...
DONK!
ROLL
SPLOSH
landing in sewage
Dohh!!
I'll give it one more go tomorrow...

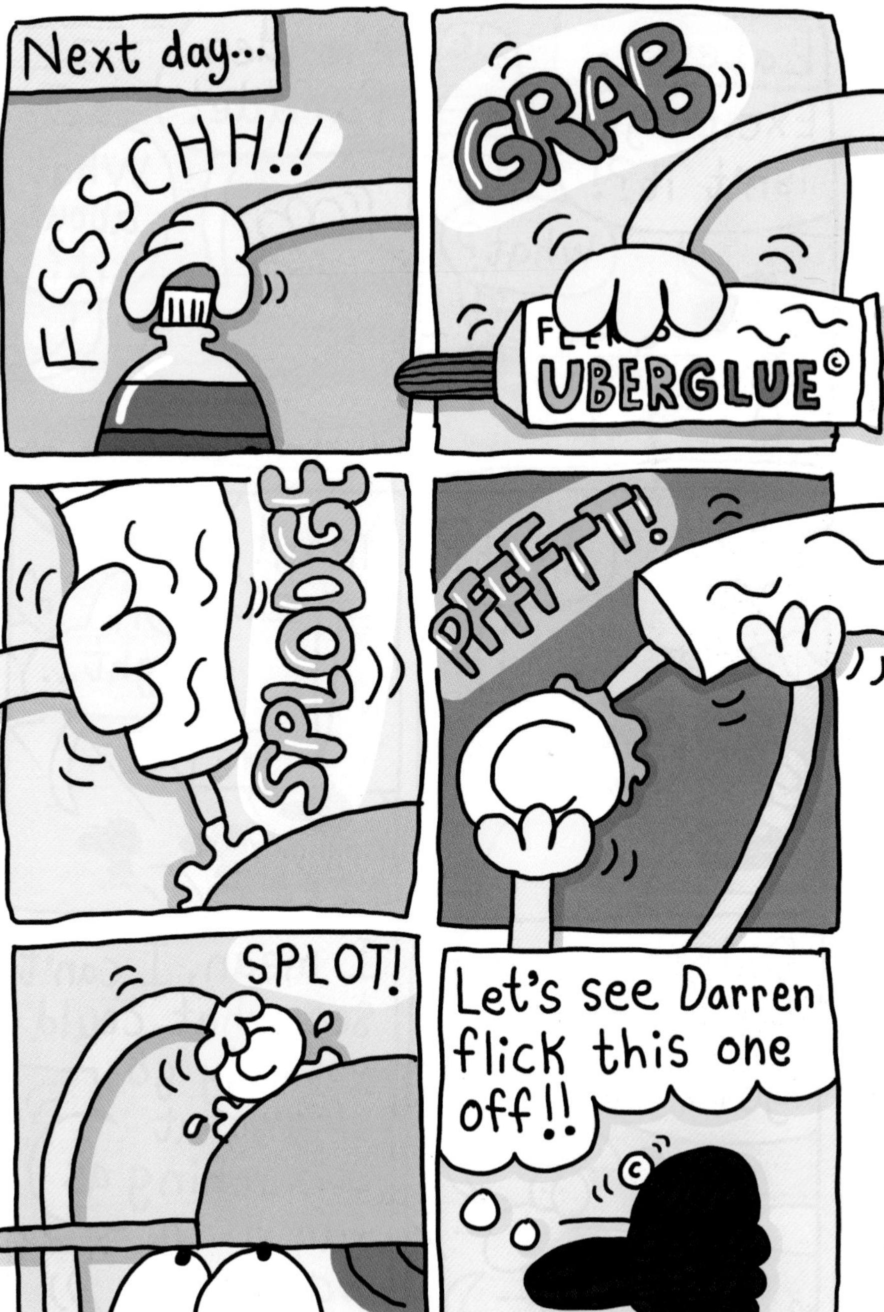

Next day...
FSSSCHH!!
GRAB
UBERGLUE©
SPLODGE
PFFFTT!
SPLOT!
Let's see Darren flick this one off!!

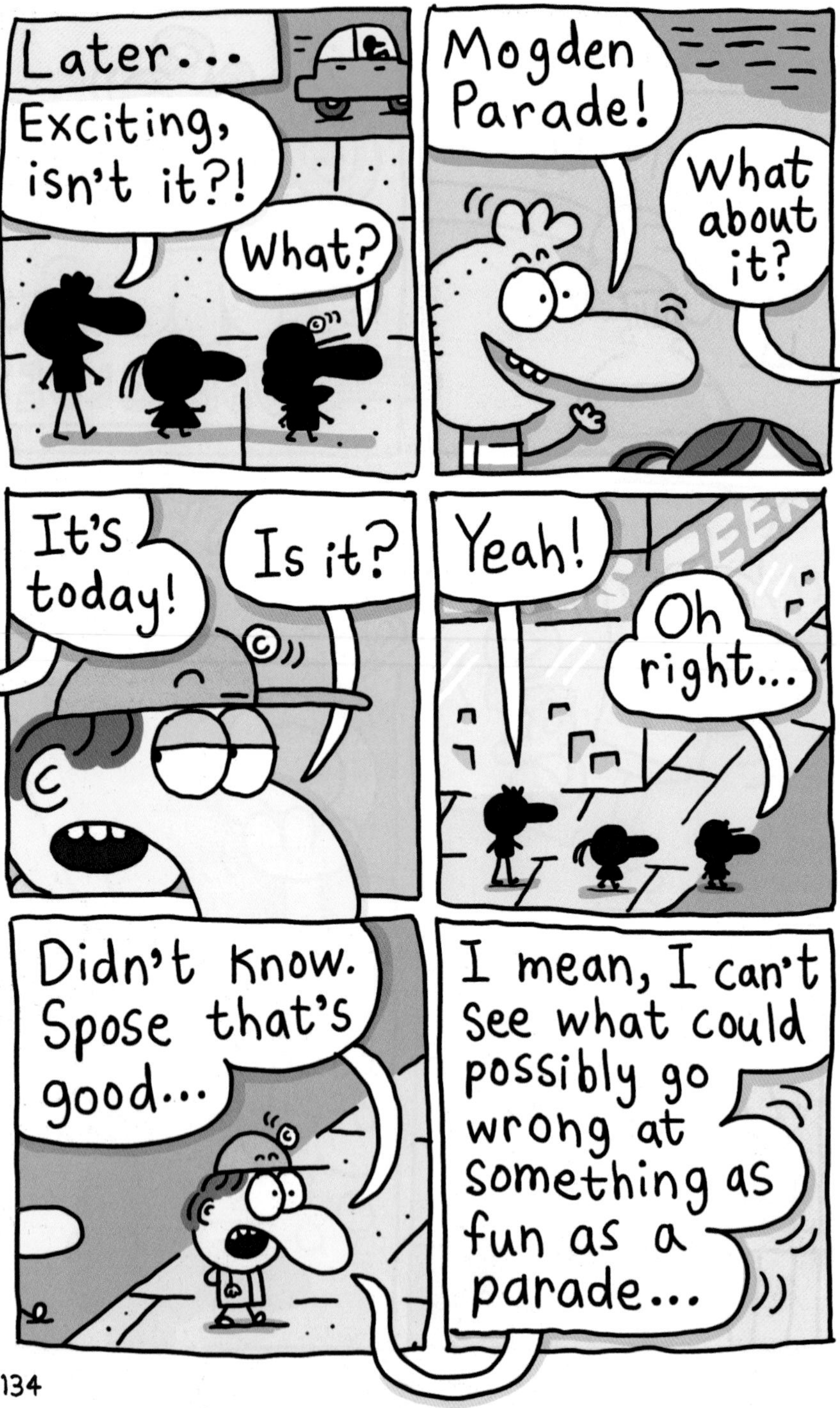
Later...
Exciting, isn't it?!
What?
Mogden Parade!
What about it?
It's today!
Is it?
Yeah!
Oh right...
Didn't know. Spose that's good...
I mean, I can't see what could possibly go wrong at something as fun as a parade...

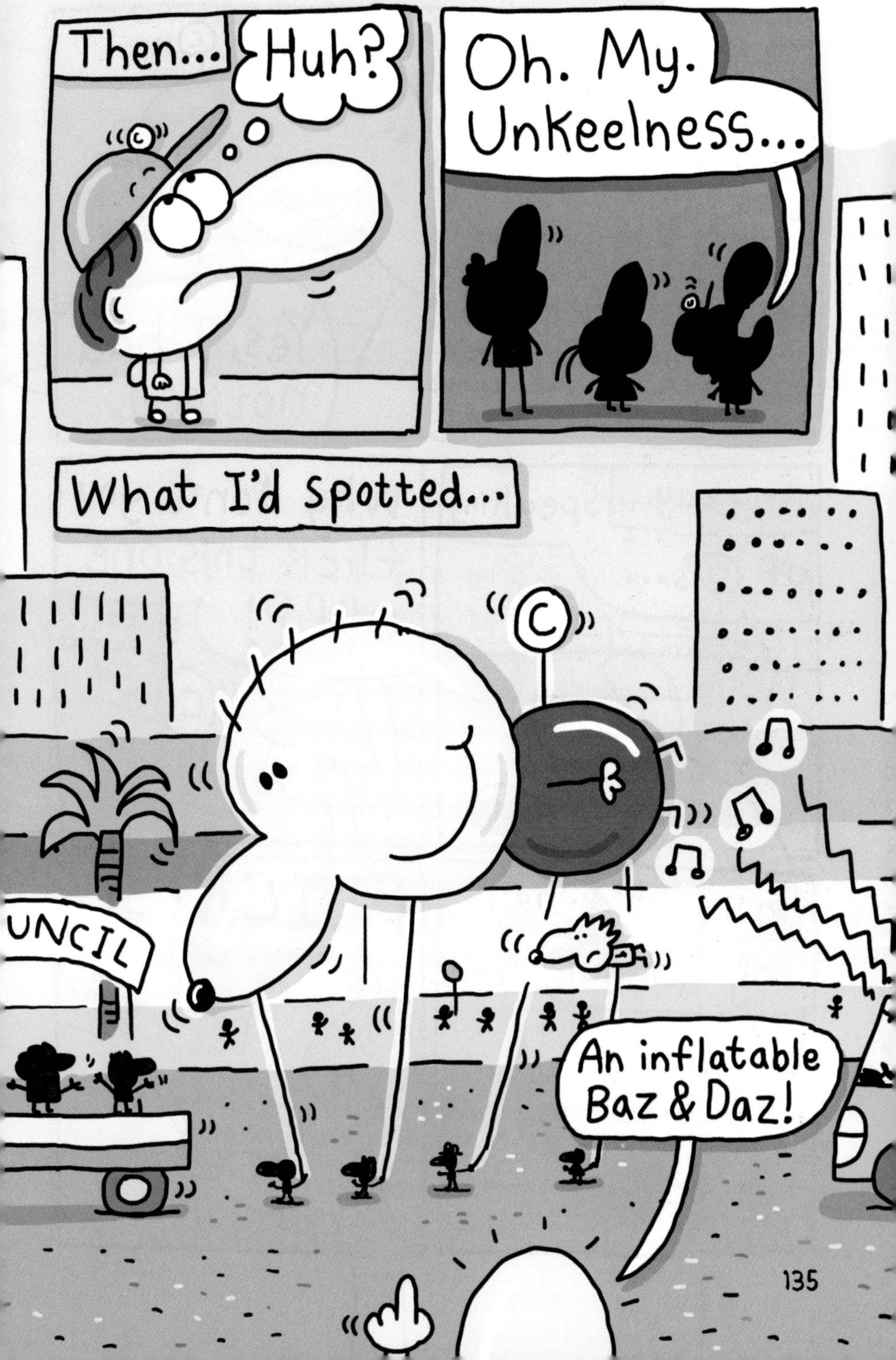
Then...
Huh?
Oh. My. Unkeelness...
What I'd spotted...
UNCIL
An inflatable Baz & Daz!

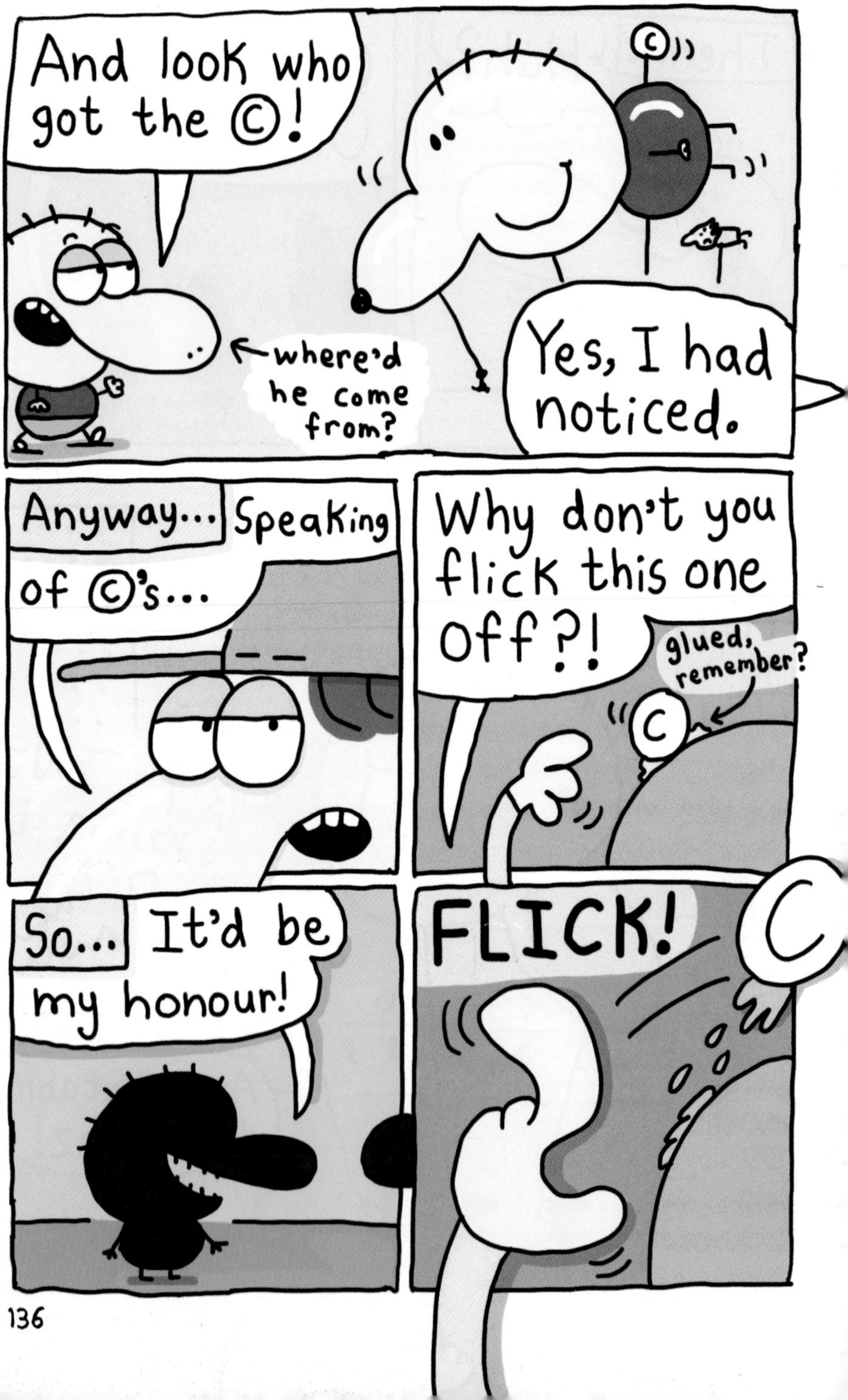
And look who got the ©!
where'd he come from?
Yes, I had noticed.
Anyway... Speaking of ©'s...
Why don't you flick this one off?!
glued, remember?
So... It'd be my honour!
FLICK!

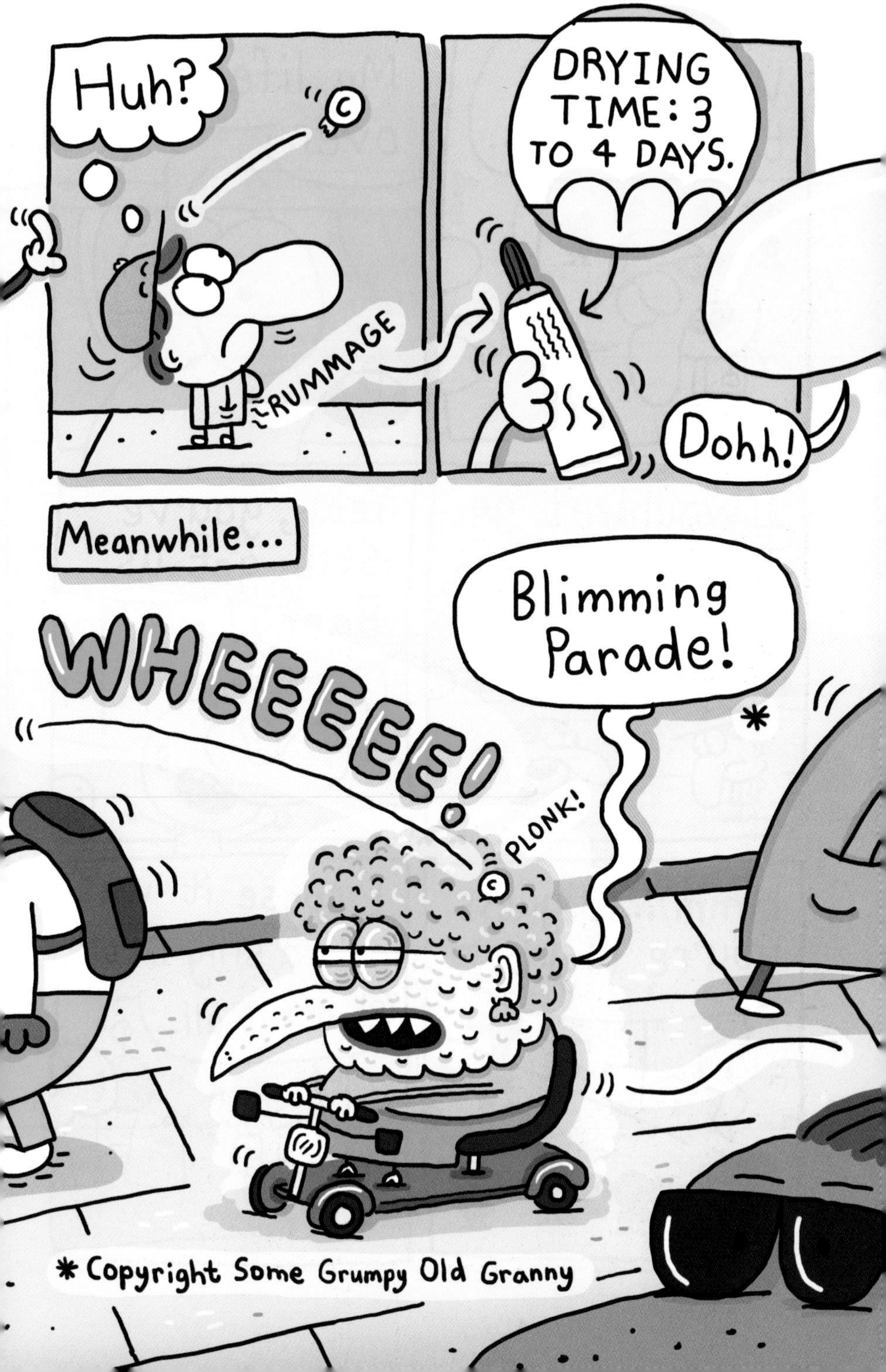

Huh?
RUMMAGE
DRYING TIME: 3 TO 4 DAYS.
Dohh!
Meanwhile...
WHEEEEEE!
Blimming Parade!
PLONK!
*
* Copyright Some Grumpy Old Granny

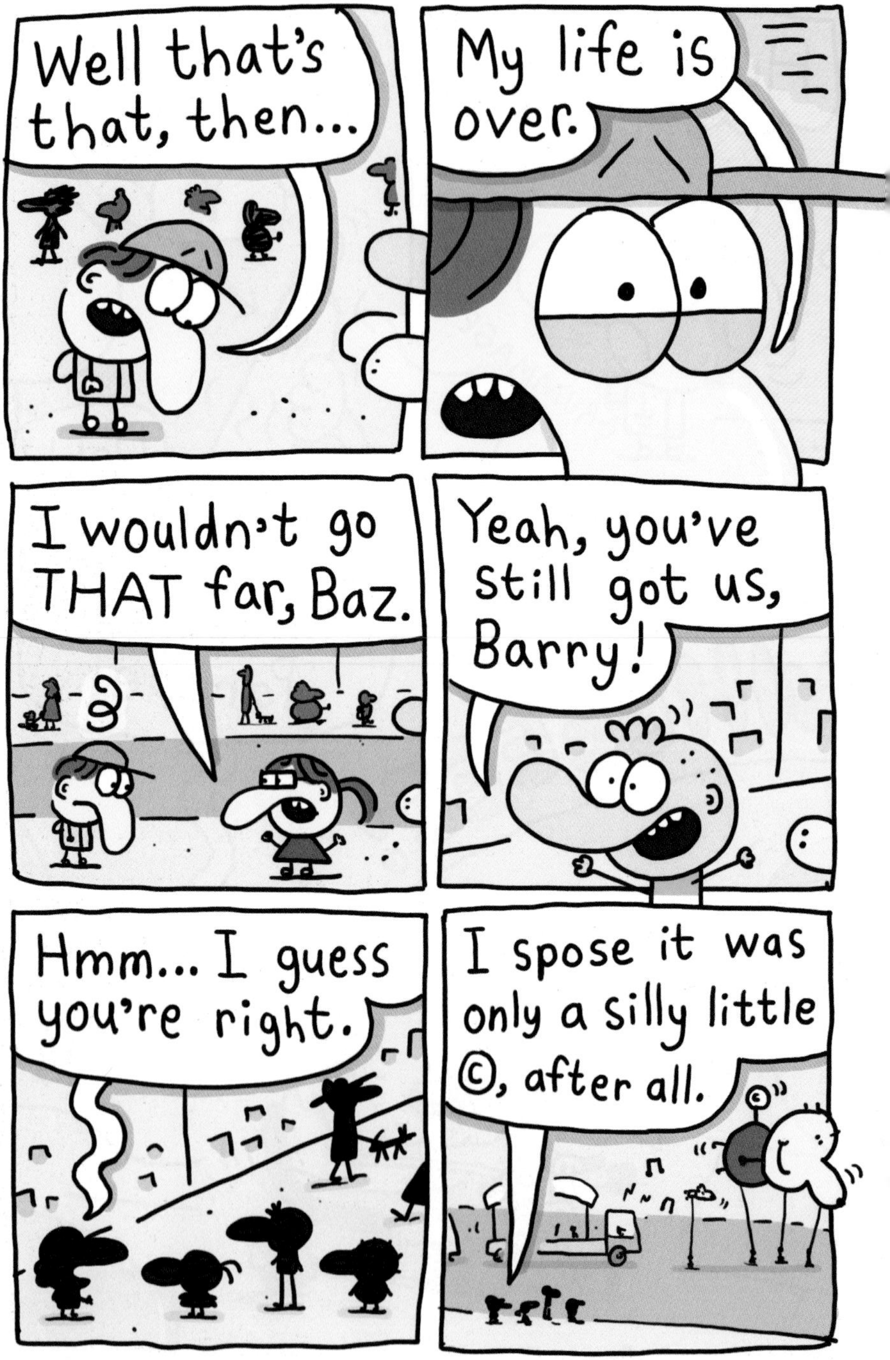
Well that's that, then...
My life is over.
I wouldn't go THAT far, Baz.
Yeah, you've still got us, Barry!
Hmm... I guess you're right.
I spose it was only a silly little ©, after all.

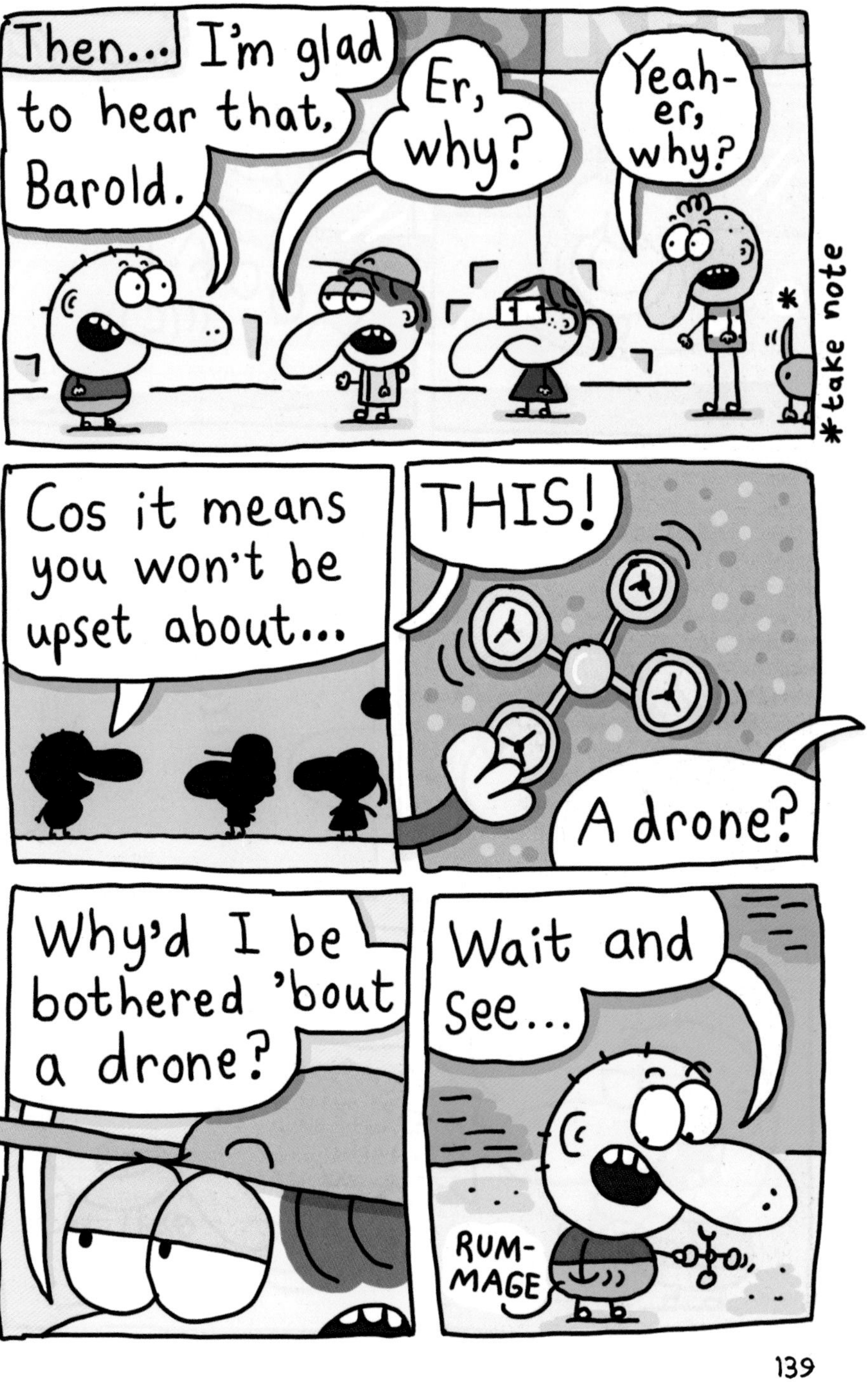
Then...
I'm glad to hear that, Barold.
Er, why?
Yeah- er, why?
*take note
Cos it means you won't be upset about...
THIS!
A drone?
Why'd I be bothered 'bout a drone?
Wait and see...
RUM-MAGE

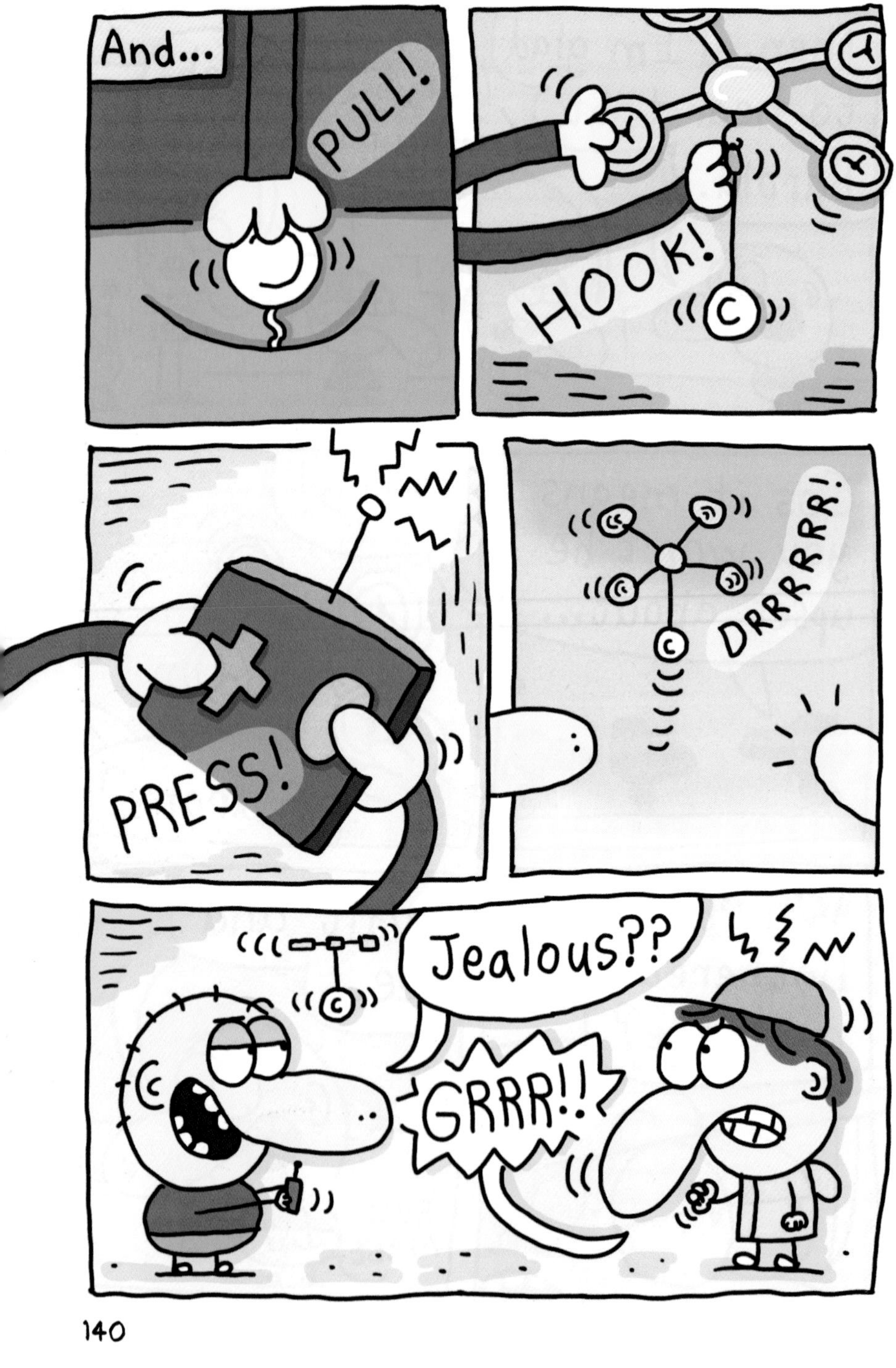
And...
PULL!
HOOK!
PRESS!
DRRRRRR!
Jealous??
GRRR!!

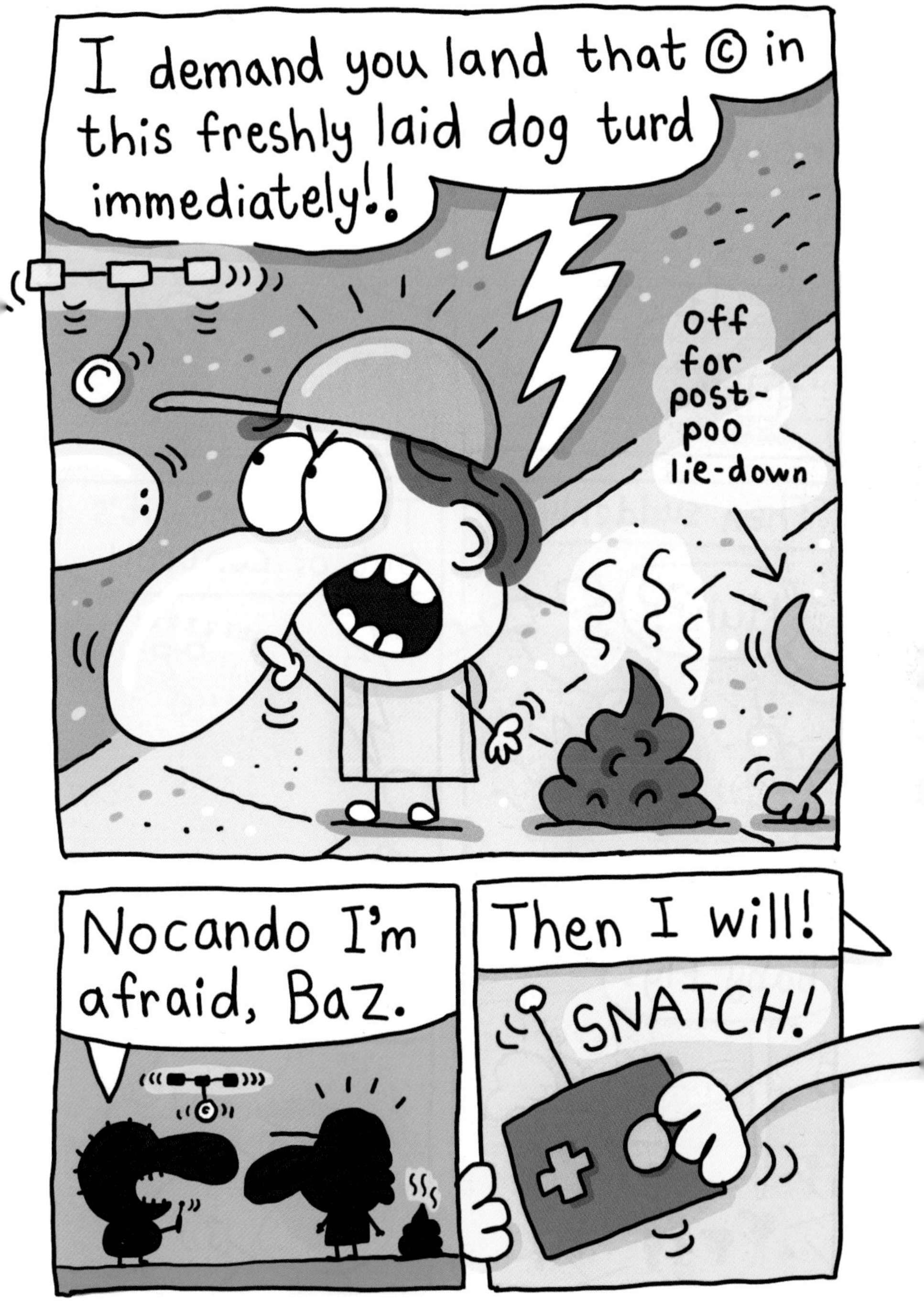
I demand you land that © in this freshly laid dog turd immediately!!
off for post-poo lie-down
Nocando I'm afraid, Baz.
Then I will!
SNATCH!

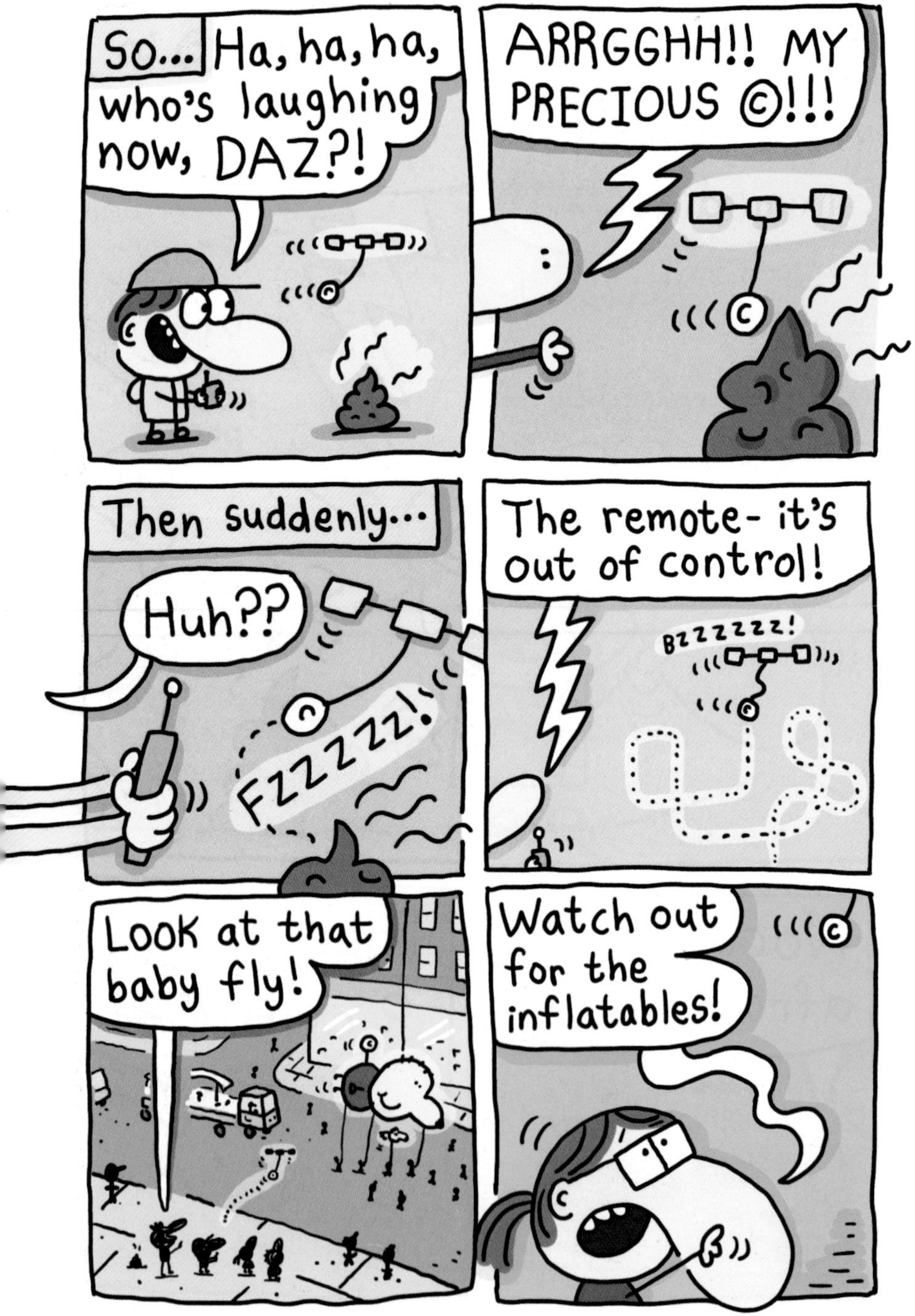
So...
Ha, ha, ha, who's laughing now, DAZ?!
ARRGGHH!! MY PRECIOUS ©!!!
Then suddenly...
Huh??
FZZZZZZ!
The remote- it's out of control!
BZZZZZZ!
LOOK at that baby fly!
Watch out for the inflatables!

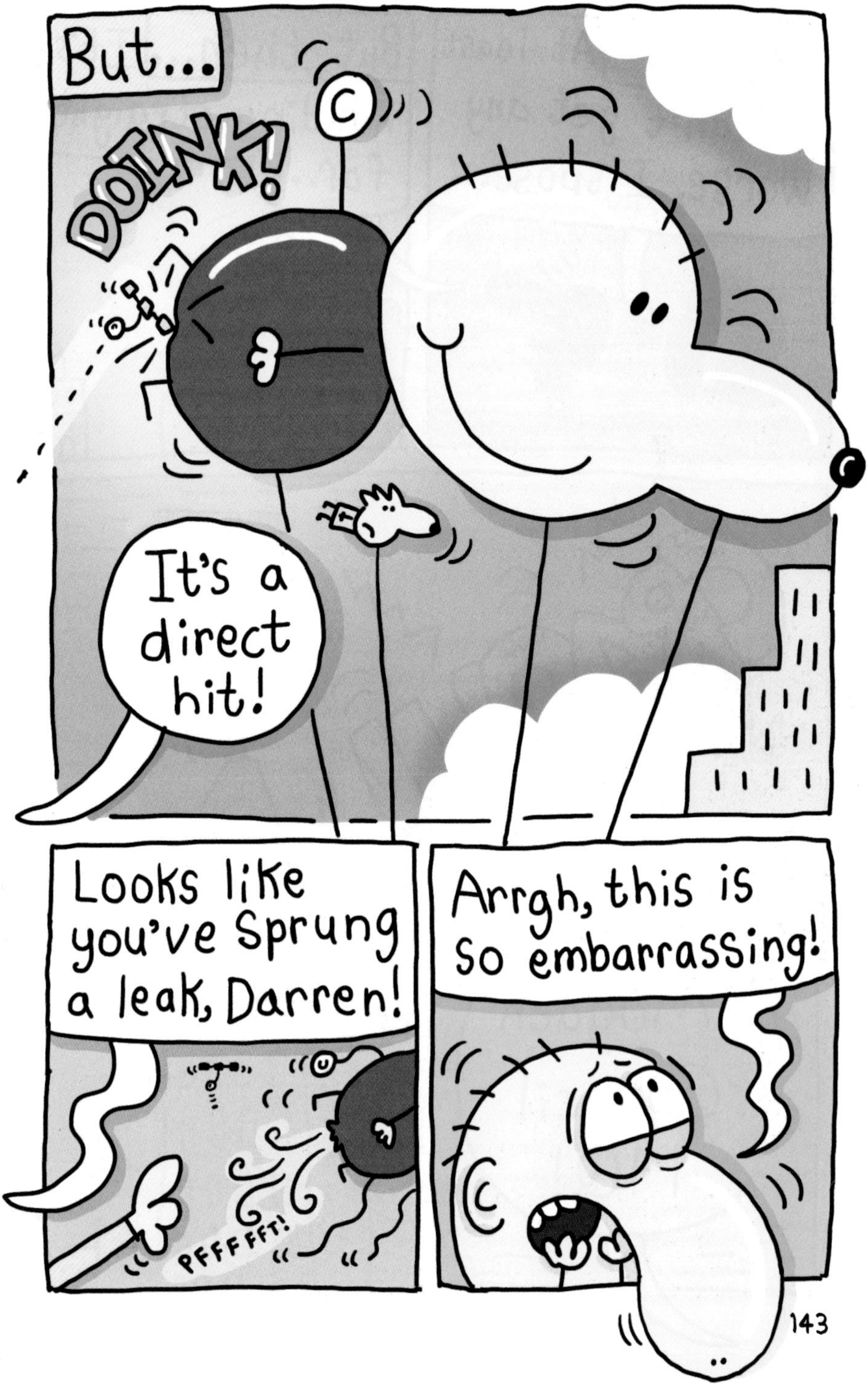
But...
DOINK!
C
It's a direct hit!
Looks like you've sprung a leak, Darren!
PFFFFFT!
Arrgh, this is so embarrassing!

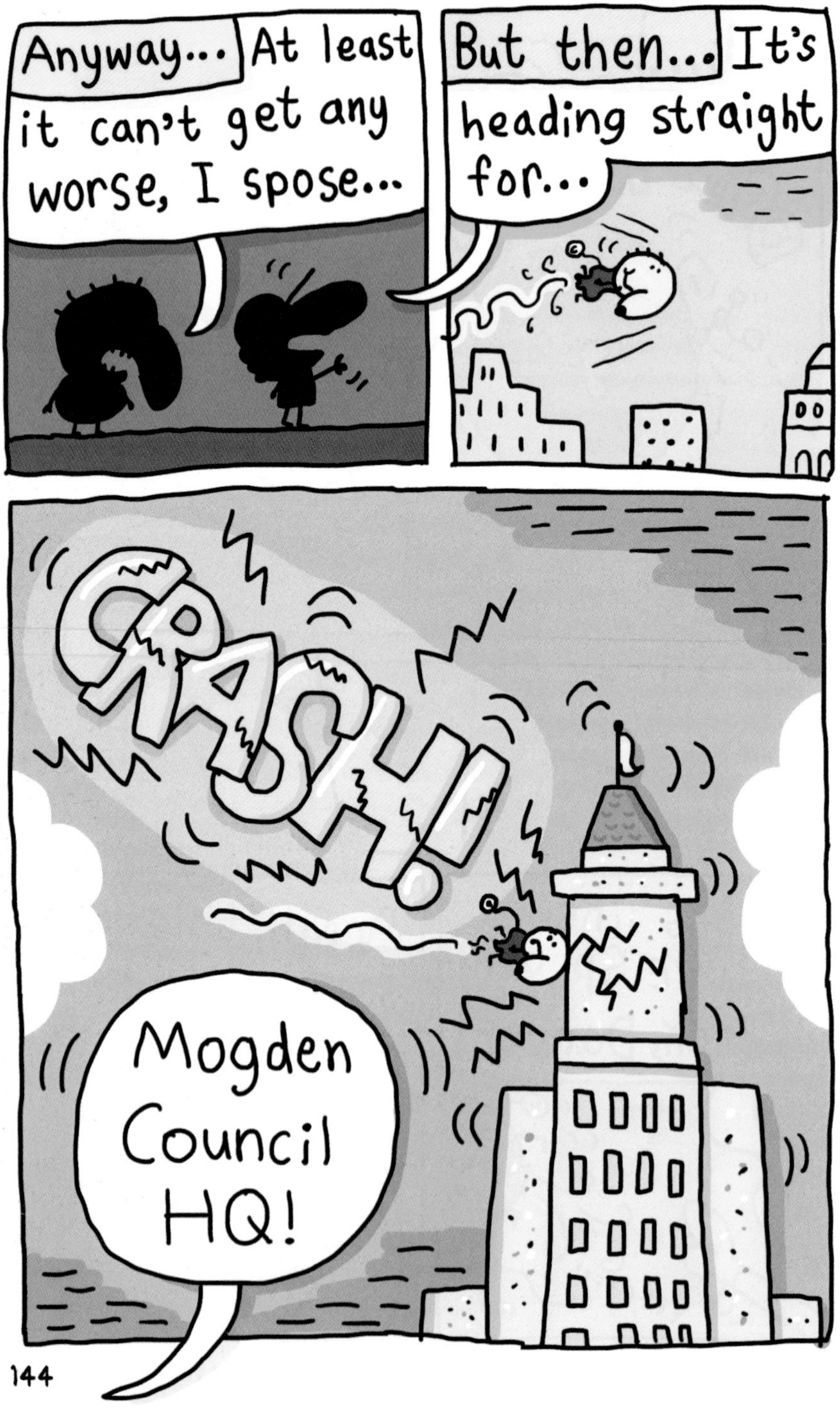
Anyway...
At least it can't get any worse, I spose...
But then...
It's heading straight for...
CRASH!
Mogden Council HQ!

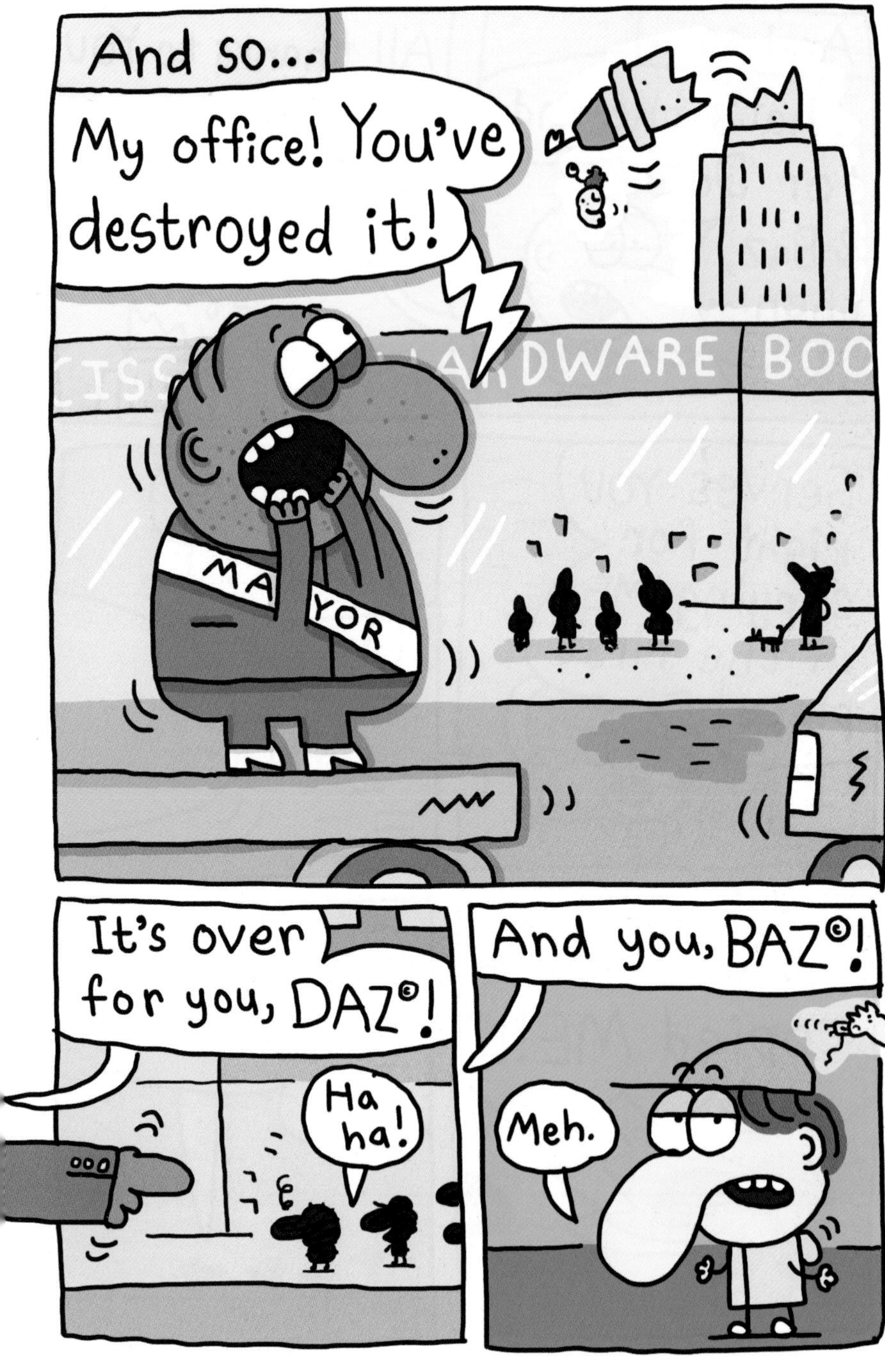
And so...
My office! You've destroyed it!
HARDWARE
BOO
MAYOR
It's over for you, DAZ©!
Ha ha!
And you, BAZ©!
Meh.

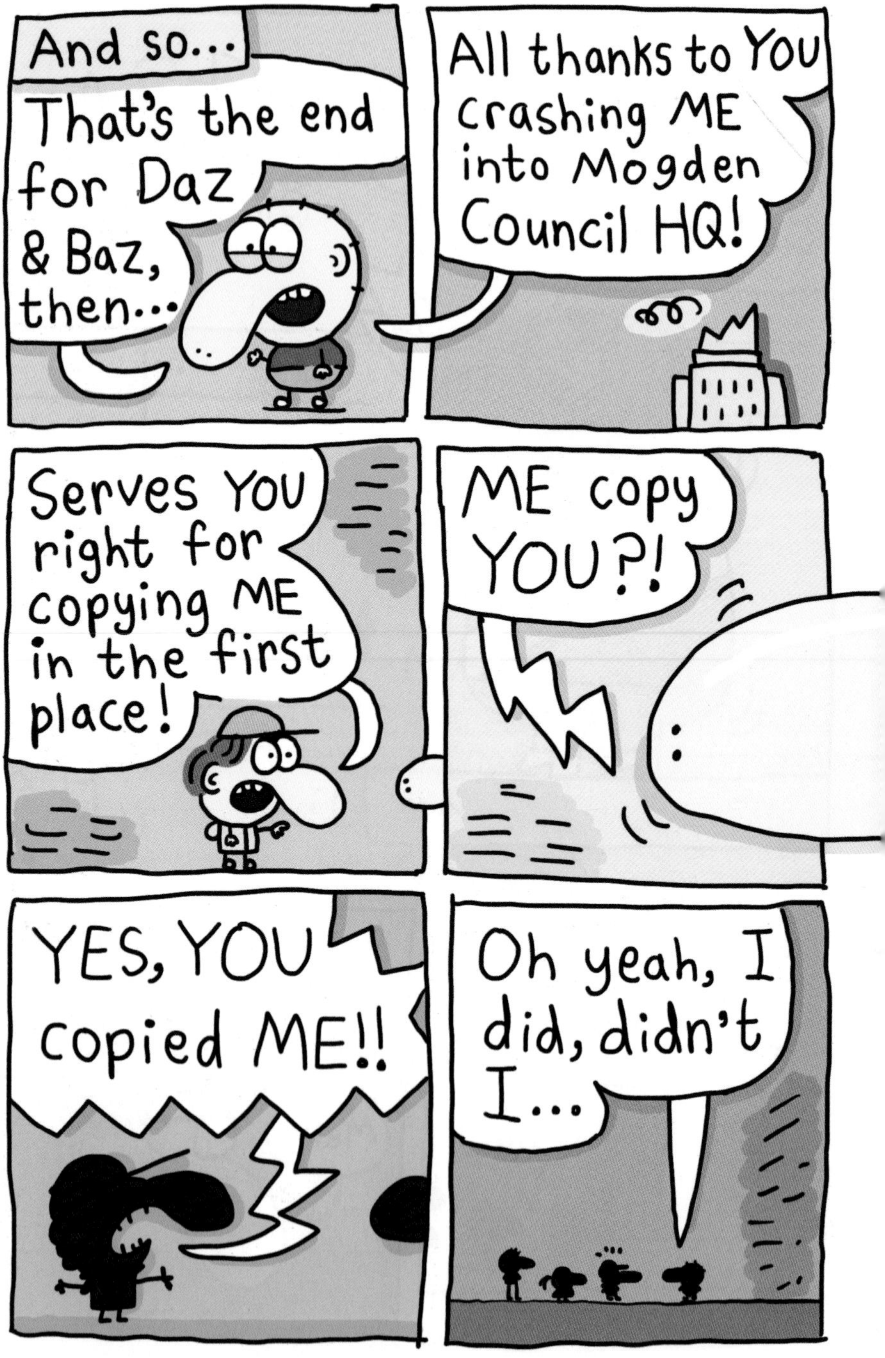
And so...
That's the end for Daz & Baz, then...
All thanks to YOU crashing ME into Mogden Council HQ!
Serves YOU right for copying ME in the first place!
ME copy YOU?!
YES, YOU copied ME!!
Oh yeah, I did, didn't I...

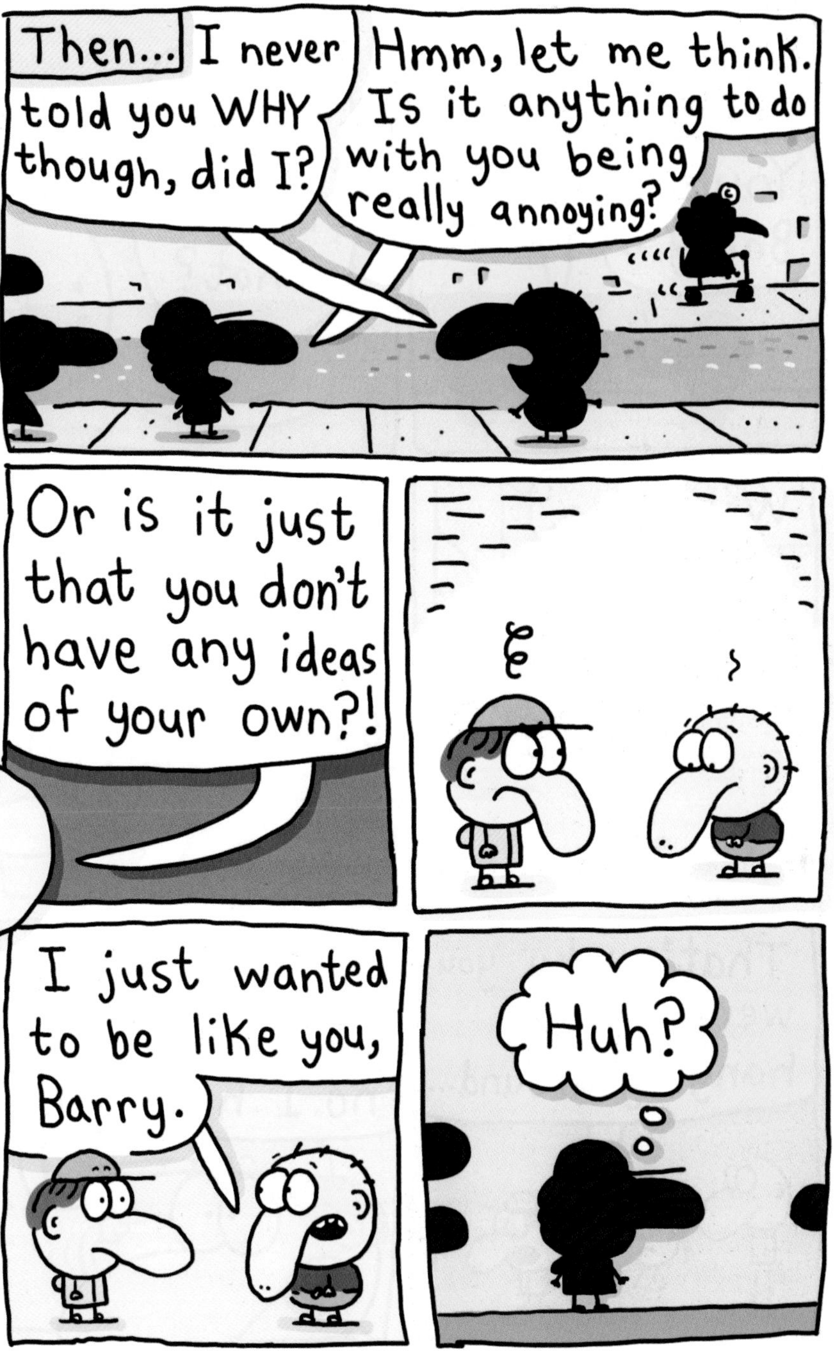
Then...
I never told you WHY though, did I?
Hmm, let me think. Is it anything to do with you being really annoying?
Or is it just that you don't have any ideas of your own?!
I just wanted to be like you, Barry.
Huh?

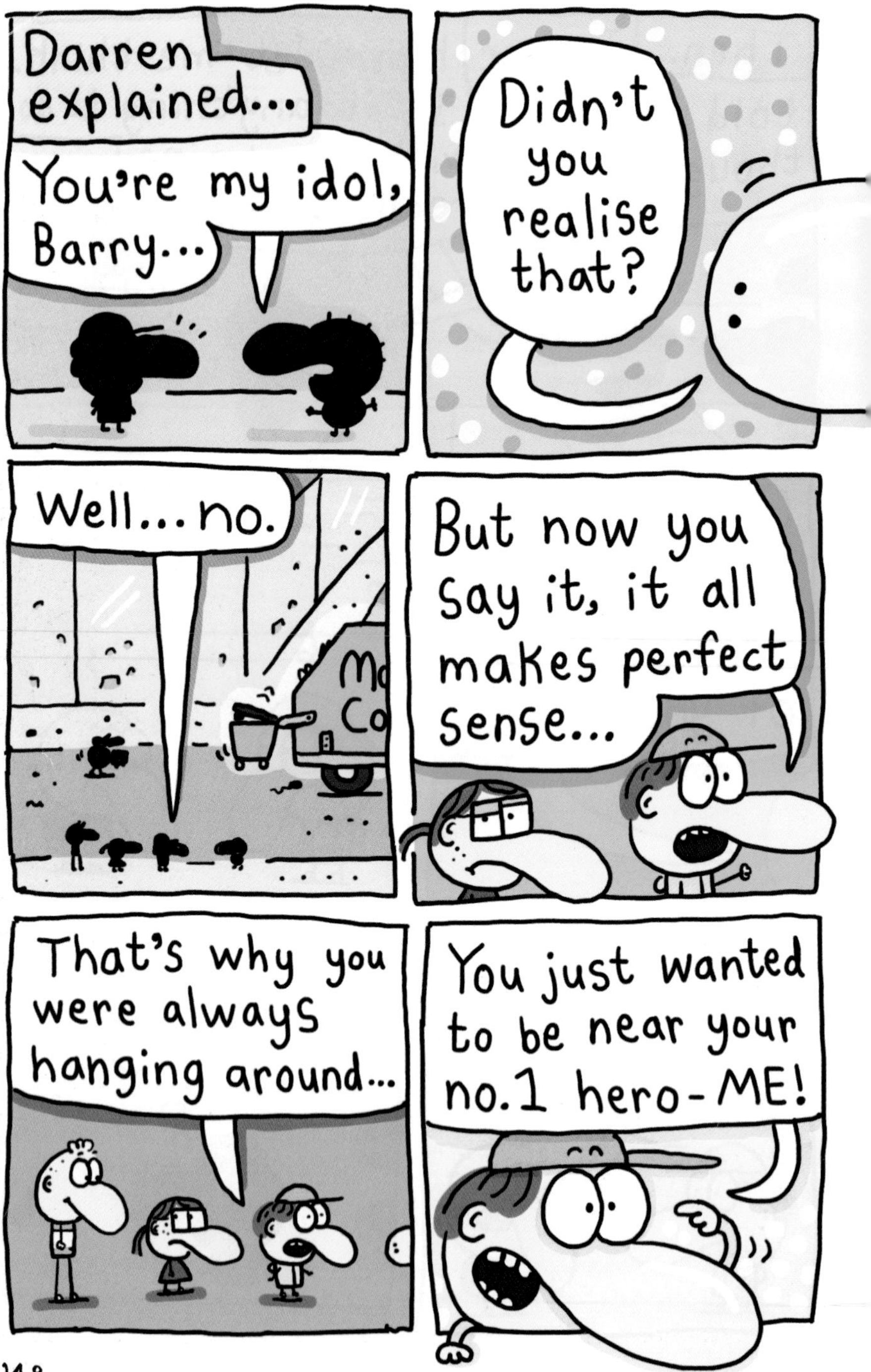
Darren explained...
You're my idol, Barry...
Didn't you realise that?
Well... no.
But now you say it, it all makes perfect sense...
That's why you were always hanging around...
You just wanted to be near your no.1 hero - ME!

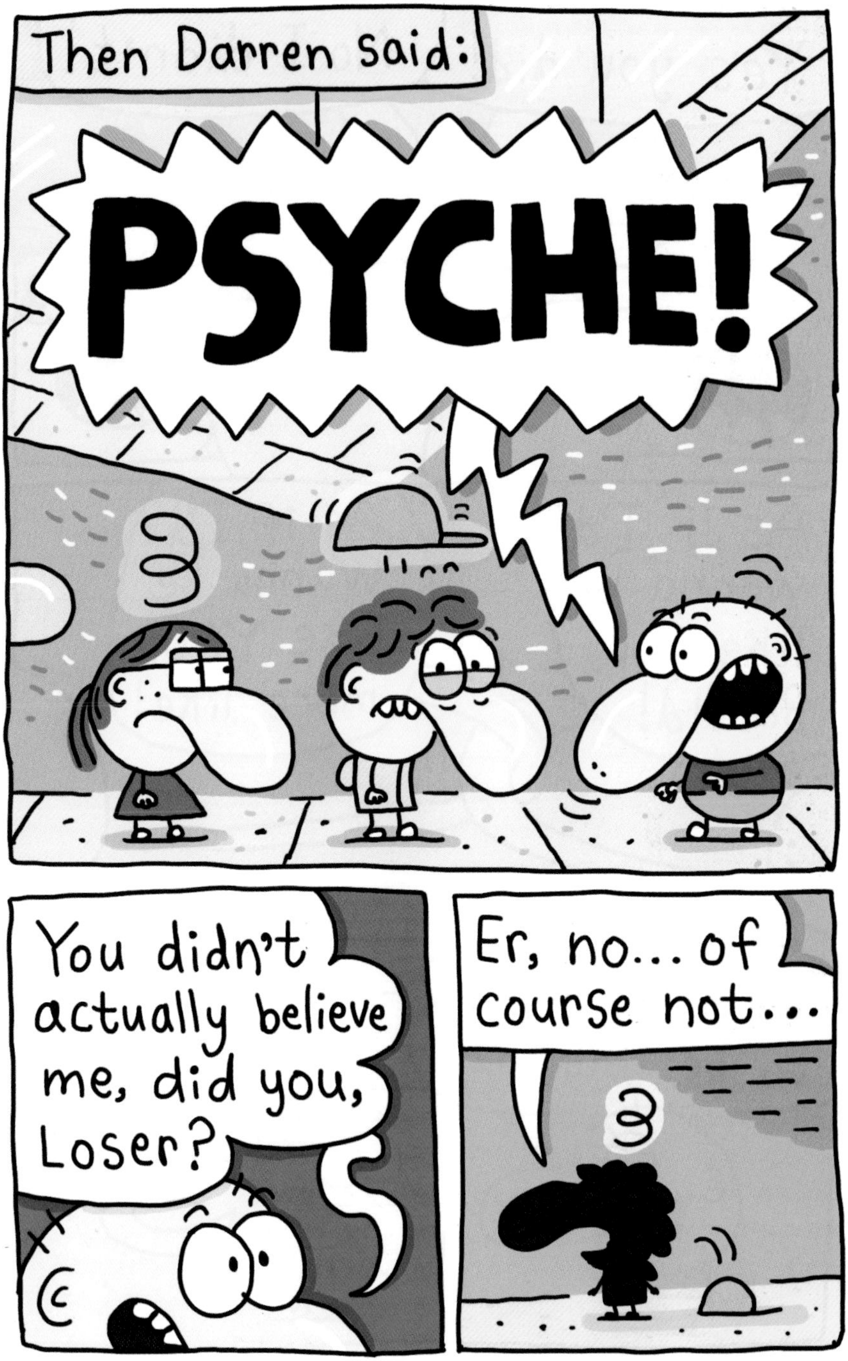
Then Darren said:
PSYCHE!
You didn't actually believe me, did you, Loser?
Er, no... of course not...

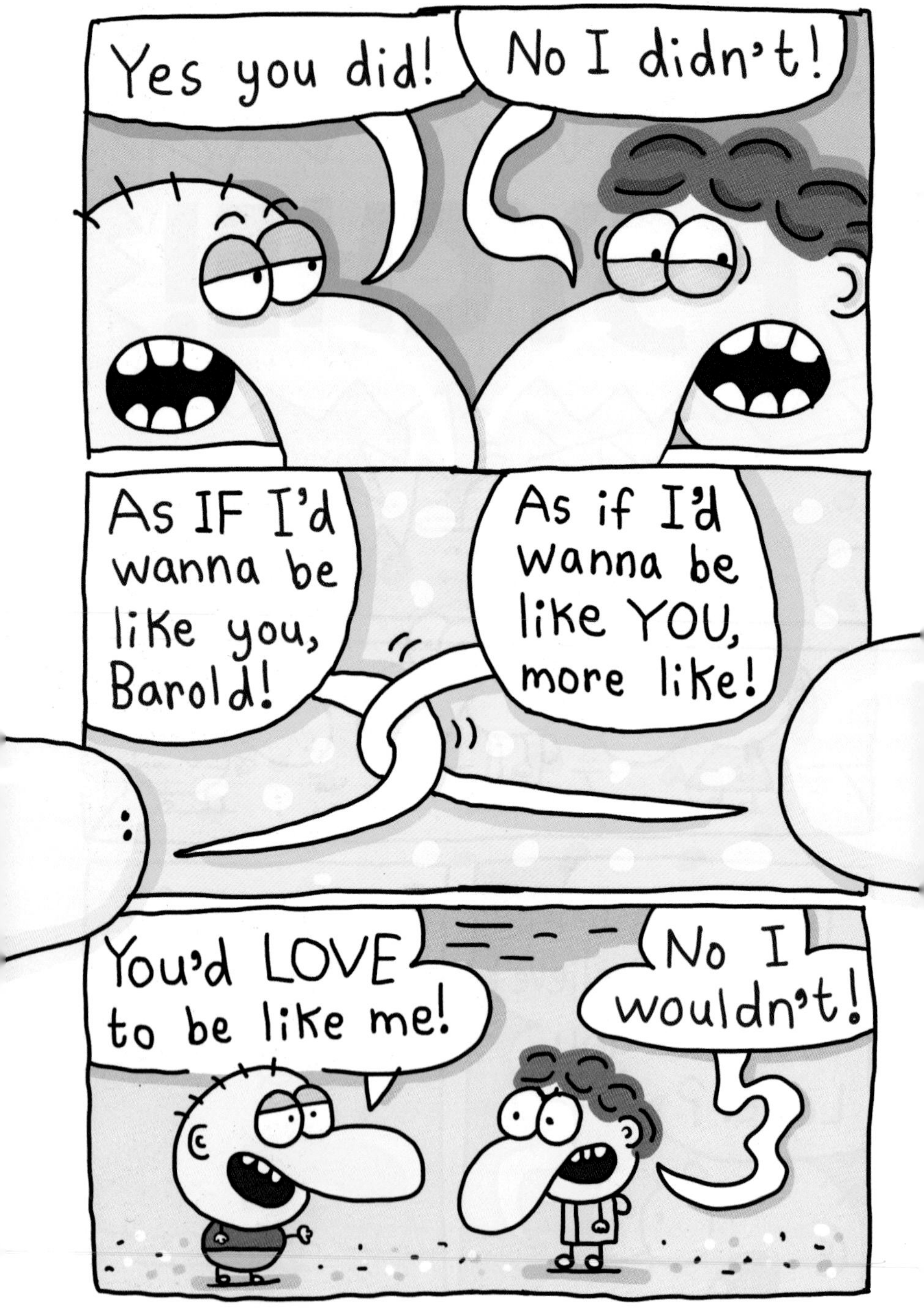

Yes you did!
No I didn't!
As IF I'd wanna be like you, Barold!
As if I'd wanna be like YOU, more like!
You'd LOVE to be like me!
No I wouldn't!

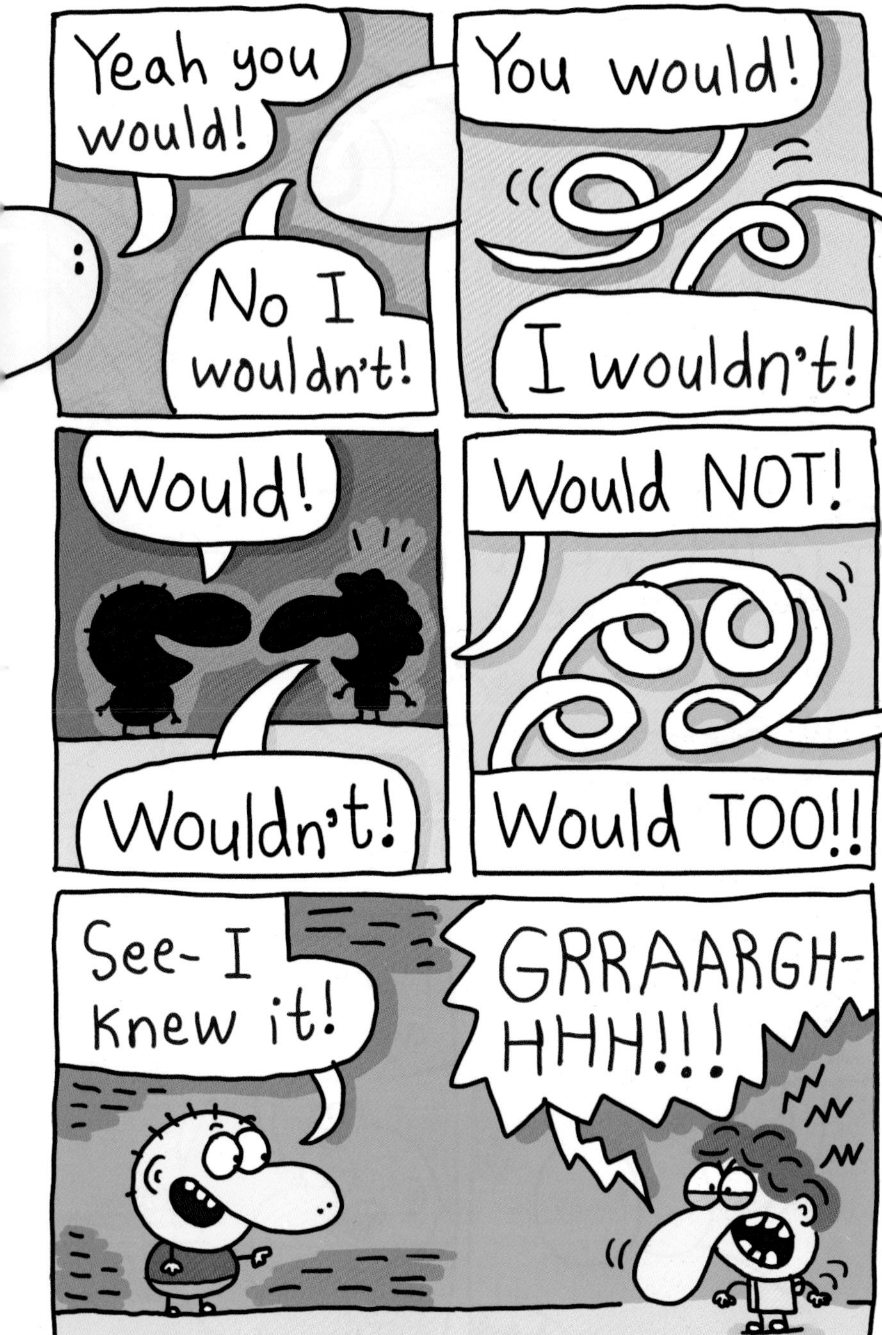
Yeah you would!
No I wouldn't!
You would!
I wouldn't!
Would!
Wouldn't!
Would NOT!
Would TOO!!
See- I knew it!
GRRAARGH-HHH!!!

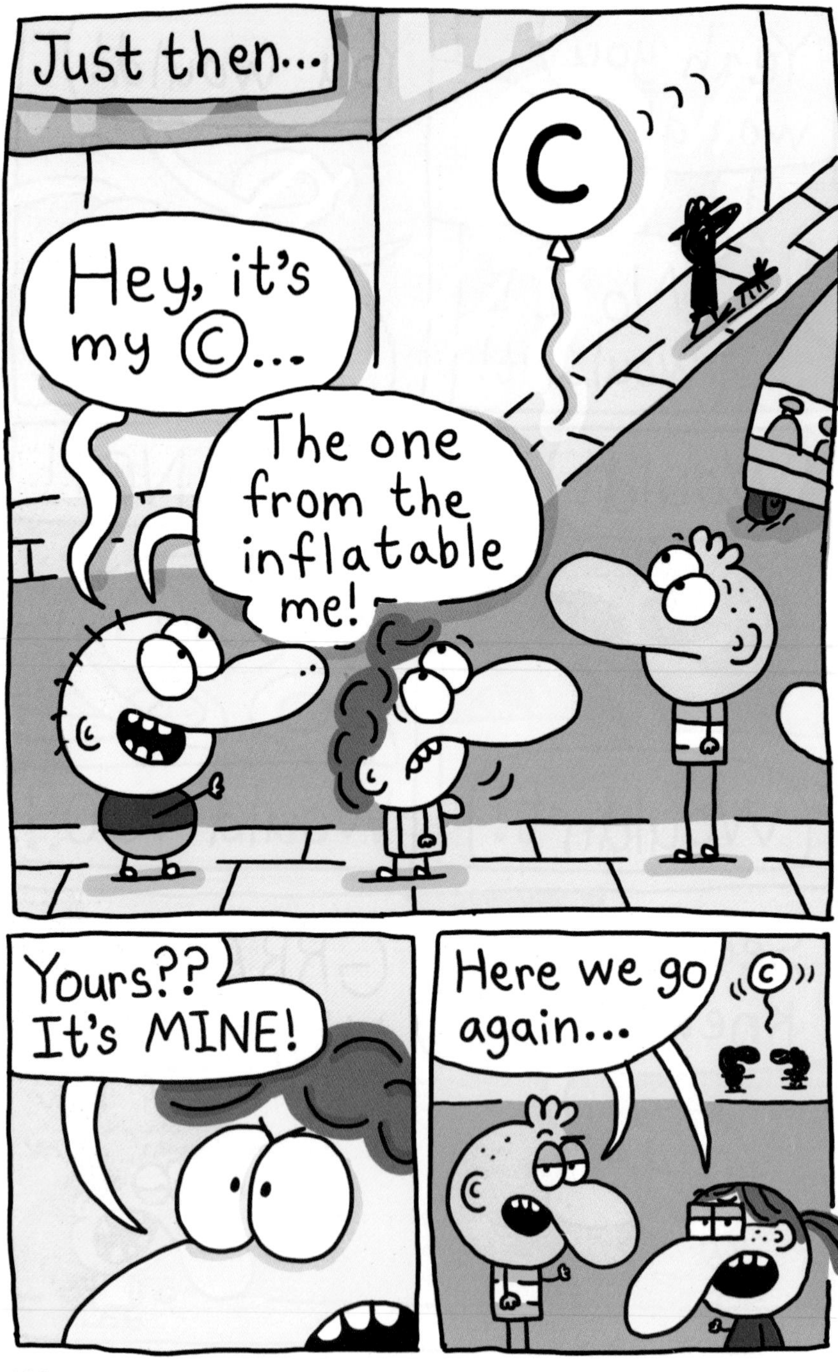
Just then...
C
Hey, it's my ©...
The one from the inflatable me!
Yours?? It's MINE!
Here we go again...
©

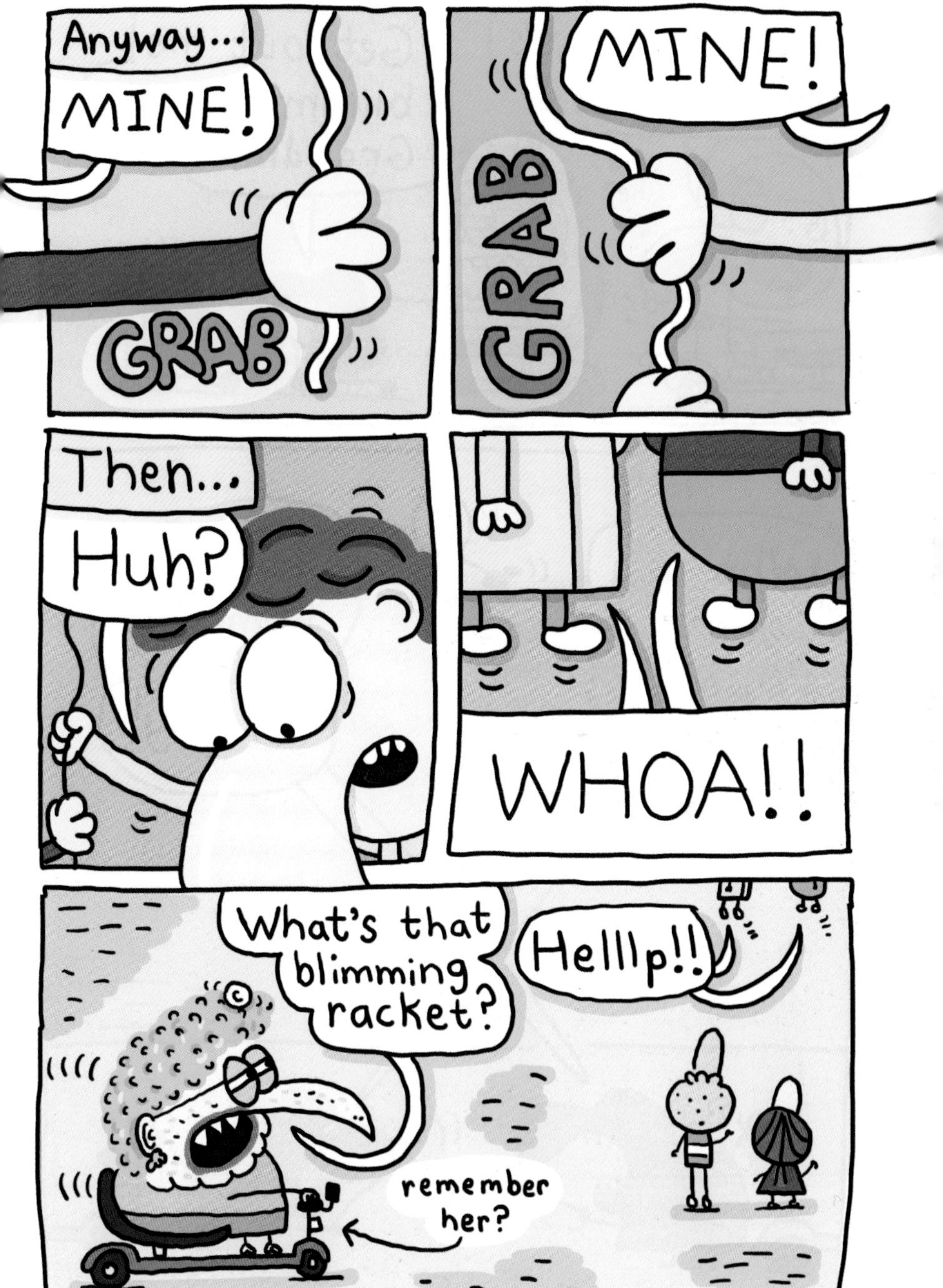
Anyway...
MINE!
GRAB
MINE!
GRAB
Then...
Huh?
WHOA!!
What's that blimming racket?
Helllp!!
remember her?

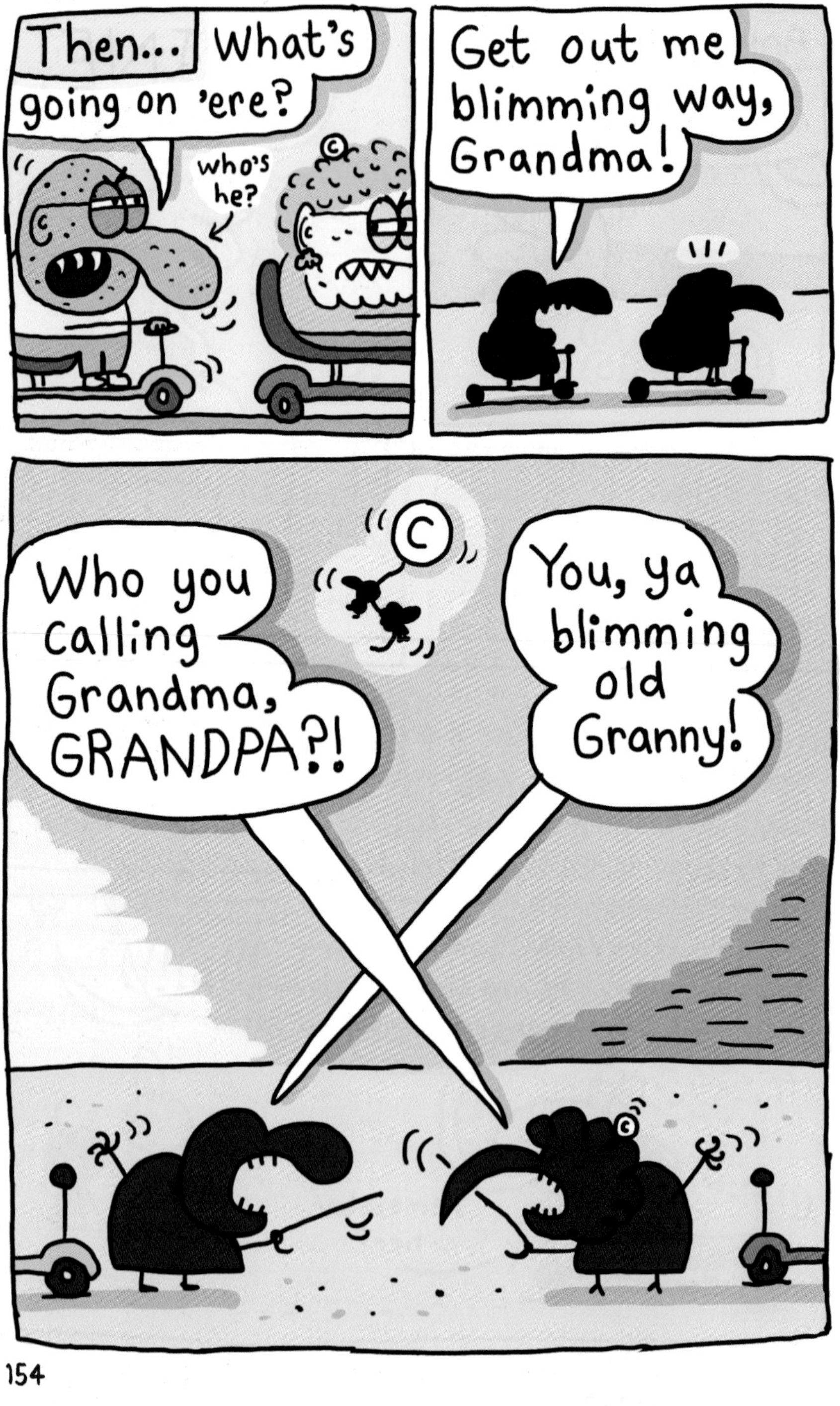
Then...
What's going on 'ere?
who's he?
Get out me blimming way, Grandma!
Who you calling Grandma, GRANDPA?!
You, ya blimming old Granny!

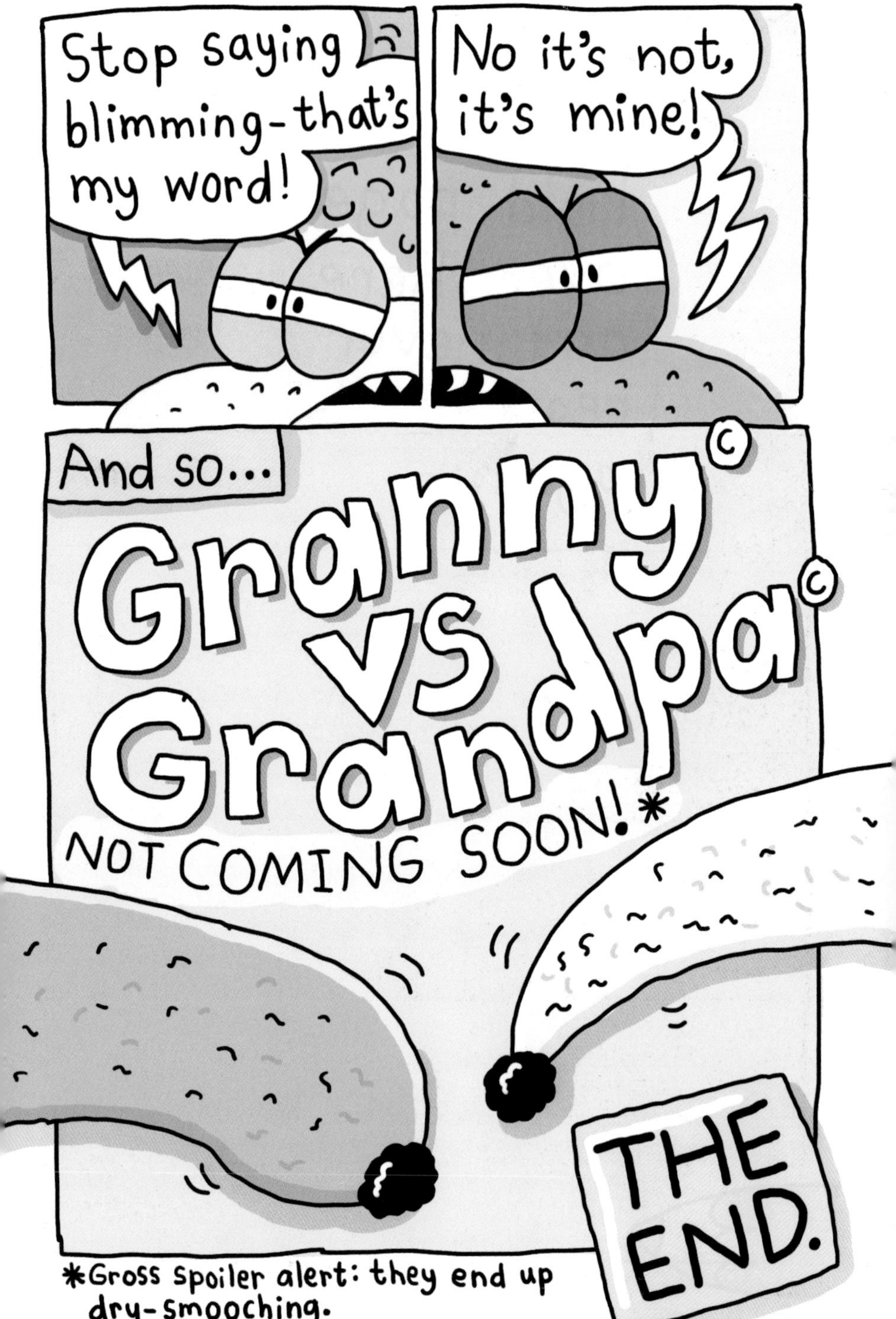
Stop saying blimming- that's my word!
No it's not, it's mine!
And so...
Granny© VS Grandpa©
NOT COMING SOON!*
THE END.
*Gross spoiler alert: they end up dry-smooching.

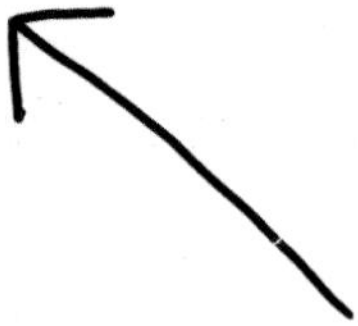

Fold page
over here
and never
read book
again.

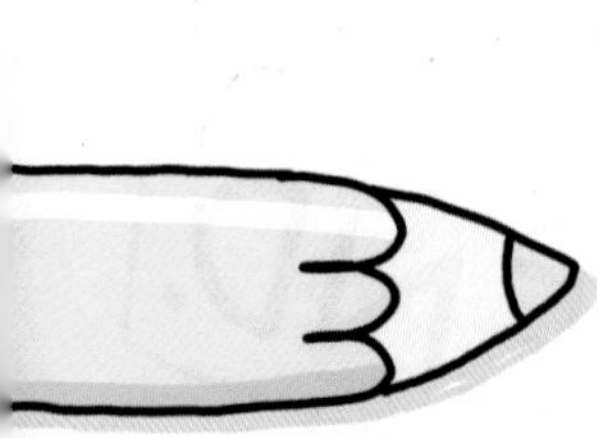

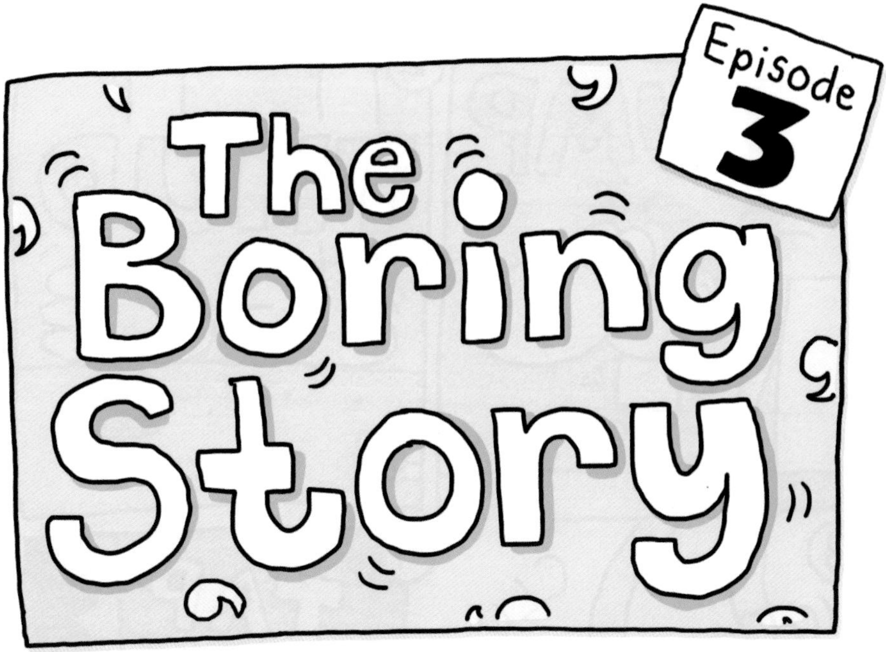
Episode 3
The Boring Story

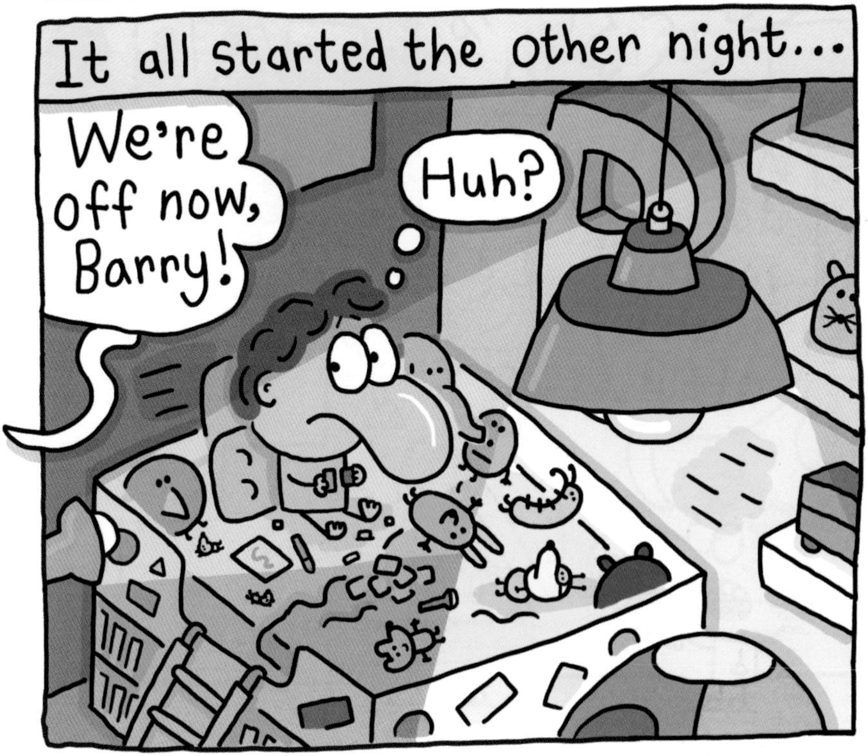
It all started the other night...
We're off now, Barry!
Huh?

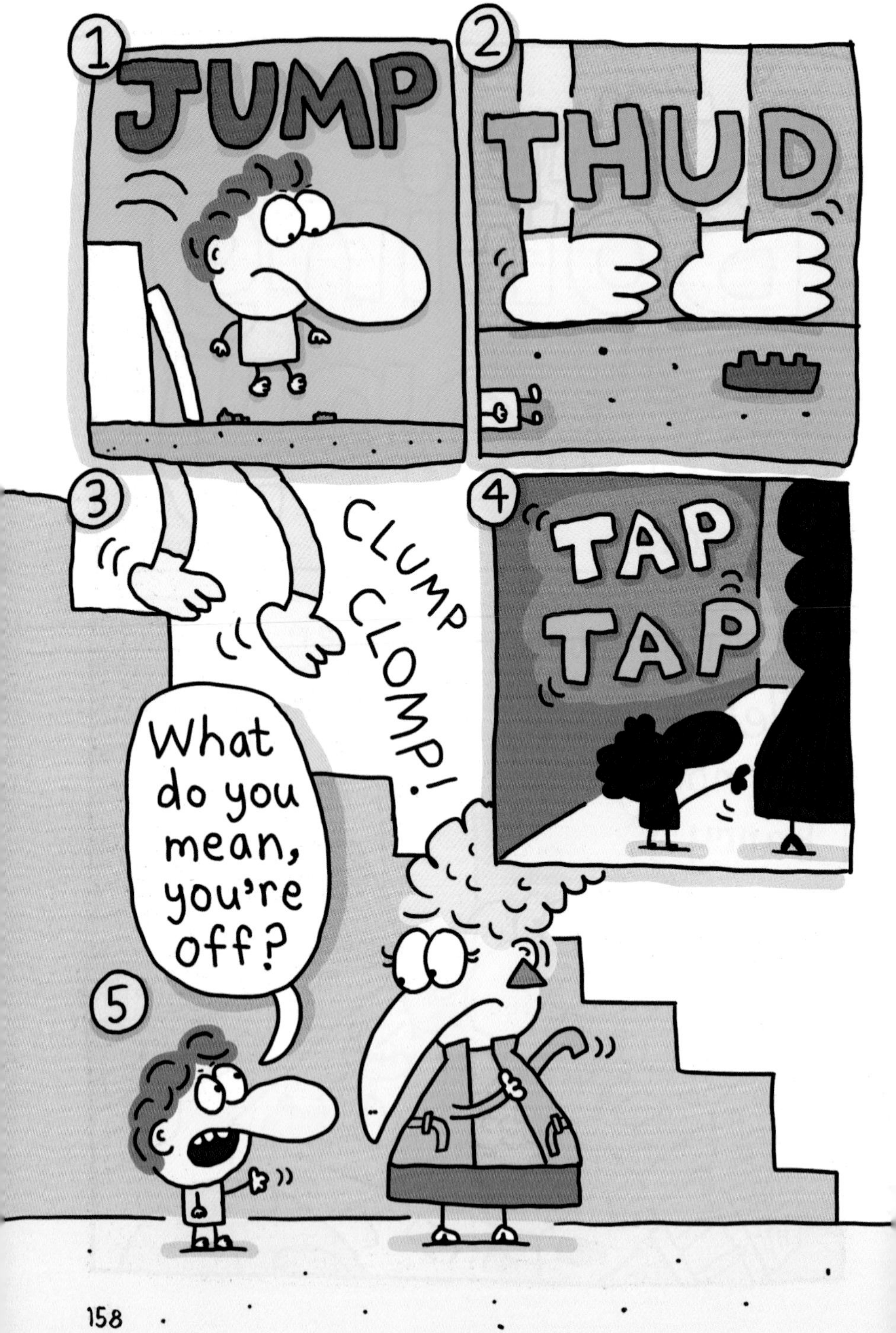
1
JUMP
2
THUD
3
CLUMP CLOMP!
4
TAP TAP
5
What do you mean, you're off?

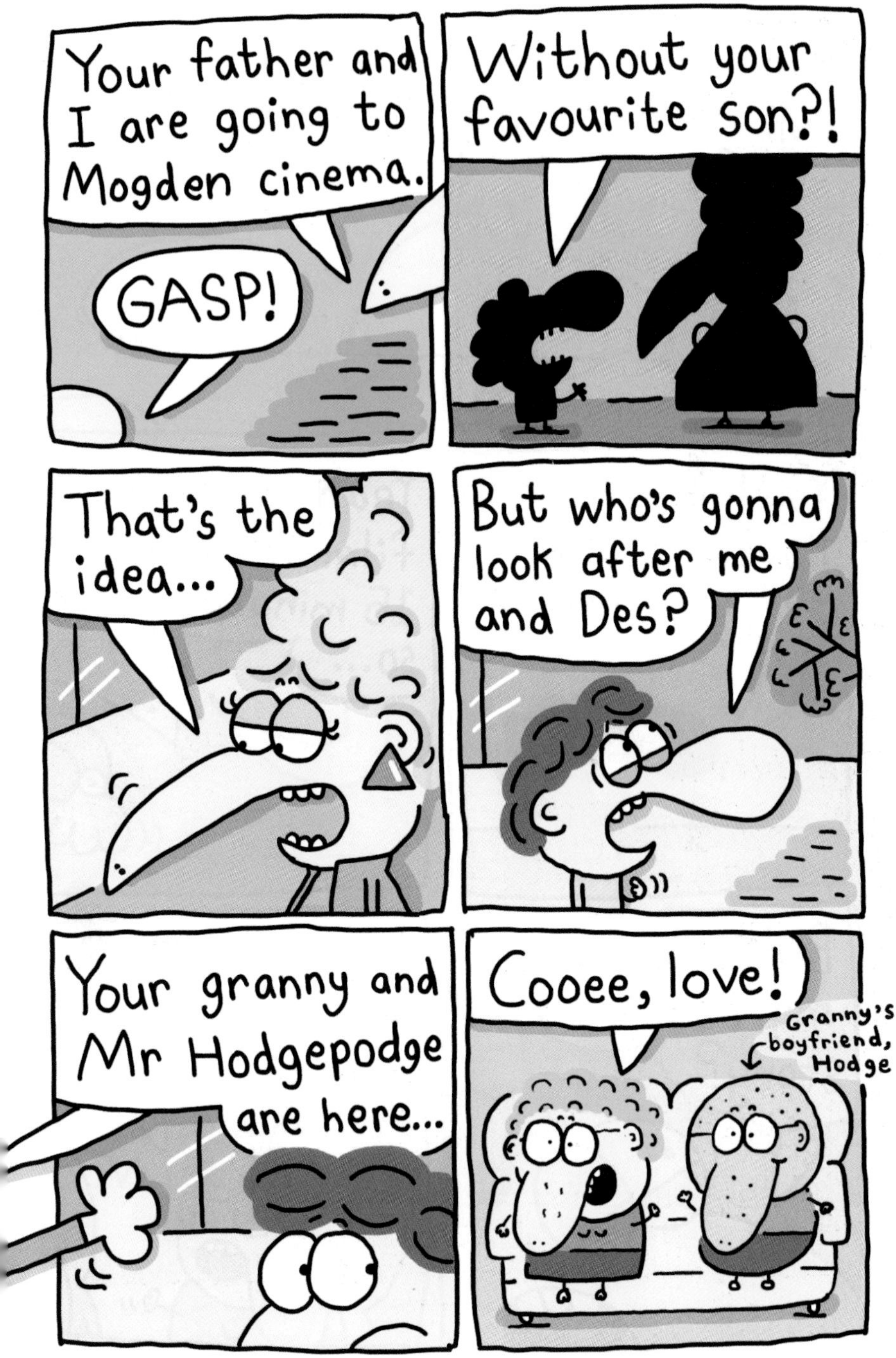
Your father and I are going to Mogden cinema.
GASP!
Without your favourite son?!
That's the idea...
But who's gonna look after me and Des?
Your granny and Mr Hodgepodge are here...
Cooee, love!
Granny's boyfriend, Hodge

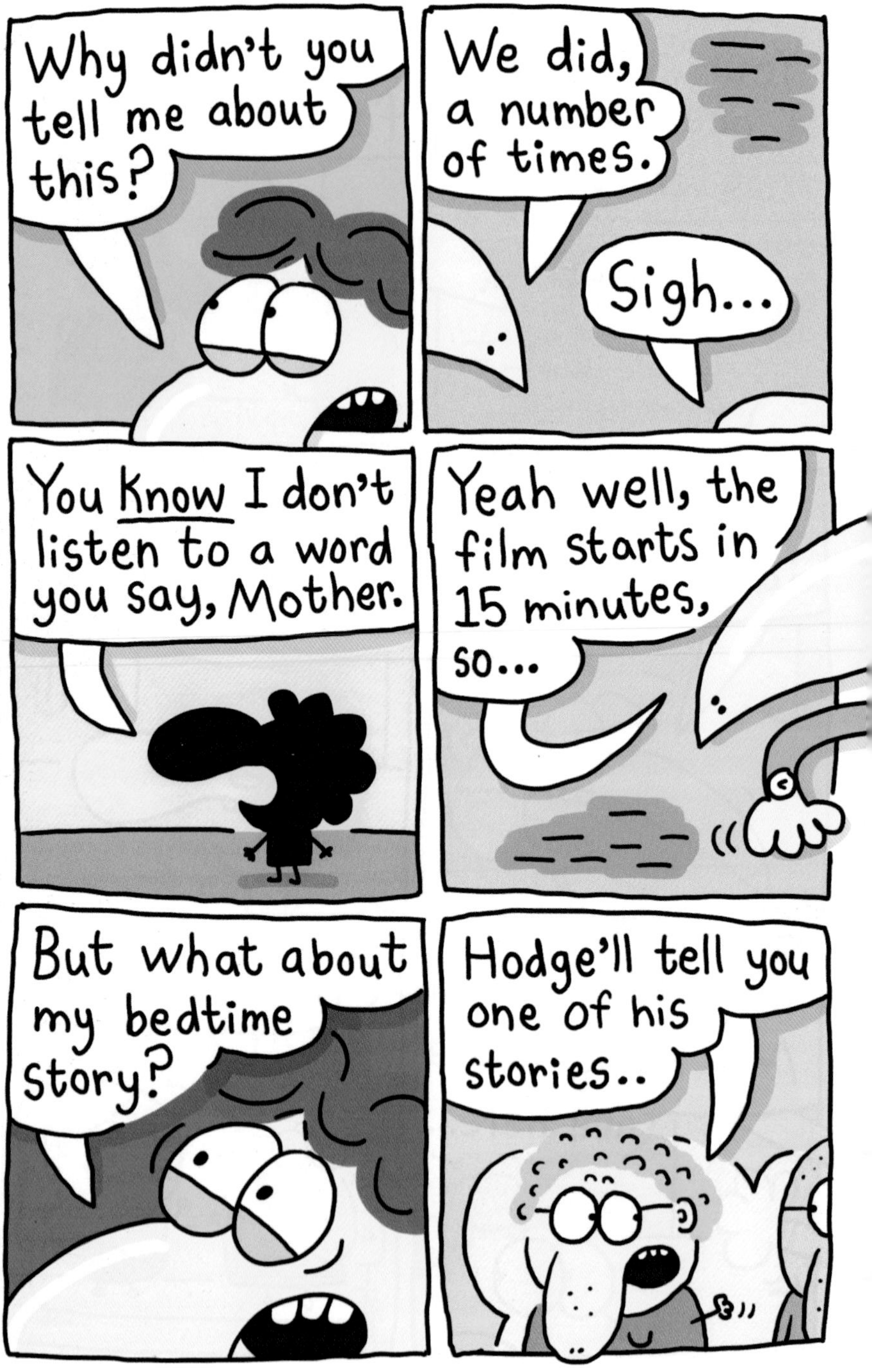
Why didn't you tell me about this?
We did, a number of times.
Sigh...
You Know I don't listen to a word you say, Mother.
Yeah well, the film starts in 15 minutes, so...
But what about my bedtime story?
Hodge'll tell you one of his stories..

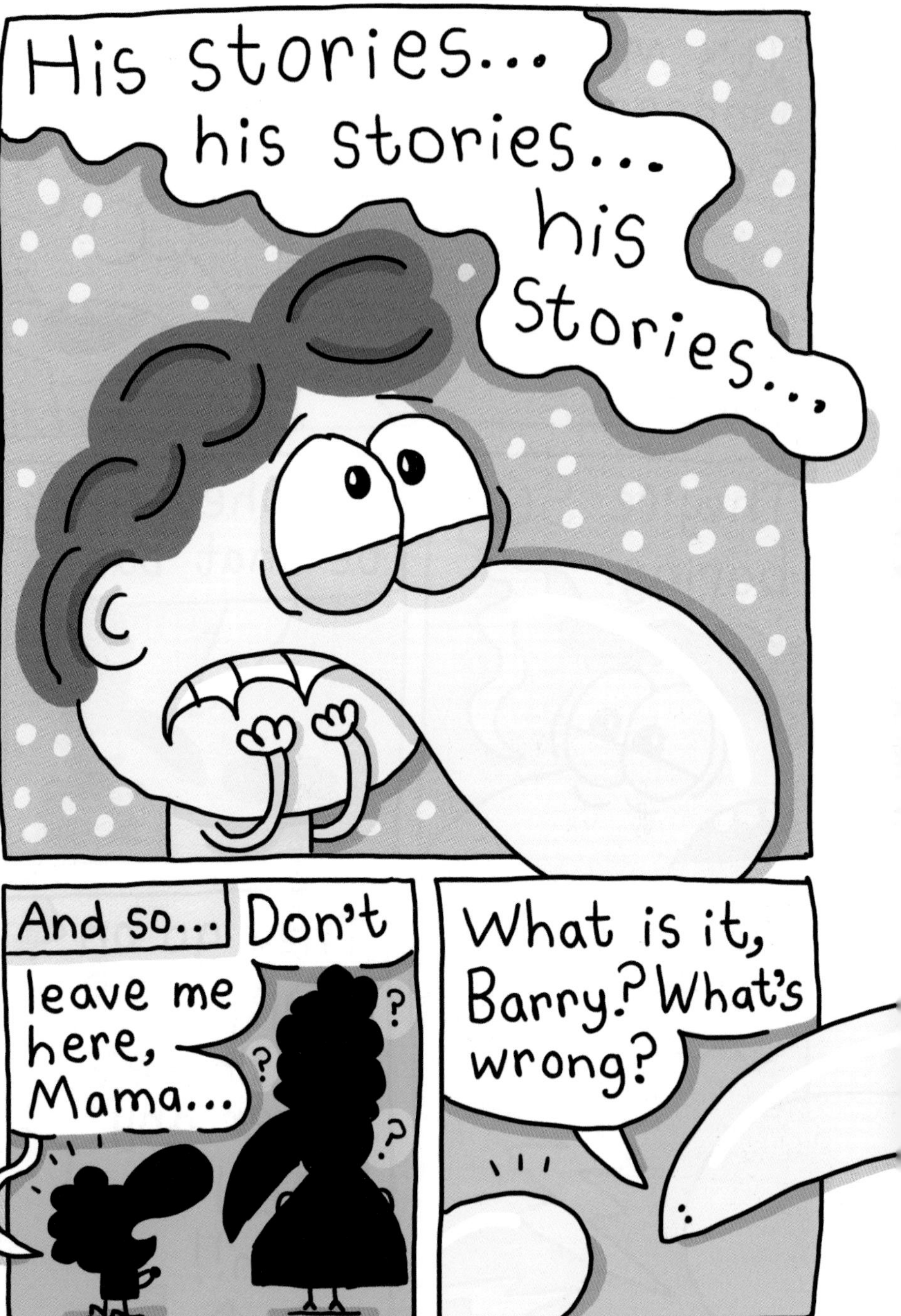
His stories... his stories... his Stories...
And so...
Don't leave me here, Mama...
What is it, Barry? What's wrong?

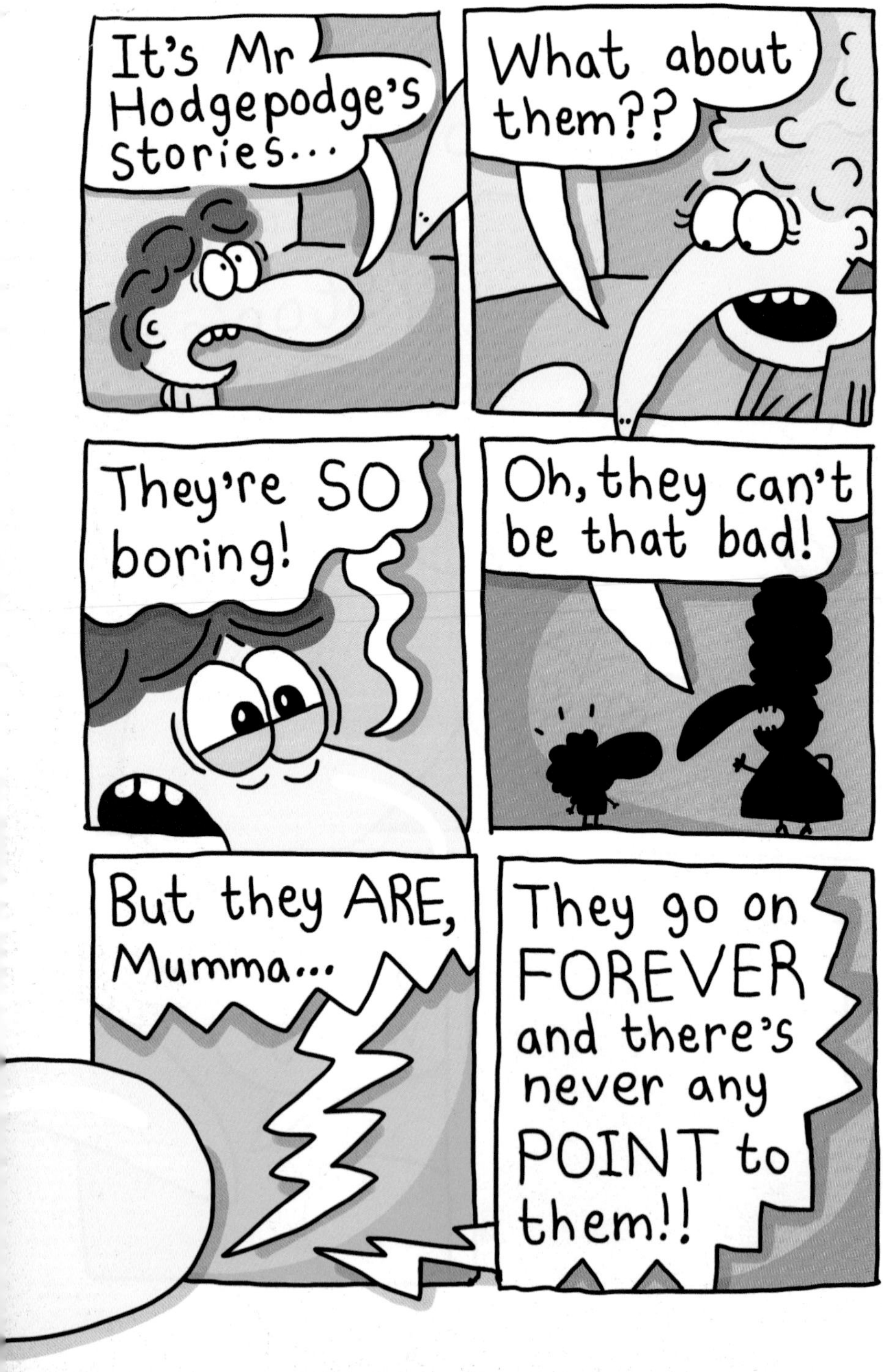
It's Mr Hodgepodge's stories...
What about them??
They're SO boring!
Oh, they can't be that bad!
But they ARE, Mumma...
They go on FOREVER and there's never any POINT to them!!

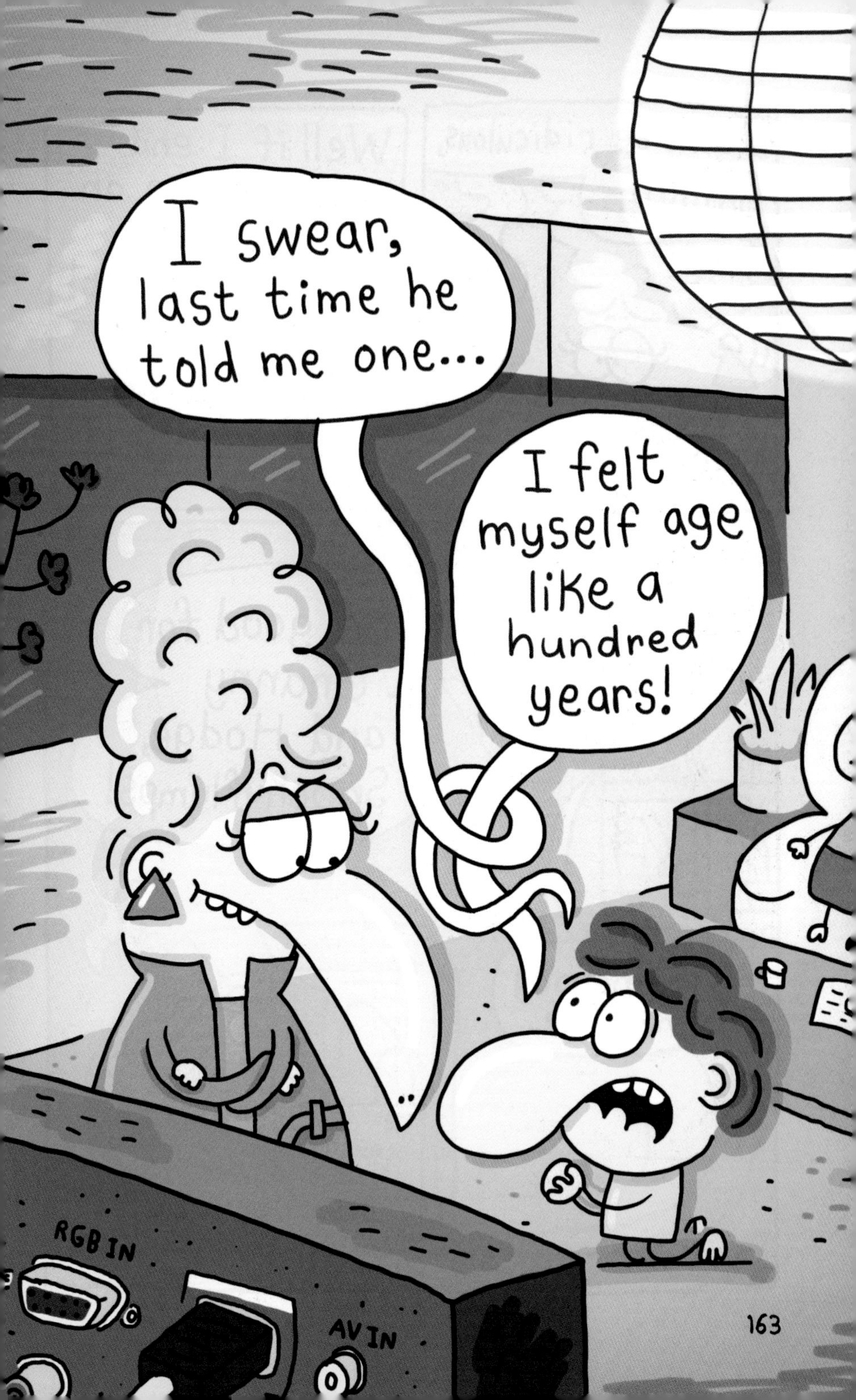
I swear, last time he told me one...
I felt myself age like a hundred years!
RGB IN
AV IN

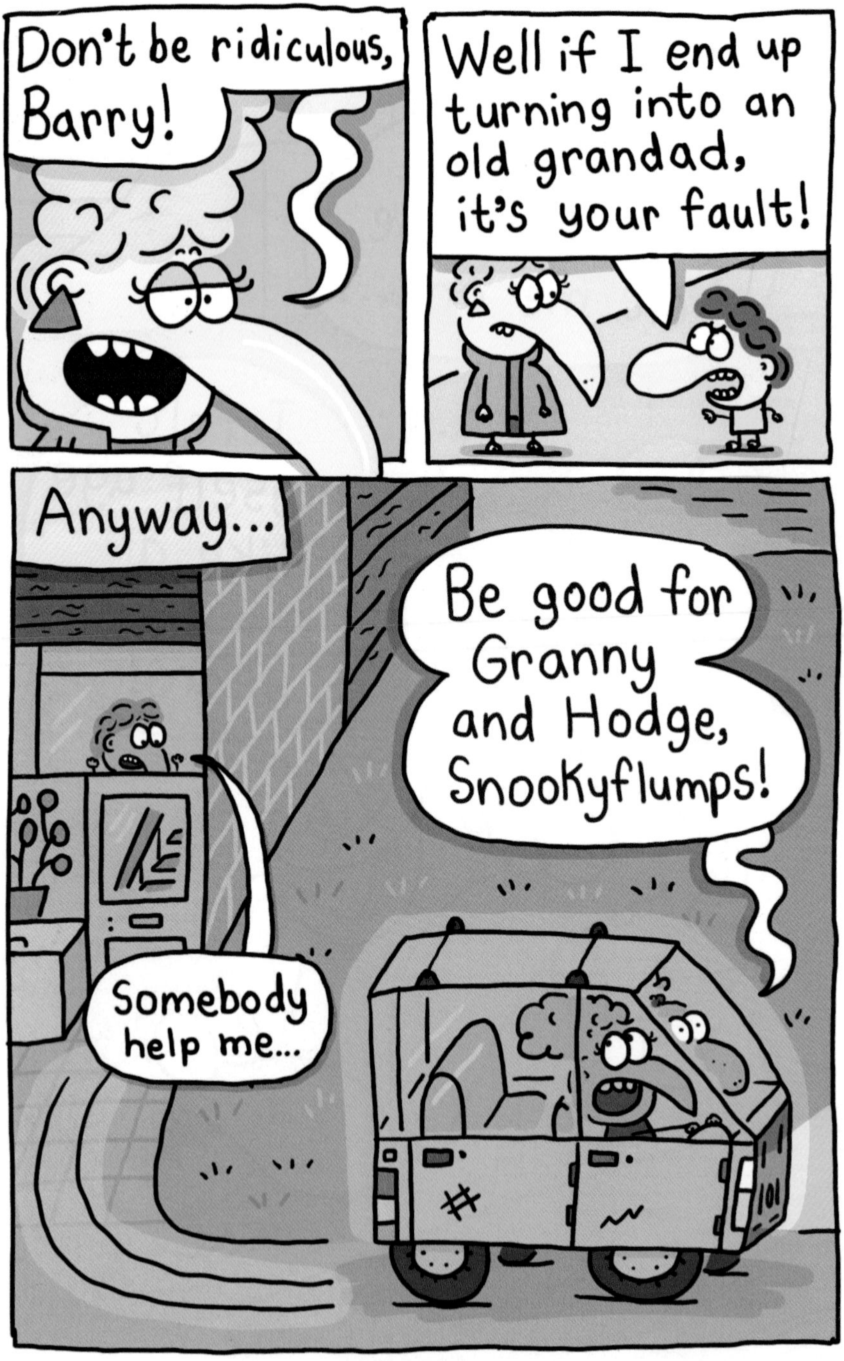
Don't be ridiculous, Barry!
Well if I end up turning into an old grandad, it's your fault!
Anyway...
Be good for Granny and Hodge, Snookyflumps!
Somebody help me...

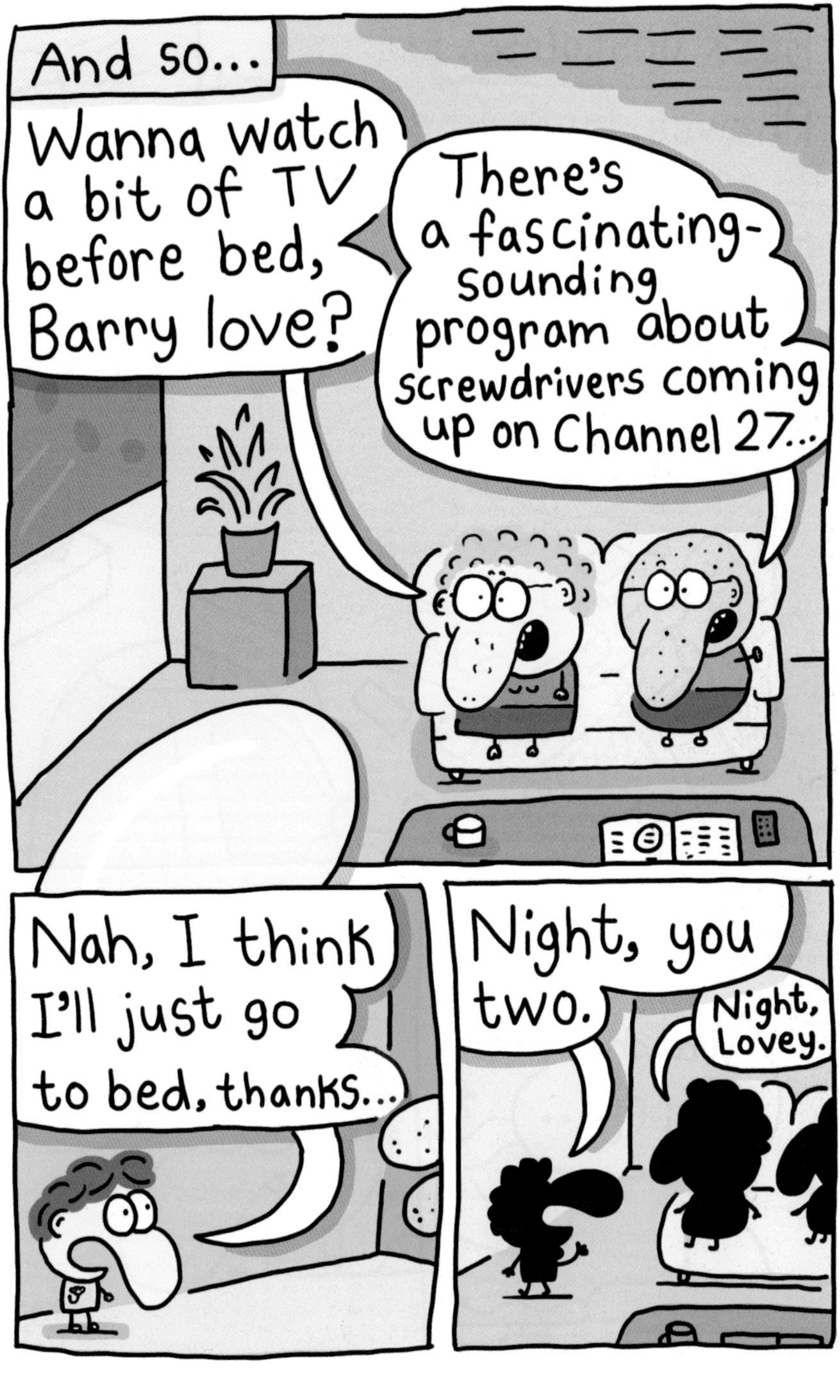
And so...
Wanna watch a bit of TV before bed, Barry love?
There's a fascinating-sounding program about screwdrivers coming up on Channel 27...
Nah, I think I'll just go to bed, thanks...
Night, you two.
Night, Lovey.

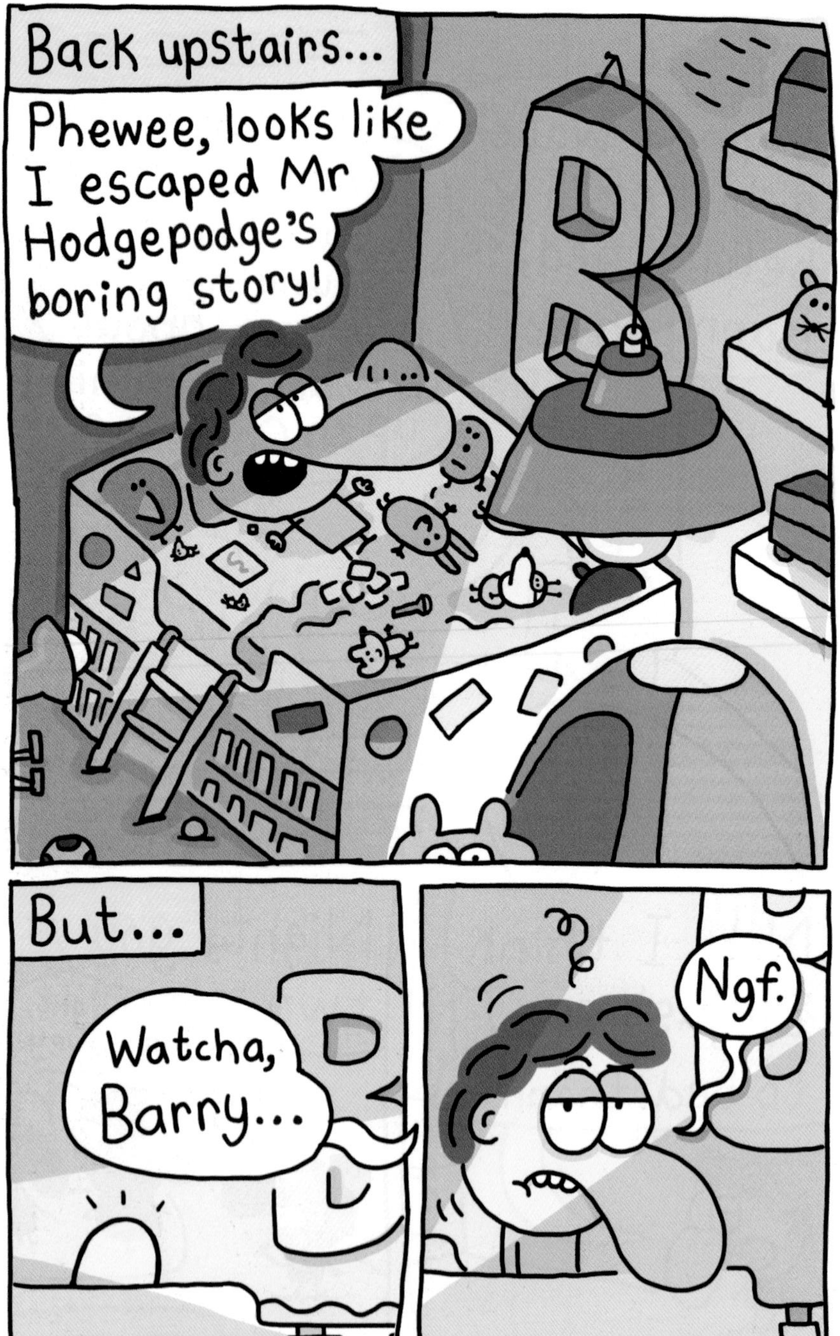
Back upstairs...
Phewee, looks like I escaped Mr Hodgepodge's boring story!
But...
Watcha, Barry...
Ngf.

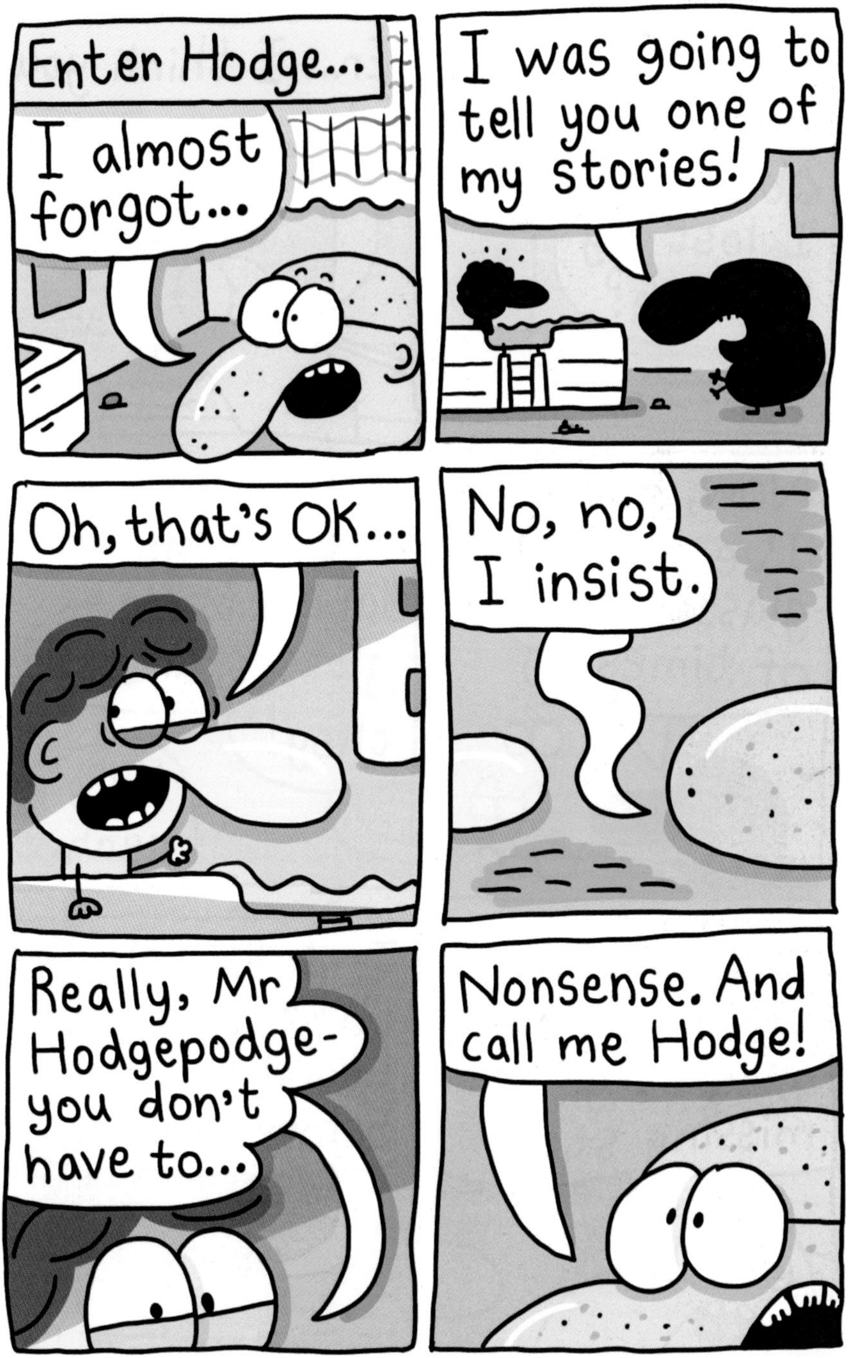
Enter Hodge...
I almost forgot...
I was going to tell you one of my stories!
Oh, that's OK...
No, no, I insist.
Really, Mr Hodgepodge-you don't have to...
Nonsense. And call me Hodge!

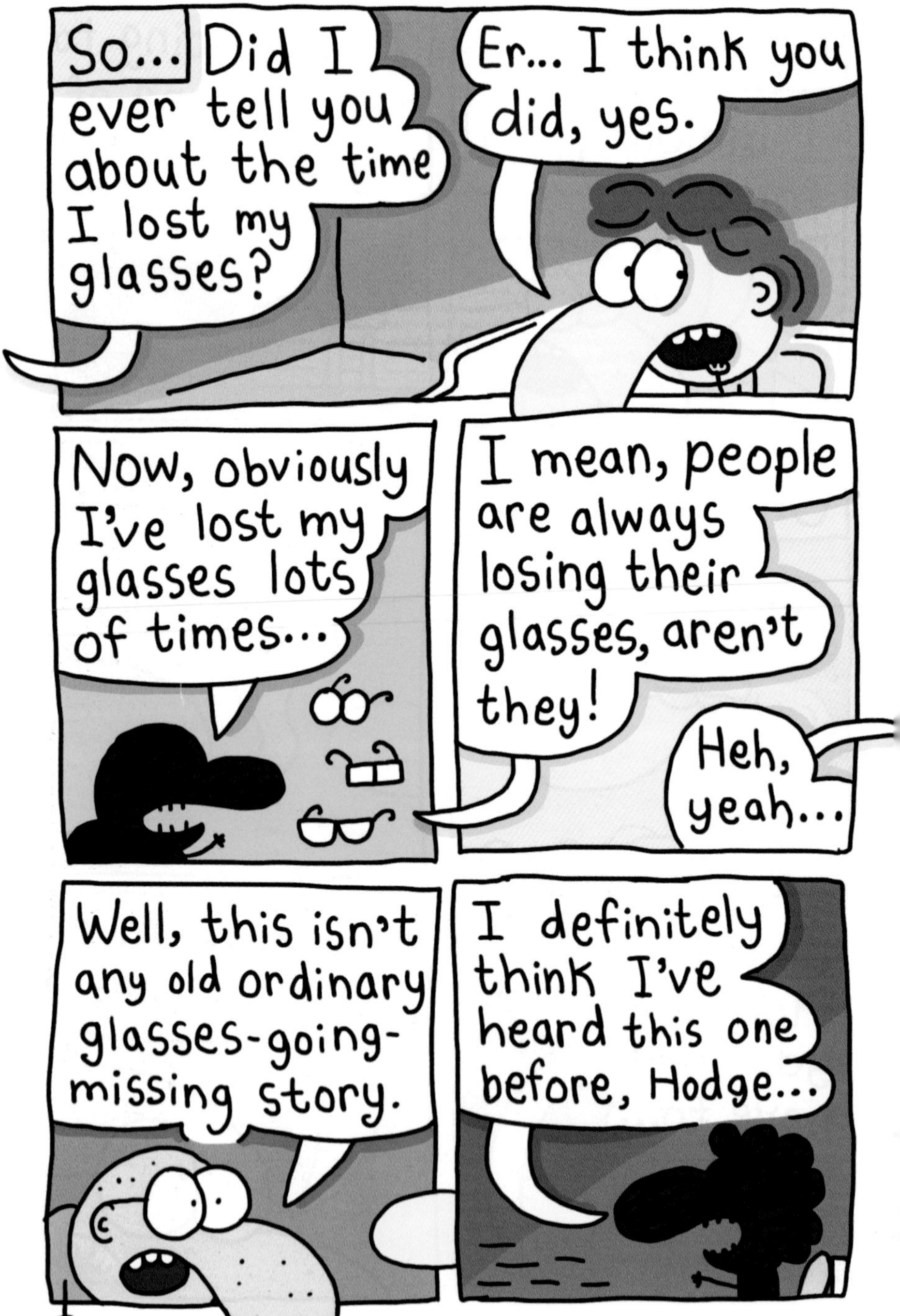
So... Did I ever tell you about the time I lost my glasses?
Er... I think you did, yes.
Now, obviously I've lost my glasses lots of times...
I mean, people are always losing their glasses, aren't they!
Heh, yeah...
Well, this isn't any old ordinary glasses-going-missing story.
I definitely think I've heard this one before, Hodge...

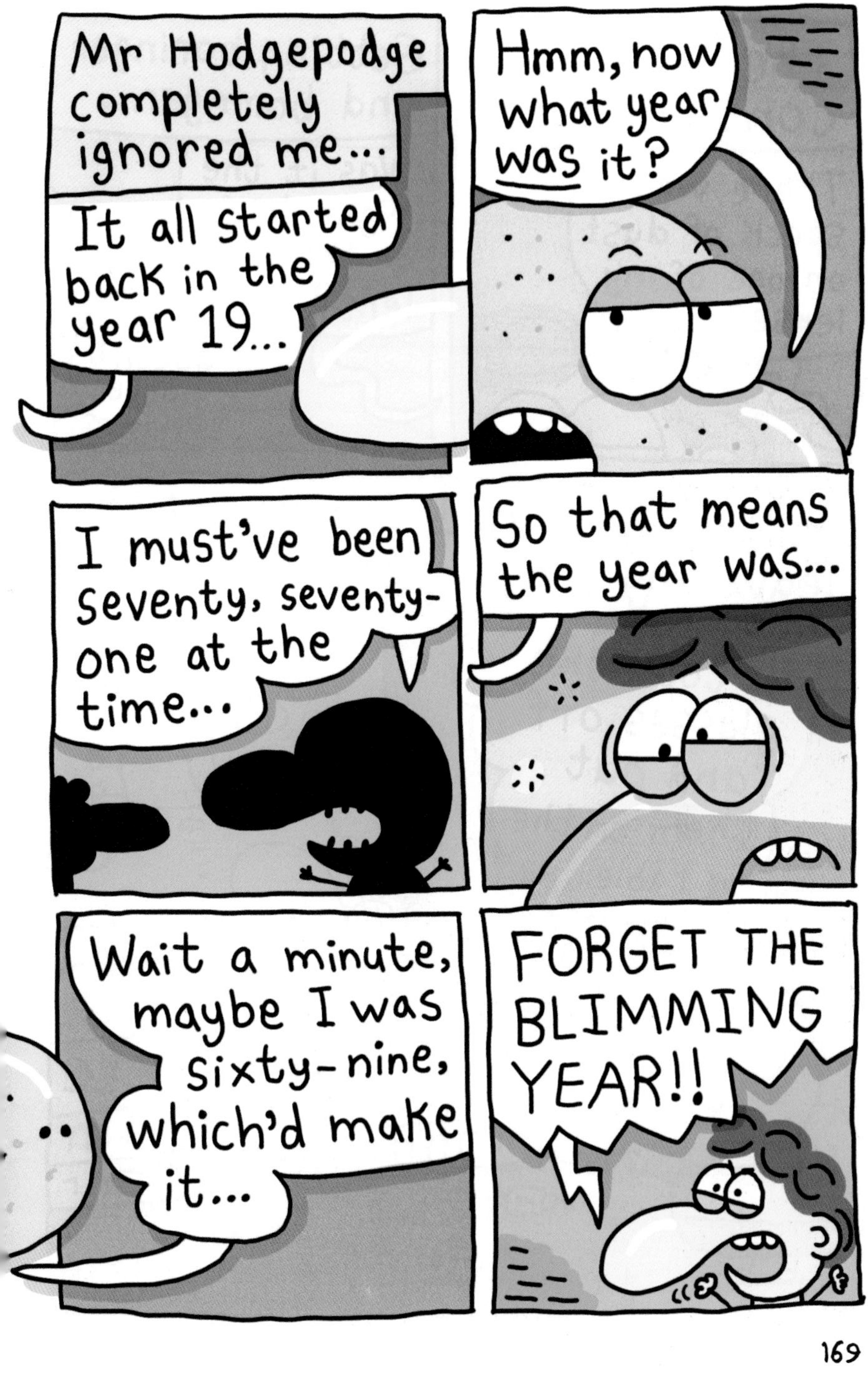
Mr Hodgepodge completely ignored me...
It all started back in the year 19...
Hmm, now what year was it?
I must've been seventy, seventy-one at the time...
So that means the year was...
Wait a minute, maybe I was sixty-nine, which'd make it...
FORGET THE BLIMMING YEAR!!

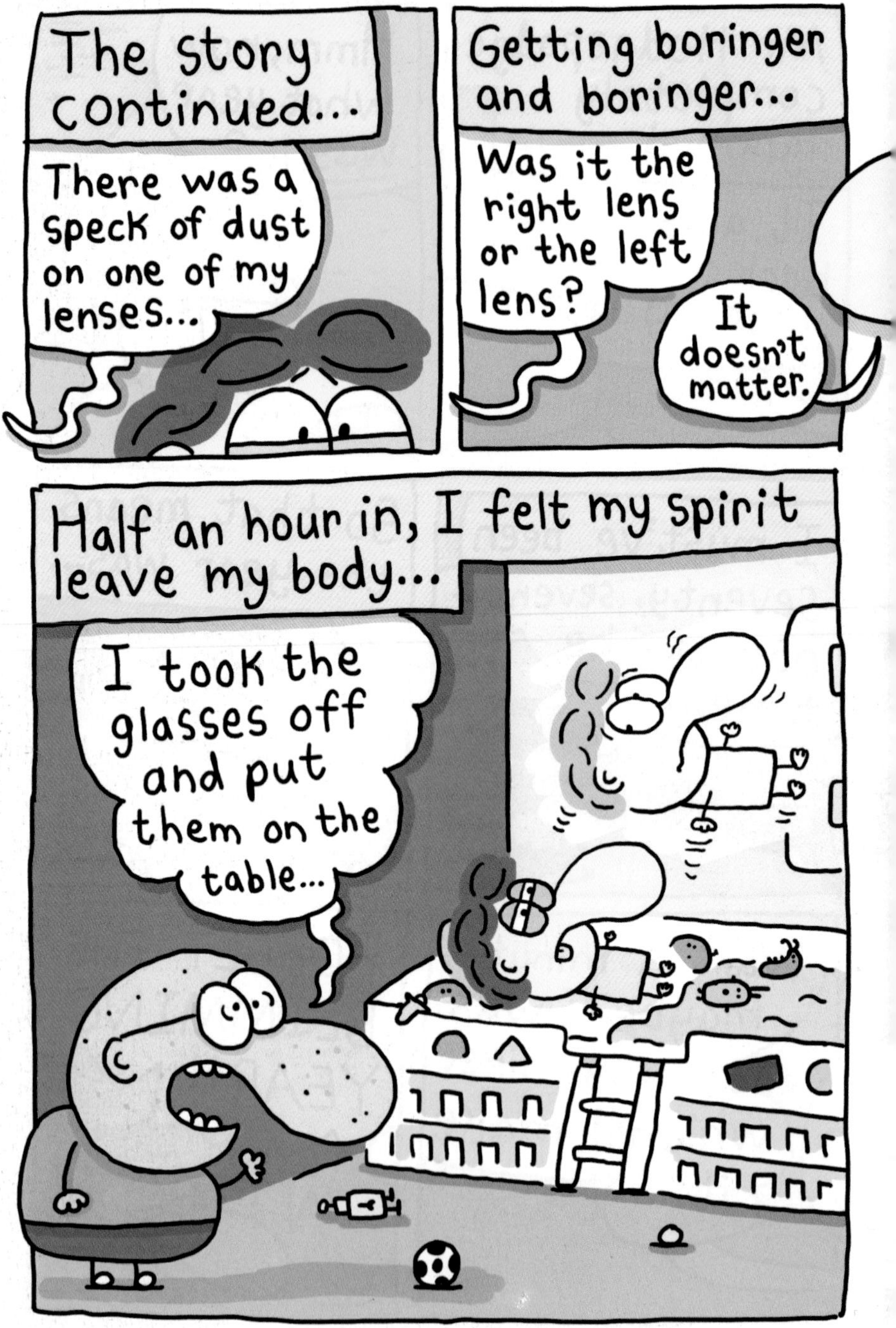
The story continued...
There was a speck of dust on one of my lenses...
Getting boringer and boringer...
Was it the right lens or the left lens?
It doesn't matter.
Half an hour in, I felt my spirit leave my body...
I took the glasses off and put them on the table...

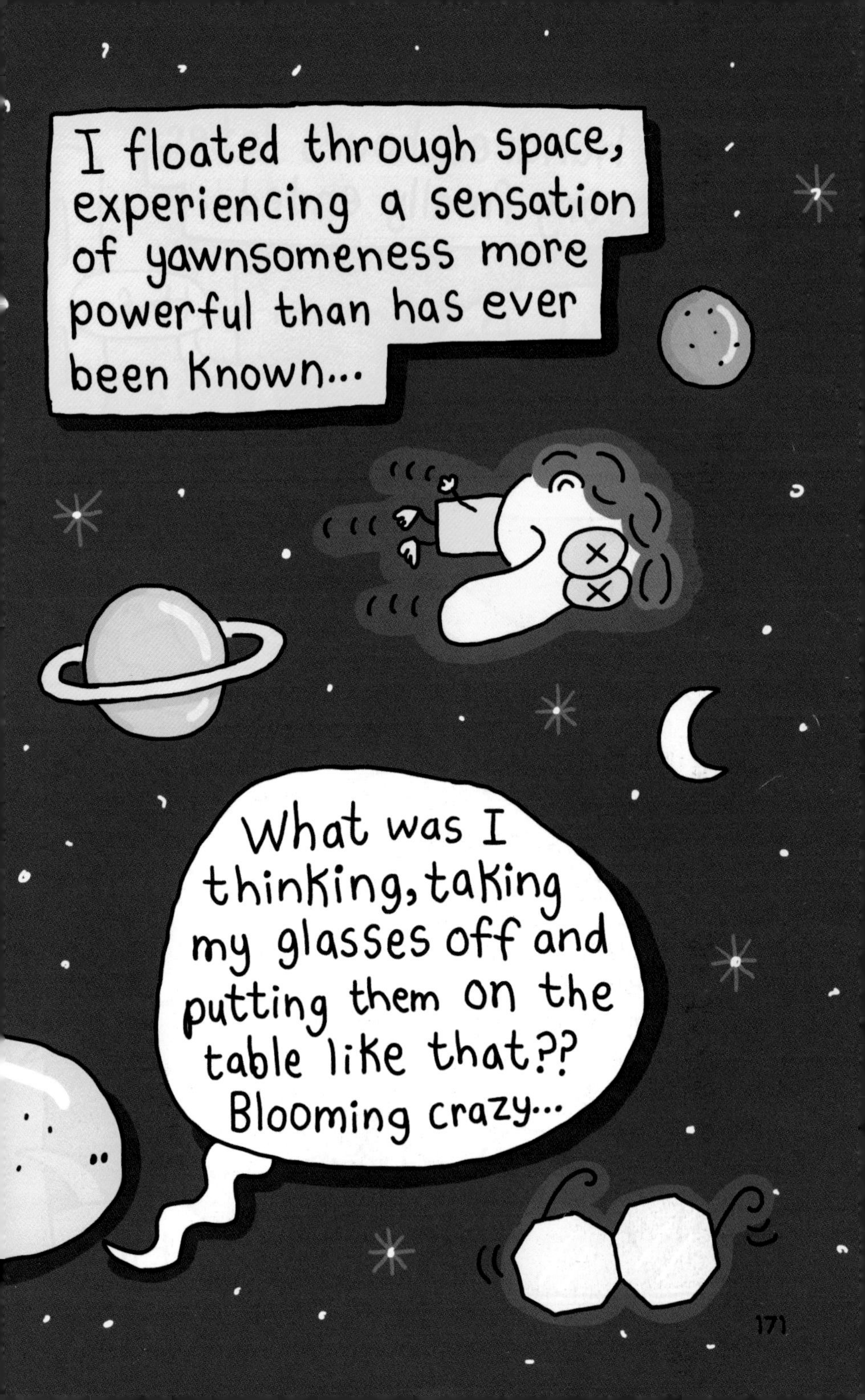
I floated through space, experiencing a sensation of yawnsomeness more powerful than has ever been known...
What was I thinking, taking my glasses off and putting them on the table like that?? Blooming crazy...

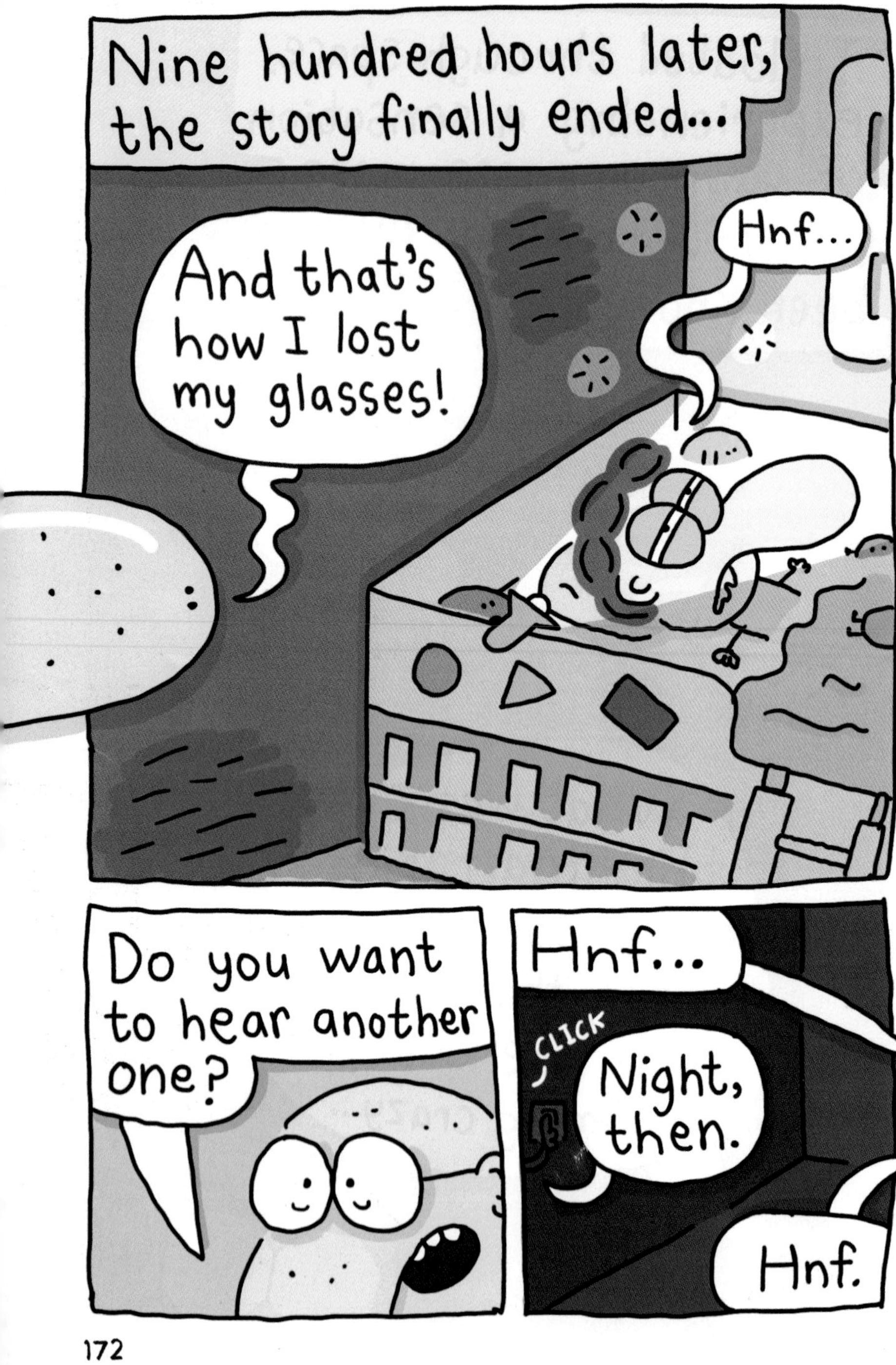
Nine hundred hours later, the story finally ended...
And that's how I lost my glasses!
Hnf...
Do you want to hear another one?
Hnf...
CLICK
Night, then.
Hnf.

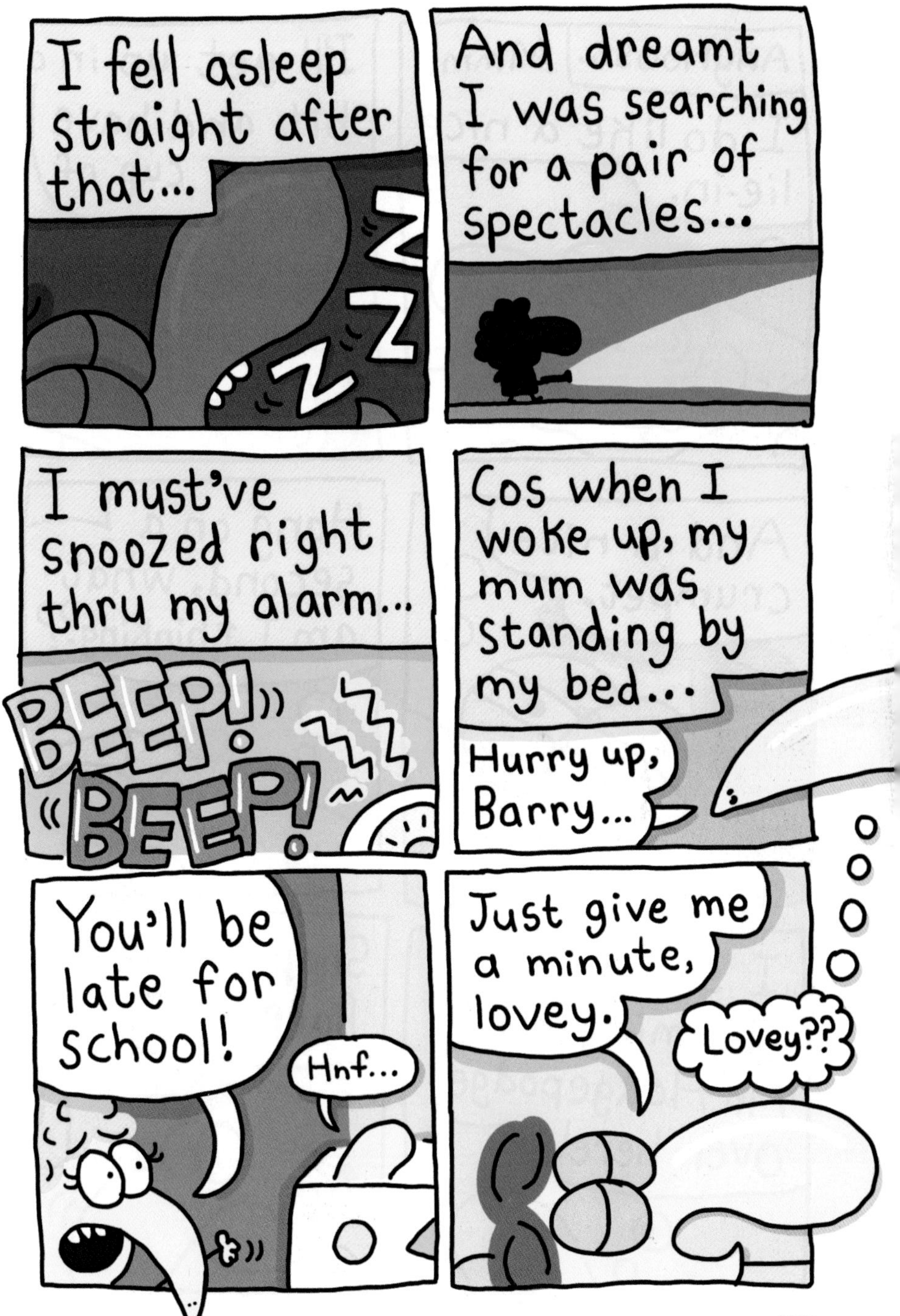
I fell asleep straight after that...
Z
Z
Z
And dreamt I was searching for a pair of spectacles...
I must've snoozed right thru my alarm...
BEEP!
BEEP!
Cos when I woke up, my mum was standing by my bed...
Hurry up, Barry...
You'll be late for school!
Hnf...
Just give me a minute, lovey.
Lovey??

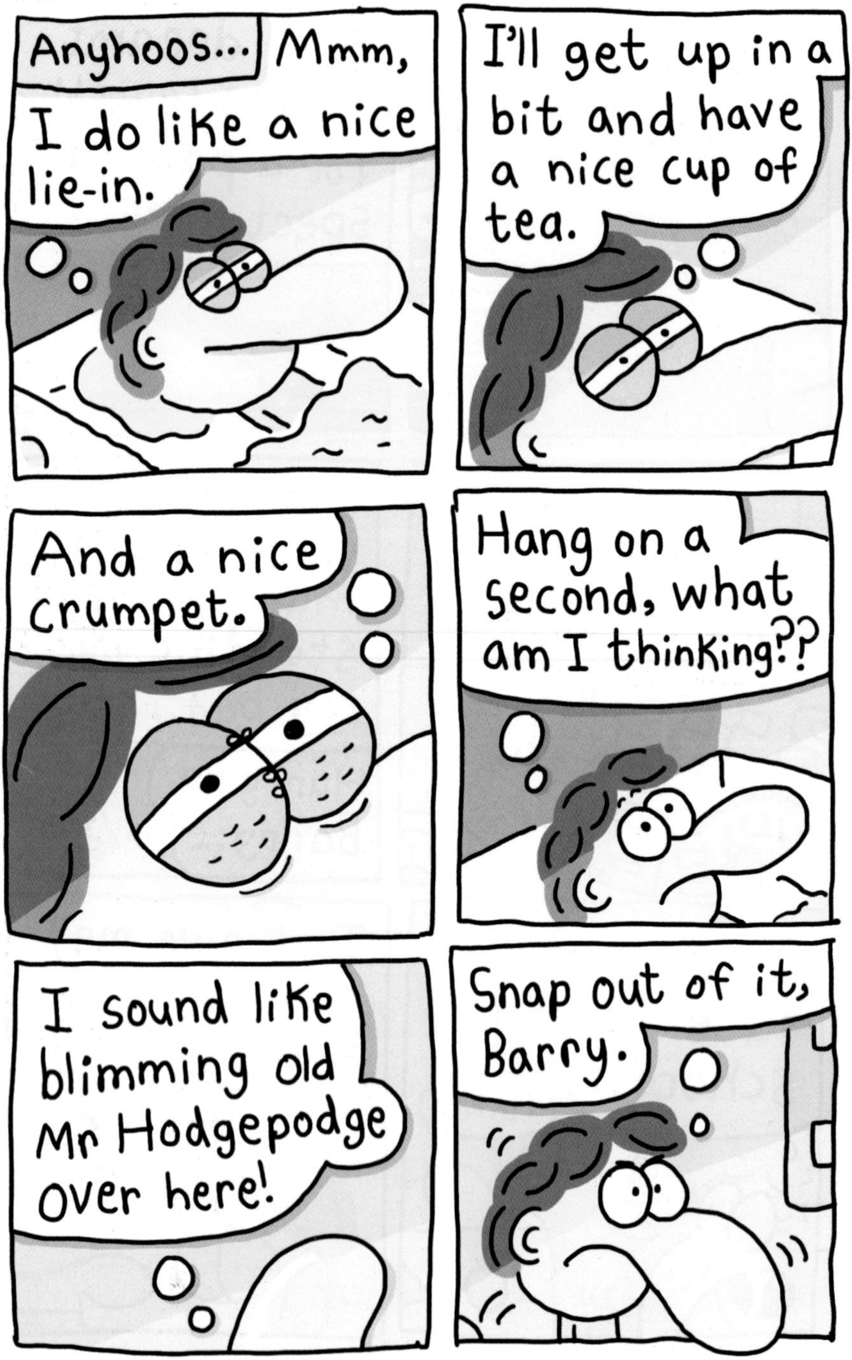
Anyhoos...
Mmm, I do like a nice lie-in.
I'll get up in a bit and have a nice cup of tea.
And a nice crumpet.
Hang on a second, what am I thinking??
I sound like blimming old Mr Hodgepodge over here!
Snap out of it, Barry.

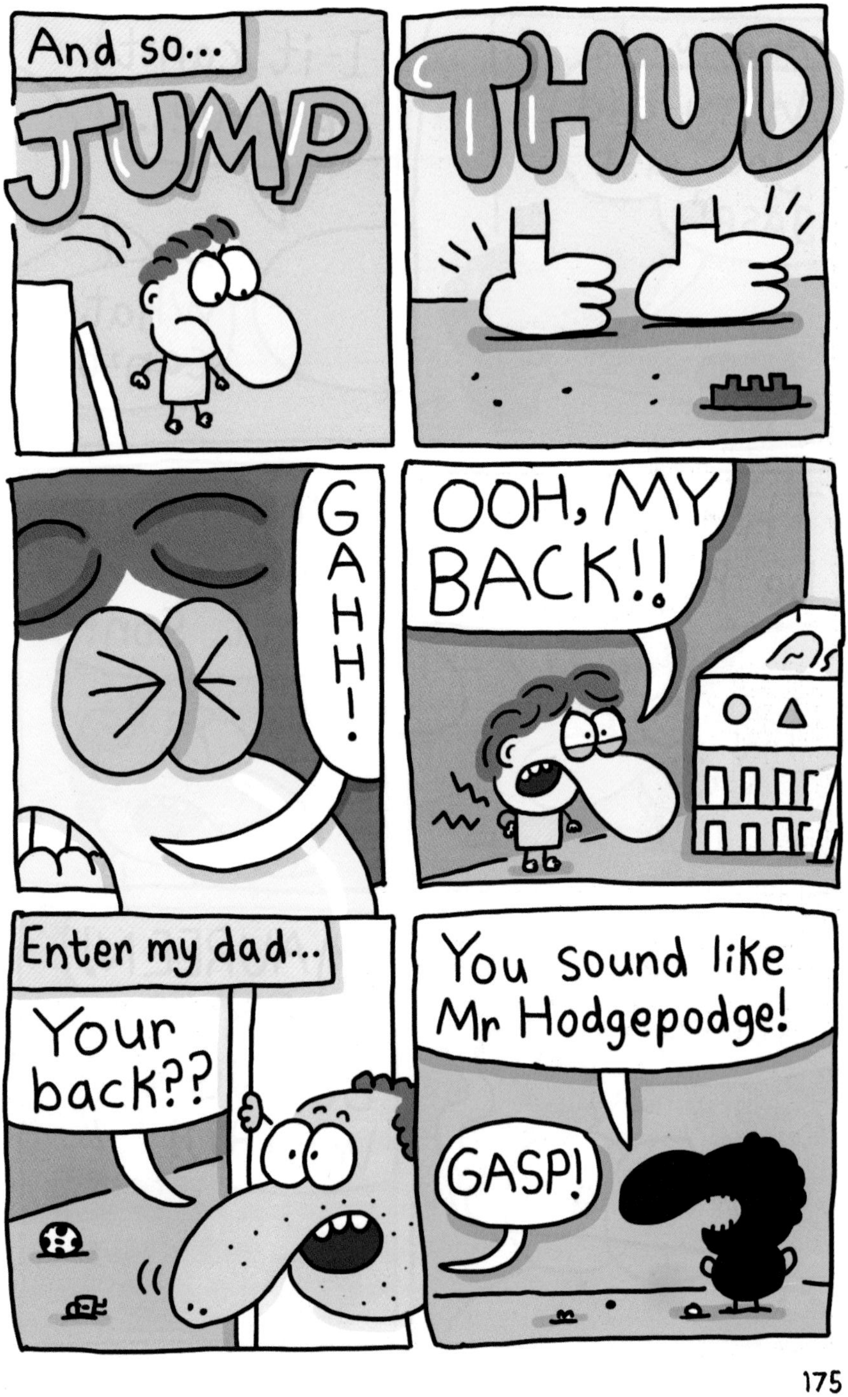
And so...
JUMP
THUD
GAHHH!
OOH, MY BACK!!
Enter my dad...
Your back??
You sound like Mr Hodgepodge!
GASP!

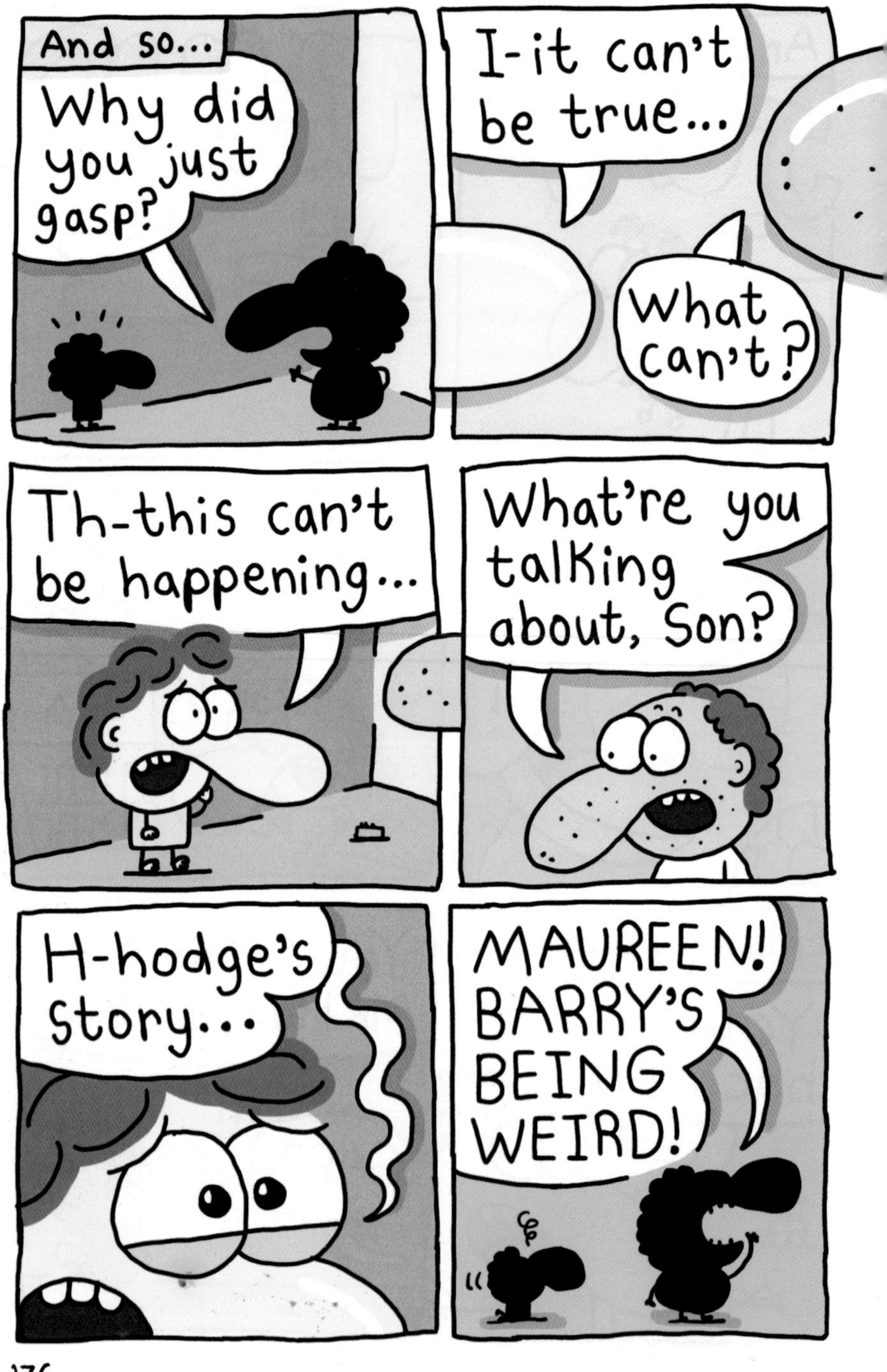
And so...
Why did you just gasp?
I-it can't be true...
What can't?
Th-this can't be happening...
What're you talking about, Son?
H-hodge's story...
MAUREEN! BARRY'S BEING WEIRD!

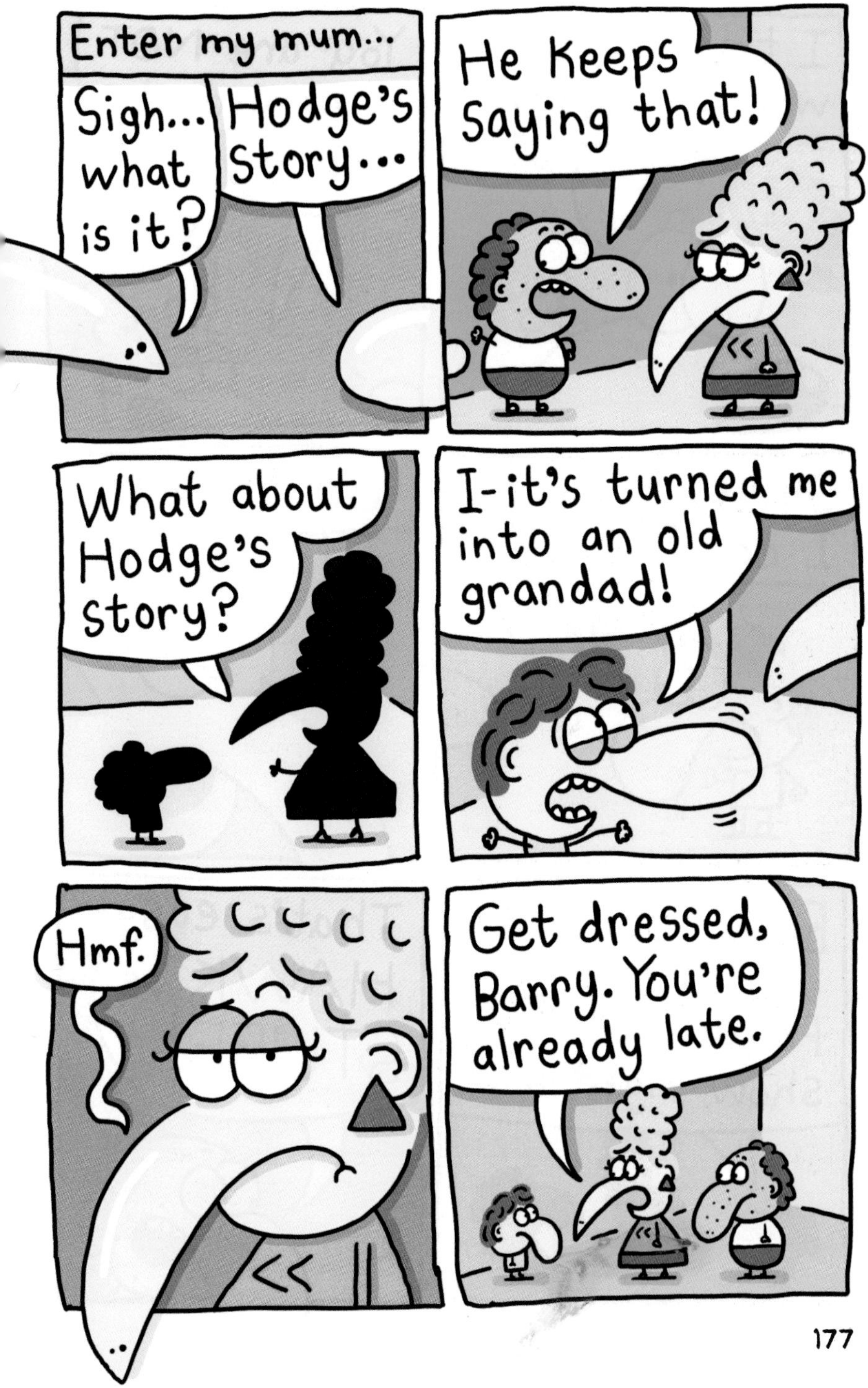
Enter my mum...
Sigh... what is it?
Hodge's Story...
He Keeps Saying that!
What about Hodge's story?
I-it's turned me into an old grandad!
Hmf.
Get dressed, Barry. You're already late.

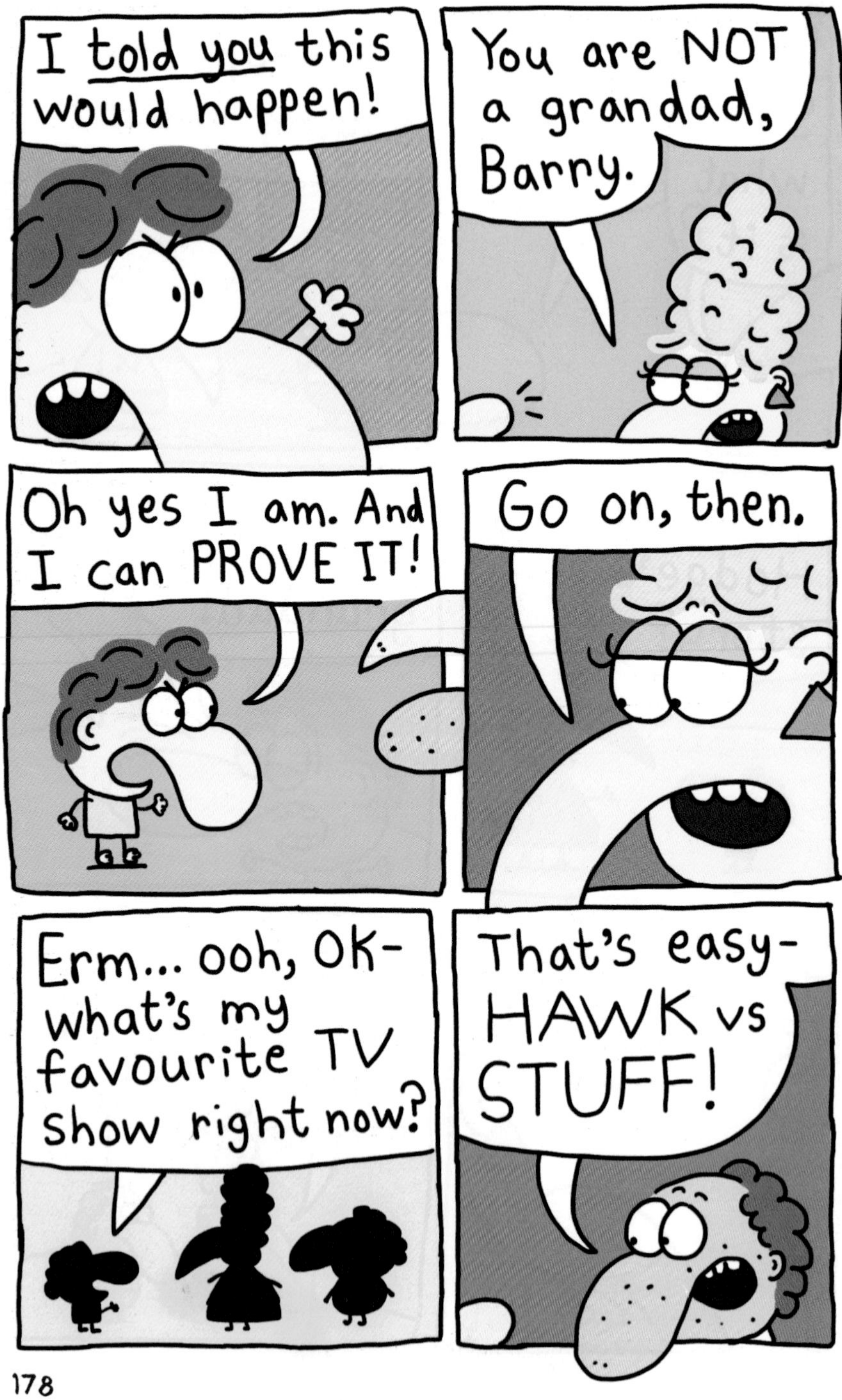
I told you this would happen!
You are NOT a grandad, Barry.
Oh yes I am. And I can PROVE IT!
Go on, then.
Erm... ooh, OK- what's my favourite TV show right now?
That's easy- HAWK vs STUFF!

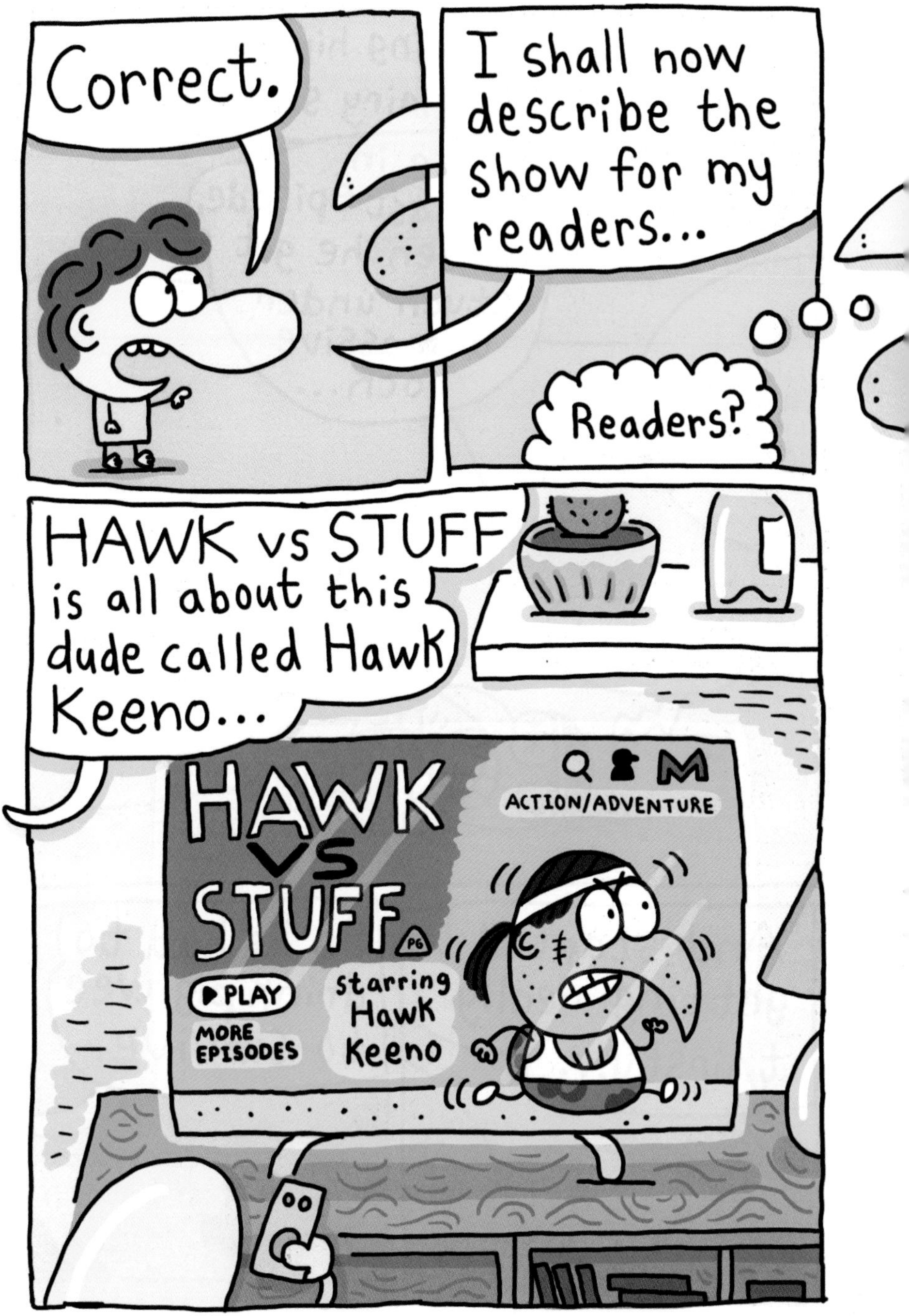
Correct.
I shall now describe the show for my readers...
Readers?
HAWK vs STUFF is all about this dude called Hawk Keeno...
HAWK VS STUFF
PG
ACTION/ADVENTURE
PLAY
MORE EPISODES
starring Hawk Keeno

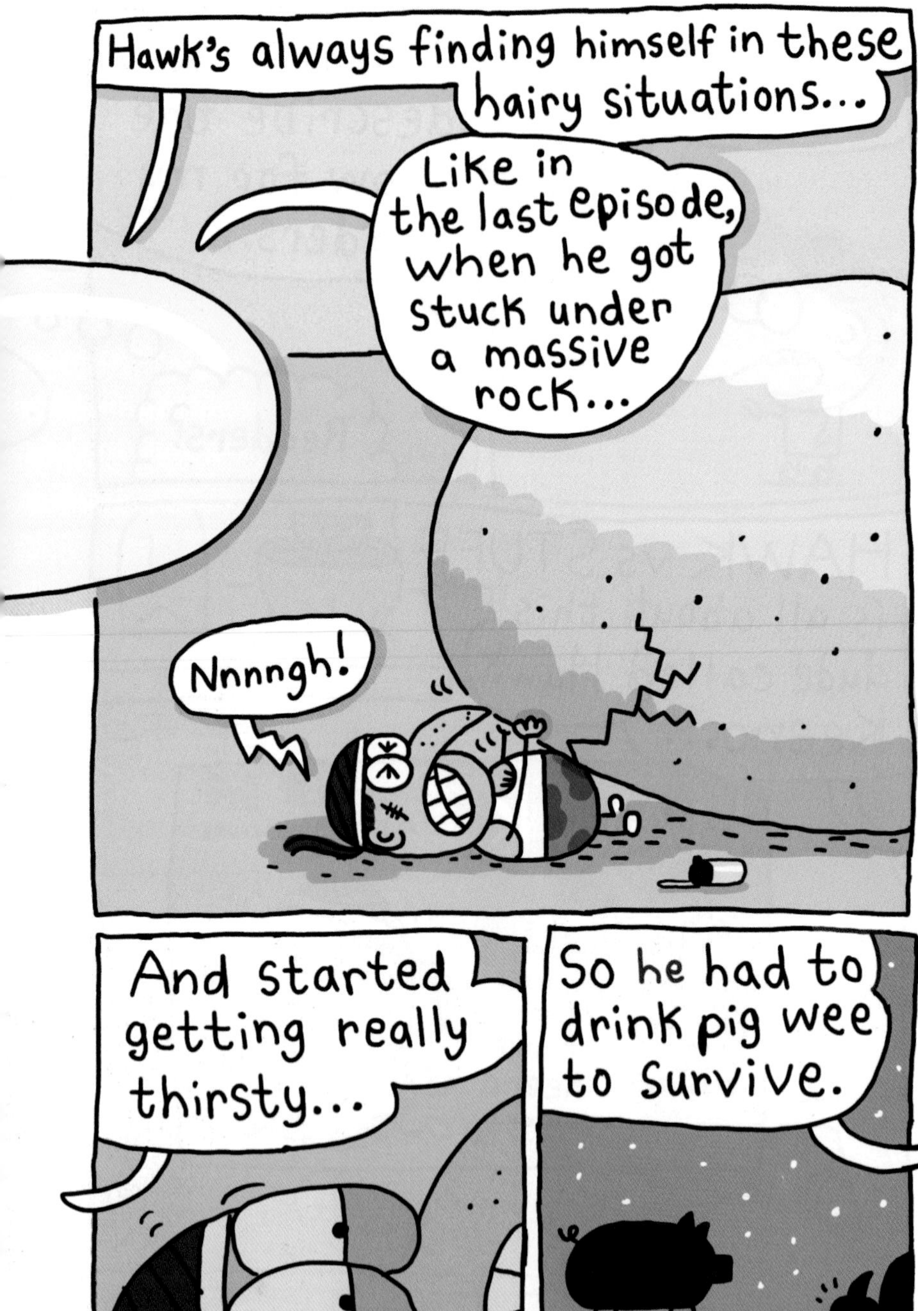
Hawk's always finding himself in these hairy situations...
Like in the last episode, when he got stuck under a massive rock...
Nnnngh!
And started getting really thirsty...
So he had to drink pig wee to survive.

(end of description)

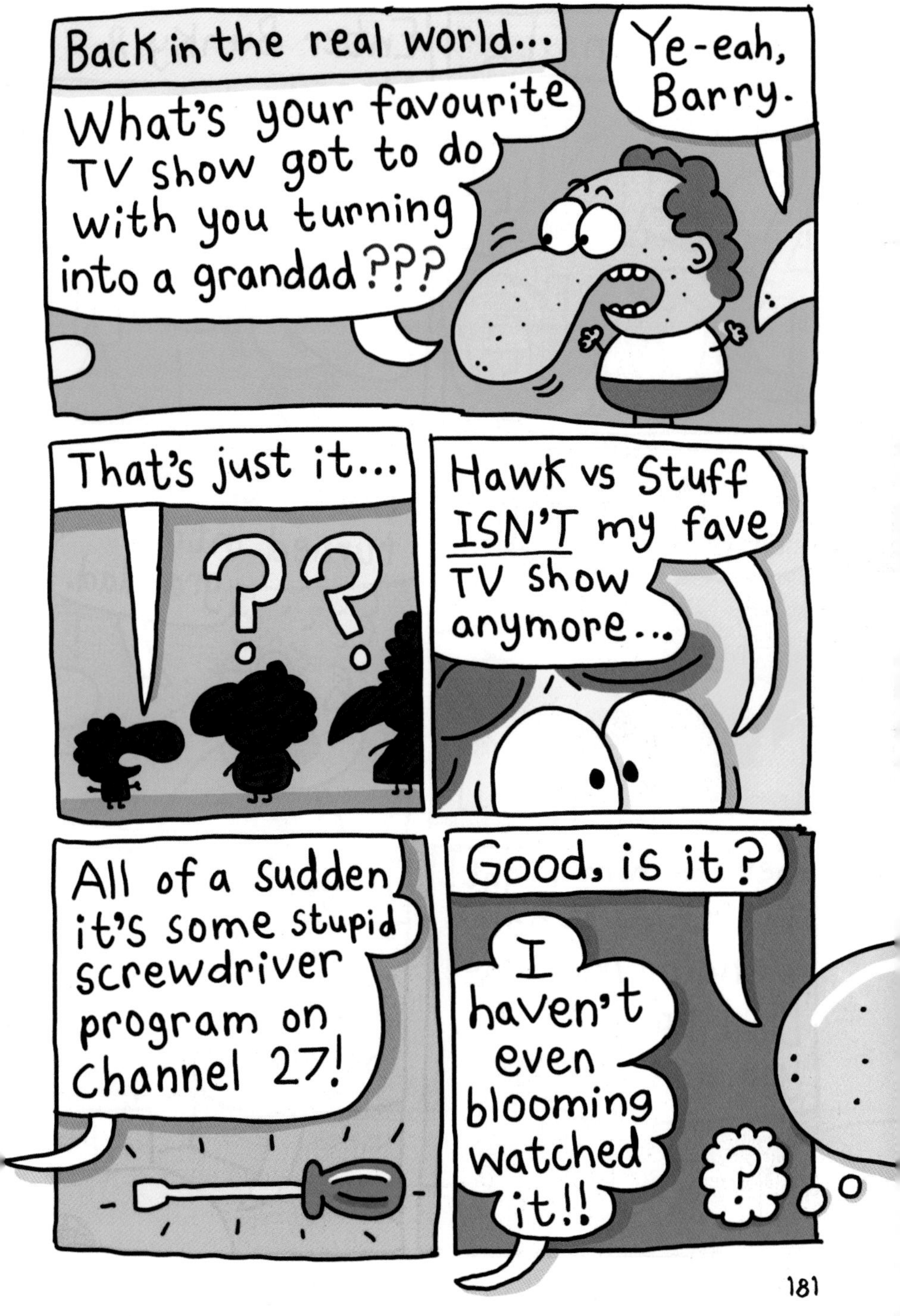

Back in the real world...
What's your favourite TV show got to do with you turning into a grandad???
Ye-eah, Barry.
That's just it...
Hawk vs Stuff ISN'T my fave TV show anymore...
All of a sudden it's some stupid screwdriver program on Channel 27!
Good, is it?
I haven't even blooming watched it!!

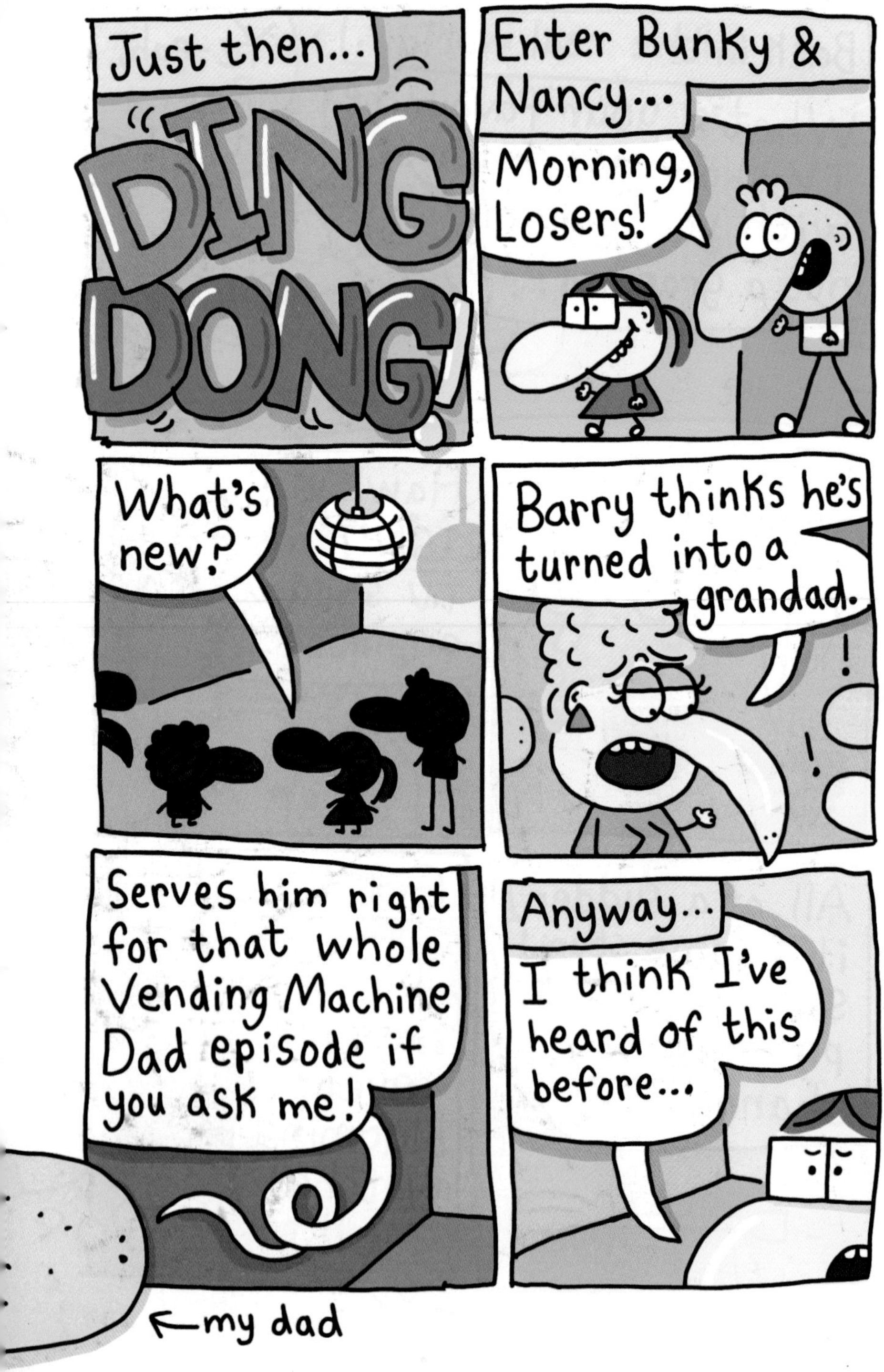
Just then...
DING DONG!
Enter Bunky & Nancy...
Morning, Losers!
What's new?
Barry thinks he's turned into a grandad.
!
!
Serves him right for that whole Vending Machine Dad episode if you ask me!
Anyway...
I think I've heard of this before...
← my dad

Nancy explained...

It happens when a normal person spends too much time with somebody really boring...

They end up catching the boringness off them.

Medically speaking, it's called 'Boringitis'.

Boringitis? Just my luck!

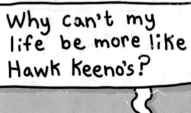
Why can't my life be more like Hawk Keeno's?

What, getting stuck under a rock and drinking pig's wee?

Chuckle

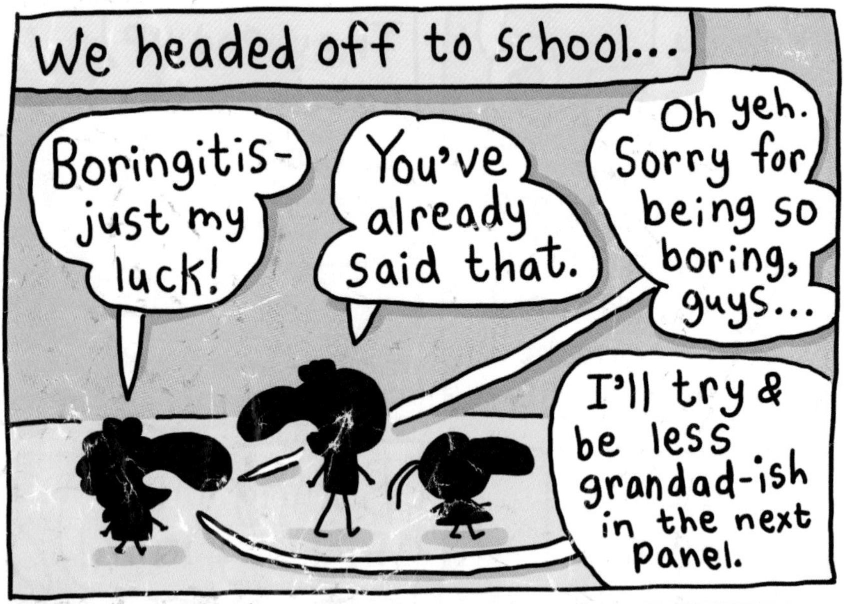
We headed off to school...
Boringitis- just my luck!
You've already said that.
Oh yeh. Sorry for being so boring, guys...
I'll try & be less grandad-ish in the next panel.

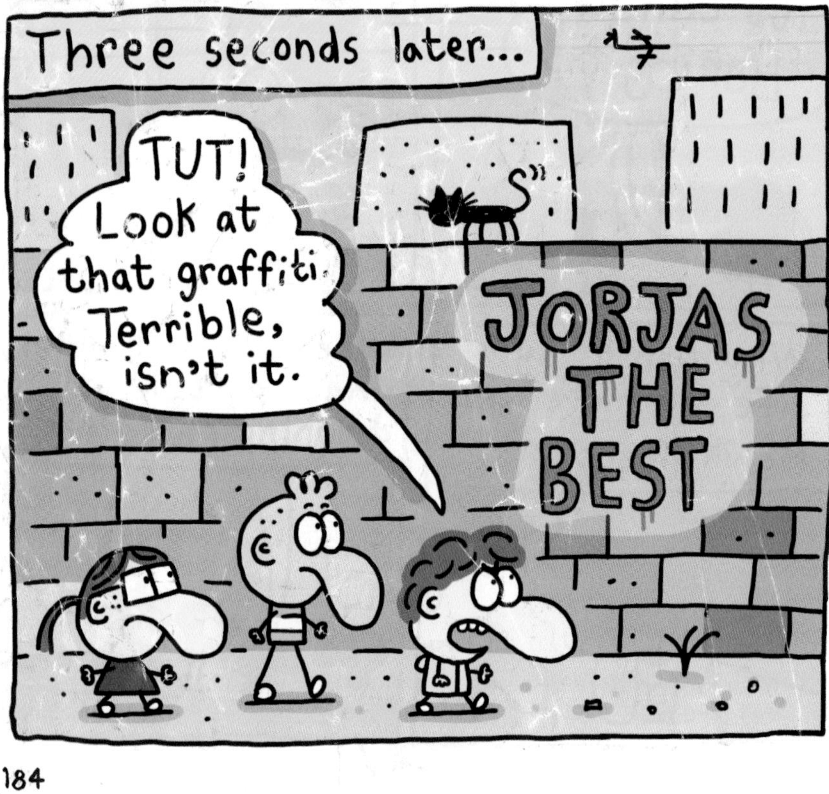
Three seconds later...
TUT! Look at that graffiti. Terrible, isn't it.
JORJAS THE BEST

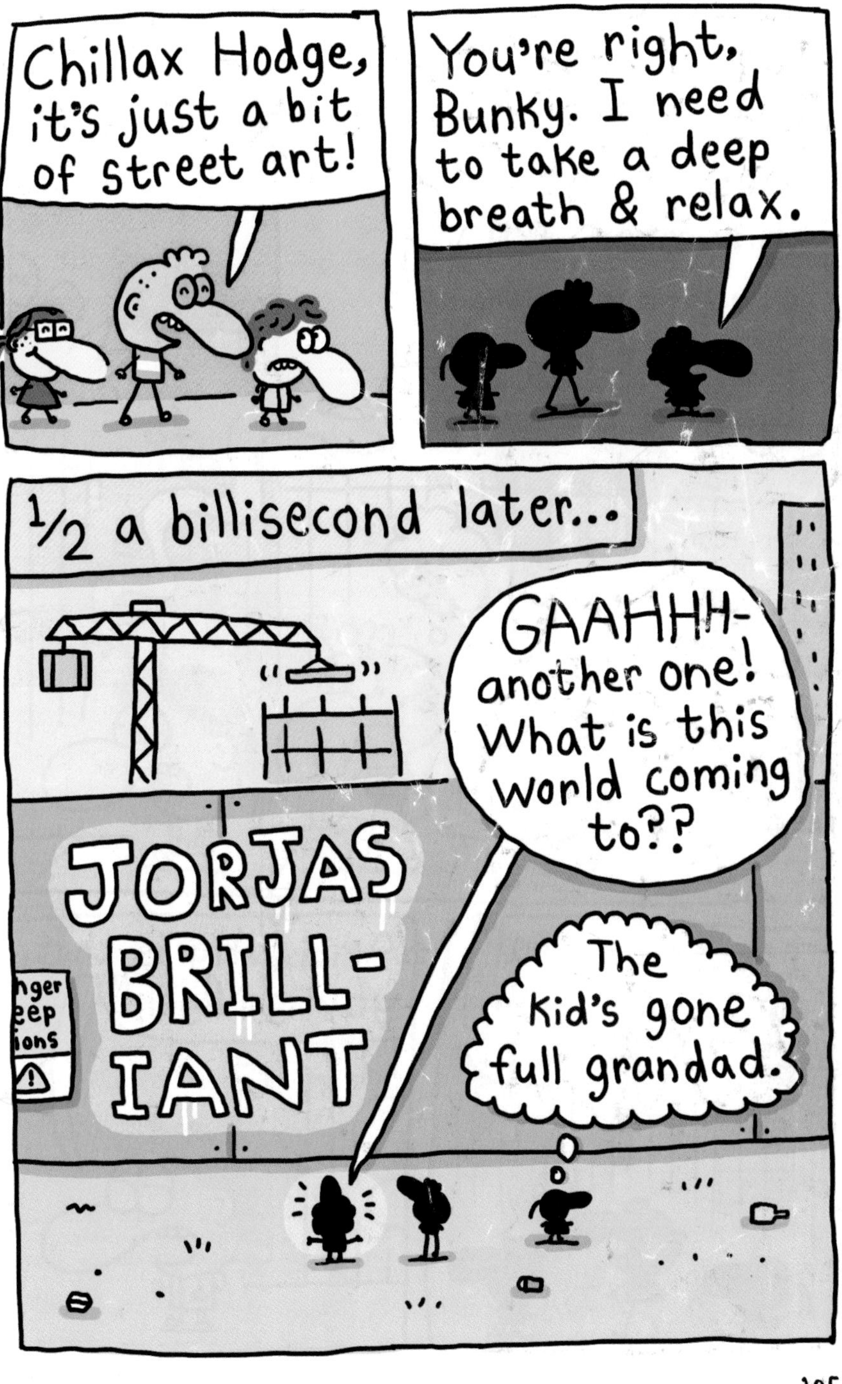
Chillax Hodge, it's just a bit of street art!
You're right, Bunky. I need to take a deep breath & relax.
½ a billisecond later...
GAAHHH- another one! What is this world coming to??
The kid's gone full grandad.
JORJAS BRILL-IANT

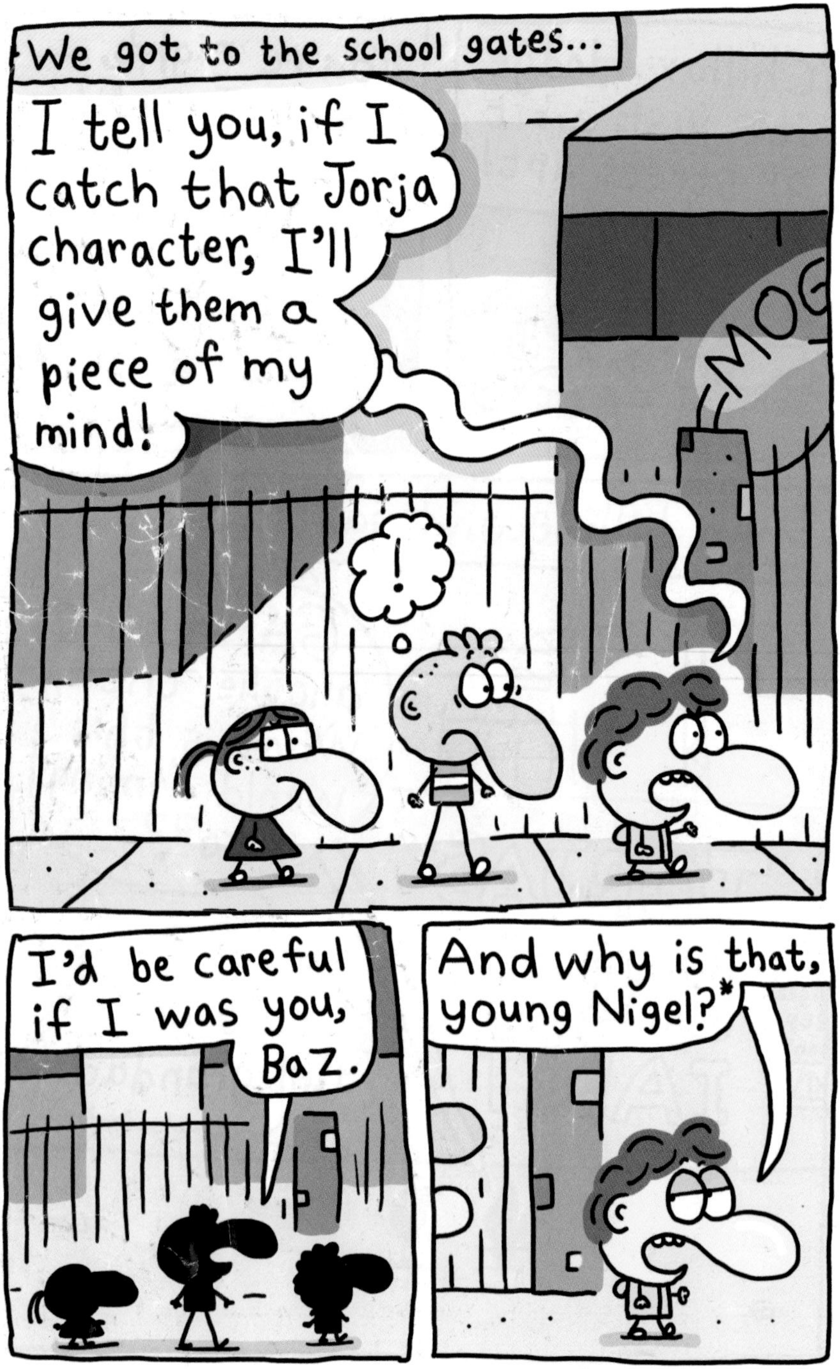
We got to the school gates...
I tell you, if I catch that Jorja character, I'll give them a piece of my mind!
MOG
!
I'd be careful if I was you, Baz.
And why is that, young Nigel?*

*Bunky's real name

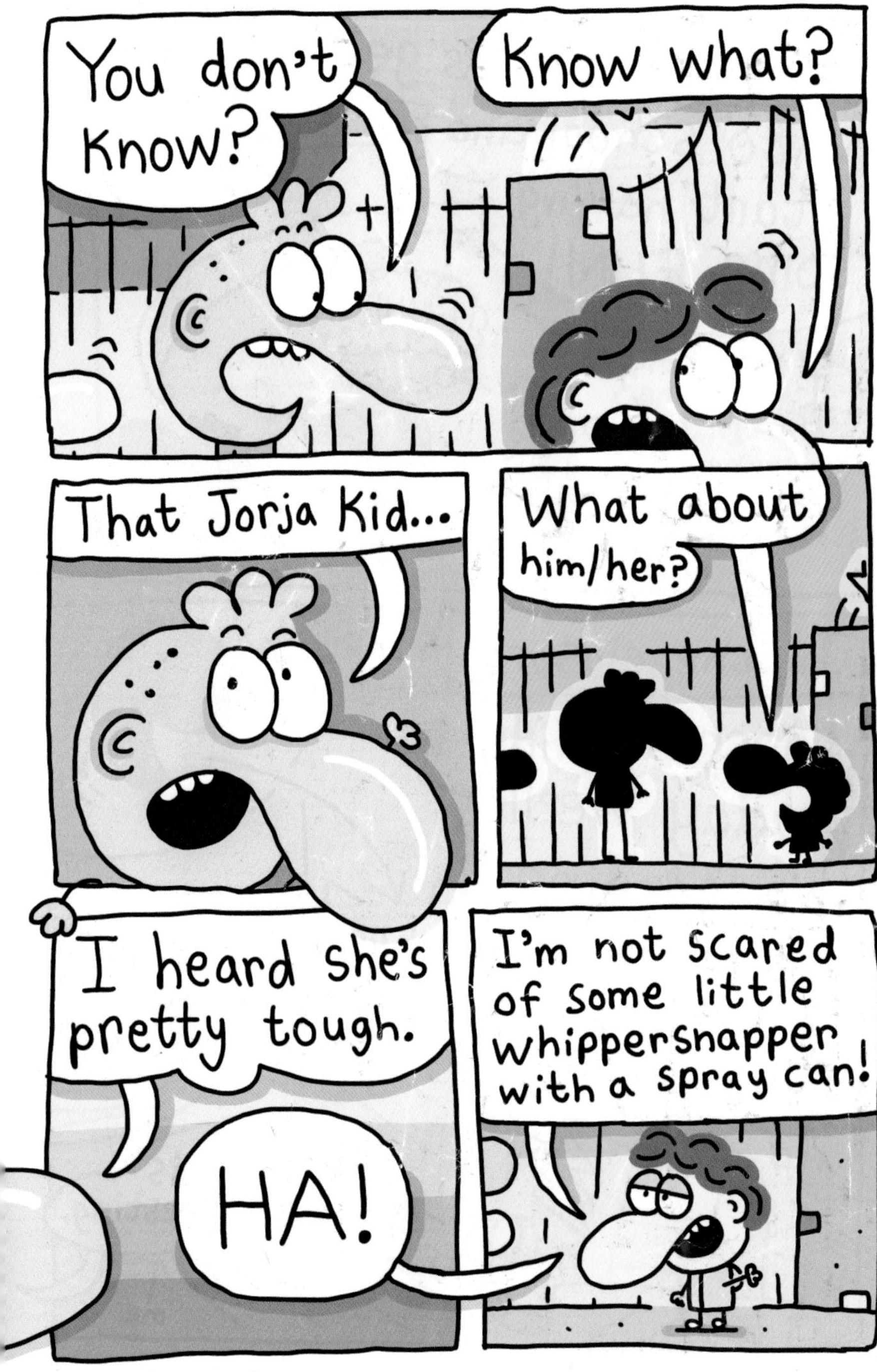
You don't know?
Know what?
That Jorja Kid...
What about him/her?
I heard she's pretty tough.
HA!
I'm not scared of some little whippersnapper with a spray can!

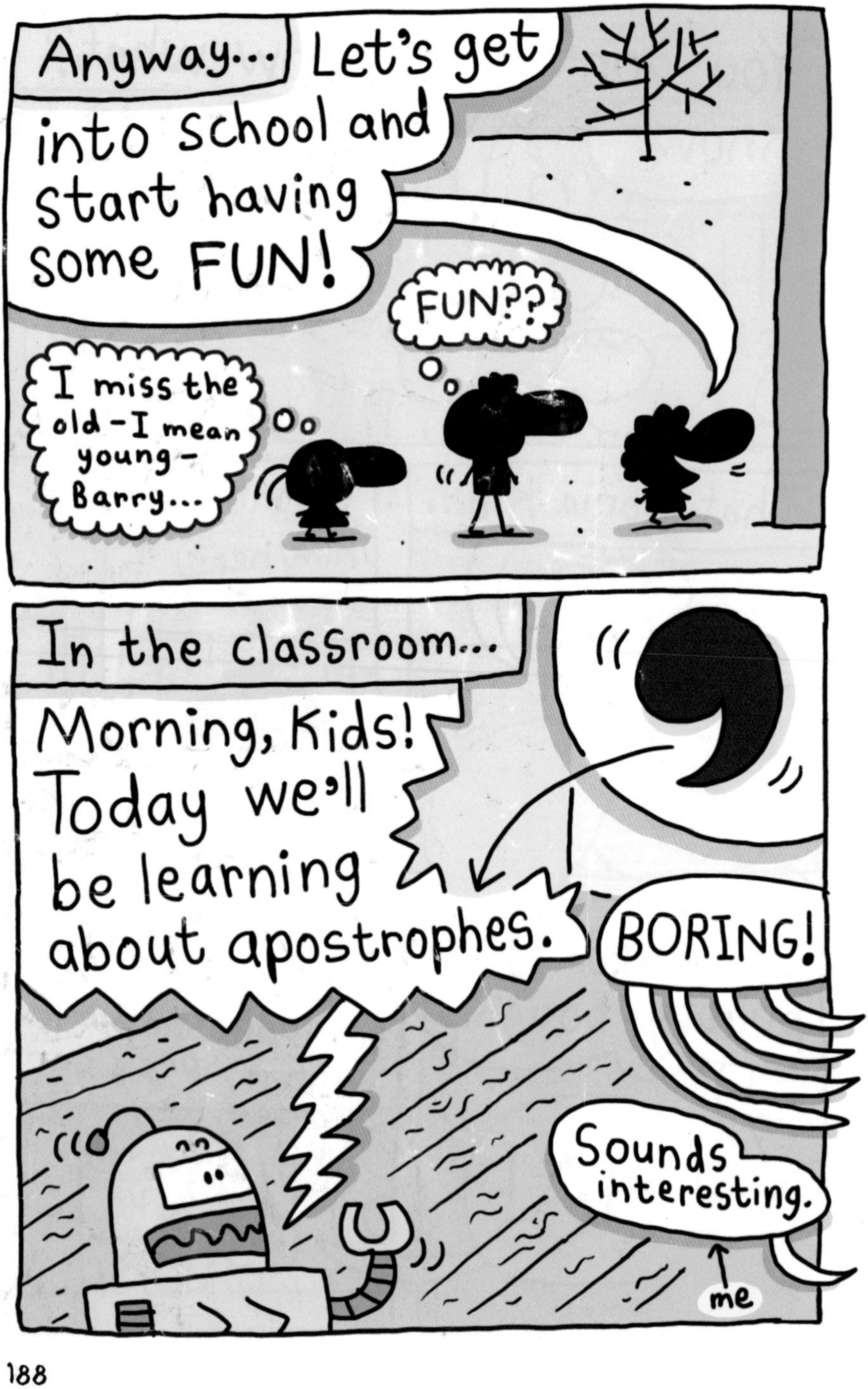
Anyway...
Let's get into school and start having some FUN!
FUN??
I miss the old - I mean young - Barry...
In the classroom...
Morning, Kids! Today we'll be learning about apostrophes.
BORING!
Sounds interesting.
me

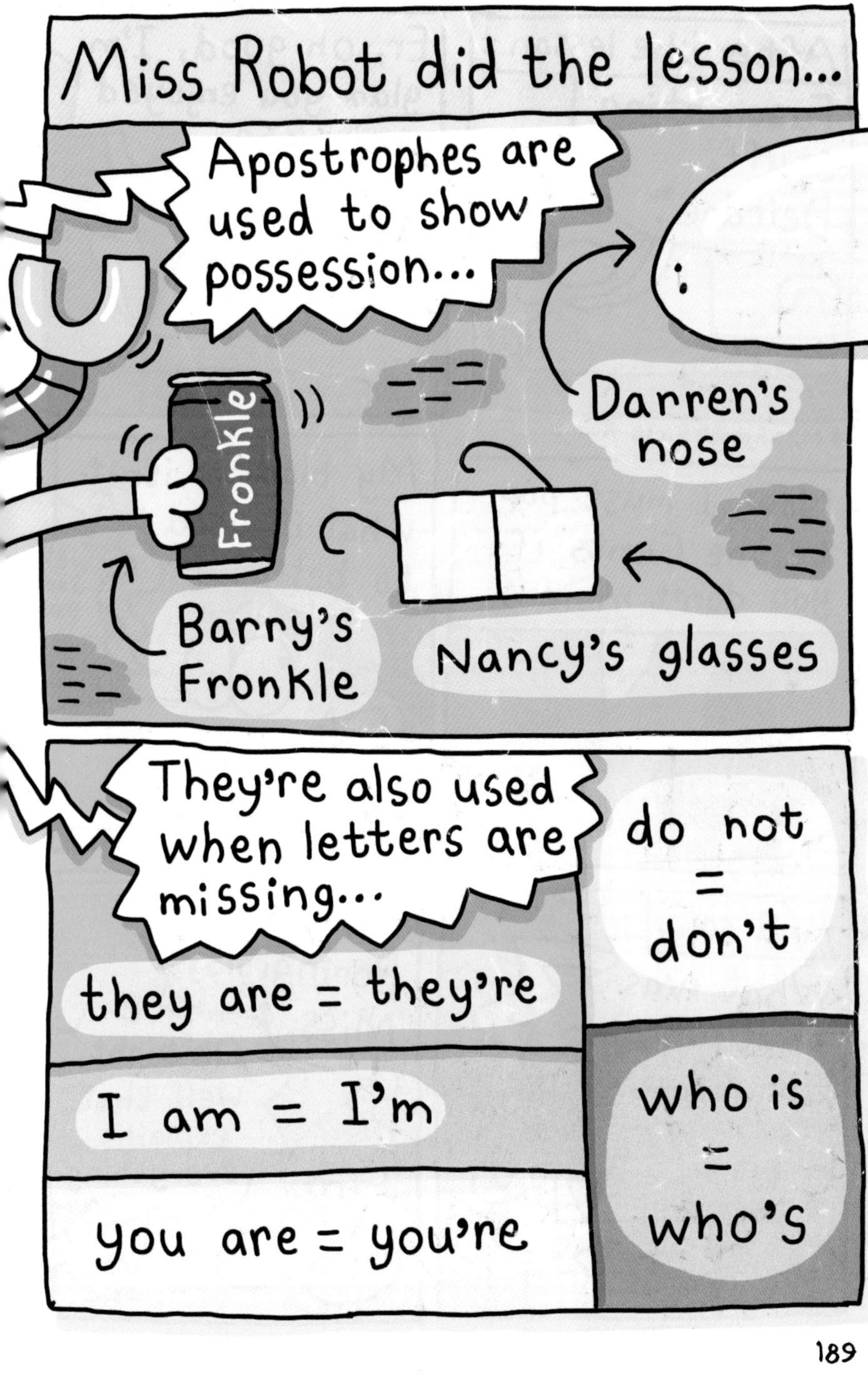
Miss Robot did the lesson...
Apostrophes are used to show possession...
Darren's nose
Frankle
Barry's Fronkle
Nancy's glasses
They're also used when letters are missing...
do not = don't
they are = they're
I am = I'm
who is = who's
you are = you're

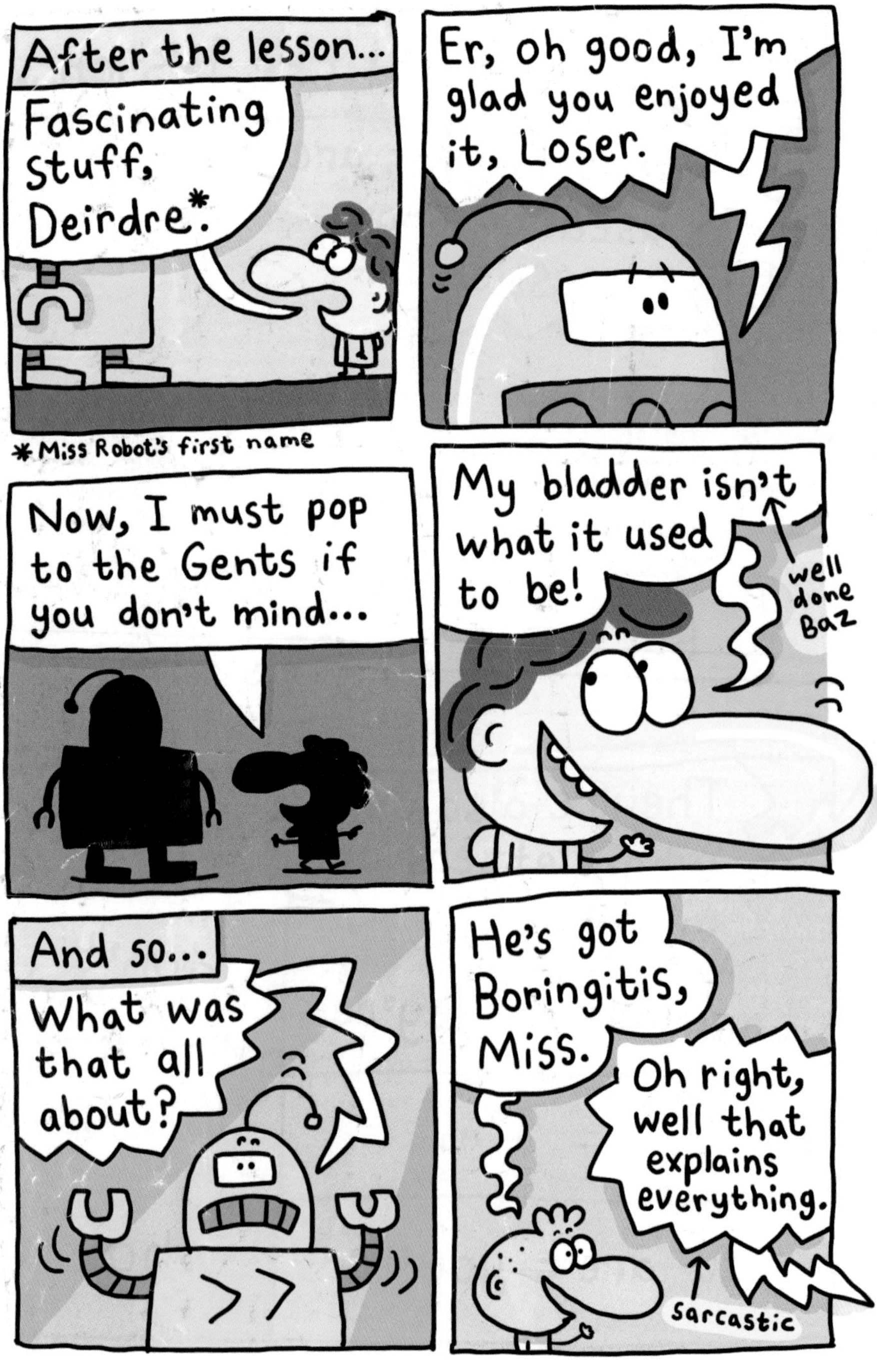
After the lesson...
Fascinating stuff, Deirdre*.
Er, oh good, I'm glad you enjoyed it, Loser.
* Miss Robot's first name
Now, I must pop to the Gents if you don't mind...
My bladder isn't what it used to be!
well done Baz
And so...
What was that all about?
He's got Boringitis, Miss.
Oh right, well that explains everything.
sarcastic

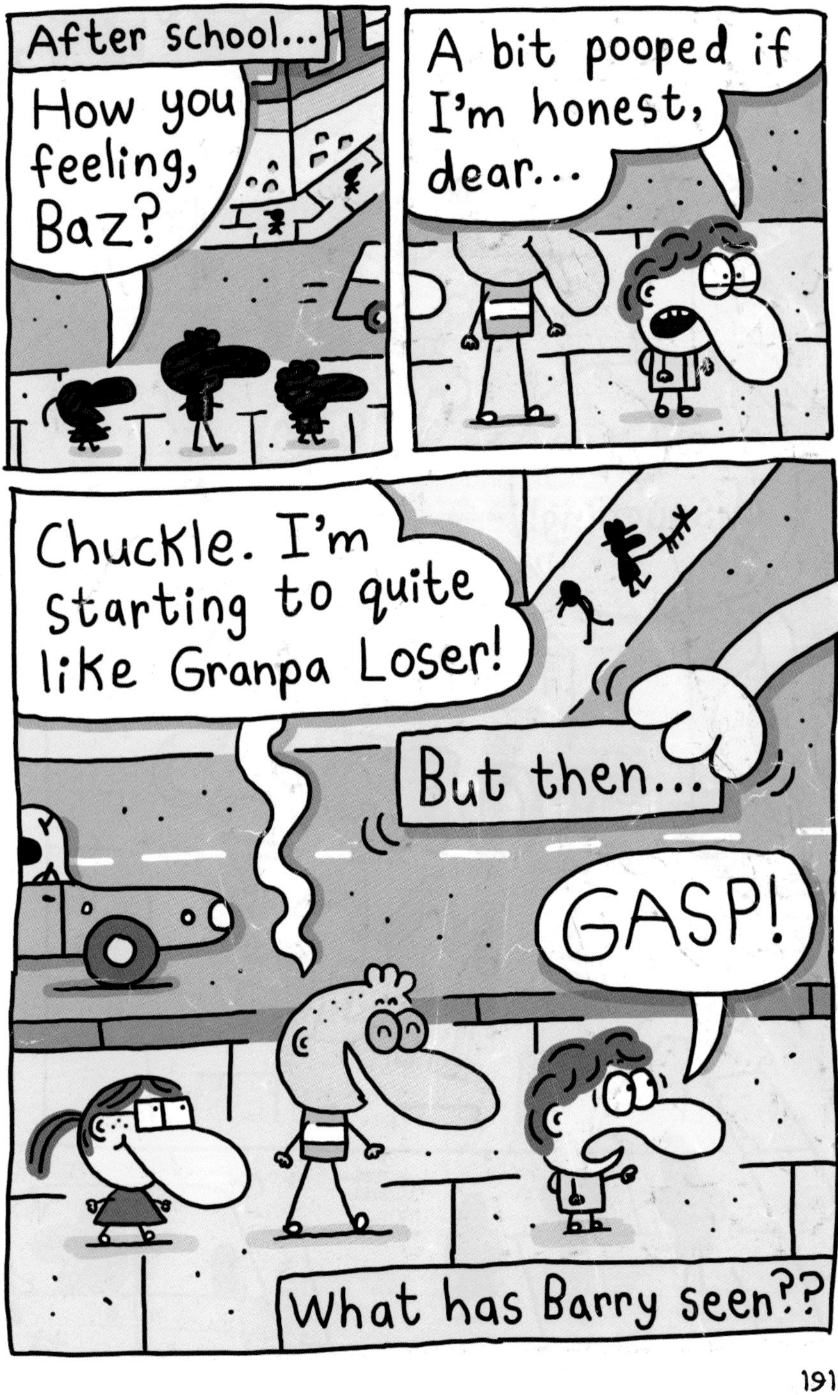
After school...
How you feeling, Baz?
A bit pooped if I'm honest, dear...
Chuckle. I'm starting to quite like Granpa Loser!
But then...
GASP!
What has Barry seen??

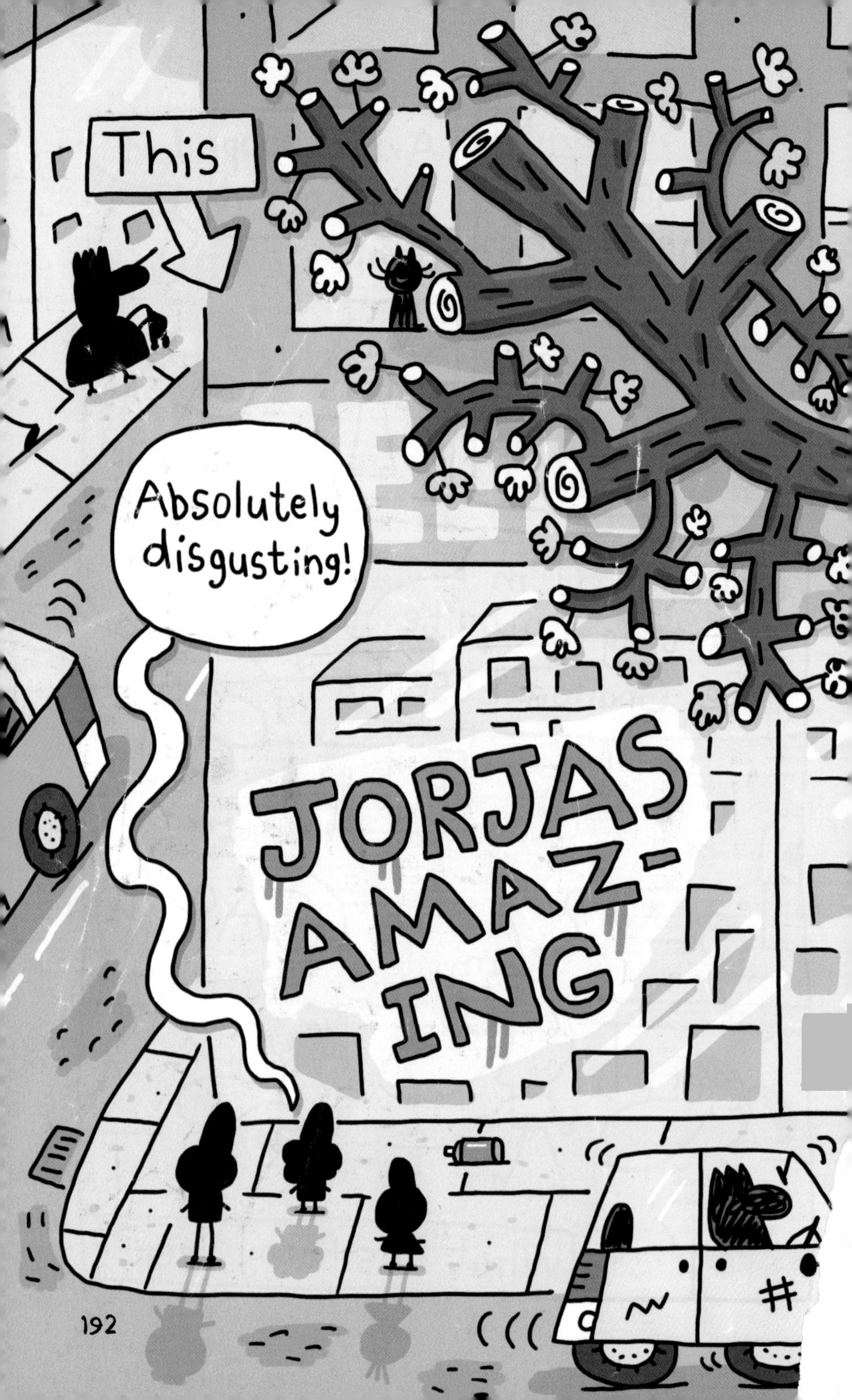
This
Absolutely disgusting!
JORJAS AMAZ-ING

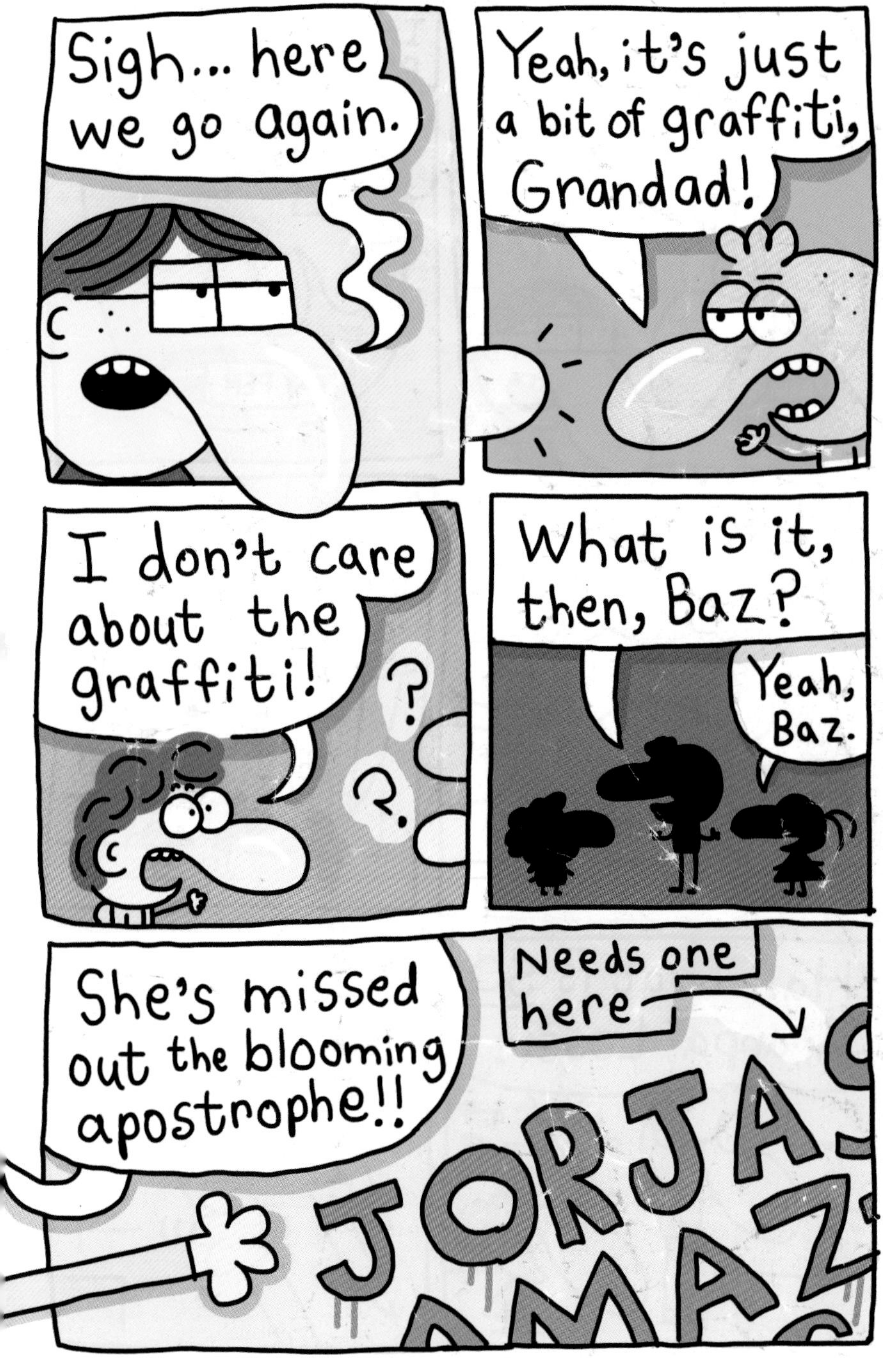
Sigh... here we go again.
Yeah, it's just a bit of graffiti, Grandad!
I don't care about the graffiti!
?
?
What is it, then, Baz?
Yeah, Baz.
She's missed out the blooming apostrophe!!
Needs one here
JORJAS
AMAZ

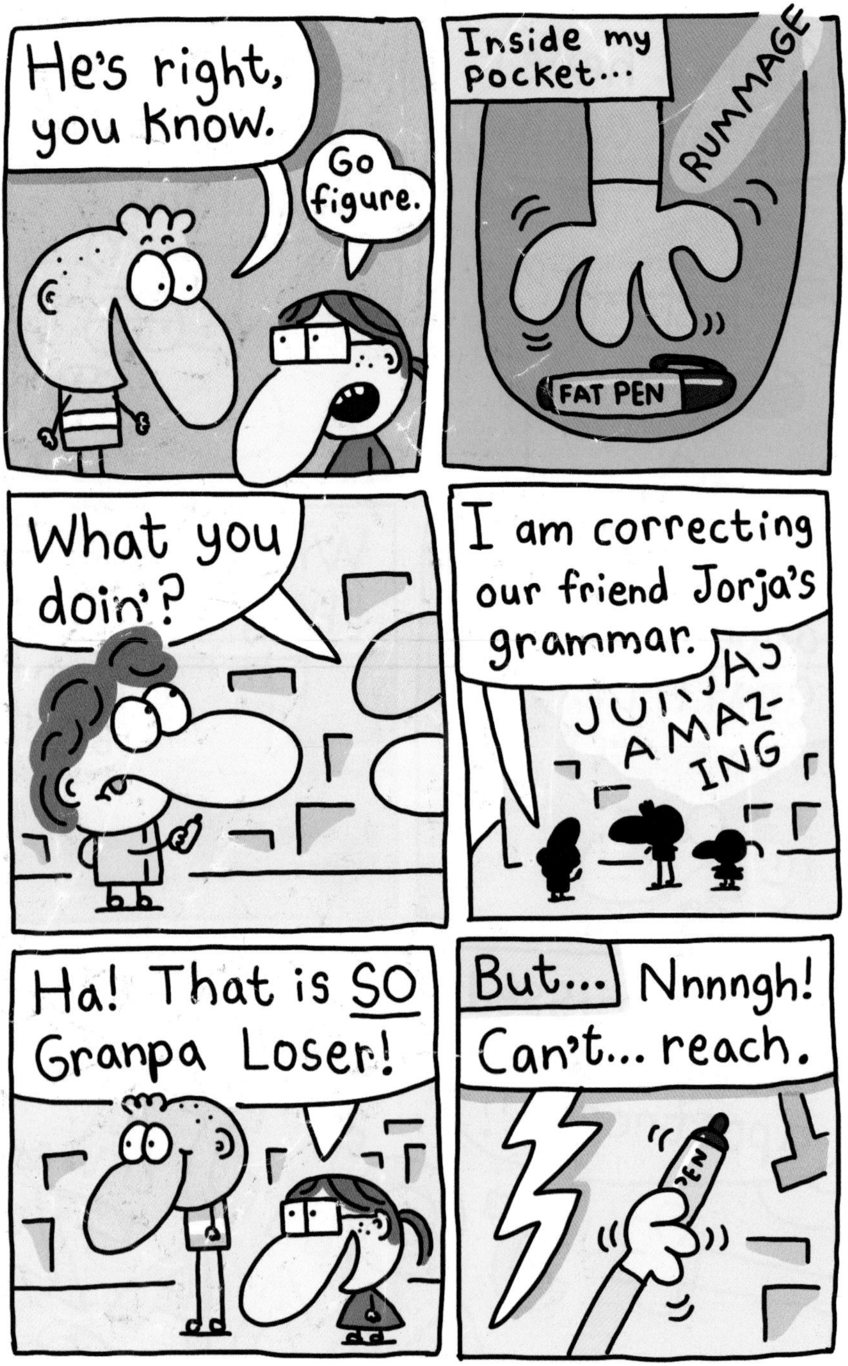
He's right, you know.
Go figure.
Inside my pocket...
RUMMAGE
FAT PEN
What you doin'?
I am correcting our friend Jorja's grammar.
AMAZ-ING
Ha! That is SO Granpa Loser!
But...
Nnnngh! Can't... reach.
PEN

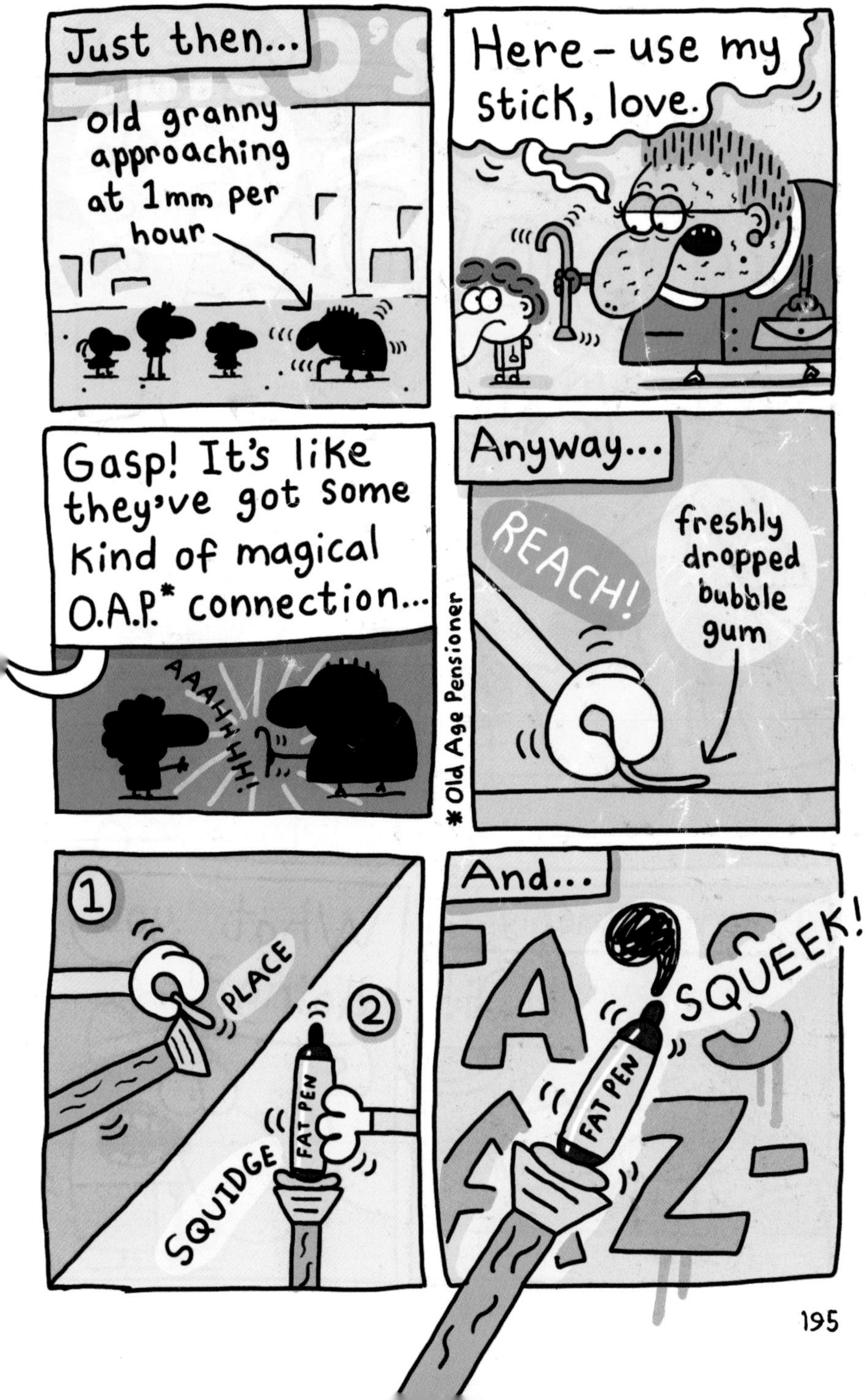
Just then...
old granny approaching at 1mm per hour
Here - use my stick, love.
Gasp! It's like they've got some kind of magical O.A.P.* connection...
AAAHHHHH!
* Old Age Pensioner
Anyway...
REACH!
freshly dropped bubble gum
1
PLACE
2
FAT PEN
SQUIDGE
And...
SQUEEK!
FAT PEN

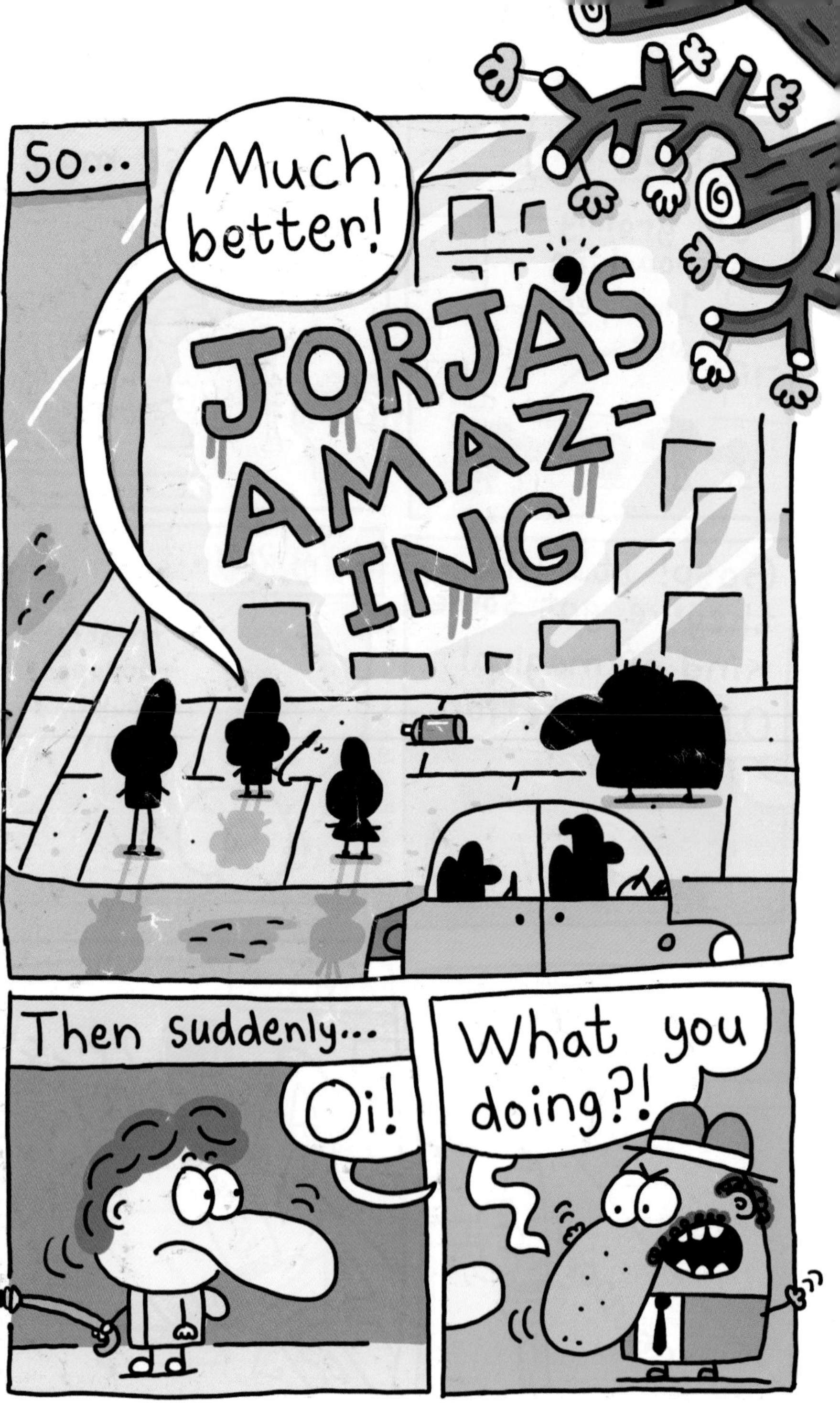
So...
Much better!
JORJA'S AMAZ-ING
Then suddenly...
Oi!
What you doing?!

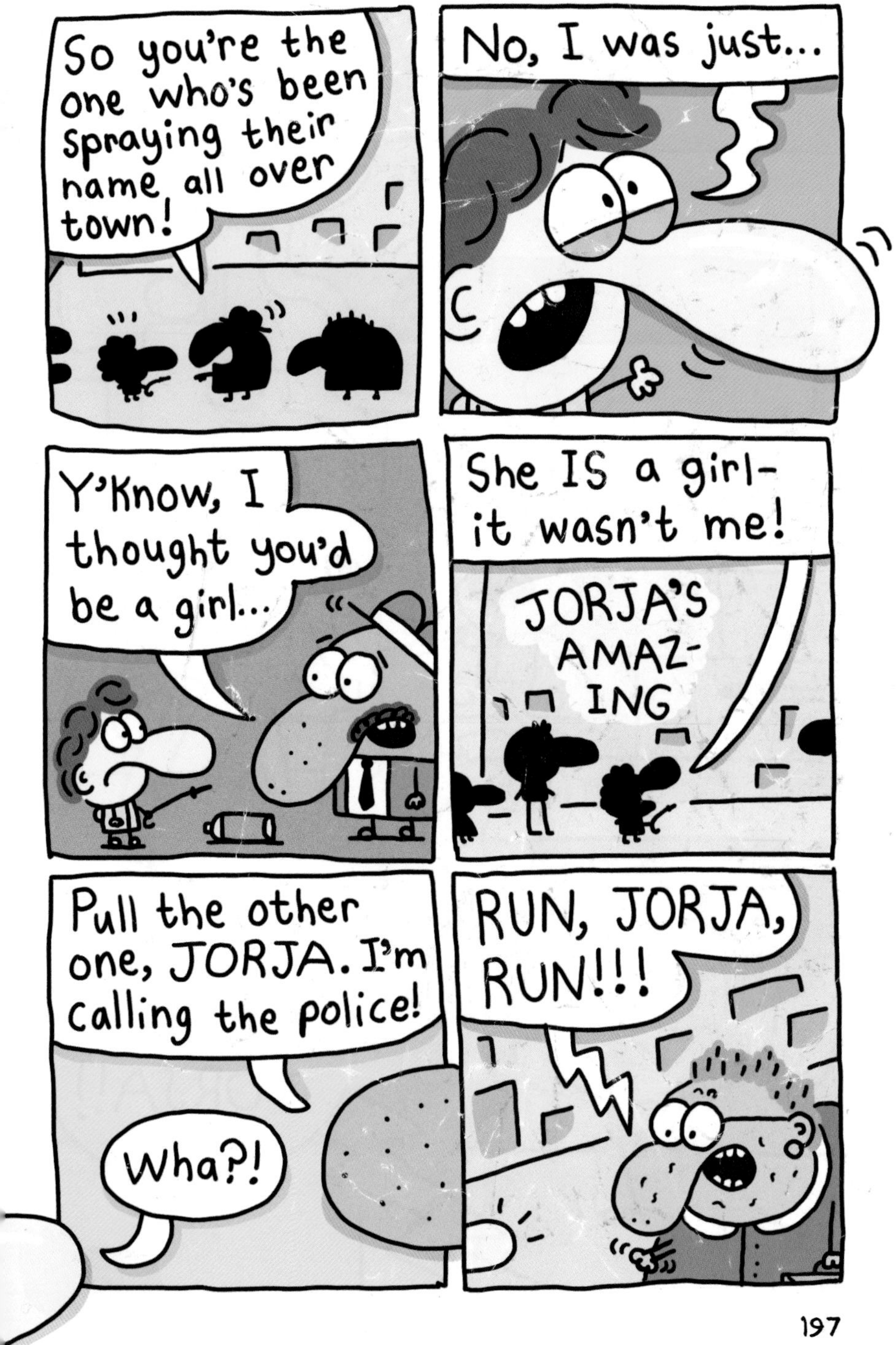
So you're the one who's been spraying their name all over town!
No, I was just...
Y'Know, I thought you'd be a girl...
She IS a girl- it wasn't me!
JORJA'S AMAZ-ING
Pull the other one, JORJA. I'm calling the police!
Wha?!
RUN, JORJA, RUN!!!

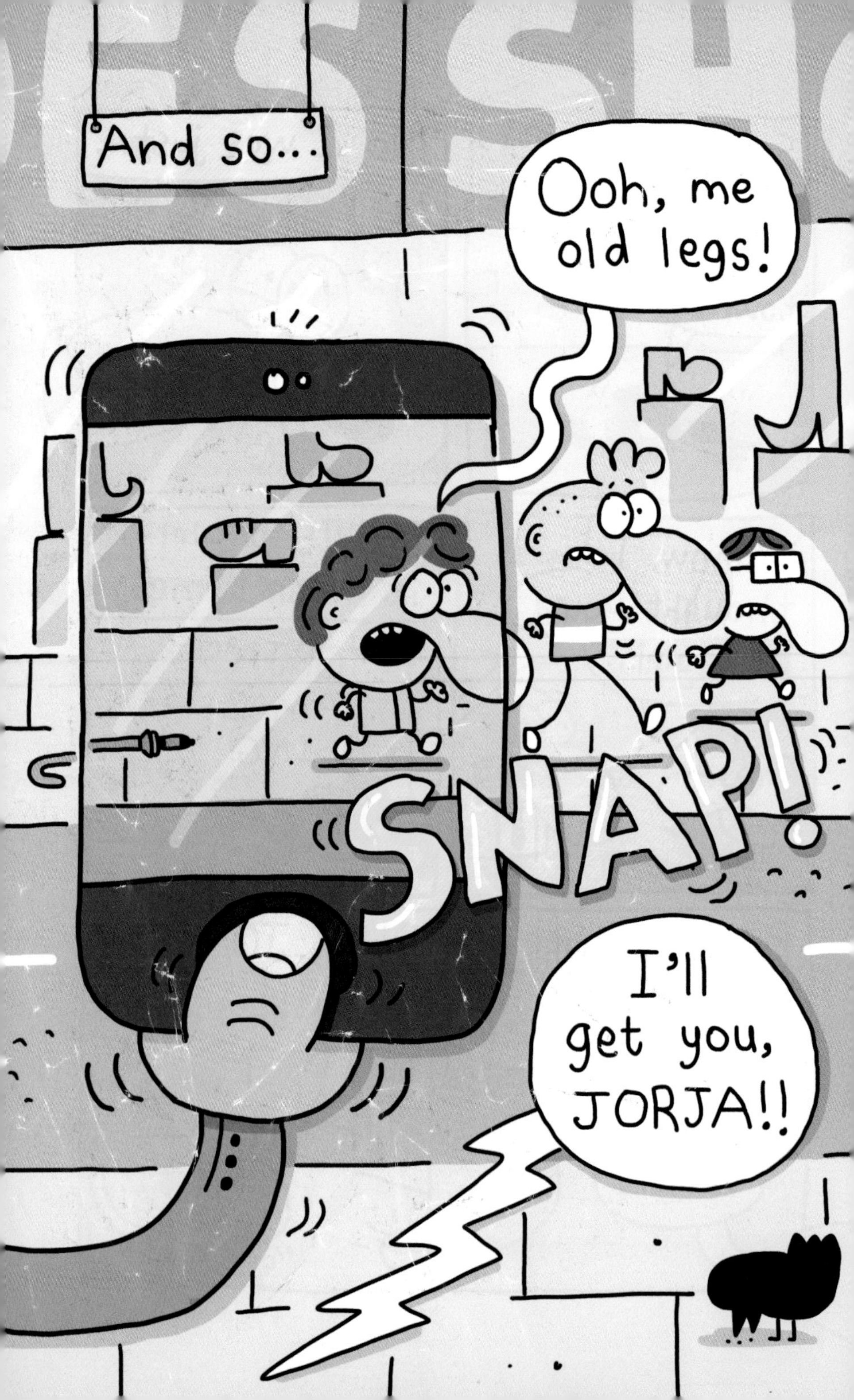
And so...
Ooh, me old legs!
SNAP!
I'll get you, JORJA!!

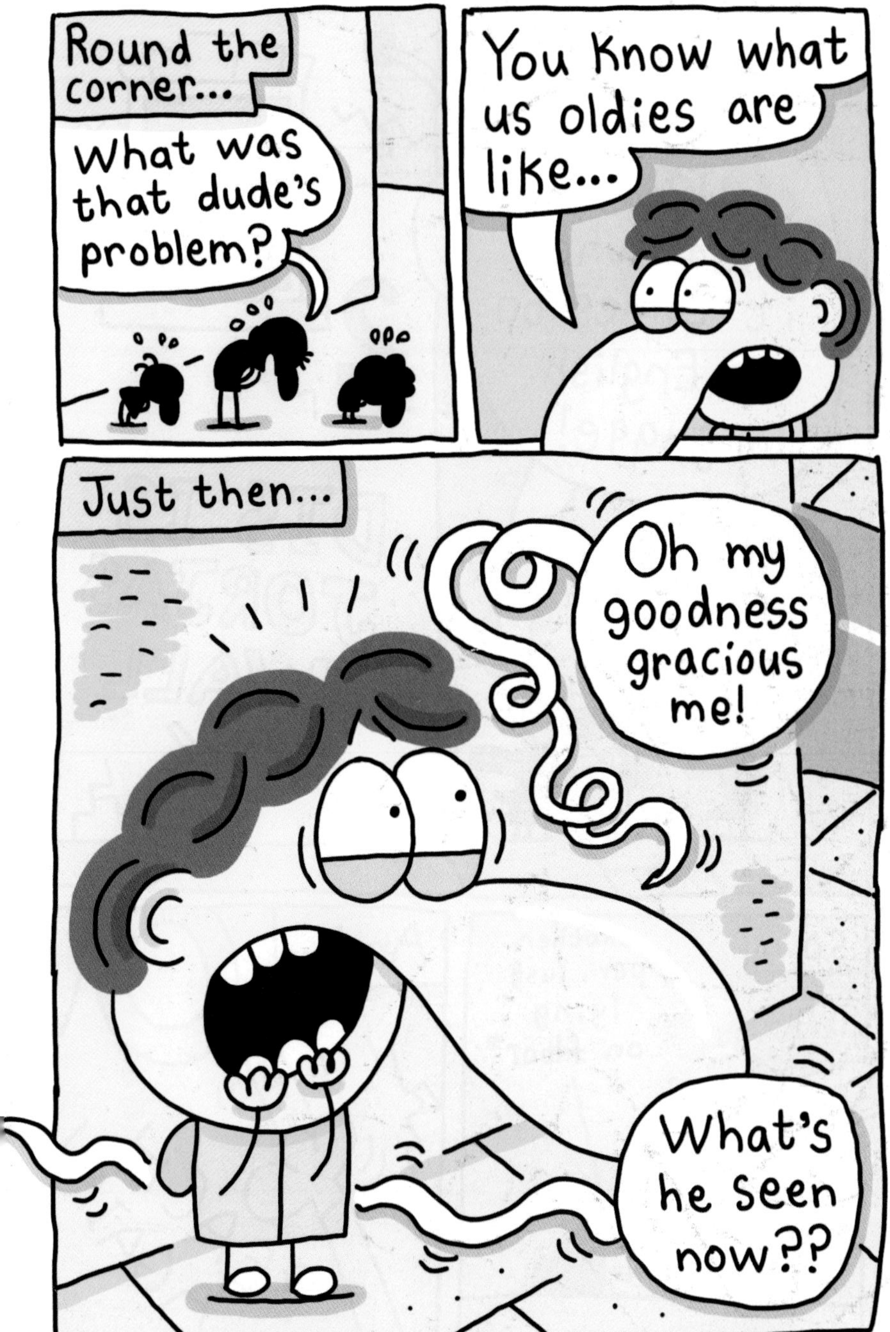
Round the corner...
What was that dude's problem?
You know what us oldies are like...
Just then...
Oh my goodness gracious me!
What's he seen now??

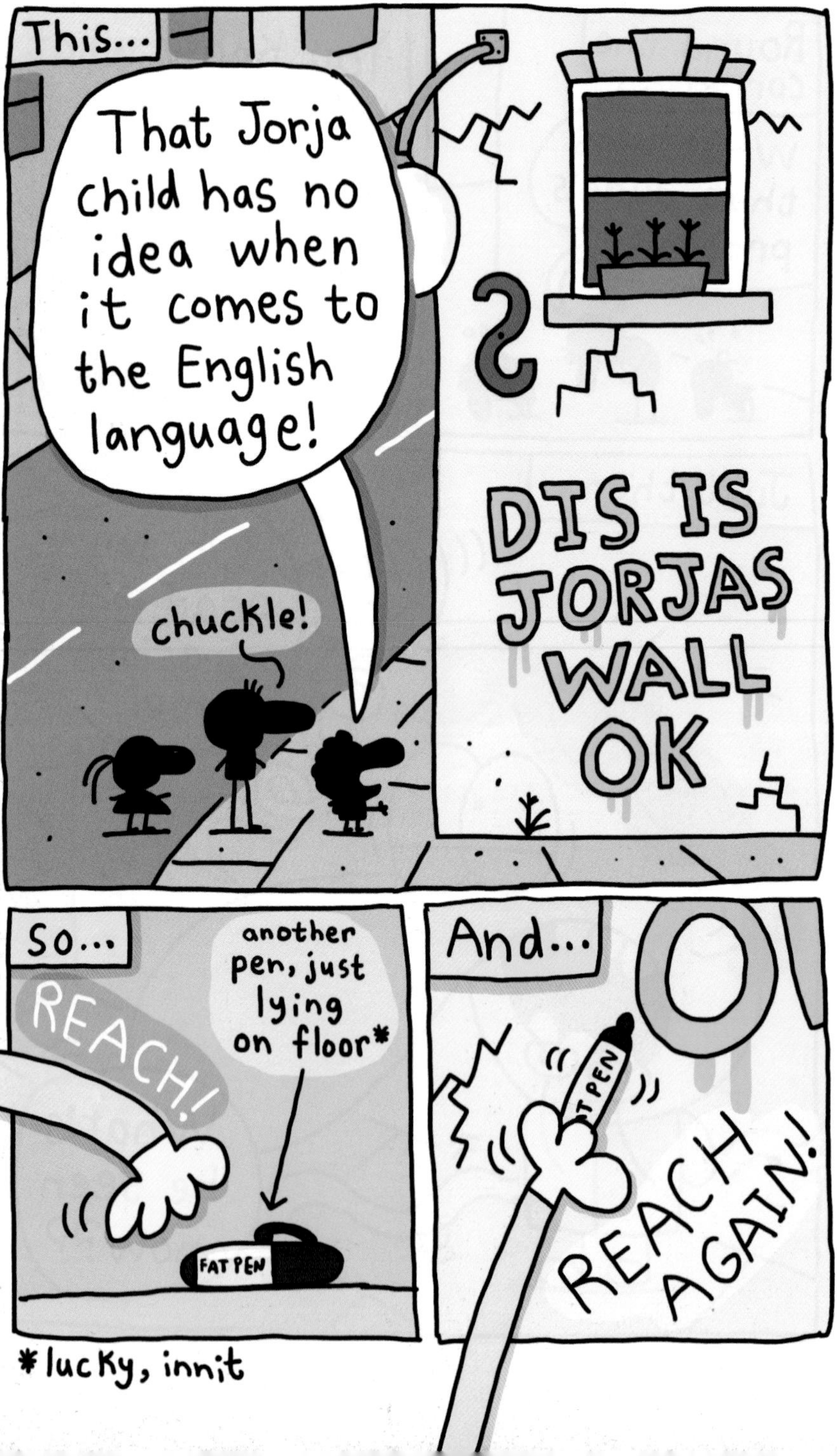
This...
That Jorja child has no idea when it comes to the English language!
chuckle!
DIS IS JORJAS WALL OK
So...
REACH!
another pen, just lying on floor*
FAT PEN
And...
FAT PEN
REACH AGAIN!
*lucky, innit

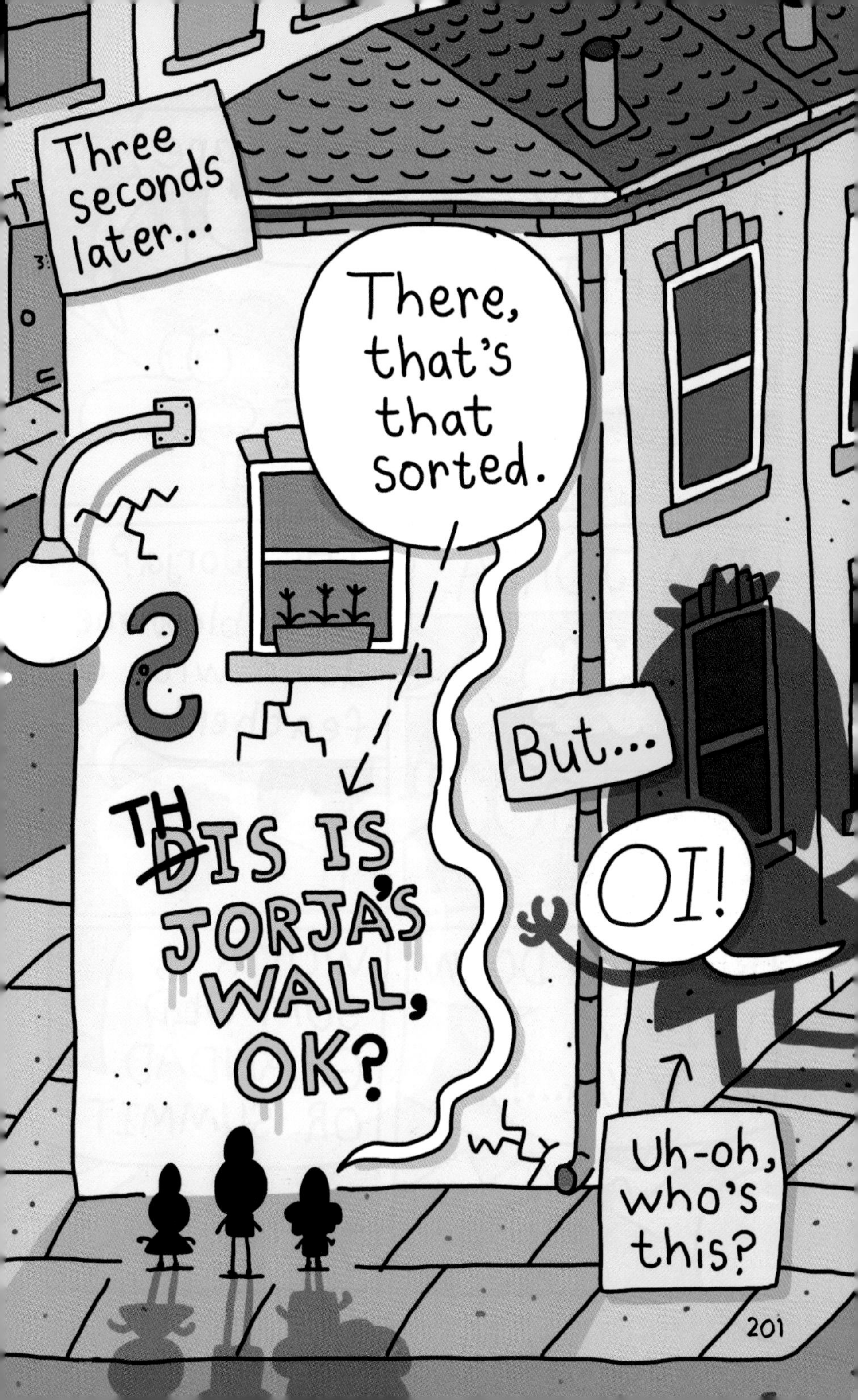

Three seconds later...
There, that's that sorted.
TH DIS IS JORJA'S WALL, OK?
But...
OI!
Uh-oh, who's this?

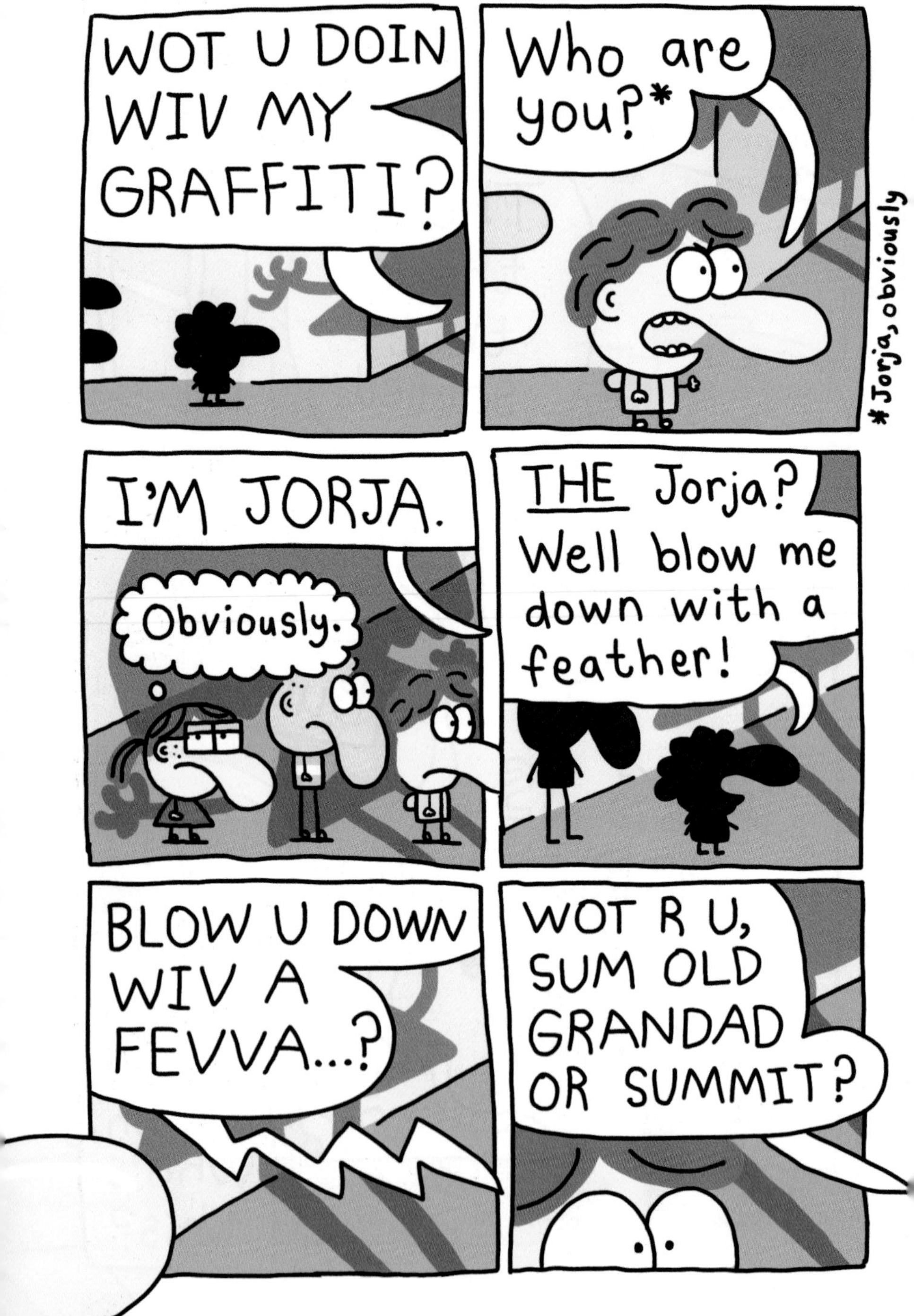
WOT U DOIN WIV MY GRAFFITI?
Who are you?*
I'M JORJA.
Obviously.
THE Jorja? Well blow me down with a feather!
BLOW U DOWN WIV A FEVVA...?
WOT R U, SUM OLD GRANDAD OR SUMMIT?
*Jorja, obviously

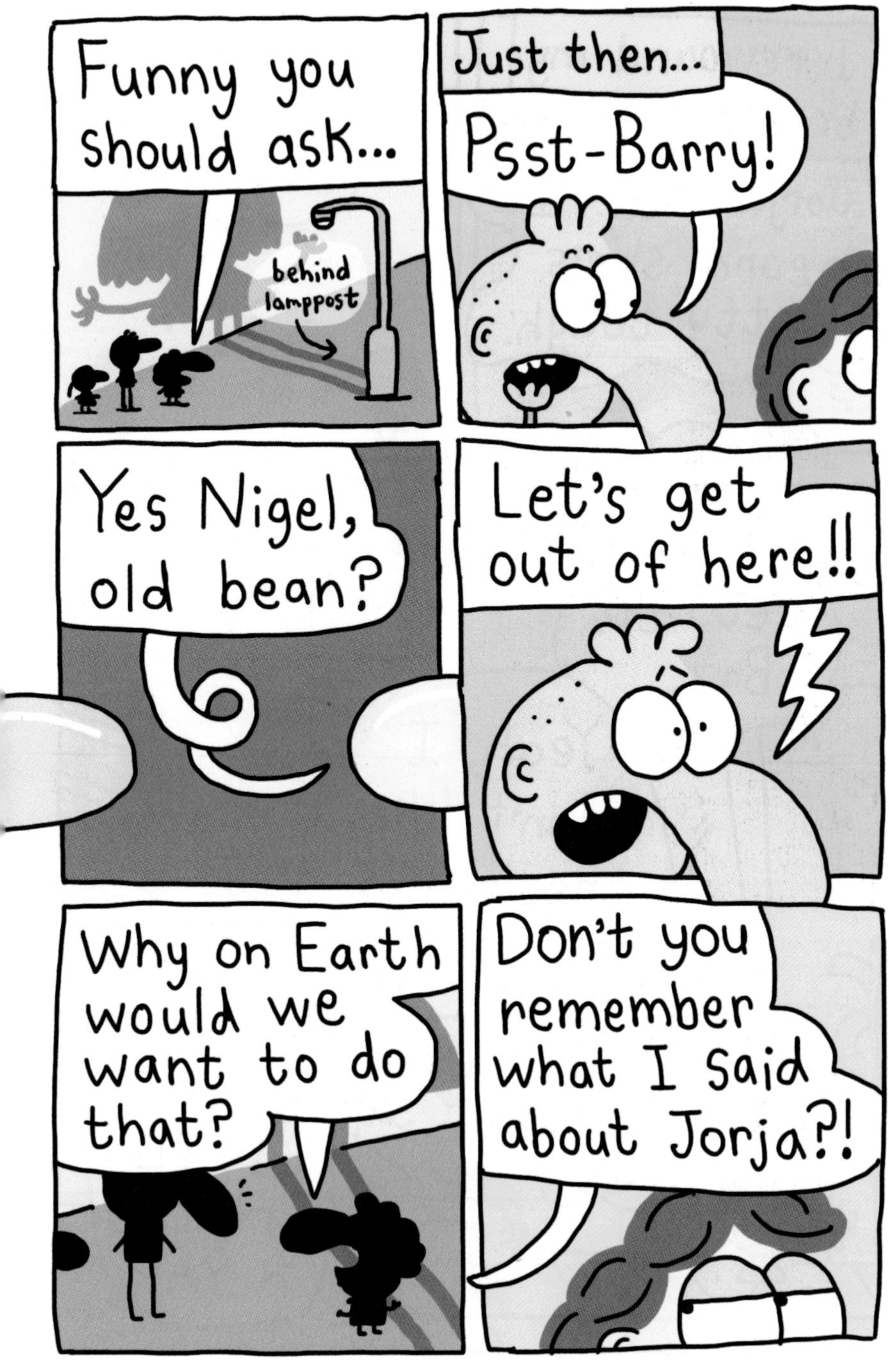
Funny you should ask...
behind lamppost
Just then...
Psst-Barry!
Yes Nigel, old bean?
Let's get out of here!!
Why on Earth would we want to do that?
Don't you remember what I said about Jorja?!

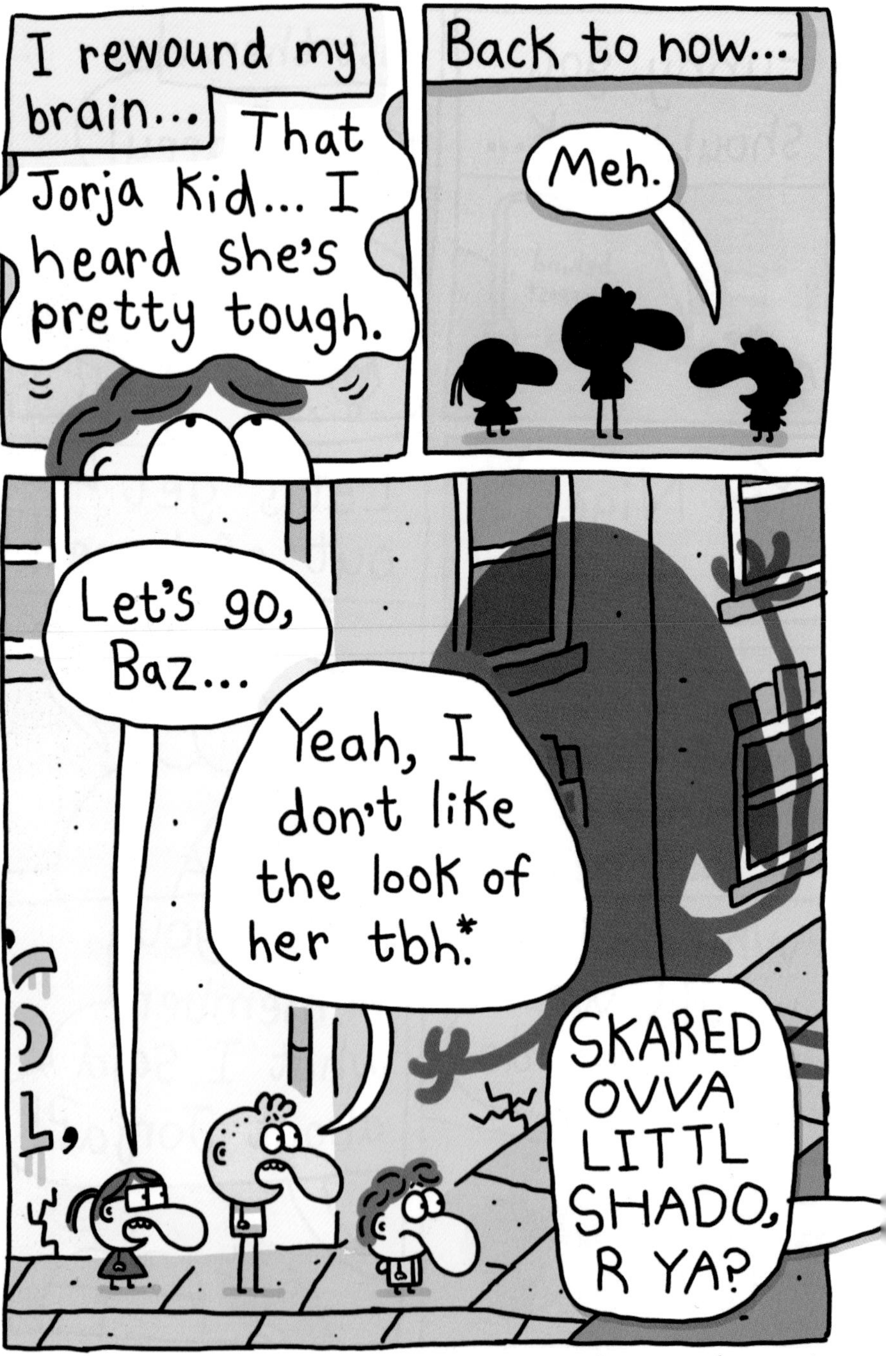
I rewound my brain...
That Jorja kid... I heard she's pretty tough.
Back to now...
Meh.
Let's go, Baz...
Yeah, I don't like the look of her tbh.*
SKARED OVVA LITTL SHADO, R YA?

*to be honest

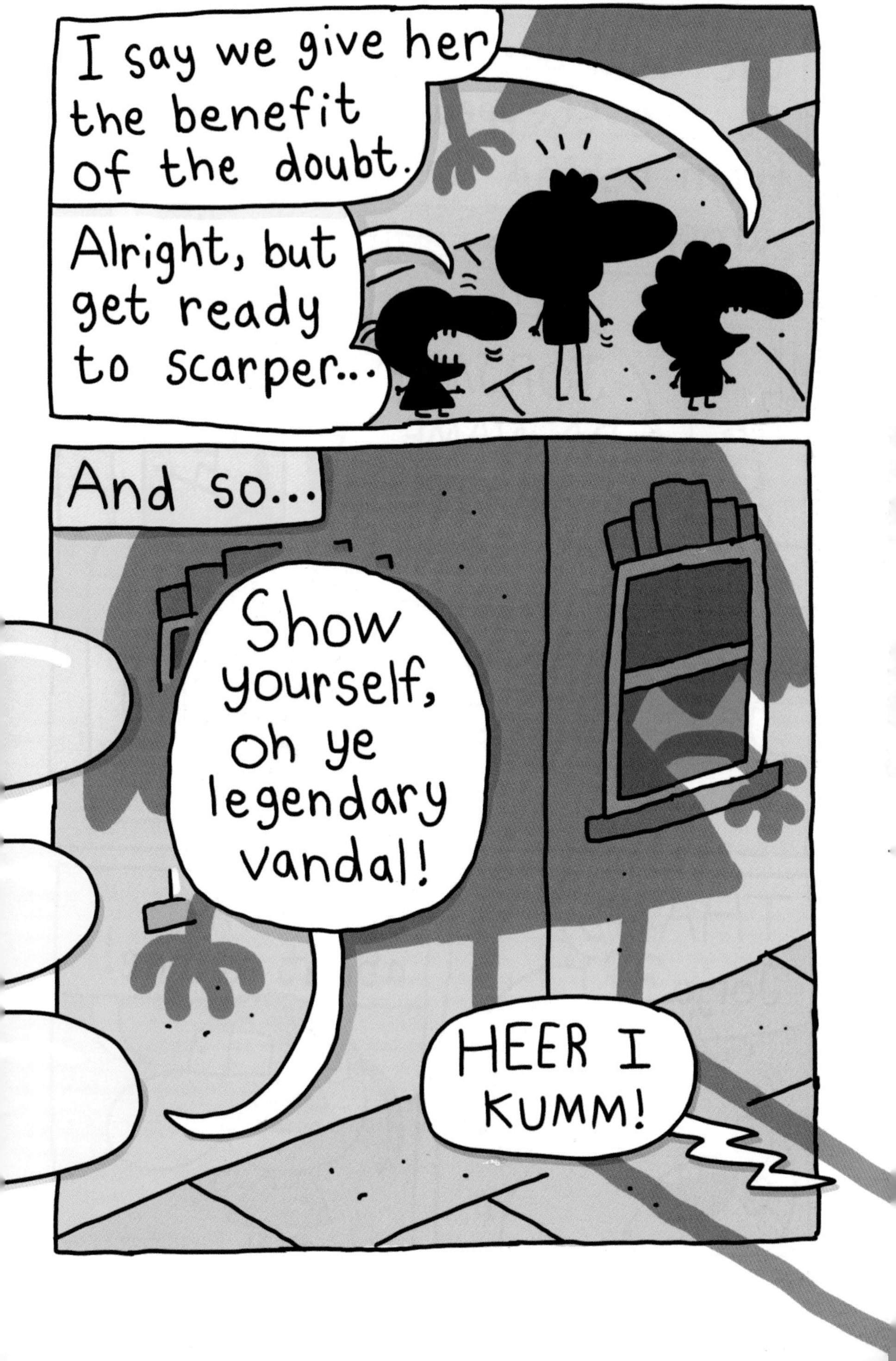

I say we give her the benefit of the doubt.
Alright, but get ready to scarper...
And so...
Show yourself, oh ye legendary vandal!
HEER I KUMM!

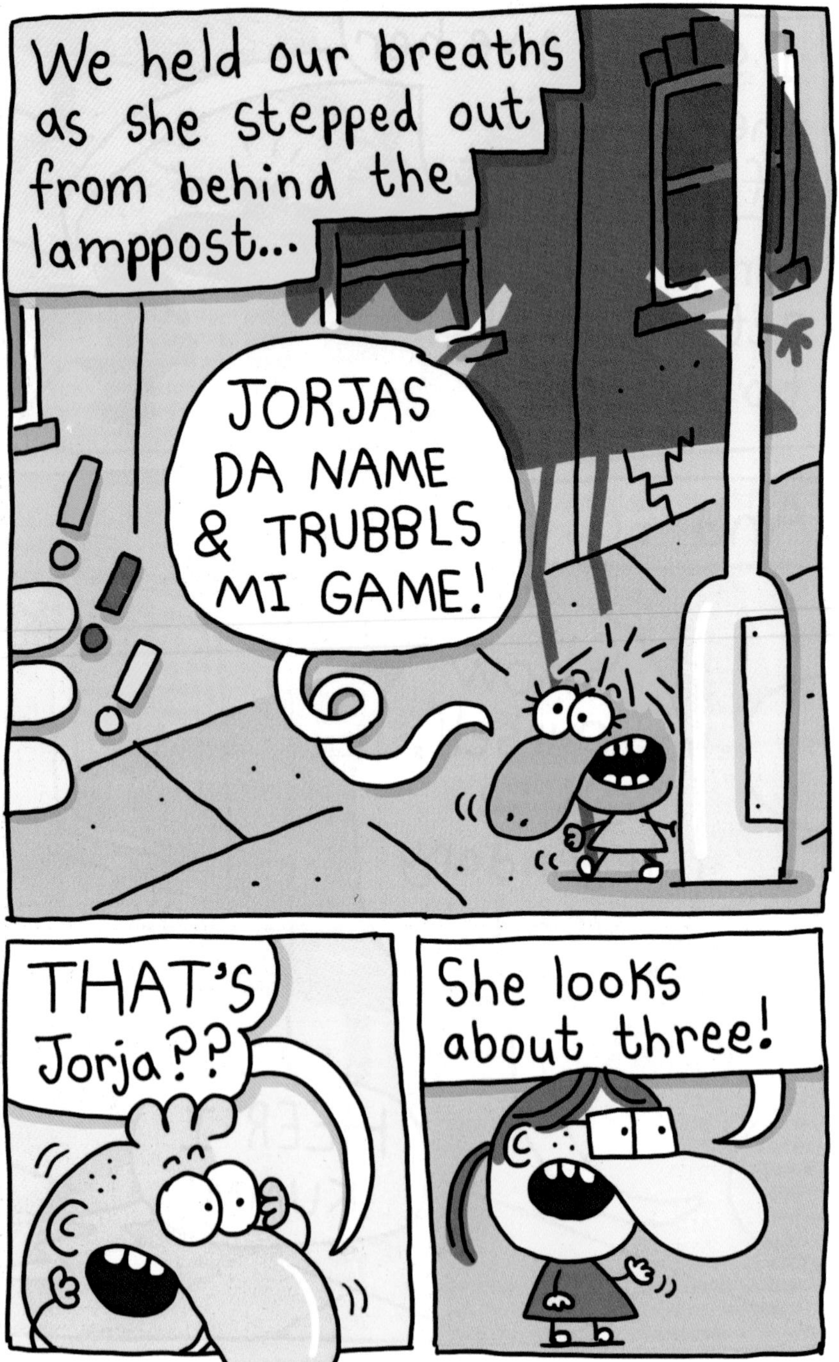
We held our breaths as she stepped out from behind the lamppost...
JORJAS DA NAME & TRUBBLS MI GAME!
THAT'S Jorja??
She looks about three!

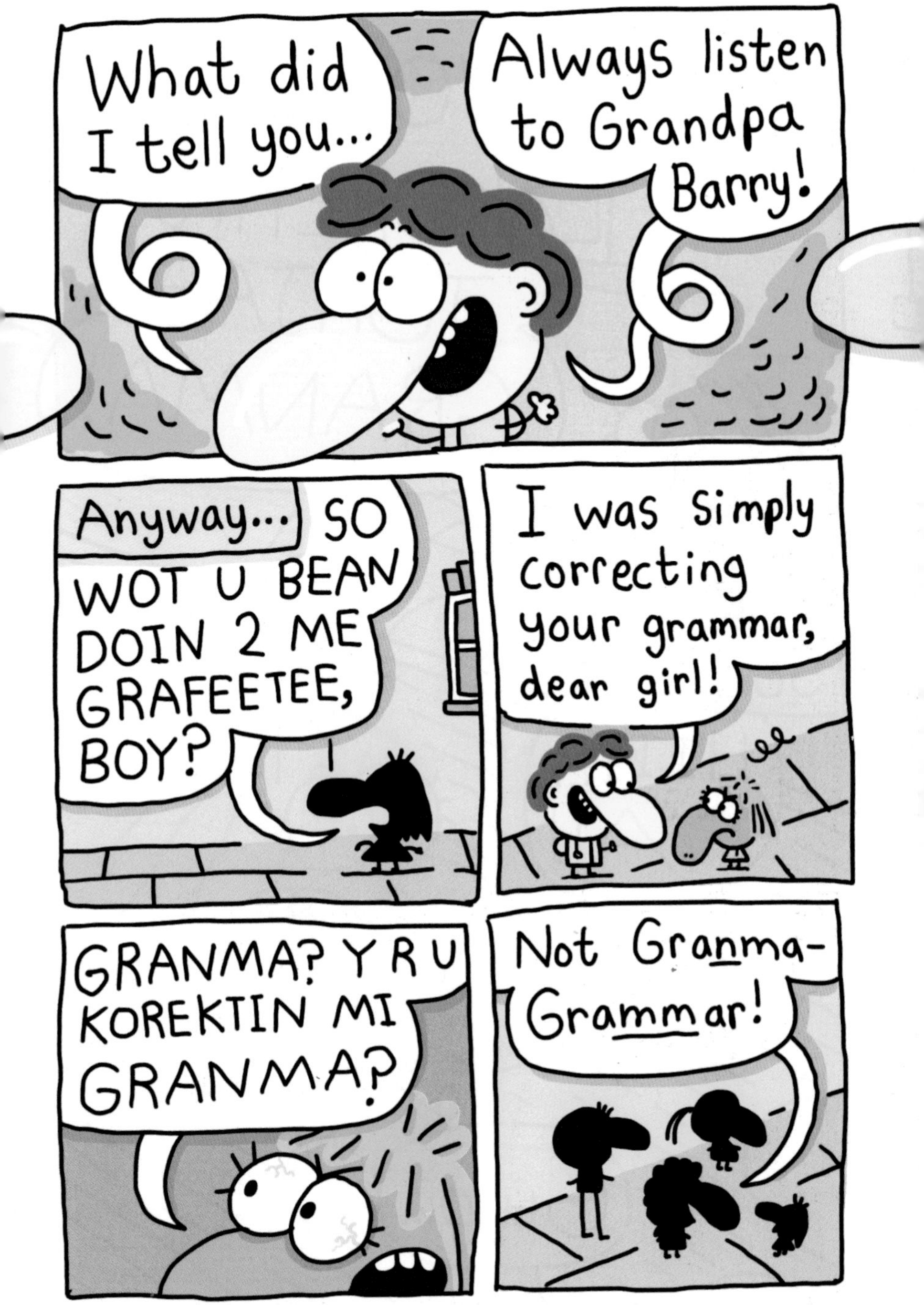
What did I tell you...
Always listen to Grandpa Barry!
Anyway...
SO WOT U BEAN DOIN 2 ME GRAFEETEE, BOY?
I was simply correcting your grammar, dear girl!
GRANMA? Y R U KOREKTIN MI GRANMA?
Not Granma- Grammar!

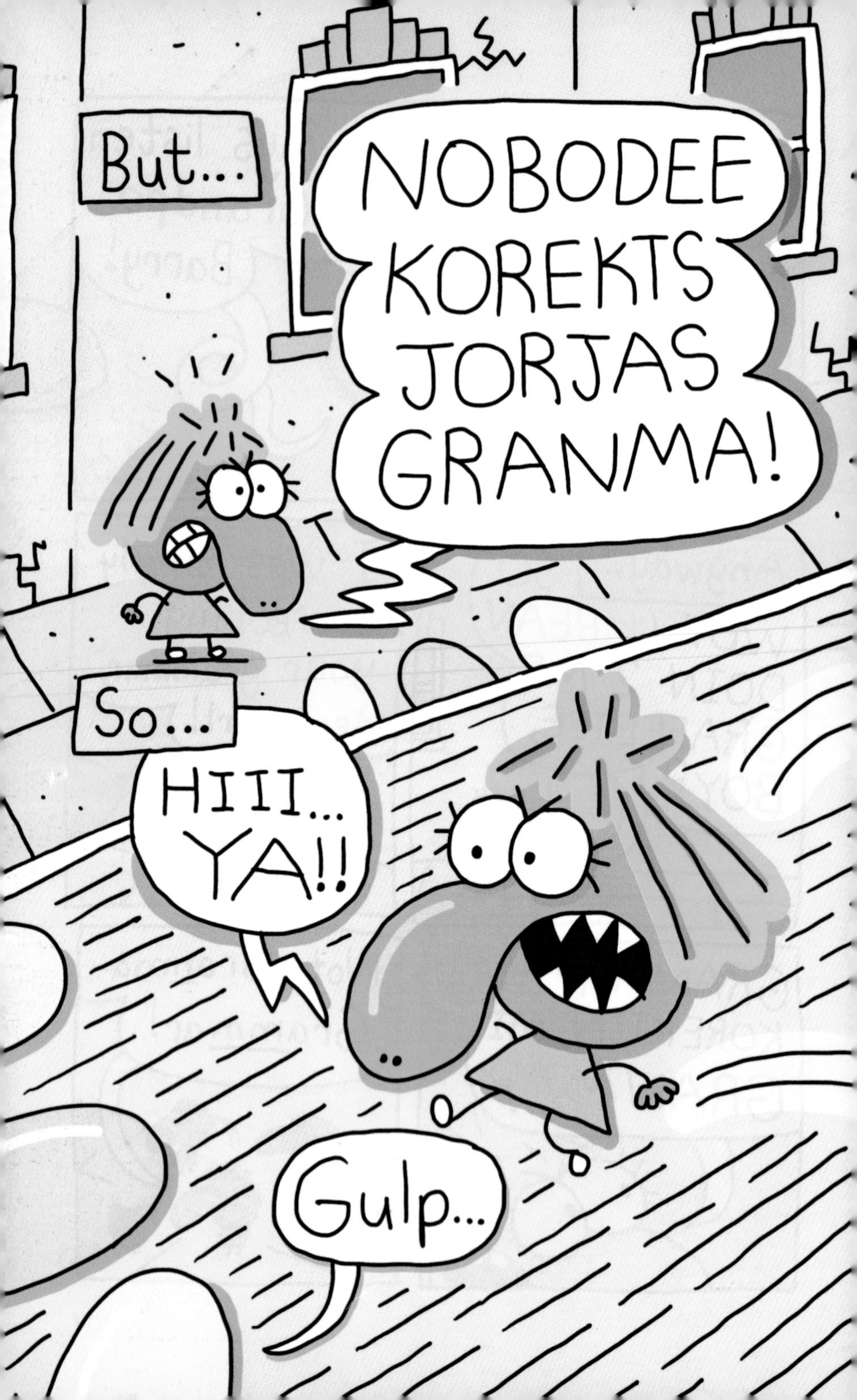

But...
NOBODEE KOREKTS JORJAS GRANMA!
So...
HIII... YA!!
Gulp...

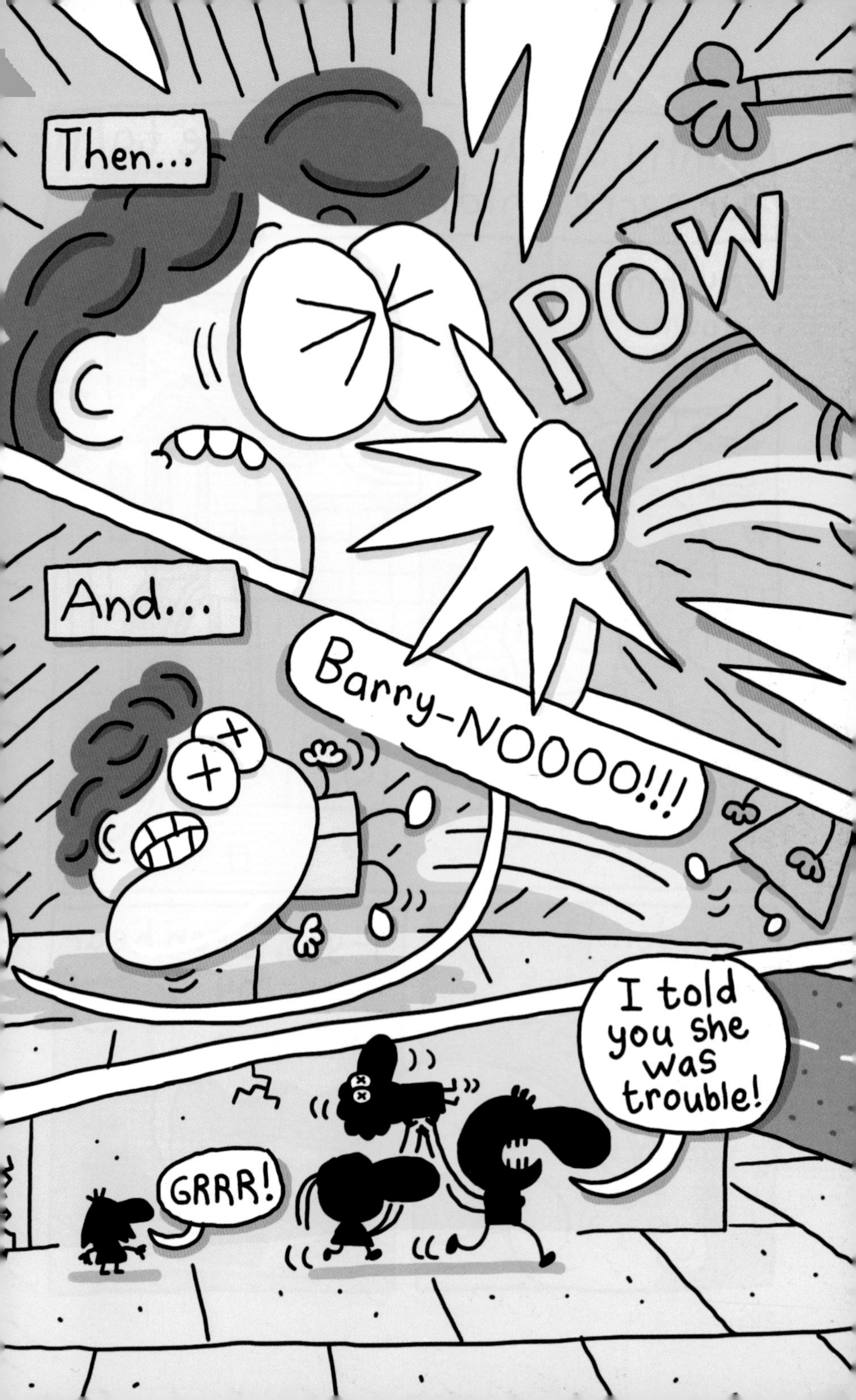
Then...
POW
And...
Barry-NOOOO!!!
I told you she was trouble!
GRRR!

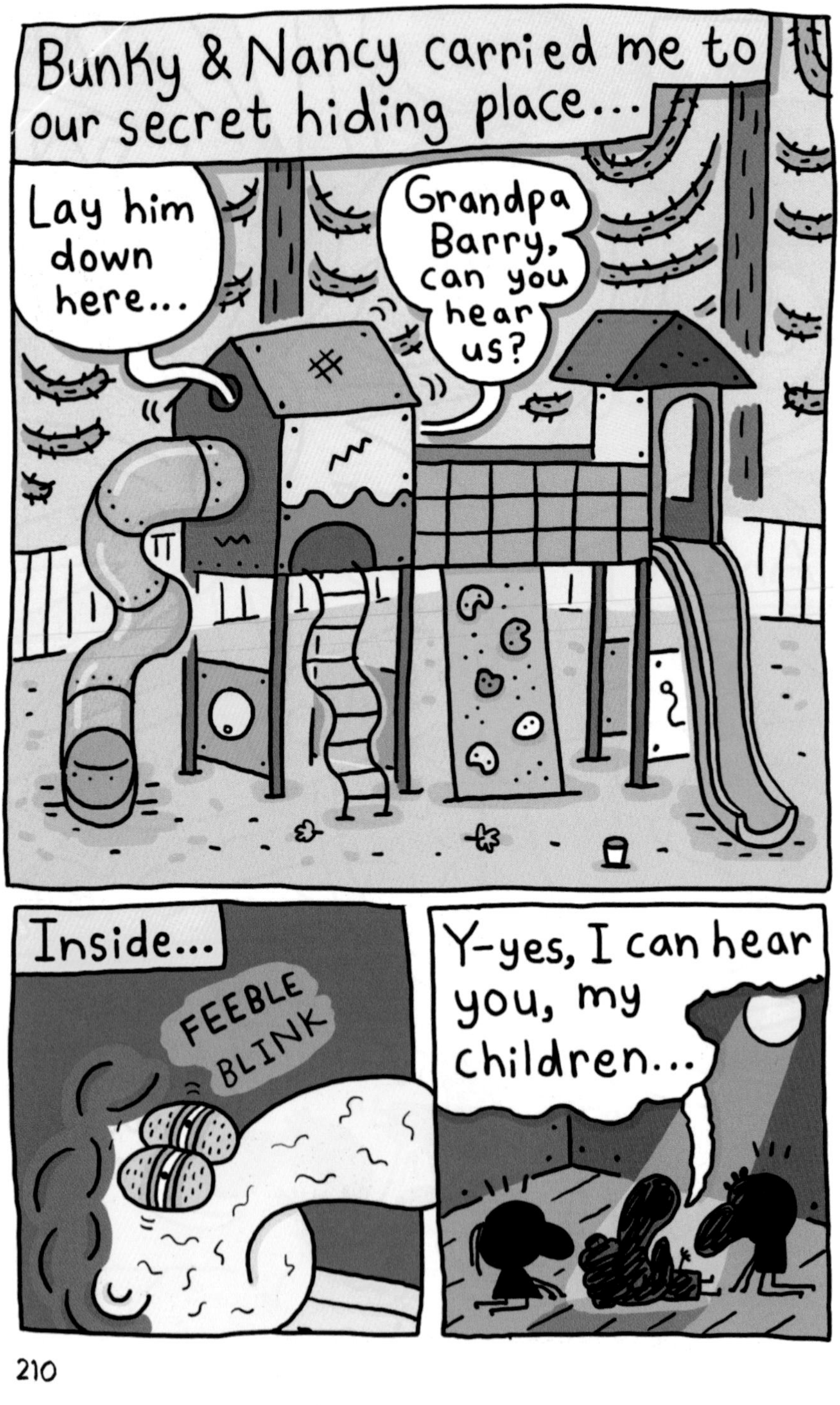
Bunky & Nancy carried me to our secret hiding place...
Lay him down here...
Grandpa Barry, can you hear us?
Inside...
FEEBLE BLINK
Y-yes, I can hear you, my children...

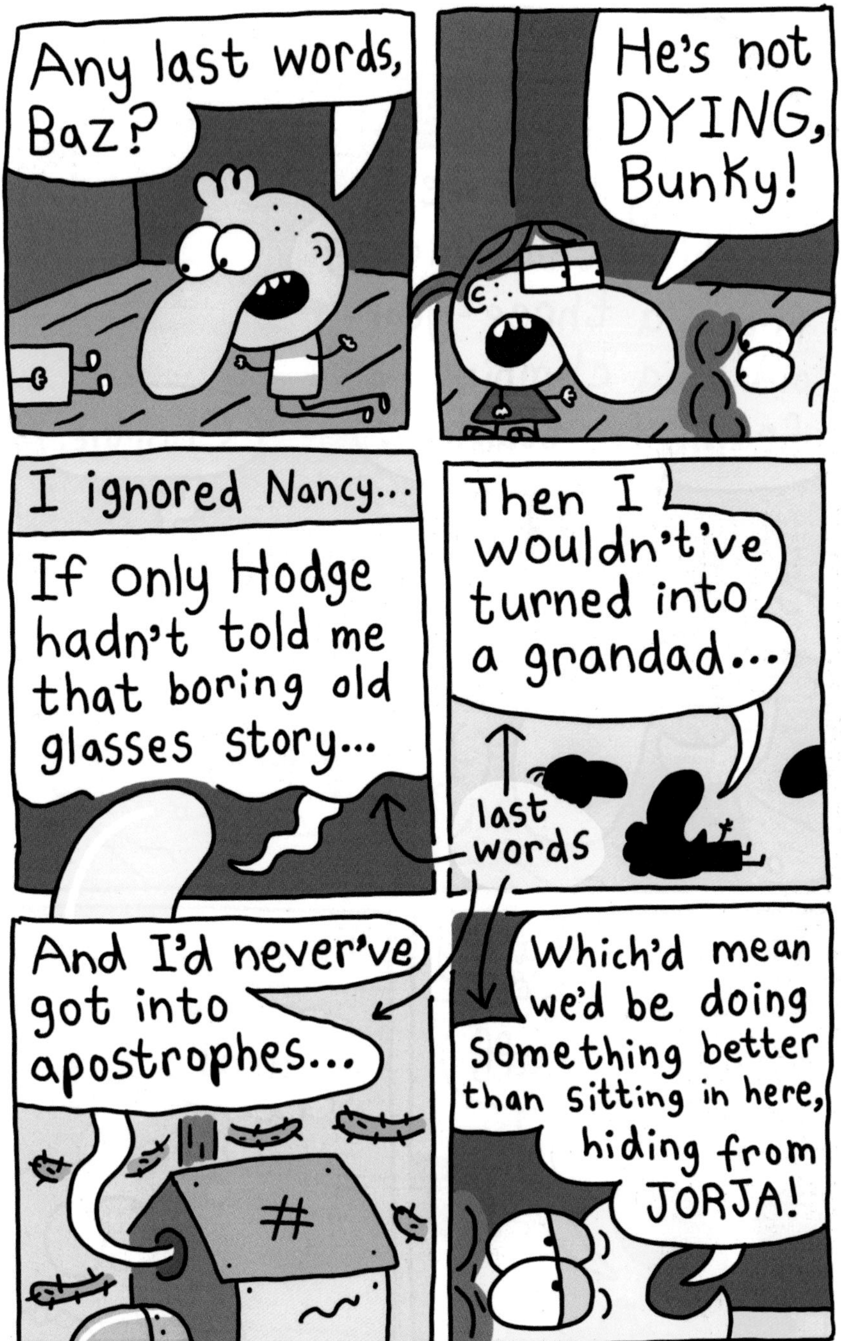
Any last words, Baz?
He's not DYING, Bunky!
I ignored Nancy...
If only Hodge hadn't told me that boring old glasses story...
Then I wouldn't've turned into a grandad...
last words
And I'd never've got into apostrophes...
Which'd mean we'd be doing something better than sitting in here, hiding from JORJA!

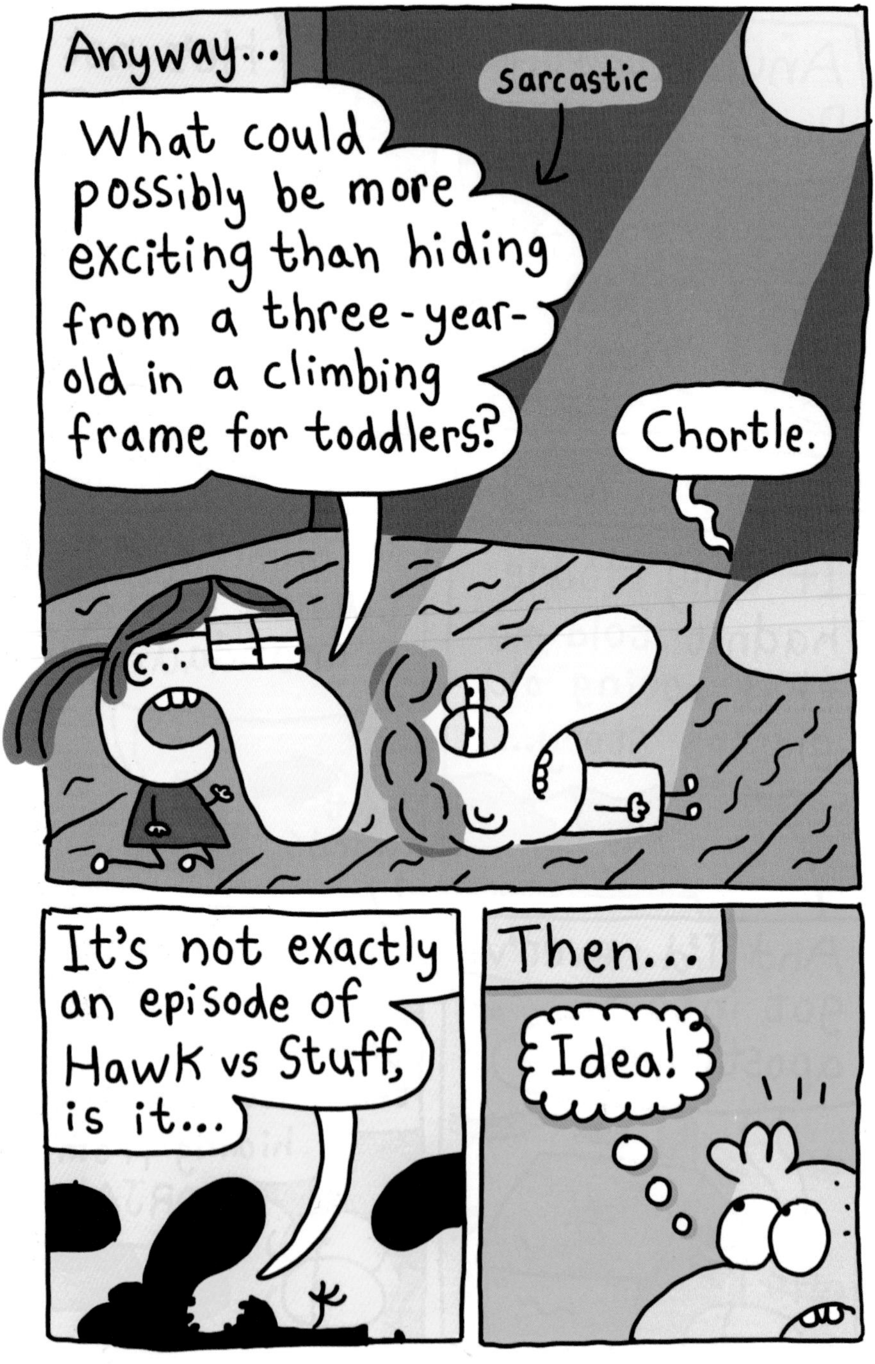
Anyway...
sarcastic
What could possibly be more exciting than hiding from a three-year-old in a climbing frame for toddlers?
Chortle.
It's not exactly an episode of Hawk vs Stuff, is it...
Then...
Idea!

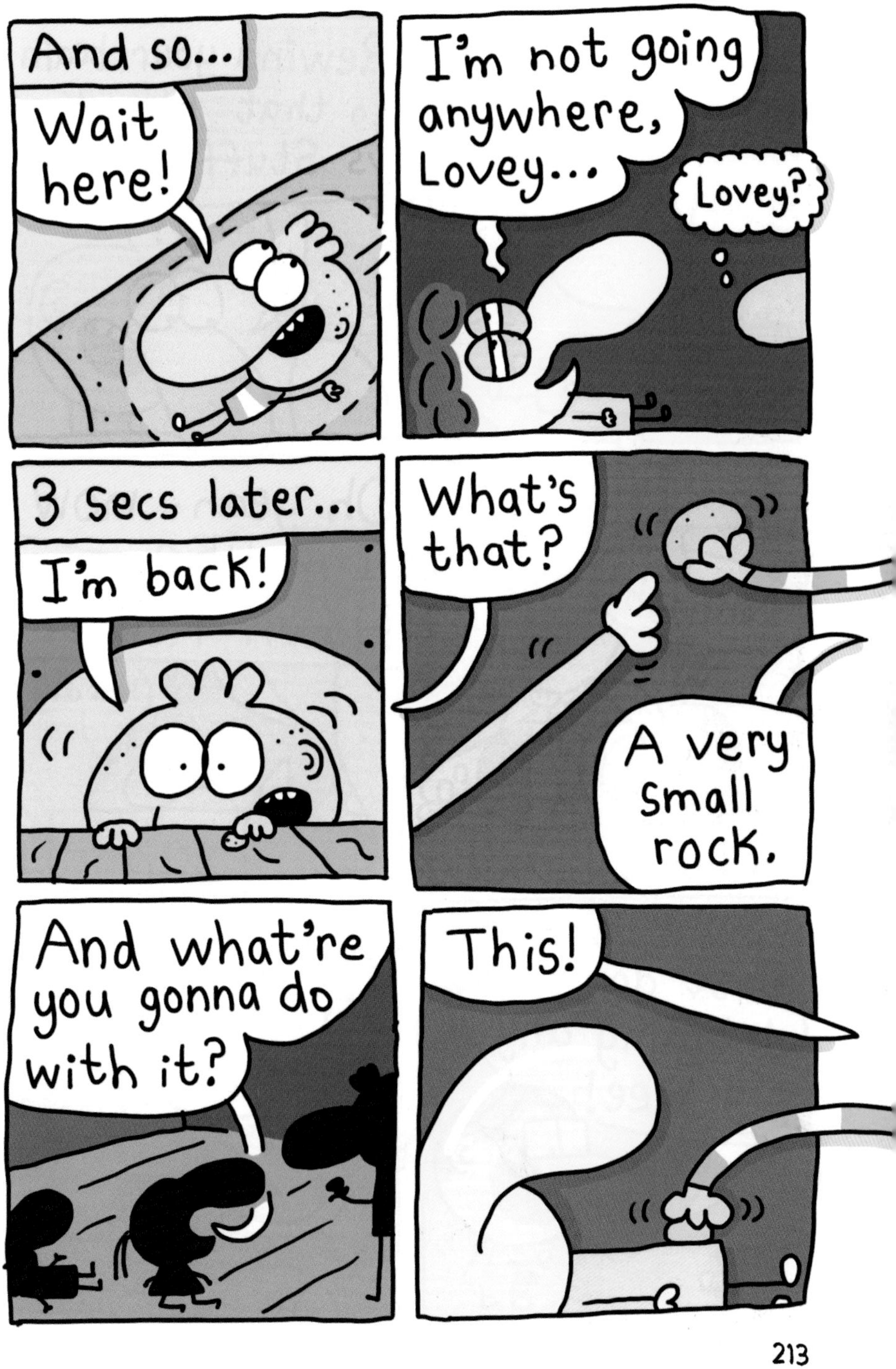
And so...
Wait here!
I'm not going anywhere, Lovey...
Lovey?
3 secs later...
I'm back!
What's that?
A very small rock.
And what're you gonna do with it?
This!

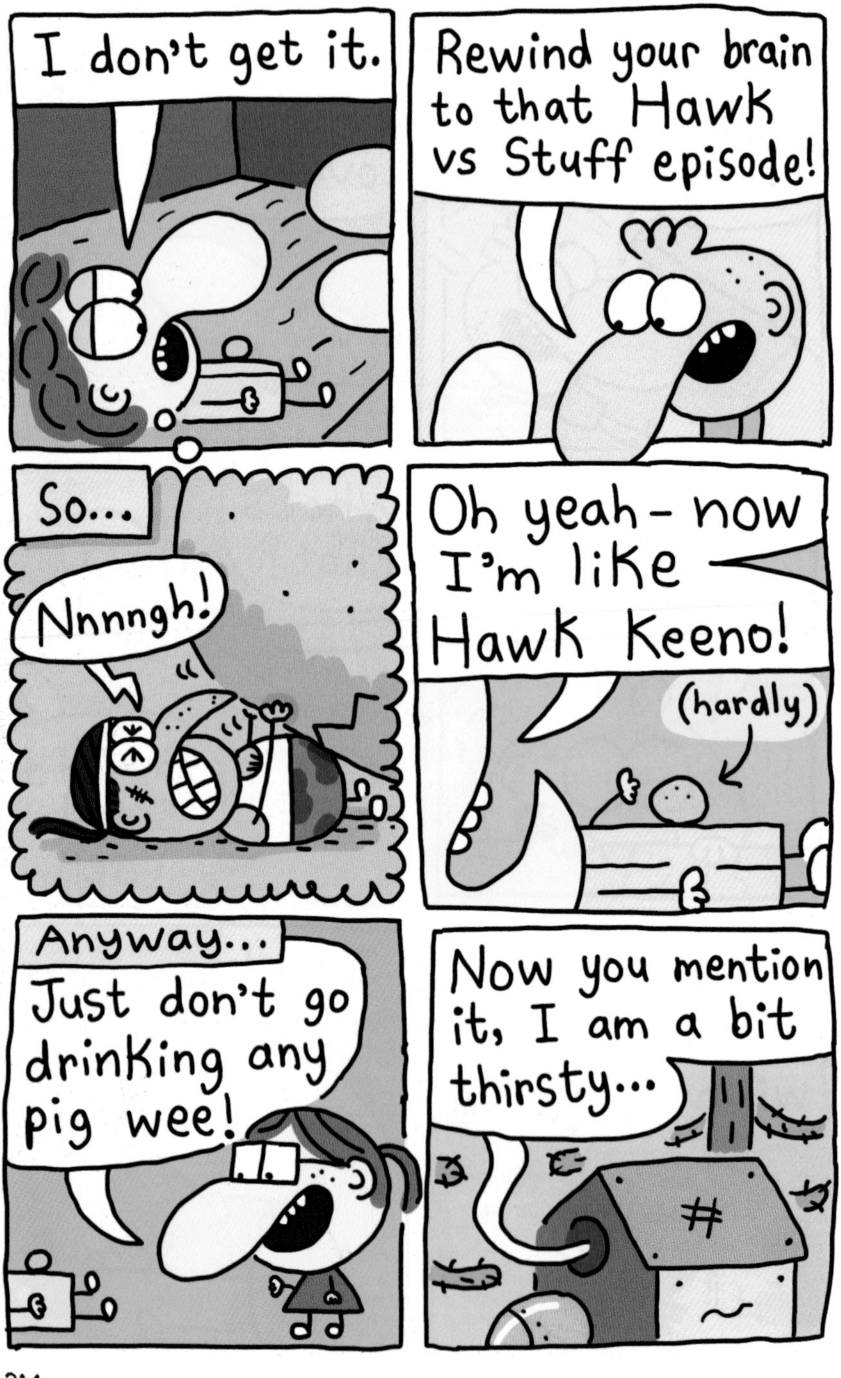
I don't get it.
Rewind your brain to that Hawk vs Stuff episode!
So...
Nnnngh!
Oh yeah - now I'm like Hawk Keeno!
(hardly)
Anyway...
Just don't go drinking any pig wee!
Now you mention it, I am a bit thirsty...

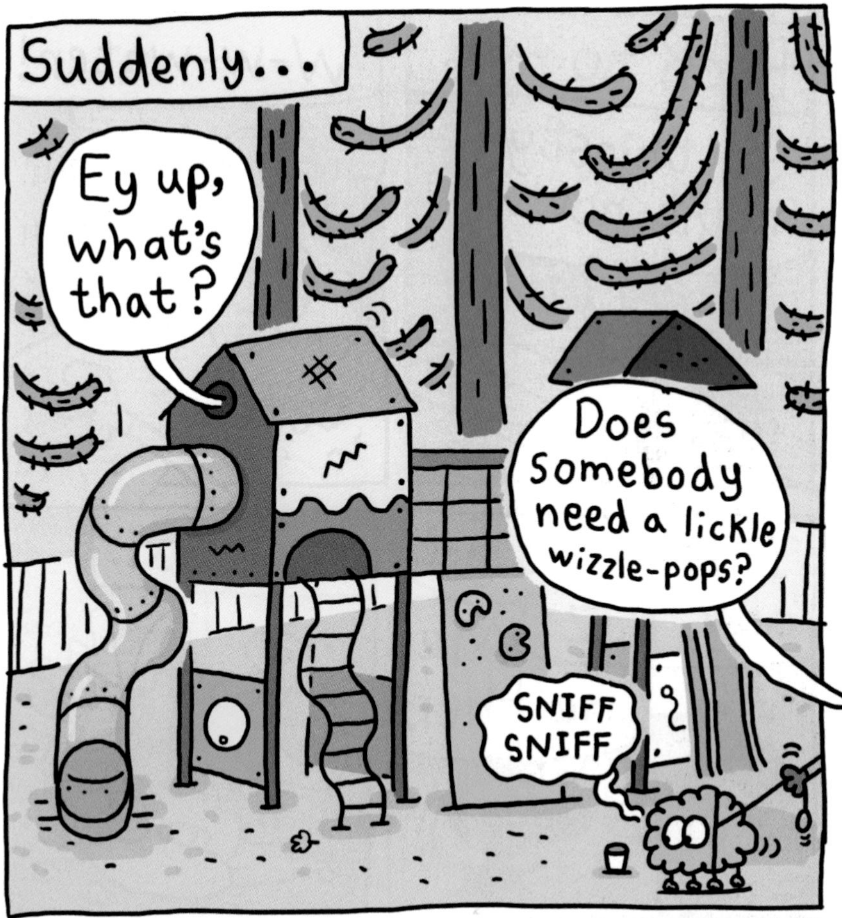
Suddenly...
Ey up, what's that?
Does somebody need a lickle wizzle-pops?
SNIFF SNIFF

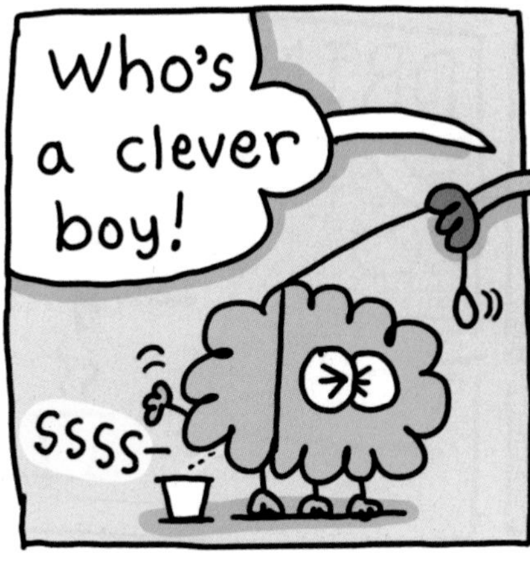
Who's a clever boy!
SSSS–

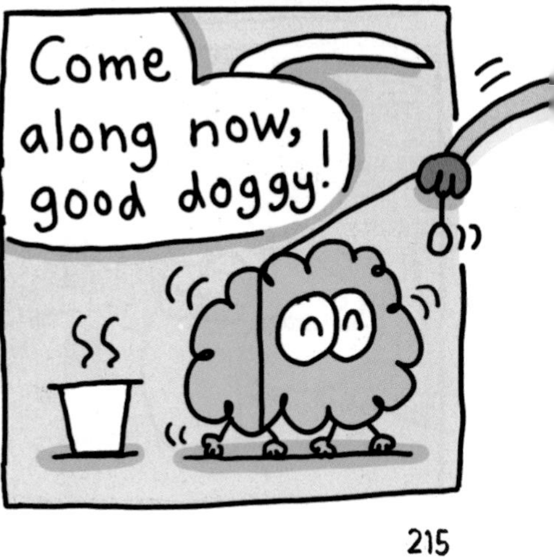
Come along now, good doggy!

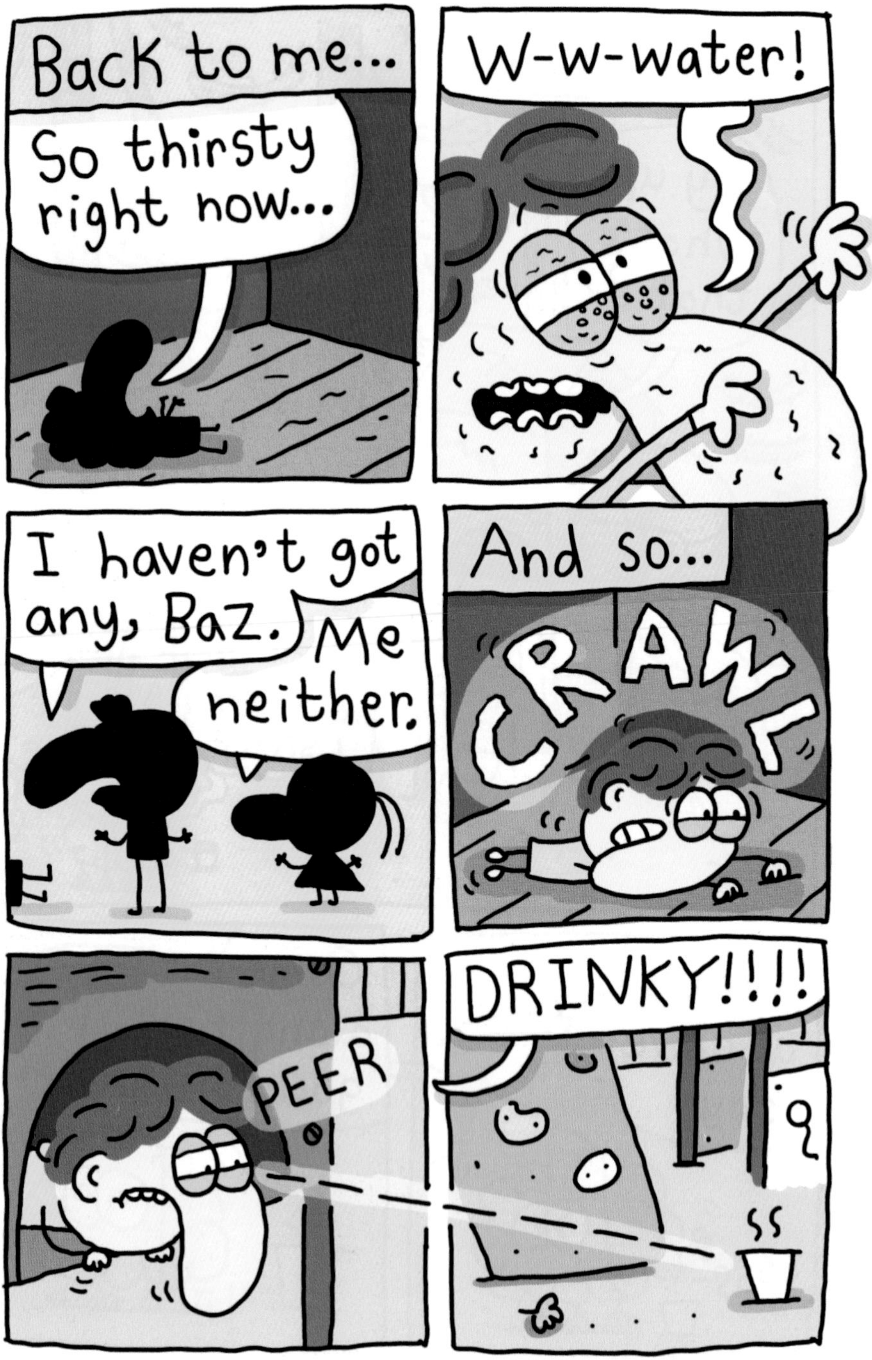
Back to me...
So thirsty right now...
W-w-water!
I haven't got any, Baz.
Me neither.
And so...
CRAWL
PEER
DRINKY!!!!

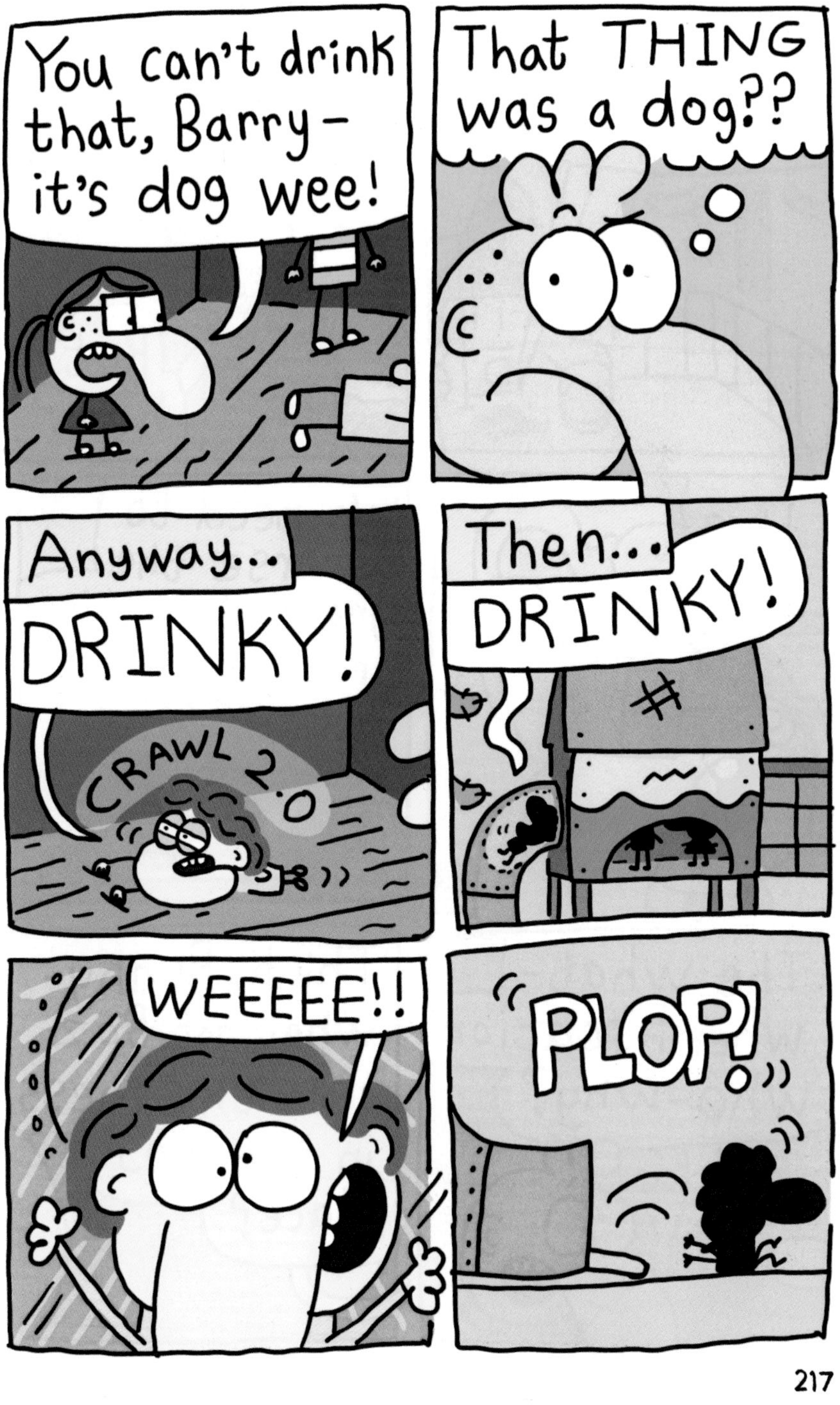
You can't drink that, Barry - it's dog wee!
That THING was a dog??
Anyway...
DRINKY!
CRAWL 2.0
Then...
DRINKY!
WEEEEE!!
PLOP!

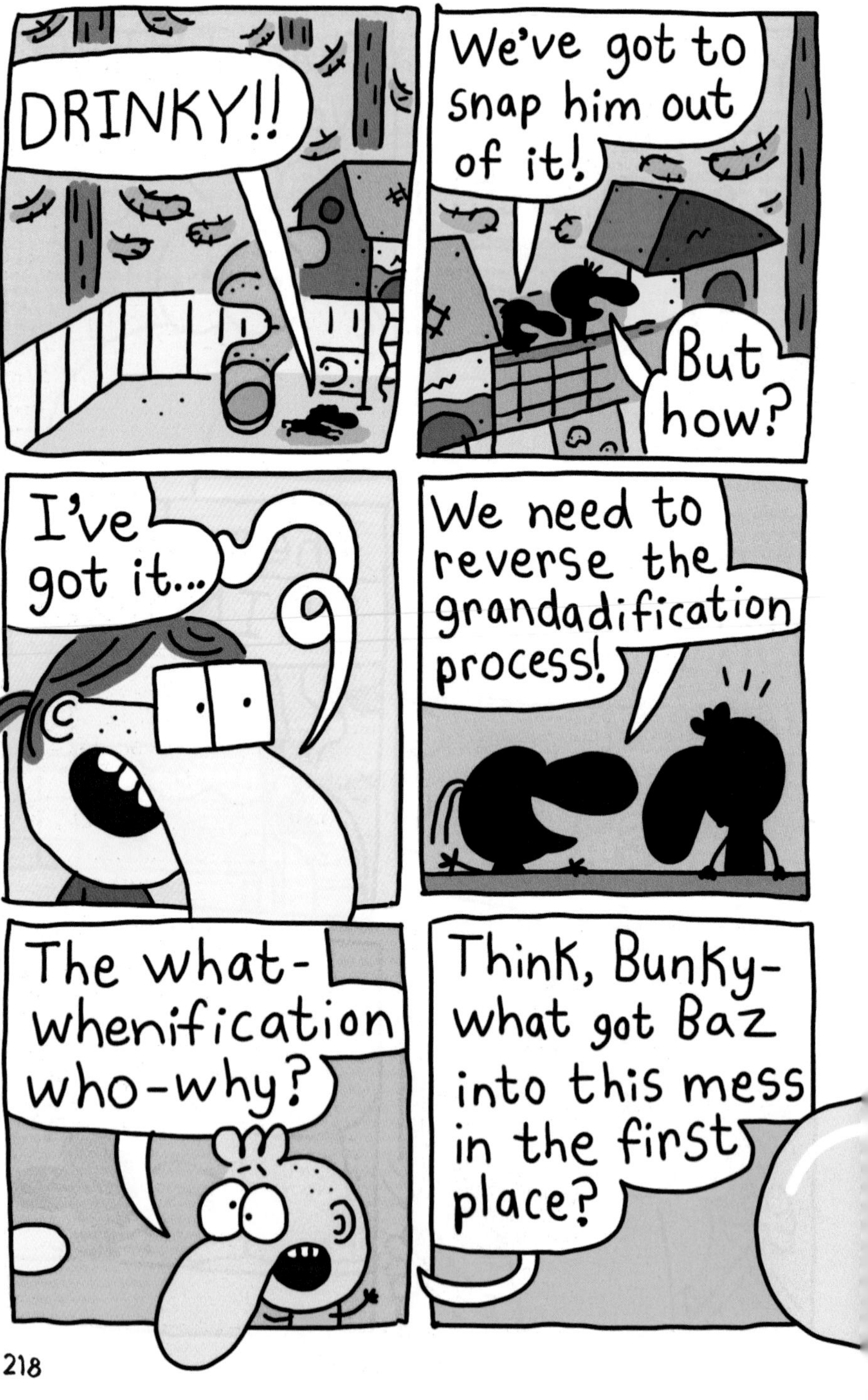
DRINKY!!
We've got to snap him out of it!
But how?
I've got it...
We need to reverse the grandadification process!
The what-whenification who-why?
Think, Bunky- what got Baz into this mess in the first place?

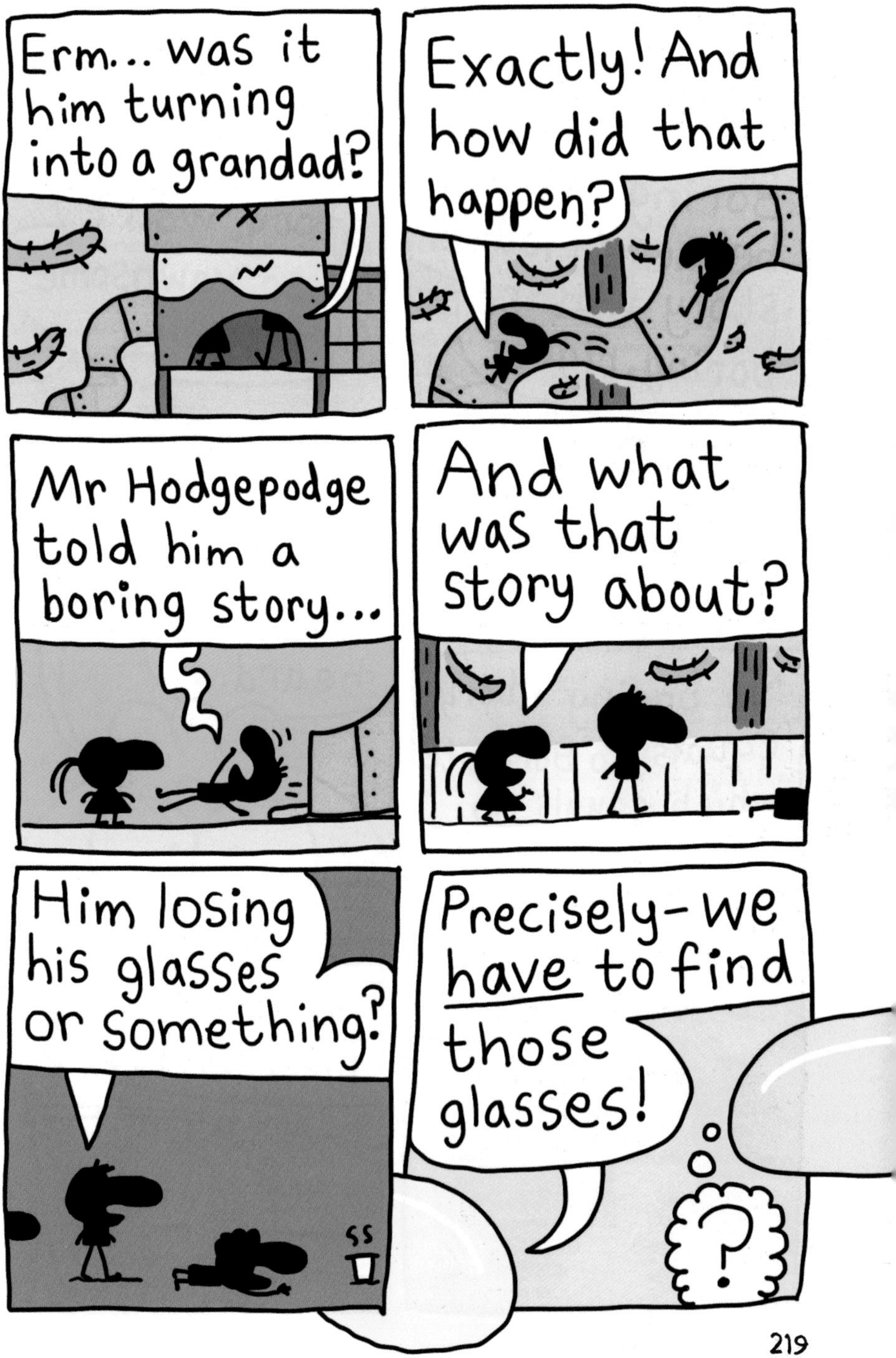
Erm... was it him turning into a grandad?
Exactly! And how did that happen?
Mr Hodgepodge told him a boring story...
And what was that story about?
Him losing his glasses or something?
Precisely- we have to find those glasses!
?

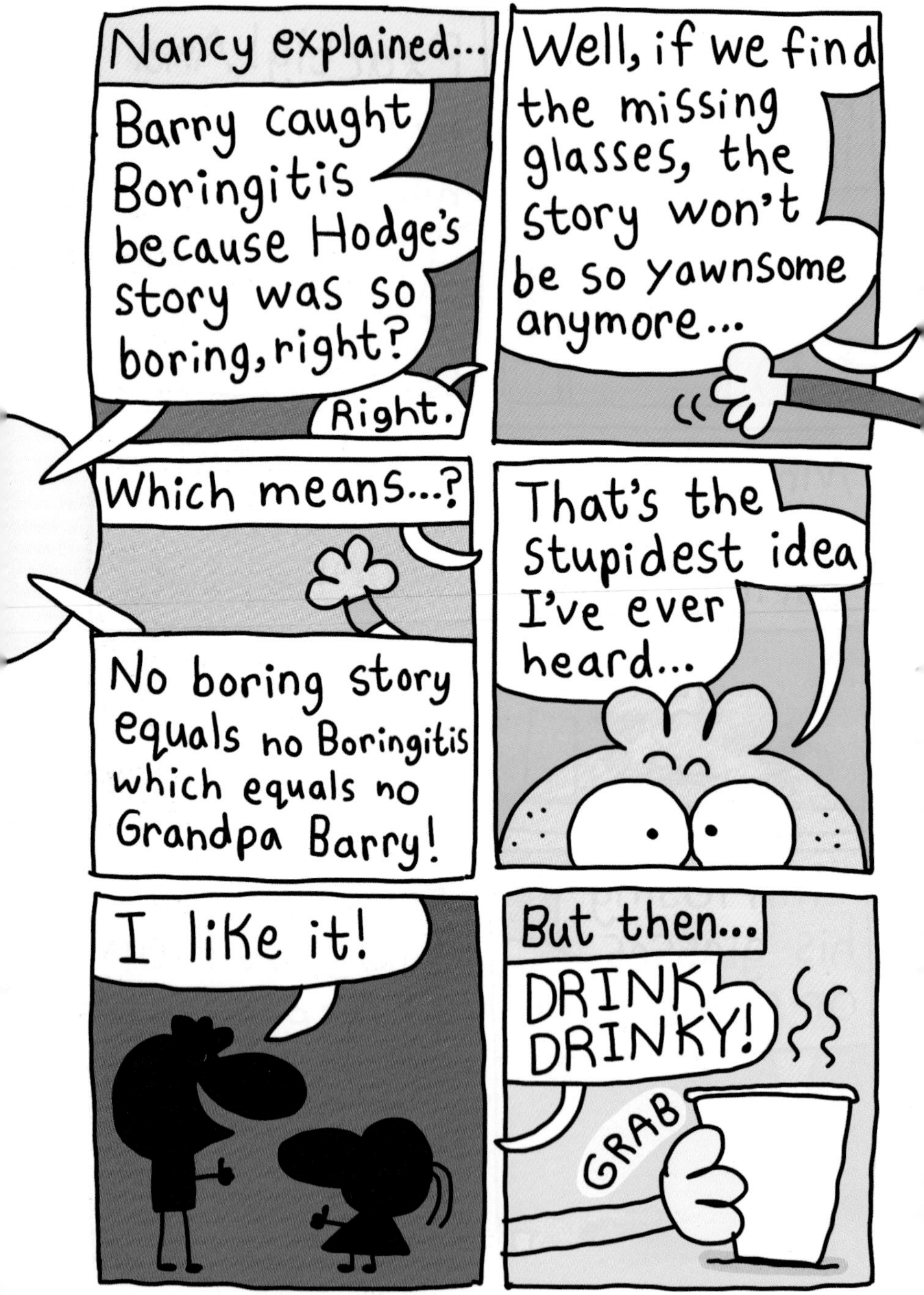
Nancy explained...
Barry caught Boringitis because Hodge's story was so boring, right?
Right.
Well, if we find the missing glasses, the story won't be so yawnsome anymore...
Which means...?
No boring story equals no Boringitis which equals no Grandpa Barry!
That's the stupidest idea I've ever heard...
I like it!
But then...
DRINK DRINKY!
GRAB

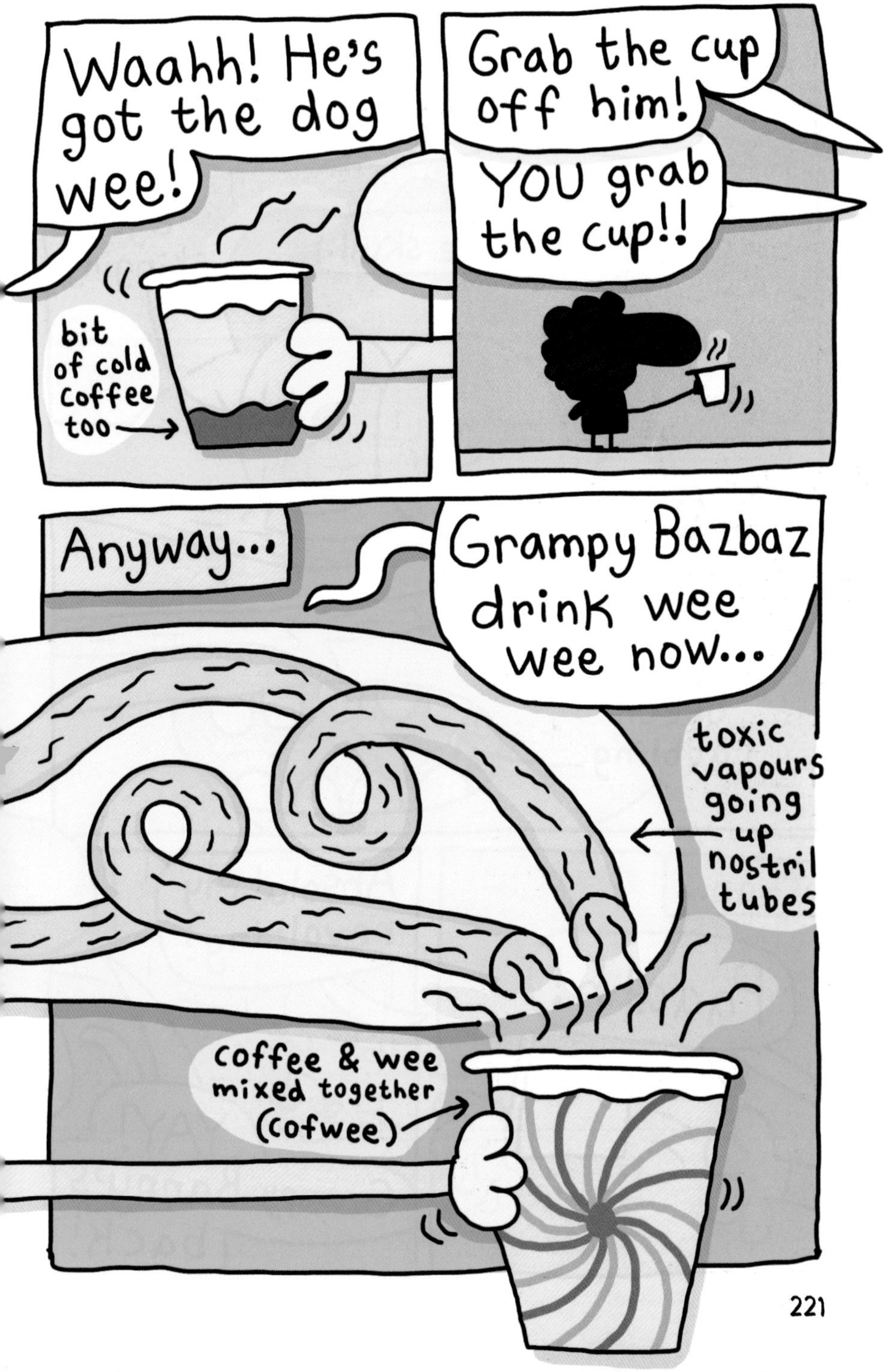
Waahh! He's got the dog wee!
bit of cold coffee too
Grab the cup off him!
YOU grab the cup!!
Anyway...
Grampy Bazbaz drink wee wee now...
toxic vapours going up nostril tubes
coffee & wee mixed together (cofwee)

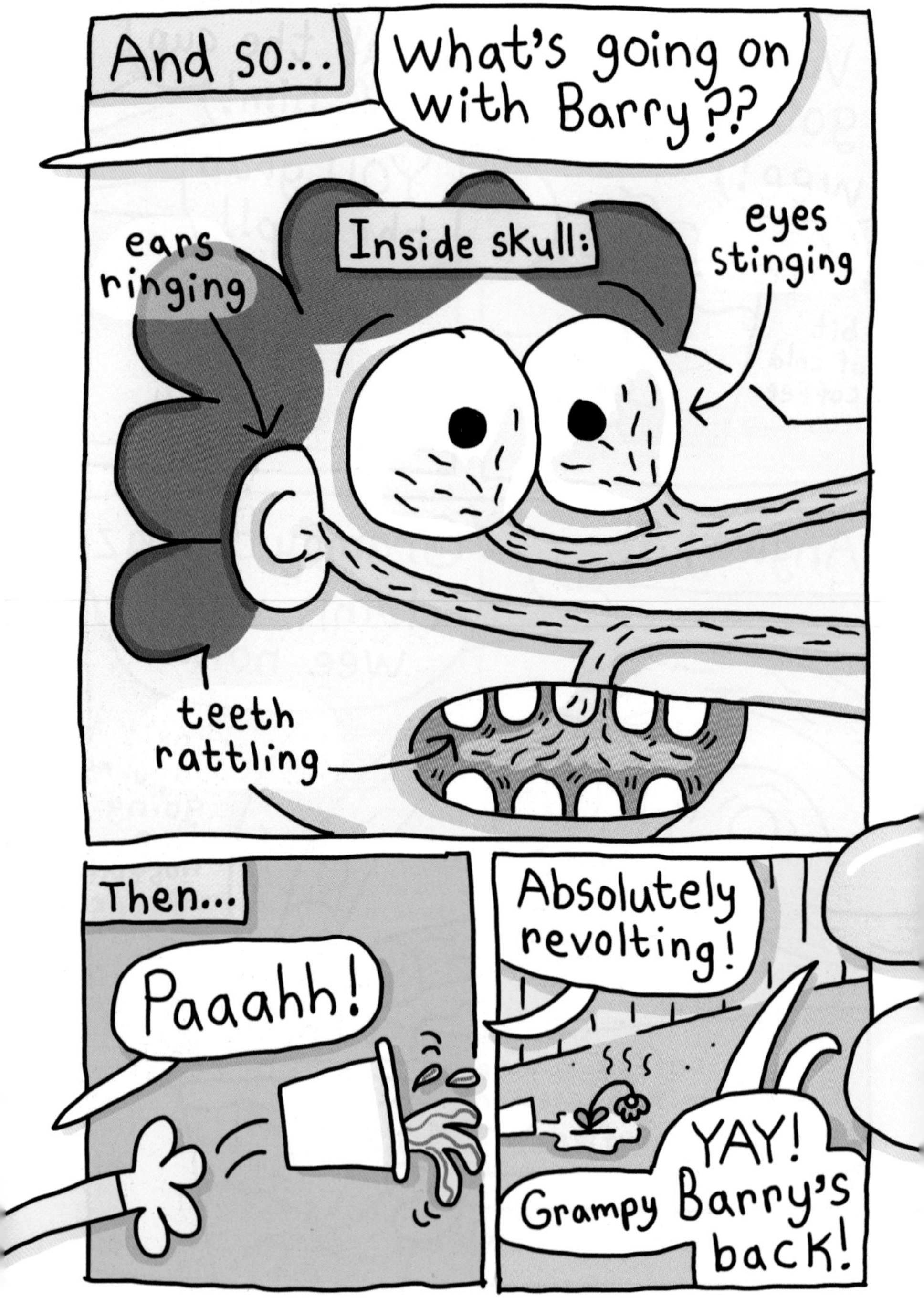

And so...
What's going on with Barry??
Inside skull:
ears ringing
eyes stinging
teeth rattling
Then...
Paaahh!
Absolutely revolting!
YAY! Grampy Barry's back!

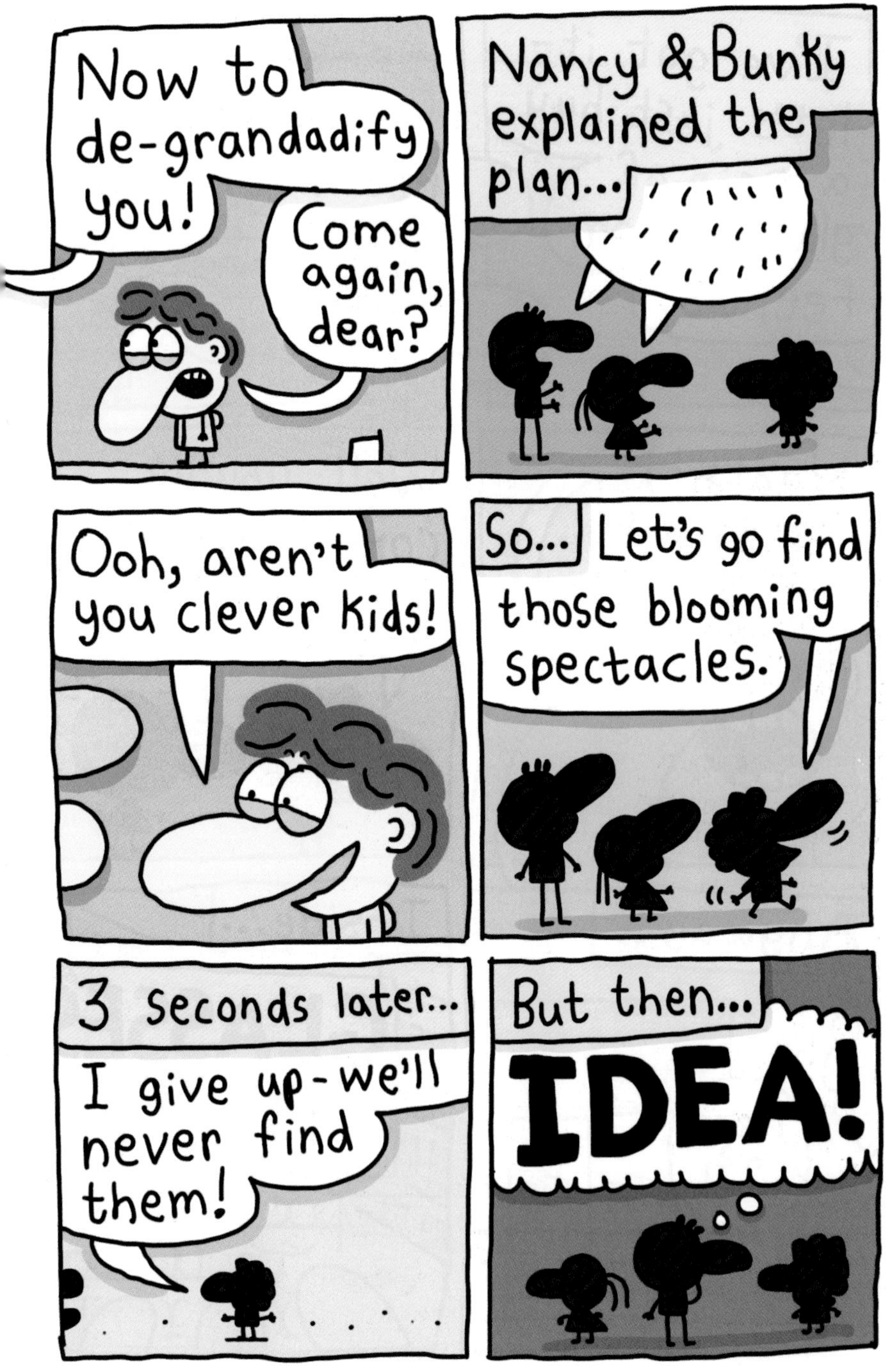
Now to de-grandadify you!
Come again, dear?
Nancy & Bunky explained the plan...
Ooh, aren't you clever kids!
So...
Let's go find those blooming spectacles.
3 seconds later...
I give up - we'll never find them!
But then...
IDEA!

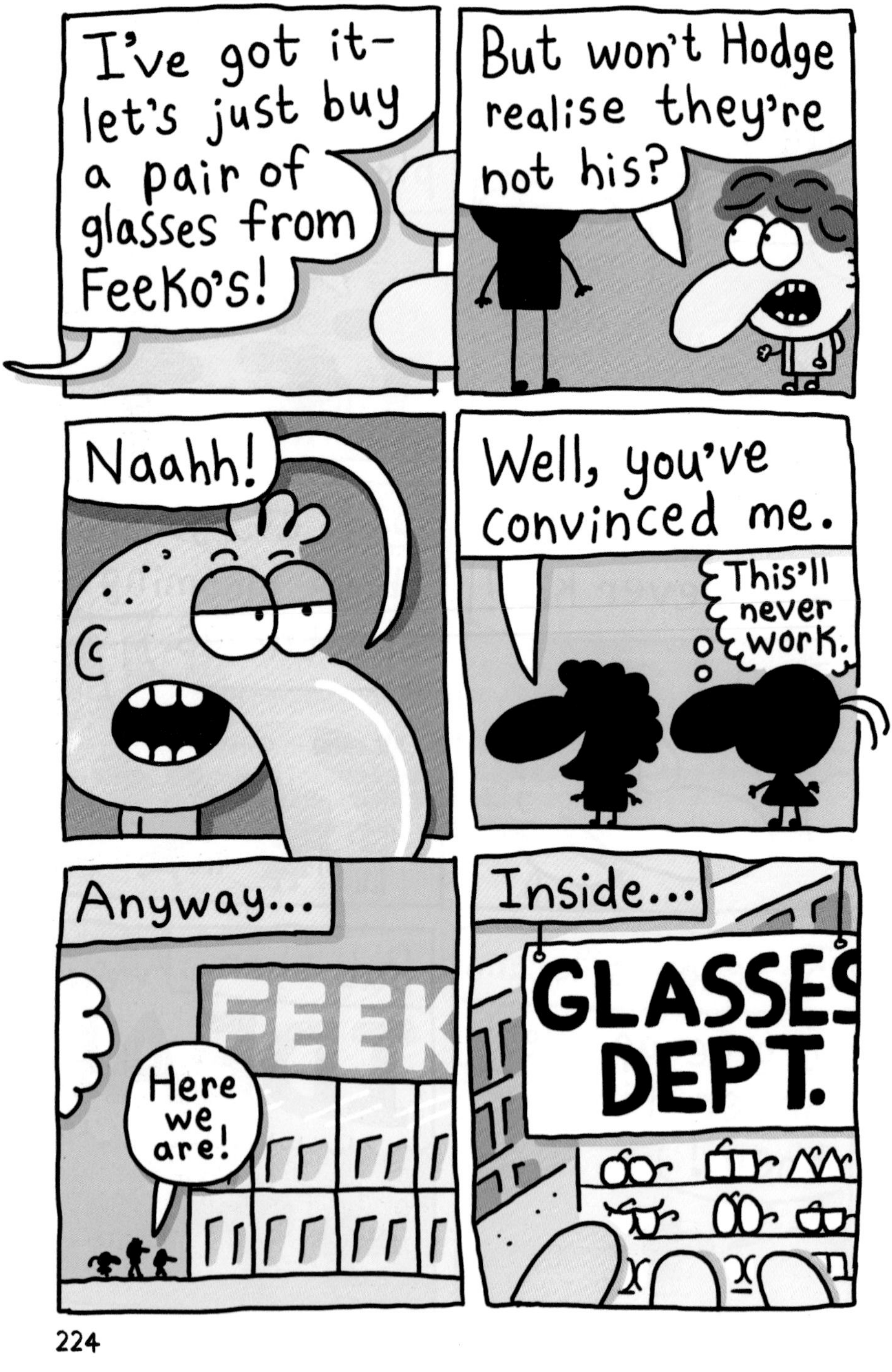
I've got it- let's just buy a pair of glasses from FeeKo's!
But won't Hodge realise they're not his?
Naahh!
Well, you've convinced me.
This'll never work.
Anyway...
FEEK
Here we are!
Inside...
GLASSES DEPT.

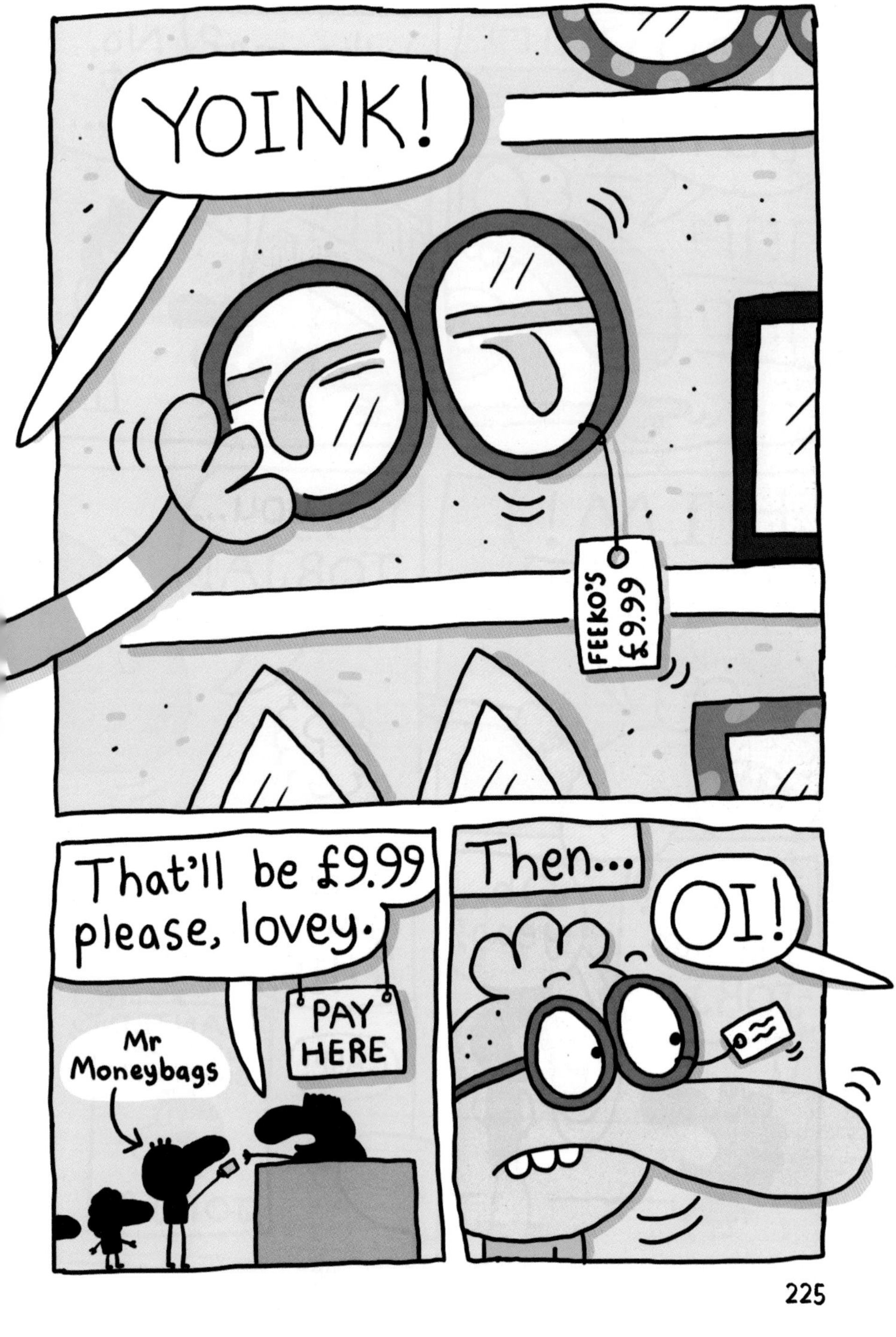
YOINK!
FEEKO'S £9.99
That'll be £9.99 please, lovey.
PAY HERE
Mr Moneybags
Then...
OI!

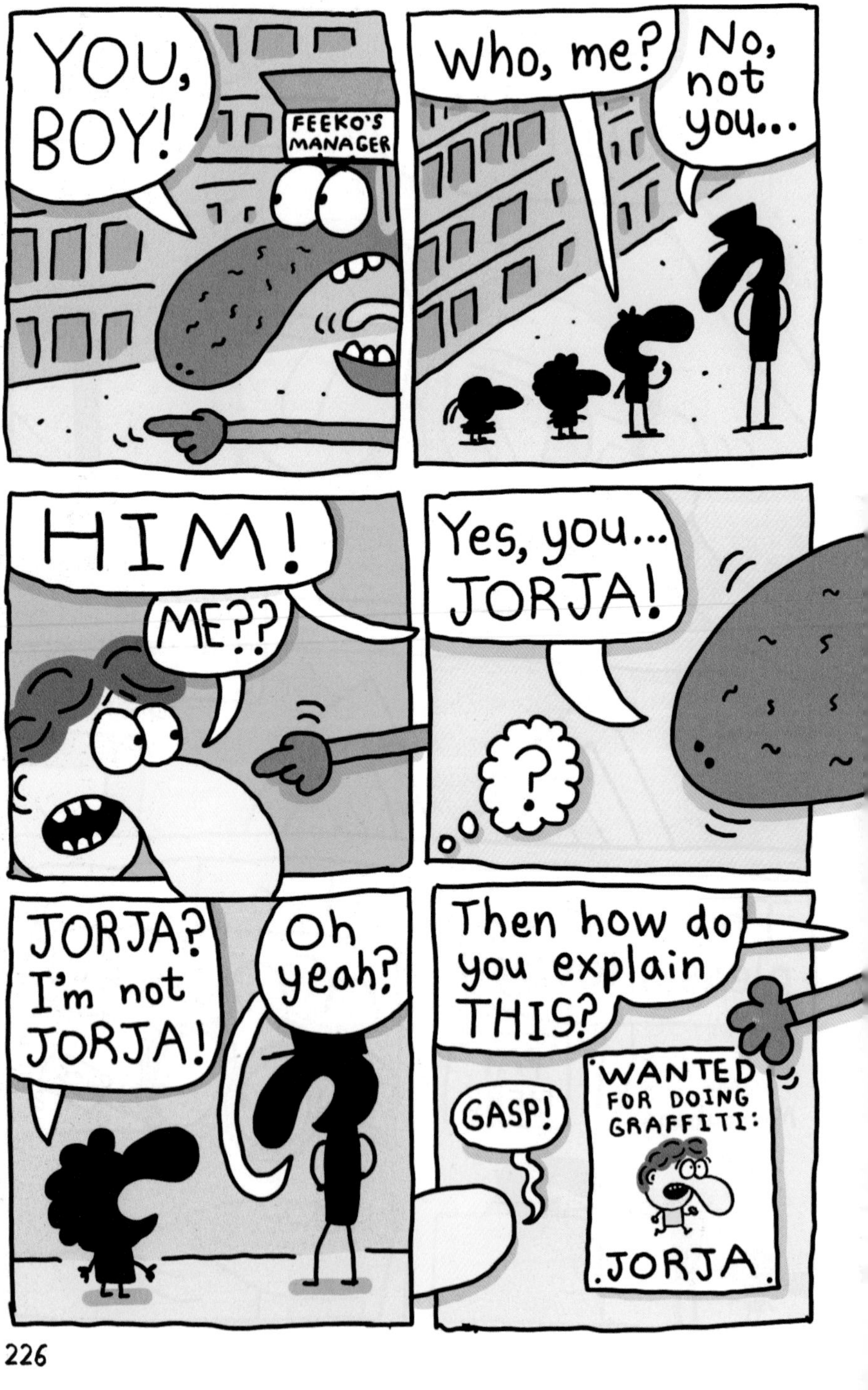
YOU, BOY!
FEEKO'S MANAGER
Who, me?
No, not you...
HIM!
ME??
Yes, you... JORJA!
?
JORJA? I'm not JORJA!
Oh yeah?
Then how do you explain THIS?
GASP!
WANTED FOR DOING GRAFFITI:
JORJA

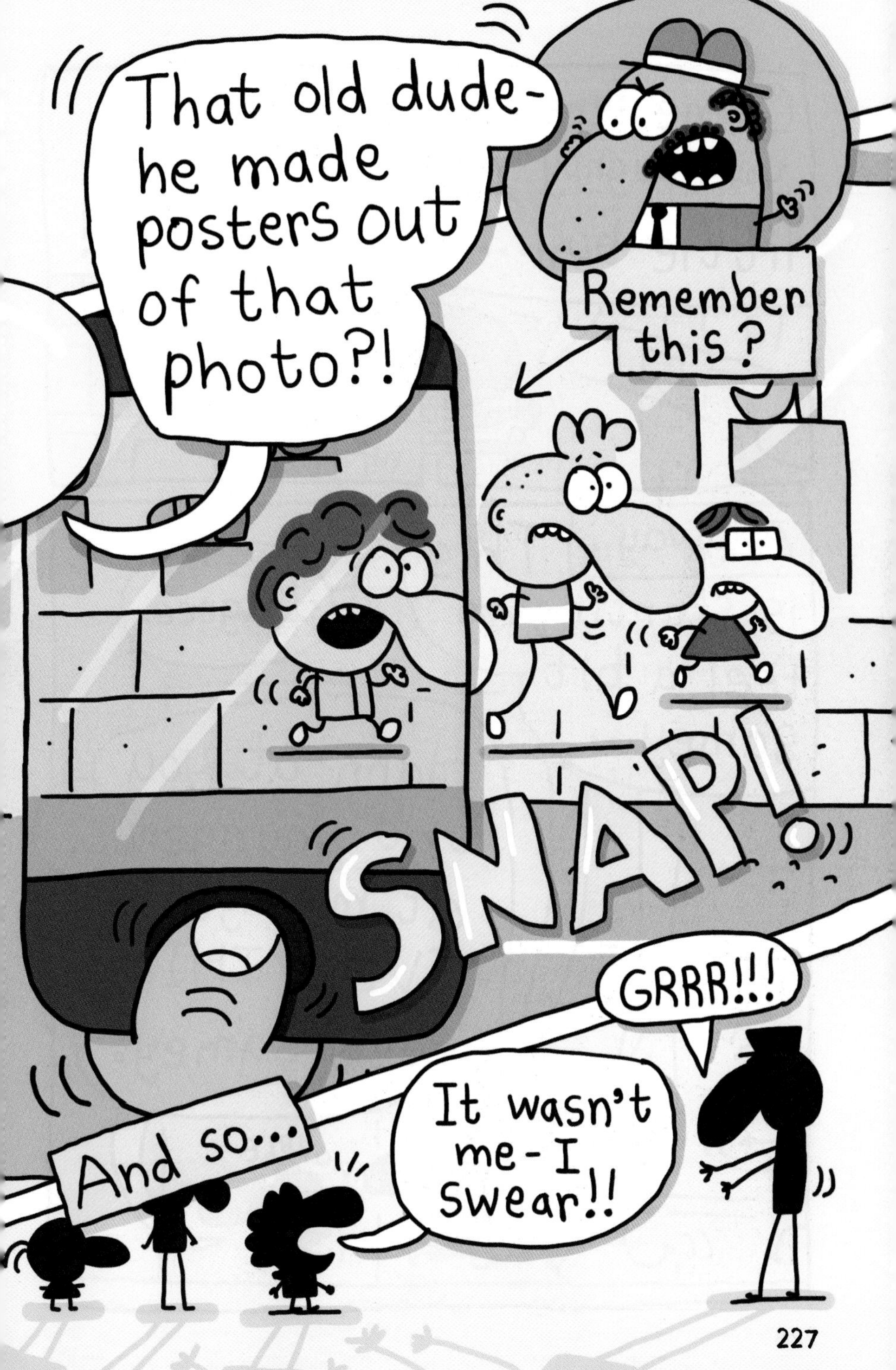
That old dude-
he made
posters out
of that
photo?!
Remember
this?
SNAP!
GRRR!!!
And so...
It wasn't
me - I
swear!!

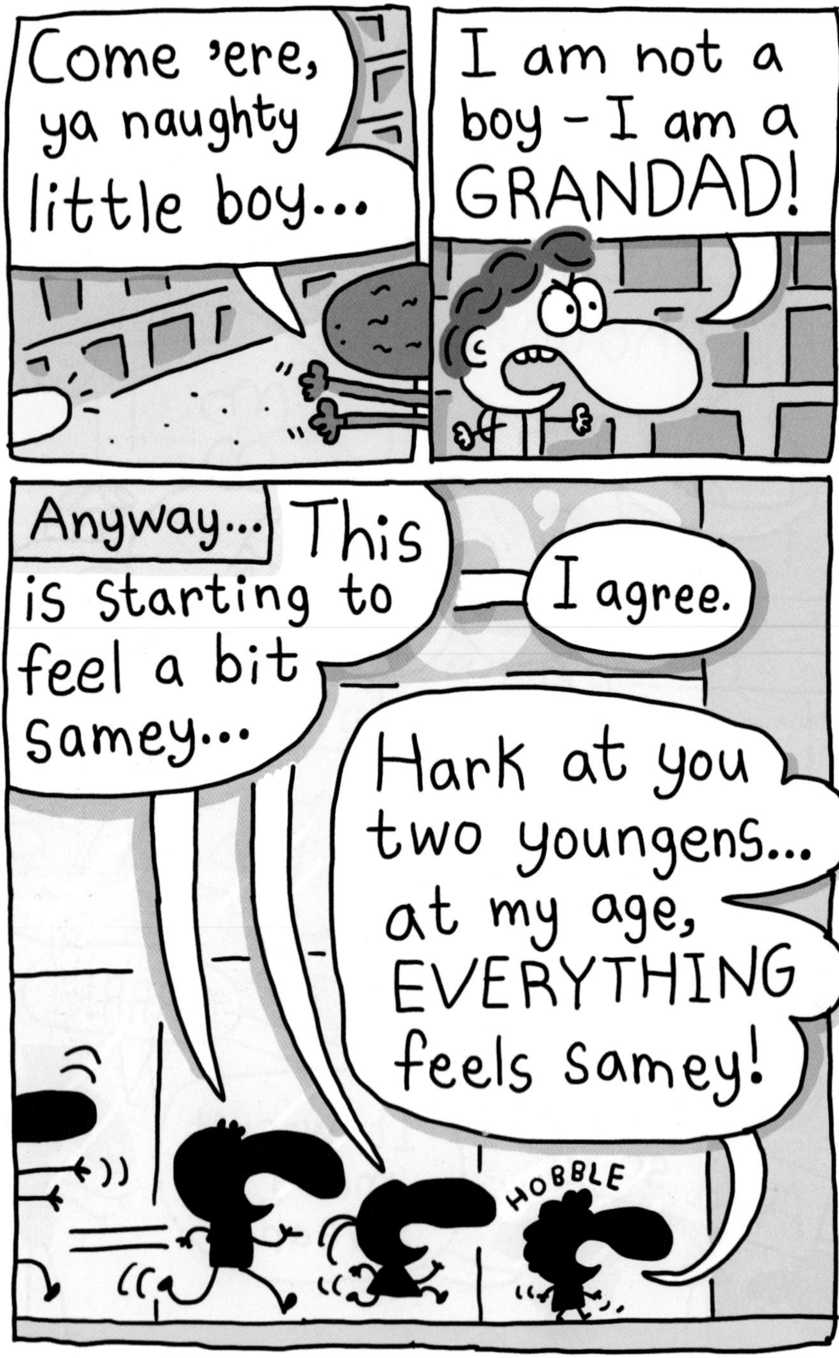
Come 'ere, ya naughty little boy...
I am not a boy - I am a GRANDAD!
Anyway...
This is starting to feel a bit samey...
I agree.
Hark at you two youngens... at my age, EVERYTHING feels samey!
HOBBLE

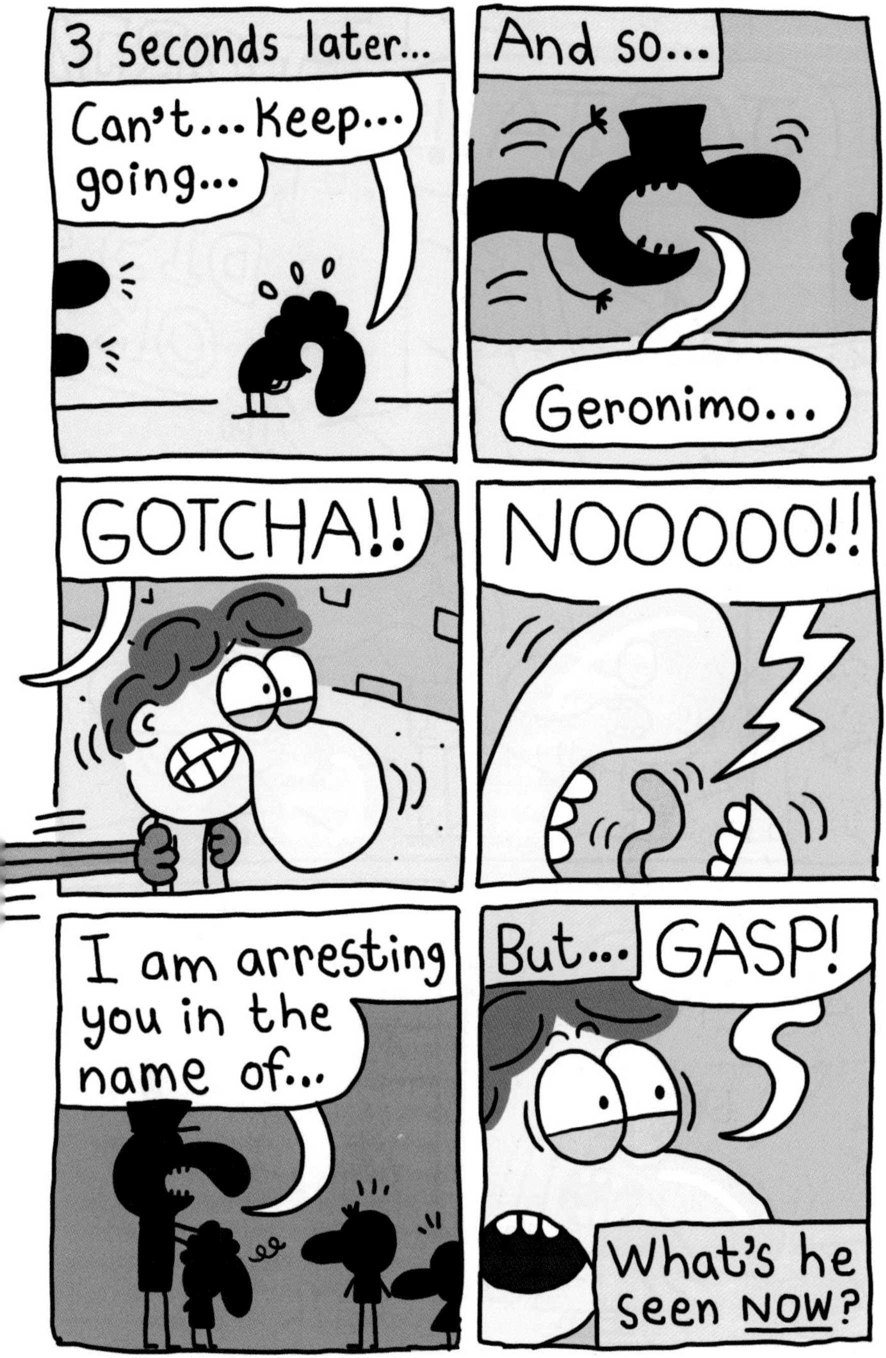
3 seconds later...
Can't... Keep... going...
And so...
Geronimo...
GOTCHA!!
NOOOOO!!
I am arresting you in the name of...
But...
GASP!
What's he seen NOW?

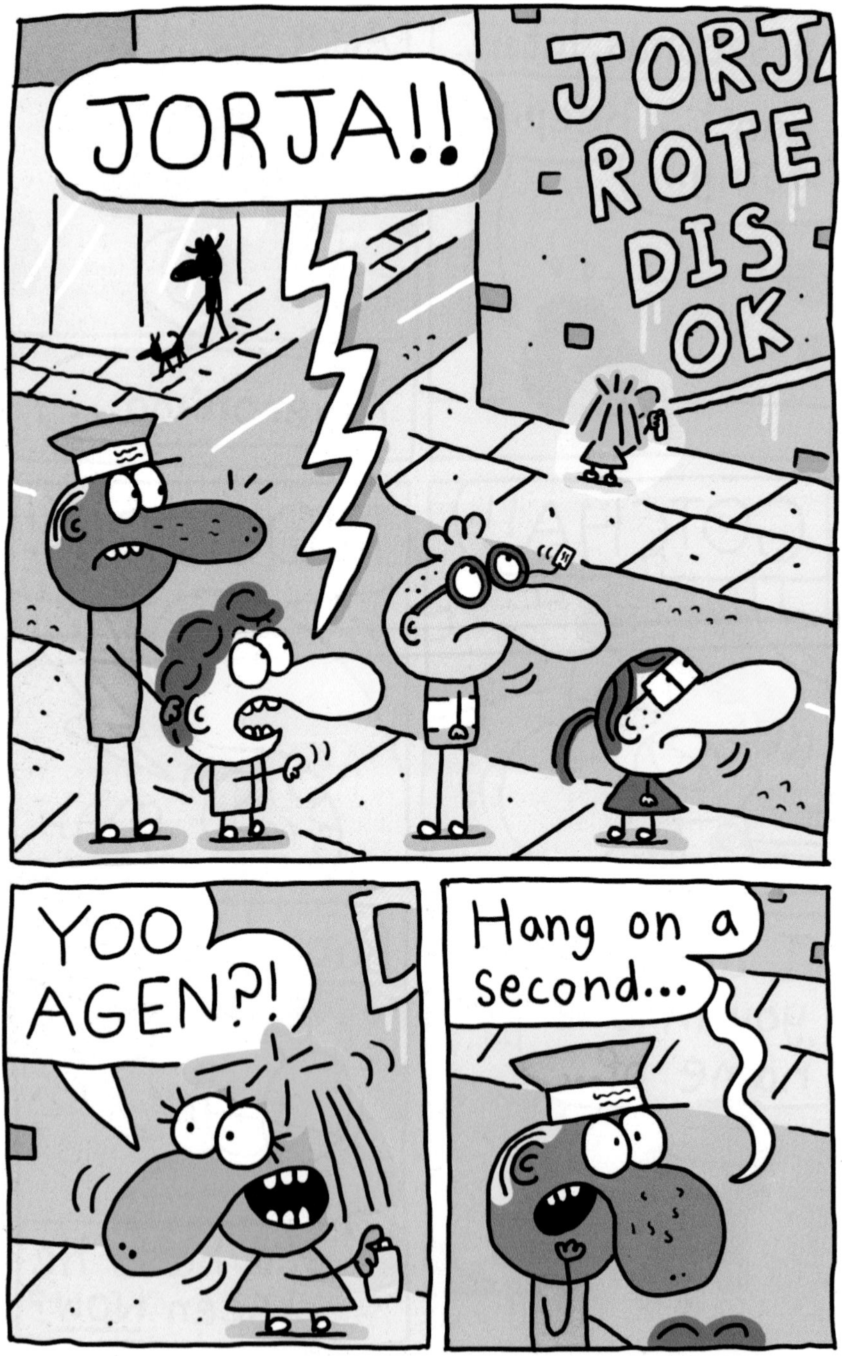
JORJA!!
JORJA ROTE DIS OK
YOO AGEN?!
Hang on a second...

Once everything had been explained...

SO U WOZ ONLY KOREKTIN MI GRAMMAR?

Yes. Didn't I just explain that?

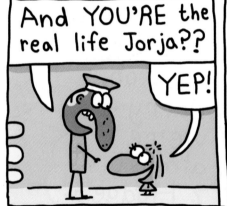

And YOU'RE the real life Jorja??

YEP!

Seriously, we've been through this already—didn't anybody listen?

Anyway, I suppose you'll be arresting her now, won't you...

Naaahh...

Wha...?!

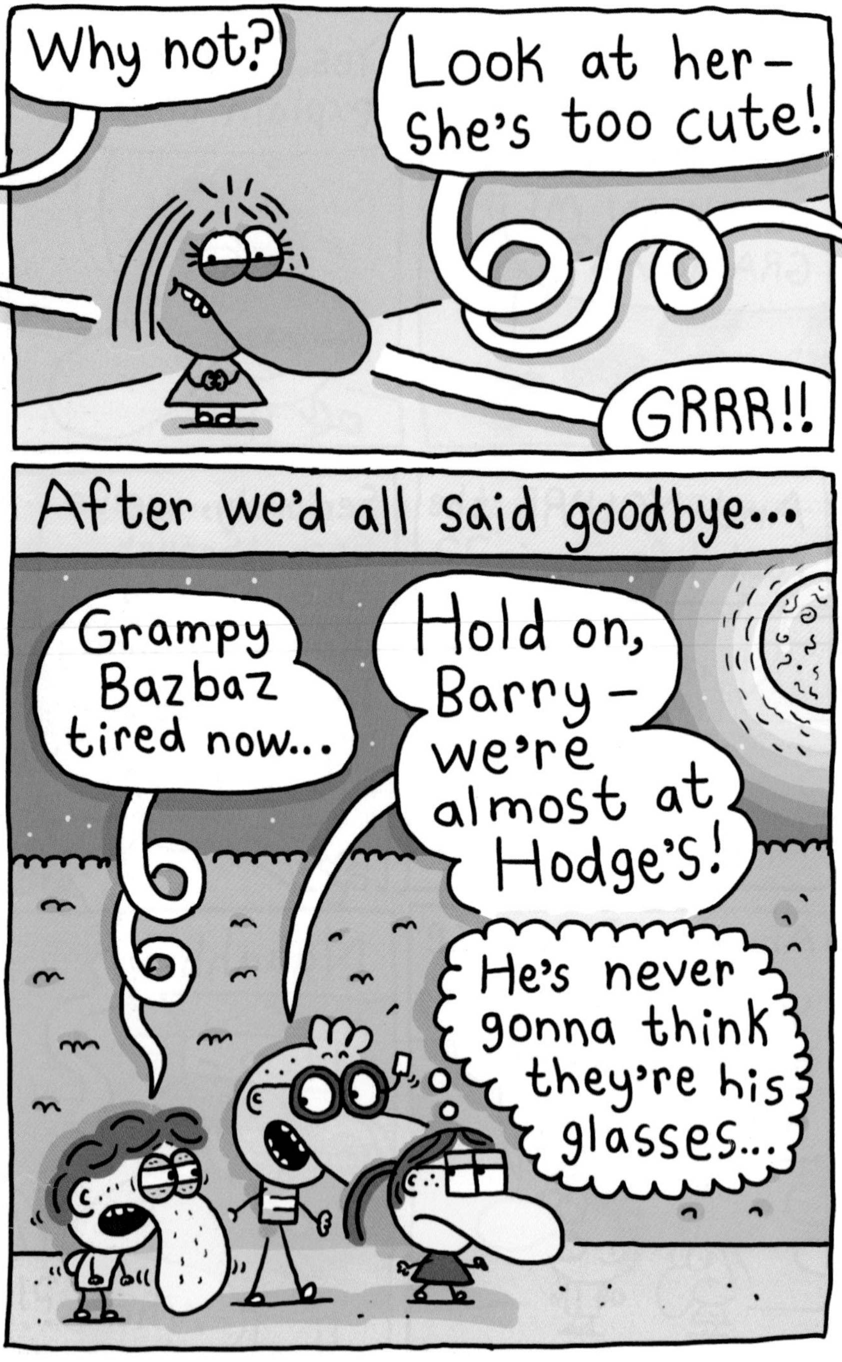
Why not?
Look at her – she's too cute!
GRRR!!
After we'd all said goodbye...
Grampy Bazbaz tired now...
Hold on, Barry – we're almost at Hodge's!
He's never gonna think they're his glasses...

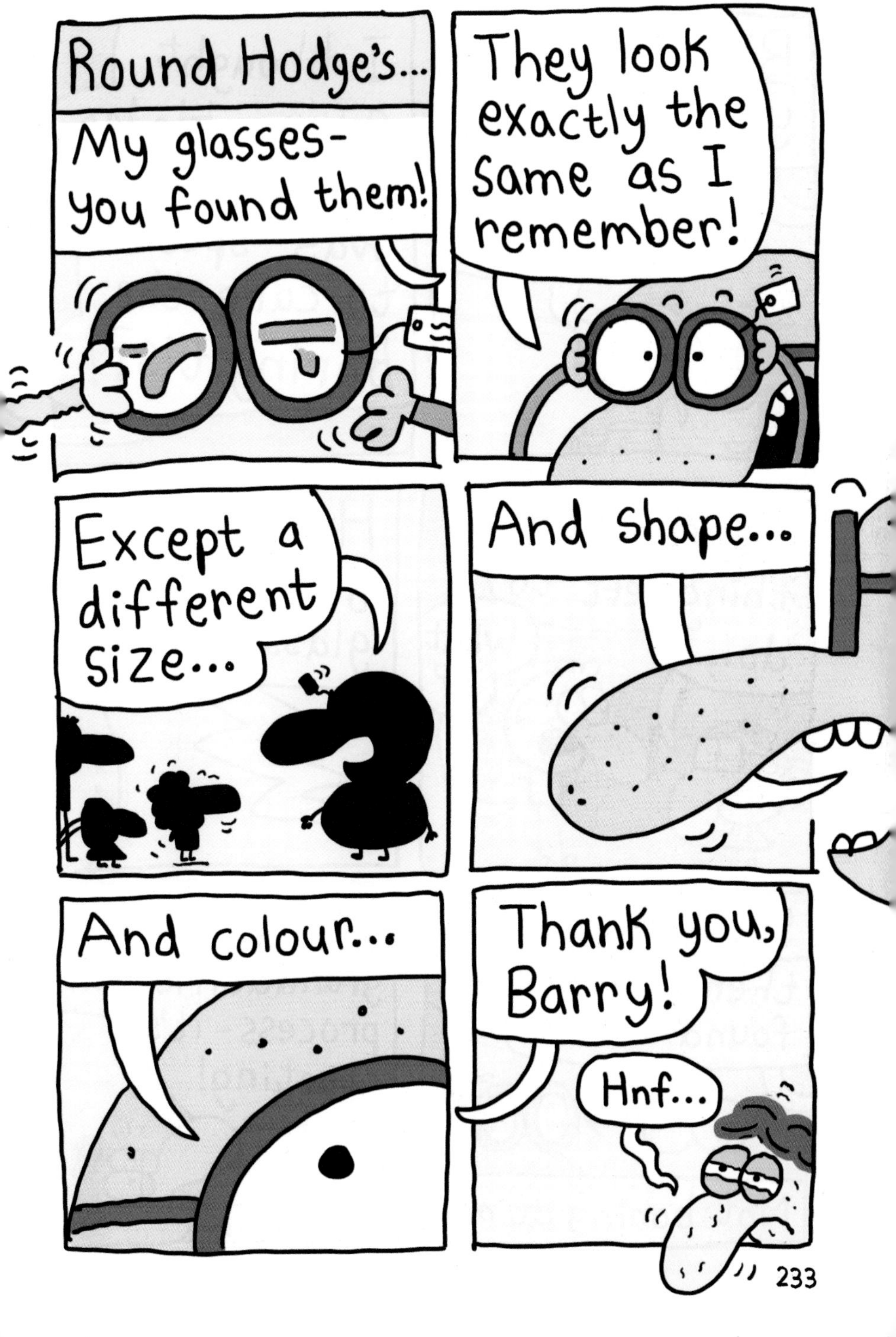

Round Hodge's...
My glasses- you found them!
They look exactly the same as I remember!
Except a different size...
And shape...
And colour...
Thank you, Barry!
Hnf...

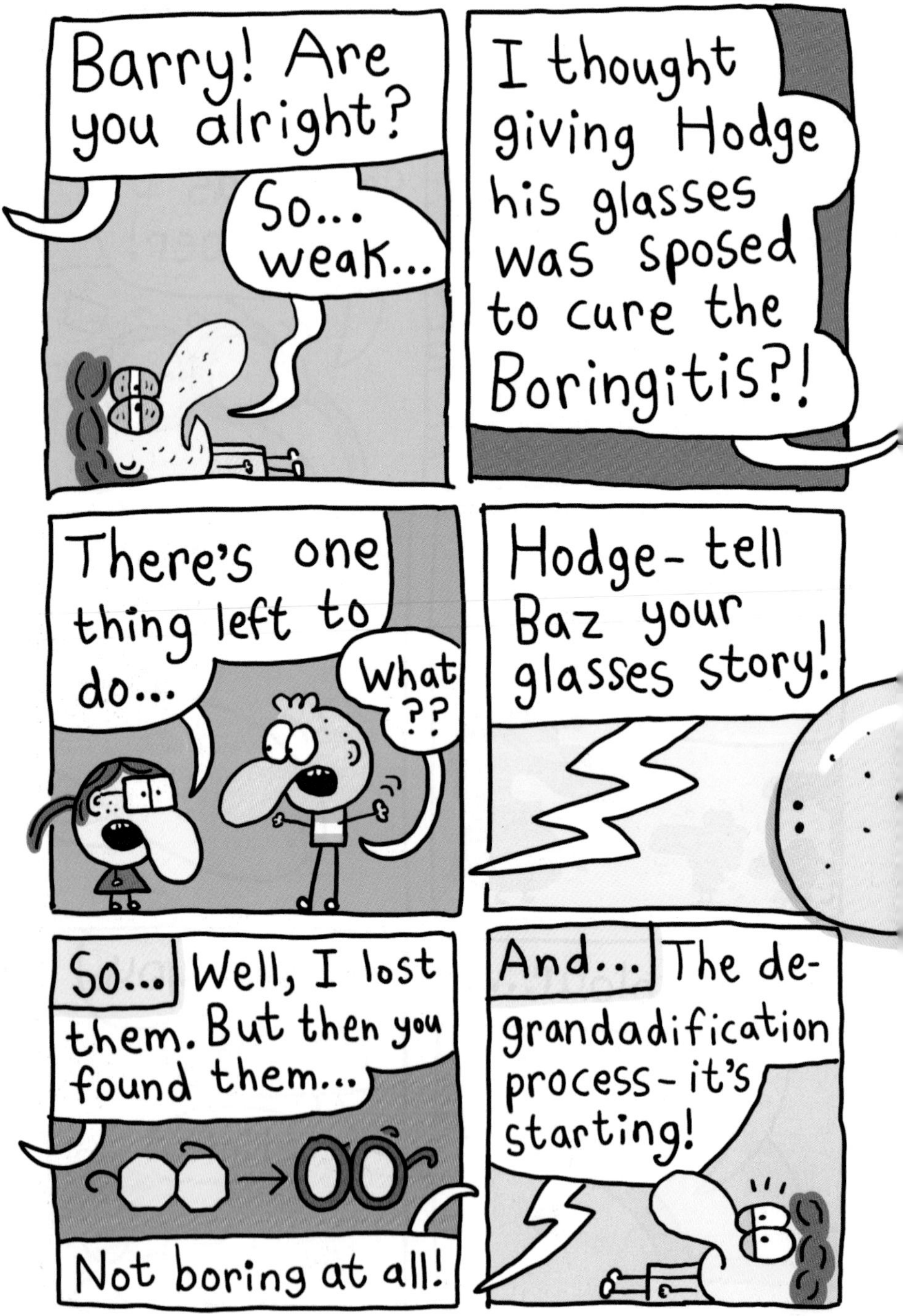
Barry! Are you alright?
So... weak...
I thought giving Hodge his glasses was sposed to cure the Boringitis?!
There's one thing left to do...
What??
Hodge- tell Baz your glasses story!
So... Well, I lost them. But then you found them...
Not boring at all!
And... The de-grandadification process- it's starting!

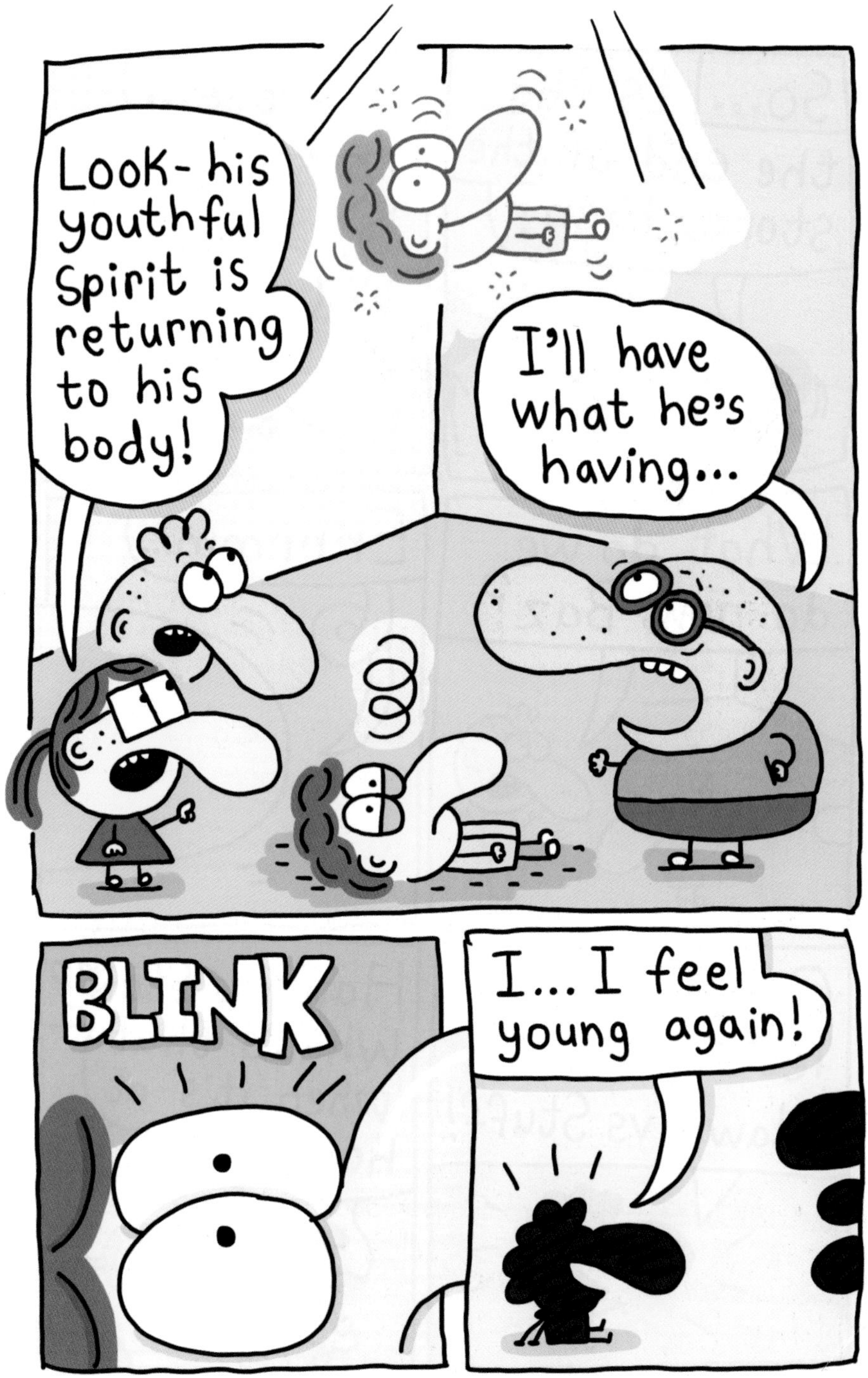
Look- his youthful Spirit is returning to his body!
I'll have what he's having...
BLINK
I... I feel young again!

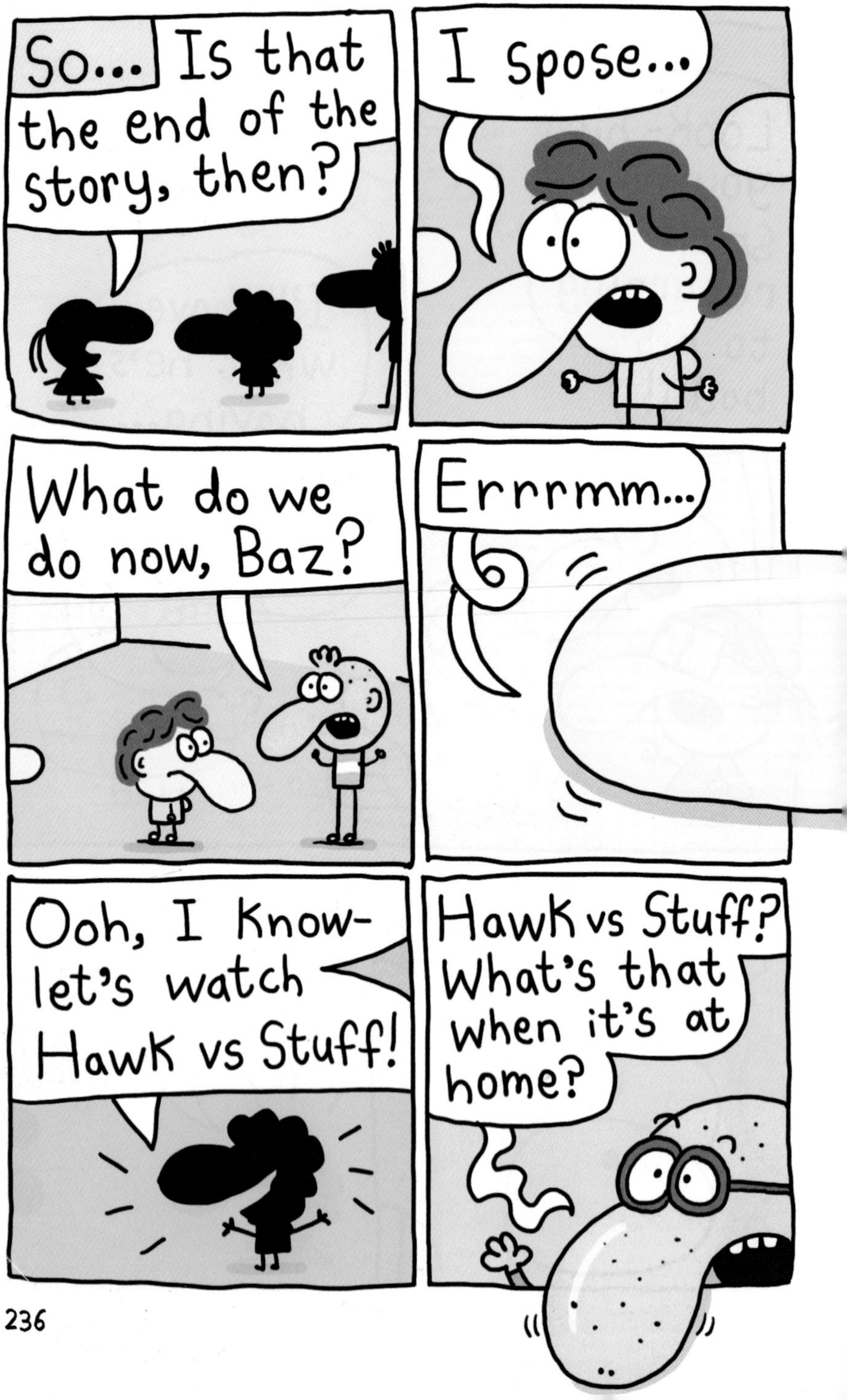
So... Is that the end of the story, then?
I spose...
What do we do now, Baz?
Errrmm...
Ooh, I know- let's watch Hawk vs Stuff!
Hawk vs Stuff? What's that when it's at home?

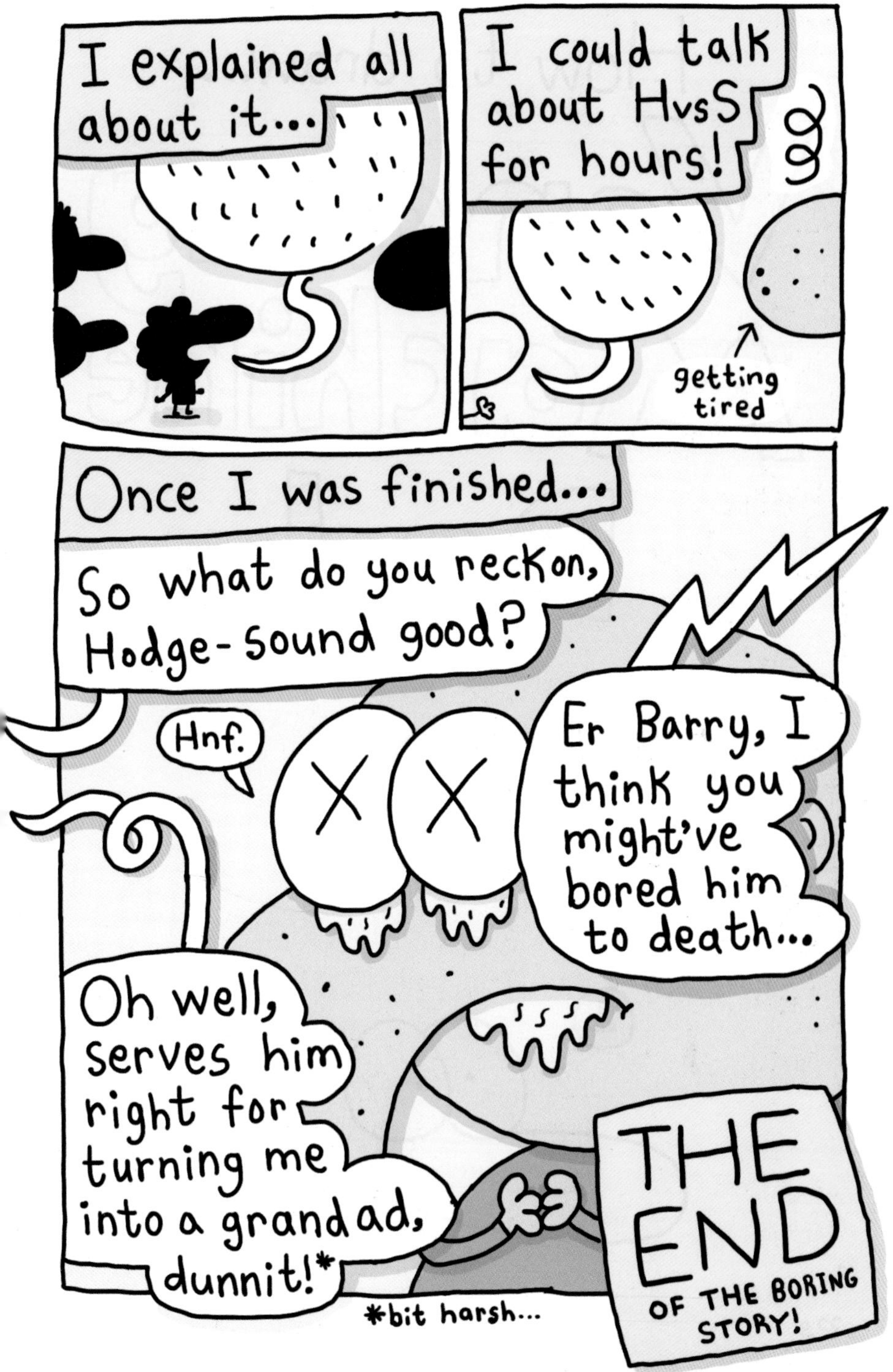
I explained all about it...
I could talk about HvsS for hours!
getting tired
Once I was finished...
So what do you reckon, Hodge-sound good?
Hnf.
Er Barry, I think you might've bored him to death...
Oh well, serves him right for turning me into a grandad, dunnit!*
*bit harsh...
THE END OF THE BORING STORY!

How to draw...

Vending Machine Dad

1

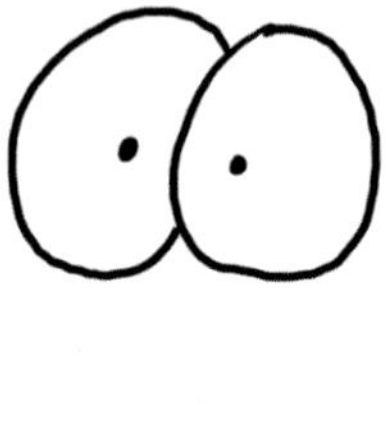

2

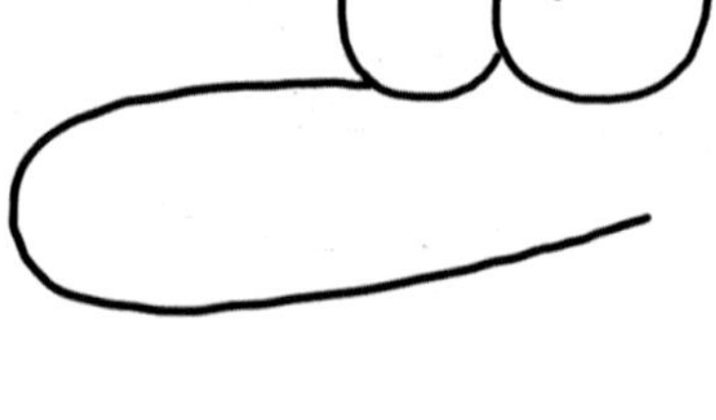

3

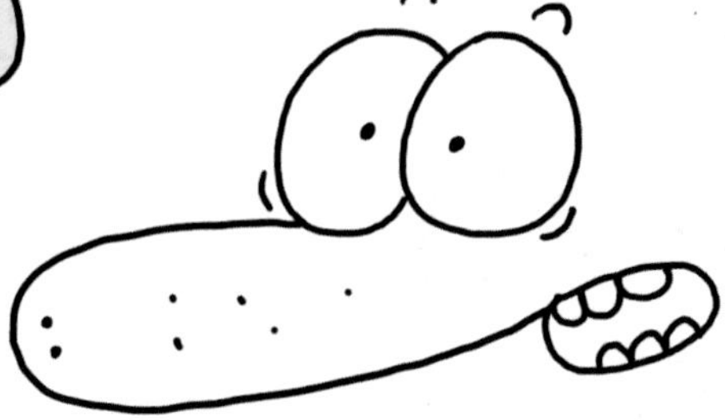

4

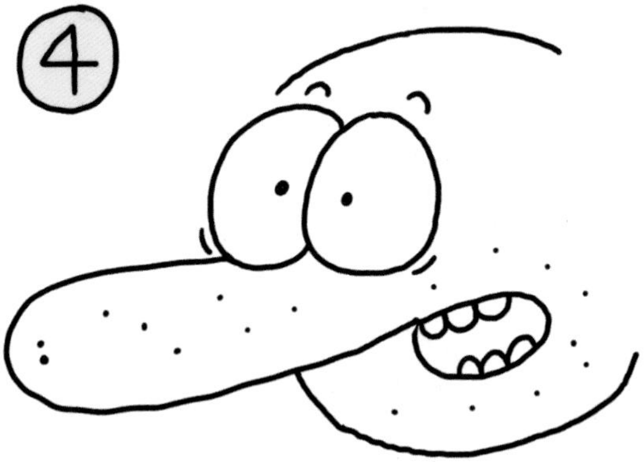

5

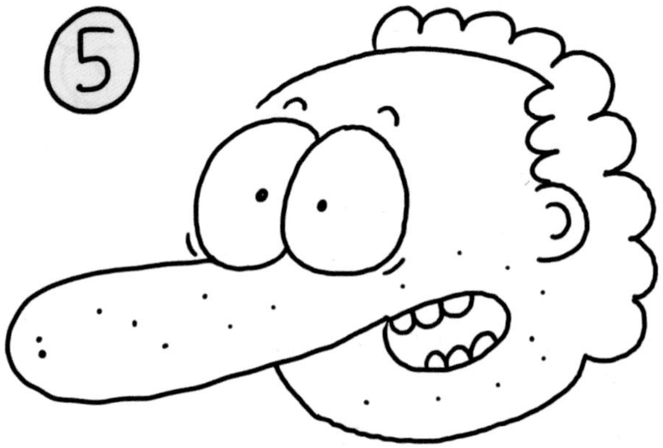

240

8

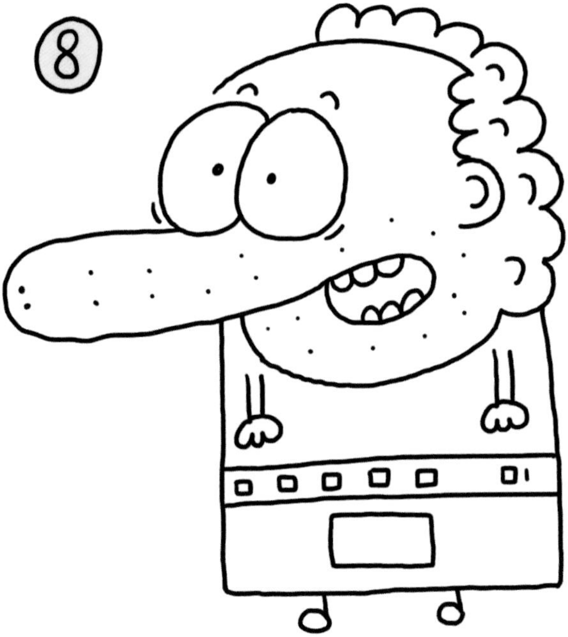

9

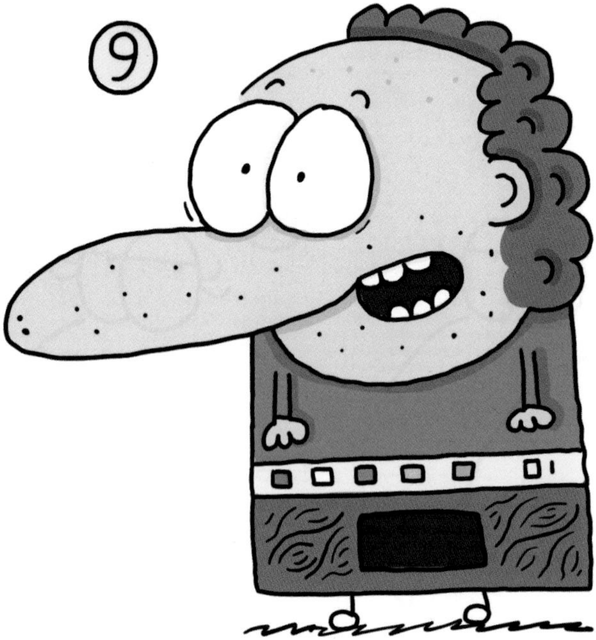

And now...
Maureen Loser

①

②

③

④

5

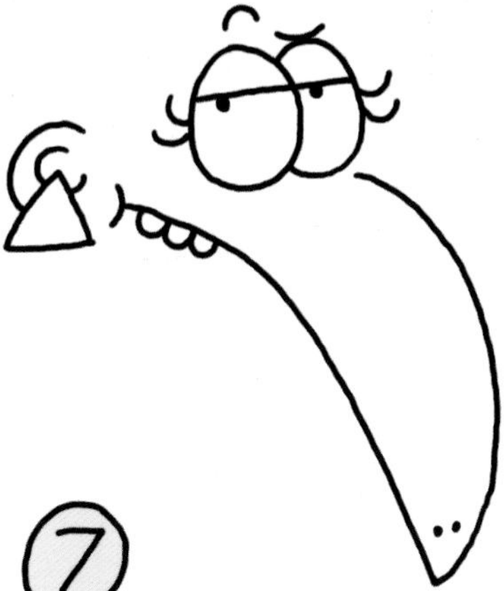

6

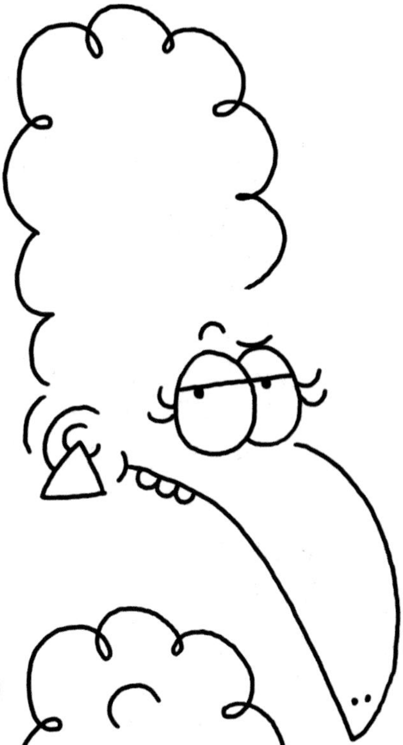

7

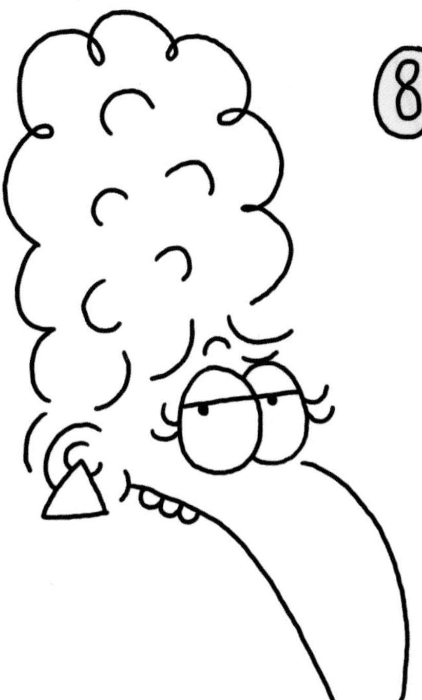

8

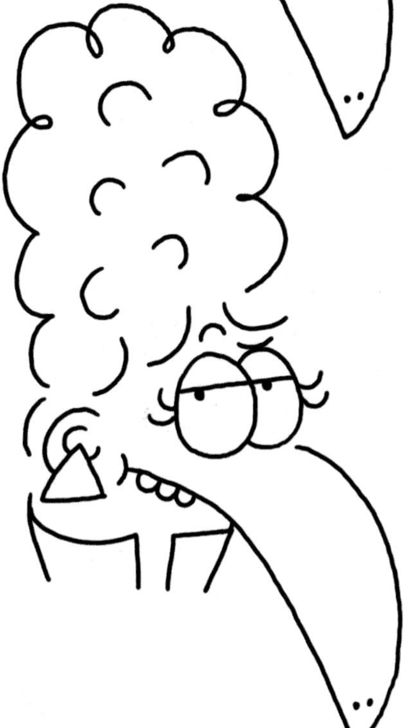

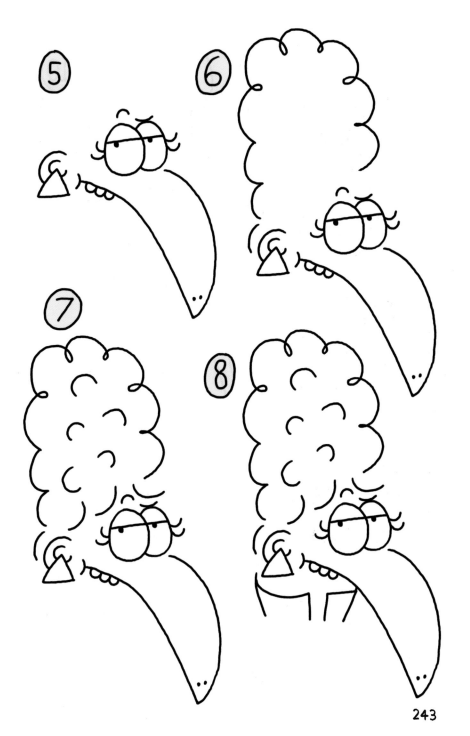

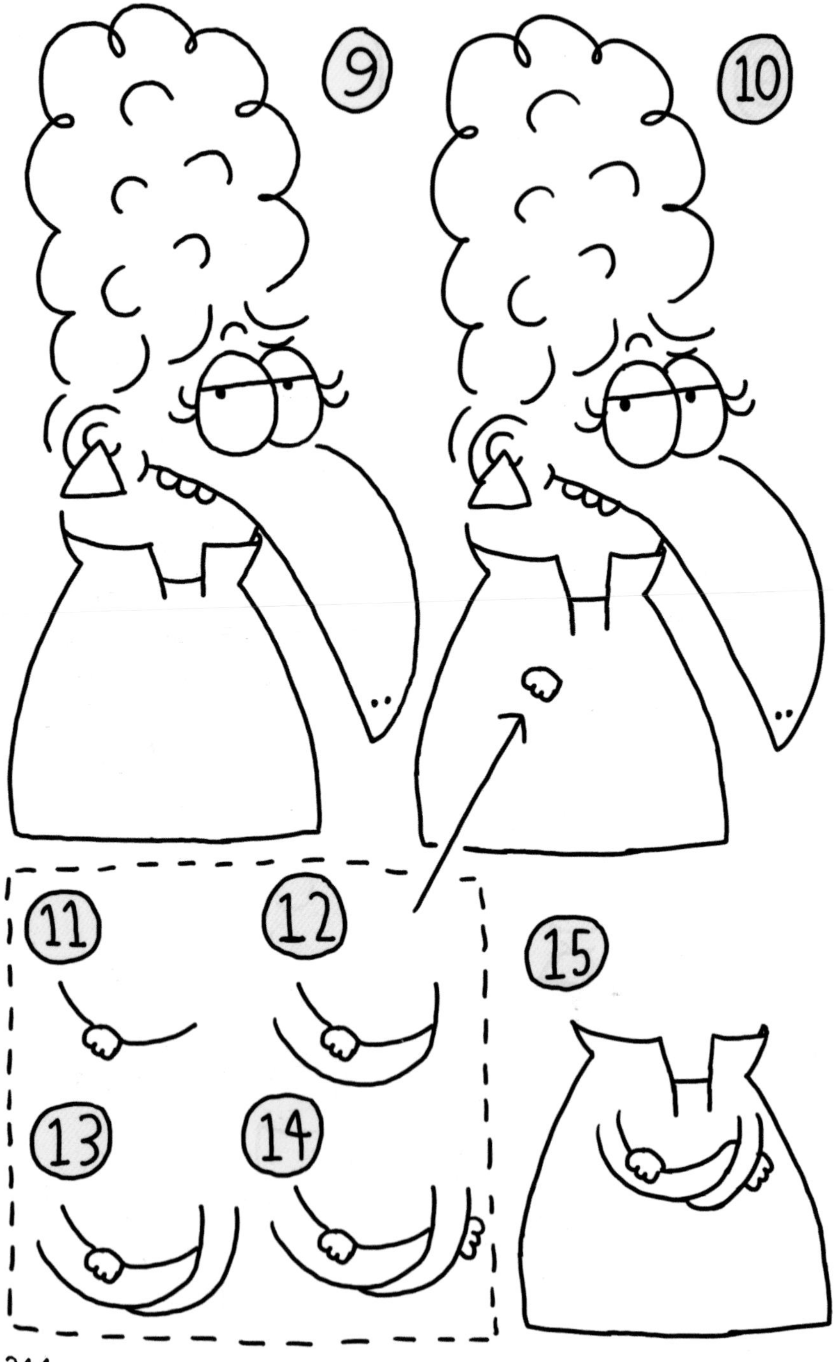
9
10
11
12
13
14
15

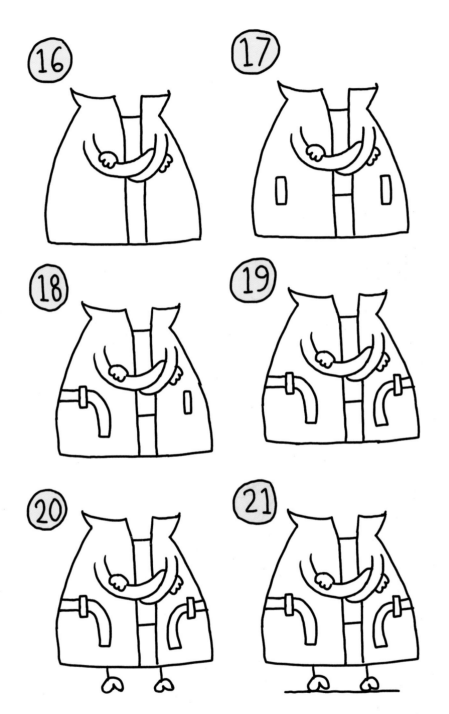

Last but not least...

Bunky & Nancy

1

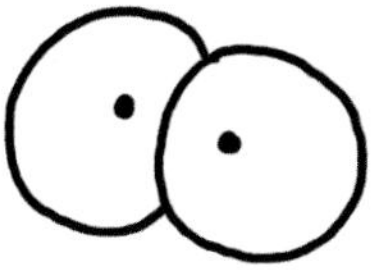

2

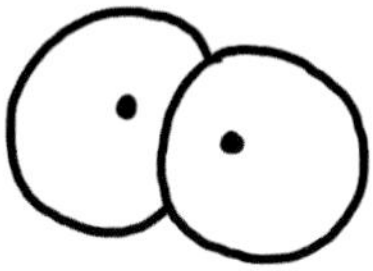

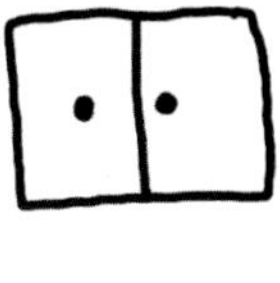

3

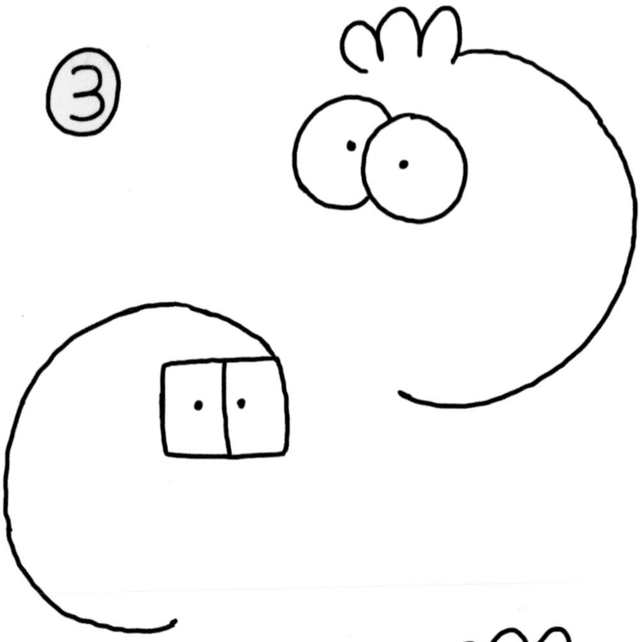

4

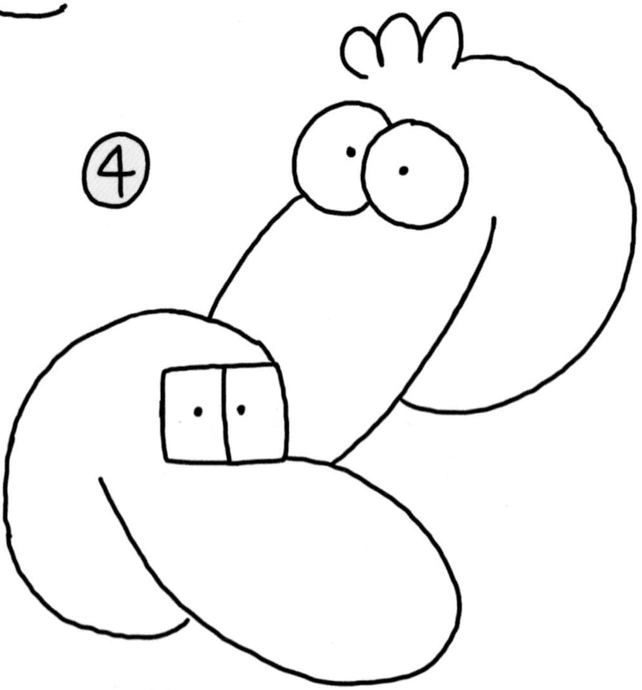

5

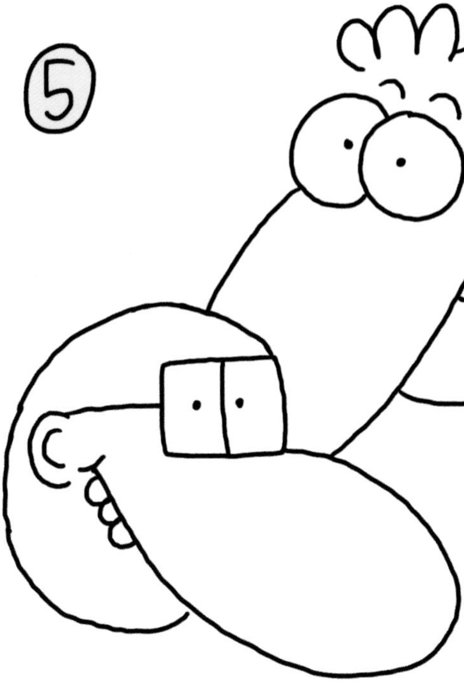

6

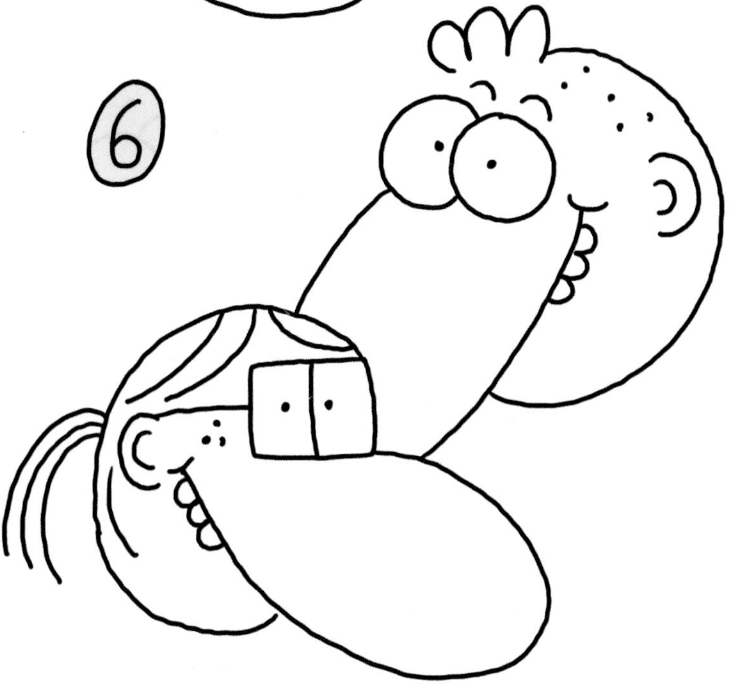

7

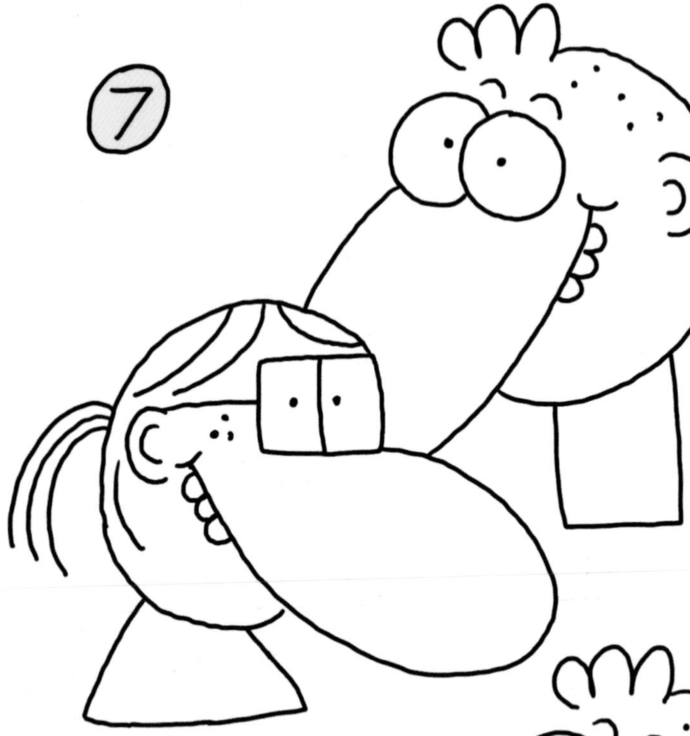

8

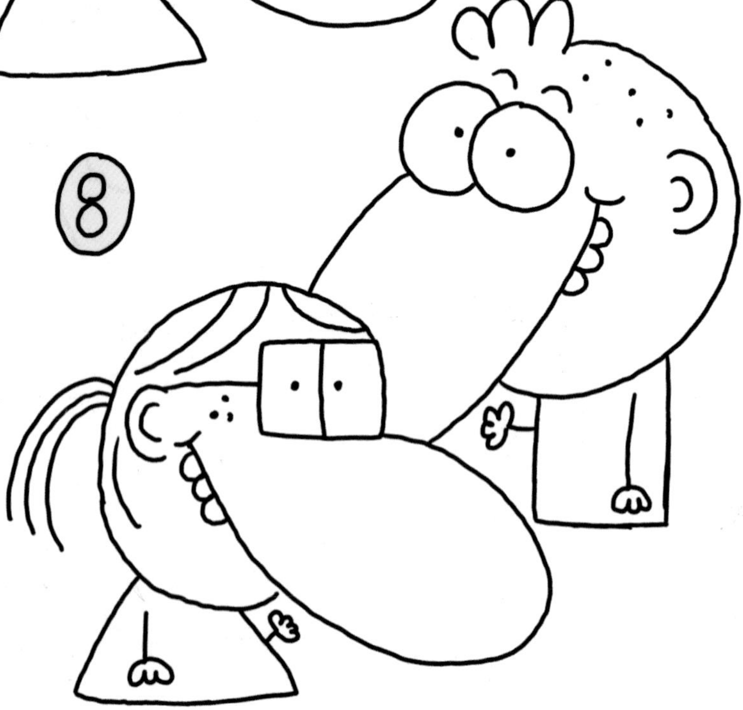

9

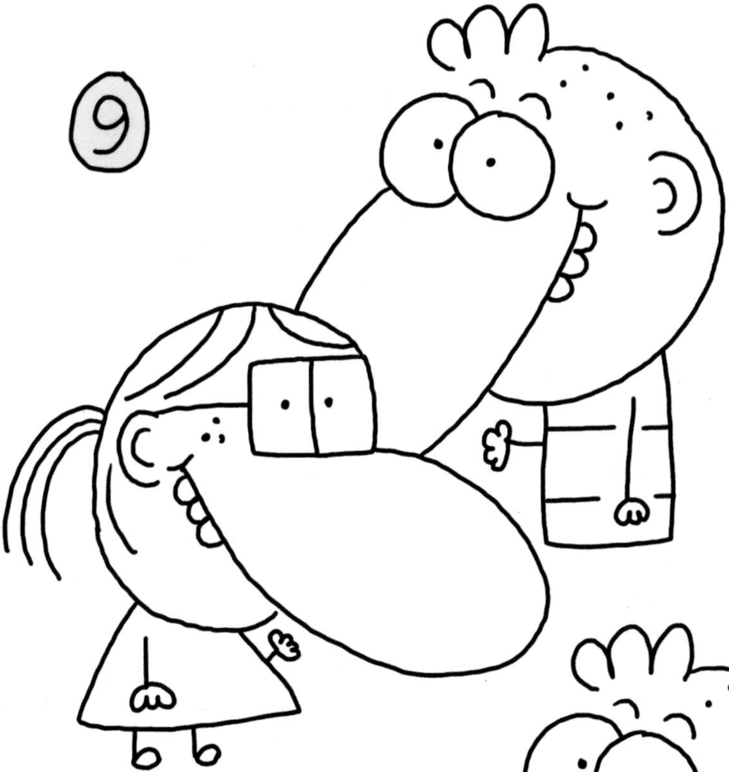

10

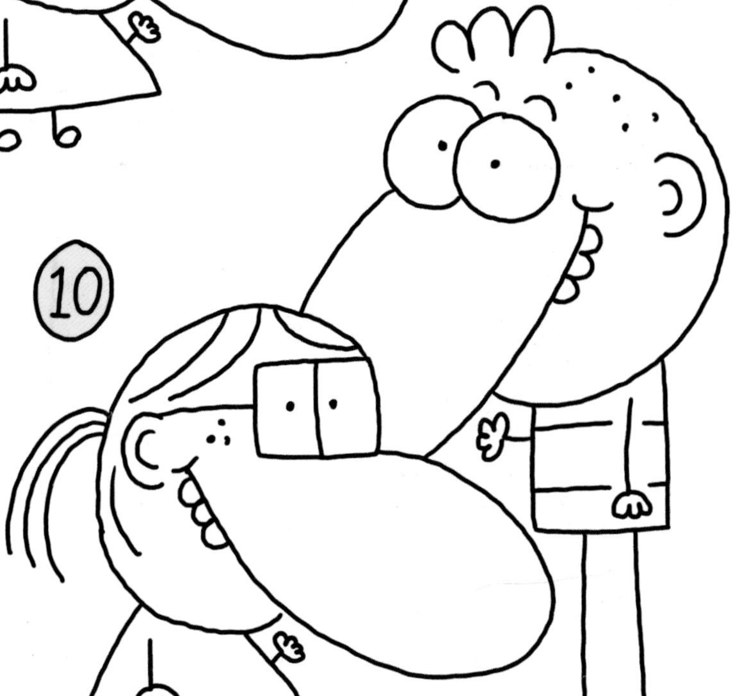

Special bonus HTD*—

DOG THING

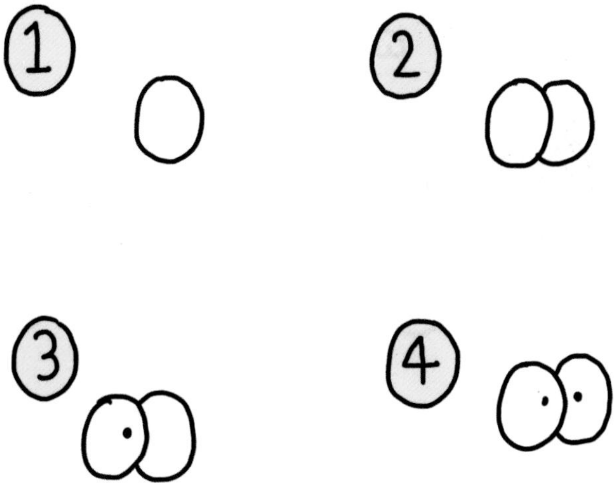

① ○

② ⬭⬭

③ ⬭⊙

④ ⊙⊙

*How To Draw

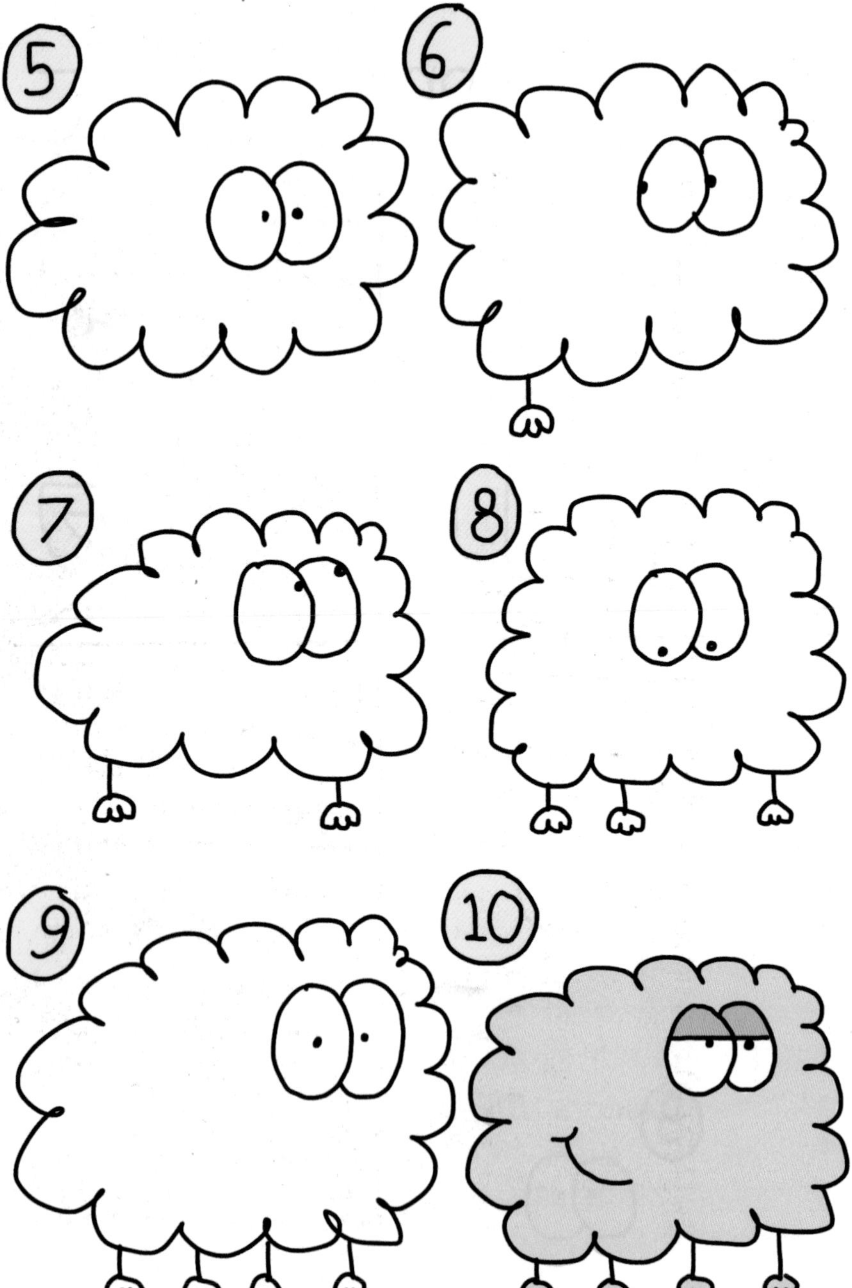
5
6
7
8
9
10

All about Jim Smith

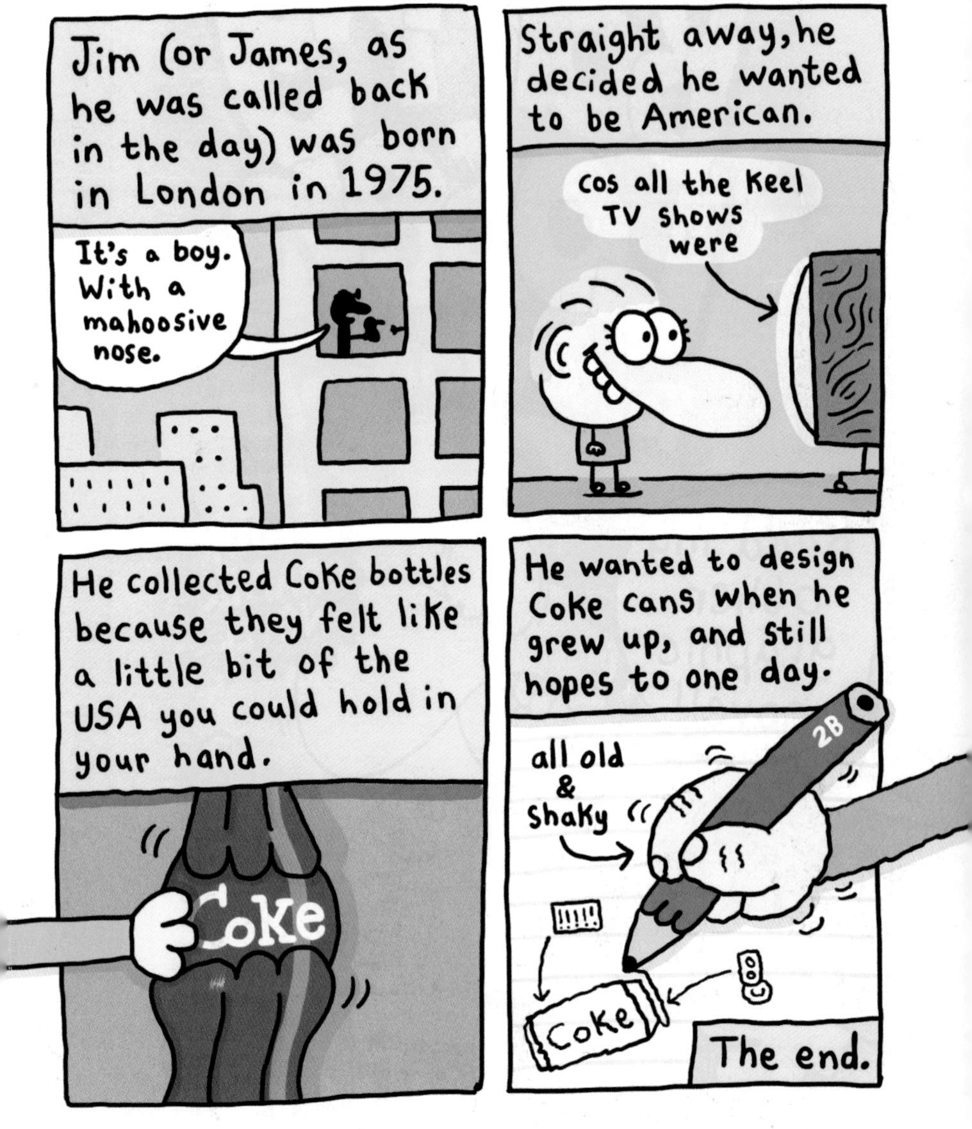
Jim (or James, as he was called back in the day) was born in London in 1975.
It's a boy. With a mahoosive nose.
Straight away, he decided he wanted to be American.
cos all the keel TV shows were
He collected Coke bottles because they felt like a little bit of the USA you could hold in your hand.
Coke
He wanted to design Coke cans when he grew up, and still hopes to one day.
2B
all old & shaky
Coke
The end.

Visit waldopancake.com for more Jim info (Jimfo).

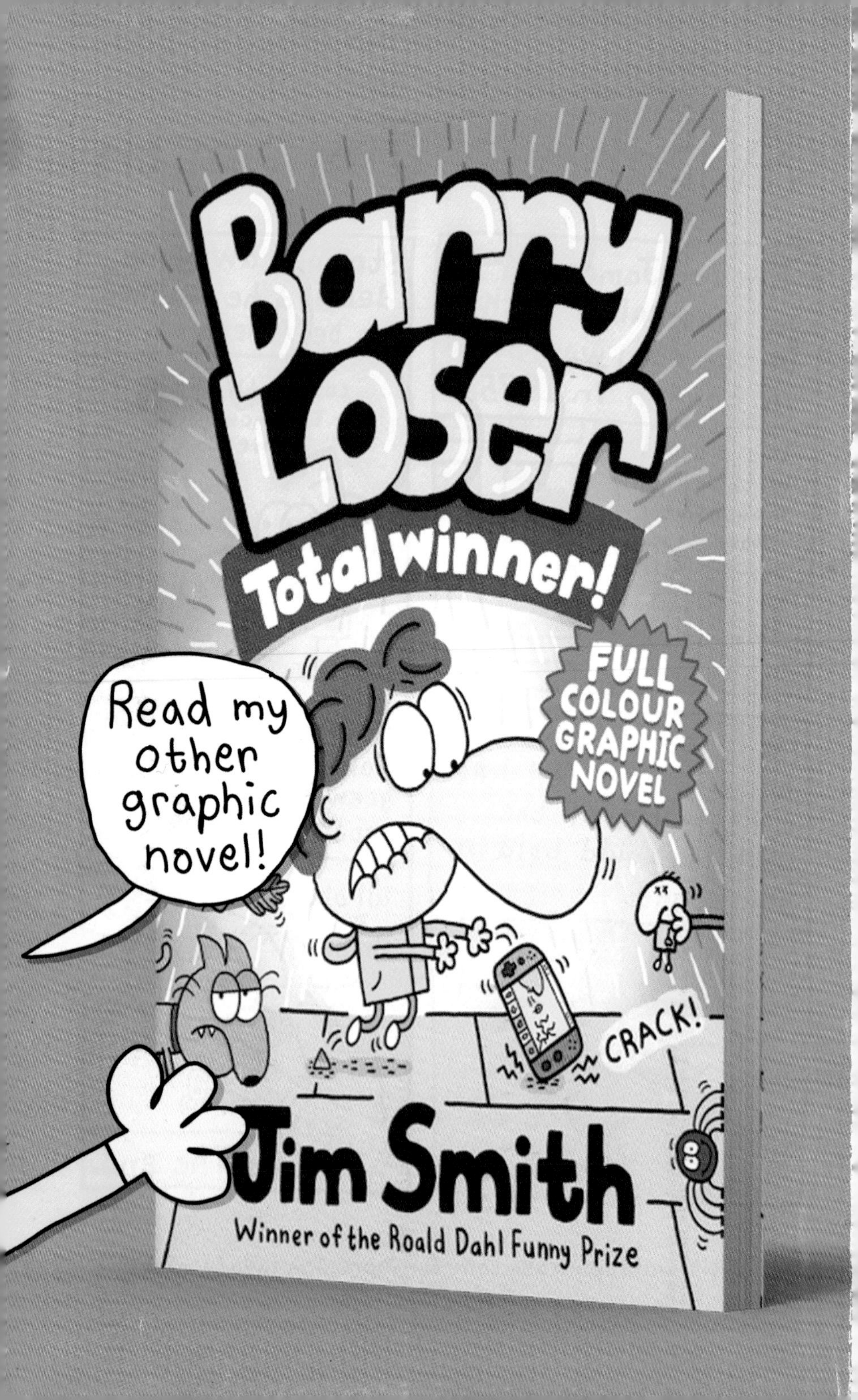
Barry Loser
Total winner!
FULL COLOUR GRAPHIC NOVEL
Read my other graphic novel!
CRACK!
Jim Smith
Winner of the Roald Dahl Funny Prize